Alex Gerlis is the author of the acclaimed Spies series of four Second World War espionage thrillers which are noted for their detailed research and intricate plots and feature two great adversaries: the British spymaster Edgar and his Soviet counterpart Viktor. The television/film rights for *The Best of Our Spies* have been bought by a major production company.

Born in Lincolnshire, Alex was a BBC journalist for nearly 30 years. He lives in west London with his wife and family and three black cats, a breed which makes cameo appearances in his books. He's a lifelong supporter of Grimsby Town, which has provided some preparation for the highs and lows of writing novels. When asked if he has worked in the field of espionage he declines to answer in the hope some people may think he has.

Also by Alex Gerlis

Spy Masters

Vienna Spies
The Berlin Spies

The Richard Prince Thrillers

Prince of Spies
Sea of Spies
Ring of Spies
End of Spies

The Wolf Pack Spies

Agent in Berlin

THE BEST OF OUR SPIES

&

THE SWISS SPY

ALEX GERLIS

San Diego, California

Canelo US
An imprint of Printers Row Publishing Group
9717 Pacific Heights Blvd, San Diego, CA 92121
www.canelobooksus.com

Printers Row Publishing Group is a division of Readerlink Distribution Services, LLC. Canelo US is a registered trademark of Readerlink Distribution Services, LLC.

This edition of THE BEST OF OUR SPIES originally published in the United Kingdom in 2020 by Canelo. This edition of THE SWISS SPY originally published in the United Kingdom in 2020 by Canelo.

Published in partnership with Canelo.

Correspondence regarding the content of this book should be sent to Canelo US, Editorial Department, at the above address. Author inquiries should be sent to Canelo, Unit 9, 5th Floor, Cargo Works, 1–2 Hatfields, London SE1 9PG, United Kingdom, www.canelo.co.

Publisher: Peter Norton • Associate Publisher: Ana Parker
Art Director: Charles McStravick
Senior Developmental Editor: April Graham
Production Team: Beno Chan, Julie Greene, Rusty von Dyl

Library of Congress Control Number: 2022934989

ISBN: 978-1-6672-0258-7

Printed in the United States of America

26 25 24 23 22   1 2 3 4 5

The Best of Our Spies

Chapter 1

Northern France, May 1940

The first time they saw German troops was around eight hours after they had left Amiens.

Fear had swept through the twenty of them, mostly strangers who had silently come together by happening to be on the same road at the same time and moving in the same direction. '*Don't head north,*' they had been warned in Amiens. '*You're walking into a battle.*'

Some of the original group had heeded that advice and stayed in the town. A dozen of them had carried on. They were refugees now, so they kept moving. It had quickly become a habit, they couldn't stop themselves.

A tall, stooped man called Marcel had assumed the role of leader and guide. He was a dentist, from Chartres, he told them. The rest of the group nodded and were happy to follow him.

Marcel decided that the main road would be too dangerous, so they dropped down to follow the path of the Somme, passing through the small villages that hugged the river as it twisted through Picardy. The villages were unnaturally silent, apart from the angry barking of dogs taking turns to escort them through their territory. Anxious villagers peered from behind partially drawn curtains or half-closed shutters.

Occasionally, a child would venture out to stare at them, but would quickly be called home by an urgent shout. Some villagers would come out and offer them water and a little food, but were relieved to see them move on. Refugees meant war and no one wanted the war to linger in their village. In a couple of the places, one or two more refugees joined them. No one asked to join, no one was refused. They just tagged along, swelling their numbers.

On the outskirts of the village of Ailly-sur-Somme a middle-aged couple came out from their cottage and offered the group water and fruit. They sat on the grass verge while the couple appeared to be arguing quietly in their doorway. And that was when they called her out.

'Madame, please can we have a word with you?'

She was sitting nearest to the house, but was not sure that they meant her. She looked around in case they were addressing someone else.

'Please, could we speak with you?' the man asked again.

She walked slowly over to the doorway. Maybe they had taken pity on her and were going to offer a meal. Or a bed. She smiled at the couple. Behind them, in the gloom of the hallway, she could make out a pair of piercing eyes.

'Madame. You seem to be a very decent lady. Please help us.' The man sounded desperate. 'A lady passed through the village last week.'

There was a pause.

'From Paris,' his wife added.

'Yes, she was from Paris. She said that she had to find somewhere in the area to hide and she asked us to look after her daughter. She promised she would be back for her in a day or two. She said she would pay us then. She promised to be generous. But that was a week ago. We cannot look after the girl any longer. The Germans could arrive any day now. You must take her!'

She looked around. The group were getting up now, preparing to move on.

'Why me?' she asked.

'Because you look decent and maybe if you are from a city you'll understand her ways. Are you from a city?'

She nodded, which they took as some kind of assent. The woman ushered the girl from inside the cottage. She looked no more than six years old, with dark eyes and long curly hair. She was dressed in a well-made blue coat and her shoes were smart and polished. A pale brown leather satchel hung across her shoulders.

'Her name is Sylvie,' the man said. His wife took Sylvie's hand and placed it in the woman's.

'But what about when her mother returns?'

The wife was already retreating into the dark interior of the cottage.

'Are you coming?' It was Marcel, calling out to her as he started to lead the group off. His voice sounded almost jolly as if they were on a weekend ramble.

2

The man leaned towards her, speaking directly into her ear so that the little girl could not hear. 'She won't be back,' he said. He glanced round at the girl and lowered his voice. 'They're Jews. You must take her.'

With that, he quickly followed his wife into the cottage and slammed the door behind them.

She hesitated on the doorstep, still holding the little girl's hand. She could hear the door being bolted. She knocked on the door two or three times, but there was no response.

She thought of trying to go round to the rear of the cottage, but she was losing sight of her group now. Sylvie was still holding her hand, glancing up at her anxiously. She knelt down to speak to the little girl.

'Are you all right?' She tried to sound reassuring. Sylvie nodded.

'Do you want to come with me?'

The little girl nodded again and muttered 'Yes.'

This is the last thing I need. She thought of leaving her there, on the doorstep. They'll have to take her back in. She paused. *I need to decide quickly. Maybe as far as the town, there'll be somewhere she can go there.*

By the time they had walked down the path and started to follow the group, the shutters in the cottage had been closed.

It was as they left the next village that they came across the Germans. They emerged from behind the trees one by one, with their grey uniforms, black boots and oddly shaped helmets, not saying a word. Slowly, they circled the group, which had come to a halt, too frightened to move. The German soldiers moved into position like pieces on a chessboard. They waved their machine guns to herd the group into the middle of the road.

She was terrified. *They are going to shoot us.* The little girl clutched her hand.

She breathed in and out deeply. Remember the training they gave you, she told herself:

When you are in a potentially dangerous situation, do not try to be anonymous.

Never look away, or at the ground. Do not avoid eye contact.

If you are in a group or a crowd, avoid standing in the middle, which is where they would expect you to hide.

If you fear that you are about to be found out, resist the temptation to own up. It is a fair assumption that the person questioning you or searching you will miss the obvious.

She heard some shouting from behind the trees and over the shoulder of the soldier nearest to her she spotted two officers emerging. One of them was speaking loudly in bad French.

'We are going to search you and then you can move on. Are any of you carrying weapons?'

Everyone around her was shaking their head. She noticed that Sylvie shook hers too.

He waited a while in case anyone might change their minds.

'Are there any Jews in this group?'

There was silence. People glanced suspiciously at those stood around them. At the word '*Jews*' the little girl's hand had tightened its grip on hers with a strength she could not have imagined. She looked down and saw that Sylvie had her head bowed and appeared to be sobbing. She realised the extent of her predicament. If they caught her looking after a Jewish child, she would have no excuses.

'My men will come and search you now. I am sure that you will all co-operate.'

Too late.

The soldiers spread the group out along the road and began searching people. Marcel was close to her and was searched before her. The soldier searching him gestured to him to remove his wristwatch. Marcel started to protest, until one of the officers walked over. He smiled, looked at the watch that had been passed to him, nodded approvingly and slipped it into his jacket pocket. Along the line, members of the group were being relieved of possessions: watches, pieces of jewellery and even a bottle of cognac.

The soldier who came to search her appeared to be in his teens. His hands shook as he took her identity card. She noticed that his lips moved silently as he tried to read what it said. One of the officers appeared behind him and took the identity card.

'You've come a long way.' He handed her identity card back to her.

She nodded.

'Is this your sister?' He was staring intently at the little girl.

She gave the faintest of nods.

'She is your sister, then?'

She hesitated. She had not said anything yet. She could do so now. They wouldn't harm a child. The little girl now placed her other hand round her wrist, stroking her forearm as she did so.

'Yes. She is my sister.' She had replied in German, speaking quietly and hoping that no one else in the group heard her. Trying to appear as relaxed as possible, she smiled sweetly at the officer who was probably in his mid-twenties, the same age as her. She threw her head back, allowing her long hair to settle over her shoulders.

If you are an attractive woman – at that point the instructor had been looking directly at her, along with the rest of them – *do not hesitate to use your charms on men.*

The officer raised his eyebrows approvingly and nodded.

'And where did you learn to speak German?'

'At school.'

'A good school then. And does your sister have an identity card?'

It was too late. She should have realised this would happen. *Does he suspect something? She doesn't look anything like me. Her complexion is so much darker.* She had lost the chance to tell them the truth.

'She lost it.'

'Where?'

'In Amiens. A Gypsy stole it from her.'

The officer nodded knowingly. He understood. *What do you expect? Gypsies. Don't we warn people about them? Thieves. Almost as bad as the Jews. Almost.*

He lowered himself down on his haunches so that he was at eye level with the little girl.

'And what is your name?'

There was a pause. The little girl peered up at her for approval. She nodded and smiled.

Tell him.

'Sylvie.'

'Sylvie is a nice name. Sylvie what?'

'Sylvie.'

'What is your surname – your full name?'

'Sylvie.'

'So, your name is "Sylvie Sylvie"?' The officer was beginning to sound exasperated. Sylvie was whimpering.

'I'm sorry, sir. She is frightened. It's the guns. She's never seen any before.'

'Well, she'd better get used to them, hadn't she?' The officer was standing up now. Not satisfied.

From the east there was a series of explosions followed by an exchange of rifle fire.

The officer hesitated. He wanted to continue with the interrogation, but the other officer was shouting out urgent instructions to the soldiers.

'All right, move on,' he said to her.

It was only when the soldiers disappeared back into the woods and the group moved on that she realised how petrified she was. Her heart was ramming against her ribs and cold sweat was running down her back. The little girl walked on obediently beside her, but she could feel and see her body trembling.

As the group walked slowly along the road, she realised that she was stroking Sylvie's hair, her trembling hand cupping the child's cheeks, wiping away the tears with her thumb.

Not for the first time and certainly not for the last, she had surprised herself.

–

They had walked for another hour. Marcel had dropped back at one stage and sidled up to her.

'And where did she come from?' He gestured at Sylvie, who was still clutching her hand.

'The couple who gave us water and fruit outside their cottage. The last village but one. They made me take her.'

'You realise…?'

'Of course I do!'

'Aren't you taking a bit of a risk?'

'Aren't we all?'

Marcel had spotted a forest ahead of them and said that the deeper they got into it, the safer they'd be. But, as she had begun to realise was the case in the countryside, distances were hard to judge and the forest was not quite as near as it had seemed and by the time they found a clearing, everyone was exhausted.

That night she found herself with Sylvie on the edge of the group, resting next to an old man and his wife. While the rest of the group slept the old man had given her his blanket, assuring her he was not cold. Sylvie was curled up alongside her under the blanket, fast asleep.

The old man had also given her the last of his water. He was not thirsty, he assured her. The moonlight poked through the canopy of the forest, the tops of some of the trees swaying very gently despite the apparent absence of any breeze. The old man moved closer to her and spoke quietly: he and his wife had lost both their sons at Verdun and had prayed they would never see another war. He had tried to lead a decent life. He went to church, he paid his taxes, he had never voted for the communists. He had worked on the railways, but was now retired. They could not stand the thought of being in Paris when it was occupied, so now they were heading to the town where his wife's sister lived, he explained. It was bound to be peaceful there.

'You look so much like our daughter,' he said, patting her affectionately on the wrist. 'You have the same slim figure, the same beautiful long, dark hair, the same dark eyes. When my wife and I saw you for the first time yesterday – we both remarked on that!'

'Where does your daughter live?'

The old man said nothing, but his eyes moistened as he held his hand over hers.

The old man was kind, but there was something about him that unsettled her. As she lay down on the cold earth, a familiar yet unwelcome companion descended upon her. The memory. The old man alongside, she realised, reminded her of her father. He too worked on the railways. The same dark eyes that couldn't hide the suffering. The same awkwardness. The reason why she was here now.

She had tried so hard to forget her father, but now the dark memories were stirred, she knew she would be troubled for the rest of the night.

She slept in short, unsatisfactory bursts, as she always did when her father came back to her. At one stage she woke with a start, aware that she must have cried out in her sleep. She looked round and noticed the old man's eyes, glinting in the moonlight, staring at her. When she awoke in the morning she felt stiff and cold. As the group moved off, she fell in with the old man and his wife, but the kindness of the previous night had gone and he ignored her.

–

'Come closer.'

It was later that afternoon and the group had paused at the edge of the forest, through which they had been walking all day. The old man, who was calling out to her, was now slumped at the base of the tree

7

and had aged ten years in the past ten minutes. His legs were twisted under him and his skin was as grey as the bark he was resting against. His wife knelt by his side, anxiously gripping his right arm with both her hands. He held his other arm out towards her, fingers urgently beckoning her to him.

'Come here,' he called out. His voice was rasping and angry. The rest of the group were moving off, leaving just her and Sylvie with the old man and his wife.

She looked down the forest path, where the rest of the group were now disappearing beyond the sunbeams. They knew that there was nothing they could do for the man and they were anxious to try and reach the town before nightfall. She could just make out Marcel, his short walking stick waving high above his head to encourage them along.

'Leave him,' Marcel had said. 'I warned everyone not to drink from the ponds. This water can be like a poison. He took the risk. We must move on.'

She hesitated. If she lost contact with the group she could be stranded in the forest, but she had made the mistake of stopping to help when the man collapsed and it would seem odd if she abandoned him now.

She knelt down by his side. Around the tree was a carpet of bracken; green, brown and silver. His lips were turning blue and spittle flecked with blood was dribbling down the sides of his mouth. His eyes were heavily bloodshot and his breathing was painfully slow. He did not have long to go. She recognised the signs. She would soon be able to rejoin the group.

'Closer.' His voice was now little more than a harsh whisper.

With a shaking hand he pulled her head towards his. His breath was hot and smelled foul.

'I heard you last night,' he said. She pulled back, a puzzled look on her face.

He nodded, pulling her back towards him, glancing at his wife as he did so, checking that she could not hear. 'I heard you cry out,' he whispered. 'I heard what you said.'

He waited to regain his breath, his whole body heaving as he did so. His reddened eyes blazed with fury.

'This victory will be your greatest defeat.'

Later that afternoon she realised how soon you became inured to the sights and the smells of war. They had a tendency to creep up on you, allowing time for the mind to prepare itself for what it was about to experience. But not the *sounds*. The sounds of war might have been no more shocking, but they had a tendency to arrive without warning, imposing themselves in the most brutal manner. You were never prepared for them.

So it was on that dusty afternoon at the end of May, where the Picardy countryside had begun to give hints of a nearby but unseen sea, and where a small group of French civilians desperately trying to flee the war now found that they had walked right into it.

It took a few seconds for her and most of the others in the column to realise that the cracking sound a hundred yards or so ahead of them · had been a gunshot. Maybe it was the shock of the strange metallic noise, that seemed to echo in such an undulating manner in every direction; more likely it was the fact that it was the first time most of them had ever heard a gunshot. In a split second, she reassembled in her mind what she had just seen and heard. Moments earlier, the tall figure of Marcel had been remonstrating with the German officer. She could barely make out what he had been saying, although she did hear the word 'civilians' more than once, as he pointed in their direction with his walking stick. Then there was the cracking noise and now Marcel lay still on the ground, the dusty, light-grey surface of the road turning a dark colour beneath him.

A wave of fear rolled through the small group that had been held up beyond the makeshift German checkpoint where the shooting had taken place. '*I know the area*,' Marcel had told them. '*I can handle the Germans.*'

Apart from the woman with four children, and three elderly couples, the group was mainly women on their own. All fools, she thought. All allowing themselves to be herded like cattle. All part of the reason why France had become what it was.

She knew that she had made a terrible mistake. She could have headed in any direction, other than east. That would have been suicide. When she looked at where she had ended up now, she might as well have gone east. She realised now that, of course, south would have been best. Due west would have been safe too; not as safe as the south, but better. But to have come north was a disaster.

9

It was not as if she had been following the crowds. Half of France had been on the move and each person seemed to be heading in a different direction. She had made up her mind when she left home that she would head north, and it wasn't in her nature to change her mind. She had tried a few weeks ago and this was why she was in so much trouble now. It was crazy though. She had passed through Abbeville when she was a girl, on the way to the coast for the only happy family holiday that she could remember. It had been an idyllic day, no more than a few hours respite on a long journey, but for some reason this was where she had decided to head.

The German officer walked over to the man on the ground, the pistol still in his hand. With his boot he rolled the body over onto its back and then nodded to two of his men. They picked a leg each and dragged the corpse to the ditch by the side of the road. A long red smear appeared on it where his body had been. The officer inspected his boot and wiped it clean on the grass verge.

One of the soldiers came over to the group and spoke to them slowly in bad French. They were to come forward one by one, he shouted. They were to show their identity cards to the officer who had shot the man, and after they had been searched, they would be allowed to carry on into the town.

The light had not started to fade yet and beyond the checkpoint she could see the outskirts of the town quite clearly. Plumes of dark smoke hung all over the town, all of them remarkably straight and narrow, as if the town lay beneath a forest of pine trees.

She couldn't risk the checkpoint. Not with this identity card. The first Germans they had encountered had not paid much attention to people's identities. They had seemed more intent on finding what loot they could lay their hands on. This checkpoint seemed to be more thorough. She had known that she would have to find another identity, and assumed she would get the opportunity in the town. She had not counted on coming across the Germans so early; no one had. The last news she had heard was that the Germans had not yet reached Calais. That was what Marcel had told them, and now his feet were sticking out of the ditch in front of them, his blood now turning black on the surface of the road.

She edged towards the rear of the column, looking around her as she did so. She spotted her opportunity. The soldiers were distracted by dealing with the mother and her four children, all of whom were crying. No one was watching the group. She leaned over to Sylvie, who was still clutching her by the waist, and whispered that she was going to the toilet in the field. She would be back in a minute. The little girl's eyes filled with tears. Reluctantly, she reached in her pocket and took out the bar of chocolate. It was the last of the bars that had filled her coat pockets and it was all she had left to eat. She pressed it into Sylvie's palm, noticing that the chocolate was soft and had begun to melt.

'If you are a good girl and keep very quiet, you can have all of this!' She was trying hard to sound as gentle as possible. She looked around. No one was looking at her. Towards the front of the column she saw the smartly dressed lady in her mid-thirties who had introduced herself as a lawyer from Paris, headed for the family home in Normandy.

'You see that nice lady there? The one with the smart brown coat? She will look after you. But don't worry, I will be back soon.'

Still crouching down, she edged towards the ditch and then through a narrow gap in the hedge. The corn was high in the field, and not far away was a large wood, which seemed to taper as it spread towards the town. She waited for a moment. She was certain that the Germans had not counted how many there were in their group and hopefully would not realise that one person had crept away. If they did come and look for her now, she was near enough to the hedge to be able to persuade them that she was just relieving herself.

It looked as if she had landed in an Impressionist painting: the golden yellow of the corn, the blue of the sky unbroken by cloud, and ahead the dark green of the wood. A timely breeze had picked up and the corn was swaying slowly. It would disguise her moving through it to the wood. If she could make it there she would have a good chance of reaching the town under the cover of the trees and the fading light.

Chapter 2

It is what comes in the wake of an invading army that is the true measure of a conquest.

The tanks and crack troops of the Panzer Group that entered the small town of Abbeville in the last week of May 1940 were quickly followed by the Wehrmacht, the regular troops with their grey uniforms and a sense of mild inferiority which they happily took out on their new subjects. And then came the camp followers: the cooks, the medics, the prostitutes and the officials. Especially the officials. It was as if the German Reich had been meticulously collecting minor officials for years and storing them in a cellar in Bavaria in the expectation that, come the conquest of Europe, they would have an army of them to promote beyond their natural station and help ensure the efficiency of any occupation.

And it was one of these minor officials, who now clearly regarded himself as anything but minor, who was to be her undoing.

She had entered the town the night before, waiting for a black blanket to drape over the Picardy countryside before she felt it was safe enough to leave the cover of the wood and crawl into the first row of ruins. From there she had worked her way through the outskirts, crossing debris-strewn roads and hurrying down streets where no building had been left unscathed. As a church bell struck ten, she had climbed into the attic above a row of abandoned shops and found a room where the window was more or less intact and there was large, dusty sofa. As the adrenaline of the escape from the checkpoint ebbed away she realised how hungry she was. Her last proper meal had been in a farmhouse the other side of Arras and since then she had managed on overpriced bread, and fruit she had taken from obliging orchards. She had been saving the bar of chocolate for an emergency. Keeping the little girl quiet had been that emergency.

In the corner of the room was a filthy sink, with a long crack running diagonally through it. The single tap, high above the sink, was stiff to turn and when she managed to release it there was a shudder and a hiss, but no water. She had last drunk water in one of the villages they had passed through the day before. Now, her throat was dry and she felt lightheaded. Not long before they arrived at the checkpoint outside Abbeville they had walked through a small forest, dotted with *étangs*. Marcel warned people against drinking the water and she knew that he was right: the surface of the little lake was still and scummy, but the old man who had given her the last of his water the night before insisted on drinking from an *étang*. They had barely walked for another five minutes before he became violently sick.

His face appeared in her dreams that night, but only fleetingly, although she couldn't get his last words out of her mind: 'This victory will be your greatest defeat.'

She dreaded to think what she must have said in her sleep to cause him to say that, but it was a good thing that he had decided to drink from the *étang*.

She dreamt a series of confused dreams that all seemed to end with her trying to catch a train or a bus that was always pulling away just as she reached it. In the final dream she found herself hiding in a warm bakery, the smell of freshly baked baguettes overwhelming.

She woke to find two boys standing in the doorway staring at her. She had no idea how old they were: certainly not teenagers, yet not so young that they could be described as children. But what mattered was what they had in their arms: baguettes, two each. The smell of them had already filled the room.

'What do you want?' she asked sharply.

'Somewhere to stay.' It was the older boy, probably thirteen now that she thought about it, thinking back to her days on the children's ward. He was trying to sound confident, but he was trembling. 'Is this your place?'

Outside she could hear the sound of the shop doors being wrenched open and then slammed shut, followed by shouting in German. 'They've gone, they're not around here,' one of the soldiers was saying.

'Are they after you?'

The younger boy nodded. He looked terrified. 'We took some food. A patrol spotted us so we ran away. They didn't see us come in here. I promise you.'

13

'You can stay,' she said, 'but let me see what food you've got.'

They laid it out on the filthy table in the middle of the room. The two baguettes, a large round cheese with a thick yellow rind and not much of an aroma, and a long, thick smoked sausage.

'Do you have anything to drink?'

The younger boy glanced nervously at the older one who nodded. He pulled a flask from an inside coat pocket.

'It's water,' he said, 'it's all we have left.' He grudgingly handed the flask over to her.

She drank all of the water in the flask in one go and then looked at the two boys.

'I'll take a baguette and half of the cheese and sausage. Then you can stay. It's your rent. Keep quiet and stay away from the windows. Understand?'

The boys nodded. They had risked their lives for this food and now had given half of it away, but they had no alternative. Crouched on the floor, shoulder to shoulder, they sat in silence, eating while sunlight swept into the room, picking out the dust and the cobwebs. The boys were exhausted and by noon had fallen asleep.

She stayed on the sofa, the remains of the bread and her share of the cheese and the sausage carefully stashed in her bag, which she clutched to her chest. By early afternoon, she had a plan. She would head for the hospital. It was the natural place for her to go. They would probably welcome her and, apart from anything else, there she would have a good chance of finding a new identity.

She left the boys asleep. She thought about taking the remains of the sausage that was poking out of the older boy's side pocket, but he was stirring and she thought better of it.

There were plenty of grey-uniformed Germans in the streets, but they weren't stopping anyone, as far as she could tell. In the distance, there was the muffled sound of artillery fire and the occasional roar of aircraft. Outside a bombed church she noticed a queue forming, which she instinctively joined. She still had some cash and, if this was a chance to buy something while her money was worth anything, she did not want to let it pass. The people in the queue were talking quietly. The Allies were trying to retake the town, she heard someone say. An attack was imminent. God would save them. It was only when she reached the front of the queue that she realised she had been wasting her time. A young priest was sitting on a chair in the porch of the church taking confession, his cassock gently blowing around his shoulders in the wind. She turned to leave, but thought that would only bring unwanted attention, so she allowed him to bless her and mutter a prayer she didn't bother to listen to.

As she moved away there was a roar of artillery, much nearer now. Two old men were discussing it.

'It's coming in this direction,' said one.

The other shook his head: 'No, it's being fired from the town.'

It hardly seemed to matter as far as she was concerned. She had no idea of which side she was meant to be on anyway.

She headed towards the centre of the town. The first bridge that she came to was intact and she joined the throng of people hurrying across the Somme. It was only when she was halfway over the bridge that she found she had been sucked into a queue, with German soldiers marshalling people into rows. This was nothing like the checkpoint outside the town, manned by just one or two easily distracted soldiers. This was a proper checkpoint. The civilians were being funnelled into one of four rows, each row guarded by half a dozen soldiers with their machine guns drawn. At the end of each row was a trestle table, where a black-uniformed SS officer sat alongside a Wehrmacht officer. Behind the trestle tables was another row of tables, laden with paperwork and manned by anxious officials. The officers at the first table were passing the identity cards they were checking to the men at the second row of tables.

There was nothing she could do. She had walked into a trap and there was simply no prospect of her being able to slip away from it. She edged along the queue, taking care to breathe slowly, look calm and, above all, avoid drawing attention to herself.

After all, why would they be interested in her? She tried to reassure herself. She had a good cover story: '*I am a nurse, heading for the hospital, ready to volunteer my services.*' Why was she in this part of the country, so far from home? She would smile, she would always smile. Her best smile. '*I was frightened. Isn't everyone? I joined other people escaping the fighting and thought I would head for somewhere quiet. I made a mistake.*' Then she would smile again.

She realised she was being ridiculous anyway. She was worrying far too much. It was hard to imagine that with everything they had on their minds, the Germans would remember anything about her. A foolish promise she had made in a rash and impetuous moment. It had been an exciting proposal they had made two years ago in Paris and one that was not hard to agree to after the wine, the flattery and the charm. The training in Bavaria. *'Go home and wait there,'* they had told her. *'We'll come and find you when we need you. Lead a normal life. Go to work, go home, and don't talk about politics to anyone. Just make sure you are where we know you are.'* She was not important. In the great scheme of things, she was barely even a pawn. Surely it would be weeks, months even, before they remembered about her, and by then she would be beyond their grasp.

'Carte d'identité… Carte d'identité!'

The soldier next to the SS man behind the trestle table was shouting at her and a sentry was pushing her roughly in the side. She had reached the front of the queue.

She fumbled in her bag and found her identity card, only just remembering to smile as she placed it carefully on the rough wooden surface. The SS man looked at the card and handed it to the soldier next to him, who spoke to her in hesitant French.

'Where are you heading?'

'The hospital. You can see that I'm a nurse. I'm going to volunteer to—'

He cut her short. 'Why are you in this town? You have travelled a long way.'

She shrugged and smiled again. 'I used to come to this area for my holidays when I was a child. I thought it would be safe. I didn't realise…'

The SS officer looked carefully at her and then at her identity card. He was turning it slowly. She noticed that his fingers were immaculately manicured, his nails quite perfect. He looked once more at the card and passed it to the table behind him.

It was then that she noticed that the men in civilian clothes behind that table were checking the cards against lists. What if her name was on one of the lists? She was being ridiculous again, but it did make her realise that getting a new identity was an absolute priority. By whatever means, she would make sure…

Something was wrong.

She sensed it before she saw it.

She could not tell which of the officials had been looking at her card, but one of them had called over a man in a long raincoat who was standing behind the table, and together they were looking at an identity card and checking it against the list. Another man, also dressed in a long raincoat was called over and he too looked at the card and then at the list. The three men nodded and she was sure that at least one of them glanced in her direction. She tried to look as relaxed as possible, but her heart was crashing against her chest. She turned round, but it was impossible. There were soldiers every side of her. Maybe if she pretended to faint, or to—

'Please...' One of the men in long raincoats had appeared at her side and was holding her firmly by the elbow.

'We need to do some more checks. Please come with me.'

–

'You are sure that you have told me everything?'

The Gestapo officer who had brought her to the Hôtel de Ville from the checkpoint had stopped circling her chair and now stood directly in front of her, his arms folded tight against his chest and looking genuinely confused. He had removed his raincoat and his hat and looked no more than thirty. His French was excellent, so she abandoned her attempts at speaking in her much less fluent German.

'I told you. I was recruited in Paris two years ago. I have been trained. My instructions were to stay where I was, but I left a week ago when the police became suspicious of me.'

'In what way?'

'What do you mean?'

He was beginning to look exasperated now. This was the third time they had been through the same set of questions. She sensed that he was primed for resistance, that he was only really at ease when interrogating people who refused to co-operate. That was what he was trained for, not someone apparently going out of their way to co-operate. He seemed uncomfortable in the face of such co-operation. She drew a deep breath, trying hard not to look put-out at having to repeat herself.

'What I mean is that I was worried that the police were interested in me. I told you, one of the nurses at the hospital said that someone had been asking her about me, whether I was ever involved in politics, that kind of thing.'

'And the name of this nurse?' He was sitting at the desk now, his pencil poised.

'Thérèse.'

He looked at her, saying nothing but raising his eyebrows, the very faintest hint of a smile appearing on his face. She knew what he was after.

'I cannot remember her surname. We weren't in the same department. I just knew her as Thérèse. In any case, that was not the only thing. I was followed home from work on more than one occasion and there always seemed to be a *gendarme* in our road. They never used to be there all the time. The day before I left, there was a car parked opposite with three men in it. I am certain they were police. That is why I decided to go. I couldn't risk staying.'

He looked unconvinced, but said nothing, tapping his pencil on the pad in front of him. They were on the top floor of the Hôtel de Ville, in a small room, with the noise seeping in along with the sunlight through the closed shutters.

There was a knock on the door and a soldier came in, handing over a small envelope. The Gestapo officer opened it, read it quickly and put the note back inside the envelope. He nodded at her. *Carry on.*

'I know that my orders had been to stay at home and act normally and I would be contacted, but I panicked. Maybe I was wrong, I don't know, but I was convinced they were after me. What use would I have been then? So that is why I escaped. I was not running away. I used my own identity, didn't I? If I was running away, surely I would have changed that?'

He nodded. Against his better judgement, it was hard to disbelieve her. Of course, he would have liked nothing better than for her to say nothing. He could cope with defiance, but he was unsure how to deal with this.

'And tell me about your recruitment in Paris.'

'Again?'

'Yes, please.'

'I met Herr Lange at the German Embassy there in February 1938. He arranged for my training in Germany. He gave me my instructions. The last I heard from him was that I was to wait for him.'

'Where was the Embassy?'

'Pardon?' It was the first time that he had asked this question.

'I cannot remember the exact address.'

He looked pleased, as if he had discovered a chink in her defence.

'You cannot remember the address. I see. Where was it near?'

'The river.'

He snorted and got up from behind the desk and came to stand in front of her. He placed his hands on his hips and leaned over her.

'*Everywhere* in Paris is near the river. You will have to do better than that.'

'It was near a station, the Gare d'Orsay – I remember that. And the National Assembly was nearby, of course.'

'Of course.' He was beginning to look disappointed. He had quite perked up at the prospect of having an excuse to hit her.

'I remember now. It was in the Rue de Lille. That's where it was!'

He nodded and returned to his desk, gathering up his papers and kicking the chair back under the desk.

'Well, you won't have to wait very long now. Herr Lange is on his way.'

–

He arrived in the middle of the following afternoon. He was shorter than she remembered, but with the same broad shoulders and thick, swept-back hair. He walked smartly into the room, accompanied by the Gestapo officer. He removed a beige raincoat to reveal a well-cut suit. Ignoring her, he neatly folded his raincoat, looked around for a coat-hook which he couldn't find and draped his coat over the back of the chair behind the desk.

The Gestapo officer was hovering in the doorway, keen to remain part of the proceedings. Lange continued to ignore both of them while he checked that the window was locked and the shutters closed.

'Thank you,' he said to the officer, who was still showing no signs of leaving.

After a moment he took the hint and turned sharply out of the door.

Lange waited until the echo of the officer's footsteps had long disappeared before going to the doorway, glancing up and down the corridor and then locking the door.

Only then did he acknowledge her, with a courteous nod of his head that was almost a bow, as he pulled a chair over and carefully positioned it directly in front of her. He sat very still, saying nothing. During the silence that followed, she realised that she could no longer hear any artillery fire. He carefully arranged his shirt cuffs so that just an inch of them emerged from his jacket sleeves. His cufflinks appeared to have a green jewel in them. He gestured at the door.

'He's angry that he never had to lay a finger on you. The Gestapo feel they have failed unless they have managed to hurt someone.'

'I never gave him cause to.'

'Apparently not.' There was a pause as he looked carefully through a typed document. 'Things have not gone exactly according to plan, have they?'

She shook her head. Two years ago, it had seemed such a good idea. She had continued to feel committed and enthusiastic until just a few weeks ago. Then the reality of what it could mean started to hit her. Perhaps, in her heart of hearts, she had never expected anything to come of it. Maybe, like a teenage crush, it had been just a passing fancy. But war had brought with it a fear that she never imagined could cut so deep. So no, things had not gone according to plan. She shrugged as if the matter was not that important and spoke in a soft voice.

'I've told him already. I was frightened. I thought the police were after me. I didn't want to get caught. That's why I left the city. Look, you know that the French authorities evacuated most of the population of the city last September. I'd only been allowed to remain because of my job. I felt isolated. I don't know what I was thinking, but I was afraid.'

'And you have not been having any second thoughts… any doubts about your mission?'

'Of course not, absolutely.' She was aware that she had replied perhaps too fast. But she could hardly tell the truth. *Of course I've had my doubts. Every night for the past few months I've gone to sleep with them and woken up to them.*

'You must not worry. It is perfectly natural to have doubts, even to be afraid. Everyone experiences that fear, they would probably not be taking their role seriously if they did not feel like that. What matters is that you overcome this fear and that you realise that doubt is a luxury you simply cannot afford.'

He leaned closer to her, his soft voice dropping slightly. He reminded her of the young priest in the porch of the church the previous day. He was so close that she could smell a strong tobacco on his breath and his hands, held together as if in prayer, lightly touched her wrist.

'Because you know, Ginette, you passed the point where you could change your mind a long time ago. The day you first came to see me, from then on, you were on our side. In our world, indecision is a luxury not open to us. Remember, you did not apply to become a waitress in a bistro. This is not the same as working in a shop. It is a vocation that you have taken on – for life.'

'I understand that, I...'

He was leaning even closer now, speaking so quietly that she had to lean towards him to hear anything. She picked up the scent of cologne on his face. He was almost whispering directly into her ear.

'And let me warn you. You have no alternative but to do everything we ask. We will always have people watching you. We will know everything that you are doing. They are there to protect you, but also to protect our interests. You know how important you are to us because we had you on that list, didn't we? The minute you arrive there you will be implicated so your only option is to do what we say. I think that you understand the consequences if you don't.'

She nodded that she understood and, with an enormous effort, she managed a smile that she hoped did not look forced.

'Of course. I was frightened, I was not acting rationally.'

He pulled away from her, leaning back in his chair.

'So you keep saying.' He straightened his suit, flicking a speck of dirt from the sleeve. 'I cannot pretend that this has not been an... inconvenience. When we tried to contact you last week, we were most angry to find you had gone. You know that your instructions were to stay put and we would find you. I know that I said it might be months before we would contact you, but I also said it could be any time. You should have stayed where you were. We have no evidence that the police were after you. I must say, when we put your name on the list of people who were to be detained, I did not expect that we would actually find you. I thought you would have changed your identity. If you were truly attempting to escape from us you would have at least travelled under a different name, so I am inclined to believe you. So, you must not worry. In fact, things have actually worked out rather well. You have headed in the right direction, without realising it. We will be able to take good advantage of the situation.'

She felt a slight sense of relief. She was trapped, of course, but the truth was that she could have ended up in worse traps. At least now she was in the hands of the Abwehr rather than the Gestapo.

'And your mother. How is your mother?'

The slight sense of relief disappeared. She started to speak, but he interrupted before she could begin.

'She was very worried when we visited her the other week. Out of her mind with worrying about you, so I am told. But don't worry. We will keep an eye on her.'

I have no doubt you will, she thought.

Her fear must have shown, because he patted her knee, speaking almost reassuringly. His hand stayed on her knee longer than it needed to.

'What you must realise is that in the world you are now in… which *we* are in,' – his hand moved between the two of them, so as to emphasise their common endeavour – 'in this world you can never be quite sure of where you belong or of who you belong to. You will move from shadow to shadow and you will soon understand that you can never be sure of who you really are. The only advice I can give you is that once you start out on this journey, as you have, keep going in the same direction. Do not hesitate, do not waver. Keep going. Do you understand?'

Without waiting for her reply he went round the chair behind the desk and picked up his briefcase. He deposited it on top of the desk and pulled out a sheaf of papers, placing them in a neat pile.

'Here,' he patted the pile of papers, 'we have your new life. Your new identity, everything. We had, of course, been hoping to have longer to prepare you, but as we are learning – in war, things happen in such an unpredictable way.'

He removed his suit jacket and rolled up his sleeves. He was ready to start work.

'We need to move fast. We will remain here for another twenty-four hours and then we will head east along the coast. I need time to brief you, and you have to learn your new identity. Ideally we would have more than twenty-four hours in which to do this but an unexpected opportunity has presented itself and we would be foolish not to take advantage of it.'

She felt sick. Although Lange was as charming as when she first met him, this did not compensate for the fact that the plan he had outlined two years ago – and which had been refined and worked on since then – was actually going to be put into action. She was not sure that she had ever believed that would happen. There was nothing she could do now. She could not run any more.

'You say we head east. Where are we going?'

Lange reached into his briefcase and pulled out a map, which he proceeded to unfold. He spread it out on the floor in front of her and pointed to a port to the north east of Abbeville.

'Here. Dunkirk.'

Chapter 3

London, April 1941

Tucked away in a small road south of Wandsworth Bridge, to the west of Clapham Common and close enough to Lavender Hill and Trinity Road to catch the hum of wartime traffic, lay the Royal Victoria Patriotic School. It had been two years since its pupils had been evacuated to Wales and the handsome greenstone building now served an entirely different purpose. It was now the home of the London Reception Centre, its hospitable name belying its true role. Following the fall of France and after Dunkirk, 150,000 refugees from Europe had escaped to the United Kingdom. They were screened at reception centres around London and the very small minority whose stories did not quite match up, became the guests of the London Reception Centre to face the MI5 interrogators.

And so it was in the Royal Victoria Patriotic School, early on an unseasonably dull and chilly April morning, that two guards unlocked one of the windowless cells in the south courtyard and its inmate had a brief glimpse of light for the first time in nearly ten hours. Familiar now with the routine, he obligingly held out his hands to be handcuffed and waited while the blindfold was placed around his eyes.

And then the brisk walk. Hurried along by the guards' hands on each elbow, he could anticipate when each turn was to be made, when steps were to be climbed or, more often, descended, carpeted corridors to be walked down and doorways to be entered. They came into the room that he assumed must be in the basement of the main building, though he could not be sure, in the same way that he could no longer be sure how long he had been there, or even which day it was.

He was guided into the room and placed in front of a chair. Only then was the blindfold removed, along with the handcuffs. He stood still, dazed and disoriented, blinking in the yellowish light that hung low just in front of him. Due to his slightly stooped posture, he appeared even shorter than he was. His most noticeable features were his long arms, which hung limply by his sides, the fingers nervously playing with the cuffs of what appeared to be a cardigan specially knitted for him, but without much affection. He could still not get out of his mind something he had overheard the guards saying on his first night here. One pair of guards was handing over to another pair and they were chatting, clearly assuming that the Belgian was asleep.

'And what's he like then, Bert, this Belgian?'

'Pathetic-looking little chap, Alan. Rat-like without the cunning.'

That had really upset him. Now one of the guards was pushing him down into the chair and then both guards moved behind him, just beyond his line of sight. He blinked again to adjust his eyes to the dimly lit room, taking in the long table ahead of him, behind which sat two men.

So started the Belgian's fourteenth interrogation in what he estimated could not be more than one week. As he had done throughout, he endeavoured to adopt the plausible manner to be expected of an innocent yet aggrieved man.

The older of the two men in front of him was the only one who ever addressed him directly. He was distinguished-looking, possibly in his fifties. The Belgian assumed from the way he spoke Flemish that he was Dutch, although he could not be sure. He was also fluent in French and English, though he had only used the former on one occasion on the first day and then it had no hint of Walloon to it. The Dutchman only had an ashtray in front of him, no notes nor even a pen. He chain-smoked and would occasionally offer the Belgian a cigarette, which he always declined. Most of the interrogation was carried out in English, not least for the benefit of the man who sat to the Dutchman's right and who never directly addressed him. The Englishman appeared to be in his forties and constantly referred to the notebooks and files spread out in front of him, in a manner which the Belgian found disconcerting, which he guessed was the idea. There were two things that the Belgian did notice about the Englishman: his height and his face that never betrayed any flicker of emotion. If you stared hard at the Englishman, with his haircut very marginally longer than the military regulation cut most people around him seemed to have, then you'd realise that he was a good-looking man, the Belgian thought. But look away from him even for a second and you would be hard pressed to recall any detail about his face. The interrogation would be punctuated from time to time by the Englishman shaking his head, or sighing, or stopping the questions to go into discussion with the Dutchman, with their heads turned away from the Belgian.

As the questioning started today, the Belgian noticed a different tone to the Dutchman's voice. He assumed it was another ruse, but he certainly sounded more confident – even slightly jolly. The Belgian concentrated on his breathing. He concentrated on trying to remember what he had been taught:

Breathe in and out deeply, speak slowly and think before you answer any question – even the easy ones – so that they will never be alerted by a change in your manner. Stick to your story. Believe in your story. That way, they will have to believe you.

If they haven't got anything to hit you with after a week, then all they will have is what you tell them. The longer you hold out, the safer you will be.

'Good morning, Vermeulen,' said the Dutchman. 'Permit me to sum up where we have got to.' The Englishman was staring at him without blinking.

'You entered England in May 1940 following the fall of Dunkirk. You were initially screened at our reception centre in Crystal Palace, where you received security clearance. You then found accommodation at a bedsit in Acton in west London, where you have lived ever since. You have worked in a variety of semi-skilled occupations, although you are, of course, a qualified lawyer in your native Belgium.'

The Belgian nodded.

'You have led a blameless life, Mr Vermeulen, is that not true?'

The Belgian nodded again, slowly, trying to gather his thoughts. He was sure that for the very first time, he could make out the trace of a smile on the Dutchman's face. The Englishman leaned forward.

'But, Mr Vermeulen, I don't need you to reassure us of that. We know it ourselves! And shall I tell you why?'

Vermeulen had no time to respond.

'You see, we have been watching you very carefully ever since you left Crystal Palace. You never received a genuine security clearance there, as you thought you did. We had been – how do they say here – expecting the pleasure of your company even before you left Belgium. Shall I tell you why?'

The Belgian found himself nodding, although his instinct told him he should not respond to a question like that.

'You are one of life's pathetic creatures.' He repeated that sentence in Flemish. The Belgian was shocked and feared he was showing it. Until now, the Dutchman had always been proper, even polite in his manner and his tone.

'Look at you, Vermeulen. How old are you? Forty-three? You look ten years older. Your skin is so pale that it looks as if you have never been in the fresh air. And it appears that a decent meal is not a habit of yours. You've never married and, as far as we can gather, you had no social life. Who would want to marry *you*, Vermeulen? Do you even *like* women, Vermeulen? Who would want to be *your* friend?'

Vermeulen felt tears swell in his eyes. Never in his life had he heard such personal remarks like these, at least not in such a direct way. He always assumed that those people in the office in Brussels made them, but that would be behind his back. And his neighbours. Even some of the people at the church. He must stay calm. This was a ruse. He had been warned about it. It was proof that they had nothing on him, he tried to reassure himself. What was it the instructor had said? *Don't react to abuse. It will be a sign that they have nothing on you.*

'You spent your time either at work, or at church, or in your small apartment playing with your radio and your gramophone. You applied to join the Free Belgian Forces when you arrived in this country, but, of course, you knew you would be turned down. You are a weak man; you are not an example of the Aryan race which you so aspire to, are you? And this story about you being a lawyer? You were a clerk at a law firm in Brussels – and not even a very good clerk. You had not been promoted in years and, of course, you blamed the Jewish partners for that, didn't you? The German Sixth Army hadn't even taken their boots off after they entered Brussels on the seventeenth of May last year before you were knocking at General von Reichenau's door volunteering your services. And what did you have in mind? Probably being a very senior clerk, with other clerks working for you. You would spend your time denouncing Jews and socialists, assisting the Nazis in their occupation of your country and, for the first time in your miserable little life, becoming someone important. But you made one mistake.'

There was a long pause. He had had no idea that the Dutchman had been aware of some of the things he was saying now.

'The mistake was to let your new masters know that you speak fluent English – probably your only real talent, Mr Vermeulen. We know that your employers had sent you over here for a while in the early 1930s to work in the office of their London associates, did they not? So when the Germans discovered that Arnold Vermeulen is not just an eager collaborator who understands radios, but also speaks excellent English and is familiar with London, they realised that you have a perfect role to play here in London!'

Vermeulen decided now to deploy the one card he had left, though he had to admit it was a creased and low-value one. The last thing the instructor had ever said to him: '*If you sense things going wrong in an interrogation, give them something. Admit to a failing, own up to a minor deceit.*' There was an outside chance that it might work, but his confidence was not strong. His voice was shaking; he knew that he sounded too eager to please.

'It is true, sir. I lied about being a lawyer. I felt ashamed that I had never had better qualifications and I thought that if people believed I was a lawyer in Belgium then they would give me a role here that would better suit my skills. My employers in Brussels had never given me a chance. They always promoted their young family friends but never me. And the radios? It was to listen to music. Is that a crime?'

'So, as we say: we were expecting you.' Again, the Dutchman had ignored Vermeulen's answer.

'You had made enough noise in the Nazi headquarters when you first turned up there to bring attention to yourself. Did it really not occur to you that we may have our own people there? And we knew what your role would be. You were not going to be doing any spying yourself. True to your vocation as a clerk, your role would be to be the conduit through which the intelligence gained by a more active German spy would be passed back to the Nazis. In other words, you would not do any actual spying yourself, but you would pass on the information of an agent who did. Perhaps someone not able to send their own messages. At this point, Mr Vermeulen, would you care to comment?'

'I am not a German spy, sir, that is a ridiculous accusation; I keep telling you that I am an innocent refugee—'

'That's right, an innocent refugee who only wishes to assist in the liberation of his country from Nazi occupation. Very admirable I am sure; we have heard it for the past week. We are very familiar with your story, Mr Vermeulen. But let me continue. Our information was that you would be what we call a "sleeper". For a period of time, you would do nothing. You arrived in this country without a radio, so we knew that only when your agent was ready to pass on information would you collect the radio from where it had been hidden. Until then you would lead, as I said, a blameless life. But then you would receive a signal that would let you know that your life as an active Nazi agent was to begin. Our understanding is that this signal would come from your agent once they had information that they wished to be transmitted to your masters. Do you wish to comment at this stage?'

The Belgian shook his head. 'It simply is not true...'

'Two weeks ago we followed you to Oxford. You were using all the old tricks to check that you were not being followed, but you were not very subtle about it. For instance, you took five different bus journeys while in Oxford and constantly looked behind you. That is how an amateur behaves. We believe that the purpose of your visit to Oxford was to collect the radio transmitter that had been hidden in that area. Of course, once you had the transmitter, we would arrest you and with such concrete evidence you would be persuaded to tell us the truth.'

'I tell you this is not true. I visited Oxford to see the sights and the—'

'—"and the architecture" which is your "special interest". Yes, I have heard that all week, Mr Vermeulen. You keep telling us. Let me continue. Our plan went wrong, did it not?'

The Englishman to the left of the Dutchman coughed and nodded.

'You are clearly a very nervous man, Mr Vermeulen. Obviously you are nervous now. That is understandable. You are being interrogated. But I think that your general disposition is a nervous one, is it not? Because what happens in Oxford when you are about, we believe, to collect your transmitter? You are sick. Not in a discreet manner. You did not find a toilet or a quiet alleyway. You were sick in the street, drawing attention to yourself. And as we all know, one of the people who came over to see what the fuss was all about was an enthusiastic member of the local police force, who decided to question you. When he asked for your papers, for some reason he was not satisfied and decided to take you to the police station so that he could check them out further. Maybe it was your nervous manner that made him suspect something, I don't know. My guess was it was because you are foreign and the British police are always suspicious of foreigners. So our plans – that is, *your* plan and *our* plan – were ruined by that overzealous police officer. If he had minded his own business, I believe you would have led us to the radio transmitter. So, once again, where is that transmitter, Mr Vermeulen?'

'There is no transmitter, I assure you. I don't know what you are talking about.'

'Now we come to the interesting developments. A radio transmitter is very important if you are to send your messages. That is obvious, as I am sure you know, Mr Vermeulen. But what is also important is the code in which you were going to send that message. And it is in connection with that, that we have some news for you today.'

The Dutchman lit another cigarette. A thin mist of grey-brown smoke now hung between the Belgian and his questioner. The Englishman leaned back in his chair, his gaze remained fixed on the Belgian, but his features faded as he moved out of the light.

'You will appreciate that once you were arrested in Oxford, we were able to search your room in Acton. You kept it very neat, Mr Vermeulen. You lead a simple life. You do not have many possessions and we were able to examine everything that you own very thoroughly. It is something that I specialise in. And until last night, we found nothing incriminating.'

He repeated the last sentence in Flemish.

Another pause. The Belgian was now feeling sick. '*Until last night,*' the Dutchman had said. What did he mean by that? He wondered whether to say anything now or whether this was another of the tricks that the Dutchman used.

'You are a religious man, are you not, Mr Vermeulen?'

The Belgian found himself nodding.

The Dutchman reached for a briefcase on the floor behind him and produced a much-used leather-bound book. The Belgian could feel his breathing quicken. He could not imagine that they could not hear it.

'*The Holy Bible*. Flemish version. Very devout. We found it by your bedside. I read your Bible very carefully, Mr Vermeulen. I must admit that it was the first time I have done so in many years. And then I spotted something, Mr Vermeulen. Little pinpricks that had been made under the first letter of the first sentence of some chapters. Very deliberate marks. They are not mistakes. And they only appear under the first letter of the first sentence of a chapter, nowhere else. And there we have it. Your code! You would transmit the chapter numbers and your controllers would understand from the collection of chapter numbers you had selected and the order in which you sent them, what the message is. It is clever, but it was not clever enough. So, you see, we have our proof.' He banged the Bible down on the table.

For the first time, the Belgian could say nothing. He did not know how to respond. He had been assured that it would be impossible for anyone to spot the marks in the Bible. He could not understand how the Dutchman had spotted them. Even he had trouble finding them and he knew they were there. He had nowhere to go.

The Dutchman now dropped his more conversational style and spoke in a firm manner in the Belgian's native Flemish.

'Vermeulen. Since the war started I have interrogated ten men who turned out to be Nazi spies. I would estimate that in half of the cases, the evidence against them was not as strong as it is with you. Eight of those men have been executed. The current interval between being found guilty of espionage in a court of law and execution is around five weeks. Do you want to ask me a question?'

The Belgian's shoulders sagged. He was terrified. It was taking all of his efforts to try to show no emotion, but he had no doubt that he was failing.

'Shall I help you with the question, Vermeulen? What you should really want to know now is what happened to the two spies who were not executed. Shall I tell you?' The Dutchman had reverted to English. His tone was markedly less aggressive. It was almost friendly.

Vermeulen nodded.

'They came to work for us. To carry on sending information to the Germans, but this time, the wrong information. Now, you would not actually do that yourself. But, of course, we do need your co-operation. We need it to locate the transmitter, to find the correct frequency and the times they would expect to hear from you and the correct use of the codes. We need you for all of that. And no tricks, no tiny changes to procedure that would alert the Germans to the fact that you have been captured. We would soon spot that, and that would be your death sentence.

'Can you imagine what it is like, Vermeulen, to be told one day that your final appeal against execution has been turned down and that you will die the next morning? Can you imagine how it feels to have to get through the rest of the day and then through that night? Who will you write to Vermeulen... anyone? Would you still believe enough to be able to pray? And then as you see the sun start to rise through the cell window, you will be alert to every sound, but even then, you will not hear them until they are in the cell. I've witnessed the execution of some of my spies. It is not a pleasant sight. The look of fear on a man's face as his hands are bound stays with you forever. If I close my eyes now, I can picture them, desperately looking round for someone to comfort them, for just a smile. They know then that – whatever drove them to be Nazi agents – it wasn't worth it. The distance from the cell to the gallows is very short, but I promise you it will be the longest walk of your life. And then they will strap your feet and place a black hood over your head and that will last another lifetime. Only you will know the muffled fear as you feel your hot breath close to you and the struggle to breathe as you wait for the trapdoor to open.'

The Dutchman paused while he lit another cigarette and the haze between the two of them thickened. For the first time, the Belgian could detect the very slightest trace of a smile on the Englishman's face, before it faded as he leaned back into the shadows again. The Belgian was sure he was on the verge of losing all physical control. Nothing that the instructors had told him had prepared him for this moment.

The Dutchman was in no hurry to continue as he carefully examined the end of his cigarette from different angles, before placing it again between his lips and inhaling deeply. He stared again at the Belgian. He could see it in his eyes now. There was a moment when their eyes told him it was over. It was usually quite sudden, the realisation that they knew the game was up. Often, this look of doom appeared before the man realised it himself. With a quiet satisfaction, he spoke again.

'So, what I need to know, Mr Vermeulen, is whether you wish to join the eight agents in unmarked graves under the walls of a British prison, or whether you want to join the two whose necks are still intact?'

Vermeulen was sobbing now, so much so that it was some time before he could speak properly. They were enormous sobs of sheer fear.

'You see, Vermeulen, I think the Germans see you as a clerk, nothing more than that. I think your role is to help another agent.

Someone more important, perhaps. I could be wrong, but that is my guess. Am I right?'

The Belgian fought hard to control his breathing before he was able to speak.

'I was never a Nazi, sir, I was fooled. There has been a misunderstanding, sir. I wanted to help Belgium. This is all such a relief, to be able to tell you the truth and to be able to help you.'

He was pleading now, his arms stretched out towards the two men in front of him. He did not know whether to be terrified or relieved. He was shaking and his voice quavering.

'I did not hate the Jews. Mendelssohn is one of my favourite composers. And my dentist – he is a Jew. I promise you, I never supplied any information to the Germans. I promise you, sir. I always intended that the minute the agent tried to give me information here, I would contact the authorities. You have my word.'

He was sobbing now, the tears streaking down the pale face, the bad skin. The Dutchman was used to seeing men fight for their life. It was his job to reduce them to this state. You break them down until they are more compliant than a baby. Then you can do what you want with them. No matter how many times he had seen it happen, it was no less edifying.

For the first time that morning – if it was morning – he stood up and walked round the table and towards the Belgian. His disposition was now friendly. He put one arm on his shoulder and spoke quietly to him in Flemish.

'What's his name, Arnold? The agent. What is he called?'

'I don't know the word in English… *pie*… it's a bird…' Vermeulen was speaking between loud sobs, struggling to catch his breath as he did so. He was desperate to finish the sentence, as if his life depended upon it.

'Magpie,' said the Dutchman. '*Une pie* means magpie in French.'

'One for sorrow.' It was the Englishman, speaking out loud for the first time.

'…and he's not a man. It's a woman.' The Belgian's voice had an eager tone to it now. He wanted to show he was doing all he could to help.

After that, the Belgian who had been so taciturn over the past week barely stopped talking for the next two days.

Chapter 4

London, May 1941

Late in the afternoon of Thursday, 1st May, five men gathered in a sun-filled room in a large house just behind Ham Common in south west London. The first hint of summer hung in the air and under a cloudless sky the day remained warm. The windows were firmly shut and barred, as they always were, meaning that silence prevailed as the men entered the room that was far larger than needed, but was the most secure room in a very secure building.

The Dutchman and the Englishman sat side-by-side, as three other men followed them into the room and arranged themselves opposite them.

A noticeably large man sank into the chair opposite the Dutchman and the Englishman, with the other two men flanking him. As with many men of his build, he moved in a careful and surprisingly dainty manner. He spoke first, addressing the man to his left.

'Jean-Louis, can I introduce Colonel Visser and Captain Edgar to you? Colonel Visser has spent most his career with your own *Deuxième Bureau* and also his own native Dutch Intelligence. He is now our chief interrogator at the London Reception Centre up in Clapham which I told you about the other day. He is our best source of new recruits. Captain Edgar is one of my top case officers here at MI5. Colonel Visser, Captain Edgar, Jean-Louis is here to represent the interests of the French Government in exile.' He nodded at the Dutchman and the Englishman in turn as he rearranged the notebook on his lap. 'Another success, I take it?'

Both men began to speak at the same time. With a generous gesture of his arm, the Dutchman allowed Captain Edgar to continue.

'Indeed, sir. Another triumph for Colonel Visser if I might say. Quite masterful. The Belgian was a miserable wretch, but he held out on us for far longer than anyone could have expected. That damned policeman in Oxford. We were quite possibly yards and even minutes away from catching Vermeulen red-handed with the transmitter. Then Vermeulen goes and throws up in the street, the policeman arrests Vermeulen and the whole operation is up the spout. Without the bloody transmitter, if you'll excuse my language, we had nothing on Vermeulen. Tricky job we had on our hands.'

'You see, Professor Newby,' Colonel Visser was speaking now, cutting across Captain Edgar and directly addressing the large man in front of them, 'he had been well-trained. To a point. They always are well-trained; the Germans know what they are doing. But what matters is where that point is. Vermeulen knew that we had no evidence on him and his confidence increased as the interrogation went on – and not without reason. Without the transmitter we had a Belgian national who had been living openly in this country for just under a year and who had no contact with the enemy in that time. All of his possessions had been checked when he entered this country and they had been cleared then. He had no reason to suspect that we had anything on him now. He had enough wit about him to do as they had told him. I come across it all of the time. "Stick to your story. If they have anything against you, you will know soon enough." You can almost see their lips moving as they repeat that to themselves.'

The Dutchman cleared his throat. He desperately wanted a cigarette but he had been warned of the professor's aversion to them.

'They even used a classic Abwehr technique by deliberately building a flaw into his story. The idea is that we think we have spotted something against him, but he is prepared for that and eventually owns up to it and then it appears not to be so important. In his case, it was pretending to be a lawyer. We made him admit that he was just a clerk. He claims that this was his opportunity to be somebody, that no harm was intended, and we are then meant to think that maybe he is not really a spy after all, just a fool.'

The Dutchman could feel the packet of Players Navy Cut getting heavier in his shirt pocket.

'So, a week into the interrogation he must have felt confident. And as he felt more confident, the more anxious I became. I was certain that he must have brought something incriminating with him into England. The transmitter would have come separately in a parachute drop or by some other route and then been cached for him, but he would have carried some kind of codebook in with him. It was impossible that he could be so clean. Our information from Brussels was so good that we knew he was an agent. So I went through all of his possessions myself. Every night after the interrogations, I went through everything, even though my men had already searched everything twice over. The Bible was the last item I looked at. It was clever. The pinpricks did not begin until halfway into Exodus and I believe that I only spotted the first one because I still had my desk lamp on as the sun rose through the window, and that combination of light somehow picked out the marks. Divine providence.'

That reference did not appear to be appreciated by the professor of theology who sat opposite him.

'There we have it. We confronted him with this evidence, and then it really was just a matter of time.'

'Will he work for us then?'

'Oh yes indeed, Professor.' Captain Edgar was speaking now. His tall frame leaning forward in the low chair, edging him closer to the other three and placing him in front of Colonel Visser.

'Colonel Visser's description of a judicial execution was masterful. It certainly did the trick. I thought Vermeulen was going to pass out there and then. Good job the chap doesn't have a weak heart.'

Professor Newby continued looking at Captain Edgar for some time after he had finished. He turned to the Frenchman on his left.

'Jean-Louis. We are called the "twenty committee" because of the two Roman numerals, XX. They represent the words double cross, hence the two Xs, which also signify twenty in Latin as I am sure you are aware. *Vingt.* Our role in the Double Cross Committee or "twenty committee" as you may sometimes hear it referred to, is to identify German spies whom we can turn into double agents. In other words, we find them and then persuade them to work for us. Colonel Visser is our best source of new recruits. So what I need to know from Colonel Visser and Captain Edgar is whether we can turn Arnold Vermeulen.'

Captain Edgar spoke first. 'You can turn Arnold Vermeulen in any direction you want, Professor. Left, right, upside down, inside out. You name it. He's yours to do what you want with.'

'Do you share this assessment, Colonel Visser?'

There was a hesitation from the Dutchman, who was weighing his words in marked contrast to Captain Edgar's enthusiasm. 'Indeed, Professor. But I would have a significant concern.'

'Which is?'

'Which is that, in himself, Vermeulen is only of secondary interest. There is very little that we can get directly from him. He has not been involved in any espionage since his arrival in this country. His only real interest to us is as a way of getting to the primary agent, whom he refers to by the code name Magpie. We must do nothing that would jeopardise our chances of getting hold of her. To do that, we have to handle Vermeulen very carefully.'

'What kind of a chap is he?'

'He is, as Captain Edgar says and as is all too obvious to any observer, a weak and pathetic individual. He is a loner. A small man, consumed and possibly motivated by resentment and envy and prejudice. He saw the German conquest of Belgium as an ideal opportunity to be someone for perhaps the first time in his life. However, we must not make the mistake of underestimating him. This man is not a complete fool, as much as we would like to think so. He has his strengths. Apart from his fluency in English and his ability with radios, he has a certain stubbornness, he has a commitment.'

'By which you mean what, Colonel?' This was the man to the Professor's right who, up to this point, had been busy taking notes.

'Despite what we think of him, he still volunteered to help the Germans. Maybe he did not envisage risking his life as a spy in this country, but he was still motivated by some kind of an ideological commitment to the Nazi cause. We have to trust him if we are to get our *entrée* to Magpie. She is our real aim. And I am not sure how far we can trust Arnold Vermeulen.'

Colonel Visser gestured towards Captain Edgar on his right. 'We have done well to obtain a confession from Vermeulen. But without Magpie, it will mean nothing.'

'What do we know about Magpie?' This was the Frenchman to the left of the professor.

'We know Magpie is important,' said Edgar. 'We know she is a woman and that she is French. Other than that, we know nothing. Nothing.'

'Narrows it down somewhat,' said the professor. The others smiled briefly. There was a long silence. The sun had dropped now, but the room was still too warm and perfectly quiet. Professor Newby was the first to speak.

'Correct me if I am wrong, Jean-Louis, but was there not a mass exodus of population after the Germans conquered France?'

Jean-Louis spoke in a resigned manner, lowering his head, which less-kind observers than those in the room might have imagined was shame. 'The population of France is forty million. We estimate that up to a quarter of the population left their homes around the time of the German invasion. The population of Paris was three million before the Germans marched in on 14th June. Less than a million were still there when they actually arrived. Cities like Chartres, where my wife's family is from, like Troyes and like Évreux in Normandy, they just emptied.'

'A picture of chaos, you see,' said the professor. 'Utter chaos. A quarter of the bloody population on the road, no civil order, tens of thousands of French refugees end up over here, and for the Germans to slip one or two agents in among them… well, it was the easiest thing in the world, and Visser has indeed caught some of them. Apologies Jean-Louis, but you get my meaning. We are searching for a needle in the proverbial haystack.'

'How do you propose we find her, Visser?' asked the Frenchman.

At this point, both Visser and Edgar smiled and eased back in their chairs.

'Oh, we know how to find her all right.' Edgar was smiling and removing a map from his jacket pocket.

'You see,' Visser added as Captain Edgar got up and spread the map out on a table near the door, 'Arnold Vermeulen has been a good deal more helpful than I think we may have given him credit for.'

–

The following day began particularly early for Arnold Vermeulen. He had been alone in his cell at the Royal Victoria Patriotic School since his interrogation had ended the previous day. Apart from the guards checking on him twice an hour, sometimes more, he had been alone with his thoughts.

At first, he had felt a sense of utter relief: that the constant interrogations were over; that they had promised to spare his life in exchange for him agreeing to work for them, and relief that his war was over. He had never meant it to go this far. He just wanted to show those Jews that they could not run things their way anymore. In his worst nightmares, he could never have imagined that the Nazis would ask him to become an active spy for them. In England. It was a ridiculous notion. His health was not up to it. He had spent the past year waiting for a knock on the door.

The sense of relief had allowed him to have his first proper sleep since arriving here, but it had been a brief one. He woke up drenched in sweat and overwhelmed by terrible thoughts. What if it was not true? What if they had deceived him? Could it be a trick? He spent the next couple of hours reassuring himself that without Magpie, he was useless to them – and he was the only person who could give them Magpie. He relaxed and even managed to eat all of the stew they brought him early in the evening, along with bread that didn't taste like bread, and a dry pudding. This time he fell into a truly deep sleep, which he remained in until the cell door burst open at five in the morning.

The small cell, with its pervading smell of new concrete, was filled with two guards, two other men wearing a different military uniform, and the tall Englishman who had sat in on all of the interrogations. He spoke.

'Get up, Vermeulen, we are moving you.'

The Belgian stood in the centre of the cell. Two of the guards had moved behind him. One of the men in the uniforms he had not seen before threw some clothes on the bed.

'Get undressed and put those on.'

Vermeulen was dazed. He looked around the cell, smiling in the forlorn hope that one person in the cell would return his smile. Slowly, he started to remove his own clothes, which he had fallen asleep in, and which were the ones he had been allowed to wear since his arrest, after they had examined them. He removed the cardigan that his mother had knitted for him a year before she died, the shirt, and the trousers from which they had already removed the belt. He stood there in his underpants, vest and socks, shivering in fear and the cold of the early morning.

'Carry on.'

Vermeulen peeled off the socks, hoping no one would notice the holes in the heels and then the vest, his spindly legs, small pot-belly, hairless chest and pock-marked shoulders exposed.

'Everything.'

Vermeulen could not remember the last time anyone had seen him naked. He felt totally humiliated. He turned round hoping for some privacy, but the guards behind could see him now. He was sure that one of them was grinning at him. He removed his underpants and tried to put on the new trousers as fast as possible in one movement, but only succeeded in slipping on the bed and exposing himself to everyone in the cell, so prolonging the embarrassment. He could feel tears welling up in his eyes again, his humiliation complete.

He stood in front of the men in the doorway, in the rough grey trousers and matching shirt and clog-like shoes without any socks. The guards handcuffed his arms behind his back and the Englishman spoke in an almost casual manner.

'Things did not work out as we had expected them to, Vermeulen. We are going to have to deal with you in a different way. Follow me.'

With that, the whimpering Vermeulen was virtually dragged out of his cell, across the courtyard – all of which he was seeing for the first time as he was without a blindfold, which he knew must be an ominous sign – and hauled into the back of a black van. He was placed on a small wooden bench which went along the side of the van, with the two men in the new uniform on each side of him.

They drove for well over an hour. At the very start of the journey he had asked his new guards where he was being taken, but the reply of '*Not a word*,' was accompanied by him being pushed back on the bench. Not in an aggressive manner, but it did mean that his handcuffed arms were pinioned against the side of the van and that hurt. He knew what was happening. They had fooled him. The English were not supposed to act like this. They were going to torture him now and he had nothing more to tell them. He had told them everything he knew. 'We are going to have to deal with you in a different way,' the Englishman had said. He spent the rest of the journey imagining every way in which they were going to deal with him, and each way was worse than the one he had thought of previously.

By the time they arrived at their destination, daylight had taken hold. The van had stopped outside enormous gates and Vermeulen was led round to the main entrance. The sign said 'Wormwood Scrubs' and Vermeulen recognised the prison from the bus. He lived just two or three miles from here, and for a while he had had a job in the hospital next door. A small side-gate half-opened and the tall Englishman walked ahead of them. His long gait meant that the guards had to hurry Vermeulen along to keep up.

40

They stopped at a guardhouse, where forms were quickly exchanged, quiet words spoken and shackles attached to his ankles. They continued their progress through the prison, accompanied now by two armed guards in front and two more behind, as far as he could make out. He was able to walk in the shackles, but not without considerable noise and some discomfort as they chafed against the rough material of his trousers. Down a long corridor with barred windows along one side, through a double set of locked doors and into an enormous room, which felt like an empty factory. In the gloom Vermeulen could make out no distinguishing features, although there appeared to be some large machinery against a far wall. The small group marched across the rough concrete floor to the centre of room, their footsteps and Vermeulen's chains echoing against the distant walls. As they reached the centre, the tall Englishman turned abruptly and walked towards the Belgian.

He had a pistol in his right hand, which he slowly raised, holding the barrel against Vermeulen's temple. The Belgian struggled, but the two guards had little trouble in holding him steady.

'You are of no use to us now, Vermeulen. The truth is that we do not trust you. You have reached the end of the road.'

There was silence in the room, broken only by Vermeulen's panicked breathing and the echoing sound of the safety catch being released. The Englishman waited. The Belgian's eyes were wide open, as was his mouth. No sound came out. Vermeulen slumped to the floor.

The Englishman circled the body, prodding it once with his shoe before turning to the guards.

'Take him away.'

–

When Captain Edgar came to visit Arnold Vermeulen later that morning, he found the Belgian lying on the metal bed, curled into a foetal position. When he saw Edgar enter the room he instinctively moved away from him, so that by the time the door shut he had forced himself into the back of the bed, against the corner of the two walls. They were alone.

'Please relax, Vermeulen.' The Englishman spoke in a quiet voice, but Vermeulen had no trouble hearing it.

'Didn't quite go to plan before, sorry about that.' He gave the impression of not being very sorry at all. He drew up a chair close to the bed, very close to Vermeulen. The Belgian was unable to get any further away from Edgar. 'Plan was to pull the trigger, you would just hear an empty click and realise that the pistol was not loaded. I would then tell you this is what would happen to you if you did not do exactly as we ask of you. Any tricks, anything less than total co-operation and that would be your fate. Except, of course, next time the pistol would be loaded. Only thing, we didn't count on you fainting down there, which is why I am making this little speech now.'

Vermeulen nodded eagerly.

'I just wanted you to realise quite how serious we are. You told us on Wednesday that you have met Magpie once. So she knows who you are. That means that without you, we cannot get to Magpie. So you are working for us now. And that means no tricks, no using the secret warning signals that you no doubt have agreed, nothing clever. When you start your transmissions, you do it by the book. If you use any device like a warning word to let them know that you've been turned, we will find out. Just do everything that we ask of you. If you don't, you now know exactly what the consequences will be.'

The Englishman stood up, looking around the room as he did so. 'Bit grim in here. This was where you were going to be staying, but instead we have decided to move you back to your bedsit in Acton. We're pretty certain that no one has been around there looking for you, so the story will be that you went to visit a friend in the north. Don't worry, for the first time in a long while, Vermeulen, you are not going to be on your own. You will have company. Your landlady has very obligingly made arrangements for my men to occupy the other three bedsits in the house. She thinks you are an important engineer and three colleagues are moving in.'

The Englishman slapped his hand a bit too hard on Vermeulen's leg and the Belgian jumped. 'So you see, Vermeulen, for the first time in your life, someone thinks you are important! Now get ready, we've got a busy couple of days.' To all intents and purposes the Englishman could have been describing the plans for the weekend to an old friend up from the country.

'Today we need to go to Oxford, don't we? Pick up the transmitter. And on Sunday... we go for a walk in the park.'

At ten minutes to eleven on the first Sunday that May, a woman in her mid-twenties emerged from Ealing Common tube station in west London. She had taken care to dress in a manner designed to attract minimum attention. Her slim figure and long legs were concealed by a slightly larger than necessary raincoat that was closer to shabby than smart, but only just. Her long dark hair was covered by a plain woollen scarf. She came out of the station and turned right, taking care to walk neither too fast nor too slowly. Everything about her was calculated to ensure that she blended in. She was grateful for the opportunity for fresh air that the short walk would afford her. A journey that she could have comfortably done in three quarters of an hour had actually begun more than three hours ago in central London. Since then, she had taken a circuitous route. Walking, buses, different tube lines, waiting at stations and then crossing to other lines. Only when she was absolutely sure that there was no chance she could have been followed, did she begin the final phase of the journey that had brought her to her intended destination.

A few hundred yards from the station, on the other side of the main road, was a narrow strip of parkland. Park was perhaps too grand a word. 'Gardens' it was called, but it seemed more like a wide strip of grass to her, buffeted between a narrow road behind and the main road. The gardens were actually split in two, bisected by a broad avenue.

To anyone watching her, her pace had not changed, but she had slowed down very slightly, enough to be able to look carefully into the larger of the two small strips of park. He was there, as he had been a fortnight ago when she first met him, and as he had been on every other alternate Sunday for the few weeks before that. On those previous occasions she had not actually gone into the park but had walked past it to satisfy herself that he would be there when she needed him.

She noticed that the little man was sitting on the bench furthest away from the station. Next to him, he had placed his newspaper, and on top of the newspaper sat his hat. He had signalled that it was safe to meet. If he was wearing his hat, but with the newspaper on the bench next to him, that would mean come back in half an hour as he was not certain all was clear. If he was wearing his hat and reading his newspaper, it was not safe to meet and she would calmly continue her walk.

The woman entered the small park and casually approached the bench. No one else was in the park; there never seemed to be anyone. It was not the kind of place where anyone would want to sit down for too long, not even the English.

'Is this seat free?' She spoke in English.

'Yes, of course, please let me remove my newspaper.' The final check. 'I am reserving this for a friend' would have been a warning, but by then it would have probably been too late. Vermeulen had done all that they had asked of him and Magpie had flown safely into his nest. He knew that at least half a dozen men were watching him, but since Friday he had been quite clear in his mind. He would do whatever they asked.

Satisfied that it was safe, the woman spoke in French.

'You have the transmitter now?' She was looking ahead of her as she talked. She was relaxed, but her dark eyes were darting left and right as she spoke, taking in everything around her. Vermeulen had felt a surge of desire when he first saw her. He knew that a woman like this would not even think about him, but even to be sitting next to her made his heart race.

She had to repeat the question.

'Yes, I collected it soon after we met two weeks ago.'

'No problems?'

'None. It had been well hidden. It is in good working order.'

'Good. You can send your first transmission then.'

'And what shall I tell them?'

'That I am well, and I am working on the main plan. I hope to have news soon. That's all. They are to be patient.'

—

Three days later, Captain Edgar returned to the large house on Ham Common. This time, Professor Newby was on his own, in a study on the top floor, behind an enormous desk, gazing out of the window and all but shielded from view by a wall of files piled up in front of him. He stood up when Edgar entered the room and pointed him towards the two armchairs on either side of an unlit fireplace.

'More success, I gather from your message?'

'Indeed, sir.' Edgar noticed that the professor was pouring two very large measures from an ornate decanter. From bitter experience

44

he knew that this would be a very dry sherry, dry to the extent of being barely palatable. The first time he had met Newby, the professor had subjected him to an unnecessarily long story about how he had brought a dozen bottles of this sherry over from Spain before the war. At the time, Edgar had thought better of affecting anything other than pleasure at drinking it. Now Newby treated him as a fellow connoisseur.

'Let us drink to it while you tell me.'

Edgar allowed the merest hint of the sherry to touch his lips before he spoke.

'As agreed, we gave Vermeulen a bit of a scare on Friday. Made it bloody clear to him what would happen if he didn't play ball. Then we made a fuss of him, gave him a hot bath and a decent meal and even some wine and a clean set of clothes, though he does seem to have a strange attachment to this filthy cardigan he insists on wearing. Took him down to Oxford first thing the next morning and found the transmitter straight away. Wrapped in an oilskin inside a suitcase, which was also wrapped in an oilskin. That had been carefully stashed in the rafters of a disused boatyard. Probably been there best part of a year, hard to tell. Clever though. All Vermeulen would have had to do was climb the remains of a metal ladder attached to the wall, pull the package out with a boathook that was left there, remove the outer oilskin and then you have a man with a case. Nothing too unusual about it at all. Would be nice to get our hands on the chap who put the transmitter there, but I suppose we shouldn't be greedy.'

'Does the radio work?'

'Oh yes. Have to hand it to the Germans, sir. Superb bit of machinery. Our chaps have had a look at it, given it a bit of a clean-up, but works like clockwork, if that's the correct phrase. Say what you like about them, sir, but they're bloody impressive engineers.'

'And has the obliging Mr Vermeulen had occasion to use the transmitter yet?'

'He made his first transmission on Sunday evening. That is his protocol, he tells us. To go to the park every other Sunday at a quarter to eleven and if Magpie has anything for him, she turns up at eleven. Appears the poor chap has been religiously turning up at the park every Sunday since he arrived here, terrified at getting it wrong. That was his downfall, of course; he had become such a stickler for routine that the moment he changed it, when he went to Oxford, we realised something was up. So, Magpie first turns up two weeks ago, tells him she is ready for her first message to be sent back to their bosses and he's to retrieve the transmitter, which he tries to do the following Sunday – the day we caught him. Luckily, we had matters neatly tied up in time for our new friend to be dutifully sat on his park bench in time for her arrival the next Sunday. As I say, he made his transmission that night. Tuned in at the appointed time, used the Bible code and told his bosses that Magpie was now active, and to expect to hear from her soon. Germans replied back that they were surprised it had taken so long, but to wish her luck.'

'Did Vermeulen behave during the transmission?'

'Yes. We had a couple of our most experienced radio chaps watching over him. They know what to look for. Selection of frequency, speed of his keying, any deliberate mistakes – anything that would suggest he was trying to surreptitiously let the Germans know that he has been compromised. As far as they can tell, he was as good as gold.'

'And how did the meeting itself go?'

'Just as Vermeulen said it would. Bang on eleven o'clock, woman turns up the main road opposite the park. Vermeulen has been sat there for fifteen minutes, all his signals on green. We've got the place well covered, of course, but keep well back. Over she comes. They have a little chat. She leaves ten minutes later.'

'And you were able to follow her?'

'Only just. Very smart lady she is, very smart. She was a textbook example of how to do it. If we hadn't put a tail of seven people on her, we wouldn't have made it. She went to Ealing Common Station and then spent the next two hours on a tour of London. Thought we'd lost her at one stage on the Strand heading towards Fleet Street but then one of our chaps spotted her on a bus going in the opposite direction. It stopped at a red light and he managed to get on. She got off in Northumberland Avenue and then walked down the Embankment, across Westminster Bridge and into St Thomas's Hospital. Magpie, Professor, turns out to be a nurse.'

'And does this nurse have a name?'

'Indeed she does. Nathalie Mercier. Aged twenty-six. From Paris. Arrived in England second of June last year. Story was that she had been treating French soldiers and was scared of what the Germans would do to her. As far as we can tell, she was certainly working in a field hospital in Dunkirk at the time of the evacuation, so nothing suspicious about her. Cleared at Balham at the end of June.'

'Is she a genuine nurse?'

'Indeed. Met her matron. They think she is wonderful. Very competent and quite beautiful, I must tell you, sir. Slim figure, long legs and long dark hair. Her eyes are jet-black, quite the most beautiful ones I have ever seen. Patients adore her, especially the chaps.'

'Naturally. And what did matron say?'

'This is where it is most fortuitous, sir. Contacted matron and said "We need to see you on a matter of national security, please say nothing to anyone," usual routine. When I arrive, I say it is in connection with Nathalie Mercier – we knew her name from when we followed her into the nurses' quarters. "Ah," says Matron. "It must be about her transfer request." Appears that the beautiful Nathalie has applied to be transferred to a military hospital. Not fussy which one, any one would do it seems, though she would prefer to be in the London area. She said she felt she wanted to give something back after France's defeat, do her bit for the Allied cause. Matron believes it, of course, which is convenient for us because we have a ready-made cover story about why we're interested in her.'

'Which presumably is the reason why she was now ready to make contact with the Germans. So you said…?'

'Yes, of course! I was indeed here to check her out as to whether she can get security clearance to work in a military hospital. No need after all to resort to the rather complicated tale I had prepared for Matron about needing to check over some paperwork. Matron would be sorry to lose her, but quite understands.'

Professor Newby sat still, holding his sherry glass in front of him with both hands, gently turning the glass and watching the slow movement of the drink. Edgar's sherry remained untouched.

'This has the makings of something most interesting, Captain Edgar. In the fullness of time we will grant Nurse Mercier her request. Until then, we have her exactly where we want her.'

Chapter 5

Surrey, August 1933

Owen Quinn had spent the summer of 1933 watching and playing as much cricket as he could manage, and also watching his grandfather die at a hospital in Guildford.

He was still a few months short of his sixteenth birthday, unaware that these few weeks would mark his transition from childhood to adulthood.

The summer had started very promisingly. His grandfather's illness, that no one discussed, meant that he was able to use his grandfather's ticket for the Test Match against the West Indies at the Oval. The ticket allowed entry every day, although the match ended early on the third day thanks to the English bowler, Marriott, taking eleven West Indies wickets. Quinn had spent the rest of the day exploring the heart of London. He had walked down Whitehall to the Houses of Parliament. He had stood outside 10 Downing Street and Buckingham Palace, and had even gone into some of the shops in Oxford Street. He had sat by a small lake in St James's Park eating his cheese and pickle sandwiches, before walking back to Waterloo Station to catch a train home in a carriage full of businessmen and civil servants. He could not have imagined being happier.

Cricket was still his passion. In the past year he had become taller and his slender figure had filled out enough for him to become a useful, quick bowler and careful batsman in the summer, and a quick defender in the winter. His grandfather had taken to coaching him and came to watch him when he could. After one game, when Owen had taken four wickets and scored a match-winning forty-three his grandfather had briefly placed an arm round his shoulder as they walked to the car. 'You played like a proper Yorkshire man then.' Owen knew it was meant as the ultimate compliment.

But other passions were creeping in, though Quinn was too naive at the time to recognise them for what they were. He was in the top French class at his grammar school and towards the end of term their teacher, grateful for such a responsive group of students, took the enthusiastic class to London to see a French film that he told them all of France was talking about. Feeling at the height of sophistication and allowed to wear their own clothes, the small group of boys travelled up from Surrey in the company of Mr Bennett who, despite his impeccable English accent which even extended to when he spoke French, still insisted on being addressed as Monsieur Bennett.

The film was *Boudu sauvé des eaux*. It was a witty comedy about a businessman who saved a tramp, and the effect that the tramp subsequently had on the businessman's family. Monsieur Bennett told the boys that Jean Renoir was a very important director, but on the journey back to Surrey it was the actresses that he could not get out of his mind. It was not just their beauty. It was the style and sophistication that he had never observed in anyone in England. At night, he began to dream of them. Accepting that they were unlikely to reciprocate his interest, however fluent in French he might become, he began to return the waves and greetings of the girl across the road, who was the same age as him and went to the girls' grammar school. He started to time his leaving the house at the same time as she left hers so that they could walk to the bus stop together. Sometimes in the evening they would stand and talk outside one of their neat semi-detached houses. They even went for walks in the park. Towards the end of that summer, he started to allow his arm to brush against hers, and on some nights she would move hers away only slowly. *If only*, he thought, *she was French*.

Owen Quinn was close to his grandfather, who had moved down from Yorkshire in search of work. He did not share the same middle-class reserve as the rest of his family. He remembered the scandalised silence in the family when his grandfather had announced that he was no longer going to church every Sunday. When his parents had asked him why he was no longer going, his grandfather asked them to give him one good reason why he should. His parents exchanged low glances, but could not come up with a satisfactory reason. Owen decided then that when it was up to him, he would not go to church either.

He was someone who the young Owen could talk openly to, so when he was moved into hospital that July, Owen visited him most days. Owen's grandmother and mother and aunt visited every day, but their visits comprised them sitting still by the bed, handbags tightly clutched on their laps, punctuating the silence with 'How are you feeling, Arthur?' or 'Is there anything that we can get you?' They would huddle together in the corridor outside his room, whispering and hoping that Owen would not see them dab their eyes.

He took to visiting his grandfather on his own and they would talk openly, though his grandfather was losing the ability to talk at any length. One day he remarked to his grandfather that it didn't seem like he was getting better. He immediately regretted saying this, but his grandfather placed his hand on top of Owen's hand. He told him he was the first person to acknowledge this and how much he appreciated it. They sat there, hand-in-hand, until his mother and grandmother arrived.

On a baking Thursday at the end of August, when the grass was beginning to turn brown, he again found himself alone with his grandfather, who was having trouble breathing now and barely ate. His skin seemed to have changed colour and was pulled tight across his face and arms. It was early afternoon and the sunbeams were darting into the room through the large window, catching a storm of specks of floating dust as they did so.

His grandfather was drifting in and out of sleep, his uneaten lunch on a tray at the side of the bed, the smell of cabbage, boiled potato and beef stew pervading the room. Owen had moved over to the window, looking down at life going on as normal below and wondering how that could be. His grandfather spoke and Owen moved over to the bed.

'Tell me, Owen. What do you want to do when you are older?'

'Play cricket for England, I suppose.'

They both smiled.

'I'd probably like to do something with my geography or my French. In fact, I think I would even like to marry a beautiful French-woman!'

Owen smiled as he had expected his grandfather to do – and he did, but only very briefly. He held Owen's hand tight.

'Be careful what you wish for.'

He then fell asleep. Owen thought he would have to ask his grandfather what he meant by that later. But then his grandmother arrived with his parents and his uncle and aunt, and Owen was ushered out of the room. He went home on his own. His grandfather died that night. He could never get out of his mind his grandfather's last words to him.

Be careful what you wish for.

Crete, 22nd May 1941

The German attack on Crete had been raging for days and it was evident that the Allied grip on the island was slipping. The night before, the Germans had captured Maleme airfield. They were now able to land troops and all the supplies they needed, as well as having a base for their Stuka dive-bombers. It was these planes that had launched wave after wave of attacks on the British naval ships that had been helping to defend the island. The fall of Crete was now just a matter of time.

The eight-hundred-man crew of HMS *Gloucester* were exhausted. Alongside HMS *Fiji* they were trying to rescue survivors from the destroyer HMS *Greyhound*, but were coming under constant German attack. The RAF had withdrawn their air cover. Only half a dozen planes remained on the Greek island and rather than sacrificing them, they had been sent to Egypt. The reputation of the cruiser, known as *The Fighting* G, meant little now. More waves of Stuka dive-bombers came and HMS *Fiji* was fatally hit. HMS *Gloucester* was running out of ammunition and defenceless when another Stuka attack came in.

Lieutenant Owen Quinn had no idea how long he had been in the water. As he slipped in and out of consciousness, he could not even be sure that he *was* in the water. There was more flotsam and debris and bodies around him than water, and any water that he could make out was black and thick with oil or stained red with blood.

He was twenty-three and too young to die. He had been in the Royal Navy for eighteen months. He had just finished his degree in geography at London University when he'd joined up and his interest in the weather, tides, coastlines and beaches had been put to good effect. He had been commissioned as a navigation officer and was having 'a good war'. He found the action they had been involved in – and there had been plenty of that – exhilarating and he feared nothing. He never thought he would die. Until now.

He lost his grip on the oil-stained plank of wood that had been keeping him afloat, but was pulled back to safety by a man who looked like one of the stewards from the officers' mess.

The steward was still wearing a white jacket, but the oil stains made it look like a black and white striped football shirt. Quinn tried to speak to the man, but his throat was too dry and there was a vicious taste of oil and salt in his mouth.

He thought he could make out a lifeboat in front of him, weaving its way through the wreckage to haul any survivors aboard. Quinn tried to swim towards it, but he could not move one of his legs and his back was in agony.

Again, he slipped below the surface and again he was hauled back by the steward dragging him up by his collar. The lifeboat was gone now. He was resigned to his fate, but without any sense of acceptance. No life flashed before him. The steward who had twice saved his life, and whose name he now remembered was Travers, let out a groan. A bloody froth bubbled from his mouth and he slipped off the plank and smoothly into the sea. Less than a minute later, behind him he heard the clank of oars and a cry of 'Here's one!' as a lifebelt tied to a rope was thrown just in front of him.

His greatest wish was for a drink of water and then to be rescued and it was about to happen.

Be careful what you wish for.

Chapter 6

Hertfordshire, November 1941

The country road was narrow and potholed and the ambulance appeared to have been specially chosen for its lack of suspension. The driver was under the impression that, after weeks at sea in a hospital ship, what an injured Royal Navy officer would most appreciate was a constant stream of jolly chatter. There were a few feeble jokes, a long story about how his wife was not coping with rationing – 'They ought to take a person's weight into account, sir' – and an account of how his mother was convinced she had seen a German spy in her church – 'He was staring at her, sir' – but for some reason the authorities had not been interested. For most of the journey from Southampton he had sustained this commentary through the small window behind his left shoulder. He had to slightly turn around as he did so and each time he did that, the ambulance lurched a bit too much for Owen Quinn's liking.

As they drove around London the driver shared with Quinn his own insight into how the war could be won – 'We need to bomb the hell out of them, sir, if you'll excuse the language, sir.' Just north of London, the nurse in the back did manage to persuade the driver to keep quiet for a while as the patient was trying to sleep. The driver then went onto a series of smaller roads. 'We'll be there soon, sir,' had been his refrain for the past hour and now the road felt like a dirt track and every movement jarred his back and leg. After a while the ambulance slowed down almost to a halt and made a sharp left turn.

'Here we are, sir. Calcotte Grange.'

The road surface for the next half a mile was surprisingly smooth.

Calcotte Grange had been many things in its one-hundred-year history. It lay in open countryside north of St Albans in Hertfordshire and was built by the family after whom it was named. They had

53

made their fortune in India and were keen to display it. As a result, everything about the house was larger than necessary. There were far more rooms than they needed and those rooms were bigger than required. The drive was longer and wider than many of the local roads and many of the side buildings and outhouses had no real purpose whatsoever and had been empty since they were built.

But what they possessed in wealth, the Calcottes lacked in sensitivity. Misinterpreting the lack of any obvious signs of gratitude or even admiration from their neighbours, they assumed this was because the house was not impressive enough. As a result they embarked upon a second phase of utterly unnecessary building. At the centre of this was a chapel. Characteristically, the chapel dwarfed the local church. Locals called it Calcotte Cathedral.

The family's lack of judgement became their downfall. A lack of funds prevented the completion of the chapel and forced the sale of the property before the turn of the century. Calcotte Grange became a girls' school before being converted into a nursing home for recuperating officers in 1916. After the war, it remained a nursing home and in 1940 reverted to its military use, becoming a hospital for Royal Navy officers.

The Royal Navy had cause to be grateful for the Calcottes' unintended munificence. The large rooms had become small wards and at last the building that had been intended as the chapel was completed, though by now it had become a physiotherapy centre. The purpose of Calcotte Grange was to treat officers who no longer needed acute care. For most of the patients, the hospital was where they were sent to recover, with the hope that they would soon be fit enough to resume active service.

It was to Calcotte Grange that Lieutenant Owen Quinn was brought in November 1941, six months to the day from when HMS *Gloucester* had been sunk. His memories of the hours and days after his rescue were a series of blurred photographs rather than a clear film. The precious drink of water just after he was hauled into the lifeboat, the excruciating agony of his back and leg, the perilous transfer to the rescue ship and then the morphine and the oblivion until they reached Alexandria.

He had since been told that for a couple of days he was touch and go. He had lost a lot of blood and there were concerns that his wounds had been infected in the filthy water. But, at the age of twenty-three, he had youth on his side and after a delirious first week he was on a very slow road to recovery. He had suffered disc damage to his back and broken his right femur, but the doctors assured him he would be back at sea within a year. Three operations later he was on a hospital ship back to England and Calcotte Grange.

He had arrived at Calcotte Grange at night and awoke on his first morning to find his parents sitting nervously at his bedside. His father was still wearing his coat, scarf and gloves. His mother had adopted the same pose as she had at her father's bedside: anxiously clutching her handbag to her lap. She allowed herself a brief display of emotion and gave her son a peck on his cheek. Her eyelashes were moist as they brushed his cheekbone. His father became uncharacteristically jolly. His conversation fluctuated between detailed accounts of cricket matches from that summer and the tedious story of how the local council had allowed him a whole two days off to come and visit his son. They remained for two hours and, confident that their only child would live, left, promising to return before Christmas.

Quinn quickly settled into the routine of the hospital. He was in a ward with three other men. One never spoke more than three or four words at a time, preferring to lean on the windowsill and stare out over the open Hertfordshire countryside. He had been in the Arctic convoys. The other two were lieutenant commanders. One had also been wounded in the Mediterranean and had been in the same hospital as Quinn in Alexandria, and there was no detail of his injuries or indeed the man's naval career of which Quinn or the other patients were left unaware. The other had been injured while supervising the loading of his ship in Devonport, which he didn't talk about very much. He spent much of his time reading Dickens.

On his second day, he had a series of consultations. He was examined by the senior medical officer and the senior physiotherapist. They studied his file and concurred with the doctors in Alexandria: he would be back at sea sometime in 1942. '*Absolutely no reason why not.*'

The physiotherapy routine was brutal and he had to go through it every day, apart from Sunday, but by the New Year he no longer needed the wheelchair and his aim was to walk without the aid of sticks by Easter.

The senior medical officer, Dr Farrow, was a kindly man who had worked in a field hospital on the Western Front in the Great War and then returned to general practice in Norfolk. He should have retired in 1940, but the war had prevented that. He had a permanent air of weariness about him.

At the beginning of January, Dr Farrow received a visit from three men, two senior Royal Navy officers and a tall man in a dark coat who never gave his name but said he was involved in intelligence planning. The two Navy officers were clearly there to make Dr Farrow understand that the visit was sanctioned by the Navy. It was the tall man in the dark coat who did all of the talking.

He wanted details of all the patients in Calcotte Grange: their names, ranks, ages, injuries and prognoses. Dr Farrow started to explain that this was irregular, that there were ethical considerations, but he was told firmly by one of the Navy officers that this was official business and his co-operation was required. '*All the ethics have been taken care of, Farrow,*' he was assured. He was unsure what that meant, but was too tired to argue.

Dr Farrow went through the sixty-three patients currently in Calcotte Grange. The tall man clearly had something in mind. Those with more serious injuries who were unlikely to recover for some time were eliminated, as were those over the age of forty or above the rank of lieutenant commander. They were soon down to thirteen names.

'Forgot. One more criterion. Any of these chaps married?'

Farrow looked at their details again. The list was reduced to eight.

'All right, let's have their files out, need to see a bit more detail.'

The Navy officers then looked at the files one by one, muttering to each other as they did so. Three more came out. Five remained.

The tall man studied the names carefully.

'What does Broadhurst do?'

'Gunnery officer,' replied one of the Navy men.

The tall man shook his head and handed the file back to Dr Farrow.

'And Bevan?'

One of the Navy men peered over the tall man's shoulder and then consulted a list of his own.

'Engineer. Same as Stewart here,' pointing to another file.

Again he shook his head and handed the files back to Dr Farrow. Three files were spread out in front of him now. He was studying their photographs. He pulled one file out.

'He seems right.'

Farrow lifted his glasses as he looked at the file.

'Yes, Beresford. Good chap. Had a rough time of it though. Having a few sessions with the psychiatrist.'

More shaking of the head. Two remaining.

'This chap. How old?'

'I think you will find that he is twenty-four.'

'Bit on the young side, but looks the part. And what does he do?'

'Navigation officer.' It was one of the Navy men again, looking through the file. 'Well thought of. Something of an expert on tides and coastlines. Even studied that sort of thing at university. Didn't know you could do that. Certainly not in my day.'

The tall man read through the file again.

'Looks like he is expecting to go back to sea.'

'Indeed,' said Dr Farrow. 'He is most keen to do so and we ought to have him ready by the end of the summer. No reason why not. Strong chap. Young and played plenty of sport. Always helps.'

'And if he was not going back to sea, when could he be out of here?'

'Well, there is no reason why he shouldn't go back to sea…'

'If he were to be based in London. No active service. Behind a desk, that type of thing. When would he be ready for that?'

'Well, he is almost there now, but a couple more months should do it.'

Silence in the room apart from the ticking of a large clock on the wall and nervous coughing of one of the officers. The tall man was reading the file carefully and nodding his head approvingly as he did so.

'He's our man. Has to be. Fits the part perfectly. I need him ready by the middle of April.'

Dr Farrow started to say something, but one of the Navy officers held up his hand to stop him.

The tall man stood and the other three people in the room did likewise.

'Lieutenant Owen Quinn. He's our man. One other thing, Dr Farrow. A new nurse will be joining you next week.'

–

Nathalie Mercier arrived at Calcotte Grange in the second week of January and for the first two weeks she was on night shifts, as was

customary for new nurses. She was due to start work in the physiotherapy department by the end of January, but the night shifts gave
her some time before then to find out what she could about all the
patients.

There were only sixty or so patients in the hospital and when all
was silent and still in the early hours of the morning she had the
opportunity she had been looking for to study their files. As a new
nurse, she was based in the same office as the night sister, which also
happened to be the office where the patients' files were kept. They
were locked away in a cabinet, but the sister had shown her where the
key was, in case of emergency only.

Between the hours of one and three in the morning, not very
much happened around her or anywhere else in the hospital. The
sister on duty would leave the wards at one 'to do her paperwork'
and would return at three, red-eyed, slightly unsteady and smelling of
cheap sherry. There were two other nurses on duty, each in separate
offices in different parts of the hospital, looking after around twenty
patients each. Nurse Mercier removed four or five files at a time,
relocked the cabinet and studied the files carefully. It was risky and she
had not touched any files on the first two nights, instead observing the
patterns of what went on around her. The office was at the end of a
long corridor and any movement on the stone-tiled floor reverberated
with the efficiency of an alarm system. She knew she would have to
be both very unlucky and careless to be caught with the files.

When she started to look at the files after the second night, the
information that she found in them was useful – some of it very useful.
As well as their medical histories, they were full of detail about the
patients' previous postings, how and where they had been injured and,
in some cases, where they were due to be posted after being released
from Calcotte Grange. She made careful notes. It was all information
that would be well received. At long last, she was playing her part.

It was not until her fifth night shift that she came to the 'P/Q'
drawer and found his file. She recognised him from the photograph
attached to the front of it. She remembered having seen him asleep
on the ward on her first night. He was no more than a boy really,
quite presentable in an English kind of way, with his fair hair and
unblemished, pale skin. But it was a note at the front of his file
that really caught her attention. It was written and signed by Dr
Farrow. 'No return to active service,' he had scrawled. 'Transfer to

Naval Intelligence requested. Approved after satisfactory completion of physio and final medical. Intelligence wants him by April. Top secret project. Tell Quinn of new posting in March. Delicate situation, Quinn anxious to get back to sea. Will be unhappy but Intelligence insist. Big role for him. Farrow.'

She read his file in detail. She read it again the next night and found it hard to believe what she had stumbled across. They would be delighted with this. More than delighted, in fact. It was a real opportunity. She had to be careful, but she also had to make the most of it. She checked him on her ward rounds. He looked innocent laying there fast asleep, his fair hair splayed out across the bleached-white pillow, mouth slightly open to reveal a perfect set of white teeth, and his pyjama top unbuttoned. She gently pulled the top sheet back over him and tucked it in. He stirred very slightly and turned onto his side, his hair falling over his eyes as he did so.

She knew what she had to do. There was no question about it. She looked around the ward. It could have been far worse, the one in the bed opposite was overweight and had bad skin and the two by the window were in their forties and looked it.

She carefully brushed his hair away from his eyes and he stirred, turning over to his other side.

–

It was towards the end of January that the lieutenant commander who had been injured in Devonport came back from his own physiotherapy session one day with a twinkle in his eye.

'You'll enjoy your next session, Quinn. They've laid on quite a treat for us.'

He had forgotten that remark by the time he arrived at physiotherapy the next morning, but now she was walking towards him through the long hall. Past the parallel bars, across the mats and with a smile, tying her flowing dark hair as she walked. She had dark eyes that had seemed alight even from the other end of the room. By the time she appeared in front of him he was quite transfixed. She was wearing a uniform that appeared to be halfway between a nurse's and a physiotherapist's. The uniform was predominantly white and pulled in tightly around her waist with a wide belt, to accentuate her already slim figure. She was above average height; her legs were long and slim.

'Lieutenant Quinn? I am your new physiotherapy nurse. My name is Nurse Mercier.'

Quinn stood still without uttering a word. He was trying hard to compose himself. She had walked out of a French film.

'*Avec plaisir*,' he replied, trying to sound as nonchalant as possible.

'*Ainsi, vous parlez français?*' she asked.

Quinn panicked. His French was good enough to hold a decent conversation, or at least the first part of one, but that would be in normal circumstances and these were not normal circumstances.

'*Un peu*,' came out making him sound unwell. 'I do speak a bit, but I am sure that your English is much better than my French.'

'Nonsense! I will help to make you better and I will help you to speak better French, and you will help me to speak better English. *D'accord?*'

'*D'accord.*'

Which was how Owen Quinn's life came to change forever.

His treatment was still supervised by the physiotherapists, but now Nurse Mercier was with him throughout all of his sessions. She was responsible for overseeing all of his treatment. He realised it was in his imagination, but he liked to think that her face lit up when he hobbled into the room and that she seemed to give him that much more attention than her other patients.

When he was practicing walking on the mats without sticks, she would be right behind him, her hands gently holding him at the top of his thighs. He had to concentrate hard on keeping his balance, which was difficult with her hands gripping the side of his thighs, sometimes seeming to slip an inch or two round to the front. He began to spend more time in the downstairs lounge, where he knew she would go and spend her morning or afternoon break. Invariably she would come over and sit with him and they would talk. She now called him 'Owen' rather than 'Lieutenant Quinn' and he began to call her 'Nathalie', certainly when no one else was in earshot.

She would ask him about his life and what plans they had for him once he left Calcotte Grange, and she would tell him about her life in France. She talked of her strict upbringing as an only child in Paris and of how her parents had died within a few months of each other when she was in her late teens. She spoke of how she became an army nurse and ended up in Dunkirk and managed to scramble onto one of the last boats back to Britain.

At the beginning of February, Quinn was moved into one of the side rooms. These tended to be reserved for the more senior officers, or those with the most serious injuries, so Quinn was surprised that one was being offered to him rather than to a more senior officer, but he did not complain. He assumed that it was because he had already been in the hospital for three months.

He told Nathalie about his new room at their next session and she began to visit him there at the end of the day. It was not unusual for the physiotherapists or their assistants to visit the patients on their wards, especially if they had a difficult session that day.

Nathalie's visits became nightly. At first, they were brief, sometimes she would just stand inside the partially closed doorway and wish him a good night and correct his pronunciation. Other times she would sit by his bed, talking of how she had no one in France and of how nursing was now her life. She would untie her hair, shaking her head to allow it to fall by the side of her face and would turn slightly away from him. Once or twice when this happened, he caught a glimpse of her jet-black eyes, moist like pools of water.

One evening he was telling her of how he hoped to go back to sea soon, how it seemed right to do so. He was not terribly close to his parents and, of course, he was not married, so he did not really have to worry about someone left behind.

Nathalie gazed at him as he spoke and then looked down towards the bed. Without looking up she spoke quietly.

'*Tu n'es pas seul maintenant.*' You are not alone now.

Her fingernail was gently tracing circles on his forearm, the fair hairs on his arm picked out against the bright red of her nail varnish. He stopped talking and she brushed her fingers down his arm. The room was so quiet that Quinn could feel a buzzing in his ear. Their fingertips touched and hands intertwined. Maybe it lasted a second, possibly longer, but for Quinn it was a lifetime. That was the first night that she kissed his lips as she left. It was not a kiss that lingered, but as she kissed him she placed a hand on his shoulder and he could taste her warm breath.

The following day he did not have any physiotherapy and did not go down to the lounge. He was confused. He knew he had fallen desperately in love with Nathalie, but was sure that it was unrequited and that she was just being kind to him. If he was honest with himself he knew that he was not bad looking, but Nathalie was a beautiful woman who was not only his nurse, but also two years older than him. He felt embarrassed at having a schoolboy crush at his age. Although the hospital seemed relaxed about allowing the patients – who were officers after all – and the medical staff to mix socially, having a friendly chat over a cup of tea was probably the limit of what they had in mind. A relationship was quite another thing.

The next day Nathalie was not in the room when he went down for the physiotherapy. He was supervised for the whole session by the senior physiotherapist and for a time he was aware that the senior medical officer and a couple of uniformed naval officers were watching him, which was not altogether unusual. Often when a patient was being considered for release back to active service he would be carefully assessed as he went through his paces.

That afternoon he sat in the lounge for an hour either side of the afternoon break, but there was no sign of Nathalie. He decided that she had realised herself that perhaps she had crossed a boundary the other night and had gone elsewhere. Or, perhaps, it was his fault. Two nights ago she had assured him he was not alone. He should have told her then that she wasn't either. Why had he missed that opportunity, to tell her that he cared for her? Why had he not held her when she kissed him, pulling her closer to him and promising never to let go. He was desolate, chiding himself for his response which she must have seen as him not caring.

That night he lay in the bath in the private bathroom attached to his side room. Nurse Slade, the large nurse who always reeked of tobacco, had helped him into the bath. He was careful to remove the towel only when she had left. She would give him twenty minutes and then knock on the door before entering, allowing him time to put the towel back in place before she helped him out of the bath.

He liked to lie in the bath with the harsh overhead light turned off. Enough light seeped in from his bedroom for him to see what he was doing, but he found lying in the warm water, in the half-light, was relaxing.

He had only been in the bath for five minutes when there was a gentle tap at the half open door. It was far too early for Nurse Slade and, in any case, her taps at the door tended not to be gentle. He had enough time to grab the towel and cover himself when the door from the bedroom opened. Silhouetted in the doorway was an unmistakable figure. Nathalie entered, leaving the door from the bedroom fully ajar, so the bathroom was now flooded with light.

62

He started to speak, but she placed her forefinger over her mouth. *Silence.*

'I told Nurse Slade I needed to see you and would help you out of the bath. The door is locked.' She was speaking very softly.

And with that Nathalie helped him out of the bath, removing his towel as she did so. He stood quite naked in front of her, the first time he had ever been like that with a woman, the water dripping fast and heavy from his body. He began to breathe deeply and opened his mouth to speak. She smiled, shook her head, placing her forefinger in front of his lips and then allowing it to move inside his mouth. *No need to speak.* She was staring directly into his eyes. In the half-light, her eyes were even darker and brighter than he had imagined.

'It is all right. Don't worry. I told you, the door is locked.' She was speaking in no more than a whisper, her face just a few inches from his. '*Nous avons seulement quinze minutes.*' Just fifteen minutes.

As she spoke she was releasing her belt and unbuttoning her white uniform. She stood as naked as he was before him but, even before that, he had already begun to respond. She moved towards him so that their bodies were now touching. She reached out, her hand sliding down his bare back and then round to the front, setting fire to every inch of his flesh as she did so. She led him towards the bedroom.

'*Venez.*'

The next fifteen minutes were everything that Owen Quinn had ever dreamed of and more.

Be careful what you wish for.

Chapter 7

March 1942

At the beginning of March, two weeks after Nathalie had come into his bathroom and his life, Quinn awoke from an early evening doze to find a tall man in a dark coat and wearing a trilby with a wide brim sitting very still in the chair in the corner of the room.

The two men stared at each other for quite a few seconds before the tall man broke the silence.

'Captain Edgar. Not your lot. Army.'

More silence before Edgar pointed to Quinn's bedside table where there was a bottle of very good malt whisky. Quinn raised his eyebrows.

'Don't worry. Officially sanctioned. Understand you prefer it to rum.' He smiled at his own joke. Quinn could not remember when he had last drunk whisky, other than in his dreams.

'Chaps here tell me that you should be out of here soon, Quinn.' The man was speaking quietly. He had taken his hat off and was turning it carefully in his hands as he did so, first clockwise, then anti-clockwise, as if checking for imperfections. Despite speaking quietly, his voice managed to fill the room. He had no discernible accent, certainly not public school. Not quite officer class, Quinn thought. Maybe even the very slightest trace of an educated northern accent, but he really couldn't place it.

'Yes, sir. I am hoping to return to active service as soon as possible.'

'Not on the cards, I'm afraid.' Captain Edgar was shaking his head. 'I'm told that they don't think you're up to it. Back not strong enough. Leg still playing up.'

Quinn was fully awake now, quite stunned. 'But when I got here they told me I would be back at sea this year!'

'Well, Quinn, the best laid plans of mice and men...'

Quinn could feel himself getting angry and upset.

'But surely this is something that the doctors would—?'

Captain Edgar held up his hat to stop Quinn speaking.

'But we do have a plan that will appeal to you, Quinn. You are going to come and work for us.'

'Us?'

Edgar waved his hat, as if batting away the question.

'All will be revealed. We are quite impressed with what you have to offer, Quinn. Bright chap. You are a navigation officer, aren't you, Quinn?'

'Yes, sir.'

'Specialising in the weather and coastlines, that type of thing?'

Quinn nodded.

'Splendid. Just what we're looking for. Couldn't find a better man. You are going to meet one of our chaps soon. Archibald. He'll tell you all then. Welcome onboard.'

As he arose to leave the room, Edgar paused in the closed doorway, his head above the doorframe.

'Just one thing, Quinn. Your nurse. Nathalie Mercier.'

Quinn felt himself turning bright red. He started to speak.

'Gather you've got rather... sweet on her.'

Quinn started to speak again, but Edgar continued.

'And her with you, I gather. No need to explain. Understand and all that. Pretty woman, perfectly natural. Bit... irregular in this kind of place, but she assures us that you both... feel... the same way about each other.'

'Yes, sir, if I can...'

Edgar shook his head as he stood up.

'No need to explain, Quinn. She'll be able to go with you. Just make sure you do the decent thing.'

The next day, he was called in to see Dr Farrow, who confirmed what Captain Edgar had told him.

Dr Farrow was clearly uneasy about having to impart such bad news and for the whole time that he spoke to Quinn, he determinedly stared at the chewed pencil he was twisting in fingers.

He tried hard to convince Quinn, while managing to sound somewhat less than convinced himself.

Leg healing nicely... but back not really holding up terribly well, not made the progress we had expected... not your fault... one of those things... too risky to let you go back to sea... know we told you we hoped to get you back to active service, but not really worked out... very sorry... accept we were possibly too optimistic... know just how disappointed you must be... look on the bright side... Intelligence chaps picked you out... big job, important etc. etc.

And that was that. As far as Quinn was concerned, he couldn't very well argue with the Royal Navy and the doctors. He was not going back to sea. He had somehow ended up in Intelligence and he had no idea why or how.

–

There are parts of south-eastern England that are so flat that at certain times of the year the harsh winds flying in from the Russian steppes manage to do so unhindered. The last week in March 1942 was one such time. In the morning, the day would be calm and there would be enough sun for those patients who were up to it to be able to gather on the vast terrace at the front of the house that the Calcottes had so thoughtfully provided.

By noon the wind would start to pick up and within minutes it would be whipping around the turrets, terraces and out-buildings of Calcotte Grange. Even the most hardy of the Navy officers would be driven indoors, with inevitable talk of 'battening down the hatches'.

On the last Thursday of March, a group of patients were in the lounge, looking out over the sweeping drive and watching the arrival of a long black car. Owen Quinn was one of that group, more anxious to see the outcome than the others. He had been warned to be ready for a visitor that day and the visitor was in the car, delayed by sheep. He had been waiting for his visitor since Captain Edgar had turned up in his room a month previously.

The car pulled up in front of the main entrance and Quinn watched the driver open the rear passenger door. The man who had got out was above average height and wearing Royal Navy uniform. One of the Navy officers who Quinn had seen around the hospital from time to time was there to salute him and lead him into the building.

It was another half an hour before Quinn was summoned into the presence of a surprisingly elderly looking man, who stood up slowly as Quinn entered the room, stiffly walked over to him, returned Quinn's salute and shook his hand in a formal manner before leading him over to two chairs by the window.

66

They were in a small room overlooking the back of Calcotte Grange. The gardens behind the house had not been as manicured as those at the front and the area closest to the house was now a large vegetable garden. Wooden fences had been erected around the vegetables to keep the sheep out and one of the gardeners was repairing part of the fence as they looked out. The muffled echoes of a mallet striking the wooden posts were the only sound until the elder man finally spoke.

'Captain John Archibald. Royal Navy most of my life. Tried to retire a few years ago, we'd bought a lovely place in Lincolnshire. Between Boston and the sea. Do you know the area?'

Quinn shook his head.

'Very quiet. My wife had been dreaming of a place like that for years and I promised her that when I left the Navy we would find somewhere like it. Cannot see a soul from where we are, but there's a splendid village just down the lane. Everything you need. Pub, shop, post office, church – in that order. Village green has a phone box next to the war memorial, but otherwise it is perfect. We'd been there a year when this war started and they hauled me back. Saw plenty of activity in my time, Jutland you know. But after the Great War I'd moved over to Naval Intelligence and I suppose that is why they wanted me back. And that is why I am here now.'

Captain Archibald was looking out of the window. Owen noticed his hands, which were enormous with thick fingers and had the appearance of the hands of a labourer. The hammering had stopped and the gardener was trying to lead a stray sheep away from the vegetables.

'I know you wanted to go back to sea and that's splendid. But the doctors here are not sure you're totally up to it. In any case, we have a much bigger job for you – greater good and all that. I work in Naval Intelligence, as I mentioned. I need people like you. You're a bright chap. Plenty of people like doing the exciting stuff, but I understand you're a bit of a wizard with maps and charts. Is that true?'

Quinn hesitated.

'Well… yes, sir. I did a degree in geography at London University. Coasts, sandbanks, meteorology – that's what I was interested in. So when I joined up in November '39, specialising in navigation was right up my street. I read maps for pleasure in the same way that other people read books.'

'Well, it is good to have you onboard, Quinn.'

Quinn noticed that while this was not a command, it was certainly not a question either. At no stage in the conversation had it been anything other than assumed that Quinn would be joining Archibald.

'But I had been hoping to return to sea, sir. The doctor said that—'

'The doctor may have thought that was possible a few months ago but he clearly does not think so now. This is why we would like you to join us.'

'And there really is no alternative?'

'To not being at sea? I am sure there are plenty of desk jobs at the Admiralty, but let me tell you, we have chaps queuing up to join Naval Intelligence.'

'I am pleased to be joining you, sir. If it really is out of the question for me to go back to sea, that is.'

'Good chap. The doctors tell me that you will be out of here in a couple of weeks. Is that right?'

'So I understand, sir. I am walking well now. Still a bit of pain, but I'll be glad to get out of here and doing a job of work.'

'That's the spirit, Quinn. I know you wanted to get back to sea and I understand that. But you need to understand that you are going to be playing a vital role in the war effort. There will be times when it doesn't seem like it. You will just think that you are pushing pieces of paper around. None of us knows how long this damn show is going to last, but it will not be until it is all over that you will have any idea of the part you've played. One other matter, Quinn: I understand that you have recently become engaged.'

'Indeed, sir. All rather sudden… not that we *have* to get married, please don't misunderstand. But when Captain Edgar came to see me earlier this month it was clear that he was aware of our… of our relationship. I didn't want Nurse Mercier – Nathalie – to get into any kind of trouble and Captain Edgar had urged me to do the decent thing so I proposed. And blow me down, sir, she accepted! I'm the happiest man in the world. She is the most beautiful woman and I love her very much.'

The hammering had resumed outside the window. Captain Archibald started to speak, hesitated, stopped and then spoke.

'I was going to say, Quinn, that your private life is none of my concern, but, of course, that is untrue. Everything you do, everything about you will be my concern once you start working in my unit. But just be careful. Love is a wonderful thing, but it does have a habit of getting in the way of things. Try to keep your feet on the ground. They're discharging you from here on Friday, the tenth of April. You start with us at Lincoln House in Duke Street at nine o'clock on Monday, the thirteenth of April. Lucky for us.'

Chapter 8

London, 1942

His wedding had not been quite as Owen Quinn had envisaged, which was hardly surprising as he had never really given much thought to getting married other than assuming that one day he would. Much more to the point, it was certainly not as Marjorie and William Quinn had ever imagined their son's wedding would be.

Over the years, Marjorie Quinn especially had frequently imagined her only child's wedding, even planned some details of it. It would, of course, be a day to remember. Their friends and some relations would all be invited and impressed. The sun would shine, the church would look perfect, the flowers would be immaculately arranged and no detail would be disregarded. It would be the height of taste and would inevitably mark their ascendancy in their middle-class community in Surrey. Ideally, the bride would be from their area and certainly from a similar background. She would be attractive and intelligent though, of course, without any unhealthy modern tendencies towards independence.

Marjorie Quinn did recognise that the war could affect her plans, but had reckoned on her son simply delaying marriage until a year or two after the war. Her cousin's daughter had married an American and that had been most upsetting, but then that side of the family were from Yorkshire.

But to marry a Frenchwoman, with no family – and a nurse, which was almost trade... it had all been too awful for Marjorie to contemplate. William had agreed at first but had soon changed his tune when he first met the girl. It was hard to deny that she was... *attractive*, one had to acknowledge that. But Owen had known her for just a matter of weeks when they became engaged *and* he was a patient of hers. It all seemed too hasty and not a little improper. She wondered whether the whole business may have been the result of any of the medication that Owen was on.

She certainly never imagined that the first time she would meet her son's bride-to-be would be when they were actually engaged. In a way, she blamed herself. They ought to have visited Owen more often after he was taken to Calcotte Grange. But the journey from Surrey involved a series of trains that took forever and the trains tended to be crowded with soldiers, many of whom were not British.

As soon as they heard of the engagement in late March they had come up. William's brother had managed to get hold of some extra petrol coupons and they were able to use his Ford Anglia. On the journey up, they had agreed that they would take Owen aside and do their best to talk him out of it. He had always been such an *impetuous* boy. William said it was because he was an only child.

The day was a disaster from the start; at least it was from Marjorie Quinn's point of view. As soon as they arrived at Calcotte Grange, Owen and the girl piled into the car and they headed off to what she had to admit was a most agreeable tea-room, where they had a small area to themselves by a roaring fire. William could hardly take his eyes off this Nathalie from the moment he first saw her. The girl and Owen actually *held hands* the whole time and even *kissed* in front of them. She drank tea without milk and smoked constantly. She ignored most of Marjorie's carefully rehearsed and very polite questions about her life in Paris and kept asking for amusing stories about Owen as a boy.

The one positive aspect of the whole sorry situation was that at least Owen was not going back to sea, which she had never been happy about. She did like the sound of the new job in London. It seemed important, although Owen insisted that he was not allowed to tell her anything about it.

The young lovers arrived in London in April. The Navy found them a tiny flat in Pimlico, from where you could hear the trains at Victoria Station on a still night. They also put in a good word to allow Nathalie to return to her old hospital, St Thomas's. She would live in the nurses' home until their wedding in June.

That took place in a grim church in Chelsea. The vicar had a streaming cold but no handkerchief and, for some unaccountable reason, was unable to pronounce 'Owen' properly. He was so slow in both speech and movement that the ceremony felt more funereal than matrimonial. It rained for the duration of the wedding and for some time after. Marjorie and William had invited a dozen friends and a similar number of relatives. Owen had invited the two or three chums from school whom he had been able to contact, along with another Navy officer from his new office. Nathalie had brought along three other nurses, none of whom she seemed to know particularly well, but who all spent most of the ceremony dabbing their eyes.

And that was it. Barely thirty of them in a damp and dimly lit church that could accommodate at least ten times that number. Marjorie Quinn did turn round at one stage during the ceremony and spotted a tall man in the very back row, well into the shadows. He was wearing a dark coat and his face was obscured by a wide-brimmed trilby. She did wonder whether he was one of the Yorkshire relatives – they were the kind of people who would not remove their hats in a church – but when she next turned round the tall man was no longer there. She decided he was simply a passer-by seeking refuge from the rain.

And so, on a wet day in June 1942, Owen Quinn, aged twenty-four, married a Frenchwoman two years older than himself.

–

Now it was September and Owen Quinn was surprised at the ease with which he had taken both to his new role in Naval Intelligence and to married life.

The Navy had been what he considered to be surprisingly helpful in finding them the flat in Alderney Street in Pimlico. He really had not realised that they went to that kind of trouble. It was a tiny flat, he had to admit that. The kitchen was little more than a galley and the small lounge which led off it had to accommodate two enormous old armchairs, a pair of rickety side tables and a stained dining table. The narrow bathroom was always draughty, but having spent eighteen months at sea and the best part of a year in hospital, Quinn had no problem with the flat – unlike his new wife.

It was an improvement on the nurses' home, but for Nathalie, the bedroom was the only room that she was happy with. Somehow they had managed to get the double bed that his parents bought them into it and from then on the bedroom became the focal point of their home life.

It was hard to predict Nathalie's shifts at St Thomas's. Sometimes it would be long days, occasionally a week of nights, which he hated.

Weekends were difficult to plan. She did seem to work more Sundays than not, which he could not really understand but she promised him that she was not being asked to do any more than her fair share. She assured him that working more Sundays meant she was not required to work so many nights. Her Sundays at work did mean that he could go down to Surrey for lunch with his parents.

There was a war on after all, and at least they were together. She more than made up for it in their time together. On the occasions when he found himself alone in the flat becoming maudlin, he would remind himself of how his life had changed in little more than a year. Clinging to the plank of wood in the sea off Crete, he had thought his life was over. Now, not only was he alive but he was married to a woman he loved and who had previously existed only in his dreams. His life, he had to admit to himself, was as near perfect as he could have wished it to be.

Be careful what you wish for, he very occasionally reminded himself. But he would chuckle when he did so. He now seemed to have what he had always wished for and there really did not appear to be anything he had to be careful about.

On the rare days when neither of them was working they would go for long walks. She liked to explore London. Owen had lived in the capital as a student, but Nathalie brought a totally different eye to it.

She would spot sights that he had walked past many times but never seen. She would be thrilled at the names of little streets, delighted at a small shop only selling buttons, or appalled at the food shops which she said were disgusting. He would remind her that there was a war on, but she insisted that the food shops and the steamy cafés they would sit and drink in were proof that the English did not care about food.

They would walk along and Nathalie would always look up. Her long hair would drop further down her back, resting sensuously in that spot halfway down it which he would always caress before they fell asleep. She would marvel at the tops of the buildings and the strange creatures carved into them or protruding from the walls.

They would be arm in arm and she would tell him long stories, some amusing, most sad, about life at the hospital. And against his better judgement, he would find himself drawn into telling her about his work. Nothing serious, of course: he knew that he was not allowed to do that. But the titbits about daily office life and the people who inhabited it seemed to amuse her and there seemed to be no harm in that. She would laugh loudly and pull herself closer to him. They would kiss and Owen would notice the looks, some disapproving, and many more admiring, of passers-by.

It would be on the occasions like this that he would feel able to again broach the subject of her life in France. He had assumed that once they were married, he would find out more about her, but he realised that he still really knew very little. He was curious about what school she went to, what hospital she had trained in, what boyfriends she had had, and about any extended family.

Nathalie was never rude and would always appear to answer his questions but, by the end of these conversations, he would realise that she had said nothing of any significance. The hospital *was a very large one, but you know what these Paris hospitals are like* – which he did not. *'But you never tell me about your girlfriends!' 'There are uncles, aunts and cousins, but we are not a close family. You are my family now.'* He would ask these questions again in bed, after they had made love and were lying face to face on the pillow, stroking each other's arms. She should have been at her most open then, but the answers would be the same and with a whispered *'Ça suffit'* she would let him know that was enough. The conversation would end.

He was not intending to pry, but he felt that he did not really know his wife and all he wanted was to be part of her life. He imagined that when the war was over they would spend time in Paris. They would stroll through the *Rive Gauche*, stopping to look at the second-hand bookstalls and the artists on the Left Bank. They would walk into agreeable bars at any time of the day and he would drink cognac. They would stop at the Café des Deux Magots in Place St Germain des Prés, drink proper coffee and hope to catch the intellectual discussions around them. If they had enough money they could even dine at Fouquet's on the Champs Élysées.

He attributed her reticence to a remark she had made one Saturday afternoon in late July when they were walking back towards Pimlico by the river. Maybe he did not appreciate enough what it meant to have to flee your country. It had been a perfect day, warm with a steady breeze and they had walked past the Houses of Parliament, crossed Westminster Bridge, by St Thomas's, along the south bank before crossing over Chelsea Bridge, heading back towards Pimlico. On Grosvenor Road there was a small group of soldiers coming towards them. As they came closer, he realised they were Free French and greeted them with a '*Bonjour! Ma femme est française.*' But Nathalie seemed shy and uncommunicative and after the briefest of pauses she moved him along, explaining that they needed to get home. As they moved away from the soldiers, he asked why. She was silent for a few seconds as they continued walking and when she lifted her head to speak her eyes had turned into those moist, dark shining pools.

'It is no longer *my* France. My France has been taken from me.'

And there was the café. It was an incident that bothered him at the time but which he allowed to slip from his mind after her apology.

It was a Thursday afternoon in August and he had finished work early. Nathalie met him in Piccadilly Circus and they walked down Haymarket towards Trafalgar Square. It began to rain in the way that it does in an English summer: a few drops without apparent warning and then a sudden and heavy downpour. Nathalie was wearing high heels and a summer dress. She was not dressed for the rain. They dived into a small corner café and sat against the wall at the end of a long Formica table. The rain had caused her dress to cling against her figure and Owen removed his jacket to drape over his wife's shoulders. Within minutes the café filled up and a family of four squeezed onto their table.

It was evident from their initial enquiry – '*Are these seats free?*' – that they were French and Owen happily introduced themselves. It ought, he thought, to have been a perfect encounter for Nathalie. '*From Paris. The 7th arrondissement. Near Les Invalides.*' The few sentences that Nathalie uttered were short to the point of being curt. The parents were in their early forties, the two boys in their early teens. They had come to London in early 1940. The father spoke to them in hushed tones as the boys flicked their straws at each other.

'I travelled a lot to Germany for business during the 1930s. I could see how...' He paused and then muttered to his wife in French.

'Dangerous,' she said.

'...dangerous it would be for us,' he continued. 'We are fortunate in having family in London. We could not risk remaining in Paris. We cannot imagining—'

'Imagine,' she corrected him.

'...imagine what is happening there now to our family and our friends. We were so lucky to escape.'

Owen looked quizzical.

'Where you involved in politics?'

Before the man could answer Nathalie, who had spent most of the time looking at the pepper pot she was fiddling with on the table, spoke.

'They're Jews, Owen. Can't you tell?'

Owen was taken aback. No, he had not been able to tell. These were the first Jews he could recall meeting. But what had really taken him aback was Nathalie's tone. She had been quiet throughout what he thought was a pleasant and even fortuitous meeting. But her tone and her manner bordered on rudeness.

Before he could say anything else, Nathalie was standing up.

'We had better leave now, Owen.'

The downpour had not abated. If anything, it was even heavier.

'Are you sure?' He knew that, if there was one thing she hated, it was getting wet.

But she was already pushing her way through. The family all had to get up to make way for them. Outside, she did not wait for him as he tried to leave in a more polite manner. He had to trot to catch her up.

'What was all that about, Nathalie?'

'What was what about?' She was walking fast, despite her high heels. Her arms folded tightly across her as if that might keep her dry.

'Why did we have to leave so suddenly? It must have seemed rude.'

She stopped and turned at him.

'You English are so concerned about manners and doing the right thing. That is all you think about. I did not want to be with those people. We were on our own. Why did they have to come and sit there and interrupt us.'

'Nathalie!'

'They're always like that, thinking they can push in and take things over as if they own the place.'

Owen was genuinely confused. They were walking next to each other now, the rain still heavy.

'Who are "they", Nathalie? I don't know what you mean.'

She paused to look at him.

'You're lucky then.'

They didn't speak again until they were back in Pimlico.

Later that night she apologised. She realised she must have been rude. She had sat with two people as they died that morning in the

76

hospital and she was upset. Sometimes being reminded of France made her even more upset and that must have been the reason for her behaviour in the café.

–

Duke Street ran from Piccadilly to the north and Pall Mall to the south. Lincoln House was about halfway down and on the eastern side of the street. It was a block down from Fortnum and Mason – where Owen Quinn occasionally wandered into the Special Officers' Department but never bought anything. A few doors along was the Chequers Tavern, a small pub which was reputed to have been the first one built in the city after the Great Fire. It was not, Owen was informed on his first day, regarded as a suitable place for officers to drink. He never found out why.

Lincoln House was a seven-storey building, more than eighty years old and difficult to distinguish from the other buildings in an otherwise elegant street. It had dutifully served some of the less exciting parts of the insurance industry until it was requisitioned by the Government in 1940. The attraction was its sheer ordinariness and anonymity. On more than one occasion, even after he had been working there for months, Quinn had found himself walking past the gloomy entrance, with its dark brown doors and grey metal shutters, with the words 'Lincoln House' picked in fading gold characters painted on a filthy strip of glass above the door. The entrance was tucked against an art gallery that rarely seemed to open and always had the same miserable, dark landscape in the window. The building was narrower than most of the others in the street, but not so much that it stood out. The white façade had weathered over the years and the exposure to London grime and rain gave the exterior a mottled effect. Now the building housed a series of offices, all of which fulfilled some security- or intelligence-related purpose. The entrance led along the length of the art gallery to a reception area and guardroom at the back. From there was a main stairwell, on one side of the building, with a door leading off it at each floor to small suites of offices. When he first went to work on the sixth floor of Lincoln House, Quinn had been told that the higher the floor, the more sensitive the work being handled there. He was not sure if this was true, but like so much of the gossip that passed for information in wartime, he did not take it too seriously – but did find a place for it somewhere in his memory.

77

The very first thing that Quinn asked Captain Archibald when he arrived at Lincoln House on Monday, 13th April, was the name of the unit. Who was he working for? What was it called? What should he tell people?

It had seemed a reasonable question, not one that he would have expected Archibald to hesitate at answering for quite as long as he did.

'That's a jolly good question, Quinn. We don't really have a name. We are part of Naval Intelligence and we handle Special Projects. You'll have your security briefing later today, but the easiest thing is not to discuss anything with anyone. You work for the Royal Navy, you're stuck behind a desk – that is as much as people need to know. It's all that I've told my wife for the last twenty-five years. Best advice I can offer is that you should give the impression to people that your job is a bit boring, that you are slightly embarrassed to be doing something as menial as this. Keep it simple. That way, they will soon lose interest. Let me show you round.'

There was not much to see. The whole suite of offices looked as if it had been recently decorated. The smell of fresh paint was evident and, that morning, boxes and charts were still being brought into the office. The central office area had a large chart table in the middle, with maps and charts stacked against it. Around the room were grey filing cabinets that were being filled by a small, well-built woman called Mary. Along the floor were what were now becoming stacks of boxes, many of which seemed to be filled with photographs.

'Time to meet the whole crew,' said Archibald. Apart from Mary, there were two other women in the office. Agnes sat in one of three side offices and told Quinn quite clearly that she *ran* the office. She was probably in her late fifties, possibly even older. Her grey hair was pulled into a tight bun and her spectacles were perched on the end of her nose. Whenever she spoke to someone, she lifted her head slightly higher than they would expect so that she could see them through her glasses. And there was Rosemary. English Rose, he thought. The kind of girl he always imagined he would end up with until his dreams had come true. He knew Rose's type; he had grown up with them. From somewhere in the middle class, somewhere in the Home Counties and somewhere between presentable and plain. Rose was in her late twenties, as far as he could tell, and had it not been for the war would have expected to have been married by now. Rose took security very seriously; it seemed to give her a sense of importance that she had never expected to have. Rose's role was to type up reports and letters.

There were two other men in the office. There was Porter, who was never referred to as anything other than Porter. He didn't wear any uniform and was stone deaf.

'Atlantic convoys,' Archibald told him, by way of explanation. Quinn had to assume that Porter had lost his hearing in an Atlantic convoy, but he never pushed the matter. He was not sure whether Porter had been Royal Navy or Merchant Navy. He suspected the latter. In so far as there was any communication with Porter, it was done by writing notes. But there was no call for too much communication. Porter's role was to manage the maps and the charts. To get out the ones that Quinn needed, put away those that he had finished with and collect new ones.

And Riley. He was never quite sure what Riley's role was, even though he and Quinn did share one of the three side offices. As far as he could tell, he provided some kind of a filter for Quinn, looking at paperwork before it came to him and checking whatever Quinn produced and Rose had typed. Riley only had one arm and the empty sleeve was pinned to the side of his jacket. No matter how hot it was – and at times it was very hot in the office – Riley always kept his jacket on.

They were not what Quinn would have described as a merry bunch. It did strike Quinn as slightly odd that the group responsible for Special Intelligence Projects comprised an elderly captain brought out of retirement and who did not seem to be in the best of health, an injured lieutenant, one deaf man, a man with one arm, and the three women. But a week into his new role, Archibald did mention that they were not the only unit in Naval Intelligence handling Special Projects, so he did not think about it again.

Quinn soon fell into a routine. A project could last a day, or a month, or longer. Captain Archibald would call Quinn and Riley into his office and outline the project and Quinn would then have Rose type a note for Porter detailing what maps and charts he required. They would all be planned naval operations and Quinn was required to put together a detailed brief on routes, coastlines, sandbanks and the like. It was work that he was good at and that he enjoyed. He just wished that he was at sea doing it.

His first project came in May. He had arrived in the office one morning and was called straight in by Archibald, who was sitting behind his desk.

'Arctic convoys.'

For a moment, Archibald said no more. Quinn wondered whether he was being sent on an Arctic convoy. A shudder of fear followed by excitement went through him.

'What the convoys are carrying into Murmansk and Archangel is keeping the Soviet Union in the war. But as the weather improves, they are sailing into waters where night never falls. It makes attacks on them too easy. The Luftwaffe and the U–Boats are sinking too many ships.

'We need the Soviets to tie the Germans up on the Eastern Front. They can only do that if we can ensure that they are properly supplied. If the supplies don't get through, the Red Army could collapse. And if that happens...'

Archibald was spreading out a large map of the Soviet Union on the chart table as he spoke.

'...then the war's over on the Eastern Front. That will make life somewhat tricky for us. Can't let it happen. Molotov is coming to London in the next week or two. He needs to be assured that we have all of this in hand. We're losing too many ships at the moment.'

Archibald had been indicating the depth of the German advance into the Soviet Union. His pencil was perilously close to Moscow. As he continued, he was straightening out a chart of the Barents Sea, placing it over the map of the Soviet Union.

'So, this is what you need to concentrate on, Quinn. Best route for getting the convoys safely into these ports.' He was pointing at Murmansk, and Archangel just below it.

'Best routes, how much sunlight there's going to be on any given day, sandbanks, any other ports we could nip into. That type of thing. Beauty of our little outfit is that we have time to think, come up with options if you like. Good luck. Remember that Riley is here to help you.'

Quinn immersed himself in the Arctic routes. He researched the weather, the amount of daylight, possible new routes, ports that some of the ships with smaller draughts may be able to dart into if they had to. Porter was forever bringing in new charts and maps, stacking used ones and rearranging the ones on the table. English Rose typed patriotically and Riley read everything he wrote. Captain Archibald seemed pleased. Quinn found the work interesting without being taxing.

At the beginning of August, Owen and Nathalie Quinn had a week's holiday. They stayed with his parents in Surrey for two days and then borrowed his father's car and – thanks to more petrol coupons obtained by his uncle – drove to Devon for their first holiday together.

He was back at work on Monday, 10th August. He was the first to arrive in the office apart from Archibald, whose presence in the office seemed to be ubiquitous. He was standing at the chart table when Quinn came in.

'Morning Quinn. I hope you are refreshed after your holiday. You are going to need to be.'

He indicated for Quinn to join him at the table. On it was a map of the English Channel, showing the southern coast of England and part of the northern coast of France.

'Here is our next project, Quinn.'

Archibald was bouncing his pencil up and down on a point on the map between Le Havre and Calais.

'Dieppe.'

Chapter 9

Berlin, November 1942

The man in the German Navy uniform pausing at the top of the steps of the SS headquarters looked much older than his fifty years. He rubbed his hands and buttoned his greatcoat before removing a black leather glove from each of the pockets. It was late in the afternoon of the last Monday in November and the arms of a true Prussian winter had started to wrap themselves around Berlin a few weeks previously, their grip tightening by the day. This had been one of those days when it felt as if the sun had not appeared at all. He had heard stories about the conditions on the Eastern Front which made him shiver in more ways than one. At least in the city you had some refuge from the cold.

He was not pleased. He had arrived back in Berlin that morning after a weekend in Rome arguing with incompetent Italians, and he had spent the past hour here in Prinz-Albrecht-Strasse arguing with the SS. In truth, he was not so much arguing with the SS as being shouted at by them. '*You don't share your intelligence with us,*' they told him. '*We never know what you lot are up to. You have people working for you that we don't trust. What's this about a Jew working for you in Madrid? If only the Führer knew, he would take a most dim view.*' And so on. He had heard it all before. It was how the SS operated. They'd shout, they'd scream and intimidate you and eventually you'd give in, or at least appear to. *Give me the Italians any day*, he thought. *As stupid as they are, at least they are not Nazis.*

If he had been able to see Himmler, that would not have been too bad. He did listen, sometimes. But the Reichsführer-SS was with Hitler in Berchtesgaden, as usual. He never liked to leave him on his own in Bavaria for too long. So he had spent the afternoon with idiots, who he knew hated him and who he knew had designs on his organisation.

He finished buttoning his greatcoat. As he climbed down the steps of the SS headquarters, he felt a sense of relief. The irony was that the former school of Industrial Arts and Crafts was one of the most handsome buildings in the city. But he knew what went on in Prinz-Albrecht-Strasse now. It was not exactly a state secret. The SS wanted people to know how they tortured their prisoners and the sense of terror seemed to radiate from the building like radio waves. He had always told his men not to forget that they were an *intelligence* organisation. '*There is nothing especially clever or intelligent,*' he would say, '*about using electrodes − as long as you get the wiring right. People would say anything just to get you to stop. But if you want quality intelligence, you use your brain.*'

He paused on the pavement and straightened his Navy cap. At least he would be able to go home now and have a proper rest. His wife was away and he could enjoy the solitude. One of the joys of living by the Wansee was the silence that lay across the surface of the lake like a shroud. You could cloak yourself in it.

Jürgen came out of the car and walked round to him. He smiled. He had worked hard to surround himself with men he trusted and Jürgen was one of those. They were hard to find now. Most young officers had joined the Nazi Party and once they did that, whatever their motives, you could not trust them.

'Sir. I'm afraid you need to return to Tirpitz Ufer. Colonel Preuss insists that it is most urgent. He wanted me to come and tell you in person. He did not want a message sent while you were in there.' There was a noticeable distrust in the younger man's nod at the building. He nodded. If Preuss said it was urgent, then it was urgent.

The car turned right into Wilhelm Strasse and then right again into Anhalter Strasse.

The man in the back of the car stared out at a Berlin that was at the same time so familiar and yet so strange. At the end of the third full year of the war the city was a cauldron of contradictions. This once liberal city was now at the heart of the German Reich. The majority of the population had happily gone along with this, but there were days when some of the four million Berliners thought they could still detect a whiff of pre-war decadence in the air. Most would shake their heads and dismiss it as an illusion. A very few would dare to see it as a sign of hope. But like everyone else, they kept quiet. It did not pay to even think too much.

They were now driving along the north bank of the Landwehr Kanal and into Tirpitz Ufer. It was like that in the regime too, the man in the back of the car thought. Contradictions and paranoia seeped into every ministry and organisation in the city, fuelled by the Führer himself. Adolf Hitler trusted no one. He would not allow any organisation to become a centre of power and therefore a threat to him. So at every level and for every function, more than one organisation would exist and inevitably they would be in conflict at worst, or an uneasy alliance at best, with a rival body. Hitler's thinking was simple and over the years it had proven to be highly effective: you don't need to worry about an organisation if someone else is doing that for you.

The car drove past the Bendlerblock, the headquarters of the Wehrmacht and pulled up outside number 76–78. It was the headquarters of the Abwehr.

The Abwehr was one of the complex patchwork of organisations operating in the area of intelligence and security. As Hitler intended, they each kept a check on the other. The *Schutzstaffel* – the SS – was perhaps the best known and most feared, although that was an honour closely contested by the secret police, the *Geheime Staatpolizei*, better known as the Gestapo. Then there was the *Sicherheitsdienst* – the security service, known as the SD.

The Abwehr was the military intelligence arm of the German Army, the Wehrmacht. The head of the Abwehr reported to the OKW, the High Command of the Wehrmacht. The man climbing out of the back of the car, going into the four-storey building and returning the eager salutes of the guards had been the head of the Abwehr since 1935. Admiral Wilhelm Canaris.

Canaris headed for the lift and his office on the fourth floor, but Jürgen touched his elbow and steered him away from it. 'Preuss thinks that we should meet in the Map Room.'

They headed down the stairs into the basement, past the rooms where the cipher clerks and radio monitors were sat in serried ranks, past the small armoury and then to a door on their right. Canaris used a key on his chain to unlock one of the locks; Jürgen did likewise with the other.

They were now in a narrow, dimly lit corridor that reminded Canaris of the submarines he had commanded in the Great War. It was only possible to walk in single file and there was a subtle but discernible sense of walking down an incline.

84

The corridor twisted slowly to the left and the gap between floor and ceiling narrowed. Both men removed their caps. The echo of the two men's boots reverberated around them, giving the illusion that there were people marching ahead of them. The corridor came to a dead end. A small flight of three metal steps, the width of the corridor, was in front of them. At the foot of the steps were two armed SS soldiers.

They parted to allow the two men up the steps. As they approached the top, a heavy door swung open. It was half a yard thick and heavily padded. No sooner had they entered than the door swung shut. It had taken the effort of two men to close it. The room was brightly lit and circular, with padded walls and ceiling. There were maps around the walls, but the room was dominated by a small circular table, around which were arranged six chairs.

Four of them had been occupied by men who stood up as Canaris and Jürgen entered the room. Canaris knew three of them very well and acknowledged them by their first names and a nod of the head.

'Hans' was Generalmajor Hans Oster. Canaris had appointed him as his deputy and Oster also headed the Abwehr's *Abteilung Z*, or Central Division, which had overall control of all the other parts of the Abwehr.

The other 'Hans' was Colonel Hans Preuss, who headed Abwehr I, which was responsible for Foreign Intelligence.

'Reinhard' was Major Reinhard Schmidt, one of Preuss's senior officers.

Like the other two, Canaris trusted him implicitly and like the other two – as with Canaris himself and Jürgen – he was not a member of the Nazi Party.

The fourth man he did not know, but he imagined that he must be the reason they had gathered in the Map Room. The very name of the room was euphemistic. It was a room that very few people in Tirpitz Ufer headquarters even knew existed. The room was completely soundproof and surrounded by enough gadgets to ensure that nothing said in it could be picked up, electronically or otherwise. For an outsider to be brought to the room was most unusual and a measure of the gravity of what was about to transpire.

All six men sat down and Preuss began talking. 'Admiral Canaris, I am sorry to bring you here at such short notice. This is Georg Lange.

He works for us in Paris and is responsible for the recruitment and the running of a number of agents.'

Canaris nodded at him.

'I have seen your name in reports, Lange. Good work,' he acknowledged.

Lange was short, but well built, giving the impression that he kept fit. His thick fair hair was slicked back and he was wearing a smart suit, which Canaris guessed was French. He was playing nervously with his watch strap.

'You can trust Georg, sir.' As in most of the corridors and offices of Berlin, as throughout Germany, people had learned to speak in code. A conversation could take four or five times longer than it needed to, because of the necessity to ensure that the person you were speaking to shared your own point of view. You wouldn't ask a friend whether they were experiencing any food shortages, which would be far too direct. But you might ask them whether they had a family lunch on Sundays, their reply might be along the lines '*Not every week*' and eventually both parties would feel able to admit that they did not have enough food.

So Preuss's 'You can trust Georg, sir' was his way of saying that the man was not a Party member.

The colonel continued.

'Georg was already working in our Embassy well before June 1940, sir. He recruited a number of agents and as you are aware, sir, we have had mixed fortunes with them. I will let Georg take up the story.'

'Thank you, sir.' Georg sounded unusually confident, in the circumstances. Canaris placed his accent from the Frankfurt area.

'We recruited an agent in 1938, sir. We had very high hopes for her. We gave her the code name Magpie... *Elster*. She was very committed to the German cause and is a most beautiful woman. Very intelligent, very quick to learn and a good temperament. The story of how I found her is very interesting. In fact, she—'

'That is for another day, Lange. Continue with the matter under discussion please,' said Preuss.

'No,' said the Admiral. 'I want to hear how you found her.'

'The point is, sir, I didn't really find her. She found us. She turned up at the Embassy in Paris. She spoke reasonable English and is also a nurse, so her cover story more or less wrote itself. We managed to slip her over to England during the Dunkirk evacuation. We were fortunate that she panicked, as half of France did, and headed north. So instead of losing her we were able to pick her up in Picardy, in a town called Abbeville. Most convenient for Dunkirk, as I say.'

'Can we trust her then?' asked Canaris. 'If she fled, that is. Presumably her instructions were to wait until you contacted her – standard procedure?'

'I am certain we can trust her, sir. Her story was credible. She believed that the French police were after her. She was travelling under her own identity. She is sharp enough that if she had been fleeing from us, she would have used another identity. Then we would never have found her.

'The plan for her was to get to England and find work in a hospital and when the time was right, apply for a transfer to a military hospital and then supply us with information. We felt that this would be a good source of steady information. She would be able to find out about casualties, what units had been posted where and where people were going to be sent when they were released from the hospital. It would be good information to have – not top grade, but it would all be very useful.

'We did have a concern about her ability to get the information back to us, so we gave her a radio man. He is a Belgian who could not wait to lick our arses the minute we rolled into Brussels. When we found out that he had a passion for radios and could speak good English, we decided to make use of him. We gave him the code name Sparrow. It is a small and common bird in England; we felt it was an appropriate name.

'So, Magpie travelled to England in June 1940. For a year, we hear nothing of her. We had told her to take her time, not to rush, but we did not expect it to be that long. Then at the end of April last year, we get our first contact.

'To be honest, sir, it was nothing much. She wanted us to know that she was working as a nurse at St Thomas's Hospital in the centre of London and that she had applied for a transfer to a military hospital. She was hopeful. Apparently she had heard that there was a shortage of nurses who could work in the area of physiotherapy. She had told them that she trained to work in physiotherapy in France.

'For a few months, nothing happened. She kept in touch with Sparrow. Every Sunday he goes to a park on his way back from church and when she has something to report, she goes to meet him there.

They bump into each other in the park. Apparently, that is a very English pastime. Then in January, she hears she is to be transferred to a military hospital. It is called...'

Georg put on a pair of reading glasses and read from his notebook.

'...Calcotte Grange. It is in the countryside, just north of London. Not a big hospital, but a specialist place where Royal Navy officers are sent to recover. Apparently the aim of the hospital is to get them fit as soon as possible so that they return to active service and fight your former navy comrades, Admiral.'

Canaris nodded: *please carry on.*

'So they have a big physiotherapy unit and Magpie is well suited. We are in business. The only problem is that it makes it difficult for her to contact Sparrow, but she can take some Sundays off, so when she has information to pass on, she is able to take a day trip to London. Not a perfect solution, but in the circumstances, a safe one.

'We start to get some good information. Not top class, but decent. You know the kind of thing: what ships are where, casualties, how well ships are equipped. Useful information on the convoys and especially on what they think of the weaponry on the ships: what guns jam, what they rate, what they dislike. No information that is going to change the war, but it all helps to build up a bigger picture and can fill in gaps in our knowledge. It has all been gratefully received by the different recipients we have sent it to – especially, of course, the Navy.'

Jürgen collected a jug of water from a table at the back of the room and poured six glasses. Georg drank gratefully from his before continuing. Canaris knew full well that everything Georg had said so far was very routine. It was the kind of information that normally would not come anywhere near him. He gestured for the man from Paris to continue.

'Then...' he was allowing a dramatic pause, during which he sipped carefully from his glass, his hands very slightly shaking '...a young Royal Navy officer falls in love with Magpie!'

Canaris nodded for him to continue. He would forgive the dramatic telling of the story if he found it justified.

'Of course, we knew that with such a beautiful woman... that men would be attracted to her. That was part of her attraction – to us! And Magpie was not a naive woman. She was experienced with men, shall we say. But this officer was different.

'He is two years younger than her and only a lieutenant. The relationship is no coincidence, Admiral. Magpie had surpassed herself. She managed to gain access to all of the patient records in the hospital and she discovered from a note in his file that this young lieutenant was due to be transferred to Naval Intelligence when he was released. On a "top secret project" according to a note on his file. Even he was not aware of it at the time, he was hoping to go back to sea. It also seems, according to his file, that he specialises in navigation and his ability to analyse coastlines and sandbanks is very highly regarded. So she put herself in a position to encourage the relationship, you might say. If you met her, Admiral, you would not be surprised that a healthy young man so eagerly took the bait.'

The silence hummed around the already very silent room. No one in it was in any doubt of the significance of what Georg was saying; least of all Georg himself, who seemed to have grown in stature as he spoke and now had a certain smugness about him as he continued.

'Magpie decided to reciprocate this officer's interest in her. She—'

'I presume we know his name?'

'Yes, sir. Quinn. Owen Quinn. Not easy to pronounce. Magpie allowed herself to be attracted to this man. She allowed him to fall in love with her and she allowed their affair to become... fully consummated, shall we say. Events then moved very fast. She feared that he would be discharged from the hospital and that he would then disappear. He would go and work in Intelligence; she would have no way of keeping in contact with him.

'Then something remarkable happened.' Lange paused again while he sipped from his glass. 'Quinn proposed to Magpie! And she, I do not need to add, accepted.'

'They allowed him to do that?' This was Oster speaking.

Major Schmidt spoke now.

'Remember, sir, that Magpie would have received security clearance to go to this hospital in the first place. She applied for a transfer to a military hospital around March, April 1941 and the transfer came through in January. Nine months. Presumably they used that time to check her out.'

'And also,' said Georg, 'she was clean when she came to England. Nothing incriminating on her whatsoever. That was the job of Sparrow. Let him carry the risk for her. She had no radio, no codebook, nothing. To all intents and purpose, she was exactly what she appeared to be: a French nurse.'

'I still find it remarkable,' said Generalmajor Oster, 'that within what seems like days of their meeting as nurse and patient, they are apparently sleeping with each other and then weeks later get married. Are we certain about this, Lange?'

'But as Lange has told us, Generalmajor, Magpie was clean. There would be absolutely no reason for the British to suspect her,' said Schmidt. 'Lange has done a good job. She had an excellent cover story and he took the very wise precaution of sending her over clean.'

'Gentlemen. Can we not argue, please. I know you find it remarkable Oster, but we need to remember this: we spend our time thinking as intelligence officers. It is our job to be suspicious of everything, all of the time. Not everyone else is like that, as we know. The British would see this girl as having had full security clearance and would hardly be surprised at a young man falling in love with her. Please continue, Lange.' Canaris was no longer tired. The Italians and the SS were a distant memory, a quiet night by the Wansee a distant hope.

'The Royal Navy are obviously a very romantic service, Admiral. They did agree to the marriage. Quinn moved to London in April and started his new job. Magpie returned to her old job at St Thomas's Hospital and in June they married and now Magpie is Mrs Quinn.'

'To live happily ever after,' said Generalmajor Oster, shaking his head.

Major Schmidt now took over.

'Thank you, Georg. Your work is of the highest quality that the service expects.' There were murmurs of agreement around the table.

'Admiral. Magpie is proving to be an outstanding agent. We are only getting small bits of information so far, but what we are receiving is top quality. We have every reason to expect that in the future, we will get more information. The lieutenant tells his wife very little, but as the months have gone on he does tell her more. She knows to take it very slowly, not to show too much interest in his work.'

'So, what do we know?'

'His unit is commanded by a captain…' Schmidt was looking through a file in front of him, searching for the name. 'Archibald. John Archibald. Saw active service in the—'

'…Battle of Jutland.' Canaris finished the sentence for him. 'I know of Archibald. Outstanding captain. Injured but continued to fight.'

'We know for a fact that this Captain Archibald worked in Royal Navy Intelligence after the war. Came out of retirement in 1940. We know that Quinn has been working on planning routes for the Arctic convoys, but we only found out about that after he finished that work. We did not get much, but what we did get was all accurate.'

'The big news,' said Preuss, taking over now from Schmidt, 'is that Quinn worked on the Dieppe raid in August. We got a whisper that he was working on something big, no details, but afterwards Quinn told Magpie that he was heavily involved in the planning. Did a lot of the work on the landings, had to put together a report of the coastline and the weather. Apparently, he was very upset afterwards. What were the figures? Six thousand Canadian and British troops went over? One thousand killed, two thousand taken prisoner, I think. No wonder he was upset.

'It is evident that he is working at the highest levels of Naval Intelligence. The projects that he works on are the most important ones. If we are very lucky, Admiral, it can only be a matter of time before the Navy puts Quinn onto working on the Second Front. All of our intelligence, as you know, tells us the invasion of northern Europe is the priority for the Allies. All their planning effort is going into it. Magpie could not be in a better place.'

Canaris got up slowly and paced around the room, deep in thought. The news from the east was bad. The Russians – aided by their great ally, the winter – were now not only holding the German advance but beginning to repel it in places. This meant that an Allied invasion somewhere in mainland Europe was increasingly likely. It was the big obsession among the planners here in Berlin and in German Army headquarters throughout Europe. When would the British and their allies launch an invasion of mainland Europe – and where would that be? To have someone in the position that Magpie was seemed, to Canaris, to be almost too good to be true.

'Is Sparrow functioning normally?' he asked.

'All his transmissions are in order. He has two or three opportunities in each transmission to let us know if he has been compromised, but he is as clean as a whistle, as they say. We would know if he wasn't,' replied Lange.

'And no one else knows about Magpie. Not the SD, no one?'

'No one, sir,' said Schmidt.

'Let's make sure that it stays that way. Excellent work, Lange.'

Chapter 10

Against his better judgement, Owen Quinn had to admit – if only to himself – that he was enjoying his work. The truth was that if he was now given the option of going back to sea, he would hesitate. It would be a dilemma, whereas back at the beginning of 1942 there would have been no question that he would rather go back to sea on active service.

It was not just that he was living with the woman he loved in what were, considering that there was a war on, close to idyllic circum-stances. It was also that, as he became busier and more involved, the more interesting and stimulating he found the work. Dieppe had been a blow, of course. Not that he had blamed himself, and Archibald insisted that nothing he had done had helped contribute to the disaster. But no one wants to be involved in an operation where half the men who go out on a mission don't return.

But if it was a setback, then it was one that seemed to act as a spur for the work of the small team on the sixth floor of Lincoln House. Their brief was to identify possible landing places for the Allies by studying the sweep of the northern coast of Europe, from the Bay of Biscay in the west to the Westerschelde that marked the Belgian-Dutch border in the east. Quinn could spend a week looking at a single port or one beach that, to be honest, he would not recommend attempting with a rowing boat in peacetime and perfect weather conditions. But they all needed to be looked at, if only to be eliminated.

Porter was forever bringing in new charts and maps and Quinn was spending less time in the small office he shared with Riley and more time at the large chart table, poring over the sheets in front of him. At times he would have Porter on one side of the table like an assistant at an operation, pulling off one map, replacing it with another or going to find another one stacked only-he-knew-where on the map shelves that had recently been installed. On occasions he would have English Rose – which, of course, was a name he never called her to her face – stand dutifully by the table as he dictated notes and observations on what he was looking at, and she would take them down in shorthand before typing them up. He would then amend the report. Riley, inevitably, would check it and Rose would type up the final version.

By June 1943 the work had taken on a different dimension altogether.

Most days he would leave work by six o'clock. If Nathalie was on a night shift he would leave a bit earlier, the incentive being that if he could get home before six she would still be in bed, where he would give in to her entreaties to join him with no resistance whatsoever. But if Nathalie was on a late shift which meant she would not be home until midnight, he was in the habit of staying late at Lincoln House. He preferred to absorb himself in his maps and charts without Rose fussing around him, without Riley's ubiquitous presence and without Porter forever trying to be helpful, but all too often getting in the way.

Archibald tended to leave the office by five o'clock in the afternoon. One evening in June, Quinn was deeply absorbed in a study of Quiberville *plage* in Normandy. The charts were particularly reliable as a resistance cell in that area had managed to obtain up-to-date copies from the Mayor's office in Quiberville itself and they had found their way to London courtesy of a returning RAF Lysander. They were especially good-quality; beach gradients, distances from shoreline at different tides. Gold dust. He was struggling a bit with the text on the chart. If *rampe* meant an upward gradient, as he seemed to remember it did, then he guessed that *pente* was a downward gradient. No point in guessing though. If only Nathalie was allowed to help him, it would save so much time. It was not exactly a word he could casually introduce into their everyday conversation. Now he would have to ask Riley to get it translated, which was an unnecessarily cumbersome process. Perhaps he could raise the matter of being able to use Nathalie for some translation again with Archibald.

'Late watch, Quinn?'

He had been so engrossed in the chart that he hadn't noticed that Captain Archibald had appeared behind him. Despite the warm evening, he was wearing his Navy greatcoat, which he was now unbuttoning. The large wall clock on the left showed it was just after seven

93

thirty. The one next to it showed it was an hour later in Quiberville *plage*.

'Useful?' Captain Archibald was looking at the chart.

'Very useful, sir. Part of that batch that the RAF brought back last month. Much more detail than we have had before. My French is not totally up to it though. Need to get some translations done. All these charts we're getting in from France are ideal, just what we need. But obviously the text on them is all in French. The translation is slowing down the whole process. There's an example here. I do need to know what *pente* means. I think it signifies a downward gradient, but I have to be sure. There's another one here – *peu profond.*'

'Well,' said Archibald, tapping a large dictionary on the desk, 'I'm sure it's all in here.'

'To an extent, sir, but it sometimes needs more of an understanding of the *context* for the words to make sense. We need to be one hundred per cent certain, as I'm sure you'd expect.'

'Ever thought of asking your wife?'

'Of course not, sir. I never discuss my work with her.'

Archibald was nodding his head in a pensive manner, as if something was occurring to him.

'Well, you're absolutely right not to ask her. Makes sense at one level: it would certainly be convenient. But not really on, I'm afraid. Essential that you keep this work and your private life completely separate. What I will do is find a decent translator for you though, someone to come in here. Anyway, I'd hoped I would catch you while no one was around. My office?'

Archibald had an ability to frame an order so as to make it sound like a reasonable question. Quinn followed him into his office.

Archibald eased himself into his chair and gestured for Quinn to do likewise on the one on the other side of the desk.

'You are not in a hurry, are you, Quinn?'

Not that it would not matter if he was. It was Archibald's way of saying this is going to take some time. Quinn shook his head.

'As you know, General Morgan was appointed as Chief of Staff to the Supreme Allied Commander in March. Three months ago. He's really got his foot on the accelerator now. His brief is to plan cross-Channel operations. That means the Second Front, the liberation of Europe. I've seen the brief. There is not much room for doubt as to what they're after. Morgan has got to plan for a full-scale assault against the Continent. Now they did want him to look into the possibility of that being this year, but he had ruled it out pretty quick. Out of the question. But they insist it will have to be in 1944. Churchill, Stalin and Roosevelt are promising that to each other, so it's hardly for Morgan to refuse. The only question is – when – and where?

'Morgan has pulled a group of senior officers together to plan it and I am on that group. About fifty of us altogether, British and American. Free French are being kept out of it. Churchill insists, doesn't trust them. De Gaulle will be furious when he finds out. We're called COSSAC: nothing to do with Russians on horseback, comes from Morgan's title, Chief of Staff to the Supreme Allied Commander. Explains why I'm not here all the time.

'The area that I am most involved in is where the landings will take place, which is where you come in. Come over here.'

The whole of one side wall of Archibald's office was taken up with a large map showing the southern coast of England and the northern coast of France and Belgium, up to and just beyond the Dutch border. Archibald had moved over to stand in front of the map. Quinn joined him.

'There are a number of factors we have to take into account. Perhaps the most important is that once we get over here,' he was holding the pencil delicately between his thick fingers, waving it in the air over France, 'then we've only just begun. There will be plenty of fighting to come and we must not lose sight of the fact that the objective is Germany. Of course, we want to liberate occupied Europe, but Germany is the key. So, the nearer we can land to Germany, the less fighting there will be on the way there. Which rules out...' his pencil was now waving above Brittany and the Cotentin peninsula around Cherbourg '...this area. Too far away.

'There are two factors we need to take in to account before deciding where to land, as you know. Many other subsidiary considerations, of course. But they will all stem from the main two. Fancy having a guess?'

Quinn was rubbing his chin with his right hand, a frown across his forehead.

'I would say distance from the British coast, sir.'

'Ten out of ten, Quinn. Distance from the British coast.' Archibald's pencil was now somewhat unnecessarily hanging over Hampshire. As a Navy man, Quinn was aware of the location of the British coast.

'Normandy is a hundred miles away. Too far, perhaps. Calais, twenty-five miles. Ideal. Belgium, getting further away again. Remember, we need to ship an army across the Channel. Morgan is talking about twenty-four Allied divisions, so the shorter the crossing, the more chance we have got of not being spotted en route and the less chance of something going wrong. The chaps have to get ashore in the landing craft and then come out fighting. Being army chaps, many of them will get seasick, so the shorter the journey, the better the state they will be in to face the bullets at the other end. Don't forget too, we need air cover. Range of a Spitfire, Quinn?'

'One-seventy-five, one-eighty, sir?'

'One hundred and fifty miles. Important figure to remember, that. Need to fly over there and back and have plenty of fuel to be of some use in keeping the Luftwaffe at bay while they are over there.

'So the favoured location is here... round the Pas de Calais.' The pencil was now drawing an imaginary circle around Calais and where the coastline dropped south, just to the west of it.

'Perfect distance. Of course, the Germans will be expecting us there, which is why they've got von Salmuth's Fifteenth Army in that area with five Panzer divisions to support him. If we go west of the River Orne, here...' Archibald's pencil pointed at Ouistreham at the mouth of the Orne and then glided left over the Calvados Coast: Lion sur Mer, St Aubin sur Mer, Arromanches, Port en Bessin, '...then we come up against the Seventh Army. General Dollman. Not in the same league as the Fifteenth and he's only got one Panzer division backing him up.

'So there is a temptation to head for the area that is not as well defended. But then even if we went to Normandy because it is defended by the weaker army, the Germans will send reinforcements over there quickly enough, so we would not hold that advantage for very long.'

Archibald stepped back from the map in a surprisingly sprightly manner.

'Would you care to guess the second important factor, Quinn?'

The younger man hesitated. There were so many considerations.

'I suppose it would be where do we land – on a beach, or a port?'

'Good. As you know, it is not just the troops we have got to land. There're the tanks, vehicles – all the supplies. So a port would be the obvious place – but if we learned one lesson from Dieppe, as you know, it is that attacking a well-defended port is just too risky. All the aerial reconnaissance photos we're getting in show just what we're up against and the resistance is telling us the same too. All the ports would be death traps. Too well defended and heavily mined.

'The solution then would appear to be a beach landing. Tricky, of course. You still have to land an army and get them and all their equipment off the beach in more or less one piece. And it is not as if the Germans have not defended the beaches. As you know, they're mined, boobytrapped – and there are plenty of bunkers and gun emplacements. Rommel has done a good job, but he has had three thousand miles of coastline to worry about. Even he cannot defend every stretch of beach in northern France. The beaches have to be our best bet. There'll be a chink in his armour somewhere. Our job is to find it.'

There was a long pause. Archibald was standing in front of the map, about a yard away from it. His arms were folded and his pencil was sticking out, waving in the air like a conductor's baton during a particularly sombre piece of music. He moved closer, until he was stood just inches from the map. Quinn moved in with him.

'Come here, Quinn. Lots of pros and cons, as you can see. Do we go for north west France?' He was tapping the Normandy coast again. 'Longer route, further from Germany, but not as well defended. Or do we go for the north east?' The pencil was now hovering somewhere south of Calais. 'Better defended, but shorter crossing and, of course, puts us much nearer Germany.

'But then it is also where the Germans will be expecting us. They have the same maps as we do, after all. But if we are going to plan a successful invasion, a decision needs to be made as to where we are going and COSSAC has made its decision. This is where the Second Front will be, Quinn, between here…' Archibald's pencil was resting on Boulogne sur Mer. As he continued to speak, the pencil followed the coast down as it fell south west. '…and here.' His pencil had rested in the Baie de Somme.

'Ever been to the Bay of the Somme, Quinn?'

'No, sir.'

'Beautiful place. Full of wildlife. Quite stunning. Hope we don't ruin it, but I expect we will.'

Another long pause.

'So that is where it will be. Between Boulogne and the Bay of the Somme. We need to decide the best stretch of beach to go for. Morgan's preference seems to be here… avoid the cliffs between Cap d'Alprech and Équihen-Plage,' he was indicating a point just below Boulogne, 'but no further south than Le Touquet. It's a seven-mile stretch.'

His pencil rested on the small town of Plage de Ste Cécile.

'But we need to keep our options open. Still need to check out the whole coast down to the Bay of the Somme, another twenty miles or so. But concentrate on this top area.'

'So, this is now your job, Quinn. By the time you've finished, you are going to know every inch of that stretch of coastline. You will get to know every grain of sand. It's about seven miles, but you will see it in your sleep and as you walk along the streets here in London. We need to know about the beach gradients, whether the sand can take tanks and our heavy armour. We need to know about tide, about unusual currents. We need to be aware of every sandbank, every rock. We need to know that even if a beach is ideal to land on, what are the exit routes like? We need to know what the weather is like. In short, Quinn, we need to know everything – and then a bit more.'

Quinn was not sure whether he was meant to say anything. He realised that everything that they had been working on up to now had been leading to this. The work had felt at times that it lacked focus, he felt like a sportsman who had been warming up for the big event. In the course of the past hour, he had been told the location of the Second Front, the biggest secret of the war.

'Come with me, Quinn.'

Archibald walked out into the central office area.

'You're not alone in this, you know. Plenty of units like this working on the planning across London. But we have something to help us.' Archibald was unlocking a large metal filing cabinet. There was a central lock and then each of the three large drawers had a lock.

'Do you remember after Dunkirk the BBC broadcast an appeal for people to send in anything they had on the northern European coast? We were after whatever they had, maps, holiday guides, postcards, photographs.'

Quinn nodded. He remembered the fuss his mother made about sending in some dog-eared postcards her sister had sent from her

French holidays. She had asked Owen to see what he could do to ensure they would be returned to her.

'Thought we'd get a few thousand. Millions of them came in. Literally millions, Quinn. I'm told that people have been driven quite crazy sorting them all out, but they've done that now. And here...' he was pointing at the now unlocked filing cabinet '...are the fruits of their labours. All the material sent in to do with that stretch of coastline. A surprising amount.'

They both stared at the cabinet, daunted by what lay in it.

'And there are more, they'll be brought in over the next few days. My guess, Quinn, is that perhaps no more than two, perhaps three per cent of all that will be of any use. But that two or three per cent will be invaluable. Look at this picture here.'

It was a snapshot of a boy and a girl standing against a wall, self-consciously close to each other, their faces partially obscured by ice creams. Archibald turned the photograph over and read the caption.

'Ian and Wendy. Le Touquet. August 1937.' Now this is exactly the kind of thing that we need. Someone in Intelligence followed this up. Contacted the parents. Sure enough, they had measured the height of Ian and Wendy every birthday, so we know how tall they both are in August 1937 – four foot nine and four foot six it says here – and from that we can get a very good idea of how high that wall is. And because we can pinpoint it thanks to this sign next to it, we know that at this point, our boys would need to get over a wall that is approximately four foot high.

'I think that you are going to be very busy, Quinn.'

–

It was not in Owen Quinn's nature to be anything other than optimistic. 'You're a glass-half-full man,' his grandfather had often remarked. He was always of a most positive disposition. But an event at the end of June did give him cause to wonder.

It was a balmy summer evening and he was enjoying the stroll home through St James's Park. Nathalie was working late at the hospital and he was in no hurry. He had just entered the park when he heard his name being called. He turned round to see a large figure in RAF uniform running across the road to catch up with him.

'Quinn. I refuse to believe it! You're alive!'

'Well, I was this morning when I last looked in the mirror!'

'It's me, Linwood. Remember?' He had removed his RAF officer's cap.

'Of course, Linwood. Good God. Didn't realise you were in the RAF. I had no idea what you were doing.'

'Don't think I've seen you since we left university, eh? Joined up in '39. Didn't fancy your lot, tendency towards seasickness. Army sounded a bit dull and flying just up my street.'

'Battle of Britain?'

Linwood shook his head. 'Bomber Command. Giving them a taste of their own medicine. Now what about you. Last I heard, you were dead. Drowned at sea?'

'Almost, Linwood. Not quite though. Was on HMS *Gloucester* when it was sunk off Crete in '41. Damn-near didn't make it. Don't remember an awful lot, to be honest. Spent months in a hospital back here. Not fit enough for active service, apparently, but serving behind a desk. You understand.'

'Of course I do, old chap. Glad to see you alive. Look, I've got to go back up to Lincolnshire tonight – getting a lift. Fancy a drink first? Bit of catching up to do.'

The pub in Victoria was emptying of civil servants and they found a quiet table at the back. Linwood negotiated his way over, doing his best not to spill the beer.

'Like navigating through German flak, eh? There you are, Quinn. Pint of best mild. Does you the world of good. Now then, tell me everything.'

'Not an awful lot to say I'm afraid, Linwood. Don't really keep in touch with many of the chaps from university. Joined the Navy, as you know. I am married though.'

'Congratulations!' Linwood had stood up to reach over the table and warmly shake his hand, spilling some of the beer in the process. 'You're a dark horse, aren't you? Never had you down as much of a ladies' man. Now, tell me all about her.'

'Well, what can I say? She's French, came over at the time of Dunkirk. And she's a nurse. She was working at the hospital in the country that I was sent to when I came back here – that's where we met.'

'What does she look like, Quinn?'

'Well, perhaps not for me to say, but...'

'Come on old chap, if *you* can't say what she looks like then who on earth can!'

'What I mean is, I don't want to appear boastful, Linwood, but she is rather beautiful. At least I think so.'

Linwood moved his large frame and fleshy face across the table. He was looking very interested. 'Description please, Quinn.'

Quinn blushed. 'Super figure, lovely long hair, remarkable eyes.'

'Too good to be true, Quinn. Refuse to believe you. Got a photograph?'

'I do actually,' he said, taking his wallet out of his top pocket. He passed over a small photograph somewhat sheepishly. 'Here we are.'

Linwood went silent and studied the photograph carefully from different angles. He turned it over. *Owen, all my love – amour – Nathalie xxx.*

'Quinn – she's beautiful. Totally beautiful. You were telling the truth.' Linwood was speaking in almost reverential tones now. 'How on earth did a chap like you...?'

'A chap like me what?' Quinn was slightly offended.

'No, no, no – don't take it like that. Just that when we were at university you were the fairly quiet type. Would never in a month of Sundays have thought...'

Linwood couldn't say much more. He just waved the photograph, before looking at it closely again. *Would never have thought that a chap like you would end up with a girl like her.* That's what he means to say, thought Quinn. I sometimes wonder that myself, if I'm honest.

'And is it true what they say about French girls?' Linwood was looking quite flushed now.

'What is it that they say about French girls, Linwood?'

His friend leaned towards him and lowered his voice.

'Oh, come on, Quinn! You know. Great lovers and all that. No inhibitions.'

'Linwood! You're talking about my wife!' Quinn had defused any tension by laughing.

'Does she have any sisters over here or friends? If so, I insist on meeting them next time I'm on leave. Tell me everything!'

'Not a lot more to say, actually. Told you most of it.'

'Where is she from?'

'Somewhere in Paris, not exactly sure.'

'And family? What about them?'

'Look, Linwood. Don't mean to be rude, but I've learned not to ask. It's different with the war. She's had to leave her own country and that's not easy. I suppose I need to be sensitive, can't ask too many questions.'

'Don't get upset, old chap. Just seems a bit… odd that you know so little about her.'

'Well, as I say, that's the war for you.'

'Understand,' said Linwood, though Quinn had the feeling that he didn't really.

They left the pub soon after, Quinn to go home and Linwood to head back to Lincolnshire. They exchanged addresses and promised to keep in touch.

For the rest of that evening he was unsettled by his encounter with Linwood.

Despite what he had said, in his heart of hearts he knew that it was odd that he knew so little about his wife.

He was determined to find out more. He needed to be more assertive – Nathalie herself had told him that.

The opportunity came the following evening. Nathalie had not been at work and when he arrived back at the flat she was walking around wearing nothing but his dressing gown. The front was open and she was smiling. An hour later, after they had finished making love for the third time, they both lay in bed, exhausted and happy. Nathalie had managed to get hold of a bottle of French wine which was meant to be very good and it now lay empty on their bedside table. Empty bodies, empty wine bottle. He felt decadent and totally relaxed.

Nathalie lay on her back naked, staring at the ceiling. Owen rolled over onto his side and leaned over her. With his finger, he gently traced a pattern across her breasts. Her black eyes swivelled from the ceiling, locked into his and she smiled.

Carpe diem.

'I want to know more about you, Nathalie.' The question sounded awkward and even his speaking seemed to have broken a perfect mood. Her eyes frowned very slightly and the smile subsided.

'What do you want to know, Owen? I've told you everything. I'm a boring person. Do you want me to be more exciting? Shall I tell you that I am secret agent who arrived here by parachute? That I am a descendant of Napoleon? Ask me whatever questions you want. Go on.'

There was a pause. Linwood's observation that he seemed to know little about her had struck a chord; he didn't know a lot about her. Try as he might, there were times when he felt that he had absolutely no idea of what she was really like. But he had no idea what questions to ask. He smiled and kissed her cheek and she took hold of that hand that had stopped tracing patterns on her breasts and started it again.

Chapter 11

London, July 1943

A fortnight after Archibald had told him about the secret invasion plans for the Pas de Calais, Owen Quinn and Nathalie were invited to dinner by Archibald.

'Mrs Archibald is on one of her rare visits from Lincolnshire and I thought it would be a good idea: we've invited two other couples. Melrose is Army, but a perfectly decent chap. Work with him at COSSAC though you don't know that, of course. And Hardisty is at the Air Ministry. Wife's French, so that ought to be jolly for your wife. Strictly nothing about work, of course.'

Nathalie, who had recently begun to complain that London was a boring city, was nonetheless not enthusiastic about the invitation.

'My English will not be good enough,' she said as they ate their supper the evening that her husband told her about the dinner.

'Your English is almost fluent, darling.'

'Almost?' She sounded angry.

'Well, yes. "Almost fluent" is not a criticism – it actually means that your English is excellent. You will have no problem in taking part in the conversation, I assure you.'

'They will all talk about work.'

'We are not allowed to talk about work.'

'Why?'

'I have explained that to you, darling. What I do is secret. I am just not allowed to discuss it. Same reason as I can never tell you anything. The same will apply to everyone else there.'

'But what is that word you use to describe how you find your work? Sounds like "tea"?'

'"Tedious" do you mean?'

'Yes. So if your work is so tedious, how can it be so secret?'

'That is how it is.'

'So it will be very boring. I suppose we will have to talk about the weather.'

'Quite possibly. And cats.'

'Why cats?'

'It's a joke, Nathalie. An English joke. You say that the English talk about the weather. Well, the other great English topic of conversation is their pets.'

'But we do not have any pets. We can be sure we will not talk about food. No one is interested in food in this country. In France, there would be riots if we had to eat the kind of food you are happy to eat in England.'

Nathalie was toying with the remains of the casserole that she had cooked. Owen was finishing his second helping while she had hardly eaten at all. With his mouth full he gestured towards his plate and gave a thumbs up sign. 'But this is good!'

'That is my point, Owen. You are satisfied with this. The meat is tough and you cannot buy the proper herbs anyway. You English think that pepper and salt is all you need. I am ashamed of this meal, even though I had to smile very sweetly at the butcher to persuade him to give me a tiny bit more of what you call meat here. Even then, it is not what I call a proper casserole. It's mostly carrots.'

–

The dinner took place in Archibald's club, which was round the corner from Lincoln House, in St James's Street. Quinn had worn his best uniform to work and Nathalie met him outside there at seven, looking ravishing. She was not allowed beyond reception, but Quinn basked in the approving looks of the guards when he went down to meet her.

She linked her arm into his, her fingers squeezing the inside of his elbow and her shoulder nestling against him. They strolled into Jermyn Street where she promised to buy him a suit when they were rich and into St James's Street, turning left, crossing the road and walking the twenty yards or so to Archibald's club.

Quinn had to agree that the dinner was hard work. You could blame the food (Brown Windsor soup, an oddly greyish beef in a thick, dark sauce, followed by apple pie) on wartime, but the conversation was somewhat stilted. And this was despite the wine, which was a very decent Côtes du Rhône.

Hardisty, it turned out, had met his wife in Paris before the war, when he had been an air attaché at the Embassy, so he was fluent in French. For much of the meal they had to listen to Melrose's wife, the extent of whose wartime deprivation seemed to be some minor problems with domestic staff. Captain Archibald and his wife talked about their life in Lincolnshire, while for much of the time Hardisty's wife and Nathalie were speaking in French.

At first, Nathalie had been solicitous enough in finding out which part of Paris Madame Hardisty was from.

'The 8th arrondissement – off the Boulevard Haussmann. And you?'

'Oh, we moved around. Usually south of the 14th.' Madame Hardisty smiled politely, clear now that it was most unlikely that their paths had ever crossed.

She was answering all their questions politely enough, but did not sustain any conversation.

It was a balmy July evening, so they walked back to Pimlico.

'Did you enjoy the evening?'

'It was fine.'

'Did you get on with Madame Hardisty.'

'She was fine. But you know, we are from very different… societies. She is a different kind of person to me. You have to learn to understand this, Owen. This kind of person, they live in a very different kind of France. The France they expect to find after the war is very different to mine.'

Quinn wanted to ask her just what she meant, but Nathalie had a way of shutting down a conversation when she wished it to go no further. By now they had turned into Alderney Street and he had more important things on his mind.

—

Two days after the dinner there was a minor disaster in Lincoln House. In response to Quinn's demands for some help with translation, Archibald had found an elderly, retired French teacher with what he described as an admirably high level of security clearance. As far as Quinn could gather, the main criterion for her high level of security clearance was the fact that both of her brothers had fought in the Great War.

So two or three days a week Miss Lean would slowly make her way to the office where she would sit at a desk and, with the aid of a large dictionary that she brought with her in a basket, laboriously translate.

The minor disaster came with a message one morning that Miss Lean had slipped on her way to work and broken both of her ankles. She would not be returning. Miss Lean was replaced by a French-woman in her late thirties who was physically stronger than Miss Lean (it would have been difficult to be otherwise), but emotionally fragile.

She only had to look at a postcard from France, or a photograph or even a map, for her to burst into tears. After just one week, Archibald had to agree that her psychological state was not conducive with working in such a sensitive environment.

'What are we meant to do?' Quinn asked Archibald. 'We need all these translations done and until then, it's just holding us up.'

They were in Archibald's office. Quinn was clutching a pile of papers that needed translating, which he had brought in for added impact. Archibald was thinking quietly, drumming his long fingers on the desk in front of him. After a while, Archibald nodded quietly to himself.

'There is a possible solution, Quinn. Not one that I am terribly happy with, but one that may work. I know that this was mentioned a few weeks ago, but now it seems that your wife...' he had put his glasses on now and was looking at a sheet of paper '...did indeed have a higher level of clearance than we had at first realised when she moved to Calcotte Grange. What we've done is check her out a bit more and we can move her clearance up another notch or two so that she has the right level to help you out with some of this. Help you shift all this stuff. You're going to be inundated with material, aren't you?'

Quinn nodded in agreement.

'No reason then for you not to take the odd low level stuff home, work over the weekend, peace and quiet, that kind of thing. And with so much in French, to be able to ask her will save a lot of time. Obviously, we keep it all hush-hush and she doesn't need to see any more than she has to. Nothing top secret, you understand. She can't know about the context of what you may ask her, but the odd word here and there – no harm in that. She doesn't need to know what all this is about and I certainly don't mean go tell her where landings are going to be, eh!'

Quinn was surprised, but agreed that it did indeed sound reason-able. It was certainly going to make life that little bit easier. Recently

Nathalie had been going on about how he told her nothing about what he did and she was wondering whether that meant he didn't love her.

–

RAF Scampton
Lincolnshire

Dear Owen Quinn,

My name is Andy Wood and I was a close colleague and friend of Flying Officer Anthony (Tony) Linwood. It is with deep regret that I am writing to inform you that Tony is listed as missing, presumed dead, after his Lancaster was lost in action in an air raid over Hamburg last month. Tony was a loyal and brave member of 617 Squadron and is sorely missed by everyone here at RAF Scampton.

I gave Tony a lift back to Lincolnshire the same night that he bumped into you in St James's Park and I know how thrilled he was to have met up with you again. He was in very good spirits that night and I am sure that is in large measure due to having met up with you. He was full of admiration for you and said what a lucky man you are. Sadly, the raid in which he was killed took place just the night after you and he met.

I am sorry for the delay in writing to you with this appalling news, but I only recently found your address among his papers.

Yours truly,
(Flight Lieutenant) Andy Wood

–

Owen's parents arrived in London on the last Sunday in July for a much-heralded and long-planned visit. He and Nathalie had bickered all morning as they prepared for his parents' arrival. Nathalie sat on the bed painting her nails: 'It is not often that I have a Sunday off,' she complained, 'and when I do, I'd rather not spend it with your mother. She reminds me of the sisters at the hospital – always critical, always checking on what I'm doing.'

But you're not doing a lot, Owen thought as he moved the furniture round in the tiny lounge. He had somehow managed to shift one of the enormous armchairs into their bedroom, which meant that they could open out the table and squeeze the four of them around it, even if that did mean him having to sit on the arm of the remaining armchair. He had little doubt that his mother would strongly disapprove of that.

'Shall I tell you how long I had to queue for the chicken?' the voice in the bedroom asked.

'You've already told me, Nathalie. Two hours.'

'Two hours.'

'Well, it does smell absolutely delicious, darling. I honestly can't remember the last time I had chicken. Must have been in the New Year at my parents'. They'll be thrilled. You can't beat roast chicken.'

She appeared in the doorway of the bedroom to inspect the rearrangement of the lounge. She was wearing his dressing gown; tantalisingly partly open at the front, revealing that she was wearing nothing underneath. Her hands were held out in front of her, the fingers spreadeagled and slowly waving as she tried to dry her nails.

'It's only just a chicken. In France it would have been living on a farm for very old chickens. Even French foxes would have the sense to ignore it. And where are you going to sit?'

'For heaven's sake, just stop it!' he shouted.

'Pardon?' She looked genuinely taken aback.

'Just leave it will you. Please stop complaining about everything. I am entitled to have my parents round and for them to have something decent to eat. I know this country is not France but I think it has been pretty decent to you. How would you like to be back in France now, with all those bloody Nazis around?' He stepped back, shocked at his own outburst.

'Owen,' she said, smiling sweetly and allowing the dressing gown to slip from her shoulders and to the floor. 'You've never spoken to me like that before. Come here...'

'Hang on, you do realise that the curtains are open and...'

She stepped back into the bedroom, where the curtains were drawn.

'And what?'

He put down the cutlery. He could lay the table later, after he had peeled the potatoes. He was inside the bedroom, his shirt already off when the doorbell rang.

'So we had to stick to the A3 even though...'

'William, I am sure Owen and Nathalie do not want to hear all about our journey today. It is not as if we had to fight our way past the Germans!'

Marjorie Quinn shrieked at her own joke and her husband and son laughed politely, while her daughter-in-law looked confused.

'Well, I must say, Nathalie, that it is a real treat to have chicken. Delicious. Cordon – what is it you call it in France?' asked her father-in-law.

'They call it cordon bleu, William, though I would not have thought that this is cordon bleu. Personally, I prefer my chicken to be roasted for rather longer, but then you probably have not had much experience recently, have you, Nathalie? Owen dear, do you really need to be sitting at the dining table on the edge of an armchair?'

'Mother, please!'

'Please what, Owen?'

His mother, father and wife had all stopped eating and were looking at him.

'Mother... this is my home and my wife... please do stop going on.'

The ensuing silence was broken ten minutes later by Marjorie Quinn's much diminished voice.

'I was only saying...' she said softly.

Her husband patted her on the wrist. 'Probably best not to say anything dear...'

They left soon after lunch: their journey that morning having been so difficult they didn't want to leave it too late.

Once they had returned to the flat after seeing his parents off, Nathalie led him straight into the bedroom.

An hour later she planted an arm firmly across his chest as he tried to get up from the bed.

'But we need to clear up.'

'Your reward hasn't finished, Owen. Why are you looking so puzzled?'

'Reward for what?'

'That you're not a boy any longer, are you?' She was brushing the long fair hair away from his damp brow, combing it back with her long fingers. 'The way you spoke to me this morning, the way you spoke to your mother… you are learning to stand up for yourself. I think I like it.'

An hour later, Owen was to be found happily tidying up the flat and merrily whistling as he washed up the dishes.

Nathalie soaked in a tepid bath for longer than she normally would have done. Life is so confusing, she thought. Everything starts off by being confused. And then you realise what you have to do and you go and do it and everything becomes clearer. And then, things get in the way. Events. People. Places. Emotions become involved, even if you don't intend them to or even want them to. So you end up being confused again.

Chapter 12

London, November 1943

'Well, all I can say is that this is most irregular. Most irregular.'

'But Leigh, everything you chaps do is most irregular!'

'I simply cannot imagine what Selbourne thought he was playing at, agreeing to this nonsense.'

Major Edgar stood up, his tall frame blocking out some of the sunlight as he did so. He was not averse to using his considerable height to help bring his influence to bear on a situation and he needed to use all of his influence now in what was a very tense situation. His recent promotion had added to his sense of confidence.

There was silence in the room. They were in the Baker Street headquarters of the Special Operations Executive, the SOE. Outside, there was a steady hum of traffic. Inside, a small ornate clock on Leigh's desk was ticking in what appeared to be an erratic manner. The clock reminded Edgar of Leigh: ornate and erratic, and from an earlier era.

Edgar was becoming exasperated. The small man he was now towering over reminded him of an ineffectual country vicar, with a high-pitched, whiny voice to match. Edgar did not understand why they picked these academics from the Oxbridge colleges where they had spent most of their lives and assumed that, because they were an authority on a medieval French poet no one had heard of, they would therefore fit naturally into the upper echelons of British Intelligence.

'The 3rd Earl of Selbourne is the Minister for Economic Warfare, Dr Leigh. He is responsible for your organisation. He has agreed to this operation.'

'I am quite aware of who Selbourne is, Edgar. No doubt Churchill twisted his arm. But it does not stop this being most irregular.'

Edgar was having to exercise considerable restraint. Leigh had used the word irregular in nearly every sentence for the past ten minutes.

His face was a bright red and his hands a pallid white as they gripped the arms of his chair.

Edgar had some sympathy for Leigh. His job could not be an easy one. The SOE had been set up in July 1940 as part of the Secret Intelligence Service, or MI6. Its remit was to work behind the lines in occupied Europe, carrying out acts of sabotage and secret warfare. Its main role was to work with resistance groups. Much of its work was done through country groups. Edgar was aware that, as far as France was concerned, it was typically complicated. There were two groups. RF Section worked with the Gaullist faction. F Section was the independent country section for France. Dr Clarence Leigh's role was to liaise with both RF and F Sections on behalf of the head of SOE. Edgar assumed that he used medieval French poetry to help resolve disputes. Or start them.

'Dr Leigh. I do acknowledge that there is a historic rivalry between our two organisations, but surely you must understand the absolute importance of this mission.'

Major Edgar believed passionately that the mission of the London Controlling Section for which he worked was of paramount import-ance. The LCS had been set up by Winston Churchill in June 1942 to plan deception operations against the enemy, and its overriding priority now was the invasion of Europe, which was planned for 1944. The invasion was fraught with risk, but one way of helping it to succeed was by persuading the Germans that the invasion was going to take place somewhere else. Edgar was the case officer responsible for handling three German agents to work on behalf of this deception. Two of them were doing so willingly, having agreed to become double agents. The most important one was not aware of the crucial role they were currently playing. It was in connection with that agent that Major Edgar was enduring a most uncomfortable afternoon with Dr Leigh.

'And you absolutely insist that there is no other way?'

The first chink was appearing in Leigh's armour. His resigned tone sounded as if he was addressing a student who was handing in an essay late.

'No. If there was, I can assure you we would have gone down that route.'

'Very well then. I'll speak to Newby at F Section. Best work with them if you don't want de Gaulle to catch wind of this.'

'Thank you very much, Clarence. I have no doubt that Winston will be most pleased to hear of a new era of co-operation between our two organisations.'

Leigh snorted. 'But one thing that I do need to make very clear, Edgar. This is a most irregular business. In everything we do in SOE, security is of absolute paramount importance, as I am sure you appreciate. For us to be asked to train a German spy in our methods and then send him over to France puts our own security at risk. It could jeopardise our whole operation. Therefore, we will have to train him at a different location than we normally use and bring new people in to do the training. We will have to incur considerable costs in the process. I do expect your people to pay for this.'

'Of course,' said Edgar. It was a small price to pay.

'Very well, then. I shall see Newby this afternoon and inform him of the situation. You ought to be able to see him tomorrow, certainly in the next few days. Are you now able to give me any details about this agent? What code name does he go by?'

Edgar was already putting on his large, dark coat.

'Goes by the code name of Magpie. And he is a she.'

'Oh!' It was a long, high-pitched and slightly surprised 'oh'. Before the war, Clarence Leigh had inhabited a world where women were little more than bit-part players and it still came as a surprise to him that they were involved at all in the world of espionage.

–

It was a bitter November night. Autumn had finally surrendered to winter and a thick, yellow-stained fog had draped itself across the city, tightening its grip with every laboured breath. Owen would have happily stayed in the warmth of the office or gone straight home, but he had arranged to meet Nathalie at the hospital so that he could walk her to their flat. When he left Duke Street, it had been not much more than a heavy mist, but with each footstep it became increasingly dense so that by the time he reached Victoria Embankment he could barely see a yard ahead. It reminded him of being at sea: the speed at which a mist would roll in before visibility was no more than a few yards and all eyes on the bridge would be on him as they sailed into the unknown. His pace slowed down to little more than a crawl as he felt his way along the wall, its surface clammy. Below him, Quinn could hear the river, the water lapping hard against the bank and the bridge ahead. The sound of the river was muffled by the thick fog and had an unfamiliar echo.

To all intents and purposes, it felt as if he was the last person left in London. No other soul was about until a policeman in his dark cape briefly came into view and then disappeared, his torch doing no more than emphasising the thick swirl of the smog. Ahead of him, he could hear the sentries outside the Palace of Westminster marching up and down, their hobnail boots scraping on the pavement, but they remained invisible. The bitter, sulphuric taste of the smog crept down his throat and he began to feel nauseous. His eyes were stinging. The air was filled with menace. The cold stone of the wall gave way and he realised that he had reached the north side of Westminster Bridge. By holding the luminous dial of his watch close to his face he could see that it was twenty past eight. He had promised to meet Nathalie outside the hospital at eight o'clock and he knew that she'd be concerned, even allowing for the fog. She was prone to impatience. Although St Thomas's was just on the south side of the bridge, it would take him another ten minutes at least to get there. He hoped she would understand, but feared that her impatience might get the better of her.

He felt a surge of optimism. He always felt like that when he knew he was about to see his wife. He'd been married for a few months before he realised what was happening, before he recognised that when he wasn't with her he was bereft and when he was with her he was whole, complete.

Owen hesitated. For some reason, he was fearful of crossing the bridge, his progress inhibited by trepidation. And he sensed that it was not the fog. From his time at sea he was well used to moving in the dark, trusting his sense of navigation. He hesitated for a good five minutes, during which time the fog very slightly lifted, but as it did so there was a sharp drop in temperature. He pulled the brim of his Navy cap low over his face and, turning up the collar of his coat, set out into the void. Progress was noticeably easier. Visibility was now as much as three or even four yards. As he approached what he took to be the middle of the bridge a woman came into view, walking on the other side of it and in the opposite direction to him. Her hands were thrust deep into her coat pockets and her head, around which was a tightly wrapped scarf, was looking down at the ground ahead of her. Owen paused. He could not take his eyes off her: a stranger, yet achingly familiar. As she came abreast of him he moved into the road so as to get a better view and as he did so, he realised that it could be Nathalie.

But there was something so unfamiliar about her that he hesitated in calling her name, settling instead for an uncertain 'Hello?'

She looked up and in the very brief moment before she recognised her husband beneath his cap and raised collar, he saw her as he had never seen her before. Her face appeared different: softer, more relaxed and, above all, unguarded. If time had stood still at that exact moment and he had been forced to use one word to describe how she looked different, it would have been that one. Unguarded. Then, as she realised it was him, her face instantly arranged itself into a more familiar look. The face hardened very slightly – and then she smiled and almost skipped over to him, before pecking him on the cheek and then moving her warm mouth to his.

'Why are you so late, Owen? I thought you weren't coming. I decided to make my own way home.'

'Haven't you noticed the fog, darling?'

Her kiss was moist against the side of his mouth. 'I'm pleased you came, Owen. You're so...' She hesitated, struggling to find the right word '...dependable.'

And with that, arm in arm, they walked back to Pimlico. Well before they arrived back at the flat, he had allowed the confused image on the bridge to fade from his memory. In years to come he would often recall that encounter on the bridge and wonder about exactly what he had seen in her expression. If he had thought about it for longer at the time, with the memory of exactly what had happened and of just what he had seen still fresh in his mind, then he would have come to the conclusion that she looked as if she was wearing a mask. But what he could not tell was whether she was wearing that mask before she saw him, or after.

–

Portman Square was a brief walk from the SOE headquarters in Baker Street and it was in a mews house just behind the square that F Section of the SOE was based. F Section looked after SOE operations in France and its primary role was to work with the French resistance.

Major Edgar had to admit that, while he was not quite sure what he was expecting, it was certainly something a bit more substantial and imposing than a pleasant mews house occupied by fewer than ten people. A woman in her mid-thirties with a vague, central European accent that he could not place led him up a series of narrow staircases to the top floor. They moved along an uneven corridor into what he assumed was a section of the adjoining house. They were now in a room converted out of the attic. A large skylight ensured that, despite the November gloom, the room was bathed in light.

Behind a small desk a man in civilian clothes was on the phone.

'*Oui, Philippe. Bien sûr, bien sûr. Je comprends. D'accord. A bientôt.*'

He put the phone down and came over to greet Edgar. The woman had closed the door, remaining in the room.

'Good to meet you, Edgar. Newby. Tony Newby. Major Newby if you're interested in that kind of thing. Everyone seems to be a major these days, eh?

'Hope you were impressed by the French. Pretty much the extent of it, I'm afraid. Rely on the likes of Nicole here. I've learned that if you keep saying *d'accord*, folks think you know what you are talking about, eh?'

Very quickly, Edgar realised that although this bonhomie was in welcome contrast to Leigh's petulance, it almost certainly masked a strong character. Edgar could see Newby's eyes summing him up and his brain playing with him. This was a man who had already sent more than three hundred agents into occupied France and was now being asked to send one more. A German spy.

'Dr Leigh has told me what you chaps are after, but how about if I hear it from the horse's mouth, eh? *Bouche de cheval* – is that correct, Nicole?'

'To an extent, sir. I would try *on l'appris de source sûre.*'

'Thank you,' said Edgar. 'I do realise that this is somewhat... irregular, but I hope you will understand that the circumstances are extenuating ones.

'In 1941 we identified a previously undetected Nazi agent. She had entered the country in 1940, after Dunkirk, but kept her nose clean for the best part of a year. She came into our sights thanks to a Belgian whom we'd been watching ever since he came into the country. We turned him, which led to her. As you've no doubt been told, her code name is Magpie. Magpie is a French nurse and by all accounts a very good one. I ought to add that she is also a most beautiful woman.'

Newby indicated his approval with one long, slow nod.

'Magpie was working at a hospital in central London when we came across her. By a sheer stroke of luck, it so happened that she had recently applied for a transfer to a military hospital, which made some sense. Plenty of decent intelligence to be picked up in that kind environment if you think about it. Morale, where people have been based, where they are being sent, casualties, what equipment works, what doesn't... all useful stuff to the Germans.

'We decided to keep her where she was for the time being. Keep an eye on her, but have her up our sleeves. Sure enough, it all worked out a treat. We thought that if we were clever and lucky, we could put her much closer to Allied intelligence than either she or the Germans could have hoped. Plan was fairly simple: send her to a hospital for recovering Navy officers, ensure that one of the patients she just happens to be looking after is due to be moved into Naval Intelligence when he is discharged from hospital. So we ensure that she has access to the files and that one of the files has a note that a particular officer is indeed due to be transferred to Naval Intelligence when he is released. Lots of references to "top secret" et cetera – you get the picture. Perfect opportunity for her. As we hoped, she starts to get particularly friendly with this young officer. He, of course, thinks she is the most wonderful woman he has ever seen – no young chap in his right mind and his position wouldn't think that. We move the young man into his own room, pretty much put the two of them into bed with each other. He's then told "no, you are not going back to sea, not up to it. Important job for you in Naval Intelligence. Oh and by the way, we know what is going on with you and the nurse so if you want to make a decent woman of her..." Not exactly a whirlwind romance, Major, but worked a treat.'

'And he... is totally unaware?' Major Newby had started to speak.

'Not the foggiest idea. Can't stress this strongly enough, Newby. He has no idea whatsoever who she is. He is unaware of what is going on. Thinks this beautiful Frenchwoman who is two years older than him has fallen in love with him. He is like the cat that got the cream – gallons of the stuff, in fact. Still is, actually.

'By the end of June '42 we've got them happily married and settled into a little flat we found for them in Pimlico. Put one of our chaps next door just in case. His bedroom is behind theirs and apparently he does not get a lot of sleep. Our man is ensconced in an office of Naval Intelligence that we have especially set up round the corner from St

James's Square. We keep it all very lovey-dovey for the best part of a year. We know that she is picking up bits and pieces from his work and is passing all this back to Paris. All useful stuff to them, but fairly low-level. They like what they get, but tell her to play a waiting game. Quinn's telling her a bit more than he strictly should be doing, but by and large he is being a bit more of a good boy than we had hoped he would be, to be frank.

'In June this year we move things up a gear. COSSAC, as you know, is planning the invasion of Europe and we in the London Controlling Section are supposed to be coming up with a really watertight deception plan. We've got two or three double agents in place already and the message we are trying to get across to the Germans is that the invasion will be in the Pas de Calais. Absolutely essential that the Germans get a consistent message from different sources. They must all complement each other. Needs to come together like a jigsaw.

'We move things up a gear with Quinn. Until then, he had not been working on terribly high-profile stuff – idea was to ease him in. Now we let him into the world of invasion planning. The Allied landings, he is told, are going to be in the Pas de Calais and that is what he is going to be working on. Oh – and we upgrade her security clearance, so that he is able to take some stuff home, that kind of thing. Intended to get him to drop his guard a bit and it works a treat. He starts taking home maps, charts, the whole bloody lot, if you'll excuse my language. She's sending it all back to Paris, Abwehr lapping it up, pleading for more.'

Edgar paused and stared up through the skylight, through which the sky had already turned a shade of grey. He was coming to the difficult part.

'The deception is absolutely vital if Operation Overlord is to succeed. We are talking about landing tens of thousands of men, tanks, armour, equipment and supplies on the beaches of Normandy. It would be tricky enough in friendly conditions. But with the beaches being mined and defended, with all the hazards of the long sea crossing and the extended lines of supply – it is a very risky operation, to say the least. So if we can convince the Germans that the invasion is going to be much further to the east, then at least that will tie up some of their defences.

'From what the boys at Bletchley are telling us they're picking up from Ultra, the Abwehr are totally buying what Magpie is telling them.

Alongside everything else we are doing on the deception front, they are convinced that the Second Front will come through the Pas de Calais.

'But there is another part of this deception operation. We don't just want the Germans to think *before* D-Day that it is the Pas de Calais. We don't want them to realise *on* D-Day that they've been tricked and then shift everything into Normandy. If that is the case, then this whole operation would only have bought us a day or two's grace and to be honest, that may not be enough. We need to persuade them *even on* D-Day – and for as long as possible after it – that Normandy is a feint, that the real invasion will take place a couple of weeks later in the Pas de Calais. That way, we tie up the Fifteenth Army and all of its Panzer divisions hundreds of miles from where they can hurt us.

'Which is where you come in, Newby. We think that the best way to persuade the Germans not only that the Pas de Calais is the target but also that Normandy will be a feint is to send Magpie over there as one of your agents. In other words, actually have her there in the Pas de Calais.'

Major Newby nodded his head in an approving manner that surprised Edgar. For a moment, he appeared to be lost in thought.

'This sounds rather interesting, Edgar. However, the way we work is to link our agents up with French resistance groups. I am not sure how I can justify exposing them to danger.'

'We have thought that through. We would want to send her out around two months or so before the planned invasion. For those two months, that group ought to be the safest resistance cell in the whole of France. The Germans won't want to touch them, they will want Magpie to stay active for as long as possible. As soon as she becomes inactive then we'll need to get the message to them, but it is a risk. I accept that – but if things work out, we ought to be able to warn them.'

'And is she aware that she could be recruited to the SOE?'

'No. It all hinges on whether you think that you can pull it off.'

'I think we can. Do you agree, Nicole? We train our agents at Wanborough Manor initially. Those that get through the three weeks there are sent to Beaulieu in the New Forest. We'll obviously have to keep her well away from these places. Can't risk her meeting other agents or even too many of our own people. We'll have to take over a country house we have never used before and are never likely to use again and get some army boys to help us with a few weeks' training. We can fly her in by Lysander, not having to train her on how to use a parachute will save time. Any idea where you want to send her in the Pas de Calais?'

'Around Boulogne.'

'Nicole?'

'The FTP is very active around there. There are some small cells that are very quiet. It's deliberate while we wait for D-Day; the idea is only to activate them when we need them. We could certainly find one to send her to – as long as we can be sure that we can get a warning to them the minute they are in danger. You'll understand that we could not possibly be associated with a plan that deliberately sacrifices any of our units. We must be satisfied that they will have some protection.' It was the first time Nicole had spoken at any length. He still could not place her accent, which was certainly not French. In the strange half-world in which he now lived, he knew better than to ask.

'And do we know her true identity?'

'No. She calls herself Nathalie Mercier, which is not her real name. Of course, now she is known as Nathalie Quinn. She says she is from Paris, but we rather doubt that. She did meet the French wife of a colleague, who said she did not think she had a Parisian accent. Of course, it is all rather tricky to check these things out nowadays.'

'Well,' said Nicole, 'we are going to need to give her a new identity anyway. By the time we have finished with her, she will not be sure who she is.'

'I would not be so sure about that,' said Edgar. 'So I can rely on you to call her in?'

Newby escorted Edgar downstairs. Together they stood in the mews courtyard, the cobblestones feeling incongruous in the midst of the busy city. Newby was filling his pipe with tobacco.

'Nicole rather rules that place for me. Quite brilliant. She can't abide smoke though, so I have to sneak out. I'll get her to look after Magpie. One question though, Edgar.'

'What is that?'

'Your chap Quinn is going to be devastated when he finds out that you chaps have married him off to a Nazi agent, isn't he?'

Edgar moved to the other side of Newby to avoid the cloud of tobacco smoke drifting towards him. He pondered the question as if it was one that until now had never occurred to him.

'I imagine he will, but I daresay that he will get over it.'

Chapter 13

December 1943

Nathalie Quinn had been hiding in the ditch beside the railway track for over an hour. Face down in the wet gravel; flecks of sharp stone pitting her face. The damp shrub that she had uprooted earlier from the hedgerow behind her was covering her, but the moisture was now beginning to work through her clothing. When she had set out two hours previously, the night seemed surprisingly warm for the time of the year, and the moon bright enough for her to find her way across the fields.

But now the chill of the December night air was eating through her and she was regretting not taking the extra sweater that she had been offered just before she set out. Enough cloud had drifted over the vast sky to obscure the moon and cast pitch darkness all around. She was grateful for that now. The last half mile before the railway line had been the most perilous. She had waited in the copse at the top of the hill for ten minutes, checking that there was no movement below. She then crept down, making sure she kept in the cover of the trees where possible. At the bottom of the hill she hid behind a high hedge for just long enough to catch her breath and check that the road was clear.

This is where they'll get me. There's a bend in the road. They'll be waiting behind that bend and come out once I start to cross the road.

But you could wait all night and still not be certain there was nothing there, so she crawled through the small gap, scratching her face in the process, then dashed across the road and jumped over the ditch into the field on the other side.

She had slipped as she landed in the field, covering herself in the chalky mud and slightly spraining her wrist – '*merde*'. But at least she was clear. She had decided beforehand that the road was the riskiest part of the journey and now that was behind her. She had a choice now: either take the shortest route by going diagonally across the field, but risk being seen in the open, or take the long route by using the cover of the hedgerow along the perimeter. Crouched in the mud, she looked up at the sky. The moon was quite obscured now by the cloud. She would risk going across the field. '*Time is never on your side,*' they had told her.

At the other side of the field she came to the mesh wire fence at the top of the railway embankment, exactly where she had been told it would be. She waited for five minutes, just in case there were any patrols on the line below. The wire was difficult to cut, much thicker than she had expected and the wet steel caused her cutters to slip. Her hands were freezing cold. She had to cut through the wire in a dozen places to make a big enough hole for her to climb through. She then tied the wire back to the fence. It would be easy enough to spot close up, but from a distance it would look like the fence was intact. She threw the shrub she had collected into the ditch and slid down into it. She covered herself as best she could and waited.

Now it was gone midnight. In the past hour she had counted the two trains she had been told to expect. Her whole body shook as the trains rushed by, just inches from her. They moved these trains in the dead of night, so that the chances of anyone spotting the amount of tanks and the equipment they were moving were minimised. Any minute now, the third one was due. If what they told her was correct, then it would be an empty train with just three carriages. She had been trained to recognise the differences in noise. After the third train, there would be exactly six minutes before the target train was due. Six minutes to emerge from her cover, make sure that the track was clear, lay the charge and be at least at the other side of the wire fence and behind the hedge when the train came past and she pressed the detonator. She would then have to rely on the confusion to give her enough time to make it back up the hill to safety.

Six minutes. Three hundred and sixty seconds. When she first started, it had taken her twice that long to set the charge.

The third train came past, travelling more slowly than the previous two. She waited until the sound of it had stopped reverberating along the track before pushing her cover away, realising just how cramped and uncomfortable she had been. She had ended up in a foetal position and she was now having trouble straightening her knees. She crawled along the side of the track – '*Keep as low as possible, all the time… they will be looking for something with two legs, not four*' – the shingle cutting into her. She rolled over onto her back and from inside her coat pulled out the explosives. With her hand, she scooped out enough gravel under the track to bury it. She connected the wire, covered the explosives with the gravel and crawled back to the ditch. She attached the wire to the detonator and then scrambled up the siding, digging her long nails into the cold earth to help her up the embankment. *Untie the hole in the fence, pass the detonator through, climb through the hole, tie it up again and move along the hedge.* As she started to do that, she could hear the low rumble in the distance of the train. She had done everything well within the six minutes. There was now maybe a minute in which to get as far as possible from the track. Crawling now on her feet and one hand, the other clutching the detonator, she moved far enough along the hedge, stopped, and started to wind-up the machine. She was covered in mud and her lungs ached. Her left hand was bleeding. She was breathing hard and could feel the sound of her heartbeat crashing in her ears. Surely, if anyone was close by, they would be able to hear her. The train was closer now. Through the gap in the hedge she could see it approaching the point where she would press the charge. *One, two, three…*

An empty click. The train passed. And now the lights were shining on her. Not just torch lights as she had expected, but large searchlights, so she could see nothing and all she could hear was the shouting. The night had turned to day.

She was hauled up by her elbows, not too roughly, and a man wearing a thick jumper and a beret was standing in front of her.

'Not bad. Better than yesterday, but not yet good enough.'

He handed her a flask of hot, sweet tea.

From the trackside, a man shouted up.

'It's fine. A decent connection. Well concealed.'

The man in the beret leaned over the hedge.

'And it would have gone off?'

'Oh yes.'

He turned to her and nodded approvingly.

'You want to know your main mistake? You had clearly decided before you set out that the road was the most dangerous part of your journey. Do you know why that was a mistake?'

She shook her head, sipping the hot tea.

'It is a mistake because *every* part of your journey is the most dangerous part. Remember that. If you decide that one part is the most dangerous, then inevitably you will be a tiny bit more relaxed in other parts, which is what happened in this field. You took the easy route across the field, even though you had enough time. You were exposed for too long. We spotted you then. And you took too long with the fence. I told you to take gloves. But you did well with laying the explosives and you were well-hidden in the ditch. We will try again tomorrow. Now, you will want a bath, no?' His sharp Provençal accent cut through the thin night air.

Nathalie brushed herself down. She knew she had done well. The man with the beret was a hard taskmaster and 'not bad' actually meant 'very good'. She was almost there. She was exhausted. There would be a car waiting at the road and she would soon be back at the house, where a hot bath and a clean bed waited.

The small group trudged back through the quiet north Lincolnshire night.

–

Christmas in London.

The man in the beret had informed her in the farmhouse when they finished the debrief late one night.

'You'll be driven to London this Friday – that's Christmas Eve. You'll be brought back here on the Wednesday. After Boxing Day.'

'And how will I be able to let my husband know I'm coming?'

'He'll be told. A condition of you being allowed home is that you avoid seeing anyone you know, apart from your husband, of course. It's too risky. Your husband knows that. He's told his parents he is on duty over Christmas and can't leave London.'

She nodded; it would be best not to show too much of a reaction.

'Do you have many friends?'

'A few – not really though. I'm friendly with some of the nurses at the hospital and Owen sometimes sees people he was at sea or at school with when they're in London, but no...'

'Keep it that way. One misjudged remark to one person could undo everything and we can't risk that. Just keep yourselves to yourselves.'

'I understand. What will you be doing for Christmas?' she asked him, trying to break through his ever-present coldness.

He carried on folding up a map. 'You don't need to know that,' he snapped, as cold as ever.

She had been subjected to mock interrogations for most of the past two days and she doubted whether the real thing could be much worse. Her cheek still smarted from where he had struck her earlier that evening, but that had been the least of her humiliations.

The previous day she had been blindfolded, driven around in a car for what she thought must have been at least an hour before being dragged into a building. A male voice that she could not recall having heard before spoke to her.

'I am going to give you a code word. Under no circumstances must you reveal this code word to anyone. Do you understand?'

She nodded.

'The code word is "ploughshares". Please repeat it to me.'

'Ploughshares.'

'And again.'

'Ploughshares.'

'That is the last time you utter that word. Understand?'

She nodded again.

'Do you understand?'

'Yes,' she replied.

She was led down some steps and into a room where the blindfold was removed.

The room was cold, windowless and harshly lit. She assumed that it was a cellar, certainly the ceiling seemed to be lower than normal. There was a damp, fusty smell. She was alone in it apart from a tall woman who was wearing a dark woollen coat. When she spoke, which was not until some time had passed, it was in French, with a distinctive Marseilles accent.

'I am very experienced. Eventually I will persuade you to reveal the code word. It will not reflect badly upon you if you let me have it now. It will show judgement.'

Nathalie raised her eyebrows and laughed. 'Really? Do you think I am stupid?'

'Some of the methods I will use are not pleasant I can assure you. What does it matter if you tell me now or later?'

It matters a lot, she thought. Everything I've been taught, both here and in Germany.

Hold out for as long as possible.

Give others a chance to escape. That is what they'll be looking for.

Even one hour can make a difference.

'You know I won't tell you.'

Focus on something else. Maybe an object in the room, or an activity you remember like a bike ride or visiting an exhibition.

Listen carefully to their questions. They will reveal how much they don't know.

Use delaying tactics: ask them to repeat a question or have a coughing fit.

Try to avoid losing your temper, no matter what the provocation.

Do not appear shocked at anything they say or do, no matter how upsetting.

'Remove your clothes.'

'Pardon?' She knew from the tone of her voice that she sounded shocked, which she knew she was not meant to do.

'I said, remove your clothes.'

The woman was holding a large cane, the kind normally seen in gardens. She decided to think about the Tuileries Gardens in Paris which she had visited the day she first went to the German Embassy. Nathalie removed her cardigan and shoes and pulled her dress over her head, taking care to brush her hair back into place with her hands. The stockings followed. The cold bit into her now. The floor was uneven concrete, covered in sharp bits of grit.

'Everything.'

The cane was being waved menacingly in front of her. She removed the rest of her underwear.

'Legs apart, put your hands behind your back.'

The woman went behind her and tied up her hands.

For what must have been an hour the woman walked in circles around her: sometimes very close, other times further away. Every so often she would ask:

'Are you ready to tell me yet?'

Nathalie would not reply.

Another hour. One more hour, they'll be happy with that.

Once you go beyond an hour, every minute is a bonus.

Buy time, it is your most precious commodity.

The sound of heavy footsteps could be heard coming towards the room and then men's voices outside the door.

'Shall I let them in or do you want to tell me? It's very easy, either for you to tell me or for me to let them in.'

One word, what does it matter?

In any case, surely she would not bring the men into the room. There had to be limits. She'd been subjected to something like this in Germany and even they hadn't gone that far. One of the instructors had felt her breasts during a mock interrogation. But she was fully clothed then. He seemed more embarrassed than she was. He even apologised afterwards.

The woman walked over, towering above her. She held the top of the cane under her chin. It was rough and nicked her chin.

'You tell me the code and they don't come in and you can get dressed. You have held out for longer than we expected. We will be pleased.'

Nathalie was on the verge of breaking. Nervously she shook her head.

'Are you sure?' The woman looked surprised.

The woman drew the tip of the cane down her neck, between her breasts and between her legs, holding it there. She could feel tears welling in her eyes and her face and neck reddening. The nick on her chin had started to bleed and she could feel a trickle of blood running down her neck.

'One last chance? I don't want to have to bring them in. Please tell me.'

Nathalie spat at her in the face.

The woman did not flinch. No expression crossed her face as a small line of spit rolled down her left cheek. She leaned close to Nathalie and whispered in her ear.

'They are not good men, you know. They can be animals. I never expected we'd have to bring them in. The code word?'

She stepped back, waiting for Nathalie to spit again. Still no response.

'Come in,' she called out. Nathalie could detect a nervous reluctance in her voice.

Two men she had never seen before entered the room. One of them much younger than her, the other much older. She had to stand there while they circled her, speaking in a language she did not recognise.

Until then the room had been chilly and she had been shivering. Now she was burning hot and could feel the perspiration trickling down her back. The men were inspecting her as if she was an animal at market and they, prospective buyers.

'Tell me the word and they will leave now.' The woman sounded exasperated, even unsettled. Nathalie stayed silent.

'Shall I leave you on your own with them or do you want to tell me the code word?'

Nathalie said nothing, defiant but also too terrified to speak. She could feel a leather-gloved hand run down the length of her back, move over her bound hands and rest at the base of her spine. The young man stood inches in front of her, slowly looking her up and down – more down than up – a cold smile on his face as he slowly licked his lips. He placed a cold hand on her chin, lifted it up and with the other hand ran his fingers through her hair. She could feel the rough hem of his coat brushing against the inside of her thigh.

The older man now had both of his hands against the back of her thighs, very slowly moving them to the inside of her legs and upwards. She could feel his breath, hot and damp against the back of her neck. Behind the young man, she could see the woman, who was beginning to look agitated.

If he moves his hands any higher up, I'm telling her the code word. This is impossible.

The gloved hands lingered at the very top of her thighs. The younger man was now standing directly against her, their bodies touching. His face was so close to hers that it was impossible for her to focus properly on him. She could feel the shape of his body.

'Don't tell her,' he whispered. 'I don't want you to tell her the code word. I am enjoying this.' He stepped back an inch or two to allow enough space for his ice-cold hands to run up and down the front of her body, his sharp fingernails scratching her.

'The code word?' The woman had moved to the rear of the room, as if she didn't want to see too much of what was going on. Her voice appeared to be shaking.

The younger man smiled and shook his head. 'Don't tell her,' he whispered again.

She said nothing.

His hands were now cupping her breasts. She was close to breaking point.

'Even...' she started to speak.

'Even what?' said the woman.

She hesitated. '*Even the Germans don't behave like this,*' was what she had been about to say.

'Even… if this goes on for another day, I won't say anything.'

The older man had now placed his gloved hands round her neck. At first, the touch was very light and he was almost stroking her. But very slowly, the grip tightened. At the same time, the younger man had taken her nipples between his bony fingers; playing with them at first and then pinching them hard. She could feel the tears streaming down her cheeks.

It is perfectly possible to withstand physical torture, they had told her.

You will be amazed at how much pain the human body can withstand.

The important thing to remember is that it is not in their interests to harm you. You will be of no use to them then.

She wasn't so sure, but it was at this point that she realised: the British would surely not expect someone like me to be able to withstand all this? If it goes on any longer then they will surely start to get suspicious. They will wonder how I was able to withstand all this.

'Ploughshares!' she spat the word out and at the same time drove her knee sharply into the younger man's groin. He crumpled to floor in agony, while the older man tightened his grip on her neck, so that he was almost choking her.

'Stop!' the woman cried out. 'It's over. Go now.'

The older man reluctantly released his grip.

The younger man slowly hauled himself up, one hand clutching his groin.

She had moved a few paces away from him now, but he lashed out at her with his fist, which she just managed to avoid.

'I said, stop!' shouted the woman. 'Enough,' she said to the men. 'You can leave now.'

The younger one in front of her looked disappointed. The older one allowed his hands to move down from her neck and brush against her breasts, holding them there for a moment.

'I said, that's enough. Go!' The woman sounded angry.

As the men left the room, she turned to Nathalie, avoiding looking at her directly. She looked shaken.

'We did not expect you to last that long. You did well. Get dressed now.'

Once she was dressed the man in the beret came into the room to put the blindfold back on.

She reckoned that having held out so well in the interrogations was the reason she was being allowed home for Christmas.

She had been dropped off at the flat in the early afternoon of Christmas Eve. Owen, she had been told, would be home by four.

It was a strange sensation, arriving home at a place that she had never truly regarded as such. The flat was still and cold, if anything it felt colder inside than out. She walked around the empty rooms, not even bothering to put the lights on. She glanced at the noisy kitchen clock. Ten to two. Another two hours before he's home. And that sensation again, the unaccountable feeling of actually looking forward to seeing Owen that had taken her by surprise when she first felt it, and which surprised and disconcerted her now.

In the lounge she picked up their wedding photo from a shelf. When she'd first seen it, she thought they looked like two strangers, randomly placed next to each other. Owen seemed to be standing in the light, his face beaming proudly. She was very slightly in the shadow and just that bit further away from him than you would expect.

In the photograph he looked little more than a teenager, young even for his years. But next to the wedding photograph was one that she hadn't seen before, taken in Hyde Park as the leaves of autumn swirled around them. A passing Canadian officer had obligingly taken the picture and there they were: faces pressed together, both smiling, both in the light. No longer strangers.

Is it me who has changed – or him?

She carried on walking around the flat.

Just visiting, she thought. Just passing through. Always, just passing through.

The place was meticulous, as she would have expected. Owen was always tidier than her. In the bedroom she noticed her slippers neatly arranged at the foot of the bed. She kicked off her shoes, the sound of them clattering against the skirting board echoing through the flat. Still wearing her coat, she slumped into an armchair.

It was only then that she realised quite how exhausted she was. The past two months had taken her by surprise. As it was, she had been busy enough with the quantity of information that Owen was bringing home. He thought he was being careful: arriving home that much earlier and then sitting at the table with his maps and charts while she cooked dinner. It was so easy to come behind him, kiss him on the neck, playfully cover his eyes with her hands and look at the chart. You could learn a lot that way. Occasionally he would ask her help with a word or phrase, never telling her what it was to do with, but she would look at it with far more attention than it needed so that she could take in as much information as possible. It might just be the odd word, but it all counted and the messages that she was getting back from that horrible little Belgian told her that the people in Paris were delighted.

And then, in November, Owen had come home to say that Captain Archibald wanted her to meet a lady. So the three of them went to a hotel behind Marylebone High Street where they were joined by a lady who spoke fluent French, but was not French. She had never worked out where she came from.

They were sat in a small annexe of the lounge, out of earshot of anyone else. The lady introduced herself as Nicole and gestured for Nathalie to join her on her sofa.

'We think that you can be of help to us,' the lady had said. 'Would you be willing to help in the cause of the liberation of France by returning there? It would not be without danger.'

Nathalie looked towards Owen, who smiled and nodded his head. She remembered that he looked terrified.

The woman continued to speak very fast and very softly in an educated accent. 'Because of the nature of his work, your husband is aware of our interest. It is important that he knows what is going on, to an extent. You would have his support, but it has to be your decision. We would train you and then you would be flown to France. You would work with your countrymen out there.

'If you indicate your agreement now, Nathalie, then we will proceed. If not, then this meeting has never taken place. But we do need to know now.'

And that was that. Would she be interested? She had looked towards Owen, who appeared overwhelmed. She asked him what he thought and he said nothing, but nodded weakly.

Just a week later she was somewhere in Lincolnshire. She actually had no idea where she was, and couldn't even be certain that it was Lincolnshire. She had feigned sleep as they drove up the Great North Road and after some three hours noticed the dark mass of a cathedral rising high in the distance, after which the car headed east. Not long after that a coach passed them going in the other direction with 'Lincoln' on its destination board. At that point Nicole had drawn the curtains in the back of the car ('*so you can get some rest*') and they arrived at the destination an hour later. From the position of the moon and the stars, she could tell that they had continued north east, so she was assuming she was still in Lincolnshire. The Germans had made her study enough of those wretched maps of the United Kingdom for her to have a reasonable sense of where she was.

Apart from the instructors, she was the only one in the isolated farmhouse. The house was set at the bottom of a large hill and surrounded by woods. It was quiet, apart from the constant drone of planes, especially at night. From what she could make out, they were mostly bombers – Lancasters as far as she could tell, dozens of them at a time, flying low and south.

The only other company in the area appeared to be starlings. Thousands of them. During the day they would gather in a dark mass in the trees, staring down at her as if they alone knew the truth. At dusk they would fly around silently, but if anything disturbed them then the sound would be deafening.

The dining room in the farmhouse had been converted into a classroom, with a blackboard on top of a large pine dresser. Upstairs there were three bedrooms. In a cupboard in the bathroom she had found newspaper lining the shelves where the sheets and towels were kept. They were copies of the *Lincolnshire Echo* from December 1942. She could not be sure if they had been left there deliberately to confuse her, or if they were an oversight. If it was the latter, it was a bad mistake.

Nicole slept in one of the bedrooms and one of the other instructors, who always wore a beret and never a coat, in the other. His name was Claude. As far as she could tell, the other instructors who would turn up for a day or two at a time would sleep downstairs. There would always be at least two of them there.

The training divided into three main parts. Firstly, there was instruction on how to use the radio transmitter. She knew she would be hopeless at that, but she could hardly tell them that the Abwehr had so despaired of her inability to use the transmitter and master codes that they had lumbered her with that ghastly Belgian. This time the instructors were more patient and she made some progress.

Then there was the explosives training. Considering that she had trouble lighting the gas on their cooker in London, Nathalie surprised herself at how she was able to cope with the explosives. What she was meant to do with them once in France was another matter. She could hardly blow up a railway track. She also had weapons training. The American Sten Mark 3 was one she seemed to excel at, and she got used to carrying the Webley revolver at all times.

The final part of her training was the hardest. Going over her cover story again and again. Knowing everything about her new self. How to conceal her true identity. What to do if captured – *hold out for as long as you can, but at least twenty-four hours. That will give your comrades a chance to escape.* How to arrange a rendezvous – *in as busy a place as possible.* What to do if the person you are meeting is not there – *keep walking at the same pace, don't come back to the same place.* And so on. It was all rather familiar. This was the only time when she felt truly compromised. She needed to have every sense primed to ensure that she let nothing slip. '*I've never had any training like this before,*' she had to keep reminding herself. '*I must make deliberate mistakes. I am an innocent nurse who had just been recruited to the SOE.*'

She must have dozed off, because she was woken with a start by the call of '*Darling*' as the front door of the flat opened.

Owen walked into the lounge, carrying a large box which he put on the table before rushing over to her.

Normally so talkative and enthusiastic, Owen said very little that long Christmas weekend. He seemed to be happy just to have her with him. They didn't leave the flat at all on the Saturday, Sunday or the Monday. It was cold and wet and they both seemed to be happy to stay in, dozing in their armchairs and listening to the gramophone. The box he had brought in with him was a hamper courtesy of Captain Archibald and contained enough food and drink to keep them replete as well as banish all thoughts of rationing from their mind. Their neighbour, Roger, could be heard in the flat next door. He was a civil servant who had invited them round the previous Christmas, but neither she nor Owen felt obliged to return the invitation. Apart from him, the rest of the house appeared to be empty for most of the weekend.

Nathalie found she was catching up on lost sleep; invariably she would awaken to find Owen staring at her, as if he'd been checking she was still breathing. And when she did emerge from her slumber, she'd smile at him and then he would come over and sit on the side of her armchair and stroke her hair, or cup her chin in his hand and pull her head towards his.

Owen never asked, not once, about where she had been or what she had been through. She assumed he must know something, but she had to resist the temptation to tell him.

He ought to know.

He ought to know, she thought, why she had recoiled when they were making love the first night she was back and he ran his fingers through her hair as he liked to do and as she liked him to do. But now it reminded her of the young man in the interrogation, running his cold hands through her hair. After they'd made love that night he was stroking her breasts when he suddenly stopped. He'd noticed that her nipples were reddened and slightly bruised.

I'll tell him. Then he'll realise.

But in the end she told an unconvincing tale about getting trapped as she climbed over a gate and no more was said about it.

He ought to know why she wanted to sleep with the bedside light on. She could not fall asleep otherwise, fearing she was still blindfolded.

The weather turned mild on the Tuesday, the day before she was due to return. In the afternoon they went for a long walk, both lost in their thoughts. Owen was as withdrawn as he had been throughout Christmas. It was so uncharacteristic, she thought. Normally he was bursting with enthusiasm and had so much to tell her. Now he seemed happy just to be with her and with little to say. She was exhausted. The journey that Georg Lange had told her she had irreversibly set out on would continue. She would give anything for it to stop.

They must have walked for hours because it had turned dark without either of them noticing the city in blackout. They were in a small road in Chelsea, a single light above a shop which, despite the blackout, was throwing out a surprising amount of light around the dark buildings, picking out windows and doorways, bricks glistening. The light caught the shape of a tall dog sitting silently at the kerb. Its dark eyes reflected the light and its head turned slowly, watching them as they walked towards a pub they had spotted at the end of the road.

The inside of the pub was dim, bathed in a yellow light and silent. A cloud of brown tobacco smoke hung just under the ceiling. Two old men were sitting alone at either end of the bar, looking suspiciously at them and at each other. The benches around the sides of the small room were occupied by half a dozen people sat on their own, all occupied in their thoughts. The only noise came from a table which an army corporal shared with two women: both noticeably older than him and wearing too much cheap make-up.

'You're just trying to get us drunk, aren't you?' one of them admonished, as she knocked back another glass of what appeared to be gin.

At the next table sat an old lady, her large handbag on it. She was swirling around the contents of her drink, an improbably short cigarette unlit in her mouth.

Owen and Nathalie sat at the only other table, which was so rocky that they had to hold on to the top to keep it still. Despite this, their drinks still slopped onto the surface.

'I'm sorry about this,' he said to her.

'Sorry about what?'

'This place. Not very grand.'

'It's fine, Owen. Don't worry. I quite like it actually.'

'Like it! I thought you hated this kind of thing?'

'What kind of thing?'

'Pubs, the English way of life – that kind of thing.'

She smiled, pulling little rivers out of the pool of beer that had spilled on their table. 'Maybe I'm beginning to get to like English things then.'

He leaned over, taking both of her hands in his.

'And does that include me?'

She leaned towards him and kissed him, to the raucous cheers of the table next to them.

Lincolnshire, January 1944

She was back in a ditch in Lincolnshire, covered in leaves, waiting for the dog to find her so that she could get back to the cold house and have a bath.

It was the end of January, the ground was frozen solid and the moon was bright. Tonight they had given her a large, weighted knapsack that she had to carry across the fields and the ditches. She had to set up the transmitter and send a brief message and then wait for the reply. She then had to scale a wall that was more than six feet high and break into a locked shed before laying explosives under a bridge over an icy stream.

She had done all that and then found somewhere to hide, all as instructed. She knew that as long as it took at least ten minutes for them to find her after she had left the bridge then she would have passed. More than twenty minutes had already passed when a large hand reached down into the ditch and hauled her up. Claude, the man with the beret, patted her on the shoulder.

'You are ready,' was all he said. There was still no warmth in his voice or his manner.

The woman was standing behind him. '*Très bien.*'

She had expected a bit more ceremony, a bit more elation but perhaps they were as exhausted as she was.

Back at the farmhouse the bathwater was only lukewarm and the bed felt cold. In a matter of weeks maybe, she could be back in France. She had expected to return in very different circumstances.

Tomorrow she would be back in London, with Owen. Her overwhelming thought as she drifted off to sleep was how surprised she was that she found herself actually looking forward to being back with her husband. The cold does strange things to you.

Chapter 14

Berlin, January 1944

The chauffeur knew to check with his passenger before this particular journey.

'Short route or long route, sir?'

Admiral Canaris looked at his watch. He preferred the long route. Anything to put off arriving in that wretched building. A pleasant drive through the Tiergarten would take the edge off his nerves. But the one thing you did not risk doing was keep them waiting. People had been shot for less.

'Better go the short way, Karl.'

The long black Mercedes-Benz Tourenwagen pulled away from the Abwehr headquarters in Tirpitz Ufer and then turned left into Potsdamer Strasse, where they slowed down for the first checkpoint. The SS guards peered into the back of the car, clicked synchronised '*Sieg Heil*'s and waved them through. Then into Potsdamer Platz, where they took the second exit into Hermann Goering Strasse. Canaris smiled. *Their arrogance means they can't even see the irony of naming a wide road after a fat man.* Moments later they came to the security barrier at the entrance into Voss Strasse. More peering into the back of the car, a check on a clipboard, a word with the driver about where to park, a '*Sieg Heil*' or two and they were through.

Canaris never ceased to be both amazed and appalled at the same time by this building. When it opened in January 1939 the myth was that Speer had built it in a year. *Imagine, how wonderful we are! This magnificent building, constructed in just one year!* Canaris knew it had taken two years, but he also knew better than to contradict people in matters like this. As he was fond of saying, people had been shot for less.

He climbed the dozen steps into the front, high-columned entrance, choosing to walk through the middle of it. In the main reception area he had to wait behind a fat SS general who was complaining that his driver was not waiting for him. He informed the woman behind the desk that he had arrived and sat down to wait for his escort, doing his best to avoid making eye contact with Heinrich Müller, who was on his way out of the building. The last thing he wanted now was to have to make small talk with the head of the Gestapo. The Bavarian was a small man with a thin face. It went without saying that Canaris did not trust him. What made it worse was that Canaris rated Müller's abilities. He was not someone to underestimate. But look at him: that was the problem with Germany these days. The country run by sergeants and corporals. People with no class.

Out of the corner of his eye he noticed that Müller was now walking towards him. This was going to be difficult. Just in time, a tall, young and appropriately blond and blue-eyed SS-Obersturmführer appeared next to Canaris. They exchanged '*Sieg Heil*'s – one more enthusiastic than the other – and set off together. Admiral Canaris always thought of Daniel at this moment. He realised that Old Testament prophets were not people that immediately came to mind in this building out of all places, but he had an acute sense of being in the lion's den.

The young SS–Obersturmführer was walking fast and Canaris was having to concentrate on keeping pace with him. Through the central courtyard and past the ridiculous statues of naked young men and towards the central part of the building.

They were now entering the heart of the *Reichskanzlei*, the Reich Chancellery. The office of Adolf Hitler.

Sentries were posted every few paces now and the corridors and the rooms off them were increasingly ornate. The SS-Obersturmführer's jackboots were echoing around off the walls. Still they continued walking, the marbled floors reflecting the light from the small windows, magnificent crests adorning the walls. It was an extraordinary building, he thought. You had to hand it to Speer. He had managed to design a building that both impressed and intimidated those who entered it. The long walk was deliberate. You were left in no doubt as to the importance of where you were heading.

The SS-Obersturmführer wheeled right, leading Canaris into a stunning reception room. He clicked his heels and gestured towards one of the chairs arranged around an unlit fireplace. He then stood at ease on the inside of the door.

Canaris had a moment to reflect and to wonder. When you were summoned to the Reich Chancellery, you could never be quite sure what it was about. It was difficult to predict. Canaris had been good at it up to now, but he was growing weary at trying to stay one step ahead of trouble.

If he was lucky, it would be about Hitler's current obsession: where the Allies would land in northern Europe – and when. At least he could tell him what he wanted to hear. He had been discussing it with Oster that morning:

'What matters is not what the Abwehr thinks, but what the Führer thinks. That stubborn bastard made up his mind months ago that the Allies would invade through the Pas de Calais. All that we have done is tell him what he wants to hear. He still believes that he is the great military strategist.'

As long as the Führer remains convinced about the Pas de Calais, then the sooner this damned war might be over, he thought.

His thoughts were interrupted by the arrival in the room of Martin Bormann. Canaris groaned inwardly, while outwardly greeting him. Hitler's Private Secretary was always rude. He never treated Canaris with respect. A few minutes somewhere near a trench thirty years ago and these clerks now thought they were important enough to be running Germany.

'Just you, Canaris?'

'Just me, Bormann.'

'Uhm. I thought you would have others with you. Are you sure no one will be joining you?'

'I am sure.'

'Very well, follow me.'

Canaris followed Bormann, with the SS-Obersturmführer following him. Through an internal door, down a short, narrow corridor, past two sentries and into an inner office. What struck him most whenever he came in here was the sheer height of the room. The magnificent, brown marble walls were as tall as a house, leading up to a splendid panelled ceiling. Having spent so long in submarines, Canaris felt lost in a room like this.

The three of them walked in single file across the long carpet. Four chairs were arranged around a large, low desk.

Bormann sat in one of the chairs and gestured for Canaris to sit in another.

'He wants me to assess your intelligence reports, Canaris. Everyone's telling him different things. He doesn't *like* you, but he respects the Abwehr.'

'And you Bormann?'

'I neither like you nor respect the Abwehr, Canaris. But I am here to do what the Führer says. Essentially, he is looking for good news. He doesn't get much of that these days. Russia, North Africa – it's all terrible. His obsession this week is with the Second Front. That is all he's talking about. Come over here.'

Canaris followed Bormann to a large table covered in maps and charts. A large map was spread out on top of the table showing the northern coast of France and the southern coast of England.

'He is obsessed with the Allies attempting to land again in northern Europe. He thinks he knows best, don't forget that. He certainly doesn't trust his generals. Look what happened when they tried to land in Dieppe. And now they will have to land a whole army, not just six thousand men. The outcome of the war will depend on whether the Allied invasion of northern Europe succeeds or not, Canaris.

'If they fail, then they will not be able to try again for years – and by then we will have re-equipped the army, the Luftwaffe will have new and better aircraft and the navy will be stronger. And while we do that, we will be able to move enough divisions away from western Europe to sort out the Russians in the east. But it all depends on making sure that their invasion fails. And the best way of doing that is by ensuring that we are ready for them when they land. What the Führer wants to know is, where do you think they will land?'

'I believe it will be in this area.' Canaris was pointing to the Pas de Calais, south of Boulogne.

'And tell me why?'

'Because it puts them nearer to Germany, because there are more places to land, because the sea crossing is shorter, because the terrain is easier and because they will have more air cover. According to Goering, the RAF have been mounting more raids over the past few weeks over the Pas de Calais than over any other part of northern France. Von Rundstedt and Rommel are trying to defend the whole of the northern coast, spreading our forces out too thinly. I believe we should concentrate our defence on the Pas de Calais. At least von Rundstedt has kept the Fifteenth Army in the Pas de Calais and most of the Panzer Group is there.'

'And what makes you so certain?'

'Our intelligence. As you know, we have at least two agents operating inside Britain – the Pole and the Spaniard. Both are extremely reliable and the message we are getting back from them is a consistent one: the Allies will invade in the Pas de Calais. They are operating quite independently of each other, of course, but they both report that General Patton's First US Army is based here in Kent, ideally placed for the short sea crossing. The landing craft are all in Dover and Folkestone. And I am pleased to report another important development which you can convey to the Führer.'

Bormann raised his eyebrows and stepped back half a pace from the table.

'I am pleased to report that we have another very well-placed agent. Her code name is Magpie. She has been in England since 1940 but has only really been active since 1942, when she entered into a relationship with a Royal Navy intelligence officer. In the past few months, the quality of material we have been getting from her has been quite outstanding – and it all points to the invasion being in the Pas de Calais. It is intelligence of the very highest quality, which corroborates all our other intelligence. And today I can report a very significant development.'

Bormann's full attention was now focussed on Canaris. He nodded towards him. *Carry on.*

'At the end of last year the British Special Operations Executive recruited Magpie. Because of her training with them, we have heard very little from her in recent months. The contact has been very intermittent. But we do know that they were training her to work with the French resistance in the area where the invasion would take place. Her role would be to ensure that the resistance group was prepared for the invasion. She has now completed her training. She will be flying to France soon.'

'And do you know where?'

'No,' he said, dismissively, allowing a pause for Bormann to reflect on his question. 'Of course, they are not to going to tell her where she is going. We will only find out when she arrives. But I anticipate here.' He pointed at the map. 'Somewhere round... here. In the Pas de Calais. Just south of Boulogne.'

Bormann nodded approvingly.

'So,' he said, gathering his papers and picking up his gloves, signalling the briefing was over, 'I shall be able to tell the Führer what he wants to hear. He'll appreciate that.'

Canaris smiled and bowed towards Bormann, gesturing for him to leave the room first.

Bormann stopped in the doorway and stepped close to Canaris.

'You had better be right, Canaris. Remember, I don't like you and I don't trust you.'

As he left the Chancellery, Canaris felt that, on balance, he was pleased he had resisted the temptation to describe the feeling as mutual.

Chapter 15

England, 20th April 1944

The door of the dark brown Humber slammed shut and even before she had a chance to wave goodbye and blow a kiss, as she knew would be expected of her, the car had accelerated down the road. Nathalie's last view of her husband was of a blurred but forlorn figure, stepping from the kerb into the road to keep the car in view even as its tail lights disappeared into the night.

Quinn stepped back onto the pavement and Captain Archibald walked over to him from where he had been standing in the entrance of the pretty, wisteria-covered safe house in Holland Park where Nathalie had stayed for almost three months. Sensitive to the mood, the older man said nothing for a while, bouncing slowly on his heels.

'Chin up, Quinn. Expect you'll see her soon enough. Could be just a few weeks the way things are going.'

Quinn walked ahead of Archibald, not wanting him to see the tears that, despite himself, now filled his eyes and were beginning to roll down his cheeks. He intended to say something suitable in reply to show that he agreed, but could not find any words. Archibald clearly sensed the situation.

'Tell you what, Quinn. Why don't you take yourself for a walk round the block? Clear your head. You can stay here tonight and take the day off tomorrow. That will give you a long weekend. As long as you're out of the house by nine o'clock tomorrow morning. Need to get the place ready for when we hand it back to the owners.'

So Quinn went for a long walk, circumnavigating Holland Park. He hadn't known the area before Nathalie was moved here when she had returned from her training at the end of January.

'Best steer clear of Alderney Street,' they had said. 'Don't want anyone asking awkward questions. This place is safer. She'll stay here until it's time to move on.'

They had had no idea how long she would be in the safe house; it could have been a few days, a few weeks, a few months. In the end, it had been three long months.

She was allowed out on her own during the day and he was permitted to visit her and even stay over some nights, though there was always someone else in the house which he found awkward. Whenever he awoke during the night, which was often, he would invariably catch her with her dark eyes open and staring into the matching darkness.

There were so many things that needed to be said, but their relationship had slipped into a kind of silence. If anything, that made things somewhat easier: Nathalie had always seemed to prefer the quiet and didn't feel the need to fill the void with conversation as Owen did. Although she was evidently nervous, she also seemed more relaxed with Owen, more prone to physical contact than before. Now, she would frequently hold his hand, or stroke his face, cupping her hand under his chin as she did so and holding it there for a while. If he ever tried to broach the subject of her going away, she would remind him that she could not discuss it. '*You ought to know better, Owen.*'

For a while he had allowed himself to imagine that Nathalie might not be sent away after all. Maybe they had changed their minds, perhaps she had not performed as well as they had hoped when she had gone away for training, possibly they were having second thoughts about her. She was certainly spending far longer than he had expected in the safe house. From the little he could gather, she spent most of her time in the house learning her cover story and practising her radio skills, but in recent weeks there seemed to be less of that and much more waiting around.

But deep down, he knew it was a forlorn hope, and by the second month of April Nathalie's movements had become far more restricted. She was no longer allowed out of the house on her own and Owen was no longer allowed to stay the night. It was clear that her departure was imminent.

Owen was still allowed to visit her after work, but he could not stay for more than an hour. He would find that, by the time he arrived, Nathalie had already eaten and was sitting in the small lounge, and he would join her on the sofa where they would talk awkwardly. Neither of them could talk about work and there was precious little else that they could discuss within the earshot of one of Nathalie's minders, who would inevitably be hovering in the kitchen. If they ever dropped their voices, the minder would come closer.

It wouldn't be long before he would be told that the car was ready to take him back to Pimlico and he would leave, not quite sure when he would see her again.

On the third Monday of April, Owen arrived at the safe house in Holland Park just after six thirty to find Nathalie waiting for him in the small entrance hall, wearing a light raincoat and clutching her handbag. Captain Archibald emerged from the lounge.

'Thought you two deserved a night out. It's a lovely evening so I suggest you stroll up to Notting Hill and find somewhere to eat there. Back by eight thirty please, at the latest.'

So they strolled up to Notting Hill. Owen kept glancing behind him as they set out.

'You won't spot them, Owen.'

'Spot who?'

'Who you're looking for. Of course, they're following us. You don't think they'd let us out all on our own, do you? They watch me like a hawk now.'

Owen put his arm round his wife's waist and pulled her closer to him. She responded by placing an arm across his shoulders and slightly inclining her head towards his.

'They'll be four of them. North, south, east and west. And we won't have the faintest idea who they are.'

'Well, that's good, isn't it?' said Owen.

She shrugged, as if she had never really thought about it like that.

'It will be any day now, you know that, don't you, Owen?'

He nodded. 'I know I shouldn't ask you this, but I don't suppose you have any idea at all of where you're going, do you? Do you know what you are meant to be doing when you get there?'

She pulled sharply away from him, their arms disentangling as she did so.

'Owen! You know that you can't ask me that.'

They were in Notting Hill Gate now, and at the end of a little alley by the side of a cinema, next door to a sweet shop, they found a pretty fish and chip restaurant called Geales, where they were shown to a table on the first floor in an area where there were just three other tables, two of which were occupied.

Despite her disdain for English food, Nathalie attacked a large piece of cod as if she hadn't eaten for a week. Owen could not remember the last time he had eaten such a large and tasty haddock.

By the time she had finished eating, Nathalie appeared slightly more relaxed. A smartly dressed couple in their sixties had taken the table next to them, so they spoke quietly, struggling to hear each other's voices.

Nathalie was holding a chip in her hand, toying with it as she spoke.

'You have to learn to accept things, you know, Owen.' She still pronounced his name as if it were two words.

'I'm not sure what you mean.'

'Like the people following us, whom we don't see. The two people who've just sat down at the next table. They're watching us. Nothing is what it seems. It's the war. People do things in war... because of the war... that they wouldn't do otherwise. That is what you have to accept. That war changes everything and when it ends, only then can you judge things properly.'

Owen was not altogether sure what she meant, but she had put the chip down now and was holding his hand, her fingers interlinked with his as she leaned over the table and kissed him on the lips. It was just gone eight o'clock and they knew that they couldn't be late, so they paid the bill and made their way back to Holland Park.

The night that Nathalie left, Archibald had arranged for a car to bring Quinn to the house from work. He was there by six o'clock. Although no one said as much, it was clear that she was going that night. Conversation had not been easy. He did not want her to go, but knew he could not allude to that. Nathalie was clearly nervous: she was physically sick more than once, but there was a steely determination in her. 'My duty' was the only thing she ever said when the much-avoided subject of her return to France crept to the surface. Owen did not need telling that the window for an Allied landing in northern Europe was a narrow one, between mid-Spring and mid-Summer. He realised that her mission to France must be linked to the Allied invasion.

At seven o'clock that night the woman called Nicole turned up at the house and took Nathalie into the small lounge. Archibald arrived and took Quinn in the kitchen.

'It's tonight, Quinn, I'm sure you've realised that by now. She'll leave in about two hours' time. You'll have a chance to say goodbye, but do keep it... what I mean is, don't make it difficult for her. She's got a long night ahead of her.'

So he hadn't made it difficult. He had actually been terribly good about it.

'See you soon. Take care. I love you,' he said when he was sure they were out of anyone's earshot. As the car arrived, a quick embrace picked out by the dipped headlights of a passing car, a final *'Whatever happens, you must know that I will always love you,'* whispered in her ear, so quietly that he couldn't be sure she heard. She said nothing, but smiled, her hand brushing his face, her fingers lingering on his lips. Her warm mouth pressed on his cheek and now he was walking quickly past the smart homes, with their white façades and their perfectly arranged flora, and along the sweeping avenues.

The tears had stopped now, but had been replaced by a sense of foreboding.

Owen Quinn wondered whether he would ever see his wife ever again.

–

Nicole had drawn the curtains in the car as soon as it set off, so again Nathalie had no idea in which direction they were heading. It was of no importance. She was heading for France, which was all that mattered.

The way she felt at that moment was about all she could be certain of. She could not really be certain of who she was. There was her real identity. Then there was Nathalie Mercier, who had come over from France in 1940. There was Nathalie Quinn who had married Owen Quinn in 1942. Then there was Magpie, for the Germans, and her new code name for the British, Rider. And her new French identity, Geraldine Leclerc. Six identities. Tonight she had become Geraldine Leclerc.

She could certainly forget about Nathalie Mercier and Nathalie Quinn; she would have no need for them again.

She did not have a watch. Everything she would be taking with her to France would be given to her later that night. She sensed that they had driven for the best part of two hours when the car pulled off the road and drove for some time over an increasingly bumpy track before pulling to a halt.

The car had pulled up close to the door of a long, single-storey building. There was a full moon, but it only showed an empty rural landscape. Trees and hedgerows on the horizon, and the smell of earth in the air. She followed Nicole into the building and into a sparsely furnished room, with a long table in the middle and chairs set against one wall. The wall at the far end had a door set into it. The windows were painted black.

On the table were clothes and various documents. Nicole stood behind the table facing Geraldine.

'Your flight to France leaves in one hour. You must prepare now. Please remove all of your clothing. All of your jewellery, everything.'

Geraldine undressed slowly, with Nicole watching her.

'You must understand, this could save your life. If you have anything on you that could not have come from France, or would reveal your true identity – that could cause you to be arrested by the Germans.'

Geraldine stood for a brief moment in her underwear before Nicole nodded for her to carry on. Her bra and knickers joined the small pile of clothes that had appeared behind her. Nicole handed her a large dressing gown.

'Put the jewellery in here.' Nicole had pushed a small box across the table for her. She removed everything, including her engagement and wedding rings.

'There is one more thing I have to do. I am sorry. Please come here.'

She walked over to Nicole. As she did so, she could hear the roar of an aircraft apparently landing near to the building. The older woman looked at her watch, nodded and produced a large pair of scissors. She pointed to a chair.

'Sit down. I need to cut your hair.'

'Please, not too short.'

'Your hair will draw attention to you as it is now. It is very long and very beautiful. You need to look as anonymous as possible.'

A few minutes later the floor around her was covered in locks of her hair. That which remained was now above her shoulders. She could not remember when it was last so short.

'Try to wear it pulled back at all times anyway. That way it will look different to your photograph. It helps if your hair is a bit different from the photo anyway. That way any Germans looking at your identity card will concentrate on the photo rather than any other detail on the card. They expect a woman to change her hair style. Now. You take a shower. Use this towel and this soap and shampoo. They are French, you probably remember them. You will even smell French when you land.' The very faintest hint of a quickly-fading smile.

The shower was in a small bathroom behind the main room. After her shower, she dressed in the items that Nicole handed her one by one. The labels showed that every single one of them was from France. The few spare clothes that were going into her knapsack were shown to her before they were packed, along with a few other items like a watch, toiletries and a torch. The Webley Mark 3 revolver she had used in Lincolnshire was there too, along with plenty of ammunition.

'You will wear these.' They were the spectacles they had made her wear when her photo was taken. An optician had come to the house in Holland Park to test her eyes and found that she could do with weak lenses anyway. The frames were thick and scratched, with a bit of tape holding part of them together. They made her look older. She glanced in the mirror that Nicole held in front of her. She was a different woman now. And not one she could imagine having much in common with.

'We are nearly ready.' For the second time that evening there was something close to a smile from Nicole. 'The paperwork now.'

She handed her the all-important *carte d'identité*, the identity card.

Nom: Leclerc.

Prenom: Geraldine.

Profession: ouvrière.

She had been born on 14th January 1914. She was a thirty-year-old factory worker from Arras. She felt like one.

Some money and few ration coupons. A letter from a friend working in Toulouse – '...*they treat us well and the weather is wonderful*'. An article torn from a magazine about fashion for the summer of 1944. And two creased photographs, of her new parents – '*avec notre amour*' – and of the brother and sister she never had – *Henri, dix ans. Juliette, sept ans.*

And that was it. Her new life stuffed into a knapsack and the pockets of her jacket.

Nicole left the room for a moment and returned with a tray, which she put on the table in front of Geraldine. One cheese sandwich, a hardboiled egg, one apple and a glass of milk. The last supper, which she didn't feel like eating.

A very plain-looking thirty-year-old factory worker from Arras was now ready to return to France.

–

Flight Lieutenant Tony Taylor of 161 Squadron of the Royal Air Force had long since given up on being confused, although tonight he was finding that harder than usual. '*In this line of work, you'd be confused every minute of every day if you stopped to think about it, so best not to think about it*' had been the helpful advice proffered when he joined the squadron eighteen months previously.

The squadron certainly made a change from flying freight in the Far East and worrying about what the Japs would do to him if he ever bailed out. His new squadron was based at RAF Tempsford in Bedfordshire. Closer to home, none of those bloody flies and a nice mix of work. Most of it was flying Whitleys on parachute drops, which suited his talents for navigation.

But when there was a full moon, out came the Lysanders, like Count Dracula. *Funny aircraft, really.* Single engine on the nose, high wing over the top of the cockpit and a strong, fixed undercarriage, attached to the wing by two improbably large struts. It had started out life as a reconnaissance plane, but they soon realised that the fixed undercarriage and general performance of the plane meant that it was ideal for landing on rough terrain, fields being a speciality, which was why they needed a full moon. *Farmland tends not to come with its own landing lights* Tony Taylor liked to joke. The Lysander had a cruising speed of one hundred and sixty-five miles an hour but could land and, crucially, take off at just eighty miles an hour. Good aircraft, thought Taylor, though you wouldn't know it to look at it. 'Reliable' was the word he'd use to describe it – and it needed to be, for what it was being used for.

They specialised in landing agents and equipment in France. The Spy Taxi, they sometimes called them, which was funny really, as his brother had driven taxis in London before the war. *No tips from these passengers, though* was another of his jokes. You could get a couple of the people and some equipment in the back, fly over to France, land in a field, drop them off, possibly bring someone back with you, and be home in time for breakfast. A few times he had brought back RAF pilots who had been shot down and hidden by the resistance, which was always nice. Good to have them back. The agents, he knew nothing about. You weren't really meant to talk to them – not that you could above the roar of the engine anyway – or even look at them properly.

There was too much to think about anyway. You had to plot your route across the Channel and then look out for the landing strip. Check they were flashing the correct Morse code signal and then come in to land. Watch out for the trees and the telegraph wires. An L-shaped flare path would have been lit on the ground. Land, turn round ready to take off again and offload the passengers and any supplies. A ladder was fixed to the left hand side of the fuselage to make things easier. Ideally, you'd be back in the air again within three or four minutes, the engine running the whole time.

They always took off from RAF Tangmere near Chichester. It was normally a fighter base, but it was right on the coast, so extended the range of the plane. The Lysander had a normal range of six hundred miles, but this could be extended to nine hundred with an extra fuel tank.

That afternoon he'd flown down from Tempsford to Tangmere as usual and waited for his instructions. Met report promised a nice clear night across the Channel and over most of France, so that was good. At four o'clock he got the call.

'You're flying just south of Boulogne, so no need for the extra fuel tank, you can take some more supplies instead.'

'Fine.'

'Oh – and you're not flying from here. There's a small airstrip about fifteen miles inland from here. Hardly ever used. Want you to fly there when it's dark, pick up a couple of passengers and off you go again.'

'Talk about a taxi service.'

Which is why Flight Lieutenant Tony Taylor was confused. They must have a very good reason for not wanting to fly from Tangmere.

He'd been on the ground for half an hour. A small truck had brought out some of the supplies, which he helped to load. Two long cylinder-like containers, which usually carried weapons and ammunition, and four smaller cases, one of which was a radio transmitter. A man came over to the plane, dressed in dark trousers, a thick jumper and a beret.

'We will be ready in thirty minutes. Myself and one passenger. Will that be all right with you?'

Probably French, he thought. Taylor told him that it was all right and sure enough twenty-five minutes later a dark Humber with curtains drawn across the back pulled alongside the left-hand side of the plane. The man with the beret opened the rear passenger door and two women got out. One briefly shook hands with the other before getting straight back into the car, which quickly pulled away from the plane. The woman stood alongside the man in the beret, handed her bag to him and climbed into the Lysander, followed by the man. Once they were settled and strapped in the back, Taylor spoke to Tangmere, was cleared for take off straight away, and gunned the Bristol Mercury engine into life. The plane bounced down the field and was soon airborne, clearing the hedges (which had slightly bothered him) with ease.

They were still climbing when the blue moonlight picked out the Sussex coast disappearing beneath them and then glinted off the sea.

'I wouldn't get too settled,' Taylor shouted into the back of the plane. 'It's only a few minutes now until we land.'

Chapter 16

She had survived as Nathalie Mercier when she came to England, because she became Nathalie Mercier. It was not who she pretended to be: it was who she was. That was the only way. She managed to lock her true identity away so successfully that she had to think carefully before she could find the key – so much so that if she ever heard her real first name, she no longer reacted instinctively to it. And being Magpie was easy enough. You treat that part of your identity as a job. When she became Nathalie Quinn, she realised it was just an extension of Nathalie Mercier. You had to believe who you are. If you don't believe it yourself, how can you expect someone else to do that? She had never had much trouble compromising her beliefs. In any case, she thought, it was not as if there was too much to miss in her previous identity.

So somewhere between the noisy and uncomfortable plane taking off from that field in southern England to it landing in a field in northern France, she knew that she had to discard Nathalie Mercier and Nathalie Quinn over the Channel and never let them enter her mind again. Any regrets or emotions that Nathalie may have had should go into the sea along with that identity. But she was unsettled. It may be easy enough to discard your identity and the details that go with it, but the emotions – they were an altogether different matter. On occasions she had surprised herself in England, and nothing had surprised her more than the fleeting glimpses over the past few months of the feelings that she had for Owen. Very fleeting at first, but recently they had been far more frequent. They had taken her aback at the time and she had attempted to dismiss them; maybe she had simply been reciprocating his very strong feelings for her, playing the part as always. It simply meant she had been doing her job well, but it would be wrong to pretend that they had not confused her and made her think. It would certainly account for why she felt so utterly sad tonight.

It was Geraldine Leclerc who climbed down the steps of the plane in a field near Boulogne. Magpie was her job, and now Rider was a second job. It was all clear in her mind. And her true identity was still neatly locked away in her mind, although it had come somewhat closer to home.

The landing had been unpleasant. The pilot had crossed the French coast south of Boulogne and then dropped altitude quite suddenly. They approached the landing zone very low and very fast. The summer storms meant the ground was wet and this caused the plane to slither as it hit the ground. The pilot struggled with the controls – 'No one told me it was on a sodding slope!' – the Lysander skidding from left to right and back again as it bounced on the greasy field. They soon came to a halt, with the engine still running. The man with her unstrapped her belt, opened the window and told her to climb down the ladder.

'Quick.' No 'goodbye'. No 'good luck'. No time.

A man helped her down at the bottom and passed her over to a woman who took her by the arm and led her quickly over to a copse, part running, part walking and part slipping over the greasy ground. She glanced round and saw that the canisters were being unloaded. Behind the copse was a narrow track, with bicycles propped against trees, and beyond that a field, with a mass of trees in the distance.

When all the equipment was out of the plane, the engine revved up and within a minute it was airborne again, its grey shape quickly merging into the black sky and soon becoming invisible. Three men were still carrying the canisters into the copse. The woman who had led her by the arm had run back into the field to extinguish the beacons. A hole had already been dug between the trees and the canisters were being lowered into it and then covered up.

A young man with dark hair covering his brow smiled at her as he spread leaves and twigs over the area. He pointed to the canisters. 'We will collect them tomorrow.'

He and another man were both carrying guns, which she recognised from her training as American Mark 3 sub-machine guns. The older man – the one who had helped her from the plane – held a Colt automatic pistol in one hand as with the other he checked the covering over the hole into which they had hidden the canisters, kicking an extra covering of leaves over the surface as he did so. When the woman rejoined them in the copse the older man motioned for them all to crouch down. The five of them sat in a small circle, surrounded by the trees. The ground around them was covered in bluebells, their colour just evident in spite of the darkness. Geraldine was fascinated by their presence. High above them, the wind was causing the leaves at the very top of the trees to rustle. There was a smell of wet earth and of France. She was conscious of her glasses and kept removing them. The bridge was hurting her nose. She was quite unused to wearing glasses.

The older man leaned over to her, offering his hand. 'Pierre.'

'Geraldine,' she replied.

The others introduced themselves. 'Françoise', the woman who had brought her over to the copse. 'Lucien', the older man, and 'Jean', the younger one with the dark hair flopping down his face and the smile.

'We wait here for a while. It is a very clear night. If the Germans head this way we will soon hear them.'

And so they sat in silence. There was a rustle in a field on the other side of the track, causing Geraldine to turn sharply.

'Germans?' she whispered.

'Don't worry,' said Pierre. 'Just cows.'

'Same thing,' said Jean. Nervous smiles and more silence.

'Do you have your pistol?' asked Pierre.

Geraldine got out her Webley, struggling to pull it out of her jacket pocket. Pierre nodded, with a quizzical look on his face. 'You prefer it? That's good.'

After what was probably only ten minutes but seemed much longer, Pierre sent Jean and Françoise out in different directions to check all was clear. When they came back, Pierre spoke in a dialect she didn't recognise.

'*Asteur.*'

He made an apologetic gesture towards her with his hand.

'Sorry. I was saying now. We use the local patois here a lot. The Germans don't understand it, so it is a useful habit to have. We leave here one by one, at five-minute intervals. Apart from you. You will go with Jean. You will be staying at his father's house. Lucien will come back with Jean tomorrow to collect the canisters. You stay in the house all day tomorrow. I will call by at some stage. I will have more papers for you then.'

They moved off into the night, like bats darting silently in different directions. She and Jean were the last to leave. When they moved out of the wood into the field, she could see him clearly in the moonlight. He was barely a man, probably not yet out of his teens, but he moved with the confidence and experience of one much older. He guided her with an arm round her waist to the side of the field and, under the cover of first the hedge and then trees, they walked for a good fifteen minutes. They crossed two roads, sat silently while dogs in an unseen farmyard reluctantly stopped barking and then climbed over a stile. Ahead of them she could just begin to make out the silhouette of the village. They edged down a gentle hill, hopped over a small river and landed on the springy grass on the other side. They were now just yards from the back of a row of a dozen cottages, with not a flicker of light in any of them. To their right the dark shape of a church was picked out against the sky. It was two in the morning. An owl hooted and she thought she heard the sound of a vehicle moving away on a distant road. A line of tall trees towered above the cottages, the tops of them gently swaying in a strange unison.

They waited while she caught her breath. Suddenly she heard a dramatic screech ahead of her, like a cat screaming out, four times in a row. A pause, then three more times. She jumped and Jean placed a reassuring hand on her thigh. He leaned close to her and whispered.

'Don't worry. It's the peacocks. They live at the château. You'll have to get used to them.' He pointed ahead of him. 'The second house on the left is my father's. I will go first. When I have been in for one minute, I will send a signal with my torch, one short flash, two long ones. That means it is clear. Come to the house then. The back door will be open. If you see no signal from me after three minutes you will have to go back the way we came as quickly as possible. When you come to the second road we crossed, follow it into Boulogne. Hide when you get to the town then go to the station when it is busy and ask for Lucien. You saw him tonight. But be careful, Boulogne is full of Germans. Everywhere.'

Within a couple of minutes, she had entered through the tiny kitchen of the little house. Jean was already in the small hall, pointing up the stairs. He took her into a tiny bedroom, checking that the curtains were shut. There appeared to be just one other bedroom.

'This will be your room. It used to be mine. I will get you a drink. Are you hungry?'

'No, I am fine. A drink would be good though. Where is your father?'

'Germany. Compulsory Work Service. Thousands of men from this region have gone, like slaves. My father is an electrician. They need people like him in their factories.'

'How long has he been gone?'

'Two years now, nearly. He writes every week. It is much harder for him.'

'And your mother?'

'She died when I was eleven.' Jean smiled, not wanting her to feel embarrassed. She realised she was probably asking too many questions, but she had one more.

'How old are you, Jean?'

'Eighteen, but I am nineteen on the sixth of June.'

As she lay down in bed she did not expect to sleep that night. Her body was exhausted, but her mind was everywhere. She had failed to completely dispose of Nathalie over the Channel; part of her last identity remained stuck inside her, which meant that Owen did too. She tried to stay awake, fearful that she would call out his name, but drifted into an uneasy sleep which only became a deep one after Owen told her not to worry, that he understood. She was woken just after seven as Jean tapped on her door and asked her to come down. Pierre had arrived. She dressed quickly and went into the small front room, which the front door opened straight into, shielded by a curtain. The room was sparse, more utilitarian than comfortable. The dark wooden floor was covered by two frayed rugs, which overlapped. An oak table with six chairs around it was the main feature of the room. There was a battered armchair in front of the fireplace. The mantelpiece held a few photographs: the young Jean; the young Jean and his parents, and a beautiful woman in her thirties. She presumed this was his mother. Like most of the surfaces in the room, they needed dusting. The other side wall of the room, opposite the mantelpiece, was dominated by a large gilded mirror. Some of the mirroring had faded away in patches, but the gold-coloured frame was ornate, sitting incongruously in the room.

There was a half empty bottle of Calvados on the table. She noticed it was the proper Calvados – farm produced. She remembered her father making a big fuss about buying some from a farmhouse when they had holidayed not far from here. It was his favourite drink. A sticky glass was beside the bottle, along with two unwashed cups that appeared to have once held coffee. A small sideboard contained a dusty

Bible, three unopened bottles of red wine, and another picture of the beautiful woman.

Pierre was at the table. She could hear Jean in the kitchen and water boiling.

'It is unusual that you stay here with another member of our group, but the situation has been helpful for us. Last month the Germans checked all the houses in the village and told people who had spare rooms that they must allow workers to stay in them. The bigger houses have Germans billeted with them. So, you are staying here with the approval of the Germans, I suppose.

'I teach at a school in Boulogne. Jean was a student of mine until a year ago. He is a bright boy, he could have continued his studies, but it was too risky for him to stay at school. He now works at a farm on the other side of the village – most of the men in the village work in agriculture, or at least they did before the war. It means that the Germans class Jean as essential labour and so he is less likely to be sent to Germany, for the time being. It also gives him good cover to move around the countryside.

'Lucien is a *cheminot*, a railway worker. He is based at Boulogne-Ville, which is the main station in Boulogne. The railway line passes just south of here. Lucien is married to Françoise, who you also met last night. Françoise is a supervisor at a factory in Boulogne. They assemble electrical equipment like light switches and plugs. Some of it is for the German Army. They are very short of staff, so it was very easy for her to find you work at the factory. You start there on Monday. Françoise was also born in the village. With all the Allied bombing of the town, she and Lucien were worried about the children when she was at work, so now they live with her parents in the village. They are on the other side of the church. This was a very small village before the war, but the bombing in Boulogne has been so bad that many people have moved out here. And then we have our guests: the Germans don't want their troops to be staying in the town either, so we have plenty of them staying here. We need to be careful, of course, but there has been very little resistance activity in this immediate area. We've only come together as a cell in the last few weeks. We assume that we were brought together as a cell to help you.

'You have a bicycle and that is how you will travel into the town. It is not safe in Boulogne. The Allies bomb it all the time. The port is important to the Germans and, of course, it is a big submarine base. You just have to be very careful there.

'Today you can cycle into the town. You will need to register with the authorities and also get your work documents from the factory. Here, I have drawn you a map of where you need to go. Memorise it, don't take it with you. If you get searched and they find something like this on you, they will find that very rewarding. Your cover is good, you should be all right when you register. It is good that you are from Arras, that was a clever touch by London; it has been so badly destroyed that it is almost impossible for the Germans to check out someone's details if they say they are from there. Try to affect a Picardy accent. It's not easy.'

Geraldine nodded. The accent was one of the most distinctive in France, so she had to concentrate on subtle differences, like pronouncing the final 's' in a word.

'The Germans will certainly believe your accent,' said Pierre. 'But it is not them you need to worry about. I am ashamed to say, it is other French people you need to worry about. Even in this area, too many people have been happy to have an easy life and go along with the occupation. And the collaborators, there are too many of them. The police, local officials. Trust no one, assume nothing. Anyone could be an informer. Say very little and just remember to keep what you say as simple as possible, otherwise you can get caught out by your own detail. Do you understand?'

She was lost in her thoughts, realising just how vulnerable she was.

'Do you understand?'

Geraldine nodded. 'Sorry. I must still be tired.'

Pierre spoke with a sense of urgency. Jean had come into the room and placed a large bowl of coffee in front of her and Pierre, along with some bread and jam. Pierre gestured – 'You must eat. Now, what can you tell us about your mission?'

She sipped at the scalding coffee, which was better than anything she had tasted in England. 'The Allies will invade through the Pas de Calais. We do not know when exactly, but it must be in the next two or three months. We will get warning of the invasion. Our main task is to take part in *Plan Vert*: sabotage of the railway lines. We will plan where to blow them up. The BBC will broadcast the coded messages that will tell us when to do it, but it will be essential if we are to stop German reinforcements coming in to the area once the Allies land. Until then, the orders are to do very little. They don't want to risk us being caught before D-Day. So we will continue to undertake reconnaissance of the area, plan the exact points where we are going to plant the explosives once we get the message, and concentrate on not getting caught.'

Pierre nodded. He understood. He stood up to leave, drinking the last of his coffee before he did so.

'Jean will leave soon. He will go to work at the farm and Lucien will join him later. They will take a truck from the farm and move the supplies you brought with you to safer locations. We have a house in the village where we can keep the transmitter. Remember this map. You will leave for Boulogne after Jean leaves for work. If you have any trouble when you register with the Germans, you must stick to your story. The paperwork you have is very good and the Germans are not always as efficient as people think they are. Just act normally.'

And then, as if as a casual afterthought: 'If they don't believe you, hold out for as long as possible. That will give us time to disappear. Good luck. I will see you later.'

After Pierre left, Jean came and joined her at the table. He had opened the curtains fully and the sun was now streaming into the room. As he pulled back the curtains he released a cloud of fine dust.

Jean smiled at her as he ate his breakfast. His eyes were jet-black, like hers, and when he smiled, he had a perfect set of white teeth. He looked uncannily like the woman in the photograph. 'You don't wear your glasses all the time?'

Geraldine realised that she had forgotten to put them on. She had also forgotten to tie back her hair. From the way Jean could not take his eyes off her, she clearly did not look as plain as she did when she left England. She realised that, in her haste to dress when Pierre had arrived, the top three buttons of her shirt were undone, and Jean was trying hard not to stare at her. His own shirt was open to halfway down his chest. Any Germans bursting in now would assume they were lovers enjoying a drink and that unspoken intimacy that comes after making love.

'I will return around six this evening. The curfew starts at eight o'clock. I will bring food from the farm for us to eat. Usually I eat with the Gironds next door, but I told them I now have a lodger. Don't worry, people know better than to ask too many questions around here these days. Enjoy your day in Boulogne.'

She was surprised at how badly damaged Boulogne was. She knew that there had been air raids and it made sense that the RAF would be attacking the area ahead of the invasion, but the scale of the damage still shocked her. Apart from what she had seen in Dunkirk, the France she had left behind four years previously had been the France she had grown up in. But this place was barely recognisable as a town, let alone one in France: buildings spilled onto the pavement and the road; road signs were in German as well as French; shops stood empty; the few civilians that were around looked dishevelled and beaten, and there were German troops everywhere.

The registration at the Hôtel de Ville in the fortified part of the old town had been easy, though it had, inevitably, taken time. All of her papers were in order. She went from one desk to another to get them stamped, then had to go to the factory to have another document cleared, before returning to the Hôtel de Ville for her final clearance. At no stage did anyone ask her difficult questions. She was treated with something approaching disdain. What she was unused to was the fact that none of the men who dealt with her gave her a second look. It made her realise that for as long as she could remember, she was accustomed to that lingering stare, the smile held a bit longer than was proper, the eyes following her around a room, the eagerness to help even when it was not required. That had been part of her life for the past ten years and it occurred to her now how much she relied on it. She only realised the extent of it now that it no longer happened. Not for Geraldine Leclerc, it didn't. The thick-framed glasses held together by tape and the uncombed hair pulled back tightly had turned her into one of the anonymous grey characters inhabiting the crowd scenes of life whom she had always despised. The British, she had to admit, had done a good job with her. No one cared about Geraldine Leclerc, the thirty-year-old factory worker from Arras billeted in a small village outside Boulogne. She was anonymous, someone who would easily fade into the background.

By now it was twelve noon. Since leaving the village she had worked on the assumption that the resistance would be following her. They had little reason to suspect her; after all, they had seen her climb out of an RAF plane with their own eyes. But at the same time, she knew just how cautious they were. Her communications with Paris had been very limited since she was first approached by the SOE, but one of the messages back from them had been that she should do everything that the resistance asked of her once she arrived in France. It was critical that they suspect nothing of her. The miserable little Belgian had given her a telephone number to memorise. Once she arrived in France and it was safe to call, she was to ring that number.

Outside the Hôtel de Ville she asked an old man how she could find the post office. He turned his whole body slowly to face her, allowing his rheumy eyes time to focus on her.

'Where are you from?'

'Arras.'

He looked around. 'Is Arras as bad as this?'

'Worse.'

He shook his head. 'Head down towards the port. The Grande Rue will take you there. Not that they call it that now.'

She looked at him quizzically. He edged closer to her and lowered his voice. His hand grasped her firmly by the wrist, pulling her nearer to him.

'They now call it Rue Maréchal Pétain.' He turned round very slowly, checking no one was watching and then very deliberately spat on the pavement.

His eyes blazed at her. She was finding this tedious, but did what was expected of her and shook her head in a mildly shocked manner.

The post office was on Quai de la Poste, facing the River Liane. She parked her bike and sat on a nearby bench eating the bread and jam she had brought with her from the house, observing what activity there was around her. She would have spotted any of the people in her cell, but what concerned her was anyone else who may have been following her. If only she could get into the post office without being observed. By the side of the post office was a narrow cobbled lane. A German sentry was posted at the entrance to the lane and only allowing a few people through. If she could get through there, it was unlikely that anyone following her would risk trying to get through too. She waited until a small queue had formed in front of the sentry. A man in a cheap suit approached the sentry.

'My office is just down there, it is easier for me—'

'Nein.'

'I have to collect a parcel from the back of the post office, here is my ticket…'

The cheap suit was gestured through.

'I need to go to the baker's—'

'*Nein.*'

And then Geraldine. She had already removed her glasses and untied her hair, shaking it as she did so. She flashed a smile at the young sentry.

'I have to collect a parcel but don't have a ticket. They told me that if I showed them my identity card, that would do and I...'

The sentry was not looking too closely at her identity card. He looked into her eyes and smiled, which she returned, at the same time allowing her hand to brush his.

'All right. But don't get me into trouble!'

She gave him another smile and wheeled her bike through, taking care to put her glasses back on and tie back her hair. At the rear of the post office was an open door, from where she could see a man emerging with a parcel. She propped the bicycle against the wall. There was no one to be seen. She removed a plain brown headscarf from her jacket pocket, wrapped it round her head and walked in.

An elderly woman behind a window asked her for her ticket.

'I am sorry. I have left it at my office. My boss will be so angry with me.'

'Do you remember the number of the ticket?'

'No, but if I could phone him then he could give me the number.'

'I cannot let you use this phone. You must use one through there. I will let you in.'

She unlocked a door into the main part of the post office. Along the wall to her left was a bank of eight telephone booths. Three were being used. She chose one that had vacant booths on either side and turned to ensure her back was to the room.

She dialled a Paris number.

'Yes?' The person answering was speaking French, but in a strong German accent.

'Is that the dentist?'

'It is. Which tooth do you have a problem with?'

'My molar.'

'And when did it start hurting?'

'Last night. Very late last night.'

'And is anyone with you?'

'No. I am phoning from a post office. No one is near me.'

A long pause.

'Welcome back to France, Magpie. So long since we have spoken! Welcome home.'

The conversation was urgent and to the point. Where are you? Where are you staying? Who are the people you are with? Where are you working? What is your identity card number? Her answers were quick and equally to the point. She turned round once, but no one was taking any notice of her. She affected a smile, as if in a conversation with a friend or family.

'Is everything as expected?'

'Yes. They are definitely coming in through the Pas de Calais. In this area. I am part of the advance guard.'

'Good. You carry on as normal. I will come up to Boulogne in the next day or so. I will make contact with you when we know it is safe. From now on, it will be easy for you to pass information on to us.'

The whole conversation had taken no more than five minutes. She returned to the parcel office, explained that her boss could not find the ticket so she would have to return and cycled back to the village alongside the river.

As she got back on her bike, a man in his early thirties casually stepped back into a dusty shop doorway. Just in case, he covered his face by cupping his hands to light a cigarette. Anyone standing very close would have seen his pale blue eyes and brown hair momentarily catch the glint of the match. Jolly good, he thought to himself. He was carrying the blue coat he had been wearing when he waited for her inside the post office. He had made sure to turn it inside out, so only the beige lining was exposed. She was doing exactly as expected. London would be pleased to hear that. Very pleased.

–

Georg Lange had lifted up the receiver of his other phone from its cradle even before he had finished talking to Magpie.

'Get me Major Schmidt in Tirpitz Ufer,' he ordered the telephonist. This development was so important that Berlin needed to know first. Who could you trust in Paris? He stood up, preparing to talk to his superior. He had once been told that you should always stand up when making an important phone call. It gave you an air of authority apparently. At his height, that was important. He called his secretary in as he waited to be connected to Berlin.

'Gertrude.' He had lowered his voice and was cupping the receiver with his hand. 'I need to travel to Boulogne this evening. I may be there some time. Please arrange for a car and for somewhere to stay. But please be discreet. The whole of Avenue Foch does not need to know.'

'Lange?'

'Major Schmidt, a very good afternoon. I have some very good news for you. Magpie has returned to her nest. The British flew her in last night as an SOE agent. They saved us the cost of travel.' He chuckled at his own little joke.

'And where is she?' The voice in Berlin was steady.

'In Boulogne, Major. She landed in a field outside the town last night. She linked up with a small resistance cell based in a village on the outskirts of the town. She is certain that she is here to help prepare for the main Allied landings in the Pas de Calais.'

'That is excellent, Lange. Excellent. And what do you propose to do now.'

'I will travel to Boulogne myself this evening. I will be able to handle her personally.'

'Well done, Lange. We have her just where we want her!'

'Indeed, Major.'

–

As Lange prepared to travel north, Major Schmidt went to pass the good news to his superiors.

Since Admiral Canaris had been forced out of office in February, the Abwehr had become part of the SD, so it was General Walter Schellenberg who was informed of this development just before he left for a briefing with Hitler. He liked to be the bearer of good news.

London, 12th May 1944

On 12 May 1944, Dr Clarence Leigh's office in Baker Street was so crowded that he had to bring in extra chairs himself from the room next door. If his secretary had been around she would have sorted it all out, but it was a Friday afternoon and for reasons that he had never quite fathomed, she had to go and do things in the country at the weekend, which meant she was allowed to leave at Friday lunchtime. Let's hope D-Day is not on a Friday, he thought as he struggled in with another chair. At Oxford there were porters to do this kind of thing.

Apart from himself, there were Newby and Nicole from F Section, along with that frightfully self-satisfied Major Edgar, who was still acting as if he was winning the war single-handed, and another chap from the London Controlling Section. Leigh had not met Captain Archibald before, but he seemed a very different kettle of fish altogether. Quite charming. Appeared to possess manners. Very distinguished Navy man in his time, apparently.

'Rider has been in France for three weeks now. Thought it would be a useful opportunity for us to have a catch-up. See how she has been getting on.' Leigh was flabbergasted. *He* had called the meeting because SOE had concerns about the whole operation. Now Edgar was trying to take it over. In *his* office. It was *most* irregular.

Leigh cleared his throat. He was determined to be very calm.

'Major Edgar, Captain Archibald. As you know we have had to put ourselves out *considerably* to accommodate this operation. We had to find a country house we had never used before, nor will be able to use again. We had to bring in a French officer to do the training and escort her over to France. Nicole here was the principal contact with Rider, which restricts her opportunities for working directly with agents again. And we could not even fly her out from our normal base, we had to use a special airstrip.'

'We are, as you are aware, Dr Leigh, most grateful—'

'But what most concerns myself and F Section now is the *extreme* danger posed to the resistance in Nord Pas de Calais. The occupation there has been especially brutal. I am unsure if you are aware, but that region is actually run from Brussels by General von Falkenhausen and they have suffered greatly. Notwithstanding that, the FTP have—'

'FTP?' Captain Archibald asked.

'I do beg your pardon. Stands for *Francs-Tireurs et Partisans*. Key resistance organisation, even if many of them are communists. As I say, they have been very active in that area. Very well organised and disciplined. Typically they work in detachments of around thirty-five men... and women. But within each detachment, they are organised in cells and the cells do not have contact with each other. That way, we cut down the risk of people betraying other cells if they are captured.

Usually, two cells of four come under a *chef de groupe*. The chief will command one group of four and his or her *adjoint*, or assistant, will command another cell of four.

'Clearly we did not want to risk the whole resistance structure in Nord Pas de Calais, as important as this Rider operation is. So what we have done is create a new cell, which was not too difficult, as the FTP is especially strong in the Boulogne area. The cell is four strong, so Rider makes it five. And that cell now has no contact with anyone else in that detachment. The *chef de groupe* has been told this is because Rider needs to be kept isolated for reasons of D-Day security. So we believe that we have managed to protect the rest of the detachment. But in doing that, we have effectively cut that cell of four loose. That means, gentlemen, that four gallant resistance fighters are at very great risk...'

Edgar shifted impatiently in his chair and interrupted. 'But as we keep telling you, Dr Leigh, they are perfectly safe as long the Germans need them. If they touch them, then they expose Rider, and if they do that then they will stop getting all of the information that she provides.'

'Oh, we do understand that, Major Edgar. But at what point will the Germans decide they don't need Rider? An hour after D-Day starts? What is going to happen then? Will they realise that they have been deceived and arrest her along with the four people in the cell?'

Captain Archibald noticed that Dr Leigh was getting red in the face and somewhat excited. He attempted to calm things down.

'That will not be the case. Rider has already been given information alerting the Germans to the possibility that the initial Allied attack on D-Day itself will, in fact, be a feint. As soon as D-Day happens, we will reinforce that message to her. The longer we can keep that going, the better. Anything to tie the Fifteenth Army and Panzer Group West down in the Pas de Calais for as long as possible. We know from Ultra that the Germans are anticipating a feint, so we believe that they will swallow this information. If we can keep them believing that for at least a week, then we will be buying valuable time, but frankly even if it buys us a day or two it could save thousands of Allied lives.'

'And are the Germans really still buying into Pas de Calais?' Leigh was trying hard not to sound too sceptical.

Edgar nodded.

'We think so. Had a bit of a scare in February when Canaris was arrested. He seemed to believe the Pas de Calais line, mainly we think because that's what his agents like Garbo and Magpie were telling him. So as long as he was running the Abwehr, then we knew that the Pas de Calais was a favourite inside German military intelligence. It's still a bit unclear about what happened in Berlin in February. Most likely thing is that Himmler finally had enough of Canaris and got Hitler to dismiss him. Canaris is now under house arrest, so he appears to be out of the picture. We'd be surprised if he re-emerges. A chap called Walter Schellenberg who runs the SD is also looking after the Abwehr. But we don't think that this is affecting the Pas de Calais intelligence we're sending them. The most important factor is that Hitler remains convinced that the invasion will be in the Pas de Calais, and so long as he thinks that, the Pas de Calais is odds-on favourite in the Berlin bookies, so to speak. Having said that, I'm not sure what the Nazi line is on gambling.'

'And how long can you – we – keep this pretence up?' The sceptical tone was still apparent in Leigh's voice.

'Well,' said Major Edgar, 'there will be a point after D-Day – probably a few days after, possibly a couple of weeks, a bit longer if the Gods are with us – when Ultra and everything else will tell us that the Germans no longer believe that Normandy is a feint. Then they will know that there is going to be no invasion in the Pas de Calais. At that point, we tell you, and you somehow get the message to the cell to go into hiding. With some luck, that should only be for a few days.'

'And what are they meant to do with Rider?'

'That,' said Edgar, 'is up to them. If she is still around.'

Silence in the room. Leigh knew what Newby from F Section was thinking and he saw the rationale of it himself. They had taken every precaution they could, but there was a very good chance that the cell of four *résistants* in Boulogne would have to be sacrificed. Greater good and all that.

'Very well. We shall proceed on that basis.'

'And how,' asked Captain Archibald, 'is she getting on over there?' Leigh waved his open hand in the direction of Major Newby.

'Major Newby is handling the case personally. Major?'

'She has taken to it rather splendidly. The new cell was a bit of a hotchpotch, to be honest. We weren't going to risk anyone very experienced, but she seems to have knocked them into shape. We're getting all your messages through to her loud and clear but, of course, we don't know what she is doing with them once she gets them. We assume that it is fairly easy for her to make contact with the Abwehr over there. One of our chaps is watching them from a distance so to speak. She seems to have rather taken a shine to a young man in the cell. How is her husband, by the way?'

'Missing her. Poring over his charts and drinking rather too much whisky,' said Archibald. 'Convinced they'll be back together soon and strolling arm in arm down the Champs Élysées.'

Chapter 17

Pas de Calais, 5th June 1944

By nine o'clock on the evening of Monday, 5th June 1944, the unseasonal storms that had been whipping down the Channel from the Atlantic all week and battering northern France had begun to relent. It now felt a bit more like the typical seasonal bad weather common to all coastal areas.

It was not just to the sea that anxious residents of the Nord Pas de Calais region would glance. For the past few weeks, the Allied bombing of the region had intensified. '*Bientôt*' was the word with which locals now tended to greet each other when they were certain they were out of the earshot of any Germans. '*Ce sera très bientôt.*' 'It will be very soon.'

In the village of Hesdin-l'Abbé, five miles south of the port of Boulogne, a young man and woman were walking arm in arm by the side of the Rue du Mont de Thunes. Although the road was normally quiet, dozens of German troops were billeted in the village and their lorries and cars had a habit of speeding along with their lights too dim, so the couple chose to wheel their bicycles along the side of the road. To their right, the grey steeple of the seventeenth-century church of St Leger loomed in the distance. To their left was Château Cléry, where the villagers swore that Napoleon had once stayed – though it would be an unusual French village if there was no property to claim a visit, however brief, from the Emperor. Now, the château was the residence of German officers. The village began to merge into the countryside and opposite one of the rich ploughed fields that sustained the area was a row of five detached houses, more substantial than the others in the village. The couple paused and fell into each other's arms, holding the embrace just long enough to be able to observe over each other's shoulders that all was clear. Satisfied that it was, they turned sharply into the narrow driveway of the second house, which was shielded from the road and its neighbours by tall rows of conifers.

As the couple approached the side entrance of the house, the door opened. They were expected. They silently acknowledged the elderly lady behind the door, propped their bikes behind the curtained alcove in the hallway and climbed two flights of stairs. On the upper landing the man picked up a broom resting against a wall and gently tapped the trapdoor above his head. Two taps, a pause and two more taps.

The trapdoor opened and a ladder lowered to the ground. The couple climbed into the attic to join an older man in there. They nodded to each other.

'You are both all right? Certain you weren't followed?' said the older man.

'Pierre, trust us. You always ask.'

'And I will continue to do so, Jean. Geraldine, how are you?'

She said she was fine as she made sure the trapdoor was firmly closed. Pierre fiddled with the dial on the radio in front of him, Geraldine adjusted the aerial in the rafters of the roof and Jean slipped the safety catch off the American Colt automatic pistol that they had only had for two weeks and were yet to use.

Within a minute they were tuned into the BBC French programme. Listening to this programme in a nearby house the previous Thursday, Pierre had heard the message:

L'heure des combats viendra.

'The hour of battle will come.' The invasion was imminent. The message was telling the resistance that the invasion would take place in the next fifteen days. That night he had risked breaking the curfew to inform as many of the others as he safely could. From then on, at least three of them would listen to the broadcasts every night.

The following night, 2nd June, they had heard the next message:

Les sanglots lourds
Des violons
L'automne.

It was the first three lines of a poem by Verlaine. The schoolteacher had questioned why the poem was not being quoted accurately. There are two mistakes, he said. '*Don't worry,*' Geraldine had reassured him. '*You're not in the classroom now.*' They knew that when they heard the next lines of the poem, that would be the signal that the invasion would take place the following day.

Now, three nights later, they were crouched in the attic, the dusty history of a family's life stacked around them. Tennis racquets, children's toys, old clothes, a chair without a seat and, wrapped in brown paper, parcels of the resistance newspaper, *La Voix du Nord*.

The three of them gathered as close as they could to the radio, the volume so low that they could only just hear it. If the Germans were going to detect them, it would be because of the radio's signal rather than any noise, but old habits were hard to break.

The dial of the radio threw up just enough yellow light to catch their faces. Pierre's lined and tanned, someone who had spent a lifetime catching the sea breeze. Jean was tense, chewing his fingers, his dark hair dropping over his eyes as he listened to the broadcast. Geraldine still wore the scarf she had been wearing outside, her hair flowing from under it, her dark eyes managing to pierce through the gloom.

The broadcasts comprised of a series of coded messages to the French resistance. Each of the messages would be meaningless to anyone else listening, even to other resistance groups. But for the particular group that each message was aimed at, the meaning would be very clear. Tonight, the messages were preceded by an announcement:

> *Today the Supreme Commander directs me to say this: in due course, instructions of great importance will be given to you through this channel, but it will not be possible always to give these instructions at a previously announced time. Therefore, you must get into the habit of listening at all hours.*

The list of messages then followed. Normally, this would last five minutes, certainly never longer than ten. But tonight, the list of messages lasted for an unprecedented twenty minutes. The final message caused hairs to stand on the backs of necks and tears to well in eyes throughout occupied France:

It was the lines of the Verlaine poem: 'Wound my heart/With a monotonous languor.'

The two men clasped each other's right hand. Pierre bit his lower lip and inclined his head away from the other two. Jean put his left arm round Geraldine, gently caressing her shoulder and pulling her towards him. She looked at him with her piercing black eyes and with her long fingernails, carefully flicked a tear from his face. She nodded and spoke one word.

'*Demain.*' Tomorrow.

From the vineyards of Bordeaux to the arrondissements of Paris, from the coalfields of the north east to the châteaux of the Loire, from the Pyrenees to the restaurants of Lyon, and from the villas of Provence to the great cathedral cities of Chartres and Rouen, groups of *résistants* who had kept the flame of France flickering – some for as long as four years – knew the same as the small group crammed in the attic in the Pas de Calais.

The liberation of France would begin tomorrow.

Paris, 5th June 1944

The *résistants* were not the only people in France listening to the BBC broadcast that night and understanding its deep significance. One hundred and seventy miles south of where the little group in the Pas de Calais were gathered round the radio in their attic, a slight, bespectacled man was doing the same in a more comfortable room in the lee of the Arc de Triomphe.

Avenue Foch was one of the twelve avenues branching out from the Place de l'Étoile in the centre of Paris, and 72 Avenue Foch housed the substantial headquarters of two much-feared organisations: the secret police, known as the Gestapo, and the *Sicherheitsdienst* – the security service, known to its few friends and many enemies as the SD. As head of the SD's radio monitoring section, Karl–Heinz Gratz was certainly no admirer of the BBC, but for the past few weeks, even months, he had been doing little else but listen to its broadcasts. Fourteen hours a day, seven days a week. He was now starting to hear the broadcasts in his sleep. Even when he was awake, he found it difficult to get the annoying *di-di-di-dah* refrain from Beethoven's Fifth that the BBC used to announce the broadcasts out of his head.

Ironic, he thought, using the music of a good German like that!

The Gestapo and the SD had tortured just enough information out of captured resistance fighters in the dungeons below Avenue Foch for

Gratz to be aware of what to listen for. Tonight he had sat through the twenty minutes of coded messages, scribbling furiously on his notepad as he did so. The messages had never lasted so long. That morning he felt he had reached a point of exhaustion, now he knew that he would certainly be up all night and probably well into the next day. He could feel a sense of excitement which he did not really understand, tempered by a feeling of fear, which he did understand.

For one brief moment he pulled off his headphones and yelled 'Jürgen!', but his young assistant was probably asleep, again. No stamina, these young people. His heart was beating so fast that he had to turn up the volume on the radio. He could hear the sound of laughter in the corridor and there seemed to be some kind of party or gathering in a nearby office. That would all end very soon.

When the broadcast ended, Gratz pulled off his headphones, sat still for a moment and then banged the desk with his fist, shouting:

'*Ja. So ist es. Das es bevorstehend.*' So that is it. It is imminent.

Within minutes, 72 Avenue Foch had sprung into life. People ran from office to office, shouting at one another, desperate calls were made to try to raise senior German officers from the beds of their French mistresses. 'Most Urgent' messages were sent to Army headquarters in Berlin and to the different German Army groups in France. Gratz stood in the entrance to his office, watching the chaos take hold around him. He was like a schoolboy who had mischievously pressed a fire alarm, not imagining what the consequences would be. Two SS colonels pushed past him. Field Marshal Rommel, it seemed, was back home in Germany, celebrating his wife's fiftieth birthday. The invasion is imminent. Some birthday present.

At eleven o'clock that night Gratz stood at the large window in his office, looking down Avenue Foch towards the Arc de Triomphe in the centre of the Place de l'Étoile. The great symbol of French republicanism now had long been overshadowed by an enormous swastika hanging inside the arch. The flag was picked out by the spotlights trained on it, swaying awkwardly in the breeze as if it knew it was an imposter. Paris was the favourite posting for Germans. Gratz knew that it could soon be over.

He took a deep breath, and as he exhaled allowed an ironic '*Heil Hitler!*' to pass his lips, although not before carefully glancing over his shoulder to be certain that he was alone in the room.

Chapter 18

London, 6th June 1944

Owen Quinn woke with a start from a deep sleep on the morning of that first Tuesday in June. He would not sleep properly again for the next eight months.

Bright shafts of light pierced the blackout and the curtains. He had overslept, and the two-thirds-empty Talisker bottle on the floor by the bed was part of the reason why.

According to the bedside clock it was just after a quarter past nine. The alarm had not been set for its normal time of a quarter to seven. He should have been in work over an hour ago.

As his body reached that moment where it was more awake than asleep, he began to remember. Yesterday had seen a never-ending stream of charts and weather reports, a sense of growing urgency, whispered conversations in the corridor, 'all hands to the pump, chaps', even more photographs arriving by the hour.

Unfamiliar faces appearing in the office, little time to chat with those he knew. Security at the highest state of alert. On Monday, he had been stopped three times by security between entering the building and arriving in his office. A military policeman was outside all day. And the WRENS – with their smart uniforms and busy manner – they were a sure sign something was up. He and the others were told they weren't to waste precious time gathering files. Then the midnight finish. The office had filled with uniforms during the evening, and it was the familiar one of Captain John Archibald who took him aside as he was about to leave.

'Good work today, Quinn. Not long now. Looks like we may have cracked it. Top brass happy. Done our part. You've been splendid. Lieutenant Commander Quinn before you know it!'

Archibald always talked a bit louder than necessary and in short phrases rather than proper sentences. It was a result of years at sea, where it was hard for someone to hear you, so he had learned to be spare with words. Owen Quinn knew the feeling. Archibald had a noisy cough and had to pause to catch his breath.

'Take this, Quinn, and enjoy it. You deserve it. Late start tomorrow. Need to let security check the place out, so best keep out of their way until noon.' Archibald had pressed a bottle into his hands.

Quinn glanced down and saw it was whisky. He was grateful, but suspected he would drink far too much of it. He checked the label. Talisker. A malt meant it was serious.

As Quinn turned to leave, John Archibald did something which at the time struck him as unusual. It would be some hours before he began to realise the true significance of it.

The elder man gently held Quinn by the elbow and guided him towards the empty cloakroom, looking over his shoulder as he did so. When he spoke, it was in an unusually quiet voice.

'Good luck, Quinn.' He was shaking his hand now, placing his left hand over Quinn's wrist as he did so.

'I may not be around here for a few weeks, but all the very best, Quinn. Whatever happens, remember you've played your part.'

In the two and a half years that he had known him, Captain John Archibald had always behaved in a proper manner. He was spare in his emotions – not exactly cold, but not very far from it either. But tonight, as he released his grip, Quinn could have sworn that he detected a catch in Archibald's voice.

Realising now that he had not overslept, Quinn's panic subsided. He stretched out, his right arm swinging over to the empty side of the bed, a cold reminder of her absence. The pillow next to him was still plump. For a few weeks after she had gone, he could still smell her on it. Now, he could not be sure if the increasingly rare hints of her scent were just in his imagination. There had been times during the torment of a restless night when he had sunk his face into her pillow and would wake up in the morning to find it still damp.

He waited for the pain in his back and his leg to ease before slowly getting up. That is what the doctors had told him. Your first movements of the day will be critical. Stretch out when you wake up, wait and then get out of bed. Slowly. No sudden movements. When the bed wasn't empty there had been less chance of that in the mornings, when Nathalie had been at her most attentive. He had even fallen into the habit of setting his alarm twenty minutes early. Since she had gone, his back had felt much better and he always arrived at work on time.

He started to run the bath in what he expected was the forlorn hope that there would be hot water actually coinciding with the time when he wanted a bath. You took your chances when you could with the hot water, in the same way that you did with everything else that was in short supply. After nearly five years of war, that covered most things.

The water ran cold. Quinn pulled on his dressing gown, unaccustomed to this enforced relaxation on a weekday morning.

This was when he missed her most, the unplanned moments when there was little to do. He was fine when he was busy, which was most of the time, or exhausted, which often accounted for the rest of the time. As long as he had a schedule to work to, he could cope. But quiet moments like this, on his own in the flat, walking by the river or awake in bed – they were the hardest. Then, he could not avoid his thoughts; there was nothing to distract him, nothing to stop him reflecting on what he would have said had she been there and how she might have replied. She had only been away for a matter of weeks, but it was beginning to feel as if it was far longer than that. At times, he struggled to remember the tone of her voice, the way her eyes dazzled as she came into a room and her scent that lingered long after she had left. He was worried that his memories of her were fading away. He would then get angry at himself for being irrational and maudlin; it was uncharacteristic. Then he'd shrug it off and get on with life. *It won't be long now.*

The tiny kitchen was just a galley area off the lounge, so Quinn was able to sit in the elderly armchair that had come with the flat, and would remain long after he and Nathalie had left it. As he waited for the kettle to boil, Quinn turned the radio on. For a while, the noise of the kettle struggling to the boil blended with the crackle of the radio as it was tuned to the BBC Home Service. For a few seconds, it merged into one confusing sound.

The kettle whistled, the music on the BBC flooded into the room and Quinn began to feel relaxed. The pains in his leg and back were still there, but the stiffness after a night's sleep was easing off, and soon he would be able to take the first of his tablets. He made a large mug of tea, shovelled in two teaspoonfuls of sugar, hesitated, and then added a third. The toast could wait. He would listen to the radio, have his breakfast, shave, try the bath again, and stroll into work with plenty of time to spare. He began to feel relaxed. From what Archibald had hinted last night, from all the activity he had seen around him and from what he had heard, it felt that the war could be over soon. Not as soon as everyone hoped and some expected, but possibly by the end of the year and certainly within a year. By then Nathalie would be back and they could lead a normal life for the first time.

The hot, sweet tea was making him feel quite optimistic and even happy. On the radio, the music was fading and a familiar voice was taking over. Quinn placed his mug on the small table in front of him and turned up the volume on the radio.

> *This is the BBC Home Service – and here is a special bulletin read by John Snagge. D-Day has come. Early this morning the Allies began the assault on the north-western face of Hitler's European fortress. The first official news came just after half past nine, when Supreme Headquarters of the Allied Expeditionary Force issued Communiqué Number One. This said: 'Under the command of General Eisenhower, Allied naval forces, supported by strong air forces, began landing Allied armies this morning on the northern coast of France.'*

Quinn could not be sure how long he had sat there. Certainly, by the time he reached for his mug, the tea had turned stone-cold and an unpleasant film had appeared on the surface. '*D-Day has come.*' Those words were going round in his head. He should have been euphoric, but instead he found himself feeling uneasy at first and then confused. D-Day was what he had been working on for more than a year. He had devoted most of his waking hours to its preparation and for the last three months his wife had been even more deeply involved in it. But any sense of relief or excitement was dampened by a sense of unease. The Allied assault, the broadcast had said, was on the '*north-western face of Hitler's European fortress*'. What did this mean? Could they really have made a mistake in such an important broadcast? It could be a deliberate mistake. Maybe he was reading too much into it. After all, the statement had gone on to say that Allied forces had landed '*on the northern coast of France*', but the northern coast of France stretched from Dunkirk on the Belgian border across to where Brittany fell into the Atlantic. The north-western edge of Nazi-occupied Europe. Every word of the first official announcement of D-Day would have been carefully weighed and considered and referred to a sub-committee. Quinn had a good idea of how these matters were dealt with. Why would they say 'north west' when, as Quinn knew only too well, the real assault was taking place many hundreds of miles further up the coast, in the Pas de Calais?

There was no point in worrying, he decided. He worried too much. The important thing was that it would be over soon.

The boiler in the large house in Alderney Street was evidently aware that it was D-Day and Quinn found he had enough water for his first deep and truly hot bath for weeks. He shaved, made himself some toast on the grill that hadn't been properly cleaned since she left, had another mug of sweet tea, and put on his dark blue naval uniform.

Owen Quinn left his flat in Pimlico just before eleven and set off on the two-mile walk to Duke Street in St James's. When he first began this job, he had been told at his security briefing to vary his route to and from work. It was advice that Quinn happily adhered to. He preferred to walk, the exercise helping his back, though he would take the bus if it was raining. Depending on when he left the flat, he could take the more direct route through the heart of Victoria, across St James's Park and then over Pall Mall. Or he could take a more roundabout route, heading for the river, down Millbank, past the Houses of Parliament and then down Whitehall. This was the route he was most likely to be stopped on, especially if he tried to cross St James's Square. Sometimes it would be for a security check, or because the road was closed, but Quinn's pass usually saw him through. Or he could take a middle route. Or a combination, sometimes doubling back on himself just to be absolutely sure he was not being followed, and occasionally darting into a turning he had never used before just to vary the routine. He was, after all, a navigation expert.

By the time he set off, any doubts caused by the wording of the broadcast had dissipated and there was a spring in his step. Even though it was the same way he had gone the previous day, Quinn broke the habit of a year and took the same, direct route. That morning he arrived at the office in Lincoln House twenty minutes before midday.

There was no familiar face among the guards on the ground floor of Lincoln House that morning. That was unusual, but not unprecedented. Sometimes they would bring in a new unit, so Quinn thought nothing of it at first. There was none of the good cheer and bonhomie from familiar faces, no 'Good morning, Lieutenant. Not too much of a crosswind I hope, sir', which he would affect to be amused by as if it was the first time he had heard it. Instead the lance corporal who took his pass handed it straight to a corporal who asked him to 'Wait here a moment if you don't mind, sir' and who then disappeared in through the door of the guardroom.

After five minutes, Quinn became mildly irritated. Never before had he had to wait in the reception area of the building where he worked, and his enquiry of the lance corporal if there was any problem was met with a dismissive 'I wouldn't have thought so, sir.'

He sat down in the small reception area, the guards managing the feat of keeping an eye on him while avoiding any form of eye contact. They were trained to do that, he told himself. That and handling clipboards. The metal chair was uncomfortable. He had walked fast and now he was feeling the familiar twinges in his back and a dull ache in his leg.

By the time he had been kept waiting for twenty minutes, his irritation had turned to an ill-concealed exasperation, which was studiously ignored by the guards.

Five minutes later, the corporal returned, along with a sergeant wearing the distinctive uniform and red cap of the military police. 'If you care to come with me, Lieutenant Quinn, we'll have this sorted in no time. Just a small problem with your pass, sir.' He was being passed through the ranks.

Quinn followed the sergeant up the stairs, past the first floor, through whose heavy doors he had once heard people talking in German, beyond the second and third floors where he had never seen the doors anything but firmly shut, past the fourth floor which always had a sentry on the stairwell, and past the fifth floor where the door was sometimes ajar and through which he had seen a mass of electrical equipment. As they approached his office on the sixth floor, two guards carrying large boxes were coming down the stairs, forcing Quinn and the military policeman to go in single file, pressed against the wall. Quinn found himself ahead of the officer, who had had to step further back to allow the guards more space to descend.

Quinn pushed his way into the entrance to the sixth-floor offices, half hearing but ignoring the sergeant's cry of 'Not in there please, Lieutenant.' By the time the sergeant had caught up with him, he realised why. He was clearly not meant to see this. The large central room, from which three small offices led, was deserted. The walls, which twelve hours before had been covered in charts and maps and photographs, were bare. The large map table in the centre of the room had been disassembled and was propped against the heavily barred windows. The filing cabinets containing thousands of photographs were gone, as were the boxes of letters, postcards and other documents. There was a box in the centre of the room full of black phones and alongside it were the two large office clocks. One of the clocks had always been on Greenwich Mean Time, the other on Central European Time. One clock had stopped just after three, the other just after four.

'Please, sir, not in here.'

'But this is my office.'

'I'm afraid we need to go up another flight of stairs to get this sorted, sir.'

'But I don't understand!'

Quinn had moved into the centre of the large room now, puzzled and determined to see what had become of his own small office. He moved quickly across the scuffed green linoleum floor to escape the attentions of the sergeant who was now at his shoulder, but as he did so he found his way blocked by a familiar figure dressed in a black greatcoat, towering well above his own six-foot frame.

'Captain Edgar!'

The tall man nodded to the sergeant. 'Leave it to me.'

And then to Quinn. 'Not happy with you bounding ahead like that, Quinn. Having a bit of a clear-out in here as you can see. Sergeant had instructions to bring you to the top floor. And by the way, it's Major Edgar now.'

From his very first encounter with Edgar in the hospital two years previously, any dealings with him had had an edge of menace to them. Had he been asked to explain that in more detail, Quinn would have struggled. He would have talked about the major's coldness, about his quiet voice with no discernible accent that nonetheless appeared to dominate the room. He would have remarked on the fact that, despite having met the major a number of times, he found it almost impossible to recall in any significant detail any of his physical characteristics, other than his height. But most of all, he would have recalled the feeling of near-fear that he instilled in Quinn. No threats, certainly no violence, but an overwhelming sense that anything the major asked or required was beyond discussion. The effect was almost hypnotic.

By now the major had led Quinn out of the sixth-floor suite of offices which had been his life for the past two years and out into the stairwell. The major hesitated, looking up towards the seventh floor, where Quinn had never been.

'I'll tell you what, Quinn. Let's go for a walk.'

Outside in Duke Street, the major fixed his familiar trilby to his head in a precise manner, twisting it carefully so it sat just right. He wore it lower than Quinn had observed in other people and the brim of the hat appeared to be wider than usual. The effect was to cast much of the major's face in shadow.

They headed south, across Pall Mall and The Mall, entering St James's Park near the bandstand. The walk had been conducted in studied silence, but throughout it Quinn kept thinking of what Captain Archibald had said the previous evening, 'I may not be around here for a few weeks, but all the very best, Quinn. Whatever happens, remember you've played your part.' And now, the abandoned office, along with the BBC announcement of D-Day and the reference to the north west of France. The sense of unease that Quinn had felt when he first heard the BBC broadcast in the flat had returned.

They strolled down to the lake, still silent as they had been since leaving Lincoln House, apart from Major Edgar's occasional cough. And so they stood, their backs to The Mall, facing the lake, silent for a good two minutes.

When the major did start to speak it was in his usual quiet voice. The noise of the city around them obliged Quinn to shuffle closer to Edgar than he felt entirely comfortable with, but he did not want to miss a word.

'Quinn. I want you to listen very carefully to what I am about to say. I don't expect you will like one word of it, and I have no doubt that by the time I have finished speaking you will hate me. But it is important that you listen, take it all in, and then forget the last two years and get on with your life.'

Major Edgar paused as two men in bowler hats got up from a bench to their right. As they moved away, Edgar gestured towards the bench and that is where they sat for the next twenty minutes.

During that time, the major spoke in his quiet, commanding tone, leaning forward for most of the time, his elbows resting on his thighs as he looked around him, anywhere other than directly at Quinn. Quinn had to lean forward himself to catch every word. To a passer-by, it may have looked as if an impromptu confession was taking place, which was perhaps not too far from the truth.

'You have obviously heard the news, Quinn. The landings?'

Quinn nodded. *Of course.*

'I need to tell you something, and from your point of view, it's not going to be very pleasant.'

There was a pause while Edgar carefully straightened his shirt cuffs and adjusted his tie, while at the same time nervously prodding away some gravel with the tip of his highly polished shoe. He coughed and shifted on the bench.

'How long is it now since you've seen your wife, Owen?'

Quinn looked puzzled. This was not what he imagined they had come here to talk about.

'Six... seven weeks? Something like that.'

'And, of course, you only saw her intermittently in the months immediately before that?'

'While she was training, yes.'

'I expect you miss her.'

Quinn looked unsure. Edgar was not the kind of person he imagined having a conversation like this with.

'Well, of course. Naturally.'

'Have you... adapted to her not being around?'

'Well, I cope, if that's what you mean. But I do miss her an awful lot. Perhaps more than I expected. Look, I'm not sure why you're asking me these questions.'

'Owen, I have to tell you that Nathalie is not who you think she is. We do not know her real name, but it is certainly not Nathalie Mercier. What we do know is that she did enter this country in June 1940 with that identity. She is indeed a nurse. There is no easy way of saying this, but I have to tell you that she came here as a German spy...'

There was silence and no movement from Quinn's end of the bench. Edgar glanced over at him; he had been expecting more of a reaction than this. The younger man had a puzzled expression on his face, as if he had trouble hearing what Edgar had said. Edgar wondered whether he needed to repeat it. The silence was broken by a pair of ducks waddling noisily in front of them, arguing furiously.

Quinn's brow was starting to furrow now as first disbelief and then anger appeared to take hold. He was shaking his head.

'No, no – don't be so bloody ridiculous, Edgar!' Quinn stood up, then rapidly sat down again, but hesitantly, as if he were about to stand up again. 'If you think I've come here to listen to nonsense like this then—'

'Listen Quinn – Owen. I know this is hard, but as it is I am telling you more than I should. Just listen. It may be the only time you hear it.' Edgar had adopted a firm tone. He could not afford to leave Quinn in any doubt about what he was saying.

'We became aware that your wife is a German spy only very recently. Certainly after she was sent to France – goes without saying, of course, that we wouldn't have sent her over there if we'd known she was a German spy. I cannot tell you much, but I can tell you this: soon after she arrived in France we came across certain intelligence that made us suspect her. You have to trust me, Owen. We checked this intelligence out most carefully. We had to be sure and I am afraid that we are. We've been back over her movements since she arrived in this country and I can tell you that there is no doubt about it. We feel pretty bad about it, as I'm sure you do. But at least we've found out now, or rather a few weeks ago. If we hadn't done so then I think the consequences could have been quite dreadful.'

Owen laughed.

'Oh, I see! And they aren't "quite dreadful", as you put it, now?'

Edgar shifted uncomfortably at his end of the bench, holding his hands out in front of him in a conciliatory manner.

'Of course they are dreadful for you, Quinn. I am sorry. We're not fools. I don't want you to think that we are being insensitive to your predicament. We can see that you are going to be absolutely devastated. But it is better to know than not to know, eh?'

Quinn was not so sure. As far as he was concerned, ignorance was bliss – at least it had been up until a few minutes ago. He didn't know what to make of what Edgar was telling him. It sounded so far-fetched as far as he was concerned, but then why would Edgar concoct such a ridiculous story? He was not sure what Edgar meant and he could not even be sure that what he was being told was true.

'And who was she supposed to be spying on – me?'

'Quite possibly. Until – if – we get the chance to interrogate her, we simply won't know. We don't know if she was spying on you, or just trying to get into a position where we recruited her. As I say, we only discovered that she's a spy a few weeks ago.'

'And is all this connected to the Normandy business?'

'What do you mean, Quinn?'

'Well, the invasion started a few hours ago in Normandy, apparently. Everything I've been working on has been on the assumption that the invasion would be in the Pas de Calais. So what's going on, Edgar? And where is Nathalie? In Normandy or the Pas de Calais?'

Edgar made to speak and then hesitated, as if he had not been expecting this question.

'She could be anywhere in France, Owen. I can't tell you any more than that and nor would you expect me to. As to the Pas de Calais, well... all I can say is that the D-Day operation is barely twelve hours old. It is far too early to say what is going to happen when... and where.'

More silence from Quinn's end of the bench. Edgar shot him another glance and noticed that his eyes were moist and he was blinking rapidly. He appeared to be in shock and was tapping his feet on the ground. Quinn pulled a long white handkerchief from his uniform pocket and blew his nose.

'So why are you telling me all of this, Edgar? Why didn't you continue to keep me in the dark like you seemed happy enough to do since you apparently discovered she was a spy a few weeks ago?'

'We are telling you now because you need to be aware of it. If I am to be absolutely honest with you, Owen, then I would have to admit that we weren't going to tell you quite so soon. But something unexpected cropped up today that meant we needed to tell you much sooner than we had planned.'

'And what is that?'

'There is a German spy loose in London. Elusive chap, this one. We've prided ourselves on having a pretty outstanding success rate in capturing German spies in this country, but not him. We've been after him since 1940, never been able to get our hands on him. From a professional point of view, one has to admire him. He is quite an outstanding operator. Caused us no end of trouble. However, a few weeks ago, we spotted him tailing you, just after we discovered your wife was a spy. What we think happened is this: the Germans wanted to be sure that what your wife was telling them was true, so they got this chap to verify you really do exist – that you work where she was telling them you worked, in the Navy – that kind of thing.

'A week or so ago, this agent disappeared into the ether again, as he is prone to do. However, this morning we intercepted a transmission he made to Berlin. Couple of hours later he's spotted near your flat. Had to wait around, of course, but once you left at eleven he followed you all the way to Duke Street. It was important that you came into work.'

Quinn was looking round the park. He had stopped dabbing his eyes now, but they were still red and damp.

'And what about if he has followed us here?'

'Of course not, wouldn't have been so foolish as to bring you here if he had, would I? We watched him follow you to Duke Street then he hopped in a taxi and headed north. My bet is that even as we are speaking he will be making his final transmission from his place in north London, then he will head off to a new place. He probably has two or three on the go at any one time. He'll be back on to you, Quinn. Probably go and check you're around this evening and then be out there in the morning. Which brings me back to why we need you to play ball with us.'

The younger man huffed and pulled a face.

'I do understand, Quinn. I daresay that is the last thing you feel like doing. We need you to do this. I am afraid that you really have no alternative – regard it as orders. Please listen carefully.'

Edgar outlined the plan. It was quite detailed. Quinn was surprised that he was able to take it all in. Edgar looked across at Quinn, as if to check that he understood.

'I'll have to be heading off soon, Quinn – you know what you have to do then.'

Edgar was leaning forward, his forearms resting on his thighs, hands pressed together in his familiar prayer-like pose and head bowed towards the ground. Quinn was very still again, speaking in a quiet voice, with no trace of either the anger or the sarcasm that he had shown before.

'You are certain about this, Edgar – Nathalie and all that?'

'I am afraid so.'

The younger man stared ahead, the emotion appearing to rise up in him again. He was biting his lower lip and clasping his hands together very tight. Another long spell of silence followed as he sank deep into contemplation. The pair of ducks walked in front of them again, their argument unresolved. Edgar and Quinn watched them as they noisily climbed back into the lake before Quinn spoke again.

'If… and I say *if*… *if* it's true what you say, where do you think that leaves me? Do you think that any of her feelings for me could have been genuine?'

'I think that only she can answer that, Quinn. We have to assume that her relationship with you was part of her work as a German spy. That doesn't mean, of course… that…' Edgar stopped. He really did not know what to say.

'I presume you had… marital relations? I mean, did you have a healthy physical relationship?'

Quinn blushed and nodded.

'There we are then. Look, you are a good-looking chap. Good personality, charming. I am sure she had feelings for you.'

When he had finished talking, the major leaned back against the bench, his hands pressed together in his familiar prayer-like pose, looking up at the white clouds picked out against the blue sky. Quinn sat perfectly still. They stayed like that while nearby bells pealed two o'clock. As if on cue, Major Edgar got up and stood awkwardly in front of Quinn, patting him gently on the shoulder before silently walking away.

Quinn waited a moment before turning round to watch Edgar walk back to The Mall. A black car was waiting and as Edgar approached it, a uniformed figure emerged to open the rear door for the major. Within seconds the car had sped off in the direction of Whitehall.

Quinn turned round and started to get up, but his legs felt so heavy that he was unable to move. He was weighed down by his thoughts. Recollections of times he had spent with Nathalie, snippets of what Edgar had said and flashbacks to his childhood, but as these memories evaporated he was left with the stark reality of what Edgar had told him. Although it seemed unbelievable, he kept coming back to the conclusion that Edgar would not have made it up. There would simply be nothing to be gained from telling him something untrue.

He stayed on the bench in a state of shock until three o'clock, and when a policeman who had already passed him twice asked pointedly if everything was well, Owen said that it was and got up slowly to leave the park.

Quinn was far too wrapped up in his own thoughts to notice anything that was going on around him. He certainly never noticed the small man watching him from the bridge to the right of where he had been sitting. He might be described as 'round' rather than 'fat' by anyone who looked at him long enough, which few would bother to do. His red face was topped by a bowler hat perhaps one size too small. He effortlessly slipped in some fifty yards behind Quinn.

Quinn never turned round as he left the park and crossed Birdcage Walk, but even had he done so, it is highly unlikely that he would have noticed that same man following him from a careful distance.

Chapter 19

London, 6th June 1944

His initial thoughts in the first few seconds after he awoke were always about who he was. A few days previously, he had attended a lecture in London on existentialism. 'Who Are We?' it was called, and he sat, amused, at the back of the hall, smiling at the thought of the earnest audience worrying about their purpose in life and who they really were.

You want to try being me. You want to know what it is like to have to be a different person every few weeks, to be constantly changing your identity. And try keeping that up for years.

After all that time, the effort of remembering who he was each day was beginning to exhaust him.

He had never before heard the telephone ring in the main hall of the house at that time of the morning. From his bedsit on the first floor the sound reverberated across the hall with its chipped and noisy floor tiles, up the pretentiously ornate staircase with its cheaply varnished banisters and missing balustrades and along the threadbare carpet to his room, the acoustics making it sound as loud as if the phone was ringing outside his door, rather than some way below it. The first ring came at six in the morning. Two shrill blasts, then silence. He turned over to go back to sleep and realised he was not alone. Whoever it was, she was fast asleep and did not look nearly as attractive as she must have done the night before, which was usually the case. Through the prism of a glass, they all acquired a flattering sheen at some stage of the evening. Daresay they thought the same of him. He would not learn his lesson, but from what he could recall, and from the state of the bedclothes, it had probably been worth it.

Something beginning with 'S', he seemed to remember. Not Susie, not Sheila – though there had been a Sheila not that long ago. Sheila from Stockwell. Sandra? Could be Sandra. Sandra was in a deep sleep, lying on her back, head tilted back on the pillow at an odd angle, mouth slightly open, the make-up which she had not bothered to remove smeared across her face and the pillow case, and probably somewhere on him too. The sheets were gathered around the top of her thighs.

He lay there for a moment, contemplating her breasts and the nipples which were somehow still hard. Maybe, if he was very...

The phone rang again. Just the two shrill blasts. He looked at his watch. Five past six. He wondered. No. Not possible. Impossible, in fact. Only in a dire emergency.

He touched the small strip of flat bone between Sandra's breasts, though he was now not sure if it was Sandra after all. Maybe Stephanie. It didn't matter if you couldn't remember the right name, just so long as you did not use the *wrong* one. He walked his fingers slowly down her body, a light touch at first, then firmer. She started to respond in her sleep, writhing at first. His hand was just past her belly button when she began to wake up, trapping his hand between her legs. She opened her eyes and turned over to face him, her wide smile revealing teeth stained with a cheap lipstick. Some of her eyelashes were stuck together with blobs of mascara and she reeked of cigarettes. He had seen better in the hardest bars in Hamburg, but once they started to respond, it didn't matter. She pulled him towards her.

Three more blasts of the phone.

This time there could be no mistaking it. Two normal rings then the phone cutting off halfway between the next two. Three rings. And exactly five minutes after the last call. He could hear Mr Fraser come out of his downstairs flat and talk angrily as he answered the phone.

'Hello? Hello... anyone there?'

There wouldn't be.

She was working hard on him now. No subtlety but plenty of experience to compensate. She made him respond soon enough. He was already inside her and could be finished in a minute if he wanted. He always could in the morning. Two more minutes and he could even satisfy her, which was not necessary but always a bonus nonetheless. Helped ensure a return visit, was how he liked to put it. But the phone calls had signalled something more urgent. He did not even have one minute.

He pulled out of her quickly, roughly pushing her hands away as she tried to coax him back in.

'You have to leave now.'

'What! At this time of the morning? Who was it who was all over me a minute ago? You woke me up for it!'

'You have to leave. You must go now.'

He was out of bed now, naked.

'I can see you still want it…'

He walked round to her side of the bed and hauled her out of it, quite roughly. He picked up her clothes from the pile by her side of the bed and thrust them at her.

'I am sorry. I suddenly realised I was late for something. You must go. Here, take this.' He had picked up his wallet from the desk and handed her a one pound note.

'What kind of a girl do you take me for?'

'I take you for a very nice girl who I would like to see again and take out for dinner. This is for a taxi.'

'Crikey. I could buy a taxi with that. Where am I going to get a taxi at this time in the morning?'

'Please be quiet on your way out. Look…' He wondered whether to try using the name Stephanie, but in the circumstances it was too great a risk, getting her name wrong. '…I promise I will come and visit you at the bar tonight, and I promise I will take you to dinner at the restaurant of your choice.'

'You promise?'

'Of course.' The easiest thing in the world was making a promise that you had no intention of keeping. You just… promised. It was what he did.

He waited until she was out of the front door and watched her disappear down the street. Of course, Mr Fraser would not be happy about this. Even now he would be writing down what time she had left in his little notebook in his spidery handwriting ('I have the evidence here, Mr White, in my own fair *hand*'). He preferred landladies; he could always count on being able to charm his way around any woman. But Mr Fraser and charm lived in different worlds.

'You know it is quite against my rules for you to have visitors…' he would say.

So far, a pound or two pressed into Mr Fraser's bony hands had worked. Probably wouldn't again, but it didn't matter. He would have to be out of this place before noon anyway. That was the procedure: if you get the emergency signal, get out within six hours. The sooner the better.

He checked that the door was locked, then slid the extra bolt into place, used his overcoat to cover the gap at the bottom of the door and moved the dresser away from the window. The floorboards opened easily enough, as he had made sure they would. The radio was on the dresser now. He hooked the aerial high inside the window, just inside the net curtains and turned it on. He was connected surprisingly quickly. He scribbled the coded message on a pad on his right. The transmission only lasted a minute. He decoded it even before he stored the radio away, which was the wrong way round.

'Large-scale invasion Normandy underway. Clarification urgently required on first sector. Urgent you check Nero to confirm movements.'

The best advice he had ever received in this business was not to panic. It was easy to say that, everyone did. It was an obvious thing to say. But the man who had taught him had been an intelligence officer in the Great War and had survived an interrogation by the British by convincing them he was a deaf mute. His advice was this – when you find yourself in a really difficult position: stop. Have a cigarette and think. Five minutes.

So he stopped for five minutes, had a cigarette and thought. He would have to leave the flat – too risky to stay. Of course, he already had somewhere to go – he would never be in the position of not having a fallback position. But the message was clear. Check on Nero. That meant being in Pimlico sometime around eight so he could follow him again. He was always having to do that. Nero was not bad, he always varied his route, but for someone in his mid-twenties he was slow, which must be because of his injuries. Not quite sure of the whole business, not that it was his business to be sure anyway. When he had first come here the work had been more varied. Travelling around the country. More excitement. Now it was just following this man and, until a few weeks ago, his wife. But it was what Berlin wanted, and what Berlin wanted...

He started to pack. Everything he needed in two large suitcases and a smaller one. He would leave the house at seven – before that would feel a bit too early. It would be pushing it a bit; he needed to get down to Clapham first, but if he then took a taxi from Clapham to Victoria

Station, that would help. It was an old trick, if you have to resort to using a taxi, take it to a train station. No one ever thought there was anything unusual about that. He could take one large suitcase with him now, drop it off at the place in Clapham and then be in Pimlico by eight to pick Quinn up on his way to work. Back here, pick up the other cases, send one last message to Germany before he left this place, pay off Mr Fraser ('No, no – please keep the deposit, for your troubles. You have been very accommodating. Thank you.') He had learned that the word 'accommodating' worked wonders with the English lower–middle class, which is what Mr Fraser clearly aspired to. It was what they spent their lives doing. Then he would take the other cases over to Clapham. Tonight he would have to start finding a fallback for Clapham. It was going to be a long day.

Funny thing was, he had never expected them to use the emergency code to get him to contact Berlin. Two rings on the phone. Gap of five minutes, two more rings. Another gap of five minutes, then three rings. That means contact Berlin. Urgent. Very urgent. The most intriguing part of it was that there was someone else in England who would have made the call and somehow Berlin would have been able to contact them. The British had picked up so many Abwehr agents that he had come to assume he was the only one left in the country. It was a little comfort that he wasn't.

'Large–scale invasion Normandy underway.' Well, there's a surprise. It was, actually. Not a surprise that the invasion was underway, although they'd taken their time about that. But Normandy was a surprise.

'Urgent you check Nero to confirm movements,' the message had said. What else have I been doing the past few months? Pimlico to St James's. And back. Two or three times a week. How often did Berlin want reassurance that yes – that's where he works, yes – he's there every day, all day.

'Clarification urgently required on first sector.' How on earth was he to find that out? Walk up to Quinn and tap him on the shoulder 'Excuse me… How come you chaps aren't on the beaches of the Pas de Calais this morning?' Follow him into the office and ask 'What's all this about Normandy then?' He'd have to work on that one.

He finished his second cup of tea, decided it was going to be a busy day and poured a generous measure from the brandy bottle before packing it in a case. He had already denied himself one pleasure that morning, so he was entitled to a small drink.

Edgar had been up since four in the morning. The initial reports were quite good, though the Americans seemed to be taking a bit of a hammering on the western beaches.

At six thirty he took a call from one of the MI5 duty officers.

'Cognac had an early morning alarm call, sir. Three calls to the house phone between six o'clock and ten past six this morning. Caller hung up after just a couple of rings.'

Cognac. The man who had caused them more trouble than entire German divisions. They knew he had entered the country early in 1940 and assumed it would be a matter of time before they picked him up, like they had with all the others. He was a well-known Abwehr agent. One of their best. He'd been spotted in the West End in May 1940 by MI5 and there were other confirmed sightings in Manchester, Liverpool and Glasgow. But they were never able to lay a hand on him. He had an ability to vanish – thin air and all that.

He had assumed almost mystical qualities in MI5 circles, but along with luck on Cognac's part and sheer incompetence from some of those following him, Edgar put Cognac's ability to evade them down to two factors: one was his sheer ability, and the second was his way with women. Edgar had sat in on one interview with one of them. A woman in her late forties whose husband was a prisoner of war in the far east. Cognac had stayed with her for a couple of months in 1941, originally moving in as a lodger. She was totally besotted with him. 'I have never been satisfied with a man before, sir. I would have done anything he asked,' she admitted, staring intently at a lace handkerchief she was twisting in her hands as she spoke. She had made a good stab at appearing ashamed, but it was not difficult to see the passion in her eyes as she spoke about Cognac.

Then a stroke of luck. In September 1943 they had been following Quinn to work, which was routine. They did it once or twice a week, as part of their monitoring of him and his wife. The man following Quinn that morning, who was especially good at his job and had the ability to follow someone from a very long way back, spotted Cognac in between him and Quinn. Instead of panicking like the rest of them had – and allowing Cognac to get away – he followed Cognac. Back to a house in Hendon, where he had a small flat. After that, it was a matter of keeping an eye on Cognac, who in turn was keeping an eye on Mr and Mrs Quinn.

Edgar assumed that the Abwehr were so pleased with what they were getting from Magpie that they had put Cognac on to them to be absolutely sure that she was where she said she was, and Quinn was doing what she said he was doing. So in turn, MI5 kept an eye on Cognac, but let him get on with it. He kept them busy enough, checking out Quinn and Magpie, and then hanging around the second- and third-division bars in the West End. He was usually lucky, Edgar noticed. He preferred to go back to their place or book a cheap hotel room where the manager was prepared to ignore the form filling for an hour in return for double the rate. It was rare for him to take one of them back to his place.

'Yes, sir,' said the MI5 man. 'Those phone calls to the house were obviously a signal for Cognac to contact Berlin. Post Office have traced the calls as coming from a series of telephone boxes in and around Waverley Station in Edinburgh. Cognac contacted Berlin around six twenty. Radio boys triangulated the transmission to his road in Hendon, but Bletchley traced the transmission anyway. Still working on the final version, but they reckon it's to do with D-Day. Seems Cognac has been asked to keep a close eye on your man today. Reference to the first sector too. Bletchley working on that.'

Edgar called Archibald.

'John. I think that you had better come over for a chat. I know that we weren't planning to do so, but I think we are going to need to tell Quinn today.'

Chapter 20

London, 6th June 1944

Quinn remembered little of the walk back to Pimlico. He was vaguely aware of a lighter mood in the air, people slapping each other on the back, strangers exchanging smiles.

'Good afternoon.'

'It most certainly is, isn't it?'

'Not long now.'

As he walked past Westminster Abbey he noticed a steady stream of people going in. The relief that people felt as they anticipated the end of the war could not be exaggerated, although the euphoria was a long way off.

Owen Quinn could not imagine feeling more depressed. The shock that had numbed him since Edgar began talking to him in the park was beginning to wear off. It was being replaced by a boiling rage against the injustice in the way his life had been ruined. The physical effort of walking was difficult. As often happened in times of stress, his back was beginning to ache.

Once he was in Alderney Street his pace quickened. He would get out of his uniform, have a bath and, most importantly, a drink. He thought about Edgar's plan. He would have to go along with it, there was no alternative. He would need to pack a case. At least it would get him away from the flat for a few days.

He climbed the steps into the house, holding the door open for the odd-looking civil servant who always wore a bowler hat and who lived in the flat next to him. *So he's come home early today too.*

Quinn checked the table in the hall for any post. The tall aspidistra, covered in a sheen of dust, stood sentry over a few bills and some handwritten correspondence. Just one letter for him, the envelope bearing his mother's distinctive script. Its theme would be familiar

– '…looks absolutely splendid, as does the front garden… so please, Owen, do make an effort to come and visit your father and I, neither of whom are getting any…'

Roger. That was what the neighbour was called. He had been useful enough when they first moved in, even offering the services of his own cleaner.

There had been a forgettable evening just before their first Christmas here when Roger had invited Nathalie and himself in for drinks. Roger, it turned out, didn't drink. Not alcohol, anyway. An evening of tea and barley water and some hard biscuits apparently baked by Roger's mother. They nodded at each other as they stood in the hall. Two men and a woman were following Roger, who held the door open for them. Quinn hadn't seen them before but he did not give it a second thought, it was a transient sort of a house anyway.

He ran up the stairs as fast as his back and legs would allow him. He decided he would have that drink before the bath as well as after it. Roger was behind him too, which was odd – he hadn't stopped outside his own flat.

'Owen – are you all right?' Roger was standing immediately behind him now. He could hear more people climbing their staircase. Owen nodded.

'Mind if I come in, Owen?' Before Owen had time to say that actually, yes – he did mind, Roger had pushed past him in his tiny entrance hall and walked into the lounge. Owen stood in the hall. The two men and one woman who had followed them into the house were now standing in the entrance to Owen's flat, waiting for the hall to clear so that they could enter too.

'Come through, Owen. Let me explain.'

Roger had sat himself down in one of the large armchairs. It was the one Owen usually sat in. It was the one he had been sitting in less than seven hours previously when he had listened to the news. Owen sat in the other armchair. No one had sat in it since Nathalie had left. He heard his front door shut and voices in the hall.

Roger was a small, rotund man, florid of complexion and given to perspiring extensively. He had obviously been walking faster than normal because he was struggling to catch his breath. His neck bulged against his tight collar, the knot of his tie concealed by the excesses of his neck. He wiped his damp face with a large handkerchief.

'Can I ask what on earth is going on with you barging into here?'

Eventually, Roger caught his breath enough to attempt conversation, though it was punctuated by frequent pauses.

'Owen. It is not simply a happy coincidence that I am your next-door neighbour. I am a colleague of your friend Major Edgar, as are my three colleagues currently squashed together in your hall. I moved in just before you did. My brief was to keep an eye on you and your lady wife. Make sure nothing odd happened. I think that Major Edgar has explained your plans for the next few days?'

'Yes.'

'Good. I have two tasks now. The first is to ensure that when you set off tomorrow, our new friend goes with you. It is vital that he sees where you are going. His code name, by the way, is Cognac. He has a taste for it, so I am told. Can't see the attraction of it myself, foul stuff actually, but then most foreign drinks are. Where were we? Ah yes. Tomorrow. The streets around here will be well covered. We anticipate that Cognac will come by here tonight just to check that you are in. Our guess is that in the morning he will also be watching out for you too. We're rather counting on that, actually. As soon as we are sure he is there, you will leave. You don't need to worry, I will be here to tell you when and where to go. Is that clear?'

'So far.'

'Splendid.'

'But—'

'Hang on, Quinn. My next task is altogether less pleasant. We need to thoroughly search the flat, and I am afraid that my orders are to ensure that any trace of your wife is removed. For reasons of security, I am told. I think that Major Edgar has explained her new... security status? Well, it rather follows that he needs to go through all of her possessions, don't you agree? Everything, I'm afraid. Apparently even the tiniest or most inconsequential-looking item could be crucial, so there we are. Not my field as it happens, but I'm told they can find almost anything these days, eh! I know this is not nice, but I am told that after a time some of it could be returned to you. If you want it, that is. My colleagues in the hall will take care of this. Did your wife have any valuables here?'

'Some jewellery – not much. Earrings, necklaces, that kind of thing. Trinkets, really, but I wouldn't—'

'Very well. I am sure that eventually anything of value will be returned. Now, if you don't mind.'

Owen spent the next hour slumped in the armchair as all trace of his wife was carefully removed from around him. A large whisky had been pressed into his hand and refilled as the two men and the woman methodically worked their way through the flat. He was never introduced to any of them. Roger fussed around the flat, annoying the other three who seemed to know what they were doing, and being unctuously attentive of Owen – 'Another whisky? Tea? Biscuit? Put your feet up old chap...'

Drawers were emptied and every item gone through. Anything to do with Nathalie or his work was put straight into a case. Other items were checked with Owen. All paperwork went into the case too. Even the bills.

As his world was efficiently dismantled around him, Owen sat slumped in the armchair, creased in defeat and resignation. The glass of whisky was refilled yet again and he was beginning to feel very tired.

By the time they were done, Owen was fighting an urge to curl up and sleep. He heard Roger telling the other three to put the cases in his flat next door. 'We can remove them tomorrow when the coast is clear.'

Roger explained the plan for the evening. The two men would stay with him – 'Don't worry, Owen, they will be fine in the armchairs!' – to make sure everything was in order. To guard me, you mean, thought Owen. Roger would stay next door with the woman 'She will have my bed! I'm on the settee.'

A supper magically appeared from the kitchen and Owen picked at it while his two protectors ate theirs with gusto. Barely a word passed between them. Conversation was restricted to the occasional solicitous remark – 'Pepper?... Salt?... More water?' After supper they brought him a mug of tea that was too strong and tasted almost bitter, but which he drank nonetheless before he ran a bath. He did not enjoy sounding like his mother, but there was no doubt that milk did go off much quicker these days. Looking round the bedroom, it was clear that there was now no evidence remaining that Nathalie had ever existed, let alone lived here. The photos of their wedding had gone along with all of her clothes, her make-up, jewellery, hairbrush, the silk stockings which hung on the inside of their wardrobe door and which he allowed to brush his face when he opened it, her few books and even the tiny, imperceptible scent of her which he would pick up from time to time and would take his breath away.

If anyone came to the flat now and he explained that his wife had once lived here, they would surely question his sanity. She had vanished in more ways than one.

He undressed for the bath, packing as he did so. 'Two weeks you'll be away,' Edgar had said. 'Maximum three. You'll be in uniform.' Not too difficult to pack then. The last item he threw into the case was a travelling toiletries bag that Nathalie had bought him in November for his birthday. He had not used it yet and she had been annoyed. He unzipped the bag. Handy little thing. Neat compartments for his razor and shaving brush, a travelling toothbrush, a soap holder, hairbrush, comb. As he picked it up he felt a rattle, coming from inside the soap holder.

He closed the bedroom door – 'Just getting undressed' – and opened the soap holder. It was empty, apart from something weighty wrapped in tissue paper. A strip of gum-paper had held the little packet in place, but one end had come loose which was why the packet had rattled.

He opened it. Carefully wrapped inside the tissue paper was a beautiful cameo brooch, the cream head of a woman with long ringlets of hair carved out of black shell, mounted on a gold base. He turned it over. Just under the pin was inscribed one word.

Toujours.

Always.

–

After his bath he had sat by the open window in his bedroom, the curtains and blackout pulled aside. The merest hint of a breeze drifted into the room, but its impact on the stifling heat was marginal. It stayed light until just before ten o'clock, but as darkness fell he began to feel angry again. He was surprised that since returning to the flat he had felt exhausted rather than upset or even angry. Perhaps he was still in shock. He remembered how he felt after being rescued from the sea. The exhaustion overwhelmed every other emotion. A packet of Senior Service lay open on the windowsill. Just two cigarettes remained. He had smoked eight since getting back to the flat. The road outside was quiet, the occasional couple returning home, one always slightly more drunk than the other. A cyclist. An elderly lady being pulled along by two dogs. An air raid warden with a limp and a dipped torch that threw out a yellowy light just a foot or so in front of him.

Which one of you is Cognac, then?

One of his two guards knocked gently on the door, opening it before Owen had the chance to tell him to come in. He was carrying a tiny tray with a large glass of whisky, another mug of tea and a plate of biscuits.

The tea was a bit weaker than before, more to Owen's liking, but it still had the bitter taste of the previous drink. It was odd. He looked again at the cameo brooch, turning it in the half-light, feeling its every contour, studying it for clues.

Was it possible that anyone other than Nathalie had put the brooch in the case? He could not imagine who. He racked his brain to see if he could picture her at any time wearing the brooch. Had she written 'toujours' herself or had she had it specially inscribed? Had that word already been on the brooch? As far as he could tell, the brooch was not new but the word 'toujours' looked fresh. The cream head of the woman looked as if it had once been whiter in colour and the gold reverse had tiny scratches. From somewhere at the back of his mind he recalled his mother and grandmother discussing a cameo brooch and remarking that tiny imperfections in the shell were a sign of authenticity. He imagined the brooch was a family heirloom that Nathalie – or whatever her real name was – had brought with her from France. For some reason, she had hidden it, wanting only him to find it. He brought it closer to his eye. At the very top of the reverse, in the centre, were two tiny capital letters. 'CT'? He pivoted the brooch in his hand. The C could be a G, part of it having faded. He went and held it directly under his bedside light. It was a G. GT. Who was GT? Were those Nathalie's real initials? Or those of her mother? And if so, was it her maiden name or married name? Or a grandmother? Or an aunt? In truth, it told him little, but it took him a bit closer to her.

On one level, the brooch gave him some hope. Would a German spy really leave a keepsake behind? Maybe she was trying to reassure him. But then he thought that perhaps it was her way of leaving him with one memento and hoping he would be satisfied with that.

He lay back on the bed, pulling an extra pillow across from Nathalie's side of the bed, and had another sip of the tea, but decided to give up on it. Whisky was always a preferable option anyway. He held up the tumbler with its generous measure of whisky. Like the cameo brooch a few minutes before, it caught the fading light. He noticed something strange. Tiny white crystals floating at the bottom of the glass. A dozen of them and only visible if he held the glass at eye level and directly against the light.

He wondered and then he realised. The tiredness and even calmness that he had felt since returning to the flat were no coincidence. He must have been drugged. The endless glasses of whisky and the bitter tasting tea. They were to make him compliant. It would ensure he was easy to handle for what they had in mind the next day.

He placed the whisky glass back on the bedside table and lay there, becoming increasingly unsettled as the effect of whatever they had been sedating him with wore off. The breeze had picked up now as the darkness took hold, and as it did so a most terrible thought came to his mind, which he dismissed as ridiculous.

He got up to close the curtains. He climbed into bed. He needed a good night's sleep.

But sleep turned out to be a hopeless prospect. The terrible thought that he had had before gnawed away, crushing him. He sat bolt upright in bed, totally awake.

What was it that Roger had said earlier when he came into the flat?

I moved in just before you did. My brief was to keep an eye on you and your lady wife. Make sure nothing odd happened.

They had moved into this flat in June 1942. Two years previously. But according to Edgar, they had only discovered that Nathalie was a spy after she went to France. It didn't make sense. If they really had no idea that his wife was a spy, why had Roger been keeping 'eye on you and your lady wife' for almost two years?

And then there were other things that had played on his mind when they had happened, and which he had dismissed. Maybe they now had a plausible explanation.

The happy coincidence of her arrival at Calcotte Grange; his being told so unexpectedly that he wasn't going back to sea despite the assurances he had received from the doctors until then; the way in which the Royal Navy had been so understanding over their relationship and so accommodating about their getting married – even helping to find them this flat.

He had thought it odd, and these thoughts never really strayed too far from the back of his mind. It was equally odd that she was allowed out on her own from the safe house in Holland Park. And then the fact that he had earlier been allowed to take secret papers home, and even use his wife as an unofficial translator. Even at the time he had been surprised that Archibald had allowed that, especially as it coincided with his starting work on the Pas de Calais landings.

He wrenched open the door to the darkened lounge where the two guards were both slumped in the armchairs.

'Get Roger for me.'

'It is rather late, sir. Perhaps in the morning?'

The shorter of the two had stood up; he had clearly not been asleep. He was adjusting his jacket, discreetly moving his hand inside it.

'I don't give damn how late it is, I want to see him now.'

The other guard got up.

'Very well, sir. Just keep your voice down though, if you would. We don't want to disturb the neighbours.'

A minute later Roger bustled in wearing a large check-patterned dressing gown over striped pyjamas. He wondered what the matter was.

'I'm not doing it.'

'Doing what?'

'Doing what you want me to do tomorrow. I've decided not to do it.'

'I'm afraid that is not an option that you have, Owen. I know you're upset, but you are also tired. Get a decent night's sleep and you'll feel fine in the morning. Be a good chap. Another whisky, perhaps?'

Quinn moved to stand right in front of Roger, towering above him. One of the guards moved towards him but Roger gestured him to hold back.

'What is it, Owen. What is the matter? Shall we talk in your bedroom?'

So he and Owen talked. Not for long. Five minutes was enough to convince Roger that this was above his rank. He opened the bedroom door and spoke to the guards.

'I need you to go and get Major Edgar and ask him to come here. It is rather urgent. Thank you.'

–

Edgar arrived within the hour, clearly none too pleased at his summons. He told Roger and the two guards to go and wait in Roger's flat.

'I gather that there seems to be some kind of a problem, Quinn?' he said with calculated understatement. His meaning was clear: '*This had better not be a waste of my time.*'

'How long have you known?'

'Known what, Quinn?'

'How long have you known that my wife is a German spy?'

'I told you in the park. We found out not long after she went over to France. A matter of weeks ago.'

'And you didn't know before that?'

'No.'

'I don't think I believe you, Major Edgar.'

'Quinn,' said Edgar, his earlier irritation now having turned to anger, 'it is not your place to disbelieve what I say. Your attitude is bordering on insolence and—'

Quinn carried on, ignoring Edgar, his voice shaking with fury. 'I'll tell you what I think, Edgar. I think that you knew long ago, before she went to France, that Nathalie was a spy. I am not sure when you found out, but I'm beginning to think that you may have known all along, certainly before I met her.'

'Don't be ridiculous, I told—'

'I think that I've been set up, Edgar. I think I've been used as part of some complicated, clever plan of yours. Your chap Roger out there, he let slip earlier that he'd moved into the flat next door just before we moved in. "To keep an eye on you and your lady wife" were his words. Why would he do that, Edgar, if you had no idea then that Nathalie was a spy? Tell me.'

Edgar said nothing. He sat still, eyeing Quinn like a boxer trying to find his way through an opponent's tight defence.

'You see, Edgar, I think that you were counting on me being in shock at first, which, of course, I was. And then when I got back here – well, Roger and his friends were busier than the waiters at the Savoy, plying me with tea and whisky. Plan was to keep me nice and sedated and calm and not causing any trouble, eh? So as soon as I realised that, I stopped taking your liquid refreshment. And then I began to think more clearly, helped along by poor old Roger's little slip. And do you know what I think? I think that you knew all along that Nathalie was a German agent. I even think that you knew that long before I met her.

'And I'll tell you why I think that. When your sedatives started to wear off, I asked myself why I believed what you told me in the park. Why didn't I just get up there and then and tell you to get lost? How, despite the fact that you gave me no evidence, did I know deep down that what you said may well be true? I'll tell you why. Because at the back of my mind, there were things that I ought to have been more suspicious about. Small things. Like the fact that I knew so little about Nathalie. Why did such an important project like the one I've been working on have such a small office with such a frankly second-rate group of people to work with? And why was I allowed to take work home with me? It was terribly convenient, of course, for me to do so, but it didn't really make sense, did it?'

Edgar started to speak, but Quinn raised his hand. *Wait.*

'So, I'll do a deal with you, Edgar. You tell me the truth. Everything. Then I'll go along with your plan. Otherwise, I'm not playing. You can arrest me, beat me up, put me in the bloody Tower of London, I don't care. But I know that you need me to co-operate with you, so I think that you are going to have to tell me everything.'

'For Christ's sake, Quinn. Stop behaving like a schoolboy who's had his bat and ball taken from him. This is war, not some silly game which you decide whether you want to play or not. I think you'll find that you have to—'

'Oh, really? And what are you going to do? Drag me along there in handcuffs? That will look good, won't it? That will convince whoever's watching. Tell me the whole truth, Edgar.'

Quinn was breathing heavily through his nose, arms folded tightly across his chest.

Edgar leaned back and removed his trilby, which he had been wearing since he came in. He looked carefully at Quinn. Maybe he had underestimated him. There was more steel there than he could ever have imagined. He slowly turned the trilby round in his hand, carefully studying the brim and flicking a piece of fluff from it. They had not expected Quinn to cotton-on quite so quickly. Roger would be made to pay for this. He would have to tell him. If he did not co-operate tomorrow – later today, actually, he thought glancing at his watch – then this carefully crafted operation was buggered, not to put too fine a point on it.

He placed his hat on the small table in front of them and turned to face Owen.

'The landings on the beaches of Normandy are our main route into Europe – our only route into Europe. There will be no landings in the Pas de Calais.'

Silence from Quinn, who looked stunned. His head had jerked towards Edgar and stayed in that position, his brow furrowed in confusion.

'What I am saying, Quinn, is that Normandy is and always has been our main choice for the landings. The Pas de Calais was an attempt to deceive the Germans. It still is. We need them to believe for as long as possible that Normandy is not our primary target and that the main landings will be in the Pas de Calais.'

'So then everything that I have been working on...'

'Everything that you have been working on is a vital part of the deception. I hope that as time goes on you will come to realise that you too have played your part. But, certainly – all the planning that you have been doing has not been for an actual invasion.'

'But what has it been for then?'

'I cannot pretend that this is not the difficult part, Quinn. Through you, we have been able to directly mislead the Germans. You have, if you like, been an unwitting but very necessary conduit for passing on incorrect information to them.

'Your wife was recruited in France before the war as a German spy. We did not pick her up when she came here. We only became aware of her after we arrested another German spy – a Belgian as it happens – in 1941. As you know, at the time, Nathalie was working at St Thomas's Hospital. By the time we became aware of her, she had already applied for a transfer to a military hospital. We had a choice at that stage. We could arrest her, but there would be little to be gained from that. We had no evidence against her for a start – just the word of our Belgian friend. Or, we could see what she got up to, and to do that we needed a helping hand. So we facilitated her transfer to a military hospital. She ended up at Calcotte Grange, where she met you.

'We knew that she had asked to go to a military hospital so she could have direct access to the kind of intelligence that you will pick up in that kind of place. It occurred to us that this gave us a perfect opportunity to enable her to meet someone who had access to top grade intelligence. She was allowed to see your file, which told her that you were going to be working on a top secret Naval Intelligence project. Even you were not aware of that, at that stage. It was not hard for us to arrange for you and her to get together. She was keen to get to know you, so to speak, and we knew that you would be keen too, though for altogether different reasons.

'We arranged for you to work in Naval Intelligence. At first the work was reasonably low-level and we knew that Nathalie would not be in a position to find out much about what you were doing. But the idea was to be very careful and very gradual about it. We did not want the Germans to get wind that this all may be too good to be true. That has always been one of the risks of this operation. But by the middle of 1943 we were well into planning the invasion of Europe, and a crucial part of this was a deception operation that would convince the Germans that the invasion would be somewhere other than where it was going to be, if you get my drift. Quite early on it was decided that Normandy was the preferred location. German defences are just too good in the Pas de Calais. They were expecting us there; everything we were intercepting from them was telling us that. So we simply told them what they thought anyway. If you like, we reinforced it for them.'

Quinn was staring down at the floor as he had been throughout the time that Edgar was talking. He appeared to be shielding his face. He was biting his nails.

'As you know, we allowed you to take some material home with you. Quite irregular, of course, but it was the best way to ensure that Nathalie was getting the information. Sure enough, she was passing it on back to her Abwehr control in Paris.

'Naturally I cannot go into any detail, but I can assure you that this was just one part of the deception. There are many other aspects of it. But what was critical was that the Germans were getting – are getting, indeed – a consistent story, whereby the different sources corroborate each other. If they know that Agent A has no connection whatsoever with Agent C, for instance, yet both are saying the same thing – then what they are both saying has added credibility.'

'If... if this is true, then why was she sent to France?'

'The icing on the cake, if you like. To help further convince the Germans. We've sent hundreds of agents over. They liaise with the resistance. In her case, she is there to prepare for the invasion in the Pas de Calais. Up until this morning, that is what we have been telling her. What she is being told now is that the main invasion will still be in the Pas de Calais, that what is going on in Normandy is actually a feint. If they believe it, even for a short while, then they'll keep their forces in the Pas de Calais and delay reinforcing Normandy. Absolutely crucial then that the Germans got that message, hence our sending her over there.'

'And what happens when it's all over?'

'If we get our hands on her then she will face the due process of law.'

Silence for a few minutes as Quinn took it all in, as far as he was able to. As much as he wanted to argue with Edgar, there was something about what he said that made sense, reluctant as he was to admit it. Despite having been with Nathalie for a year and a half, deep down, he felt that he had never really known her. The questions that he constantly asked about her life in France, the answers that told him nothing. The times when she appeared briefly distracted to the extent that she seemed to be a different person, only to snap out of it and return to him with a smile. On the other hand, her affection for him did not feel forced. When he came home, she appeared genuinely pleased to see him. She was an enthusiastic lover, he could not recall many occasions when she had rejected his advances and often she had instigated lovemaking.

'But you deceived me!'

'Unfortunately we did. We had to. It was the only way. Your wife has been such an important source for the Germans that we had no alternative.'

'Why are you telling me all this, Edgar? What if I do something about it?'

Edgar laughed. 'I'm telling you, Owen, because you insisted, rather had me over a barrel before, didn't you? Not sure that you're better off knowing what you do, ignorance being bliss and all that. But what are you going to do, Owen? Go to the police? Tell the newspapers. Come on, old chap. There's a war on. No one will believe you. We won't let anyone believe you. They'll assume you are mad. Anything you say will be denied. It never happened. Not true. Wife working for us, went to France and not heard of again. Happens in war.'

'But you just said that if you catch her she will go on trial.'

'I think that what I said was that if we find her, she will face due process. *If* we find her.'

'And if not?'

'Then that may be better all round. Look, Quinn. I've taken a calculated risk telling you now; you didn't really leave me with an alternative. But we need you to play ball with us. We are sure that they are still keeping an eye on you and, if that is the case, we need you to be doing what they'd be expecting you to do. May have been better for you to carry on drawing your maps, which was the original plan. But you would have found out in a matter of days anyway that there was to be no invasion in the Pas de Calais. Better this way: we can tell you in a controlled manner. We owe it to you. You have every reason for feeling that you have not been treated well.'

'But she deceived me – you deceived me! What am I to do now?'

The anger was coming now, Edgar thought. Long overdue.

'You get on with your life. Look, Quinn. No one is pretending that this is nice for you. But look at it from our point of view. We get one shot at D-Day. If it fails, it could be years before we can try again. We have to use every trick at our disposal to ensure that it does not fail. You, I am afraid, are one of the tricks. You'll get over it. The Navy will look after you, do the decent thing. Just play ball with us for a few more weeks. Come on. Busy day tomorrow. Try to get some sleep.'

–

After Edgar left, Quinn demanded a new bottle of whisky, so he could be sure of having a drink that had not been tampered with. A strange calm came over him. Maybe it was the whisky, maybe it was the quiet of the night, maybe he was still in shock. Quite possibly, it was a combination of all three. But most of all, the calm came from a determination to find his wife. Whatever happened and however long it took, he would find her – and the brooch was the first step.

One of the men in the lounge was snoring loudly and he could hear the other one shuffling around.

He climbed back into bed naked. For the first time since she went away, he rolled over to her side of the bed. Once again, he imagined he could smell her on the pillow case and feel her indentations on the mattress. He woke up frequently during the night and each time he stared at the cameo brooch on the bedside table before drifting back to sleep.

He awoke at four o'clock on her side of the bed and lay there thinking until the first hint of dawn, when he drifted back to sleep again. He thought of his grandfather, the only other person whom he had loved and lost. He remembered that last conversation with him, when his grandfather asked what he wanted to do when he was older and he had replied that he would like to play cricket for England, at which his grandfather laughed. And then he said he would like to marry a beautiful Frenchwoman. That really was what he had wished for then. 'Be careful what you wish for,' had been his grandfather's reply.

Those words had come back to haunt him now.

Chapter 21

Owen Quinn was woken by the sound of voices coming from his lounge. He had not slept for more than an hour at a time that night. It was seven o'clock.

He stayed in bed until there was a knock on the door. It was seven thirty. One of his guards, for want of a better word, came in with a mug of tea.

'Roger suggests we may need to think about moving in around an hour, sir. No sign of anyone outside, but just in case, before you open the curtains we'd better wait in the hall. Take your time, sir.'

He did take his time. Checking to see if anything else had been overlooked, drinking his tea, repacking his case and listening to the news. As far as he could make out, it was good news. More than one hundred and fifty thousand Allied troops had landed in Normandy the previous day, plus something like twelve thousand vehicles. It was the latter figure that impressed him. You could do all the planning in the world, but until you put a tank on a beach, you would not know what was going to happen.

At eight thirty Roger came into the lounge. Quinn was dressed in his uniform, in his armchair and drinking a third mug of tea. By the side of his bed was the bottle of Talisker that Archibald had given him, less than a quarter of the bottle still to be drunk.

'Good news, Owen. Cognac popped by last night on his bike. Had a quick look up, and back to Clapham. And the even-better news this morning is that he is back in the area, so he's behaving exactly as we were expecting – now we just need to give him the bait: you. Shall I just run through the plans one more time?'

Quinn left the house at a quarter to nine, after Roger had run through the plans. The exodus was carefully choreographed. Roger left at his normal time of ten to nine, though he would make his way via a circuitous route to Owen's destination. One of Owen's two guards, whose name he now discovered was Andrew, left the house immediately before him, the other man and the woman just after him. As he locked the door of his flat, the couple were waiting on the landing. 'We'll look after the key for you,' the man said, his hand held out towards Owen. He hesitated before handing over the key.

He paused at the bottom of the steps, looking back once at the house, not certain when he would enter it again and not sure that he wanted to. It was a pleasant day. Just the perfect weather for his trip. Carrying his case and so walking a bit slower than usual, he set off. A few minutes later he entered Victoria Station from Bridge Place.

'Take your time when you get there, Owen,' Roger had told him. 'Give Cognac a chance to catch up with you and get his bearings. Go and buy a paper, look at the departure board – that kind of thing – and then go and buy a ticket. First class. Whatever you do, make sure you get on a train that is not just about to leave. Can't risk him losing you.'

There was little chance of that. The station was a heaving mass of people, far busier than he would have expected. A crowd was gathered under the departures board and small but noisy groups formed around any member of the station staff who made the mistake of standing still. As he passed one group he overheard the plea from a harassed ticket inspector.

'If we all shout and push at the same time, we won't get anywhere today, will we? For the one hundredth time: there are severe delays on most of our services to the south coast. Some of you may have heard the news. It means that we are running far fewer trains. Now madam, if you care to...'

Quinn walked over to the departures board. It was now five past nine. It was clear that there were delays on all routes, especially those to the south coast. Some services seem to be cancelled altogether. The next train to Dover was scheduled for nine thirty, which would have been ideal, but that was showing as 'delayed'. Another harassed-looking ticket inspector walked by, doing his best to avoid any questions. Owen stepped in front of him and asked about trains to Dover. A small crowd joined him round the ticket inspector; people were anxious to find out what was going on. He just hoped that whoever was meant to be following him would catch what was happening.

'No trains to Dover so far and I doubt if there will be any through trains all day, sir. If you want to try your chances, I would go to Maidstone East and then see what they can do there. If you're lucky, you'll then get a connection via either Faversham or Ashford. Good luck, sir.'

A train was about to depart from platform three: a cloud of pure white steam travelled more or less horizontally into the station concourse. The guard's shrill whistle, a cry of '*Come on now!*' and a sudden rush to the gate as it swung shut. A Canadian soldier put down his bag and tenderly stroked the face of the girl he had been hugging next to Quinn, before picking up his bag and vaulting over the gate. Three sailors hurried past, saluting him as they did so. On a small bench a woman was bent double, her face covered. A young boy, no more than ten, stood next to her. He looked confused; his hand uncertainly placed on her heaving shoulder.

It was going to be hard for Cognac to keep tabs on him in this chaos, Quinn realised. He walked slowly over to the newspaper kiosk, to join a long and disorderly queue. People were keen to read whatever they could of D-Day, and that had led to a run on the papers.

'As I have just told the gentleman in front of you, sir, we have no copies remaining of either the *Daily Herald* or the *Daily Mail. Daily Telegraph?* Very good, sir. Yes, sir?'

Quinn bought one of the last copies of *The Times*. He was careful not to look around. 'Avoid the temptation. You won't spot Cognac, of course, but he may well spot you looking around. Just act normally.'

As instructed, he waited until a small queue had formed by the first class window in the ticket office and went to join it.

'First class single to Dover, please.' Again following instructions, he spoke softly.

'Where to?' the ticket clerk asked.

'Dover, please. I understand I may need to go via Maidstone East. Is that correct?' Quinn repeated, a bit louder this time for the benefit of the clerk.

'It will have to be Dover Priory, sir. No trains to Dover Marine today or the rest of this week. Security. You'll understand. Head for Maidstone East. Next train due to depart ten o'clock. Probably another delay on top of that. Platform four, sir.'

An hour later he was wedged into his first class compartment as the elderly locomotive pulled the eight-coach train out of the station.

He had boarded the train as soon as it was announced as the one for Maidstone East, but even so he was lucky to have found a seat in the rush. There were even three people standing in his six-seat compartment. He had noticed a man bearing a distinct similarity to Roger, but wearing a trilby hat that was far too big. The man pushed his way through the crowded corridor, briefly glancing into his compartment. Owen opened his newspaper. He noticed that it was just eight pages today. It was rare these days for it to be more than that. By the time the train pulled out of Victoria Station he had already answered six of the clues in *The Times* crossword.

'He'll be following you,' Edgar had told him in the park the day before. 'What the Germans will want to know now is whether Normandy is a feint. Will there still be a main invasion through the Pas de Calais? That's what preoccupying them. So we've decided to send you to the seaside'.

Edgar and Roger had both explained his role in some detail. The Germans believed that Quinn was involved in planning the Pas de Calais invasion, so they would now be looking at his behaviour after D-Day to see if it was consistent with that. The Germans had also been relying on intelligence that a massive Allied army was gathering in the south east of England. This would be the army that would invade through the Pas de Calais.

'FUSAG,' Edgar had told him. 'Stands for First US Army Group. It's the US Fourteenth Army and the British Fourth Army, at least that is what the Germans think it is. Commanded by General Patton. Totally fictional, of course, apart from Patton. Although, as I understand it, quite a few of the top brass wish he was fictional. Tricky chap, apparently. We have every reason to believe that the Germans have bought it. Some of their agents – now working for us, of course – have spent quite a while in the south east, spotting the formations, tanks, landing craft. The whole place has been buzzing with radio traffic. Based around the Kent ports, short hop over to the Pas de Calais.

'So it makes perfect sense for you to get down there today. They'll think that the main invasion is imminent, so your moving down to Dover will fit in with what they expect. Cognac will be able to follow you to the Castle and watch you go in. Won't be able to go any further, but that doesn't matter. Our guess is that he'll then head back to London and let Berlin know that one of the Pas de Calais planners has moved down to FUSAG.'

Twenty-four hours ago, all had appeared to be well in his world. Then it collapsed. Now, like this train being led along on the tracks, he was being led along, with little control over his destination.

—

Cognac prided himself on his composure. He had always considered that to be a secret agent's most important asset – staying calm, making careful judgements, avoiding silly mistakes. His composure had been fully tested this morning.

The previous day had been hard enough. After the early morning excitement, he had taken the tube down to the bedsit in Clapham where he had deposited his large suitcase and then taken a taxi to Victoria. A short walk so as to be near Quinn's place for eight o'clock – and, of course, it was a full three hours before he emerged. He followed him to Duke Street, watched him go in, waited five minutes – which was as long as he could risk – and then took a taxi back to the house in Hendon for the last time. He made his final transmission to Berlin, letting them know that Quinn was at work as normal, then he packed up his remaining bags.

He settled the rent with Mr Fraser. The stooped figure of his landlord had opened his door before Cognac had finished knocking on it, no doubt he had been peering through the spy-hole as was his habit whenever the front door of the house opened. Mr Fraser's slightly hunched back made him appear shorter than he was. His accent had the very slightest trace of Scotland from where he had moved many years ago. As ever, he had a cold and was constantly dabbing at his nose with a crumpled handkerchief that may once have been white. Whatever his landlord's intentions had been, they soon changed. Not only did Cognac tell him to keep the deposit – 'I am sure there will be the odd scratch and chipped saucer' – but he also pressed a five pound note into his grateful hands – 'Just in case any of my lady friends or their fathers come looking for me! If you could tell them as little as possible. I am a married man myself, you'll understand.' A knowing nod from Mr Fraser, who would very much have liked to be a married man himself, but was flattered that the gentleman thought he would understand. He left Mr Fraser a fictitious forwarding address and then embarked on a series of criss-crossing bus journeys to Clapham. They confused him and hopefully would have the same effect on anyone following him. As the day wore on he had the occasional pang of regret: Stephanie, which he was now sure was her name, had been an enthusiastic lover – far more responsive than most women he'd come across in this country. It was a shame, he could have had a few more days' fun.

Later that night he cycled up to Pimlico, a journey vindicated by seeing Quinn's distinctive profile by the window.

Back there at eight o'clock the next morning. Good job that the warren of roads afforded plenty of discreet places to wait. Street corners were always good, a couple of small blocks that he could walk round, sure in the knowledge that if Quinn left his flat he would not have gone very far by the time he came back round the block.

The round little civil servant with the red face and the funny hat had come out as usual. Quinn left at a quarter to nine, but today he was carrying a suitcase – and not a small one either. This was interesting. He turned left rather than going right or straight on as he normally did. Cognac was not altogether surprised to find himself following him in the direction of Victoria Station.

The crowds in the station were helpful. Plenty of cover. Of course, he had to work that much harder to keep an eye on Quinn, but that was not too difficult – his quarry was tall and his Royal Navy peaked cap distinctive enough to be very helpful.

He stood in the queue alongside Quinn. The best way of following someone, he had been taught all those years ago, was by not being behind them all the time. People take too much notice of what's behind them. You would never be expected to be followed by someone in front of you. Bit of a risk, if he reaches the ticket window before Quinn, but he is a Dutch refugee today and his English is poor, so his failure to understand the clerk could delay matters long enough until he hears Quinn's destination.

Dover. He had never been there, though in the past few months he had had to make a few trips to Kent to see what he could find about all the Allied forces gathering there for the invasion. 'Lots of them' had been the essence of his subsequent reports. 'All over the bloody place,' as the English would say. Lots of security though. You needed to be careful down there. He was pleased he had chosen his Dutchman today, it was his most robust identity.

The journey ought to have taken just under two and a half hours, but by the time they changed at Maidstone East and then Faversham, it had taken them the best part of four hours. He had nearly lost his man at Maidstone East, the platforms were so crowded. On the final train, from Faversham to Dover, he had ended up sitting in the compartment next to another young navy officer. He chose a seat right by the door so he could keep a check on his movements.

But the journey itself had been most useful. Tanks parked in fields in the distance, hundreds of them, literally. Around five miles outside of Dover he noticed heavy guns mounted on rail wagons parked in some sidings. They were covered in camouflage and would have been hard to spot from the air. He counted five of them in total. He memorised all the details. Large troop camps were just outside the town. When the train pulled in to Dover Priory, the station master's announcement:

'This train terminates here. All change please. There are no services to Dover Marine.'

Even if he lost Quinn now – and there was a chance he would have a car waiting for him – he would still have plenty to report back tonight.

He made sure he went through the ticket barrier ahead of Quinn and then paused to light a cigarette. The station appeared to have been bombed quite heavily. The end of one platform was fenced off and one of the buildings had been reduced to a pile of rubble. Quinn waited outside the station, looked around, glanced at his watch, looked up at the skies and then set off.

The station was at the top of a hill. Quinn walked down the hill into the town centre, stopped to ask directions of a policeman and then carried on, this time up another hill. Around half an hour after leaving the station he arrived in front of Dover Castle. The security was very high. Cognac knew he had reached the end of his own journey. In the reflection of a tea shop window, he saw Quinn pass through the security barrier in the road outside the castle, and then through the heavily guarded main entrance, being saluted as he did so. Cognac would have to go into the tea shop and have a cup of disgusting English tea, in case anyone wanted to know the purpose of his walk up the hill. Then it would be back to London.

Cognac was weary by the time he arrived back at Dover Priory Station. It was four o'clock and the station was quiet. Three policemen were on duty outside the station, taking care to check everyone as they entered it. This was going to be too risky. Cognac had taken care to remove his coat and hat, but he still needed to be careful. It would be difficult to have to explain to a policeman why he had come to Dover for less than two hours to purchase a cup of tea. 'Don't they sell tea in London then, sir?'

He decided to go cross country. They taught you to do that, of course, but it was notable how tempting it was to disregard it. If you are in Manchester and need to get to London, it is very easy to take the direct route. But if you are being followed – and you must always assume that you are – then you are making it so easy for whoever is following you that you may as well have a sign on your back saying that you work for the Abwehr. Cognac had once left Manchester at seven in the morning and not arrived in London until nine o'clock that night. Four trains and six buses. Three department stores visited in between buses and trains. Hard to beat a good department store for losing someone in, with their lifts, back-stairs and gloomy corridors.

There was a small bus station across the road and he headed there. One of the three buses that displayed any sign of going anywhere that day showed Deal on its destination board and the driver had just started the engine. That would have to do. It was the opposite direction from where he was heading, but that was not a bad thing in itself. He knew the map of Britain better than his own country now.

He paid the fare and slumped in a seat at the back. A mother and two noisy girls were occupying most of the back row and Cognac chose to sit in front of them.

They arrived in Deal just after five. There was another bus waiting as they pulled in showing Ramsgate as its destination. That would still be heading away from London, but he could catch a train from there. Ideally he'd have tried to spend an hour or so in Deal, just in case he was being followed, but it was beginning to get late so he got on the bus.

The journey was another long hour. The bus stopped in Sandwich for a while, where it filled up with people, and then wound its way to Ramsgate. He went straight to the train station. The restricted service on the south coast routes that had been so evident this morning had not improved. His best chance, the man at the ticket office told him, was to go to Chatham. From there he ought to get a direct train back to Victoria.

The journey back was punctuated by a series of delays. Not long after the train left Chatham it pulled into a siding to allow three trains laden with troops and equipment to pass. He carefully counted the number of carriages on each train and even managed to spot some serial numbers on tanks. He closed his eyes as he tried to memorise the numbers, fighting sleep as he did so.

It was about nine thirty by the time he walked out of a now-quiet Victoria Station, buying a copy of the *Evening News* on the way. It was still light, although night was not too far away. He noticed four taxis waiting at the rank, but knew he must resist the temptation. He'd pushed his luck with taxis the previous day. Two bus journeys would be four times longer, but safer.

It was a quarter past ten by the time he arrived at the bedsit in Clapham. He would encode his message and keep it as brief as possible, though there was plenty to tell Berlin tonight.

He sank onto the narrow bed, with its greasy candlewick bedspread and a gentle tilt towards the wall. Not the kind of place he could bring anyone back to. He would have to find another place soon anyway. He fought sleep.

He knew he was good, quite possibly the best, which was why he had survived so long. From the little that he could gather, he was one of the few German agents still active in Britain. Maybe now that the woman was in France, he was the only one still around, though he did suspect that she possibly had a radio-man somewhere out there, and of course whoever had made the phone calls the day before. He had been careful today, he always was. But in his heart, he knew that they would catch him sooner or later. A policeman would be lucky, or he would make a mistake. He had been so exhausted on the journey back that he did not like to think what would have happened if he had been stopped by the police in Deal or Ramsgate, or if some officious train guard had decided to be difficult.

And all for what? Germany was going to lose the war. Even allowing for the Allied propaganda, the evening paper made it clear that the invasion of Normandy seemed to be a success so far.

What would happen then?

Where would he go?

Would someone in the Abwehr turn him in during an interrogation?

And had it been worth it?

For the first few years, of course it had been. He'd been a believer then. But now it was just a matter of survival. Maybe it was now time to put himself first. To contemplate retirement. He hauled the transmitter from under the bed. *Ask me if it has been worth it when they lead me from the cell, condemned. Ask me if it has been worth it when they slip the noose round my neck. Ask me then.*

Chapter 22

Pas de Calais, 5-7th June 1944

Just before ten thirty on the night of 5th June, Geraldine and Jean left the house on the edge of the village where they had been listening to the BBC broadcast. The curfew was well underway, so they left their bikes in the house and returned to Jean's cottage via the covered bridle path at the rear of the house. It brought them out into a country lane which they had to cross before entering the churchyard through the back gate. The graveyard was wrapped protectively around the church, the moonlight picking out some of the inscriptions on the gravestones. They crossed the graveyard, past the bleak memorial – a large cross on top of it and the names of the twenty-five villagers who had fallen in the Great War picked out in metal characters. In her less composed moments, she had imagined them pointing accusingly at her. The memorial had even started to appear in her dreams. The stone angels that adorned the gravestones had developed a habit of flying into her dreams, quick to arrive, reluctant to leave, like the worst type of guest. She could barely sleep at night for the noise they made on the windowpane. When she entered the churchyard these days she looked down all the time, doing her best to avoid the accusing looks. When she was very young, her father would take her to the cemetery where his parents were buried. 'The people here,' he would say, pointing at the statues and the graves, 'they are the only ones who know *everything* that is going on.' It had taken her nearly twenty-five years to come to believe it.

The peacocks in the château grounds could be heard in the distance as they entered the Impasse de l'Église and Jean's cottage.

The curtains in the front room were drawn tight and they sat around the table in darkness, apart from a band of pale light coming in through the half-open door that led to the kitchen. Jean poured two glasses of wine.

222

'What do we do now, Geraldine?'

When she had first met Jean, she had seen him as little more than a boy, deferring to her, seeking her approval and enjoying having a woman in the house. At other times, he was a man, strong and fast, and when they were out in the fields or woods at night, there was no one she would rather have with her. He never panicked and displayed a rare courage. She could never anticipate whether the Jean she was speaking to would be Jean the boy or Jean the man. The previous week she had got up in the middle of the night to fetch a glass of water and caught sight of Jean in his room, towelling himself down. What had unnerved her that night was not the sight of Jean, but the memories seeing him like that evoked of Owen. She lay in bed that night, not knowing what she would not give up for the chance to have him there with her for just one unsettled night. By the time dawn pricked through the thin curtains, she wished she had spent the night with the stone angels.

Now he was Jean the boy, relying on her to know what to do.

'You heard the message tonight. Plan Green, the railways. Tomorrow we will need to contact London, so we will have to use the transmitter. Then we will know when we are to begin the sabotage. They will also give us more information. We need to sleep, Jean, the invasion could be starting very soon. It could even be underway now.'

Neither of them slept well that night. Few people in the Pas de Calais did either. The Allied planes overhead were incessant. The sounds of bombs exploding in the direction of Boulogne and further to the north was deafening. At one stage Jean knocked on her door and asked whether they should be doing anything.

'Like what, Jean?'

'Maybe we should take to the hills, if the Allies are coming in tonight, they will need help.'

'We stay here. Try to sleep.'

He hesitated in the doorway. For one tense moment she wondered whether he was going to come in. She could not possibly risk that happening.

Pierre stopped by the house early the next morning. There were rumours that the Allied invasion had started, but much further west, perhaps in Normandy. The priest had told him that some villagers had reported seeing British paratroopers. No doubt there were other reports that General de Gaulle was already marching down the

Champs Élysees. Was the tricolour flying over the Hôtel de Ville in Boulogne?

'We will meet again this evening. By then we will know if anything has happened. Until then, we go about our lives normally. I go to school, Jean, to the farm. Geraldine, you go to the factory.'

There were more roadblocks than usual on the road into Boulogne and in the town itself. Each roadblock had at least one extra soldier on duty. One soldier who examined her card in the last roadblock before the factory looked no more than eighteen. His helmet was a size too big, but what was most noticeable was that his hands were shaking as he examined the identity card, holding it upside down at first. Geraldine gave him a smile when he returned it and he looked as if he was about to burst into tears of gratitude.

She could see plumes of smoke rising from the port area in the distance and she cycled past one block that had been reduced to rubble overnight. But if the invasion had begun, it was not in this area. Apart from the normal sounds of the town, there was none of the noise and activity she would have expected with an invasion. But the coded messages on the BBC had been very clear. The invasion should have begun by now.

The cacophony of noise in the factory made it difficult to talk. It also made it difficult to be overheard, which was always an advantage in her passing conversations with Françoise.

'Have you heard anything?'

'Just the same rumours that everyone has heard. Philippe says there has been a broadcast on the BBC that the invasion has begun, but no one has heard anything or seen anything.'

An hour later Françoise brushed past, pushing her slightly against the bench. Geraldine did not look up but carried on assembling a plug. When she had finished, she went to the toilet. Françoise was washing her hands, they huddled closer together. Françoise turned up the tap to help muffle her voice.

'One of the drivers has just returned from Calais. He says that German radio has announced a big Allied invasion in Normandy – on the beaches. They say that their forces are defending successfully.'

'They would do.'

'Surely they wouldn't report something if it hadn't happened. I thought that the invasion was supposed to be in this region?'

'I thought so too. It still could be. This could be an attempt to trick the Germans – to get them to move their forces away from this region.'

'We will see tonight.'

At lunchtime Geraldine went out, telling Françoise she was going to ride into town to buy some bread and to see if she could find out any information. A block past the factory she stopped, dismounted, and knelt down by the side of the road to tie her shoelaces. An open-top lorry full of troops drove past. She was used to them calling out to her, but this lorry drove by in silence, the troops all looking sternly ahead. Assured that no one was watching, she felt under the saddle and sure enough, a note had been secreted there. Lange had been in touch, she was not surprised. She glanced at it and hurried off to his meeting point.

She passed a bakery and noticed a smaller-than-usual queue and stopped to buy the bread, thankful that she had remembered her coupon.

The church of St Nicholas was halfway between the Hôtel de Ville and the post office. Barely one building around the church remained intact. Women were hunched in the rubble, picking through it as if it was harvest time, not knowing quite what they were looking for. There would have been a time when you could have seen the church from far off, but the top half of the steeple had disappeared during an RAF raid in May. Miraculously, all the stained-glass windows had somehow remained intact and the church still functioned, shrugging off the damage as an expected inconvenience.

Although he varied his meeting places like the experienced Abwehr man he was, this was Georg Lange's preferred rendezvous. He liked the mixture of noise and silence and the contrast between the damage, which shocked people, and the magnificence of the architecture, which left them in awe. People came to the church to pray, or to seek shelter, or just to sit for a few minutes. Some came to meet friends. Many, no doubt, liked to believe that its sanctity gave them a temporary immunity from the war, even if they knew that was fanciful.

Being lunchtime, the church was busy, but not packed – more people would be at the Notre Dame in the centre of the town. Lange was on a pew at the front of the church, to the side. He had taken care that no one was sitting around him and was on the seat closest to the aisle, apparently deep in prayer. Few people would feel able to disturb him and ask to be let through. Geraldine positioned herself in the row behind him, just to his left.

She crossed herself and was seemingly lost in prayer too. Lange leaned back in his seat, taking care to look around. There was no one anywhere near them.

'You have heard the news? The Allies have landed in Normandy. They are on the beaches, many of them have broken through. Tens of thousands of them. This is not Dieppe.'

'Is this the main invasion then?'

Lange turned round, looking directly into her eyes with the faintest hint of a very brief smile.

'That is what I was hoping you would tell us.' He turned back to face the altar, where an elderly and overweight priest with a dirty cassock was hobbling with the aid of a stick that threatened to snap at any moment. He picked up a candle holder and disappeared behind a curtain, releasing a shower of dust as he did so.

'The information you have been giving us was very clear – that the main invasion will be in this region. It is probable that this is still the case and that the invasion of Normandy is just a diversion, but we need more hard information. I cannot tell you what it is like today. Some generals want to move troops from here to Normandy now, others think it is a trap. The Führer is convinced that the main Allied forces will still land in the Pas de Calais. One minute they want me back in Paris, the next I am to remain here. You are very important to our intelligence, I hope you realise that. What are your instructions?'

'One of the coded messages last night was for our group. We are Plan Green, which means we have to sabotage the railway system. Heaven knows, we checked out the likely spots often enough. But we have to contact London tonight, we should get more detailed instructions then. We are going to the woodman's hut in the forest. Can you arrange for the patrols to keep away from there?'

'That is so difficult. I have not been able to tell anyone the real reason why I am here. The Gestapo just think that I am here for general intelligence duties, but they suspect something. They know that I am running an agent, they aren't complete fools. You know what those boys are like. They have no subtlety. They would just arrest the whole cell. They would ruin the operation. Lieutenant General Heim is the garrison commander here. I know him well enough, we've dined together a couple of times, we have mutual friends in Frankfurt. He has some idea as to why I am here. I will talk to him this afternoon and suggest he put extra patrols on the shoreline tonight. That ought to draw people away from inland patrols, but it would be too risky to ask for much more than that. You're just going to need to be very careful. And Magpie…?'

'Yes?'

'I don't want you blowing up railway lines, you understand?'

'I understand, but our orders are to attack the railway lines. How is it going to look if we don't do it? I am the one who has had the training. If we don't carry out the attacks, the group will get suspicious.'

'I know. You will have to be clever. But if the Gestapo finds out that one of my agents is blowing up a railway line, that will give them all the excuse they need. As it is, they would love to meet you. In any case, we can't risk damaging the railways. We need them to transport troops and equipment. It is the best way to move tanks. We must not shoot ourselves in the foot. I will see you the same time tomorrow. Notre Dame.' Lange had stood up now. As he walked past her he tapped her baguette and smiled.

–

The Forest of Boulogne lay to the north east of the village, across a range of upwardly sloping fields. The first line of birch and ash could be seen from the village itself and at night the forest gave the impression that an enormous black cloud had floated down to earth. There were some small roads and tracks through the forest, but its sheer size did afford them some safety. It was very rare for German patrols to venture beyond the roads and tracks. You needed the lifetime experience of the woods, such as Jean and Pierre had, to be able to find your way around it in the dark. Within just a matter of yards from a track, the trees stood improbably close together and the undergrowth was heavily carpeted with bramble and ferns.

Four of them went into the forest that night, the 6th of June. The plan was to travel in pairs, taking different routes to their destination. Geraldine would travel with Jean, Pierre with Lucien. Once they met up, Jean and Lucien would rig up the aerial then fan out to stand guard, while Geraldine and Pierre looked after the transmission. It was always perilous. There was the ever-present danger of German patrols, added to the risk of their transmission being intercepted. They would take the right precautions: keep the transmission short, change frequency if it went on for more than five minutes and then dismantle the equipment quickly as soon as it was over.

The Germans would almost certainly intercept the broadcast and then triangulate its location, but if all went according to plan, by the time the Germans arrived in the forest the group would be safely back in the village. The danger was either a passing patrol stumbling across them by chance, or if a mobile detection unit was in the area that night.

They met at a disused woodman's hut in what had once been a small clearing in the centre of the forest, well away from any track. The hut had not been used for years, but it was a good place to meet. The clearing was now overgrown and the forest had begun the process of reclaiming the small parcel of land.

The little moonlight there was that night struggled to penetrate the canopy of the forest as a steady stream of cloud streaked across the sky. It was as dark in the forest as Geraldine could remember. She and Jean were waiting in the lee of the hut for the other two. She shivered. Instinctively he put an arm round her. She moved closer to him, placing her palm on his chest. He was about to speak when silently the other two came upon them. A brief conversation. Pierre knew every inch of the forest. They would walk five minutes to the east. The trees were very thick there, but there were a few that were easier to climb.

When they found the spot, Pierre and Geraldine prepared the radio. Jean removed his jacket, strapped the aerial to his back and, with Lucien's help, climbed the tree – lowering down the cable so they could attach it to the transmitter. They were all carrying Sten sub-machine guns. Pierre and Geraldine lay theirs on the ground next to them. Jean and Lucien fanned out on either side. Within seconds they were out of sight.

Pierre hated this business. He much preferred to rely on receiving messages via the BBC, but recognised that there were times when they needed to contact London. As soon as they established contact he shone his torch on his watch. It was eleven thirty-three. If they were still transmitting at eleven thirty-eight then they would need to change frequency. The Germans would be able to pinpoint a position with an accuracy of around ten miles. That ought to be safe enough. It was the vans with the mobile receivers that bothered him.

Geraldine was tapping away hard at the Morse code key and scribbling down the response on a pad which Pierre was illuminating with his torch. At eleven thirty-eight he signalled to her – 'Need to change frequency'. She held up one finger: one more minute. Three minutes later she pulled off the headphones and turned off the transmitter. Pierre made a soft owl hoot and within a minute they had been rejoined by Jean and Lucien.

Pierre nodded at Geraldine.

'What do they say?'

'The main invasion will still be in this area. Soon. We are to be patient. They want us to begin the sabotage.'

Five minutes later the aerial had been dismantled and the transmitter packed away. They would bury it nearer to a track and Lucien would collect it in the morning in his father-in-law's car.

Pierre and Lucien left first, taking the most direct route back to the village. Geraldine and Jean stood silently against the trees. They would wait for three minutes and then leave in a different direction, which would take them to the north of the forest, further away from the village, at first. They would then skirt back round the outside of the forest, making sure to stay inside the tree line. They ought to be back by half past midnight. Geraldine stumbled once in the undergrowth and fell over. She allowed Jean to pick her up and he had continued to hold on to her.

It may have been because of this, or possibly because the cloud cover had grown thicker, that they did not see the Germans until it was too late. They were approaching one of the tracks that threaded across the forest. The normal procedure would be to halt well short of the track, and Jean would creep forward until he could see it properly. If all was clear, he would signal Geraldine forward, she would cross the track while Jean covered her and he would follow, with her providing cover for him.

For some reason, they stumbled across the track before they noticed it. They only came to a stop when Geraldine was on the track itself with Jean right behind her. It was too late. A German motorbike and sidecar was parked on the other side of the track, no more than five yards from them. Standing with his back to them, lighting a cigarette was a soldier. Jean and Geraldine froze. Jean made a reversing gesture with his hands. They would move back into the cover of the trees and hide. At that moment the soldier stepped out into the centre of the track and turned casually towards them. They had the advantage of having had their shock a crucial two or three seconds before his. In the second that he stood there, stunned and transfixed to the spot, momentarily unable to react, they both rushed him. Jean threw himself at the soldier, diving at his hips and using his speed and momentum to bring him down in a rugby tackle. The soldier's rifle fell as he went over. On the ground, the soldier and Jean struggled. The soldier was a large and strong man. Once he had got over the initial shock he seemed to regain his strength and worked his way on top of Jean, pinning him to the dusty ground. He was reaching for his holster.

'Help me,' Jean called out.

From her side belt Geraldine pulled out the knife that was standard SOE issue. The only time she had used it before was on a straw dummy in a barn in Lincolnshire. Now she plunged it into the soldier's back. There were two things that struck her in that moment. The first was that nothing had prepared her for the amount of bone that the knife would hit. She thought it would just go straight in. The other was the blood. She must have hit an artery, because a fountain of blood spurted up.

As this happened, Jean threw the soldier over and pinned him down with his hands round his neck. He held them there, tightening his grip. The soldier's eyes seemed to double in size and a look of utter terror was etched into every line on his face. Even in the dark, she could tell that he was turning blue.

'Watch out, there will be another one,' Jean panted.

She turned round. Of course. A motorbike and sidecar. There would be two of them. The other one was coming towards her. He must have gone into the woods to go to the toilet because he was now running out with his trousers flapping loose around his thighs. He was using one hand to try to hold them up. Geraldine lunged at him with the knife, but he parried her blow, sending the knife skidding across the track. She remembered she must have put her Sten gun down when she got out the knife. The soldier was raising his rifle to her, his trousers now round his ankles and his finger on the trigger.

The bullet that she thought would kill her came from behind and sent the second soldier crumpling to the track. She turned round. Jean had one knee firmly on the throat of the now-still soldier. In his hands was his sub-machine gun with which he had shot the second soldier just before he was able to fire at her.

He checked the pulse of the first soldier, nodded and walked over to her. She was now kneeling on the track, drained of all her energy. He picked her up, holding her close to him as he did so. At that moment he shrieked. The second soldier had lunged at Jean. He must have found Geraldine's knife and, despite his wounds, was able to attack. Geraldine grabbed Jean's sub-machine gun. The soldier and Jean were in a frantic struggle. She took aim, but in the dark it was hard to see who she was aiming at. She stepped over to the two of them, held the gun at the soldier's back and pulled the trigger. His body muffled the noise and he slumped onto the track, a dark pool emerging from under his body.

For one moment she feared that she had also hit Jean as well. His shoulder was covered in blood, but he climbed out from under the second dead German. It was a knife wound.

'Quick,' he said. 'We have to move them. Now.'

They dragged each soldier as far as they could into the under-growth. They would be difficult to find at night and that would give them enough time to get back to the village. But the track was covered in blood and in any case the dogs would find them soon enough. Then there was the motorbike and sidecar. They wheeled it into the undergrowth on the other side of the track, but could not move it more than five yards in before the undergrowth made it impossible to go any further. They spent a minute or two pulling branches and shrub on top of it. That might just about cover it during the hours of darkness, but at first light the search parties would spot it easily enough.

Geraldine checked Jean's wound. The knife had penetrated the front of his shoulder, but it did not appear to be too serious. She gave him her scarf. 'Keep this pressed against it.'

It was nearly one o'clock when they crept into the house on the morning of 7th June. Within hours the whole area near the forest would be teeming with search parties. Fortunately for them, they had killed the soldiers on a track on the eastern edge of the forest, which was in the direction of Boulogne. Other villages were nearer. There would be nothing to link the attack with this village. They went upstairs. Both of them were covered in dirt and blood. She needed to deal with Jean first. He sat on his bed. The curtain in his room was very thick, so they could risk lighting a lamp. Even in the dim light she could tell that he was pale.

'Remove your shirt.'

He peeled off his shirt. The wound had stopped bleeding, but it would need cleaning up before she could tell if it would need stitching. She was worried that he might need medical attention. A couple of years before a doctor from nearby Isques had been shot for helping a wounded *résistant*. From the bathroom she fetched a bowl of cold water and a sponge. They would need to burn their clothes. She cleaned the wound and then put ointment on it from the small first aid box that she had found in the bathroom. She placed a pad over the wound and told him to hold it while she found something to keep it in place. The wound did not seem too bad. The real concern now would be to make sure that it did not become infected.

The priority was to remove all trace of the dirty clothing. If the Germans did a house-to-house search they would find them both filthy and covered in bloody clothing. She was trying to remain calm. When Lange realised what had happened he would be furious, but she had no alternative. The most important thing was to maintain her cover. She knelt down, untied Jean's shoes, and removed them and his socks. 'You need to remove your trousers, Jean.' He couldn't do that while still holding the pad over his wound, so she undid his belt and unbuttoned his trousers before pulling them down. She sponged the filth and blood from a now-naked body.

A small pile of filthy clothes was now on the floor by the side of his bed. When she turned round, Jean had pulled over the bedspread to cover himself.

Pas de Calais, 7th June 1944

She was woken that night by the muffled noise of more bombing raids. They did not sound as close as Boulogne this time, but it had made for a strange and urgent background. She remembered she had to do something with the clothes. She tied them into a bundle and hid them in the loft. They would survive a random house-to-house search, but nothing more thorough. Jean would have to take them with him to work and destroy them. She was aware of vehicles speeding through the village, which was unusual at this time of the morning. The search was on for the missing soldiers.

In the morning she checked Jean's shoulder. It couldn't have been more than a glancing blow. She cleaned it once more and dressed it. He would be fine.

They went downstairs for breakfast. Jean prepared the coffee and they sat together in silence at the table. Neither of them felt like eating bread and jam. Yesterday had been Jean's nineteenth birthday, which they had celebrated by killing two Germans.

Pierre stopped by on his way to work. He commented on the amount of Germans on the road and they told him what had happened. Pierre paced up and down the small front room, trying hard to arrange his thoughts.

'And there is nothing that could link the deaths with you... with us?'

'Only the clothes and Jean will destroy those at work today.'

'No, too dangerous. There will be roadblocks everywhere. They will search everyone. Keep the clothes where they are for the time being. You didn't take their weapons?'

'No, we didn't think,' said Jean.

'Don't worry. Maybe it is safer anyway. There will be reprisals when they find the bodies. Just stick to your routine. We had better delay the sabotage until later in the week.'

So they stuck to their routine. Jean left as normal for the farm. He wore one of his father's jackets; the extra bulk would help conceal his shoulder dressing and any awkward movements.

Geraldine cycled into Boulogne. There were fewer troops at the roadblocks, so she assumed they had not found the missing soldiers yet and were still out searching for them. She did not say anything to Françoise at work. It would be too risky.

At lunchtime she left for her appointment with Lange at the Notre Dame inside the fortified old town. There were roadblocks everywhere and they were stopping and searching everyone. Maybe they had now found the bodies.

She was a few minutes late when she got to the church and there was no sign of Lange. She found an empty side chapel and went in, lighting a candle before sitting down. What if the Germans turned on her for this? Maybe they thought she was now an Allied agent who had misled them over the invasion and was killing German troops. Why had she told Lange yesterday that they would be transmitting from the forest? He was bound to know she was in some way involved in the deaths.

Lange shuffled into the chapel and sat down in front of her before turning round.

'You had better explain.'

She did her best. If she had done nothing then she and Jean would have been arrested. Her cover would have been blown. She would have been useless after that. 'You would get no more intelligence from the Allies. No clues about the invasion. Nothing.' What was she meant to do? And wasn't he meant to make sure that there were fewer patrols inland last night? It was not her fault. It was bad luck.

Lange calmed down. He was not so much worried about the deaths of two worthless conscripts, but if the Gestapo or the SD found that there was a connection with the Abwehr, well that was a different matter altogether. '*But they needn't find that out, eh?*'

What mattered to Lange was the information that she had received when she spoke with London. So there *would* be an invasion through the Pas de Calais after all. It would be soon. They were to be patient. The sabotage was to start.

An old woman dressed in black came into the chapel. Lange left as she did so, Geraldine following behind.

They walked down the steep flight of steps from the Notre Dame, turned left and then down a narrow alley, with tall buildings flanking either side. Lange was walking a few paces ahead of her. As they emerged, they could hear a commotion in front of them, from the direction of the Hôtel de Ville. She hesitated, unsure of what was going on. Lange stopped and waited for her to catch up with him.

'You ought to watch this,' he said as she came alongside. 'It may teach you to be more careful in future.' With that he doffed his cap, smiled and wheeled away.

She was in the Place Godefroy de Bouillon now, immediately in front of the Hôtel de Ville. It was teeming with German troops, who had ringed off the perimeter of the square. Crowds of civilians were being forced to assemble around the outside of the square. In the centre there were a dozen SS, dressed in their black uniforms, laughing and joking with each other. Standing separate to them was a detachment of around ten Wehrmacht soldiers, guarding a small group of civilians.

She was pushed to the front of the cordon. The sun was quite glorious now, streaming down into the square and bouncing off the neat rows of cobblestones.

An SS officer moved up to a large lorry, took a megaphone from the dashboard, tested it, and then addressed what was now a large and tense crowd in fluent French.

'Last night, two German soldiers were murdered in the Boulogne area.'

Murmurs in the crowd.

'These murders could only have been carried out by French criminals. Therefore, in accordance with the military orders governing the Nord Pas de Calais region, two French citizens will now be executed. If there are any further criminal acts, *two* civilians will be executed for the death of every *one* German soldier.'

She could hear sobs and gasps from within the crowd. Geraldine noticed some people surreptitiously crossing themselves. A woman behind her tried to walk away. A soldier shoved her back.

From the group of civilians held at gunpoint in the centre of the square, a young man was dragged out. As he was pulled nearer to where Geraldine was standing she could see that he was probably not much older than Jean, quite possibly younger. His shirt had been torn and his face was bruised. Two SS men went over to where he had been pushed to the ground. One of them said something to him and he shook his head and screamed '*Non.*' The other SS man lashed him across the face and kicked him hard in the stomach. The boy crumpled to the ground. The first SS man was now behind him, his Luger revolver drawn. He drew it slowly round, leaned down, held it against the back of the boy's head, and fired. The body lurched forward, the head contorting at a strange angle so that it was turned to the sky. Small streams of blood began darting through the cobblestones with surprising speed.

Shocked silence in the crowd. Geraldine could hear the man next to her mumbling a 'Hail Mary'.

There was more screaming from the group of hostages. A woman was pulled out, her shrieks reverberating around the square, bouncing off the walls and through everyone standing there. She was dragged towards the still-laughing SS men and pushed to the ground in front of them, no more than a yard from the body of the dead boy.

She rose up to a kneeling position, begging the soldiers, her hands clasped in prayer in front of her. The SS men were circling her, laughing and smoking. One of them grabbed hold of her dress and tore it. She held her head in her hands as two soldiers drew their revolvers. They both shot her at the same time, but they were body shots and her body was still moving after it hit the ground. Soft groans floated across the silent square. Even some of the soldiers guarding the cordon seemed shocked. After a minute, a Wehrmacht officer walked over and said something to the laughing SS men. They shrugged and the officer walked over and finished her off.

The crowd was ordered to disperse. Geraldine went to collect her bike. It would be easy to justify where she had been and why she was late. She had better remember to buy some bread.

Berlin, 8th June 1944

General Walter Schellenberg did not know what to make of these Abwehr types. Ever since Hitler had sacked Admiral Canaris in February, Schellenberg's *Sicherheitsdienst* – the SD – had taken over the intelligence functions of the Abwehr.

They certainly knew plenty about intelligence, with impressive networks of spies everywhere. But Schellenberg could see how Hitler had come to mistrust them. It almost seemed to be a badge of honour among the top brass of the Abwehr that you were not a Nazi. Indeed, Schellenberg was aware of a fair amount of evidence now emerging that some of them were actually *anti*-Nazis. He did not understand it.

One of the few Abwehr officers still in place was Major Reinhard Schmidt from Abwehr 1. This was the department that looked after foreign intelligence, not without some success. They were responsible for some very useful intelligence, not least in the immediate aftermath of the Allied invasion of Normandy.

Major Schmidt had now asked to see him in connection with that. His timing was good. He would have trouble naming one of the French-based generals or one member of the General Staff here in Berlin who had not contacted him in the past forty-eight hours.

They all wanted to know the same thing: is this the real invasion? I thought you told us it was going to be in the Pas de Calais.

Schellenberg did his best to reassure them. Normandy is a diversionary tactic and the main invasion will still be through the Pas de Calais. That is our assessment. *'We stand by it. Do not panic and, certainly, do not abandon the Pas de Calais. We must remain at full strength there.'*

But it's not easy, thought Schellenberg. They want *me* to tell them what to do with the Fifteenth Army and where to send their wretched Panzer divisions.

All he could think was that, for a feint, the Allies had landed an awful lot of troops in Normandy. It was not looking good. This damned Abwehr intelligence had better be good. Schellenberg did not fancy having to explain it away to Hitler.

There was a knock at the door and Major Schmidt entered.

'It had better be good news, Schmidt.'

'I think it is, sir. You remember I briefed you on our agent in London – Magpie? She is the one who ended up marrying the Royal Navy intelligence officer, and from whom we have been getting such good information about the Allied plans to have their main invasion in the Pas de Calais. It strongly corroborates the information we have been getting from our other agents in Britain.'

'I remember. Continue, Schmidt.'

'As you know she was then recruited to the SOE and landed in France in April, on the Führer's birthday as it happens. My man, Lange, has been up in the area since then to liaise with her. Magpie was in contact with London last night. She was told still to expect the main invasion through her area. We have also been following her husband. He went to Dover yesterday. He was seen entering Dover Castle, which we believe is General Patton's main base for the First US Army Group, FUSAG. So he is behaving exactly as we would expect him to behave.'

Chapter 23

Pas de Calais, June 1944

When Jean heard the news of the executions in the centre of Boulogne he was inconsolable. There was no doubt whatsoever in his mind that he was responsible for them. Try as she might, it was impossible for Geraldine to persuade him otherwise. The boy who was murdered was just seventeen and Jean had been at school with his brother. The woman was a mother of two young children; her husband had been sent to work in Germany. If he had been in the square at the time, Jean insisted, he would have given himself up to save the lives of the hostages. He could not understand why she had not done that herself. He wanted to give himself up now to stop any more hostages being killed. They were responsible for this.

Their arguments had to be conducted in whispers in case the neighbours heard. That night, she could hear him pacing up and down and the sound of gentle sobs.

It was only when Pierre came round the next morning that they managed to convince Jean that there was nothing they could do. They had not set out to kill the German soldiers, so they had not been deliberately reckless with the lives of civilians. And they were far more use by remaining an active resistance unit.

By the Friday, Jean had calmed down. The prospect of beginning the sabotage at the weekend concentrated his mind.

The tension in the area had heightened since D–Day. Before then, the Germans who were billeted in the village had mainly used it as a place to sleep, restricting themselves to the occasional patrol, but now the Germans were constantly asking people for their passes. On the Friday evening they even saw a German radio detector van driving through the village. Pierre decided they must do everything to reduce the risk to the group.

'Our job is simple: sabotage the railway lines. If we are caught before then – doing something like breaking the curfew for example – that would be irresponsible.' He would listen to the BBC broadcasts on his own in the old lady's attic. Her house was just a few doors down from his and he could slip in and out without being spotted.

On the Saturday afternoon they all met in the house where Françoise and Lucien were staying. Her parents had taken the children to Samer, where Françoise's sister lived and was expecting a baby any day now. Her husband had also been sent to Germany.

They gathered round the table in the large kitchen. The cooker and oven were laden with food in different stages of preparation. If the Germans turned up when they were all there then they would say they had all come round for a meal. It would not be much of a defence, but even after four years of occupation, the Germans were still bemused at the French obsession with food. They might just believe it.

The kitchen was suffused with the aroma of roasts and baking and the noise of bubbling soup as Pierre opened up a large map of the area. It had been drawn on the reverse of a picture of cows and ducks painted by Françoise and Lucien's young son. If the Germans came in, the map could be flipped over. It would give them a small chance of persuading the Germans that they had happened upon an innocent gathering of friends.

From Boulogne, the railway headed in three directions. There was one route to the north, to and from Calais. That route then headed south out of the town. Just to the south of where they were sitting now was the village of Hesdigneul-lès-Boulogne, on the other side of the main Calais to Paris road. At Hesdigneul-lès-Boulogne, the line split: one track continued east towards Lille and then Paris. The other track headed due south, to Abbeville and into Normandy.

'The railways are the quickest way for the Germans to move large numbers of troops and vehicles. If the invasion is going to take place in this area, then they will want to send reinforcements, especially from here…' Pierre pointed to the east and the centre of France, '…and here.' Normandy. 'At the moment, they must be uncertain – as we are. They are not sure if Normandy is the main invasion area. If they decide it is, then they will want to move the Fifteenth Army from this area down to Normandy, along with the Panzers. If there is an invasion here, then they will come in the opposite direction. Either way, the railways are vital to the Germans. Without them, their options for moving around are much more limited. They will be restricted to the roads and remember that other resistance groups will be carrying out Plan Turquoise, which means they will have the task of sabotaging roads.

'So, our job is to stop the Germans being able to use the railways to either get in or out of the area. Lucien?'

Lucien was a man of few words. He had a large moustache and was built, Geraldine thought, like a locomotive. A typical *cheminot*.

'The RAF have been bombing the area, as we know. They have obviously been aiming at the railway lines, but with very limited success. It is difficult, they are flying at night and from their altitude it is hard to be accurate. Any damage they do cause tends to be fairly superficial – maybe a siding will collapse – but it is all repaired fairly easily, no matter how inefficient we try to be!'

The others laughed. They knew that the railway workers, the *cheminots*, were at the heart of the resistance movements throughout France. Thousands of workers risked their lives every day by doing their best to compromise the system. It was not always the acts of sabotage that counted. As Lucien liked to point out to them, if five workers were sent to repair some track and they took two days over a job that they could have done in one, then the Germans had lost five days' labour. Multiply that by what was going on across France and the effect was significant.

'You see, what would really cause major disruption would be a direct hit on a track, and that has not yet happened in this region. The only way to be sure, is by planting explosives in exactly the right position.'

'And,' added Pierre, 'doing that just before a train passes over.'

'Indeed,' said Lucien. 'That way it takes many more days to remove the train before you can even begin repairing the track.'

'Not forgetting, of course, that if it is a military train then you will kill troops and damage vehicles,' said Pierre.

'Our instructions are to concentrate on this area.' Pierre was using a fork to trace a small circle around Hesdigneul-lès-Boulogne. 'Where the line splits. That way, we disrupt the routes to and from Lille and the centre, and to and from Normandy. Other groups will look after the Calais line.'

'Will there be reprisals against civilians?' asked Jean.

Françoise placed a hand on Jean's arm. 'Jean. Everything we do will help to end the occupation. How much longer can people be allowed to suffer? If we stop and consider all the consequences of our actions, then there will be no resistance and without the resistance, the occupation will continue.'

'Tomorrow night,' said Pierre 'we will hit the track through Mourlinghen – where the Lille line goes through the woods. Geraldine, how much explosive do we have?'

Geraldine asked Pierre to repeat the question. She had been thinking. She had no way of contacting Lange today or tomorrow to warn him of the attack. They had agreed that when she knew the location of an attack, he would arrange for a German patrol to be on the line, which the group would spot and therefore abort their mission.

'Is Sunday really such a good day to do it, Pierre?' she asked.

'Why?'

'Maybe it will be... too quiet?'

'But the attack will be late at night. It will not matter what day it is. In any case, Lucien is working tomorrow and finishes at six in the evening. By then he will have a good idea of what movements there will be on the line that night. How much explosive do we have?'

'Enough for three major explosions. Maybe we could split some up and go for two major attacks and two or three smaller ones – like junction boxes or signalling equipment.'

'Very well,' Pierre was folding the map now and placing it back into the lining of his jacket. 'We go for a major attack tomorrow night at Mourlinghen. We will meet at Jean's house at eight. Be careful.'

–

They left Jean's house between nine and ten o'clock the next night.

Lucien's information was that a supply train would be leaving Boulogne just before eleven, heading towards Lille. He was unsure what was on the train – it didn't do to ask too many questions – but the important thing was that they had an opportunity to blow up the track with a train on it. As Lucien pointed out, if they could blow up the track where it went through the woods, it would be even harder to remove the train. With any luck, it would put that line out of action for three or four days at least, quite possibly a week.

The night before, Jean and Geraldine had retrieved the explosives and the detonation equipment from where it was hidden in the forest and concealed it in a culvert under the Calais-Paris road. They left the house one by one, at ten-minute intervals. Jean went first, heading due north and then working his way round anti-clockwise to Mourlinghen. It was a long route, potentially hazardous, but Jean knew the countryside so well that he could take the risk. Pierre also headed north from the back of the house, taking a clockwise route to the woods. The other three fanned out in a southerly direction.

By ten thirty they had all crossed the River Liane as it flowed across the gently sloping countryside and were at their meeting point in the Bois du Quesnoy. They crouched close together as Pierre carefully went through the instructions one more time. The railway line cut through the top of the woods, most of which was on the southern side of the railway track. Pierre and Françoise would guard the north east and north west corners, Jean would look after the south. Lucien would go down with Geraldine to the track. If all went well, four of them would be north of the track at the moment of detonation. From the position they had chosen, it was a relatively short distance across the fields back to their village, although it was uphill. Hopefully they would be back in the village before the Germans appeared on the scene. The real danger would be if the Germans billeted in the village heard the explosion and came out to investigate. There was no discernible wind that night and Pierre was concerned that the sound of the explosion would carry to Hesdin. They would just have to be very careful when they returned.

As Geraldine scrambled down the steep bank to the track, she remembered her training in Lincolnshire. It had been much colder then but, strangely, she felt calmer now. Back then she had been concerned that the training was a trap, that maybe they would discover her true identity.

If tonight's explosion worked, the SOE and the resistance would be pleased; if it failed, the Germans would be pleased. She still had no idea what to do; she would have to wait and see what opportunities were presented to her. In a strange way, it seemed to sum up her predicament; increasingly she felt that she had slid into a state of limbo. She knew which side she was meant to be on, but she was no longer convinced how distanced she was from the other side.

There was little cloud in the sky, but the tall trees made it difficult to see. She and Lucien waited by the side of the track, scanning up and down the line with their binoculars to see if there was any movement. They waited five minutes, listening carefully for any warning signals from the other three. *All clear.* Lucien crossed the track, crouching down by the southern side of the line. Geraldine got to work from the north side. Scooping the gravel away with her hands, she pushed the explosives in and then attached the wire. Until that moment, she was not sure which course of action to take. She thought of what Lange had said. She imagined what the reaction of the group would be. Lucien seemed more concerned with scanning up and down the track than with what she was doing. Once she had made her decision she finished her preparations, smoothed the gravel back over the wire and then ran it back towards the siding, taking care to scatter some stones on top to keep it in place. Lucien joined her and together they climbed up the bank and back into the woods. Geraldine had taken care to bring plenty of wire to enable them to reach the far edge of the woods. They had chosen a position that gave them a view of the line, so she could see the train as it was about to enter the woods. Two seconds after that, she would detonate the charge.

They had only just settled into position when they heard the first distant rumble. It was hard to work out where it was coming from at first, but within a minute it was the unmistakable sound of a train coming down the line from the direction of Boulogne. They heard the clatter as it slowed down and crossed the points at Hesdigneul-lès-Boulogne and seconds after that the dark mass loomed into sight. As the train entered the woods, they counted, '*One, two...*' together, and Geraldine pressed hard on the detonator. Instinctively, they all covered their heads – not so much because of the noise they were anticipating, but more because of the danger of any flying metal or exploding ammunition.

But there was nothing. Just the rush of wind as the train sped through the woods and the noise of the birds disturbed by it. In front of them, a small creature scurried through the undergrowth.

Pierre looked at Geraldine. '*What happened?*'

'I don't understand. It makes no sense. What do we do now?' she asked.

Pierre looked shocked. 'It's too risky to stay. We can't even risk getting the explosives back. We must try to pull in as much of the wire as possible and then go. There must have been a faulty connection. I don't understand. Did you check it, Geraldine?'

'Of course I checked it! What do you think I was doing down there, Pierre? We checked it, didn't we, Lucien?'

The railwayman nodded.

Pierre shook his head. This was close to a disaster.

'Lucien. You go down and recover as much of the wire as you can. I'll cover you. You two, back to the village. Jean will guess something has gone wrong, he'll make his own way back.' He was clearly angry and was muttering to Françoise in the local patois, something which he had avoided doing in her presence since her first night back in France. He shaking his head and saying '*dinon*'.

Jean arrived back just after midnight. Geraldine was already in her bed when he silently entered the house. He came into her room, leaning exhausted against the doorframe.

'What happened? Why was there no explosion?' He was angry, his tone almost accusing.

'I cannot explain, Jean. How do you think I feel? When I was training in England, sometimes it happened, the explosives didn't work. Maybe a rat got to the wire, maybe Lucien or I pulled it by mistake with our feet – I just don't know. It's possible the explosive got damp when it was stored. I did my best, I checked the connection carefully. I don't understand either.'

'Such a wasted opportunity. We cannot risk getting those explosives back.' He stood there shaking his head.

–

The 13th of June was a Tuesday, exactly one week after D-Day. Lange had left instructions in the usual place under her saddle telling her when and where she was to meet him. She had wheeled her bike up a narrow alley just beyond the old town and came across a shop with a dusty façade, improbably squeezed between two larger shops. She paused there, exhausted. She was getting tired these days and after the exertions the other night, her back was hurting. The shop sign said '*Levy – Chapellerie*'. There had been a clumsy attempt to scrub out the word '*Levy*', but the outline of the name remained visible, like a ghost haunting the new owner. Geraldine was looking at the tired display of just a few men's hats when a man materialised on her right. When he was sure no one was around, Lange spoke quietly in the direction of the window.

'Do they believe you?'

'Pardon?'

'Your comrades, who do you think I mean?' Lange said sarcastically. 'Do they believe you? About Sunday night?'

'What do you know about Sunday night? I was going to tell you about it.'

'Do not forget that I am an *intelligence* officer. I am trained to deduce matters. Yesterday morning a patrol found some loose wire by the track in Mourlinghen. They are aware of my interest in any matters relating to railway sabotage so I was called in. We found the explosive. You had not connected the wire to the explosive. It was not even subtle, was it? If one of them had gone back to check the connection that would have been obvious to them too.'

'Of course, I didn't connect it. Did you want me to blow up the train?'

'Absolutely not! All I'm saying is that you need to be careful. You did the right thing, but what I want to know is this: do they suspect you?'

'I don't think so. Pierre is angry, but I think he just believes I was either incompetent or unlucky. Lucien was near me but he never saw the actual connection being made, he was too busy watching the track.'

'Just so long as they don't suspect you. They'll kill you, you know. We infiltrated a man into a cell near the Belgian border. He was useful for a time, very useful. But he must have made a mistake. At the end of May he was found hanging from a tree. His ears and nose were not the only parts of the body they had cut off. Before they hanged him.'

'I am sure they don't suspect me.'

'The minute you think they do, you come to me and we'll get you out of the area. The Gestapo will be very keen to get their hands on your "friends".'

Geraldine looked shocked.

'Don't worry. You will be well out of the way. It won't matter to you, will it? It won't be long now. Soon we ought to know for sure whether there is going to be an invasion in this area. Once we know that, your job is done.'

The shopkeeper opened the door and gave them an unctuous smile, hopeful that their lengthy spell at his window might result in some much-needed business. No one was interested in hats these days. All they were interested in buying was food. He thought it had been too good to be true when he was offered the chance to take the shop over when the owner was sent away. His wife told him it was a mistake. 'It can only bring bad luck,' she had said. He regretted it now, of course, but it was too late. Even his own brother wouldn't talk to him. The neighbours crossed the road when they saw him. All these rumours he was hearing. He had nightmares about what would happen to him when the war ended. What about if the old owner returned? He shook his head sadly as the couple walked down the alley in the direction of the cathedral. It was a pity. They would have been his first customers that week.

–

Boulogne and the whole of the Nord Pas de Calais region continued to be battered by the RAF. One night just over a week after D-Day, three hundred RAF aircraft took part in a raid on the Boulogne area. Geraldine and Jean watched the sky turn black with swarms of Lancaster and Halifax bombers. By 20th June Boulogne was barely recognisable as a town, its identifiable infrastructure of roads, traffic signs, shops, houses and places of work all but destroyed. Its landscape now took on a strange dimension, the rubble resembling mountains formed over thousands of years.

Even hours after a bombing raid, the air would still be heavy with dust, and the streets running with water where the drains or sewers had burst. Geraldine was no longer going into work; the factory had been blown up in the big overnight raid. Half the remaining population of the town now seemed to be homeless. Many were living in cellars or the ruins of their houses. Food was in short supply. Any illusion of normality, which the Germans had been so desperate to encourage during the occupation, was now gone. Children were seen begging in the streets for food. Lucien told them that when he was leaving work one day he had seen a young Wehrmacht soldier slip a piece of bread to a young boy who could barely stand. A few minutes later, he saw a passing SS officer kick the same boy into the gutter.

There was a sense that law and order was breaking down. There were reports of looting in some areas and some German soldiers no longer appeared to be quite as rigorous as before, though no less brutal. The Germans weren't stupid. They would have an idea of what was going on, they would gossip in their barracks, rumours would be rife. They would know that the invasion of Normandy had not been repelled. They would suspect that defeat might not be long coming.

And it was not just the Germans that knew that. Françoise met a woman from the factory in a bread queue who told her about a young woman in her street who had done very nicely out of her relationships with a succession of German soldiers. People had been frightened of her, but recently they had started to laugh at her. Two nights ago she had thrown herself from the roof of an abandoned ruin.

One of the teachers at the school where Pierre taught had bumped into an official at the Hôtel de Ville. Before the war he had been a minor official, but his eagerness to co-operate with the occupiers had seen him promoted to a senior position. '*Rising like scum,*' they had said. He had been particularly efficient in carrying out their orders. In the autumn of 1942 the Germans decided to round up all the Jews in Nord Pas de Calais. He had been especially assiduous in tracking down the few Jewish families in Boulogne, a role he repeated in January 1944 when the Germans rounded up the Gypsies.

Now, according to Pierre's colleague, he was acting like a man condemned: pleading to be understood, desperate to assure anyone he met that he had acted in the best interests of France, that he was only doing what he was told.

Françoise did find the factory manager. He was telling any workers he could find that they should stay put. He did not know if the factory was going to reopen. So the people who still had homes stayed in them.

And that was the pattern for the remainder of June and into July. People trying to survive, the air raids, the anarchy of the occupiers, and the rising fear of the collaborators.

They were still getting messages from London that they were to prepare for the landing: very soon now. It was always 'very soon'. Lange continued to be encouraged by this and told her that in order to maintain her credibility she needed to carry out some limited but successful acts of sabotage. They successfully blew up some points and a branch line. The damage did not seem to be enormous to the group at the time and Pierre was disappointed, but Lucien reported that, according to the Germans at the station, the damage was far worse than at first appeared to be the case.

By the end of June, the BBC was reporting that half a million Allied troops had landed in Normandy. The coded messages were still telling them that the Pas de Calais was the main target. *Soon. Very soon.*

But a month after D–Day and with such a bitter battle still raging in Normandy, even from where they were, it seemed hard to conceive that the Allies could be holding even more men in reserve to invade the Pas de Calais.

One night in the second week of July, Geraldine and Jean were eating at the table in the front room. Food was in short supply in the whole area, and although Jean usually brought a bit extra back from the farm, he insisted on giving most of it to the family next door, where the children were noticeably hungry. Geraldine was toying with a watery stew that mostly consisted of thin carrots and turnips, with only a gristly hint of the rabbit that Jean had caught the previous night.

It was an unusually quiet night. The group had not been out for a night or two, they were very low on explosives and Pierre had decided that they should keep what they had until the invasion. For a few days now, it had not been a matter of 'when' the invasion comes, but 'if'. She wondered if it was her they disbelieved or the British. She was no longer sure who to believe herself.

'Pierre does not think that there will be an invasion here, you know,' Jean told her. He was staring at the plate, moving a piece of carrot around in the watery gravy with his fork.

Geraldine shrugged. 'None of us know, do we? We only know what the British tell us. The Germans must still think that there will be something going on. Otherwise, they wouldn't still have so many troops in the region, would they?'

Jean's turn to shrug now. 'I just know that Pierre is suspicious. About everything.'

He was trying to avoid eye contact with her, instead glancing uncomfortably around the room.

Silence.

'What will we do after the war?'

Geraldine was shocked at the question. 'Who?'

'Us. You and me. After the war. Will you go back to Arras?'

'I will have to. My family. They… what will you do?'

'I would like to go to college. Pierre always said I had the ability. I would like to be an engineer. I will wait until my father returns from Germany. I don't know…'

'You are assuming the Germans will be defeated, Jean!'

'Don't you think they will?'

'I don't know.'

They went to bed after that. Geraldine could not sleep. It was not the heat, nor the silence. Jean had said something that she could not get out of her mind: 'I just know that Pierre is suspicious. About everything.' She knew that he was. She had seen the glint of suspicion in Pierre's eyes. He now openly used the local patois in front of her and she suspected that he was often talking *about* her. She had seen his lack of trust in her on the night the explosives had failed and she had seen it since, when she kept reassuring them that the invasion would come. She knew that the moment they realised who she was, she would be finished. The best she could hope for would be enough time to make her escape. She thought of the man hanging from the tree near the Belgian border with most of his extremities hacked off. Maybe one of them had seen her with Lange? Could she have been followed from the factory one lunchtime?

That night she made up her mind.

–

For some reason she decided that a Monday would be best, though she was not sure why. The others would be at work and not back in the village until the evening. Lange had started worrying about how to contact her and had taken to leaving messages under some bricks by a farm gate between the village and the town. The last time she had seen him he was tense and blaming her. He was talking about having to go back to Paris. He was no longer even sure whether he was supposed to be working for the Abwehr or the SD. She was almost as afraid of him now as she was of Pierre. She was unsure of whom she was really escaping from, the Germans or the resistance. The very fact that she was so uncertain only made her more confused.

A message had been waiting for her on Sunday. Lange wanted to see her on the Tuesday morning near the post office. If she left on Monday, she reckoned, she would have a day to get away from all of them.

She waited until Jean had left before going to the farm that Monday morning and then packed a few belongings. She had some extra money from Lange and an identity card in the name of Hélène Blanc that she had found in the rubble of a house near the factory when she had been helping to dig for survivors a few days ago. The identity card came from the purse of a corpse she had helped carry from the building. Nathalie had made a great play of placing the body carefully by the side of the road, removing its coat to cover her and using that opportunity to remove the purse from the coat. The woman was older than her, thirty-seven, but she could just about pass. The glasses were similar. It would have to do. She would just take a knapsack to carry some food, a jumper, some underwear, and a spare pair of shoes. And the Webley. She would not be able to take the revolver very far, but she might need it for the first part of her journey.

She paused in the front room and looked at the photograph of Jean with his parents. They were all smiling. He was still a boy. She hesitated and then opened the drawer where Jean kept writing paper. She paused for a while, then closed the drawer. She must not allow sentiment or emotion to get in her way. She was being foolish. She half opened the drawer again and pulled out a yellowy sheet of paper and started writing. She left him a note on the table, under the bottle of wine. He was sure to see it when he got in that evening.

And then she left, not looking back once. She was well used to this, leaving one life behind, plunging uncertainly into another one. Now she realised that it was never without a cost, there was always a small part of her that remained. And the more a part of her remained, the more diminished she was as she moved on. She cycled out of the village, heading south east for Samer on the N1, the main Paris road. This was the most dangerous part of the journey. If one of the others had seen her then, she would have probably needed the Webley. The ride took longer than she had expected; her cycling was definitely slower now. After about three miles, with Samer in view, she pulled into a small wood and buried the pistol along with her old identity card, after ripping it up into small pieces. A few weeks ago she had abandoned Nathalie Mercier along with Nathalie Quinn, somewhere over the Channel. Now, the remains of Geraldine Leclerc were buried under a tree. The wood was quite dense and showed little sign of being used, so she shoved the bicycle deep into the undergrowth and did her best to cover it.

It was Hélène Blanc who walked the last mile into the market town of Samer.

In Grand Place Foch a contingent of grey-uniformed Wehrmacht troops were climbing into lorries. She waited in the shadow of the *Mairie* until the lorries sped off. It was silent in the large square, even though it was still the middle of the day. Outside the church she spotted a woman of her age, struggling to push a pram across the cobbles. 'If there are any buses today,' she said in answer to her question, 'they'll go from just over there.'

She was worried now. She had not thought what would happen if she couldn't catch a bus from Samer. Not wanting to draw attention to herself, she walked slowly round the square. After about forty minutes, a bus pulled noisily into the square.

She approached the bus as the driver was changing the destination sign from Samer to St Omer. She asked for a ticket to St Omer.

'We'll see,' said the driver without looking at her. 'First, we go to Desvres then we'll see if they let us continue.' An exhausted-looking *gendarme* checked her identity card and allowed her onto the bus.

She was lucky. After a short stop in Desvres the bus continued on to St Omer, arriving there in the middle of the afternoon. She had planned to move on as quickly as she could, but the town was teeming with Germans and one of them looked at her and the identity card two or three times before nodding her through a checkpoint. Maybe the card was not good enough. She was concerned that it might attract attention if she caught another bus straight away, so she walked around the town for a short while and sat quietly on a bench in the Square St Bertin. On a bench directly behind her were two women of a similar age to her. One of them not only looked a bit more like her than Hélène Blanc, but even seemed to have a hint of the accent from her own region. No one noticed as she leaned quickly under the bench and swiftly got up, heading back to the bus station, where she was relieved to see that the sentries had been changed.

She was already on the bus to Lille before the woman on the bench in Square St Bertin realised that her handbag had been removed from under her seat.

When the bus pulled into Lille just after six that evening, she had two identity cards on her: Hélène Blanc and Nicole Rougier. She had been having serious doubts on the journey to Lille. Nicole Rougier would almost certainly have reported her handbag missing by now. The French police would have reported the fact that it contained a missing identity card to the Germans. It would be too risky to use. She had become careless. She would have to stick with Hélène Blanc.

She glanced at her watch: Jean would be arriving home around now and would see the note. 'Go to the forest as soon as you get this. Stay there,' she had written. 'Do not tell the others. It is not safe. I will find you.' The last part was not true, but it ought to keep him away from the village for long enough for her to escape. She owed him that much, but she still found it hard to believe that she had allowed sentiment to get the better of her. So out of character.

She went into the toilet of a small café and looked through the handbag. She took money, a clean lace handkerchief and some perfume from the handbag, tore up the Nicole Rougier card into tiny pieces and flushed it down the lavatory, then stuffed the empty handbag behind the cistern, where it couldn't be seen.

She only thought briefly about what she had left behind her. There was too much that she had left behind too many times to give much thought to it.

—

It all would have worked out if Georg Lange had not been so impatient, and Lange was only so impatient because Berlin was so impatient. Now that the show was being run by the SD there seemed to be a sense of panic about everything. They had been on the phone that Monday morning. He knew it was urgent as they were communicating in the clear, no attempt at code.

'We must know what is going on... situation in Normandy is desperate... What is she being told?... Can we still trust her?... What do you mean you were waiting until Tuesday?'

So he agreed he couldn't wait until the Tuesday as they had arranged. He would go and see her now, in the village. He would pretend to be an official from the factory. They had reopened, he would say, in another location, and needed her. That would be his cover if he saw anyone else. But she was not in. A woman in a cottage at the end of the row said she had seen her heading east on her bike earlier in the morning. He began to get concerned, so let himself into the house. 'Don't worry,' he told the neighbour, 'I'm from the factory.' She did not look reassured. Inside the house there was no sign of anything. Maybe she had just gone out.

He was about to leave when he noticed the bottle of wine on the table and under it a sheet of paper. His hands shook when he read her note. Apart from any other consideration, this could mean the end of him. He realised that somewhere very deep down inside him he had never completely trusted that woman.

Long before Hélène Blanc arrived in Lille, the Gestapo had got to work.

Jean was arrested as he walked home from the farm: a Traction-Avant Citroen slewed across his path and he was bundled into the back before he could react. Lucien was arrested at the station: in the noise of the engine shed, he didn't hear when they came up on him from behind. They never arrested Pierre. He was in an upstairs room when he saw the Traction-Avant pull up in front of his house. He knew this was the favoured car of the Gestapo. He reached for his pistol as five men rushed into the house. He heard his wife scream. If he had been able to get to his Sten sub-machine gun, he may have stood a chance, but he must have known that this was hopeless. He put the barrel of the pistol into his mouth and pulled the trigger as the first Gestapo man reached the top of the stairs. He was not quite dead when they found him, but he was by the time they had carried him downstairs.

Françoise and her father had been visiting her sister, who had just given birth in Samer. When the Gestapo raided her parents' house in the village, she was not there, so they took her mother and her two boys. When it became apparent what had happened, a neighbour went to tell the priest. Father Raymonde cycled all the way to Samer, where he told Father Pierre, who was able to warn Françoise just in time. Father Raymonde was back at church in Hesdin to say Mass that evening to a larger than normal congregation.

Chapter 24

Berlin, August 1944

Admiral Wilhelm Canaris had seen it coming. It was inevitable, which did not make it any easier. The irony of his situation now was that he had always found visits to 8 Prinz-Albrecht-Strasse distasteful enough, even when he was head of German military intelligence and had to deal with the SD on a regular basis. However unpleasant, it had been part of his job. After his meetings, he had been free to leave, even if it was with an unpleasant taste in his mouth.

And now he was back here. This time, it was not for meetings on the ornate top floor. Now it was as a prisoner of the SS in the cellars.

The truth was that he had been playing a dangerous game since the beginning of the war. If there was one event that set him off on the path that led to this cell then it had been in Będzin in Poland in 1939. He had been in Poland just after the start of the war to visit the front line. And it was in the small town of Będzin that he had witnessed SS troops push two hundred of the town's Jewish population into the synagogue and burn it down, killing everyone inside.

After that, he made sure to appoint non-Nazi Party members to the senior positions in the Abwehr. He did not stop there. There was discreet support for non-Nazi Wehrmacht officers who had got into trouble. He had helped some Jews to flee Germany. Earlier in the war, his intelligence reports overstated Britain's defences, which some in Berlin believed helped delay and eventually stop any German invasion of the British Isles. There were discreet contacts with the British. Some of these had been through trusted intermediaries, others direct. He used his frequent visits to Spain to meet with British Intelligence. He passed on information. And then in 1943, he started to co-operate with other senior non-Nazi officers who knew that the only way to save Germany from utter humiliation and ruin was to get rid of Hitler and his cohorts.

And that had been his motivation. He wanted to save Germany. He could see what would happen. Germany would career madly towards total defeat and then the communists would take over. The sooner the war ended, the better.

The SS and the SD had had their eyes on him, of course. The beginning of the end was in February 1944. Hitler sacked him, and most of the work of the Abwehr then came under the SD and General Schellenberg. He had ended up with a desk in some anonymous ministry, but it was only a matter of time. He could have escaped, but he stayed. The plots against Hitler were thickening now. The big one was Operation Valkyrie on 20th July, but somehow Hitler had survived the bomb planted under a table in the Wolf's Lair. Canaris was arrested three days later, along with dozens of others, and taken to the Border Police Academy at Fürstenberg. To add to the irony, he was not even directly involved in the 20th July plot. Maybe if he had been, he thought, it would not have failed.

He had been roughed up a bit in Fürstenberg, nothing too bad. Maybe he would be able to cope with it; there might even be a chance to escape. But once they brought him here to Prinz-Albrecht-Strasse, he knew there was no chance.

He had been here a couple of weeks. Every day and sometimes at night, he was tortured. It was never clear what they wanted him to tell them. Perhaps everything, but the secret of surviving interrogation was to work out what the interrogators did not know. Once you knew that, you knew what not to tell them. And when you knew what they did know, there was no harm to be done by telling them that. That is what they had taught the Abwehr agents. But what made sense in theory was difficult in practice.

It did not take into account what the lack of sleep did to your mind. They kept the sharp lights blazing day and night and if he ever fell into a deep sleep, he would be woken up with slaps or by cold water being chucked over him. Then there was the hunger. They must have put him on reduced rations, because there was hardly anything to eat. If you had any chance of getting through an interrogation you had to concentrate and it was difficult to concentrate when all you could think about was food.

Nothing, of course, that the SS did came as a shock. Since that day in Poland when he had seen them herding men, women and children into the synagogue without a flicker of emotion on their faces, he knew that these people were capable of anything.

They kept him in chains and on occasions, to amuse themselves, the SS guards would take him into the corridor, force him onto all fours and walk him around like a dog.

For most of the time, he was in solitary confinement. Some of the 20th July plotters were being interrogated there too, and Generalmajor Oster, his former deputy in the Abwehr, was also a prisoner.

But from time to time there was contact with other prisoners. Such contact as there was tended to be fleeting, but two mumbled sentences could sustain you for days. You had to be careful, of course – make sure they weren't SS stooges, planted there to get you to reveal something.

This man hunched on the floor next to him was no SS stooge, he was certain of that. He had known Franz Hermann before the war. A very clever lawyer, an expert in banking law as far as Canaris could recall. Canaris was aware that Hermann had been a social democrat in the early thirties, but not very active. He had continued to practise during the war and had kept a low profile, but Canaris knew that he had been involved with the resistance in Berlin. The last time he had come across him was when he had been sent a report suggesting that Hermann had arranged for a Jewish family in hiding in Berlin to escape to Switzerland. Luckily the report had come to the Abwehr rather than the Gestapo, which is really where it should have gone. It was conveniently filed in the wrong place and forgotten.

Now Hermann was slumped next to him, his face badly bruised and blood crusted around his nose and mouth. He was trembling.

'When did you get here, Hermann?'

The lawyer turned and looked at Canaris through swollen eyes.

'Canaris? I didn't recognise you. They brought me here two days ago, maybe three. I don't know. I have no idea anymore.'

'What for?'

'Better to ask what *not* for.'

'What is happening outside?'

An ironic laugh from Hermann.

'Haven't you heard? We've won the war and Hitler is calling free elections. The Social Democrats are favourites to win.'

Canaris pulled a wry smile. Hermann dropped his voice and through broken teeth and a badly split lip he spoke urgently.

'The last I heard was that the Allies have broken out of Normandy. They're racing through France now. Our defences aren't holding. All this talk about the main Allied invasion being further east along the French coast, apparently it was not true. It was never going to happen.'

Canaris nodded his head. A guard had spotted them talking and was marching over, twirling a long truncheon in his hand.

'Of course not,' said Canaris. 'It was a clever deception all along. It is a good job we persuaded Hitler to believe it as long as we did, eh?'

Chapter 25

London, August-September 1944

There was no single moment when Owen Quinn knew for sure that it was over. There was no single moment when he knew that there would be no Allied landings in the Pas de Calais, even though he had been told as much on D-Day. There was no single moment when he finally realised that Edgar had not made a dreadful mistake. There was no single moment when he knew that his wife had indeed deceived him, as had the Allies. In short, there was no single moment when he gave up hoping he was having a nightmare and realised he was living through one instead.

He remained in Dover until the end of July, which was far longer than he had anticipated. Edgar came down to see him once a week, visits which were certainly not occasioned by concern for his welfare. Quinn got the impression that Edgar came to check that he was neither being too difficult nor going mad. He felt quite close to the latter. He had precious little to do in Dover Castle. The Royal Navy were perfectly happy to have him there, and he was able to help with the weather reports, but it was obvious that work was being created for him.

He had far too much time to contemplate his pitiful predicament. After a while, he realised he must have been in shock for the first few days. If he had that time again, he would have attacked Edgar or tried to do something about it. Quite what, he didn't know, but he resented himself for the way he had sleepwalked home from the park, and allowed Roger and his friends to remove all traces of Nathalie from the flat, and then be led like a compliant beast to Dover.

His visits to the edge of insanity were driven in part by the sheer injustice of his situation. He was a loyal Royal Navy officer who had come within minutes of losing his life on active service, and who was then denied the opportunity to return to sea so that he could be used as part of some secret scheme, the efficacy of which was uncertain. He had been deceived by the people whose side he was meant to be on. But far worse than this injustice was the grief that he felt. Had Nathalie been killed, that would have been bad enough. But now, not only had he lost her, he knew that she too had deceived him. He doubted that she had ever loved him; she probably never even cared for him, and her only interest in him was for the information she could supply to the enemy.

When he reached the very edge of madness one thing stopped him inexorably tipping over. The cameo brooch. It was hard to conceive of any circumstances in which it could have been secreted in the soap dish by mistake. It must have been a sign from Nathalie of something. Possibly it was a way of saying sorry, or she could have thought that leaving him one little memento like that might be a way of filling some emotional void. He did not know. He doubted it was meant to offer any clues as to either her identity or her whereabouts. The brooch was not especially distinctive and the initials 'GT' not particularly helpful. He could hardly walk round France asking strangers if this brooch meant anything to them.

But what the brooch did do was allow him the slenderest of reasons to believe that maybe there was some point in his searching for her. At the very least he might get an explanation. Beyond that, he had no idea.

Edgar seemed satisfied that Quinn was not going to do something stupid. Quinn was tempted sometimes to stand on the ramparts of Dover Castle and shout out what had happened. But he could not be sure what they would do to him. The first night he arrived at the castle, a Navy doctor came and had a chat with him. It was an 'understand you've had a difficult time, old chap' kind of chat. The end result of this chat was a large pill being pressed into his palm. 'One of these each night, you'll soon be as right as rain.' He slept twelve hours that night and when his lethargy began to wear off the next afternoon, he found himself craving the next pill. He took it, slept just as well, felt just as lethargic the next day, and the craving for the next pill was even stronger than the day before. After that, he took no more pills. He accepted them all, of course, very gratefully, even eagerly. But they all ended up down the sink, every single one of them. He did not sleep well and there were many times during the day when he would have happily traded his rages, the insomnia, his anxiety, and his grief for a spell of lethargy, but at least he felt he was in some kind of control of his own feelings. He was not going to end up in some military nursing home shouting at passing clouds, and telling anyone who would listen that the sheep were Nazi spies and, by the way, my wife was one too.

Just play along with them.

On his first visit Edgar told him that the trip to Dover on 7th June had worked out well. The German spy had obligingly followed him up to the point of his entering the castle. They did not know whether anyone was still watching him, so a routine was agreed just in case they were. Quinn would leave the castle between nine and nine thirty every morning to walk down the hill to buy a newspaper. At around five in the afternoon he would emerge from the castle to stroll around its perimeter. Anyone watching him could be sure he was still there.

By the end of July, Quinn knew that the deception game must be over. From what he could gather from the BBC and what he overheard in the castle, more than half a million troops had landed in Normandy and now they were breaking out of the region into other parts of France. After a bitter battle, Caen had fallen, and that convinced the divided German military that there would be no invasion in the Pas de Calais after all. By the end of July, the powerful German Fifteenth Army and its Panzer divisions were moved from the Pas de Calais, but it was too late. The generals – on both sides – could only ponder at what would have happened had these forces moved into Normandy straight after the invasion. The Germans had been well and truly deceived. It was no consolation to Quinn.

On Tuesday, 1st August, he left Dover Castle. Major Edgar came to collect him in a black car very similar to the one in which he had been driven away from St James's Park on D-Day.

'Look on this as the first day of the rest of your life, Owen. You seem to have put what happened behind you. Well done for that. There is almost no family in this country that has not suffered during the war. You have lost your wife. Imagine she was killed in a bombing raid. But how old are you now… twenty-six, twenty-seven?'

'Twenty-six.'

'Well, that's no age, Quinn. You have years ahead of you. Plenty of time to start a career, find a new wife, have a family, nice house somewhere. Mark my words, you will just look back on this whole business as something unpleasant that happened in war. You'll be in the same boat as thousands of other people.'

'I doubt it.'

Edgar was gazing out of the window of the car as it sped through the Kent countryside, but was slapping Quinn's knee in a jolly manner.

'I know it is of no consolation to you now, Quinn, but you have played your part in a hugely successful deception operation. Can't go into too many details of course, Quinn, but all in all we must have saved tens of thousands of Allied lives. Germans have been giving us a hard enough time as it is in Normandy. We've picked up over two hundred thousand casualties in the Battle of Normandy. Something like 35,000 of those killed. If we had not helped persuade them to tie up forces round the Pas de Calais, the casualty rate would have been much, much higher – and it is possible that Normandy may even have failed. If that had happened, we would not have been able to invade again for years, and with all this talk of the Germans getting new weapons... who knows? It doesn't bear thinking about.'

'So the end has justified the means?'

'If you put it like that, then yes, I am afraid that in your case, it has.'

'And what happens after the war?'

'What do you mean?'

'With Nathalie, or whatever her real name is. Will she be arrested? I mean, where is she now?'

Edgar furrowed his brow. The thought of her being arrested had not occurred to him and he hesitated while he contemplated it.

'She disappeared a couple of weeks ago, Quinn. No contact, nothing. Hard to make out what is going on in the Pas de Calais, as it is still in German hands, but we do know that the resistance cell that she was with was pulled in by the Gestapo. There has been no contact at all. My guess is that once the Germans realised that there was going to be no invasion through the Pas de Calais, she had outlived her use to them. They may have arrested her, who knows? She's a smart young lady, as you know. Maybe she just left the area. We just don't know. Whatever happens, I cannot see her hanging around for when our chaps roll in, coming running up to one of our tanks waving the Union Jack and shouting, "Oh, by the way, I was a German spy", can you?'

Be careful, you are talking about my wife. 'But what about if she is arrested elsewhere in France, Edgar?'

'For that to happen, we would have to be very lucky and she would have to be very unlucky. We do not know her real identity, never could

261

crack that. We don't know where she is from. Owen, we are talking about a country twice the size of this one, with a population of forty million. Once the whole country is liberated, it will be chaos over there. We would not know where to start.'

'But just say she is caught. Then what?'

A long pause from Edgar.

'Then we shall cross that bridge when we come to it, eh?'

'And if she turns herself in?'

Edgar laughed. 'Nazi spies tend not to do that, Quinn.'

'Sounds to me that it would be rather inconvenient to you if she was caught. Am I right, Edgar?'

Edgar stared out of the window. They were now entering the southern London suburbs.

'Possibly. But have you thought how you would feel if your wife were to go on trial as a Nazi spy? Anyway, I thought you'd pretty much got over it. No signs of you being too bothered while you were down in Dover, I'm told.'

'Indeed,' said Owen.

The rest of the journey back to London was taken up with the plans that had been put in place for Owen's life.

'The Royal Navy are going to look after you.' They had rented a very nice flat for him behind Marylebone High Street – 'Assumed you wouldn't want to return to the old flat, all the memories and that.' He could live there until the end of the war, and then for a few months after until he sorted himself out. He was to be promoted to lieutenant commander, with a desk job at the Admiralty that he would keep at least until the war ended, and longer if he wanted. A generous stipend was to be paid when he did decide to leave. His new flat was a bit further away from work, but it had been chosen carefully: he would have no need to return to Alderney Street or even go anywhere near it. They clearly did not want to risk him getting any more upset than was inevitable. And everyone would agree on an official line regarding his wife: missing in action while on operational duties in France. Not allowed to discuss any details.

'Try and stop feeling so sorry for yourself Quinn,' were Edgar's parting words, delivered with a thin smile.

–

Cognac gave up at the end of July. He could not see the point of carrying on. He had performed miracles by keeping going as long as he had, but the trip to and from Dover had a valedictory air to it. 'Living on borrowed time' was the English phrase. He had delayed sending his final message to Berlin on the night of 7th June because he had no back up, nowhere else to go in case they managed to trace the transmission to that miserable bedsit in Clapham. So he found a room in a house in Kew and moved in there, making the final transmission to Berlin just before he left Clapham for the last time. Immediately after that last transmission he burned everything incriminating in the hearth. He took the transmitter to Kew, but only briefly. It disappeared into the Thames at high tide one night from a footpath under Kew Bridge. He took a risk throwing it in, but it was a calculated risk of the kind he had been taking every day for the past few years. Once the transmitter sank silently he knew that there was nothing to incriminate him. He had some money left and a decent identity that he had been keeping for this eventuality, which even the Germans were unaware of. But his prize possession was his ability to outwit and outthink the British, an ability which had served him so well up to now.

He would stay in Kew for a few weeks and then he had a plan. But most important of all, he had retired.

–

Owen Quinn behaved in the compliant way that he realised was expected of him that summer. He moved into his very pleasant flat in a neat street between Marylebone High Street and Portland Place. He turned up at work every day at the Admiralty, where he found himself in an office full of charts and maps, and was fastidious in ensuring he caused no trouble. He was suspicious of everyone, of course. He had no idea whether the charming neighbour in the flat next to his really did work at the Colonial Office or whether he was there to keep an eye on him. The three or four people who worked with him at the Admiralty were all pleasant enough, but whether they were really who they said they were, he had no idea. He always checked whether he was being followed, but was never sure. The truth was that what he did and where he went probably did not matter to anyone now.

He had a plan. *Keep your head down, do not cause any trouble, and when it's all over, go to France and try to find her.*

Sitting on his own in his flat in the evening he would go through the plan, fuelled by his first glass of whisky. He would go to the Pas de Calais. He would find people who knew her there. He had the brooch. Somehow, he would trace her. But by the second or third glass, he worried that it might be a fanciful plan. Edgar was right. He would not find her. '*Needle in a haystack and all that. It would be impossible.*' She had disappeared.

By the fourth glass of whisky he would start thinking about what he would do in the unlikely event of him ever finding her. That varied according to whether he ever got onto the fifth glass, but in truth it was never really a question he could begin to answer.

On Saturday, 26th August, Owen went to visit his parents in Surrey for the first time since May. His contact with them had been minimal: he had told them he was leaving London for a while, and that Nathalie was away too. That was all that they needed to know, and his father at least knew better than to ask.

It was a glorious weekend. The day before, Paris had been liberated, and that was another significant milestone towards the end of the war. He took the train down in the morning and was planning to stay overnight. After lunch they sat in the garden, bathed in the warm sunlight and the still of the afternoon. Conversation during lunch had been easy enough; he just let his mother talk about life in Surrey and the lives of their friends and relations. But there was obviously an unspoken presence that could not be avoided.

'So, Owen,' said his father, trying to be as matter of fact as possible, 'what have you been up to?' The question was framed in very much the same way as when his father came home from work and enquired of Owen's day at school.

'Been away for work, told you that in the letters.'

'And you cannot tell us where?' his mother asked.

'You know he can't, Marjorie.'

'We are your parents, Owen, and we have been worried sick that you may have been in France. We had no idea of what you were doing and what was going on,' said his mother, close to tears.

'Well, wherever I've been, I'm here and I am safe, so there's no need to worry now, is there?'

His parents shot worried glances at each other. This attitude was so uncharacteristic of their son. *That woman*, thought his mother. *She has a lot to answer for.*

'You must have done something right if they have promoted you. We are so proud of that. If only you had let us invite some people round today, we could have had a small celebration.' A son who was a lieutenant commander would clearly do his mother's advancement in her social circle no harm whatsoever, if only he would play ball.

'And this new job, Owen, at the Admiralty. Good prospects?' said his father.

'Possibly. Let us see what happens at the end of the war.'

'Both your mother and I do feel that the Navy has treated you in a splendid way.'

'Absolutely, father. I could not have been treated better.'

Time now for the other unspoken beast to emerge.

'And… er… Nathalie? What news there? Is she still away?'

Thank you so much for asking. Everything is fine! Turns out that she is a Nazi spy and the Royal Navy who have treated me so splendidly, as you put it, arranged for her to get together with me so that they could use me as a conduit for her to pass false information on to the Germans. Then she was sent as a British spy – please keep up – to France to work with the resistance, but has now disappeared and I doubt that I will ever see her again. But don't worry, it's fine. At least I have a brooch, and many people are far worse off than me, or so I am told.

'No – I mean yes. No, there is no news and yes, she is still away. I think… I think I have to… to tell…'

'Yes, Owen?' His mother was leaning forward anxiously.

'I think I am going to have to ask you not to raise the question of Nathalie again, if you don't mind. It is very difficult, you see. She was sent back to France on operational work and has… well, she has disappeared.'

A long silence.

'Owen, how dreadful. I am sorry.' His father got up and somewhat awkwardly placed his hand on his son's shoulder. His mother said nothing, unclear how she was meant to react.

'I mean we just don't know what has happened, and I can really say very little, I hope you appreciate that. I just have to accept the fact that she has gone. Maybe… who knows…?'

He struggled to hold in the tears now. Somehow, crying in your childhood home was much easier, having done it there before.

His father plied him with whisky, which was not something he tended to do in the afternoon and, after a long and awkward silence, his mother was as tactless as ever.

'What do we tell everyone?'

'As little as possible please, mother. Just say she had to go back to France. Just say you cannot discuss matters, which I would rather you didn't anyway.'

'I always thought that a foreign marriage would not last.'

'Marjorie!' His father's tone towards his mother was reproachful.

'Well, I did,' Owen responded. 'Wouldn't have got into it if I hadn't thought it would last.'

His mother stood up, smoothing out the front of her dress and adjusting her hair after catching sight of herself in the mirror. 'At least there are no children. I suppose, Owen, that is one small blessing for which one ought to be grateful.'

And so on. For the first time since Nathalie had gone to France, Owen felt that there was a danger he was losing control in front of other people, even if these other people were his parents. It was out of character. He shouldn't behave like that. He realised he needed to get a grip. If he carried on like this – the drink, the open displays of emotion – then the only thing that was certain was that he wasn't going to find Nathalie.

By dinner that evening his parents were taking heed of his request for them not to raise the subject. His mother was back to her inconsequential tales of local life and his father talked about cricket. He suspected that his mother's overriding emotion was one of relief. She had never really liked Nathalie and would now no doubt consider that dislike vindicated, not that she would say so in as many words.

He left after lunch on the Sunday. Before he did, he found his father standing by the mantelpiece in the lounge, looking at Owen's wedding photographs.

'Not sure whether you want us to take these down?'

Owen realised that he did not have his wedding photographs anymore. After Roger and his friends had so thoughtfully cleared out the flat in Alderney Street and helpfully moved his possessions into the new flat, the wedding photographs were not included with all of his other photographs. He had repeatedly asked for their return, and had been assured that that was imminent, but he doubted it. He had no photographs of Nathalie, apart from an increasingly creased one that he kept in his wallet.

'Don't worry. Maybe best if I take them.'

Towards the end of September, he recognised that he quite possibly might be heading towards depression. He had seen people behave oddly at Calcotte Grange, especially when they thought no one else was watching, and he was concerned that when he wasn't with other people and having to act normally, his behaviour was not natural. When he returned home from work it was the whisky that helped him through the evening and into the night. If he thought about it, he realised that he was drinking too much, but he didn't bother to think about it often. Too often he would wake up in the early hours of the morning slumped in his armchair, still dressed, the lights blazing and the cameo brooch lying on the floor from where it had slipped from his grasp. Most times he would haul himself up, have a wash and brush his teeth and climb into bed, but there were nights when he would curl himself into a ball and wait for a restless sleep to return.

He was functioning well enough during the day. A couple of strong cups of tea, a bath and a shave and brisk walk to the Admiralty helped with that, and his work was not too demanding either.

At the end of September, he realised he needed to sort himself out. The emotions that had surfaced at his parents' were still there and, if he was to find Nathalie, then he needed to get back in control. Most of the Pas de Calais was now in Allied hands: the Canadians liberated Boulogne on the 22nd and Calais on the 25th. Quinn realised that if he was to be of any use when he did manage to get over there, he needed to pull himself together.

He could not remember the last time he had visited the doctor. They had registered at a surgery in Pimlico when they moved into the area, and he been there a couple of times for prescriptions for painkillers when his back or leg had been playing up. Nathalie had been there more often, but in his case it must have been a good year since he had visited.

They would sort him out. Something to help him sleep, nothing like the heavy-duty stuff they had tried to get him addicted to in Dover. Then he would just be able to get away with one drink after his evening meal and have a decent night's sleep.

He left work early one afternoon and walked all the way to the surgery. It was a pleasant day and he was feeling buoyant. Not quite optimistic, but he had a feeling that he could soon be in France, and until he did that, he would not be able to move on.

The surgery was crowded. An elderly receptionist with tiny glasses perched improbably at the end of a very long nose asked him twice whether he had made an appointment. '*No, I didn't realise I was going to be unwell.*' She tilted her head so as to be able to shoot him a disapproving glance through her glasses. '*Very well, you'll have to wait your turn.*' It had not occurred to him that he would have to do anything other than that.

He waited the best part of an hour, leafing his way through *Punch* and *Country Life* and being forced into conversation with a ten-year-old boy who wanted to know what ships he had sailed on and what battles he had taken part in.

'Quinn. Owen Quinn?'

He followed the GP into his surgery. He recalled having seen him before when he needed some painkillers. Dr Peacock had spent much of the time then explaining how his retirement golfing plans had been disrupted by this 'wretched war'. They also serve, thought Quinn. Delaying the doctor's retirement would have to be listed as another Nazi war crime.

His surgery was a fug of cigarette smoke. The small window was locked and the ashtray was full of spent cigarettes, some of the ash spilling onto the desk. A lit cigarette was stuck in the side of Dr Peacock's mouth, and every so often he paused to move it to the centre of his mouth, inhale deeply and then return it to its resting place. Dr Peacock was a tall man, with bright red braces, a matching tie and frayed cuffs. Owen noticed damp patches spreading under his shirt armpits.

'Now then, Quinn. How are you? Having a decent war?'

'Based in London now, Dr Peacock. Haven't been back to sea. Promoted though.'

That would appeal to Dr Peacock, who had now perched his glasses on his forehead and was studying Owen's file.

'Splendid. Very good, well done. And how's the back? Is that why you're here?'

'Back's not too bad, thank you. I have come about something else.'

'As long as it is not in-growing toenails. That is all I seem to have this week. Why people can't go straight to a chiropodist, I don't know.'

Owen explained he was having trouble sleeping, '...nothing serious you understand, but you know, Doctor... probably to do with the back...'

Dr Peacock understood. No problem. Quick listen to the heart and look at the blood pressure, no problems there. Hard for everyone to sleep these days. The German rockets didn't help. Had to send Mrs Peacock up to her sister's. Here's a prescription. Should help. Good long walk in the evening helps too. Go easy on the booze, not that I'm much of a one to be telling you that. Come back and see me in a month.

And that was that. Owen slipped his jacket back on and Dr Peacock stubbed out his cigarette, but not before removing a new one from the pack.

'And how is Mrs Quinn getting on these days?'

Owen was momentarily taken aback. Nathalie.

'Oh… she's, you know… the war and that…' He had not really expected Dr Peacock to ask about his wife, but his response was the standard anodyne one he had ready for whenever he was asked about her. He relied on people's reluctance to pry.

'As long as she is keeping well.' Dr Peacock was glancing down at his file. 'Beginning of April I last saw her. Told her I only needed to see her if there was a problem, so I'm assuming no news is good news, eh? She must be what… seven months pregnant now? Anyway, not long to go. Make the most of the peace and quiet while you can!'

Chapter 26

Lille, August 1944

The bus ride from St Omer to Lille in the middle of July had been more hazardous than she had anticipated. The elderly man sitting next to her on the bus held her arm as he spoke and looked at her carefully through moist eyes. 'Lille and the countryside around it have been moved into Belgium by the Germans,' he told her. He looked around, making sure no one could overhear them and moved closer to her, his whisper even louder than his hushed voice.

'This all comes under Brussels now,' he said, gesturing outside the window. 'All of it.'

He shook his head and coughed violently. 'To think...'

He remained lost in his thoughts, but still clutching her arm, until they reached a checkpoint on the outskirts of Lille. Her confusion gave her an air of genuine innocence which seemed to help with the exhausted-looking German sentry, who appeared to be having problems with his feet and was probably the wrong side of fifty.

Hélène Blanc, the identity she was now travelling under, had a blank against 'Profession' on her identity card, but she was able to persuade the sentry that she was a nurse. 'For some reason it has been omitted from the identity card,' she told him. She was going to visit an elderly aunt in Lille, and maybe find work there as a nurse.

'You look like you could do with a rest,' she told him, managing her sweetest smile and allowing her forefinger to brush very slightly against his hand as she handed him her identity card. She had switched to German now and he returned the smile.

Behind him an officer was laughing inside the guardroom, a phone pressed to his ear. He was leaning back in his chair with his jackbooted legs on the table.

'You can say that again,' said the elderly sentry. 'We're on double shifts now, you know. Shouldn't be telling you that. Half our lot have been sent to either Normandy or the east. I just sleep and then stand here. That's my life. "If you don't like it," they tell us, "then you can go out east."'

He continued to scrutinise her identity card. She could tell from his eyes that he was not inclined to believe her, but he seemed too tired to probe.

'I'll tell you what. Because you're a pretty nurse I'll believe you. You really should have had the papers sorted before you set out, but the curfew starts soon and I just want to go to bed. How long were you planning to stay in Lille for?'

A day, a week… a year? She had no idea.

'I'm not sure. A few weeks, certainly.'

'The longest I can do myself is one month.' He had pulled a sheet of paper out of a folder and was organising some rubber stamps. 'More than that and he'll have to get involved and we don't want that, do we?' He gestured to the guard on the phone behind him.

She shook her head. Behind her the bus driver hooted. All the other passengers had been cleared and he was waiting to continue the journey.

'Hey!' The officer had sprung out of the guardroom and was shouting at the bus driver. '*You* don't hoot *us*. Do you understand? Otherwise you'll find yourself driving buses in some very unpleasant places.' He turned to the sentry. 'Get a move on, Schmidt.'

The sentry was busy stamping a permit.

'If he finds out, I'm off to the east – but he won't find out, will he?'

She shook her head. *He wouldn't find out. She was very grateful.* She turned to climb back on the bus.

'And you take care, won't you? How long now?'

She was confused, until she noticed he was glancing at her stomach. She looked down and realised how much she was showing now. It was the first time that anyone had noticed, or at least commented upon it. She was surprised no one had said anything at the village, though in the past few weeks she had made an effort to wear looser-fitting clothes.

–

From that very first night, Lille was close to a disaster. All of her ingenuity and luck, her ability to anticipate trouble, seemed to desert

271

her in this strange city which seemed to be French one minute and Flemish the next. Possibly, it was because it was like her: not sure of what it really was. First one thing and then the other.

She had found a small guest house a few roads from the enormous Grand Place. The sign in the dirty window said there were rooms vacant, but she had to keep knocking until the door was opened by an enormous landlady whose body seemed to fill the hall.

'Yes, we have a room. You wait here while I finish my dinner.'

She had to sit in the narrow front hall while the landlady and her husband, who seemed to be half her size and twice her age, finished their meal.

She could see them through the open door into their small kitchen, peering out at her.

'How long are you here for?' The landlady was speaking with her mouth full.

'Perhaps a month.'

'You have papers?'

She nodded, taking the permit out of her handbag.

'Because I don't do anything I shouldn't do, you understand? The authorities keep an eye on these places, and I don't intend getting into trouble for anyone.'

She nodded. She understood.

'Got money?'

She nodded.

'Let me see it then.' A long piece of dark green cabbage was dangling from the landlady's mouth.

She opened her purse and waved a wad of notes towards the open door. Behind the landlady she could see the husband helping himself to another potato while his wife was distracted.

When the landlady had finally finished her meal, she followed her up the narrow stairs to the top floor. The landlady was so wide that once or twice it looked as if she might get wedged between the walls. The room was tiny, with a bed against one wall and precious little else. A grey net curtain hung in front of the small window and there was a smell of dust and mice. The floor was just bare floorboards with an old rug next to the bed.

'What do you think?' The landlady was leaning against the door, struggling to catch her breath.

She couldn't begin to say what she thought.

'It will do me fine. Thank you.'

'I want a week's rent in advance.'

'But what if I only stay for a few days?'

The landlady remained impassive, shrugging her broad shoulders. Beads of sweat dotted her forehead. 'A week's rent.'

She handed the money over. The landlady noisily licked her thumb before carefully counting it.

'No visitors, you understand?'

'Of course.'

'Your husband?' She had removed her coat and the landlady was staring at her stomach.

'Taken away... a couple of months ago.'

The landlady nodded. She would have liked to know more about her new tenant, but there was plenty of time.

That night, she lay on the bed fully clothed, unwilling to crawl between the greasy sheets which had evidently not been changed since the last occupant. She removed her shoes and covered the pillow with the one jumper she had in her bag. The bed itself was not uncomfortable, though it felt as if it would not be able to withstand too much movement. Despite the narrowness of the window and the state of the curtains, the moonlight filled the room. She could hear scratching under the floorboards. In a room somewhere below a couple were having noisy sex that lasted an improbably long time. She tried hard to avoid imagining that it was the landlady and her husband.

For the first time since leaving the village she was able to stop and think. She lay on her back, her hands crossed over her stomach and she could clearly feel the kicking inside her. She thought of the couple below her and of the trail behind her. And to her surprise, she thought of Owen. Part of him was moving inside her and perhaps for that reason she realised that her thoughts about him were now so different from before.

She imagined that he had entered the room, as pleased to see her as always: the broad smile showing his white teeth and hardly creasing his smooth face, the blue eyes sparkling and the fair hair flopping down over his forehead. She'd shift over slightly to allow him to sit at the end of the bed and he would perch there, taking care not to disturb her and taking her foot in his hands and gently massaging it.

Previously, she had always had to think of Owen in strictly practical terms. How to inveigle him, how to be sure of where he was at any given time, how to convince him of who she was and that she cared, how to find out what he was doing and trying to remember where she had told him she was going to be.

His presence in the room was very real now.

'I've never thought about you like this before, Owen,' she found herself saying. She had started to sob gently now and the kicking in her stomach was growing stronger.

'Everything I had to do, I was forced to. Do you understand?'

And he would have nodded. In an innocent way, as if he didn't fully understand, but couldn't see what all the fuss was about.

'I couldn't tell you how I really felt about you because I could not even allow myself to contemplate such thoughts. But you were always so happy, so grateful for everything, so keen to show how much you cared about me. And I couldn't give anything back to you. At first, because I didn't really want to. You were just my work. But then I couldn't because the one thing I could not do was give in to my emotions.'

Her crying was so strong now that she turned her face to the pillow. She thought of the first time she had been waiting for him to come back from work and had realised that she was looking forward to his arrival. That had shocked her and worried her. That evening they had made love three times before either of them properly spoke to the other, and she had lain in bed afterwards wanting to tell him that she loved him. That was when she knew she had to get a grip on herself. Carry on that way and she would make mistakes. She had convinced herself that she was deluded.

'I'm not sure now, Owen. Maybe I wasn't deluded.'

The crying had subsided and her stomach was still. She hauled herself up into a sitting position against the bedstead. At this point, Owen would finish massaging her feet and slide his hands up her legs.

'I must have cared about you. And what will become of us now?'

She had no idea. She was beginning to feel the chill of the night now and crawled under the dusty bedspread which smelled of tobacco and human bodies. She was still fully clothed.

She was utterly confused. She was shocked at her expression of feelings about Owen. At that moment, she would have given anything for the opportunity to return to him, with all the consequences that that entailed.

The hospital in Lille had enough nurses, the matron told her. Hang around, she told her, when the fighting starts we'll need more. She was desperate, she said, following the matron down the corridor. She had spent most of her money on a week's rent and some food. She had been to the cobblers that morning to get her shoes repaired. Before the war, she could have bought a decent pair for the amount she'd just paid for these to be repaired. She would do anything. The matron paused and looked her up and down.

'How many months are you?'

'Five or six.'

'Fit and healthy?'

She nodded.

'Husband?'

'At war,' she answered without hesitating.

'Aren't they all,' said the matron, who was staring at her left hand. She realised she was not wearing a wedding ring and that that was going to be a problem. She felt the need to explain and held out her left hand.

'A German soldier took my ring from me at a checkpoint.'

The matron wiped her hand on her apron, her eyes showing that she was not entirely convinced by that explanation.

'You can start on Friday night. We always need more help then. I'll give you a trial for a few days to see if you're really up to it. I'll put you on the wards. You clean and help the nurses out. When we get busier there may be more for you to do, if you are still able to.'

For three weeks, the best that could be said of the work was that it allowed her to eat and paid the rent. For that privilege she was able to grab the few hours' sleep that the daylight and the noise would allow her in that rank-smelling room, where the landlady seemed to resent her coming in or going out.

Whenever she could, she would take refuge in one of the small cafés behind the Grand Place. She avoided those in the Grand Place itself; they were more expensive, even if the coffee tasted very slightly more like coffee. The main problem, though, was the number of Germans in them. Previously, their presence would not have bothered her. She would have been wary not to draw attention to herself, but would have done her best to ignore them.

But the atmosphere was very different now. Maybe it was Lille, but she doubted it. The news from Normandy that people discussed in corners and behind their hands was not good for the Germans. The Allies would be moving through France soon. She sensed that the German troops knew it and their presence had an added air of menace to it.

In a café one morning she watched a young SS officer deliberately barge into two local women who were negotiating their way towards a table, causing them to spill their drinks and plates over a group of young Wehrmacht soldiers.

'You animals!' the SS officer shouted. He was in his early twenties and his face was flushed and sweating as if he had been drinking. With the back of his hand he lashed out at the women, connecting with the one nearest to him, causing her to stumble and then crumple to the ground. One of the Wehrmacht soldiers put his arm out, to stop her falling further.

The SS officer was incandescent.

'You,' he said to the women, both of whom were white with shock, 'will pay for this damage. Give me your purses.' They handed them over and he emptied the contents of both straight into his jacket pocket. 'Now go away. And you...' he was pointing to the soldier who had helped the woman up '...come with me. Now!'

On the Thursday evening of her third week in Lille she had given up on sleep early. The house was hot and the top floor unbearable. The landlady was shouting at her husband and a band seemed to be rehearsing nearby. The aroma of dinner rose up through her window, which was by far the most disconcerting sensation of all.

She was not due at the hospital until nine, and by the time she reached the small café on the corner it was only just seven thirty. She had more than an hour to kill, but she found solace in these small cafés, where she could always find a seat alone and an obliging *patron* who would allow her to move the food around on her plate for an hour and sometimes refill her drink with a wink and a smile. And then she would talk to Owen. His imagined presence would comfort her. She had decided on the first night in Lille that Owen would forgive her. He would be angry, perhaps even furious, but in time he would understand. So on those evenings in the cafés of Lille she would revisit their relationship; the little things he had said, the questions he had asked but she had not answered, the nuances that would have made another man uncertain or jealous, and the episodes of affection.

Alone with these thoughts, on this night she was startled by the *patron*, a large man with an enormous moustache who had decided that the price of an occasional free drink was that he could confide in her.

'Not long now. They'll be running with their tails between their legs before the autumn, mark my words,' he would mutter at German soldiers on the other side of the glass. 'Another drink?'

Shocked, she glanced at her watch. Ten to nine. The hospital was a fifteen-minute walk away. She paid and left in a hurry, running across the cobbled streets, straight across the Grand Place and towards the hospital. She was no more than five minutes' walk away when she passed an abandoned industrial building. There was not a soul in sight.

'Hey. Pretty girl. Come here.'

She looked round. In the doorway of the building was a young soldier wearing the black uniform of the SS. She looked around; maybe he meant someone else, maybe there would be other people around.

'Yes, you. Come here.'

If she took her shoes off and ran fast, she might make it to the main road before him. But the ground was scattered with debris and she remembered her condition. Any thoughts of escape ended with the distinctive metallic click of a catch of a gun being drawn.

'Where are you going?'

'Home.'

'And where have you been?'

'At work. I'm a waitress at a café in the Grand Place.'

She realised she was panicking. Maybe she should have told him the truth about where she worked. She was so used to avoiding the truth that to lie was now her natural response.

'And where is home?'

She panicked. She did not know Lille well enough to know what to say. She pointed in the opposite direction that she had come from.

'Change of plan. Follow me.' He pointed his long-barrelled Luger revolver straight at her and then, using it as a finger, waved her towards him and into the building.

He waited until she was inside the building before opening a door off a dark corridor and pushing her into a dim room. It must have been an office at one time. The only windows looked out onto what would have been a factory floor. A desk had been pushed against the wall, a half-full bottle of brandy on it and an empty one next to it. A torn leather office chair was in the centre of the room, circled by a collection of empty beer bottles. A calendar had stopped at January 1943 and there were the remains of a dead pigeon in the fireplace. In one corner was a large pile of sacks with two or three torn blankets on top.

'Over there.' He was pointing to the sacks with his revolver. 'Get over there and get undressed.'

'I can't.'

'Really?' he asked sarcastically. 'And why is that?'

She opened her jacket to show him her swollen stomach.

'Oh, don't worry. That really doesn't bother me. If anything, it adds to the pleasure. It would be my first time with a woman in your condition!' He was leering at her, slightly unsteady on his feet.

'Look…' She was breathing heavily and could feel herself panicking. She was not thinking rationally. Should she tell him that she was on his side really, that he was making a terrible mistake? *I have the name and telephone number of someone important in Paris who would vouch for me.* But she knew it was hopeless. He would not believe her, and anyway, she was no longer sure whose side she was on now. And if he did believe and act on what she said, she would be in even worse trouble than she was now.

Having been in the unusual position of having been trained by both the Germans and the British, she felt she was prepared for this. Not prepared for being raped in an abandoned building, or for the extreme fear that she felt now, but prepared for a confrontation of this nature. Treat it like an interrogation, she thought. She tried to remember her training.

You are an attractive young woman. There may be occasions when men may try to take advantage of you. If so, appear to go along with them. Do not encourage them, but do not antagonise them either. Do anything to take the edge off a situation. If a man tries to rape you then he will not be thinking about his own security during the act. This will be when he is at his weakest. That is when you must act.

So she calmly removed her jacket, taking care to fold it and remove a handkerchief from the pocket, which she used to dab her face, and she sat down on the coarse sacks. Her tactic seemed to be working. The young SS man smiled and removed his own jacket, placing it with his cap and revolver on the chair. He took off his boots, undid his belt and lowering his trousers, crawled on top of her. He was breathing deeply now, his hand inside her skirt and beginning to hurt her. She could smell the alcohol on his breath as he became rougher. *If he carries on like this I am going to miscarry.* With his other hand he had been holding her down, but now he paused while he removed his trousers altogether and started to pull down his pants. Her head was pushed back against the rough skirting board, its dull green paint peeling, revealing damp wood underneath.

'Don't be so rough,' she whispered, 'there's no need.'

And with that she pulled him closer to her, feeling the skin of his back, hot and clammy, through his shirt. She kept one hand, with the handkerchief inside it, on his back, stroking him with it. With the other hand she started to caress him. He reacted straight away, breathed in sharply and started to moan, his body relaxing and tensing at the same time.

With her fingers expertly working at him, she carefully moved the handkerchief to her other hand. Now was her chance.

At first he didn't realise what was happening and for a very brief moment carried on moaning as before. She pushed the nail file in far as it would go and then twisted it. As his moan turned into a childlike high-pitched wail she rolled him over and crawled away from him as fast as she could. He was already doubled up into a foetal position, his face white and his body shaking. She had seconds to act before the immediate shock wore off.

She gathered up her shoes and jacket. He was starting to react now. Blood was pouring through the hand that was clutching his groin and he was trying to get up. She grabbed the revolver from the chair and thought about using it, but feared that the noise would attract attention. *As long as he doesn't have it.*

She fled the room, taking time to jam a plank of wood against the outside of the door. It would buy her a few seconds. The Luger disappeared through a hole in the floorboards. Before she left the building, she put on her shoes and jacket and straightened her skirt. There was some blood on the hand that had plunged the nail file into him, but not enough to attract attention.

She was almost twenty minutes late at the hospital, but the ward sister believed her story about being given a hard time at a checkpoint. Much later that night she was sitting alone in the canteen, as she always did. Two nurses moved to the table behind her, discussing their shift in casualty.

'No more than twenty-five, I'd say.'

'Really?'

'Yes. They had to bring him in here, he was so bad. Didn't have time to get him to the military hospital.'

'You don't say!'

'Surgeon operated on him straight away. They've had to remove both of them.'

'He won't be prolonging the master race then!'

'We shouldn't laugh really. There'll be hell to pay when they find out who did it. Probably one of the prostitutes who hang around there.'

The other nurse lowered her voice. 'Or the resistance.'

It was a monumental effort of will for her to remain at work for the rest of her shift. When she finished at six she returned to the guest house on a long route that kept her well away from the abandoned building.

She lay still and wide awake on the bed until she heard the landlady stir at eight o'clock. Already packed, she went down and explained that she had received some bad news. Her aunt in Amiens was gravely ill and she had to go to see her immediately.

Grateful that she had so many aunts around France, she pressed a week's rent into the landlady's outstretched palm.

The Germans were checking everyone's papers at the bus station, but hers passed a quick inspection.

When you have to escape from somewhere, get on the first bus or train out. Don't wait for a preferred destination. Do not look around a station as if you are unsure of where to go. They look out for people behaving like that. You can plan where to go next on the journey. When you are queuing for a bus, try to get behind a family or an elderly person. The guards will be relieved to deal with someone straightforward. It is a good idea to act slightly annoyed at the delay, but blame other passengers, not the guards. If the situation allows, pretend you recognise someone on the bus or in a queue as your pass is inspected. It will make you appear more credible.

She couldn't remember which side had told her that, probably a bit of both.

A bus was about to leave for Lens and her priority now was to get out of Lille.

Chapter 27

London, October 1944

'It just does not feel right to me, Edgar. I am afraid that I don't see how we can help you. I'm sorry, but you have to understand that it's a mess out there and I cannot see how this is going to help anyone.'

A silence ticked away the seconds in Major Newby's office in the mews house off Portman Square. Major Edgar had listened to what he had said and had yet to respond. He was sitting in a low chair in the corner of the room, still wearing his coat and trilby and staring intently at Newby through his hands, which were held together as if in prayer, his fingertips touching.

Newby was unnerved by the silence and felt obliged to break it.

'Look, Edgar. You have to agree that we did all that we could to help. We sent her out there, we linked her up with the resistance – we did all that you asked. We—'

'I simply feel,' interrupted Edgar, 'that if we allow him to go over in a supervised and, above all, controlled manner, then hopefully he'll get it out of his system. He can meet the people she knew, see where she lived, ask a few questions and then realise that he is never going to find her. If he goes over on a semi-official visit, so to speak, then we can control what happens. What we don't want is him rampaging around the French countryside, shouting her name from every hilltop. We want him to realise that it is a hopeless task. Of course, we can stop him doing that while the war is still on and he's in the Navy. But once it's all over, then there's nothing to stop him going over there and causing all manner of problems.'

Major Newby walked over to the window and had to bend down to be able to look out of it. An unlit pipe was in his mouth, bouncing up and down as he spoke.

'As I said, it is a bit of a mess over there, Edgar. You chaps had promised us that when she was no longer needed we would be able to get a warning to the resistance group. That never happened, did it, Edgar?'

'No it didn't, but then we didn't know that she was just going to disappear – and from what we gather from the boys at Bletchley, neither did the Germans. Something probably spooked her and off she went. Wherever she is, my guess is that it is an awfully long way from the Pas de Calais, so he's not going to find her.'

'As I say, Edgar – it is a bloody mess out there. Gestapo moved in on her little group as she moved out. There are only two of them left now and I don't think that they are going to welcome Quinn with open arms.'

'Do they suspect that she was a German spy?'

'No. They have enough on their minds as you will find out. They are just suspicious, but I think that they are suspicious of everything, to be frank.'

Newby turned round to face Edgar.

'And you say that he's being a bit difficult?'

'That's a recent development. Up until a week or so ago he was as good as gold, in the circumstances. Remarkably so, actually. Took it much better than we could have hoped, to be honest. We have looked after him, of course; nice desk job at the Admiralty, promotion, comfortable flat. But something happened at the end of September. Don't know what, maybe the enormity of it all just dawned on him. But something made him snap, in rather dramatic circumstances, as it happens. Read this.'

From a thin briefcase Edgar had produced a sheet of paper, covered in dense type. He handed it to Newby.

Belgravia Police Station
202–206 Buckingham Palace Road

Crime Report

My name is Neville Priest and I am a police constable with eighteen years' service in the Metropolitan Police. I am currently based at Belgravia Police Station in Buckingham Palace Road.

On Wednesday, 27 September 1944, I was on a routine patrol in Pimlico Road. I was on the south side of the street, heading in a westerly direction towards Chelsea

Bridge Road. The weather conditions were unremarkable: there had been some light drizzle around lunchtime, but visibility was clear.

At around 4pm I was alerted by a passer-by to a commotion that was coming from a street on the other side of Pimlico Road. I made good haste to the scene of the disturbance, which I discovered to be halfway along Passmore Street.

Upon arriving at the scene I saw that a small crowd numbering approximately seven persons had gathered outside number 25 Passmore Street, which is a residential building. I observed that a long ladder was on the pavement along with two empty buckets and a pool of water. A gentleman approached me to explain that he was a window cleaner who had been retained by the owner of number 25 to clean the windows of the house. He had placed his ladder against the small first floor balcony and gone to collect water. When he returned, he found that a man had used the ladder to climb onto the balcony and had then thrown the ladder down to the pavement.

I then observed that a man in his mid-twenties wearing a Royal Navy uniform was on the balcony. His uniform was in a dishevelled state and he appeared to be distressed. I noticed that his Royal Navy cap was on the pavement. He was holding on to the wrought iron railings to the side of the balcony and appeared to be trying to climb onto the ledge.

I asked him what he was doing and he shouted that he wanted everyone to get out of the way as he was planning to jump from the balcony and did not want people to get hurt when he did so. I urged him not to jump. The window cleaner, who I now know to be a Mr David Osbourne, thereupon shouted abuse at the man and said he would sue him for damage to his ladder. Mr Osbourne also told the man that he should go ahead and jump, but from that height he was unlikely to do much damage to himself.

I told Mr Osbourne that were he not to desist he would find himself under arrest. A lady in the crowd asked the man on the balcony why he was up there. The man started shouting in an incoherent manner. He did, however, keep repeating the phrase 'Why didn't she tell me?' At this point I asked a young man in the crowd to go and find other police officers. I asked the man on the balcony to come down and he replied in an abusive and offensive manner which I do not intend to repeat verbatim in this statement. He then shouted 'It's not Normandy – they are all lying. Edgar is the biggest liar.' He repeated this a number of times and I was able to write it in my notebook.

The balcony railings must have still been wet from the earlier rain because the man slipped as he moved along them.

I noticed that he was crying now and after a while he climbed down from the railings and sat on the floor of the balcony, holding his head in his hands. At this point three Canadian army officers passed by, and with their assistance I was able to place the ladder against the balcony and climb up. The man did not acknowledge my presence; he was just staring ahead and not responding to anything that I said. I was able to escort him through the doors of the balcony into the house. At no time did I form the impression that the man was acting under the influence of alcohol. By this time assistance had arrived and I was able to arrest him for breach of the peace and take him to Belgravia Police Station.

Upon searching him at the police station we discovered that he was a Lieutenant Commander Owen Quinn of the Royal Navy, based at the Admiralty. The matter was then referred to Inspector Page, who I understand liaised with the Admiralty. I am told that the man was released without charge that evening.

Neville Priest (Police Constable)

Addendum to above report

With reference to the very thorough report by PC Priest: I was informed that a Royal Navy officer was in custody at the station and I rang the Admiralty. Within twenty minutes two gentlemen presented themselves at the station and said that they had come to take Quinn away. I told them that this was a police matter. At this point one of the men used my telephone to call Scotland Yard. Within five minutes I received a call from a senior officer at Scotland Yard telling me to do as the men asked and release Quinn without charge. I was informed by the men that Quinn had recently lost his wife in an air raid and was under some pressure. I was asked to instruct PC Priest not to discuss this incident further and was told that I myself should regard the matter as closed. Quinn was released into the gentlemen's custody at a quarter to six that evening.

Frank Page (Inspector)

Newby finished reading the statement and handed it back to Edgar, knowingly nodding his head as he did so.

'Poor chap. I rather see what you mean, Edgar. And you say that you have no idea what may have triggered this off?'

'None whatsoever. As I say, he'd seemed to have taken the whole business terribly well, once he found out what was going on. We gave him some pills at the time to calm him down and I can only surmise that they must have been working. Whether he was relying on them and then stopped taking them, I just don't know.'

'And I presume you were one of the two gentlemen who turned up at the police station?'

'Indeed. Carted him off to a safe house in Surrey. He didn't say a word. Stared out of the window the whole way there. Doc then pumped him full of something that sent him to sleep for the next twenty-four hours. Calmed down a good deal when he woke up, quite apologetic, actually. Desperate to find her, though. Has to go to France – that kind of thing. "Before it is too late" he kept saying; not sure what he meant by that. If I told him once, I told him a dozen times, "You are not going to find her, Quinn". But he wants to go. So, as I say, let him go out there, get it out of his system.'

Newby walked back to his desk and toyed with a pouch of tobacco and a box of matches.

'And any idea as to what caused this behaviour?'

'Told us he had run out of his tablets and thought he could cope. Doctor gave him another batch and he promised to take them. Seems to be more or less back to normal, apart from this obsession with going to France to find her. One of our psychiatrist chaps came to have a look at him and said we need to let him get it out of his system. Quite bonkers.'

'Who? Quinn?'

'No, Newby. The psychiatrist. So that's where we are. Apparently if we send Quinn on a trip to France then he'll be as right as rain.

'I am prepared to sanction him going out there, but it does have to be controlled. Nicole is in France pretty much most of the time now, looking after the SOE agents we sent out there, finding out what has happened to those who disappeared – the genuine ones that is, Edgar – so I would remind you that this is a sensitive situation. I ought to tell you that the FTP leadership are hopping mad about all this. They suspect that we may have put a German spy in their midst, so they may want their pound of flesh.'

'Meaning what, precisely?'

'Ideally, they would like to get their hands on Nathalie, or whatever her real name is. Failing that, you may want to consider giving them… someone else? Would certainly help us if we could get them off our backs for a while. If you could offer up some other sacrificial lamb, that would help. The atmosphere is pretty vengeful out there, I can tell you. Can't say that I blame them. Have a think about it.'

A thought occurred to Major Edgar. 'I think I may have just the right person for them. In time.'

'Very well then. Quinn can go out there, for what it is worth. I will tell Nicole to meet up with him and she can take him to meet the surviving two members of the group. Let him wander around and realise he is not going to find her. With some luck, he'll appreciate that it is a hopeless situation. As you say, let us hope that he gets it out of his system. One thing occurs to me though, Edgar.'

'What is that?'

'It is not exactly in your interests for him to find her, is it?'

'Meaning?'

'What is going to happen if he does find her, Edgar? Are you going to put her on trial? Let the whole world know what happened? I doubt it.'

It was Edgar's turn now to walk over to the small window. He had to go down on his haunches to be able to peer through it. Sacks of coal were being hauled off the back of a lorry in the courtyard below and two dogs were fighting over an empty sack.

'I really do not think that is going to happen. Certainly not if I have anything to do with it.'

Pas de Calais, October 1944

Edgar managed to find Owen Quinn a seat on an RAF flight to Le Touquet in the last week of October. He fixed it up on the Monday afternoon, but did not want Quinn to have too much notice; he certainly did not want him going round broadcasting his trip to anyone who would listen. So he let his man at the Admiralty know on the Tuesday that Quinn would be away for a few days on official business, perhaps a week, certainly no more than that.

He waited until Quinn returned home from the pub at around eight o'clock. He was staying longer there each day now and Edgar was getting concerned. *Sooner we get him out there and back here, the better.* And then he called. 'Good news – going to France in the morning. I'll pick you up. Be waiting outside at seven thirty. Only room for a small case. Get a decent night's sleep.'

Edgar duly picked him at the appointed time. Quinn cut a forlorn figure, standing alone at the bottom of the steps leading up to the main entrance of the house where his flat was, anxiously studying his watch, a small Navy kitbag resting against his leg.

Within a couple of minutes they were on the main road to Oxford and by nine o'clock they were at RAF Benson in Oxfordshire. Two hundred and seventy-one Squadron were flying de Havilland Dragon Rapides into France and Edgar had called in one or two favours to get him aboard, along with a lot of documents, a crate of whisky which he was concerned that Quinn might think was for him, an army padre and a couple of Canadian Army officers. Edgar looked after such formalities as there were, which seemed to comprise having a chat with a group captain in a Nissen hut.

At quarter to ten they were led out across the tarmac to the plane. Edgar came with him as far as the steps and shook his hand – 'Good luck and bon voyage!' – and by ten o'clock he was airborne.

Owen Quinn left England for his first ever visit to France with the last vestiges of summer hanging uncertainly in the air. When he landed in France an hour later, the winds had a colder edge to them and the sky was more grey than blue. The plane landed and taxied back to the small cluster of buildings.

'Don't worry, Quinn, you'll be met at the other end,' Edgar had told him.

'By whom?'

'Don't worry. They will know who you are. You will be well looked after. It has all been taken care of.'

A light brown Renault was parked between the De Havilland and the buildings. As he climbed down the steps a woman climbed out of the car, struggling to tie a scarf around her head as the wind took hold. As he came past the car she asked him whether he was Owen Quinn and he told her he was. 'How did you recognise me?'

'The Navy uniform. My name is Nicole. Glad to meet you.'

Nicole was immaculately dressed and extremely proper. Quinn realised after just a few minutes that she was one of those people who would say as much as she needed to and then no more. Her silences were not to be interpreted as rudeness, it would just be that she had said what she needed to. He suspected that it was a natural trait, reinforced by years of secret work.

'We will head straight for Boulogne sur Mer. It should take an hour, but it is difficult to judge,' she said as the car headed north from the airport. 'The roads are a bit of a mess. There are some good stretches though and apparently this machine can do seventy miles an hour, although I've not yet managed to get up there yet.'

'What car is it?'

'A Renault Primaquatre. Courtesy of a German official in Calais. Apparently, he purloined it at the beginning of the war in Paris, so as long as I don't drive it down there I should be all right.'

Owen was shocked when the car entered Boulogne just after one o'clock. He had not been expecting the extent of the damage that he saw all around him. Groups of German prisoners of war in their grey uniforms were clearing rubble away without much enthusiasm.

Nicole glanced over at him in the passenger seat and smiled. 'We're responsible for most of this you know. RAF. Hit the town very hard. Big submarine base in the port. Lots of bombs went astray, as you can see. Canadians had a bit of a battle coming in, but luckily we are being treated as liberators so there is not too much ill feeling.'

The Renault pulled up in front of a small hotel in the town centre, which appeared to be the only undamaged building in its block.

'You're booked in here. I'll give you an hour to check in and get unpacked and then I will meet you in reception.'

By two o'clock they were the only customers in a café near the Notre Dame in the main square, apart from a young Canadian officer talking intently in French to the waitress. When they were finally able to attract her attention they ordered one of the two dishes remaining on the menu and ate their omelettes in silence. When Nicole had finished, which was some time after Owen, she neatly arranged her cutlery on the plate. She could now start talking.

'Very well. I do understand that this is a very difficult situation for you. I hope that you will appreciate that it is also a very difficult situation for the people out here, especially those that I will be taking you to meet this afternoon. People here do not know the truth about your wife, and it ought to remain that way. As far as they are concerned, she was an SOE agent who came out here and who then disappeared. It is best that they do not know she is your wife. I have told them that you are a British officer who has come to find her. They are suspicious, but then suspicion is endemic at the moment. It is everywhere. Do you speak French?'

'Some.'

'Are you familiar with the word *épuration*? No? It means purge, or purification. There is plenty of it going on at the moment. This country was occupied for four years, parts of it still are. The Germans could not have managed such an orderly occupation without a good deal of co-operation from the French population. Most people just got on with their lives, did not want to cause trouble. A few collaborated with the Germans, far more than the French would have you believe. And then a few joined the resistance – but this time far fewer than the French would have you believe. Do you realise that it was almost a year into the occupation before the first German soldier was killed by the resistance? A bit of a myth has grown up around the resistance, I ought to tell you. For most of the occupation, *résistants* were seen as a nuisance by the general population. They just wanted to get on with their lives. Then as the tide of war changed, suddenly everyone is in the resistance. The *résistants* even call them the *Septembrists*, the people who only emerged once the invasion of Normandy began.'

289

Nicole stood up and left some money on the table and put on her coat. She did not continue talking until they were back in the car. They had to drive slowly. Enough rubble had been cleared to make the roads passable, but in most cases the road was not yet wide enough for two vehicles to pass. As most of the other vehicles were military, the Renault was constantly having to pull in.

On the outskirts of the town she halted in front of a badly damaged building.

'This is the factory where your wife worked, or at least the remains of it. She assembled electrical parts.' They paused for a few moments and then drove on. The road became easier outside the town. Quinn noticed that they had entered a village called Hesdin-l'Abbé, where they appeared to be the only car on the road. Just by the church they pulled up outside a row of cottages.

'And this is where your wife stayed while she was in the area. This house here.' It was the only one in the row where all the curtains were drawn. 'She lodged here with another member of the resistance group. They were all based in this village. We are going to meet two of them now. You need to know that while she was here, your wife was known as Geraldine.'

'Was that her real name?'

'No, of course not. No one knows her real name. Geraldine was the name we gave her. Geraldine Leclerc. And remember. They do not know the truth about her, whatever they suspect. They wanted to be able to tell you what happened themselves and I agreed to that. We owe it to them.'

The house was larger than some of the others that Quinn had noticed in the village and it was set back from the road, behind a low stone wall and a pretty though slightly unkempt front garden. It was on the outskirts of the village and Owen could see a forest rising in the distance. Nicole signalled for Owen to pause halfway down the path while she went in. A minute later she signalled for him to enter.

A man and a woman in their late thirties, or perhaps early forties, were sitting around the table in a large kitchen. Neither of them smiled when he entered the room, though the man did point to an empty chair where he should sit. Through the kitchen window, Owen could see an older man in the garden.

'Françoise, Lucien – this is Lieutenant Commander Quinn from the Royal Navy.' They both nodded. Owen noticed that the man was sitting in a wheelchair and winced whenever he moved. 'He has come to France to try to find Geraldine. He may have a few questions for you, but first, please could you tell him what happened?'

Lucien made a hand movement towards his wife. She would speak. Owen noticed that her eyes were red and she was tightly clutching a large white handkerchief, twisting it as she spoke.

'We were not really an active resistance cell until March or April this year. Pierre had joined the FTP earlier in the war but was not very active. In March they asked him to put together a group in this village. The FTP operates in cells of four people, a leader and three others. So he asked Jean to join him. He was one of his pupils and was a bright boy, very strong and knew the countryside very well. And then he asked us. In fact, he did not want a husband and wife to be in the same group, but he needed us both. Lucien is... was... a *cheminot*, he worked on the railways. I was a supervisor at a factory in Boulogne. Because it was supplying equipment for the German Army I had good security clearance, it was easy for me to get in and out of Boulogne. In any case, this village is not exactly full of people queuing up to join the resistance. Geraldine joined us towards the end of April, I think it was. Lucien?'

Her husband nodded.

'At the end of April then. She landed not far from here and brought a transmitter with her, and explosives. I got her a job at the factory and she lodged with Jean in his father's house. It was only Jean there as his father had been sent to Germany and his mother is dead. It was fine, there were no problems. We would make transmissions to London and Geraldine would get the information that we were to prepare for a landing in this area. We carried out some sabotage on the railways.'

Lucien muttered something. His wife continued.

'Geraldine had been trained in explosives in England, so she was our expert. Lucien wonders how much of an expert she really was. What would have been our biggest act of sabotage did not happen. It was near here actually. Lucien had information that a German supply train was going to be passing through a wood late at night. If we could have blown it up it would have caused major damage. Because of the position, it would have taken days for them to recover the train, and then they would have had to repair the track. Lucien went down with Geraldine to lay the explosives while the rest of us stood guard.'

'I never saw her make the connection, so I do not know the truth,' said Lucien. 'All I know is that afterwards, Pierre was very suspicious.

He just could not understand why the charge had failed. But I never checked the connection, that was her job. I was keeping an eye on the track.' He shifted himself uncomfortably in his wheelchair and continued.

'But we did carry out some successful sabotage after that. Not very big jobs, we had lost too much of our explosives already on that first attempt, but it was enough to cause a bit of trouble.

'We carried on through June and July. Transmissions, sabotage. Our main job was to wait until the invasion here and then do what we could to help. But then in the middle of July, Geraldine disappeared.'

'Do you remember the date?' asked Owen. He was looking up from the small notebook he had in front of him.

Both Françoise and Lucien laughed bitterly. Françoise's eyes filled with tears as she carried on speaking.

'Oh yes, we remember the date. The 17th of July. It was a Monday. Monday, the 17th of July.' There was a long and complete silence, apart from the thud of wood being chopped in the garden.

'I had gone to Samer to see my sister who had just had a baby. My father came with me.' She nodded towards the older man in the garden. 'We were about to return when Father Pierre turned up. He is the priest in Samer. The priest from this village, Father Raymonde, had come to see him. The Gestapo were raiding our house and looking for me.' She broke down into a sob. Lucien continued.

'I was at the station in Boulogne when they arrested me. The Gestapo. I was taken to their headquarters in the town and thrown into a cell. Jean was already in the cell next to me. He had been badly beaten. I think he must have fought with them. There was blood everywhere. They took it in turns that day and through the night to torture us. Who else was in the group, where was Geraldine, what did we know about her, where is the transmitter, our weapons. They wanted to know everything.

'Pierre told us that if we ever got caught, to hold out for as long as possible – even a few hours will give the others time to get away. Of course I did not know that Pierre was already dead.'

Quinn looked up, raising his eyebrows.

'Yes, he shot himself when they came to arrest him. And, of course, I had no idea whether Françoise was safe. But I said nothing. Jean, he argued with them the whole time, he fought them. At about six in the morning – that would be the Tuesday – they must have been doing the most terrible things to him. I heard him cry for his mother. He let out this terrible howl and then there was silence and soon after that I saw them carry his body from the cell. I don't know what they did to him in the end, but it was terrible. I have heard animals caught in traps and this was far worse.

'Of course, they could concentrate on me after that. They broke every toe. They pulled out my fingernails. They broke my knees. They put electricity in places I can't tell you about but the pain was so bad that I passed out. When I was coming round on one occasion I heard them talking – they must have thought I was still unconscious. They said something like "We just need to find his wife now". So I reckoned that meant Françoise was the only one who had escaped, which meant I could tell them about Pierre. So I took a risk and when they tortured me next, I told them about Pierre. I also told them that I had no idea where Françoise was. There had been an argument I said and she had left home. I don't think they believed me but they weren't sure. I had told them about Pierre and they were not to know that I had overheard them talking. Then I just collapsed. It was like a coma. They could not wake me up. I was taken to the prison near Calais. I was freed by the resistance there just as the Canadians came in.'

'And you, Françoise. What happened?'

'My father and I went into hiding. There is a lot of forest and marsh in that area and my father knows it very well, it is where he was brought up. We survived. It would have been better if I had not survived.'

Owen started to ask a question, but Nicole put her hand on his arm to stop him. Françoise continued.

'When they came to this house to find me, my mother was here with my children.' She gestured to a photograph on a shelf of two boys. 'They took my mother and the boys. They took them to a barn, where no one could hear anything. They must have tried to make them to say where I was, we do not know exactly what happened. But we do know what happened next, one of the workers on a nearby farm was hiding in the trees and he saw it. They locked the three of them in the barn and set fire to it. He heard their screams. Apparently, they lasted for ten minutes.'

For a full five minutes Françoise wept into her handkerchief before she could continue.

'Georges was ten, Charles was seven. My mother was in her sixties. So you see, Lucien and I survived, but for what? We have each other and we have my father, but we now have no life. We have entered the winter of our lives and it will only get darker, it will never be warm again. People do not know what to say to us. They are very nice, they bring us food,' she pointed at a kitchen top with bread and baskets of vegetables on it, 'but we have little appetite. They say things like, maybe you can have more children.'

Lucien shook his head.

'After what the Gestapo did to Lucien, that is impossible. Ten and seven they were. Georges and Charles. A life without children, it is unimaginable.'

Another long pause. He was shocked beyond belief at the grief and the dignity in this room. His own problems now seemed so irrelevant that he felt embarrassed. Françoise's father came in from the garden; he walked over to his daughter and placed a hand on her shoulder, and she reached back to place her hand on his. When he spoke again, Owen tried to sound as sympathetic as possible.

'And what do you think alerted the Gestapo? Was it Geraldine? Did she inform on you?'

Françoise spoke now.

'We don't think so, because they were so desperate to find out where she was. From what we have found out since, a man went to Jean's cottage to look for her. He said he was from the factory but, of course, he was not. One of the collaborators who was working for the police was arrested after the liberation and he gave some information before he was... dealt with. He said that this man was from German Intelligence. The Abwehr I think it is. We do not know what he was doing there, there must have been some information that she was a British agent. But apparently, he found a note Geraldine had left for Jean. We do not know exactly what it said, but it was a warning of a type, telling him to escape. Jean thought a lot of her and he protected her. Maybe it was her way of thanking him.'

–

Nicole waited until they had left the village before she pulled off the main road and parked on a verge. To either side of them were rolling fields and trees. A flock of sheep was grazing in the field closest to them.

'It is Wednesday today. I can assist you until the weekend and then I have to continue my work.'

'What do you do?'

'You don't know what I do?'

'I have an idea.'

'My section of the SOE trained agents to work in occupied France and then sent them out here. Nearly five hundred of them. Over a hundred of them have not returned. Some of them, we know, were killed, but others are missing, some are still in occupied areas like Alsace. My job is to try to find out what happened to them.'

A shepherd had now joined the flock in the field to their right and his dogs were herding it up the hill. The shepherd bent down to pick up one of the lambs. Nicole continued.

'You know, I often accompanied these agents to their plane before they were flown out to France. Many of them were parachuted into France, some landed in Lysanders, like your wife. But it was always a difficult journey. I often felt that I was sending people to their deaths. But they were all so brave. They all thanked me, you know.'

'With your wife, it was different. Did you know that I was with her during her training too? We had to make special arrangements, we couldn't let her be trained with other agents or at the places we normally used. I tried not to get close to her, but that was not difficult. She never gave anything of herself. She was as cold as steel. I always thought that if she had been one of ours, she would have made a very good agent. Did you love her?'

Owen was surprised by the question.

'Yes… I did. More than anything else in the world. I know that I shouldn't, that it's wrong, but I…'

'Don't worry. It is not a crime to love the wrong person. Most people manage it at least once in their lives. I can see you need some answers.'

'Do you think that we will find her?'

'Honestly? No. The Abwehr were good, very professional. Probably only one or two people in it were aware of her true identity, no more than that. She has shown how resourceful she is and how she copes under pressure. Can you imagine living the lies she has led – here and in England? I mean, did you think you had a normal relationship?'

'Of course.'

'Exactly my point. You are an intelligent young man. You believed that it was a normal relationship, and maybe in some respects it was.

She was clever. Come on now. We go back to the hotel and tomorrow we resume our search.'

Owen Quinn felt humbled by the grief and the dignity he had encountered at Françoise and Lucien's house, although it had done nothing to diminish his determination to find his wife. But he was equally determined to do what he could to help Françoise and Lucien.

–

Quinn came down for breakfast at eight the next morning. Nicole was waiting in the tiny reception area. 'We are going to Samer,' she said. 'We will talk in the car. There is no time for breakfast.'

'Françoise contacted me last night,' she said as they headed out of Boulogne. 'She felt guilty, I don't know why. Maybe she picked up that there was a connection between you and her. She has one clue that she didn't bother to tell us about, but she has now. She hasn't told anyone about it, which is lucky for you. Apparently, Geraldine was seen in Samer the morning she disappeared. She was seen getting on a bus to St Omer.'

'By whom?'

'By one of the villagers from Hesdin who happened to be in Samer that morning. She knew that Geraldine was staying with Jean, but she only mentioned it to Françoise last week. This villager did say that a local *gendarme* was checking people's identity cards as they boarded the bus. So now we are going to the police station in Samer.'

The small police station was inside the *Mairie* and it did not take them long to find the policeman who had been checking the passes that day. There were not many policemen in Samer.

'Yes, I think I remember,' he said.

'Please look at this photograph.'

'Yes, probably.'

'Where was the bus going?'

'Desvres first, then St Omer.'

'You sure? Yes? And what was her name?'

'Hélène something or other.'

'Not Geraldine?'

'No! I told you, Hélène.'

'You sure?'

'Yes, of course I am sure. My mother is called Hélène. And my wife. I don't forget a Hélène, as much as I might try!'

So they drove to St Omer, the roads crowded and progress slow. They tried all the hotels in the town. No one recognised the photograph. They had split up by now to try to cover more places. Owen slipped into a couple of jewellers on Rue Carnot.

'Does this brooch mean anything?'

'It's cameo.'

'Thank you – other than that?'

'No, nice example, good quality, nothing exceptional.'

'And the 'GT' on the back?'

'Maybe someone's initials, sir.'

'Thank you. Thank you very much.'

It was getting dark now and they booked into one of the hotels. It would give them the evening to ask in the restaurants and bars. When they emerged from the hotel to do that, Nicole had an idea. 'We know the date, don't we? Let's check at the police station.'

The sergeant was having a quiet evening and was very happy to help, especially an officer from the British Army and such a beautiful lady. 'Thank you very much sir, even our darkest hour, you never forgot France.' He was puffed up with his own self-importance. As long as they didn't ask any awkward questions about what he was up to during the war. He was only doing his duty. He had a family to consider…

Quinn bit his tongue. He thought better of explaining the difference between the Army and the Navy. At least we have one of each, he thought. And he decided not to ask the *gendarme* what he did in the war.

'The seventeenth of July, you say?'

'Yes, it was a Monday.'

'It was. That's what it says in my book too.' A loud, toothy laugh. Both Owen and Nicole briefly joined in.

'And you say an identity card was stolen that day?'

'No. We are just wondering whether one was reported as stolen that day. We are not sure whether one was.'

The sergeant looked puzzled, but carefully studied the book.

'Ah yes. Two reported missing that day.'

'Can we have the details?' asked Nicole.

'Were they your cards? Because if not, this would be most improper.'

Nicole smiled very sweetly as she palmed a couple of folded bank-notes across the desk.

'Of course, for the British Army, this is not a problem. Henri Laporte from St Omer reported his card missing that day.'

'Age.'

'Sixty.'

'And the other?'

'Nicole Rougier. Aged twenty-seven.'

Nicole Rougier. 'And where is she from?'

'Place of residence, Béthune. That is near here. Place of birth, let me see… Mulhouse. In Alsace.'

It was a breakthrough. Of sorts. They had done well to trace Geraldine from the village to St Omer and now, acting on Nicole's instinct, they had established that the identity card of a women of a similar age to Geraldine had been lost, presumed stolen, in St Omer on the same day. It didn't prove anything, of course. It was probably complete coincidence. But Nicole had a growing regard for Geraldine's prowess as an agent. It was possible that she had stolen the identity of Nicole Rougier.

She was quite probably going to continue her journey home in stages and at each stage would try to assume a new identity. She would presumably target women of a similar age and, where possible, from a similar part of the country. It was a risky strategy in the short term, but once you had stolen a new card, it would help keep the scent cold.

They returned to the hotel. Had they bothered to turn round after they had left the police station that evening, which, of course, they had no reason to do, they would have seen a tall figure wearing a long dark coat and matching trilby enter it.

–

Friday was the last day that Nicole could help Owen. They decided to stay in St Omer to see if they could trace where she had gone from there, possibly as Nicole Rougier. But they drew a blank. No one at the train station or the bus station could recall seeing her. They asked in shops and cafés, they revisited the places they had tried the day before.

The truth was, she could have gone anywhere. Nicole had to continue with her own work. They sat in a small bar by the train station. She was heading back towards Normandy. Where would he go?

'Paris. I will try there. I am not sure why. She said she came from there, but I suppose that was a lie like everything else. But it seems like the best place to go next.'

Nicole had torn a scrap of paper from her notebook and was writing on it. Truly professional, thought Owen. Avoiding leaving an impression of the writing on the blank sheets underneath. Impressive.

'Here. I didn't give this to you, understand? If you are going to Paris, visit this man. That is his address. I met him when I was there last month. He will be very helpful. Tell him that I sent you. See how you get on with him and then judge for yourself how much you want to tell him, but if I were you, I would trust him. You don't have many other options.'

'Why are you helping me like this?'

Nicole thought long and hard.

'I was wondering that myself. I am certainly doing more than I was told to do. I was meant to keep you with me all the time, not let you out of my sight and deliver you home in one piece with no harm done. If I am honest, Owen, I don't think they want you to find her. I was asked to report any leads we found. So why am I helping you? I'm not sure. Maybe I am helping you because you aren't after revenge. I think it is because when I asked you whether you loved her, you admitted you did. "More than anything else in the world," I think was what you said. I admire honesty. You deserve to find her. But you had better think carefully about what you'll do if you do find her.'

Chapter 28

Lens-Reims-Nancy, September-October 1944

Like a river, she meandered without any obviously logical route down the eastern edges of a France steeling itself for liberation. She knew where she was heading but was seemingly reluctant to arrive there. Like a naughty child afraid of facing up to punishment, she procrastinated throughout her journey, looking for excuses to avoid moving on.

To a great extent her journey was dictated by the circumstance of war. She had arrived in Lens to find the town in a state of panic in the aftermath of an Allied bombing raid. The bus was stopped by a German tank pulled across a road just before the town centre. A soldier came onboard and shouted at everyone to get off, although few passengers needed to be told.

The German garrison was in the process of evacuation. An army truck had pulled up on the other side of the road and soldiers were loading it with food and other provisions from a large shop with broken windows. The owner was pleading with an officer not to take everything.

The officer walked over to the entrance and told his men to stop. The owner, a thickset man in his late thirties with a large, clean, white apron, smiled and put his arms round a couple of children who were standing with him on the pavement. The officer adjusted his gloves, briskly walked over to the owner, removed his pistol from its holster and shot him through the temple. He nodded at his men for them to carry on.

Hélène Blanc was shocked – not so much at what she had just seen, but rather that she was no longer so shocked by it. She had been considering staying in Lens but, from what she could see, she would soon be on her own. On the journey from Lille she had realised

300

that she had to regard her Hélène Blanc identity as compromised. It was likely that when the Gestapo started to investigate the castration of the soldier in Lille they would be looking at reports of anyone matching the description of the attacker who had recently left town. They could identify her through the hospital and certainly through her landlady, who would have registered her with the authorities while she was staying at the guest house. She doubted the landlady's capacity or inclination not to co-operate with the Germans. Her priority in Lens, she decided, was to find a new identity but, judging by the speed at which the town was being deserted, that appeared to be futile.

The army truck had pulled away and a small group of people had detached themselves from the stream of civilians wending their way out of the town. The two children were howling and a woman was bending down asking them where their mother was. Another woman and two men carried the shot owner into the shop. Hélène followed them in and, feeling she at least ought to do something, knelt down by the body and felt for a pulse.

'I wouldn't bother. He was dead before he hit the ground.' The man who was speaking was about her age and height. The collar of his jacket was turned up and he was not wearing a tie. As he lit a cigarette the match briefly illuminated a thin and unshaven face. His green eyes appeared translucent. He looked as if he could do with a good meal and a few days in the sun.

'I'm a nurse.'

'Congratulations,' he said, bowing slowly and grinning. 'You ought to have known he was dead then. Not many people survive a German bullet through the head. I'm a teacher and even I knew that. My name is Laurent, by the way.' He stretched over the corpse to shake her hand, as if they had been introduced by friends while strolling. Ash from his cigarette floated onto the body.

'And do you have a name?'

'Pardon?' She was lost in her thoughts, unsure of whether to stay or to leave, to take some food from the shop or not.

'My name is Laurent,' he said slowly, as if she were hard of hearing. 'What are you called?'

'Hélène. I arrived here just before from Lille. I really don't know where I'm heading. What is the latest news?'

The shop was quiet now. The other people who had helped carry the body in had left and the hysterical children must have been taken away. Flies had begun to buzz around the dead body and the food that had been strewn across the floor by the Germans in their haste to take as much as they could. A smashed jar of jam was getting particular attention.

'The Allies are pushing in from the west, mostly Americans and Canadians. In most places the Germans are staying and fighting. I wouldn't stay around anywhere like here where there is going to be fighting. People seem to be heading into the country to hide until they can then go to somewhere liberated by the Allies. Hard to think it will all be over soon. That is when life will get interesting. Why don't you join me? We can go for a long walk in the country together.'

They headed south and stayed together as travelling companions for a month. Laurent had made the most of his asthma, he told her, to avoid being sent away as forced labour and he was able to remain in Lens throughout the war as a teacher. He made a passing reference or two to helping out the resistance. Nothing much, he emphasised, just passing messages and things like that. He wasn't brave enough to do much else, he assured her.

'You watch though,' he told her. 'Soon everyone will have been in the resistance. It will turn out that France was a country of heroes while the Germans were here. It wasn't at the time, that's all!'

On their third day together, as they looked over Cambrai from a nearby hill, she confided that she had been involved in the resistance too, in Lille. Like him, nothing too important, but there had been 'an incident' with a German soldier and she had decided to leave town.

Laurent nodded, not probing any further. He didn't ask too many questions, preferring to have her as an audience to whom he could give the names of the trees and plants they saw, and for whom he could recite poems, tell her about medieval French history and the books he'd read and reread during the war.

They headed south, following the Reims road, and by the second week in September they were deep into the Champagne region.

'If the Germans had any sense they would have taken it all with them,' he said. 'The true taste of France.' But they hadn't. Just to the north of Reims they came across an abandoned château by the banks of the River Aisne where the liberation of the city was being celebrated by anyone who was passing by.

An elderly gardener, wearing his Great War medals for the first time in four years, told them that the château had been requisitioned by the Germans in 1940. Before that it had belonged to a family with German connections, so none of the dozens of people who had converged on the château seemed to have any qualms about partaking of its hospitality.

'They never treated me well,' the gardener confided in them as he led them through the cellar.

On their second night in the château, Laurent and Hélène were sat by the banks of the river, halfway through their second bottle of Mumm Grand Cru. Their shoulders were touching, though during their time together, Laurent had made no attempt to go further than a friendly arm around her shoulder.

'You are married, Hélène?'

She was slightly startled. He asked so few questions and when he did, nothing intrusive. She was about to say no, but realised that she was playing with the cheap wedding ring she had bought in a second-hand shop in Lille. It was something she had felt obliged to do after being questioned by the matron in the hospital.

'My husband was killed. A few months ago, by the Germans in the Pas de Calais. It was in a forest near Boulogne. I had no idea I was pregnant at the time.' She held out a hand in front of her, palm down. Enough.

Laurent was silenced by the amount of detail along with the lack of it. Hélène was drawing jagged patterns in the grass with a twig. He pulled her close to him as the tears began to streak down her face, their lines illuminated by the moonlight bouncing off the river.

'I suppose that at a time other than this, it would be a consolation. When is the baby due?'

'Late October, maybe early November.'

Her head was bowed down, her hair covering all of her face and the tears flowing quite freely.

'At least your baby will be born in a free France. You must have loved your husband very much.'

For the next few minutes she was so inconsolable that even Laurent, never lost for the right thing to say or to do, was helpless. All he could do was apologise, rub her back and pour her another drink.

When she regained her composure she assured him that she was fine. He was not to worry. It did her good to cry. She felt better. In any case, it was more of a wartime romance than anything else. Probably wouldn't have lasted.

What had disconcerted her so greatly was her reaction to Laurent's statement that she must have loved her husband very much. She had not hesitated to think about his question, because there was no doubt in her mind that she did love her husband very much. Not the fictional French husband apparently killed in a French forest, but the real one in England, who she could only wish was here with her now.

They remained at the château for two more days. By then it had been drained of champagne and American troops had arrived to take the estate over.

They took a circuitous route into Reims: not long after leaving the château they came across a platoon of American soldiers who told them that there was still some danger in the area. Small pockets of Germans remained and it was especially hazardous around the airport. That was their most direct route into the city, but the Americans advised them to head east. That side of the city was safe. 'Once you've crossed the River Vesle you know you can enter the city.'

Which was how they arrived at the small village on the banks of the Vesle. On the outskirts of the village a group of around thirty German prisoners of war were being led away in a column. An American Army jeep pulled up alongside them and a sergeant leaned over, shouting above the noise of the engine.

'Speak English?'

'A little,' said Nathalie.

'You planning on going into the village?'

'We're passing that way.'

The sergeant stood up in the jeep and looked back at the village.

'Just be careful. They're in a vengeful mood. We had to do a deal with them. They've let us take these prisoners in return for leaving the officers behind.'

The village opened out slowly in front of them: the houses were large with small plots of land between them. The road leading through the village and the two or three that they passed leading off the main road were all wide, with well-kept verges. They could not see any people, and so headed in the direction of the church steeple. Ahead of them was a commotion that grew louder as they approached.

Next to the church was a large house, set back from the road and linked to the church by a high wall, which appeared to have been recently whitewashed. A row of trees peered out from behind the wall, some of the leaves beginning to turn brown. A large crowd was facing the wall. Standing with their backs to it were two men in steel-grey German uniforms.

'What's going on?' Laurent asked a man at the back of the crowd.

The man took a step back so as to talk to them away from the others.

'The Germans carried out a reprisal shooting here two months ago. The resistance blew up a German truck just outside the village and the Germans shot four local men against that wall. The Americans captured the German unit that carried out the shooting and brought them back here so they could be identified. There was almost a riot: people want revenge. Eventually it was agreed that the two officers who were in charge of the unit would be left behind.'

'What's going to happen to them?' she asked.

'What do you think?'

An elderly man wearing medals and holding a rifle was shouting at the two officers.

'You have to answer our charges!' he kept repeating.

'No comprehends,' the older of the two officers replied, shaking his head. He was around fifty and plump, his face a deep red and his eyes imploring. His hands were tied behind his back and his nose bloody. He was trembling violently. His companion was much younger, perhaps in his twenties. He stood very still, his face impassive and with possibly the faintest trace of a smile, as if he was a man resigned to his fate. His trousers were bloodstained and he was jacketless, the front of his white shirt ripped.

A woman came and joined the old man who had been shouting at them.

'You cannot pretend that you don't understand. We know that you speak French well enough, you bastards. You certainly spoke it when you shot those men against this wall.'

Between the two Germans and the crowd an elderly priest stood to the side. He was holding a tall cross in his hands. The priest appeared to be terrified and he was leaning on the cross for support.

The man turned to Laurent.

'The Germans have been pretending that they don't understand us. Some of the villagers are insisting that we cannot do anything to them until we know that they understand what we're saying. Others just want to shoot them straight away. It's crazy.' He lowered his voice.

'It is anarchy, to be honest. We would have been better letting the Americans take care of them. You don't speak German by any chance?'

Laurent shook his head and looked at Hélène. Purposefully she strode to the front of the crowd.

'I speak German. I can translate for you.'

There was a murmur of approval.

'Tell them,' said the old man, 'that they are accused of shooting the four hostages here. We want to know if there is anything they have to say.'

She stepped forward and translated what the man had said into German.

The older officer leaned forward.

'Please, *madame*, you must understand. We were acting under orders. I actually managed to persuade my superiors that we should only shoot four people: they wanted us to kill one hostage for every German soldier killed on that lorry – twelve! We should be treated as prisoners of war. This is not a proper way to deal with us.'

She translated back into French.

The woman and the man with medals conferred. The man then spoke.

'Tell them that is as good as an admission. They are going to be shot.' Behind him two men emerged from the crowd carrying what appeared to be German machine guns.

'No!' said the older officer. 'This is a terrible mistake. *Madame*, please... I have a wife and children... you must tell them to save me. I would have been shot if I had not taken the hostages. Please...'

He was weeping and had sunk to his knees. The younger officer next to him spoke for the first time.

'Get up, sir, and shut up. You know what they are going to do to us. Let them get on with it. We're finished.'

'Do not speak to me like that! I am your commanding officer!'

'Then act like it, sir. Where is your dignity?'

The two men with machine guns had stepped forward now.

'Ask them,' said the woman, 'if they have any last words.'

She translated.

The younger officer shook his head and looked slowly around him. The older one spoke quickly, looking at the priest as he did so.

'I am a practising Catholic, even during the war. Please allow me to confess. Please.'

She glanced over to the priest who appeared to have caught the gist of what the German had said. He looked quizzically at her, the cross quivering in his hands as he did so.

She allowed the silence that had descended to linger. In that time a small flock of ravens descended on the trees behind the white wall.

She stepped towards the two officers. As she got nearer, she could smell the fear.

'You've lost, haven't you? Accept that.'

With that, she turned round and walked back towards the crowd.

'What did he have to say?' the woman asked her.

She shook her head. 'Nothing. He just said to get on with it.'

One of the two men had trouble releasing the catch on his machine gun. When they fired, it was clear not much had been planned. Both fired at the older officer, leaving the younger one still standing – unscathed and shocked. There was no smile or defiance on his face now, just a wide-open mouth, unseeing eyes and a look of utter fear. The two gunmen stepped towards him. One man's gun jammed and the other only let out a short burst before stopping.

Above them, the sky had blackened as the ravens flew off en masse, their panicked shrieking merging with the ring of the machine gun fire.

The younger officer had slumped to the ground, where he was groaning loudly and writhing on the bright green strip of grass. The old man with the medals stepped forward. He was holding a pistol and stood no more than two feet from the officer. He was taking careful aim at his head, but he was shaking violently. His first shot missed completely, ricocheting off the white wall. One of the gunmen put his machine gun down and went over to grab the pistol from the old man. The officer had lifted his head off the grass and was trying to say something, blood seeping out of his mouth. The gunman knelt down next to him, placed the pistol against his temple and fired.

No one in the small crowd moved for a good minute, shocked at what they had seen and shocked at what they had done.

Hélène and Laurent were offered a bed for the night but decided to move on.

'Victor's justice,' said Laurent as the village began to fade behind them.

'What other kind is there?' she asked.

They moved on to Reims, where they stayed until the end of September. Laurent had decided that he wanted to return to Lens. By now, he was beginning to be open about his desires towards her. The occasional friendly arm around the shoulder became more frequent, pulling her closer to him and trying to hold her there. The kiss on the cheek moved closer to her mouth and there were references to 'we'. She realised that he was beginning to assume that 'we' had a future. She allowed herself to contemplate the prospect for a while. It was not without its attractions. Laurent was a decent man; intelligent, witty, and resourceful. She could disappear into the anonymity offered by being a schoolteacher's wife in Lens. Life there would be dull but safe, something that she could not contemplate.

She also realised that she needed to head on. He had no idea where she came from and she needed to escape his attention and his affection before it became a problem. One morning when he was helping to clear roads she fell into conversation with an American officer who couldn't believe she spoke such good English. The officer was about to head down to Lorraine and if she wanted a lift, he would be happy to oblige.

–

Nancy had been liberated by the US Third Army on the 15 September after a ten-day battle, but in other parts of Lorraine the war continued.

She had intended to stay in Nancy until it was safe for her to move eastwards on the last leg of her long journey. Lieutenant Larry Jones had spent much of the first half of the journey from Reims to Nancy with his hand on her knee, and most of the second half of the journey with it on her thigh. She wondered if she had made the right decision to abandon Laurent. But she needed Lieutenant Jones, even more than he apparently needed her.

'Civilian control, ma'am. My mom is French–Canadian and I speak it as well as all of you, so I'm running the office in Nancy making sure everyone has the right documents.'

His French was not as good as he thought it was, but it was passable.

'I'll let you practise on me later,' she promised, which was all the encouragement he needed to book her into the one hotel that was still standing and pay for the room.

But more importantly, she needed new documents. He bought her story that her papers had been lost in Reims without too much difficulty and so the first thing he did when they arrived in Nancy was fix her up with an impressive new set. She was exhausted now; tired of moving, tired of not being sure of who she was meant to be, and in no real physical state to do much other than rest.

She thought hard about the new identity Lieutenant Jones was fixing her up with. She could be anyone, apart from the one person she wanted to be, and be with. Instead, she decided to revert to her real identity, which was something she had never given much thought to. It seemed to make sense. She had come full circle.

The hotel ought to have been the perfect place for her to stay: the sheets were clean and the small bathroom always had water. Downstairs there was a bistro attached to the hotel which had some food, if you liked potatoes, and Lieutenant Jones had assured her that her bills would be taken care of. He had even arranged for her to have a check up with an army doctor. All was well, she was assured. If only it was, she thought.

But there was an air about Nancy that made her uncomfortable. She had imagined that liberated France would be euphoric, that people whose dreams had come true and whose suffering had come to end would be happy. Yet all she could sense was an edge to the city. A tension that she found hard to describe flowed in on the River Meurthe and attached itself to the elegant but war-scarred buildings on the Grande Rue.

On her second night in Nancy she was in the bar adjoining the bistro. It was ten o'clock and Lieutenant Jones had just left. He had joined her for dinner and, realising that he was going to get no further than the ground floor of the hotel, reluctantly but politely bade her goodnight.

The barman was polishing a beer glass in an extravagant manner.

'Not your boyfriend then?'

'No. He'd like to be. I'm married.' She held up her left hand and wriggled her fingers.

The barman smiled. 'What brings you here?'

'The war. I got a lift here. I'm moving on soon.'

Outside there was a crashing noise, the sound of glass breaking and people shouting. The barman went into the street and returned, still polishing the same glass.

'They've found another *collabo* then. It's not a nice sight. Go and have a look if you want to see what a free France looks like.'

She got outside just in time to see a crowd of people disappearing down the small road outside the hotel. She followed them into the Place Stanislas, where a larger crowd had gathered.

A young woman, perhaps in her early twenties, had been pushed to the ground and was being made to kneel. A man was tying her hands behind her back while another had yanked up her long hair in his hands.

The crowd was quiet, muttering disapproval of the girl.

'What is going on?' she asked the woman next to her.

'You don't know? Sleeping with Germans. And she's one of the lucky ones. They shot six men two days ago for helping the Germans.'

She was fixed to the spot, appalled at the spectacle in front of her, yet fascinated by it too. It was carried out in silence, the girl bowed and compliant, accepting of her fate. The older man finished tying her hands and then produced a pair of large tailor's scissors and proceeded to hack away at her hair. The younger man had his hand under the girl's chin, keeping the head upright. When most of the hair had been removed the younger man took out a cut-throat razor and scraped away at her scalp, nicking it and causing it to bleed. All along, the girl kept quiet and still, with not a tear in her eye.

She backed away from the crowd as it nodded its approval. A fear was gripping her now. She had been deluding herself over the past few weeks. She was worse than a collaborator, she was a traitor. If the truth were known about her, a far worse fate awaited her.

She ran back to the hotel, her worn shoes sliding against the cobbles. Outside the hotel she held herself against the wall while she vomited. She knew she must move on.

Inside the barman was holding the same beer glass, the bar still empty.

'Not pleasant, is it?' he said.

She nodded. A large cognac was on the bar in front of her.

'I imagine you'll want this. On the house.'

The next morning she told Lieutenant Jones that she was leaving Nancy. He understood. He had already realised that his interest in her was not going to be reciprocated. Frenchwomen looked like a lot of trouble anyway.

—

By the time she realised she had made a mistake it was, of course, far too late. If only Lieutenant Jones had tried to persuade her to stay in Nancy. He wouldn't have had to try too hard. She would have been comfortable there, there were hospitals, and it was away from the fighting.

The lorry that Lieutenant Jones had arranged to give her a lift had left Nancy early that morning, hugging the line of the Meurthe towards the Vosges Mountains. She was only about sixty miles from home. The front line was nearby and the lorry was delivering supplies to it. The driver apologised in the way that she had discovered Americans were good at. 'I can't take you any further. Sorry ma'am.' He sounded genuinely sorry.

The late summer sun was streaming down into the square of the village where she had been dropped. There was no shade in sight. Some of the trees were beginning to lose their leaves and a pyramid-shaped pile of them had been swept into a corner of the square. She deeply regretted leaving Nancy: she had been impetuous again, driven on by some kind of nesting instinct. She was feeling exhausted – weighed down by her pregnancy. She had underestimated how tired she would feel. Her back was hurting as it had been on and off for the past few weeks and her ankles were swollen. If only Lieutenant Jones had not been so obliging in helping her leave Nancy.

The *Mairie* next to the church was decorated with a row of bullet holes. Stacked up on one side of the square was a collection of dismantled German road signs. At first she assumed that the village was deserted, given its proximity to the fighting, but then an old lady dressed in black left a building ahead of her, slowly walking round the square, never taking her eyes off her. A family left the church, followed by a young priest with a wide-brimmed hat and a long black cassock, who carefully locked the door with a key on a long chain tied around his waist. A *boulangerie* looked as if it had closed for the war and was yet to be informed it was over.

She sat on a bench at the edge of the square for a while. Her eyes filled with tears. Until a few weeks ago she could not remember the last time she had cried. Now, she seemed to do so most days.

She couldn't stay in this village, she must keep moving. *I can't draw attention to myself.* A large black cat had circled her bench and was now sitting in front of her, its head cocked as if it was expecting to be fed, the yellow eyes burning into her. A gentle breeze rolled across the square. If she was going to move, she'd need to do so now while there was still plenty of daylight.

She carried on walking. Heading east, always heading east. It did not take long for the village to fade behind her as if it had never existed, like a strange dream, and for the countryside to open up. Ahead of her, far in the distance, was the crump and smoke of artillery fire. Her urge to go home was instinctive, but she had no idea where she was going to spend the night. She wondered whether there was any way she could get back to Nancy.

She was climbing uphill and her pace had slowed to a near-crawl. As the incline became steeper, she stopped every few paces. There was no breeze now and she felt lightheaded. Although the sun had dropped, she felt unaccountably hot and nauseous. She paused, leaning against a narrow tree. She peered up through the branches; the sun appeared enormous, its yellow edges bleeding into the sky. As she looked down she was sweating profusely and felt unsteady. She had to hold the tree trunk tightly as she was violently sick. Strange, she thought: she had, mercifully, avoided morning sickness in the early part of her pregnancy. She carried on walking painfully slowly. The birds were silent and the land swayed gently around her. She was concentrating so hard on reaching the top of the hill that she never heard the car until it stopped alongside her.

The last thing she remembered seeing was a tiny black car alongside her, with a man dressed in black in the driving seat. The words 'Where are you going?' were the last ones she remembered hearing.

Chapter 29

Lorraine-Alsace border, October 1944

That night she was back home, being dragged through the Place St Étienne, stripped naked by an angry crowd hacking at her with razors.

That night she was curled up in bed with Owen in a large London house, their children sleeping peacefully in adjoining rooms.

That night she had her hands round the neck of the German soldier in Lille, her well-practised smile fixed on him as she squeezed the life out of him as slowly as possible.

That night was the fourth in a row in which she had endured an interrogation by the British in a dank basement, insisting that she regretted what she had done and had been looking for an opportunity to tell them, but please let me rest now.

That night she was chased down the Avenue Foch; she knew that when she reached the Place d'Étoile she would be safe, but the faster she ran the further the enormous arch slipped into the distance.

That night she told Owen that she loved him and begged for his forgiveness, over and over again, but his face faded away as he began to speak and she never heard his reply.

That night stretched over three days and two nights.

She woke bathed in sweat, with an elderly man and a middle-aged woman at each shoulder, both looking anxiously at her. As far as she could tell, she was in large dark room, with a high, beamed ceiling and no windows but the sun leaking in through a part-open door. There was an earthy smell about, and outside the noise of a farm. She tried to get up, but the man held her down. His touch was firm, but not harsh.

'Lay still. A moment, please.'

He spoke French, with a heavy accent she couldn't place. He had a kindly face, with deep wrinkles, silver eyebrows that gave him an owl-like appearance, and just a few wisps of white hair. Her head was spinning. The woman wiped her brow while the man placed a stethoscope on her chest and told her to relax. He moved the stethoscope around her chest, placing it in different positions, listening carefully.

'Good. You're strong,' he said after a while. He was holding the pulse on her wrist as he spoke to her.

'My baby?'

He patted her stomach. 'Strong too. But you must rest. You were found just in time. Drink.'

The woman held a flask of water to her lips. The water was cold and she drank the whole flask quickly before slumping back on the pillow.

'What happened to me?'

'The priest found you collapsed by the road – *collapsing* to be more precise. He brought you here. We are about five miles east of the village you stopped in. The priest saw you in the square there. He is a good man and has been keeping an eye on us. You have a fever and exhaustion. I gave you a dose of sodium barbiturate and you've been asleep for two days, nearly three, in fact.'

He spoke to the woman in what sounded like a strange dialect of German. She nodded and went away.

'We'll get you something to eat, but you must be careful. Not too much for now.'

'What about the baby?'

'Don't worry. The baby is getting all the nutrition it needs from you. It's you we need to worry about. For now, you must rest. You will stay here with us. When are you due?'

'Maybe a month? I'm not sure. Soon.'

He moved his hands from her wrist and held them around her stomach.

'It could be sooner. Have you been healthy throughout the pregnancy?'

She nodded.

'And active?'

She laughed. 'I think that you could say that I've been active.'

'Well, now it is time to rest. I'm a doctor, by the way, in case you were wondering.' He lifted up his stethoscope and dangled it. He was smiling, his eyebrows dancing as he spoke.

'What kind?'

'Before the war, I was a cardiologist in Kraków. In Poland. I studied in Paris for a while.'

'And during the war?'

The smile dropped and his long fingers drummed on the side of her bed. 'You don't want to know. Not now. Here, some soup and bread. Thank you, Rachel. Sit up and drink it, then we'll talk.'

The woman helped her drink the soup and spoke to the doctor in the German dialect.

'*Ask her about...*' the woman seemed to be saying.

'Ah yes,' he said. 'I meant to ask you. Who is Owen?'

'What?'

'You kept shouting it out in your sleep. You were delirious. It sounded like you were calling the name of someone.'

She shook her head, doing her best to look puzzled. 'It's not a name I know,' she reassured them.

—

It was four days before she was well enough to get up and only then did the doctor tell her how ill she had been.

'Another hour and I think you would have lost the baby. You were very sick. The fever was strong, but the priest found you in time. He was pleased. It helps confirm his beliefs. They were quite challenged after he met us.'

They were sitting around a large table in the dining room of the farmhouse. The top floor of the house had been destroyed by either a bomb or a shell, but the ground floor was functioning, despite the lack of glass in the windows and long cracks down the walls. The atmosphere was heavy with dust. The barn and another out-building alongside the main farmhouse had been made habitable, and now she was learning who else was in the odd community she had ended up in.

The doctor was sitting across the table from her.

'Do you want to tell me about yourself?'

She hesitated. 'I'm French – a refugee. I was working in the north. Now I'm heading home... south.' She felt the tears welling again.

'Don't worry. In time. Everyone here has a story too big to tell. That's the story of Europe now. Let me tell you who we are.'

Before he started talking he walked into the kitchen and came back with two apples, handing one to her. 'Eat. It's from the orchard. You need to eat more.'

There was a pause while he ate his apple, including the core and the stem.

'Imagine, four years I went without fruit,' said the doctor, shaking his head. Another pause.

'Let me tell you about your new companions. The girl who looks after the animals. Elisabette. This is her farm, or her family's. Her parents and brothers were killed when it got caught in tank fire. A shell took out the top floor when they were all asleep. She was the only one who survived.

'The rest of us, we had been inmates at a German camp near the village of Natzweiler, which is further into Alsace. The camp is about fifty kilometres south west of Strasbourg. Until 1943 they kept mainly political prisoners and resistance fighters there. You see Hans and Ludwig over there?' He was pointing at the two Germans, both sitting on a low wall, surveying the surrounding countryside. 'Both socialists who refused to help with the war effort in Germany. They were sent to the camp in 1940. It shows. They're both insane now. It's probably how they survived this long.'

The doctor got up and stood at the glassless window, his back to her.

'The rest of us – well, we were taken to the camp from Poland over the past few months. You know about me. The woman who was nursing you, she's called Rachel. From a city called Łódź. The four boys, they were all in the Warsaw ghetto. The Jewish ghetto. Last year there was an uprising in the ghetto, which the Germans crushed. These boys were found in a sewer weeks later. All six of us were at a camp in the south of Poland called Auschwitz. It's near Kraków. If you imagine hell on earth, you won't even come close to what happened there. Not even close to it. We're all Jewish, you probably gathered that.'

She nodded, though she was not sure that she had gathered that.

'The two women, the mother and daughter. They're Roma – Gypsies. The Nazis hate them as much as they hate us. They were also in this camp in Poland.'

'So how come you're now in France?'

'The Germans did not bring us to France for a holiday; I can assure you of that. It was not for the mountain air. When I arrived and they found out that I was a doctor, I was sent to work in the camp hospital at Natzweiler. From working there, I discovered why people had been sent to Alsace from Auschwitz. A German doctor was – still is, as far as I know – running an Institute of Anatomy at the University of Strasbourg. He's a proper Nazi, this doctor. His work is to help prove that people like the Jews and the Gypsies are a subhuman race: inferior to the Aryans. You have heard that theory, of course.'

Her eyes were wide open and she nodded just once. Of course, she had heard those theories. It was not that long ago that...

'What this so-called doctor was doing, I am told, was conducting experiments on the bodies of Jews and others to try to provide medical evidence for the Nazis. But he needed his bodies to be fresh, if you understand what I mean. So the Nazis arranged for people to be brought alive from Auschwitz in small groups, thirty or forty at a time. They were then kept at the camp and when their bodies were required, they were killed and taken to Strasbourg to be experimented upon.'

'How were they killed?'

'One day, maybe everyone in Europe will know. Maybe not. The Germans do not like to waste bullets, so they have devised this method of killing a lot of people at the same time. It's called a gas chamber. They force a group of people into a large, sealed room and then pour lethal gas in. The people suffocate within minutes. They didn't have a gas chamber at this camp, so they converted a nearby building. I don't know how many people died there altogether. What I do know is that we were next. Then one day, a few weeks ago, the Germans evacuated the camp. With no warning. Some of us just wandered out. Prisoners were heading in every direction. The French ones wanted to head for their homes, the Germans were heading for anywhere but home. And us... we somehow randomly came together as a group and just walked. I didn't think we would survive; the Germans still controlled the area, but near a small town called Raon-l'Etape a farmer hid us in his cart and put some distance between us and the Germans. We then carried on walking and came across this place. We should really head towards the Americans, I suppose. We'll be treated as refugees. If it was just me, I would. Rachel too, I imagine, and the Roma women. But the boys, they are terrified. I think if they saw another person with a gun, it would finish them. At the moment, they would not be able to distinguish between Germans and Americans. They would only see men in uniform. They trust me, so I'm trying to make them understand what is happening. They may be ready to move on in a few weeks. That is my hope. Maybe they are young enough to recover. They are the main reason we are staying here, for the time being.'

'And the Germans?'

'Look at them.' Hans and Ludwig had climbed onto the roof of the barn now and were scouting the sky with their hands turned into the shape of binoculars.

'I don't know what their countrymen have done to them, but it has had an effect on their minds, you understand? The taller one, Ludwig, he was an architect before the war, apparently. A very intelligent man. In his sane moments, he will talk passionately about Bauhaus. Now he tells me that the owls have been sent to spy on us. He passes onto me confidential messages from the chickens.'

She did not know what to say, and was not certain she was able to speak. Her throat felt tight. She was staring down at the table, drawing patterns on it with her fingers. Between them, she noticed through blurred vision that the light surface of the table was darkening with her tears.

She felt guilty. If she told the doctor the truth now, would he believe her? And if he did, would he then forgive her? It was not as if she had no idea. As much as she would like to believe that she had made one mistake, that there had been a misunderstanding, that she was not aware of what the Nazis were really like, she knew that was not true.

The doctor was sitting opposite her again, his soft hands gently placed on top of hers.

'Don't be upset. The people of France are not to blame. You look so guilty! It's not your fault. You look like a good person to me.'

Later that night she was sitting in the barn with the doctor and Rachel. The Roma women were in the house, the sound of the folk tune they were humming floating across the farmyard. The Germans were asleep and the four boys were cautiously walking around the farm, their heads looking in every direction.

'What happened to your families?' she asked them.

There was a long silence. Eventually, the doctor translated her question for Rachel. His translation lasted a long time and then a conversation between the two of them followed.

'We don't know.'

More silence.

'No idea at all?'

Another long pause as the doctor carefully straightened his shirtsleeves.

'When a transport arrived at Auschwitz, people were separated. The old, the very young, and the sick — they were sent to these gas chambers straight away. People who looked fit and who had a skill — they would be spared, for a time. I was with my wife and my son. When we came off the train, it was chaos. I have no idea what happened. I just don't think about it. Rachel, she had five children. She has decided in her mind that at least one of them must have survived, but she can hardly bring herself to think about it. Your question was a difficult one for us to answer.'

'How old was your son?'

'Twelve.'

'I'm sorry.'

'I keep telling you, you don't need to be. You're not to blame. And what about you? Do you have family?'

So far, he had not asked where she came from, or where she was going or what she did and she had told them as little as possible. They knew her as Hélène and had no idea that she was a nurse or that she spoke English and some German.

'My mother...' She could not say much more. Rachel spoke to the doctor, who replied at length.

'She asks about your husband, your baby's father. Where is he, is he alive?'

She gazed through the open door of the barn where the moon had lit up the farmyard, casting a silvery glow on the four boys as they silently walked round in a circle, one behind the other.

'I hope so.'

The night before she gave birth, she was woken by a commotion in the farmyard. Autumn was in full grip and, outside the warmth of the barn, a frost had already taken hold. She gathered a blanket around her and went out. Rachel beckoned her to stay back but she pushed past her.

At the end of the yard was a gate; beyond that was the farm track which, in turn, lead up to the road. Some twenty yards beyond the other side of the gate, standing on the uneven track were three men. They were all tall, standing stock-still in the shadow of the night, so it was not possible to make out any features. The two Germans were at the gate, pointing excitedly at them. The four boys were petrified, cowering in the middle of the farmyard. The doctor walked towards the gate.

'What do you want?' he called out in French.

The three men remained perfectly still. There was no breeze that night, but the noise had started to disturb the farm. The dark shape of a cow could be seen moving in the field behind the men. One of the chickens clucked its disapproval.

'Who are you?' The doctor's voice was firm, but his French was not convincing.

The three men moved forward by one step, staying within the shadow.

She walked up behind the doctor. 'Please go away,' she called out loudly, making sure they would be in no doubt that she was French. 'We are a French family. This is our farm. We have nothing of value here.'

The three men remained motionless.

To her left, she could see Elisabette in the broken doorway of the farmhouse, out of sight of the men. She had a rifle in her hands and was carefully releasing the safety catch.

'I don't think they are French,' the doctor said very quietly to her. The air was steamy with his breath.

'What are you after? We are French,' she called out in English. The doctor glanced quizzically at her.

Still no response. Had she been on her own, she would have wondered whether it was an illusion. But there was no doubt that the three men were there.

'Who are you?' the doctor cried out again, this time in German, his voice trembling.

The men stirred and appeared to be muttering to each other.

'God help us,' the doctor whispered, taking two or three steps back, fear etched onto his face.

She walked right up to the gate and called out in German.

'We are French. Leave us alone. There are Americans nearby. In one of the fields next to our farm. They will come if they hear anything. They promised us that.'

More muttering from the three men. Two turned and started to walk away from the farm. The third waited a moment and took one step forward. The moonlight caught his body and the lower part of his face. He was dressed all in black, in uniform. She leaned forward to get a better view of him.

'*Dreckige Juden,*' he said. Filthy Jews. It was said softly enough for just her to hear; his voice did not carry as far as the doctor. She had no doubt as to what she had heard. He paused a moment and then turned sharply and joined the other two walking away from the farm.

Shaken, she walked back to the doctor. SS renegades, she thought, evading capture, just realising that their dream was over. There was the sound of whimpering from inside the outhouse where the four boys had shut themselves in. Elisabette had put the safety catch back on the rifle.

'What did he say? I thought I heard him say something?' asked the doctor.

She looked at the doctor, at Rachel, at the two Roma women, at Hans and Ludwig who were both smiling, and beyond them at the outhouse door, where the four boys were now peering anxiously from behind a half-open door.

What could she say to them?

'Nothing,' she said, her hand reassuringly stroking the doctor's forearm. 'He didn't say anything.'

Chapter 30

Paris, October 1944

Owen Quinn had the first of a number of lucky breaks on that Friday afternoon in St Omer, not that he realised it at the time.

After Nicole had left, he had planned to take a train to Paris, but when he went into the station there were long queues and very few trains. He stood very little chance, they told him in the ticket office, of making it to Paris by train that day.

Then he remembered that, at the café where he had been with Nicole just before she left, there had been a couple of US Marine officers who were talking loudly about driving down to Paris that day. He returned to the café and they were just about to leave.

'Sure kid, as long as you don't mind a jeep ride.'

Had he taken the train, it would have been possible for the very tall man in the trilby watching him from the back of the station to have followed him. When he saw him leave and then hitch a ride in a jeep, he realised he was beaten, for the time being.

Half an hour later, and Quinn wished he was back on the platform at St Omer, going nowhere. The two Marine officers had a driver called Bob. Owen thought that Bob drove very nicely, if a bit too fast. The officer who was called Bill thought that Bob was driving too slowly, but was not complaining. The other officer, Earl, thought that Bob was driving far too slowly. As Earl outranked Bill, Bob had to drive very fast. Owen hung on to a side-rail with one hand and an overhead bar with the other as their death-defying journey gathered pace. On a number of occasions they came across groups of refugees heading in one direction or the other, clogging up the road with handcarts. Bob would drive round them by cutting into a field and then back onto the road. It was, without doubt, the longest one hundred and fifty miles of Owen's life.

They entered a city apparently unscathed by war. The French had General Dietrich von Choltitz to thank for that, Bill shouted at him. Hitler had appointed von Choltitz as commandant of Paris just a matter of days before its liberation with orders to destroy the city. Von Choltitz instead negotiated an orderly surrender and thus saved it.

'Where do you want be dropped, kid?' The jeep had slowed down to a speed one degree below suicidal and Earl had turned round from the front passenger seat to shout at him. 'Want some girls? With that uniform, kid, and your accent, you'll get a very good discount. I know a good place. Here's a card. Mention my name. Earl from Chicago.'

'The centre will be fine thanks.' Owen was now able to breathe normally and remove one numbed hand from the rail. He was not sure if his wrist was broken; he would need to wait until some feeling returned to it.

Five minutes later and they were picking up speed again down a very broad avenue, before screeching to a halt under the Arc d'Triomphe. He had said that he wanted to be dropped in the centre of Paris, and they had taken him at his word. Some passers-by were shaking their heads disapprovingly. They did not want to appear ungrateful, but...

'OK, kid. Guess this is as near as you're going to get to the centre of Paris. Good luck.'

It was six o'clock now and he decided to find somewhere to stay. Twelve avenues emerged like spokes from the Arc de Triomphe. Avenue de la Grande Armée was the nearest and felt appropriate, somehow. He passed a number of hotels and eventually found one that was much the same as the others he had walked past, and checked in.

That evening, he walked up and down the Champs Élysées, with the infatuation common to all first-time visitors to the city, and an aching sense of regret that this was where he had planned to come with Nathalie. This was where they were going to walk; this was where they would have eaten. Lovers, some recently reunited, others quite probably newly acquainted, sat quietly in the bars, not needing to speak. He could only be a spectator.

What was most noticeable was the number of men in uniform. Americans, British, French, Canadian, Polish. Not many Royal Navy, he had to admit. The River Seine had not been too much of a military problem. He was saluted by a couple of Royal Navy ratings, who looked as surprised to see an officer in the Champs Élysées as he was to see their salutes.

The photographs of Nathalie he now carried in his pocket were not to prop by his bedside, but to help trace her. But what was he meant to do in this city? Show them to every shopkeeper, every bar owner? Would the police help? He had heard all about the Paris concierges who knew everything that went on in their block and even their street. Should he try some of them? There would be tens of thousands in this city. It would be hopeless. The one clue he had to go on was from when they had had dinner at Archibald's club and Mrs Hardisty had asked Nathalie where she came from in Paris. And what had been Nathalie's reply? 'Oh, we moved around. Usually south of the 14th.'

He had picked up a map of Paris in the hotel and settled into a bar to study it. He bought a *Pastis* because he imagined that was the thing to do, a decision he quickly regretted. The 14th arrondissement was a large area in the south of the city, criss-crossed by large avenues and boulevards like St Jacques, du Maine, and Raspail, with the Montparnasse cemetery at its heart. If he knew for sure that she had a connection with the 14th then he could base himself there for a week, or even a month, and work his way through it systematically. He would need a lot of luck, but it was not impossible. Some shopkeeper, concierge, or schoolteacher might recognise the photo. No one can live in a city and not leave a single trace, he thought, though he was beginning to realise that if anyone was capable of doing it, Nathalie would be.

But Nathalie had not actually said she lived in the 14th arrondissement. She had told Mrs Hardisty that they lived *south* of it. *Usually*. Quinn shook his head and downed the *Pastis* in one go without thinking. It was hopeless. *The Pastis* – and the situation. Two thirds of France was south of the 14th – for heaven's sake.

–

He woke up early the next morning to the rank smell of drains that he had noticed throughout the city the previous day, and more sun streaming into the room than he imagined possible. That was because he had forgotten to draw the curtains, and he had forgotten to do so because of what had happened in the bar after he had downed his *Pastis* in one go.

He must have pulled a face because a couple of corporals from the Royal Northumberland Fusiliers came over to join him. Reg and Ron, or it could have been Ron and Reg. They were from the Fourth Battalion and had fought in the Battle of Normandy, and wanted him to know it. They had fought hard and now they were drinking hard. 'You don't want to be drinking that muck, pal.' For one dreadful moment he thought they might have found a supply of Newcastle Brown Ale in Paris and he would have to make his excuses and leave. But no, Reg and Ron had found a wonderful drink. Made with herbs. Absinthe they called it. 'Good for you.' And that was pretty much all he could remember. Maybe if it made you forget, it *was* good for you. Something about it not being legal, but they had befriended a bar owner. He remembered little more than that.

He did remember a taxi back and promises of lifelong friendship, and now he was on the bed, fully clothed.

He bathed, shaved, and went out in search of coffee and his wife. His first inclination was not to wear uniform, but as a non-Frenchman he would have stuck out like a sore thumb in civilian clothes, and in any case, the uniform of an Allied officer counted for something in this city, and that wouldn't last long.

It was a glorious autumn morning and in a noisy café on the Avenue Hoche where everyone was smoking strong cigarettes, he had a coffee and the first croissant of his life. He was surprised to see a couple on the table next to him already sharing a bottle of wine.

From his wallet he took out the piece of paper Nicole had given him with the name and address of her contact. It was in Rue Taitbout in the 9th arrondissement. He found it on the map. There were some Metro stations nearby, but he decided to walk. He didn't have a schedule, and by walking he might get a feel for the city. At the end of Avenue Hoche he turned right onto Rue Faubourg St Honoré and then left into Boulevard Haussmann. It was a long walk, much further than he had imagined – and he was supposed to be a maps expert. He imagined his map was not drawn to a proper scale. Despite having been occupied for so long, Paris felt more at ease than London. Maybe, he thought, it was *because* it had been occupied. It had not suffered air raids, and the city itself had remained intact. The buildings are the heart of a city. The people come and go, and give it its soul, but the fabric of the buildings, the style and atmosphere that they evoke – these are what gives a city its character. He admired the sweeping boulevards and the height of the buildings, which made it feel as if he was walking through an elegant ravine. He had been in the city for less than twenty-four hours and could already see why people were besotted by it, even though it smelled entirely different to anywhere he had been before. The smell of drains and the ever-present aroma of strong cigarettes. If only his first visit here had been for a different reason.

Just after the Opera he came to the junction with Rue La Fayette, and then turned on to Rue Taitbout. He noticed small groups of people, in twos and threes, dressed smartly in dark clothing, moving hurriedly to his right. They all seemed to be going in the same direction, and appeared to be glancing anxiously at him. There was an atmosphere that he could not put his finger on. It felt like a classroom which all the children had suddenly left, although the sense of noise remained. The area felt abandoned.

The building he was looking for was four blocks to the north, just before Rue de Châteaudun. The front door was open and the ground floor comprised the mailboxes for the flats. He checked the note and studied the names on the mailboxes.

'Can I help you?'

The old lady was peering at him from inside her concierge's room. 'Who do you want. Are you police?'

After all these years of occupation even a Royal Navy uniform obviously had these connotations.

'No, I am looking for... André... Koln?' She turned away, speaking as she did so. 'Top floor. Number nine. The lift is broken, so don't bother with it.'

He walked the eight flights of stairs. These days, his back and leg were fine, but a climb like this could trigger stiffness. He paused on a landing halfway up, before continuing, eventually ringing the bell for number nine. There was no reply. He rang again, still no reply. He had walked a long way to find no one in. He would leave a note and return in the afternoon.

He was not sure whether '*I am a British officer, and a friend recommended I come to see you*' would be of any use, but that is what he wrote, and slid it under the door. He would return in the early afternoon.

He had descended one flight of stairs when a door above him opened and a voice called out, 'Wait! Come up!'

The figure, leaning against the door of apartment nine and eyeing him coming up the stairs, was tall and thin with a dark complexion, but an unhealthy pallor, and a couple of days' growth of beard. His hair was long and he had a bohemian air about him that Quinn felt was in keeping with the surroundings. He held out his hand, taking care to do up his shirtsleeve as he did so.

'André Koln. Hello.'

'Owen Quinn, I am glad to meet you.'

'Come in.'

The main room of the flat was chaotic, books and papers piled everywhere. On the sofa was a stack of framed pictures and photographs. The floor around the sofa was dotted with used cups and wine glasses. The table by the window was piled high with papers and a typewriter. Those surfaces that were still surfaces were covered with a veneer of dust. One wall of the room was dominated by a large glass-fronted cabinet, part-covered by a dust sheet. Where that sheet had slipped down, ornaments were visible. On the walls he spotted a series of square and rectangular dark patches, outlining where pictures or mirrors had once been.

Yet despite the chaos and the untidiness, there was a quality to the room. A woman must have lived here, Quinn thought. The curtains were clearly good quality and they matched the carpets and the wallpaper.

André sat at the table, next to a large ashtray which contained the remains of a number of packets of cigarettes. His hand slightly shook as he took one out of a packet, and he had to use two hands to light it, closing his eyes briefly as he inhaled deeply.

'What's the uniform?' He pointed at Quinn with the now-lit cigarette.

'The Royal Navy. The British Royal Navy.'

'Really?' He laughed. 'The Royal Navy. Have you jumped ship?'

'Not exactly. Nicole gave me your name. She said you could help me.'

'The reason I didn't answer the door when you kept ringing is that I have a problem with uniforms – I could see you through the spy hole, you see. When you have been through what I have been through, you'll understand.'

'Can I ask what have you been through?'

A long stare at Owen through the white smoke.

'When I know you a bit better. You obviously need help. I can help. It is what I do. It is all I can do, now. Nicole would not have sent you along if I was not the right person. So you tell me what you need. But I warn you. Tell me everything. If you miss something out, then it is your problem.'

'Can I ask first what it is you do? What is your job?' Owen risked.

'I have had many jobs – you can choose which one you want. I'm a lawyer. And a journalist. Now I put all these skills together and I find people. Go on, tell me your story.'

It took Owen Quinn an hour to tell his story to André Koln. The whole story. He left nothing out. He had no idea why he was able to open up so freely to a stranger. And not just a stranger: André Koln was a *strange* man. Sitting in his peculiar flat, in a foreign city, with his distrusting eyes, which darted around as if there were things that only he could sense. Possibly it was because Owen was in such a different environment that he felt able to let down his defences, for the first time since June. At one stage, he found himself weeping and not feeling the need to apologise for it. Only once in that hour did Koln react, and that was when he told him that Nathalie – which was the name he was using for the want of anything else – was pregnant.

When he finished, Koln disappeared into the kitchen and came back a few minutes later with a strong pot of coffee and poured them each a cup.

'So your child will be born very soon?'

'Yes. She was two months' pregnant at the beginning of April, so nine months is the end of October. So, yes. Any day now. It may have been born already.'

'So, you are going to be a father. Congratulations. It is good. It's the best thing in the world.'

It was an unusual reaction. Not the one he had been expecting. In return for being so frank over the past hour, he was expecting a bit more than this. '*How can I help?*' was what he had in mind. Or better still, '*I can help, I know how to find her*'.

Koln walked over to the window, which looked onto the Rue Taitbout, and flung it open. It was now noon. It had turned grey outside and a cold blast swept into the room.

'I'll tell you my story, Owen. Then you can decide whether you want me to help you.'

He pulled his chair directly in front of Owen's, so the two men were sitting virtually knee-to-knee.

'You are in the 9th arrondissement. A lot of Jews lived here before the war. Some still do – you may have seen them going to synagogue as you walked here. But not as many live here now as did before the war. It's not a ghetto like you have in other parts of Europe, or used to have. We don't have these in France. No need for it. Not everyone is religious. My family is not religious. I'm certainly not. My family have lived here for over a hundred years, they came from Germany originally. My wife, her family came here more recently, from Poland. Sophie.' André paused, taking a sip of coffee before concentrating on his cigarette for a moment or two.

'But before the war, it was fine. I was a lawyer, and I was also a journalist. I was active in politics too, with the socialists. My wife taught literature at the Sorbonne. We had a good life. Our son was born in 1940. Daniel.'

He leaned over to the sofa and selected a picture from the pile stacked there, and showed it to Owen. André Koln looked ten years younger, with a beaming smile, standing next to a beautiful woman with long, dark, wavy hair and amazing eyes. She looked not unlike Nathalie, and was holding a tiny baby.

'A happy family, eh? That's what I thought. You should know that something is going to go wrong when everything is going right. We were very happy, but not for long. The Germans entered Paris in June 1940. It all happened so fast, we couldn't believe it. Half the population left the city, but where could we go? To Germany? In any case, we had a young child. Look Owen, I am an intelligent man. I am resourceful. I know what to do. I know people. I'm not religious, I didn't think everything would be fine, that God would sort it out. But in this case, we had no idea what to do. We were like rabbits caught in lights. We just stood still. And by the time the shock had worn off, there was nothing we *could* do. We were trapped in the city. There was nowhere to go.

'Life became difficult – but then it was for everyone in this city, apart from those who collaborated with the Germans. And let me tell you something, Owen, there were plenty of those. Everyone you meet in France now will tell you they were in the resistance, and for most of them that is a lie. Most people did nothing, perhaps you can't blame them for that. But those who helped the Germans, they deserve everything they're getting.

329

'Sophie lost her job at the Sorbonne, so she stayed at home to look after Daniel. I was not allowed to work as a lawyer, and funnily enough there was not much demand for a socialist journalist, so I worked for my uncle. He had an electrical repair workshop in the Marais, and I used to help him in the holidays when I was a student. I had my one stroke of luck, if you can call it that. I had to get a new identity card to show that I was a Jew, and on it I made sure that my occupation was shown as "electrician". So, I was no longer a troublesome lawyer or journalist, but I was an electrician.

'Then, in 1942, things got worse. In May we were told that we had to wear yellow stars to show that we were Jewish. Everyone over the age of six. We had to buy them from the police station, three each. Let me show you.' He opened a drawer in the cabinet and took out an envelope and put two pieces of cloth on the table.

'Here we are. This was one of mine – "*Juif*", and this was one of Sophie's – "*Juive*".'

Owen noticed again that André's hands were trembling slightly.

'But worse was to come. In July that year they started the deportation of the Jews. They called it the *grande rafle*. It was terrible. That first day, they rounded up more than ten thousand people. After that, hundreds more every day. Old men who had fought at Verdun, babies, everyone. Some people did not go. In the next block, a woman threw herself and her baby out of a top floor window as the police hammered at the door.

'I made plans for us to escape to the country. A lawyer friend of mine had moved his family to his family's farm in the Loire and he said we could stay there too. It was complicated, it was in a different zone, but I managed to sort papers, and as long as we could get there, we would stand a chance.

'We were going to go on the 19th of August. They came for us on the 17th. I don't know why. Maybe someone informed, maybe it was our turn. I will find out one day. I had made plans for when they came. I thought we would hear them coming, and I would hide Sophie and Daniel in the apartment next door; they were away and we had the key. I would be able to get out across the roof. But they hammered on the door at four in the morning, and by five o'clock we were in Drancy.'

'Drancy?'

'It was a housing estate they were building near Le Bourget airport. It was only half-built, so there was no sanitation, no electricity. It was very primitive, the conditions were terrible. Everyone was sick. People died. One morning they put us on trains. Not ordinary trains, these were like cattle trucks. Thousands of people stuffed together. We were on them for days. When we got out, we were in a place called Auschwitz. Have you heard of it?'

Owen shook his head.

'You will. It is in Poland. It is a death camp, where Germans murdered the Jews and other prisoners. I will tell you something now, Owen. It was only when we fell out of the train at this terrible place that I saw German soldiers. Until then, from the moment we were arrested here, to when we were taken to Drancy, and to when we were put on the train to Poland, it was all French policemen.

'There was a selection process once you came off the train. Old people, children, anyone who looked less than fit and healthy, they were sent to the gas chambers and murdered. You look shocked, Owen? I know. You don't understand? You will. I never saw Sophie and Daniel again, I did not even get a chance for a last look. It was so chaotic as they sorted everyone out, but I know they were murdered that day.'

Owen was aware that he was rigid, as if any movement might appear inappropriate. There was a pause as André flicked the long piece of the ash off his cigarette, checked whether it was still alight, and then lit another one. Owen noticed that André had to hold the lighter with both hands to steady it.

'I was fine, which sounds odd to say. I was fit and I was an electrician, so I was able to work. At first, I didn't care, actually. I knew that my wife and my child had been murdered, so what was the point of struggling to stay alive? But there was a man from Lyon in the bunk next to me; he was about ten years older. He had lost his wife and all four of his children, and he looked after me. He said that I had a simple choice to make: whether to give up or to carry on. And he said that we owed it to our families to carry on. So, I made that choice and I decided I had to carry on. I worked in a quarry like everyone else, and then I was sent to work as a slave labourer for a company called Siemens – they were using a lot of the prisoners at Auschwitz. I survived that first winter and then, in late summer of 1943, myself and some other prisoners who were electricians – or so they thought – were moved. We were taken to a place called Nordhausen, which is in the centre of Germany. And there they were building another concentration camp, which they called Dora. This was also a factory to make rockets. So I became a rocket engineer – can you imagine!

'I had the advantage of speaking very good German; remember my family were originally from Germany. My friends and I were clever; we had to be to have survived so long. We did our best to ensure that they were not very good rockets. But then, at the beginning of this year, a few of us were moved again, this time back to France. The Germans were building a new rocket factory, underground at a place called Helfaut-Wizernes. It is in northern France, very near to where you were yesterday in St Omer. So, the Germans brought me back to France. They abandoned the site in July, and we managed to escape. I returned to Paris.

'The concierge, she had moved her nephew into this apartment. She assumed we weren't coming back. They looked like they had seen a ghost when I returned. He said he was looking after it for me. So I threw him out, literally. Down the stairs. He broke his shoulder and both his legs. The concierge does not like me, and I do not like her. I suspect she may have tipped off the police that we were leaving the apartment. If I find that out, I will deal with her too.

'So, let me finish my story. I remembered the policeman who came to arrest us. He was a sergeant. I remembered his number, I memorised it. When I got back here, I decided to look for him. It seems that I was not the only person who was looking for him – the SOE were too. He had arrested one of their agents who had then disappeared. This is how I came to meet Nicole. When I found him, I handed him over to her. By the time she had finished with him, they found out what had happened to their agent. He was murdered by the Gestapo, apparently. I am not sure what happened then, but this policeman is not around anymore. I now use my skills as a lawyer and a journalist to find people. I have good contacts, but the truth is that people feel obliged to help me. I seem to have acquired a certain moral authority; I don't know how long that will last. Perhaps one day, I will find myself. I can't live here properly, there are too many memories. That is why everything is piled up. I don't want the apartment to look or feel like it did before. One day, I will move out, but at the moment I can't do that either. So you see, Owen, our stories are similar!'

'Not at all, André. I cannot begin to compare what I have been through with what you have.'

'Maybe not, but we have both lost a woman we loved, and a child...' He shook his head then looked up. 'That is why I will help you. You need to find your child. Come, let's get to work.'

André soon realised that there was precious little to go on. Owen gave André a photograph of Nathalie and the cameo brooch, and they went through all the details again. It was agreed that Owen would return to England and see what he could dig out, and then return to Paris, perhaps in December. 'You need to find one small fact to help me, Owen. Anything, just one decent clue to help me.'

Owen started to write down his address in London, then decided better of it and gave him his parents' address in Surrey. He had no special reason to, but it did no harm to be cautious.

They walked up into Clichy for lunch, which did not finish until after four in the afternoon.

Walking back to his hotel Owen came across an RAF crew who were flying back to RAF Northolt that night and said he could hitch a lift if he bought them all one more drink.

By six that evening, and three drinks later, he had checked out of his hotel on the Avenue de la Grande Armée and was on his way to Orly Airport. His timing was impeccable. Just half an hour after he left, a harassed and very tall Englishman wearing a long dark coat and a trilby entered the hotel to enquire of an Owen Quinn, only to find out that he had just left.

It was most annoying. The man had been checking the hotel registration cards that recorded the names of all guests in the city's hotels since early morning and had only come across Quinn's at five o'clock. He was proving to be an unexpectedly elusive quarry.

–

Owen Quinn had returned to London buoyed by a sense of his own resourcefulness and his meeting André Koln. At last, he now felt in control – or at the very least, no longer *not* in control. He felt that if anyone could help find his wife, it would be André. Over lunch in Clichy that Saturday it had become clear that André had, if anything, played down his influence. It transpired that he was well connected in resistance circles and would be able to tap into that enormous body of people who were now effectively in control of much of French society.

'Don't keep asking me why I'm helping you, Owen,' André said. 'It's a challenge for me. It's good to help someone. I need to be doing things all the time. If not, then I have too much time to think.'

And Owen knew what he had to do. So far, he had given André precious little to go on: a couple of photographs and the cameo brooch along with the names Nathalie Mercier, Geraldine Leclerc and Nicole Rougier, though all of these identities would have been discarded long ago. Without something more substantial, it was going to be a hopeless task.

There were all of Nathalie's possessions that Roger and his team had removed from the flat on D-Day, but he had little hope that there would be any clues there, and in any case, they were hardly likely to return them to him. He could imagine Roger and Edgar and the lot of them sifting through everything to try to find some clues themselves.

He reflected on something that Nicole had said to him: putting aside whatever personal feelings he had for Nathalie, and whatever one thought of her as a Nazi, her skill as a spy and at leading a double- and then triple life had to be admired. She had managed to enter England undetected, had remained that way for a year, and then conducted herself as an active German spy with poise and bravery for the best part of three years before going to France. She had then managed to disappear. The idea, thought Owen, that this careful and clever person would have made the mistake of leaving some meaningful clue as to her real identity among her possessions was fanciful. The cameo brooch was, if anything, he now thought, probably designed to put him off the trail.

He had flown back to London on the Saturday night and, leaving the Admiralty after work on the Monday evening, found himself walking down Whitehall with Edgar, whose distinctive figure had materialised alongside him out of the early evening fog.

'Welcome back, Quinn. Any souvenirs from Paris?'

Quinn ignored him and carried on walking, attempting to quicken his pace.

'Not very happy, Quinn, have to tell you. I organised that little trip to France for you to answer one or two questions for yourself. I had to pull a number of strings with the SOE to get you over there. The idea was that you would play ball, not go gallivanting all over France. And did you get any answers?'

'No. Which is probably why I went gallivanting all over France, as you put it.'

'I see. Part of me is quite impressed, Quinn, actually. You obviously have some skills that you had previously kept well concealed, that at a different time we could do well to tap into. Avoiding the train in St Omer, palling up with those Americans, managing to fall off our radar in Paris for the best part of twenty-four hours. Very impressive, I have to say.'

'How did you know about all that – I mean the Americans, Paris and that?'

'It's my job to know, Quinn. And out of interest, what did you get up to in your lost twenty-four hours in Paris?'

'You know, the usual sightseeing, like half of the British and American armies – that kind of thing. I seem to remember having a drink or two. Anyway, why are you asking me – I thought it was your job to know?'

'Now look, Quinn.' Edgar was angry. 'Let me get something clear. We have all acknowledged that this situation with your wife is unfortunate, to say the least. We are sorry. But we really cannot have you going off on some freelance operation to find her. And in the highly unlikely event of you actually finding her, what are you going to do?'

'As you say, Edgar, that is highly unlikely, so...'

'But you may just be lucky. Very lucky. If that happens, we don't want anything embarrassing happening. We would rather matters were dealt with in a quiet manner. Diplomatic. We can help you. I am not sure what happened in Paris that Saturday, but mark my words, we will find out. So the minute you get a whiff of where your wife is, I am the first person you call. I can help you. Do I make myself clear?'

'Perfectly.'

And with that, Edgar peeled away into the fog filled night. For the first time, Owen Quinn had a sense of perhaps holding the upper hand over Edgar.

Chapter 31

London–Lincolnshire, December 1944

It was now December and London was just a few days away from what everyone hoped would be the last Christmas of the war. Owen had only a vague memory of what it was like before the war. Before the war, there had been plenty of cheer on the streets, of course, and you could sense a jollier atmosphere. Nowadays, it was altogether more restrained, but inside the pub around the corner from work there were some decorations and some attempt at cheer.

Owen had stopped in for a quick drink after work. Another week at work, and as short a time as he could get away with down at his parents' over Christmas. It would be dreadful, of course, and the New Year would be awful. André Koln had written to him at his parents' address. 'I really don't know why you didn't give these people your own address, dear,' his mother had said, eager to know who the letter was from and what it was about. Although there was no news, Koln suggested a longer visit in January. Thousands of collaborators had now been arrested, and Koln had some thoughts about how they might be able to find out something. It was all a long shot, but that was all he had, and he needed that to get him through the festive season.

He pushed his way towards the bar.

'Quinn, isn't it?'

Owen's face was clearly a picture of confusion. He could only just about hear the man he was shoulder to shoulder with in the pub.

'Hardisty? Don't you remember me? Air Ministry? Met up for dinner at Archibald's club? Both our wives are French.'

'Yes, yes, of course! I remember. Sorry, not quite with it today. How are you?'

'Can't complain, and wouldn't do much good if I did, would it!'

They both laughed. They agreed it wouldn't.

'I see you got promoted. Well done. Back at sea?'

'Not quite. At the Admiralty, round the corner. And you?'

'Still at the Air Ministry. Was hoping for a posting back to Paris, but there is some talk of sending us out east when that show is over. And how is your wife?'

He still didn't know how to deal with these questions. They always took him aback. Mumbling tended to help.

'Oh, you know – the war and that. She's over in France at the moment. Can't say a lot, you understand.'

'Of course, of course. My wife did enjoy meeting her though, that evening. Nice for her to be able to have a good old chinwag in French. Good for her. She hates London, actually. She was a bit confused though.'

'About what?'

'Where exactly your wife is from. She told my wife she is from Paris, but Amée noticed that once your wife had drunk a couple of glasses of that rather decent Côtes du Rhone her accent had a definite ring of Alsace to it, rather than Paris. She's a bit like that, Amée. Prides herself on being able to spot where people are from. Difficult in France, because they have less regional accents than we do, apparently. She can spot an Alsatian accent though: her grandfather was from that part of the world. It's got a slightly Germanic ring to it and sometimes they'll use German phrases, but in French, if you get what I mean. It was draughty in that room and Amée noticed that your wife said "*ça tire*". Apparently her grandfather used to say that too. Means "it pulls" and stands for nothing in French, but the German does. Maybe she had an Alsatian boyfriend, eh! Before you, of course, old chap.'

'Quite possibly.' He felt his breathing tighten. The first chink of a possible clue.

'Must push off, Quinn. We'll have a proper drink in the New Year, shall we? I say, it's bad news about old Archibald, isn't it?'

He had not seen or heard from Archibald since the night before D-Day, but didn't want to let Hardisty know that. He furrowed his brow and leaned towards him, adopting a confidential tone.

'What have you heard, Hardisty?'

'That he's taken a turn for the worse. Thought you'd know more than me. Apparently, he has been poorly on and off for a year or two, but since the autumn there's not been much they can do.' He lowered his voice. 'Lung cancer, I believe. Lost his son on D-Day. Must have been a blow, can't have helped. Bad show all round really. He's at home in Lincolnshire apparently. Anyway, you're more likely to see him than me, so when you do, please do give him my very best.'

'Of course, I will, Hardisty.'

–

He had to wait until the gap between Christmas and the New Year before he had an opportunity to head up to Lincolnshire in search of Archibald.

He had already booked a couple of days' leave and did not want to arouse any more suspicion than necessary. He decided that it was inconceivable now that Edgar did not have someone at the Admiralty keeping an eye on him. A few days' leave at his parents after Christmas would seem innocent enough.

He would also be able to use his uncle's car. He had hinted to his parents that there might be a lady in Lincolnshire whom he wanted to visit. He did not tell them as much, but when he was reluctant to disclose his reason for wanting to drive up there – other than an unconvincing 'I fancy seeing the countryside' – his mother optimist-ically jumped to a conclusion that he did nothing to discourage.

'We're so pleased for you, Owen. A chance to put everything behind you.'

On Christmas Day itself, he pored over maps of Lincolnshire. His only clue was his first meeting with Archibald, at Calcotte Grange. Archibald was telling him about how he had tried to retire to Lincolnshire. 'Between Boston and the sea,' he had said. He studied the map. It was a start, but not much more than that. There was quite a lot between Boston and the sea, but much of it was fields. Due east of Boston, there were around a dozen villages. He could certainly work with that, but then there was the possibility that 'between Boston and the sea' could also be north of Boston and south of it.

On his many solitary walks that Christmas, he racked his brain to try to remember what else Archibald had said in describing his idyllic life in Lincolnshire. They didn't live in a village, but near it. He remembered that much. There was something about a telephone box next to a war memorial on a village green. That would narrow it down. A bit.

He drove up to Lincolnshire the day after Boxing Day in a Ford Anglia borrowed from his somewhat reluctant uncle. Uncle Jimmy had bought the little black car when it first came out, just before the war started in 1939, and it was his pride and joy. But given that he managed to run it on the proceeds of his black market activities, he was not in a strong position to resist his nephew's increasingly firm requests over Christmas.

Boxing Day was a Tuesday and he was not due back at work until the following Monday, which was New Year's Day. He would need to head back to Surrey on the Saturday at the latest, so that he could return to London on the Sunday.

He set off at six in the morning. His parents had both decided to get up and wave him farewell from the front porch, his father already wearing his tie and his mother wrapped anxiously in her dressing gown.

By eight o'clock he was on the Great North Road, driving through grey sleet and slush, struggling to coax every bit of the 900 cc horsepower out of the Anglia. By eleven o'clock he was in Peterborough. He stopped to fill up the car with petrol and then had a cup of tea in a café, eating his mother's sandwiches and feeling thoroughly miserable. He headed towards Spalding and into Lincolnshire, wondering whether he was on a pointless journey. The chances of Archibald having any idea as to his wife's real identity were remote, but given that he had been involved in the case from the outset, he had to at least ask him.

The countryside had turned grey, the weather was showing no sign of improvement and, even before he reached Spalding, it was beginning to get dark. It was noticeable that all around him the land was flat, completely unbroken by hills or any interesting geographical features. As he got nearer to Boston he could sense that the Wash was just to his east. In reality, he knew that it was some miles away, but with little to keep his attention other than the long road and empty space all around him, it felt as if he was driving on the edge of the world.

It's possible, thought Owen, that Archibald may be too ill to help, even if he did know anything, and even if he did want to help.

He arrived in Boston at four o'clock and decided he would go no further. It all felt so bleak that it almost seemed as if there was nowhere to go. The town appeared to be deserted. It may be the largest town in the area, he thought, but that was about as much as you could say for it. He could see why the Pilgrim Fathers were so keen to leave.

If anything, the sleet was heavier now and he drove round what he took to be the town centre in an attempt to find somewhere to stay. He stopped at a small police station, where the desk sergeant insisted on seeing some form of identification. 'Satisfied' was not the quite word to describe his reaction, implying as it would some evidence of a positive attitude. But he did, at least, scrawl down the name of a hotel with the most basic of directions.

The hotel was approached down a narrow side street which was only just wide enough for the car to pass. At the end, the road widened into a small square, which had probably been a coaching stop. Any thoughts of a comfortable room and a roaring fire were soon disabused.

The owner wanted to know why Owen was up here. 'Having a few days break' sounded unconvincing enough to him when he said it, so he had no idea what it sounded like to someone else. The owner was a tall man who had to constantly stoop to avoid hitting his head on the broad beams in the low ceilings. He also seemed to be oblivious of the fact that he needed to wipe his nose. There was no evidence of a roaring fire, just a faint smell of gas and boiled vegetables. It was a good two minutes before the owner informed him that they were full. All twelve rooms. He helpfully informed Owen that it was the time of year. Quite why he could not have told him as soon as he came in, Owen was not sure. Or even have invested in a 'No Vacancies' sign. But Owen was partially relieved. He was feeling miserable enough without risking either his dinner or breakfast being served by a man who needed to wipe his nose.

The owner did at least give him details of a nearby pub, which ominously 'always' had vacant rooms. It was only 'round the corner. You can leave your car here. Please tell them Clifford sent you. Remember – Clifford.'

He never bothered to tell them Clifford sent him. If the hotel was strange, the pub was downright peculiar. Owen was wearing civilian clothes but, had he walked into the pub wearing a Waffen SS uniform, the reaction could not have been any less friendly. He had barely stepped inside the door, clutching his small overnight bag, when the whole pub fell silent. In itself, that was not too difficult; there were no more than twelve locals in there. But all of them stopped talking and drinking and stared at him.

With the whole of the pub intently listening in, he asked whether there was a spare room, was informed that there was, and gave his details. He had to spell 'Owen' twice and 'Quinn' three times and eventually offered to fill in the registration details himself. Otherwise, he risked checking out before he had checked in.

The room itself was basic, but not as dirty as he feared. It was lit by a single, low wattage light bulb with no shade, had a single bed that seemed to rise in the middle, and a wardrobe that only had three legs but somehow stayed upright, the back balanced optimistically on the skirting board. Most of the floor was covered with a large rug, but around the sides were just bare floorboards. The curtains closed with some difficulty, but even when they did, there was little to prevent a vicious draught.

He lay down on the bed, and was just thinking how tired he was after all the driving when he must have drifted off to sleep. He was woken by a gentle knocking on the door. When he opened it, a girl who could have been no more than sixteen carried in a tray, which she placed on the small dressing table by the window. He had paid for dinner, bed and breakfast, but was nonetheless surprised to find a plate of stew and some grey bread being deposited in his room at six in the evening.

He needed little incentive to be up early in the morning to start his search for Archibald. He had two full days, maybe part of Saturday if he really needed it. He spent the whole day driving around the villages between Boston and the sea. Not just the villages: if he passed through hamlets or even went past isolated farmhouses, they too were scrutinised.

By mid-morning, the foul weather of the previous day had been replaced by some quite pleasant sunshine, and he began to revise his opinion that this was the bleakest place he had ever visited. True, there was an ever-present biting wind, but the isolation of the countryside did have a certain attraction to it. The sky seemed to go on forever, and you did not need actually to see the sea, or even hear it or smell it, to be ever aware of its enormous and constant presence.

Not quite the end of the world, he thought – *but you can certainly see it from here.*

He subjected every village to a mental checklist. Was there a village green? A telephone box? A war memorial? Most of them had village greens of sorts, and telephone boxes. Only three that whole day had war memorials, and none of those had a telephone box near it. From what he could recollect, he was certain of two things: that the location was between Boston and the sea, and there was a war memorial with a telephone box next to it. On the village green.

In one village, he did make further enquiries. The village had a green and war memorial. The war memorial was near the village green, but across the road from it. Further down the road was a telephone box.

He had prepared a line of enquiry during the long journey up. 'My father served in the Navy in the Great War, under a Captain John Archibald. Told me he's retired to these parts. Married, possibly living just outside the village.' Much shaking of heads in the village shop, where the combined age of the shopkeeper and her two customers must have been well in excess of two hundred years.

By late afternoon he realised he had driven in pitch darkness for the past hour and his chances of spotting a village, let alone a telephone box, had diminished. He headed back to Boston, and this time when he entered the pub, one or two of the regulars even carried on speaking.

The next morning he decided to head up the coast road in the direction of Skegness. He had looked carefully at the map the night before: he had visited all the villages in a corridor directly between Boston and the sea. South of The Haven, it was more The Wash than the sea, so north seemed a better bet.

The weather was somewhere between the sleet of the first day and the previous day's sun. It was grey, but the wind was not as biting as the day before, and for the best part it was dry. He had not been driving long when he came to a road that he knew from the map that led to a cluster of three villages, so he came off the main Skegness road and headed in that direction. The complete absence of road signs had probably added hours to his search: he was constantly having to refer to his map, checking the tell-tale stumps by the road that indicated a road sign had once been there.

The first thing he saw in the first village he came to was a village green, with a war memorial very definitely on it. *Next to a telephone box.*

He pulled the car up outside the church, just as the priest was unlocking the large wooden doors. He followed him in.

'My father served in the Navy in the Great War, under a Captain John Archibald. Told me he's retired to these parts. Married, possibly living just outside the village.'

The priest shook his head.

'Is your father close to him?'

'Not terribly, they were in the Battle of Jutland together and he has always talked fondly... I just happened to be in the area you see, thought I'd look him up.'

'He's not in a good way, I'm afraid. Very ill. He is at home and I visit most days. Iris takes good care of him. They are a bit isolated. You would have passed their lane as you drove into the village without spotting it. I'm sure he would be happy to have a visitor. Here,' he guided Owen out of the church, 'let me show you how to get there.'

The sound of the car coming down the lane must have alerted Mrs Archibald, because when he parked up in the drive of their very pretty cottage, she had come out to see who it was. The location was certainly isolated; the lane petered out just past the cottage, and there were no other houses or buildings in sight.

She was wiping her hands on her apron, looking at him quizzically, as if she was not sure whether she could remember him.

'Good morning, Mrs Archibald. I am not sure if you remember me. I am Owen Quinn. Lieutenant commander Quinn. I am – was – a colleague of your husband's.'

'Yes, I remember. What a surprise – you ought to have let us know you were coming up. Do come in. You know he is ill, don't you? He is actually quite comfortable today, so you are lucky. The doctor was here earlier. Let me see if he's awake now and I'll see if he wants any visitors. Please do sit down.'

He was in a large lounge that opened from the hall. The room was replete with sofas and armchairs and a large piano, on top of which was a display of framed photographs.

He was about to walk over to the window to admire the view from the large picture window when Mrs Archibald returned.

'John was surprised you'd come, but he will see you. I cannot let you stay long. It doesn't take much to get him tired, and in any case the district nurse is due here at twelve.'

She led him into a large downstairs bedroom. Captain John Archibald was propped up on a number of pillows in a large bed, next to which an array of tablet bottles and other medicines lay on a small table, along with a jug of water and a half-full glass. His appearance was transformed. He looked gaunt, he had clearly lost a lot of weight and his skin was drawn tightly over quite visible bones. He appeared to move with some difficulty, but did hold out his arm when Owen came in to shake his hand.

'Owen Quinn. Owen Quinn.' There was a long pause after Captain Archibald repeated his name. 'Good chap. I always wondered whether you would find me. Rather glad you did. Thought you'd come looking. We underestimated you, I think. How are you?'

'I am all right, sir. I am sorry that you aren't.'

'So am I. Damned thing started a couple of years ago. Doctors thought they had it under control, but it turned out to be something nastier than they suspected. Thank you, Iris, I'll be all right, dear.' Mrs Archibald left the room.

'I've not got terribly long, Owen. I'm glad I've had Christmas here, and if I can hack it through to the spring, I may get a bit longer than the doctors said I would, but I know it is not too long. Tell me, why did you come here?'

'I heard you were unwell, sir, and I thought—'

'Now come on, Owen. You and I know each other well enough. If you are honest with me, I can be honest with you. Tell me the truth. You're not going to be allowed to stay terribly long, you know. Iris will have you out in half an hour. She seems to have this rule, thirty minutes per visitor. Go on.'

'You obviously know the full story about my wife, sir. I have not come here to discuss the whys and wherefores of what happened. I have come to ask for your help. I need to find her, and I need to know if you can help me in any way.'

'I've thought about this. Why do you want to find her, Owen? What good can it do?'

'Because I need to know why she did it, sir. I loved her with all my heart, and I need to know whether she ever had any feelings for me. Edgar keeps saying that I should just get on with the rest of my life, move forward. Maybe I should but, until I've seen her, I am not sure that I am going to be able to do that.'

'Owen, I am sorry about what happened. I did have reservations about the whole operation. In the end, the deception was so successful that perhaps anything we did to bring it about was justified, but from a personal point of view, the way we treated you, I'm not so sure. But I cannot see what useful purpose can be gained from finding her. Edgar and his lot are ruthless. He's always been determined that the truth about her should never get out. They won't want her put on trial, either here or in France. On the other hand, if you actually find her then they're not going to let her go. There will have to be some kind of justice. She is a Nazi spy, after all. But you have to think carefully about this. Do you want to see her strung up from a tree in some isolated wood?'

'But do you have any clue who she really is?'

Archibald shook his head. He started to cough and pointed to his water for Quinn to pass it to him. Mrs Archibald half opened the door.

'I am all right, Iris. Don't worry.'

'There is another reason, sir. Why I want to find her.'

'And what is that?'

Owen hesitated. He had decided earlier not to utter a word about this to anyone in England, but he was prepared to risk doing so now.

'She went to our GP in April, sir, not too long before she left for France. She was two months pregnant. She would have had the baby by now. My child. I have a right to know. I must see my child.'

Archibald sank back into his pillows, his eyes filling with tears and his head moving slowly from side to side.

'I can see why you're so keen to find her.'

'No one else knew, sir, apart from her GP, and he has no idea what Nathalie has been up to. And now you, of course.'

'We lost our only son in Normandy, you know. William. He was a second lieutenant in the Royal Scots Greys. Fourth Armoured Brigade. Killed on the 10th of June somewhere near Bayeux. Iris wept the night we heard, and has not mentioned his name since. Lord knows how she will cope when I'm gone. God Almighty, this war... what has it done to all of us?'

Archibald slumped back in his pillows and closed his eyes, silent for a few moments while Owen wondered whether he'd fallen asleep. The door opened and again Mrs Archibald's head popped through.

'John?'

'I'm all right, dear, just a few minutes. Pass me that notebook, Owen.'

There was a small notebook on the bedside table. Archibald leafed through it and eventually found what he was looking for.

'Here we are. Come here.'

Owen moved closer to the bed as Archibald dropped his voice and gripped his visitor's arm.

'Edgar came to see me in November. Never really liked the man. He warned me that you may try to find me, to see if I could help you find your wife. He wanted to know if I had any idea about who she really is. He insisted that if you came here I was to call him. I told Edgar that I had no clue about who your wife really was or where she was from. That was more his side of things. Annoyed him a bit. Told him he should have found out more himself. Every week or so one of his chums pops by. Just happens to be in the area, they say. Checking to see how I am. But they always ask me two things: have I heard from you, and have I thought of anything that could help them identify who Nathalie really is.

'Edgar does not know what I am about to tell you. And I hadn't planned to tell you this. I felt that it would not serve any purpose for you to find your wife. But when you told me about your child... and then, having lost William... I think you have a right to know, and I have no right to withhold it from you.

'The SOE are a funny lot. Your wife came under F Section, which looked after France. But there is actually another section in the SOE which looks after France too: RF Section. They worked with de Gaulle's lot over here. Never the twain could meet, I am told. Lord knows how that country is going to get sorted out once the war's over, but that's their business. A friend of mine works for RF Section, and they got wind of the operation with your wife. Of course, they would not do anything to jeopardise it, things were not *that* bad.

'Because of the connection I had with them, I was sent over to RF Section to try to patch things up, warn them off this case. They trusted me. Less confrontational than Edgar, so they said. Turns out that they had a woman in Paris who had very successfully infiltrated the Abwehr – that's German military intelligence, the people your wife was working for. They came across a reference to Magpie, the code name that the Germans use for your wife.'

'So do they have her real name?'

'No. They had very little, and because they weren't aware of the operation, they weren't able to put two and two together. But they did have something that I think could be most helpful to you. It's something that until now I had decided to keep to myself.'

Owen's eyes widened as Archibald painfully leafed through the pages of the notebook.

'Here we are. It is the name of the officer who recruited your wife and seems to have been her liaison. I wrote it down here. Take it.'

346

He ripped out a page from the notebook and handed it to Owen.

'I never thought I would do anything with this information, but there we are. If you find this chap, he will most likely know Nathalie's true identity. Whether he cares to tell you is quite another matter.'

Owen looked at the sheet of paper, which contained the name of the Abwehr officer written in large block capitals.

'I wouldn't bandy that piece of paper around, if I was you. Be careful with it. Destroy it once you have memorised the name. Never let on to Edgar that you got this name from me. Not that there is much he can do about it now, but still. He never really trusted me. I think he suspected that I might be disposed to helping you one day. Be careful though, Owen. Edgar will do everything he can to stop you finding your wife. He doesn't know about the child, does he?'

'No, sir.'

'Maybe that's as well...' Archibald's eyes were slowly closing as tiredness visibly crept over him.

'Thank you, sir. I do hope you...'

'What? Get better?' He laughed and coughed at the same time. Iris opened the door.

'Owen is just leaving, dear.' He beckoned him to come closer and grasped him by the wrist. The older man's touch was cold and bony.

'I felt bad about what we did to you. You were deceived. I know that we saved thousands of lives, no doubt about that. But you suffered. This,' he tapped at the piece of paper in Owen's hand 'clears my conscience. This is my absolution.'

–

Owen was away from the isolated cottage by noon. He drove straight back to Boston, checked out of the pub and headed west along the Holland Road towards the Great North Road.

He felt quite elated as he drove along, the expansive countryside to either side glistening under a cloudless sky. He had got the breakthrough he needed. Coming up to Lincolnshire had been a long shot: he'd had no idea whether he would find Archibald, or then whether Archibald would have either the information or the inclination to help him. He would pass this name onto André, and then see what happened. He kept repeating the name '*Georg Lange, Georg Lange, Georg Lange*' out loud. Back in the pub in Boston he had decided that

347

this was a name that he would never forget, so he had burned the piece of paper and flushed the ashes down the toilet.

Georg Lange, Georg Lange, Georg Lange.

He had slowed down now behind a tractor caked in mud, its wide plough taking up the width of the road and allowing him no space to overtake. After a mile or so, a small convoy of cars had built up behind him as the tractor slowed them all down. A mile later and the tractor turned right onto a farm track. He tried to get as much out of the little Anglia as possible. It would start getting dark soon and he needed to be on the Great North Road soon if he was going to find a petrol station open.

He was struggling with the Anglia on the greasy surface and slowed down to allow a car and a van to overtake him. One car remained behind him, seemingly in no hurry. He wound down his window and waved to indicate that it could pass. But the car stayed with him, dropping a bit further behind.

I know that it's the mood I'm in, he thought, *but it's unsettling me.* As far as he could tell, it was a large black car, certainly one that could overtake him with ease on the empty country road. Ahead was a lay-by. *Pull in there, get out to check a tyre or something, let him carry on, and stop being so silly.*

The black car stopped too, some way short of the lay-by. He could see at least two people in the car, apart from the driver. The front seat passenger appeared to be wearing a black coat.

His heart was beating fast and his breathing heavy. *This car has been following me for miles, it won't overtake me and now it's pulled into the lay-by behind me. Either I get out now or drive on, or...*

He could feel the sweat under his shirt and his face was burning. This was no coincidence. He sat still for a moment, tapping his hands on the steering wheel as if in time to music. *Maybe it's all in my imagination, Archibald going on like that and getting me worried. Let's give it one last try.*

He pulled out without signalling and hit the accelerator as hard as possible. The little Anglia swayed a bit on the surface, but he was travelling much faster than he had done before. The black car pulled out and within seconds was close on his tail. Ahead he could see a turning to the left. He slowed down without braking and turned left without indicating. In his rear-view mirror he saw the black car shoot past.

He pulled in to the verge and breathed a heavy sigh of relief, allowing his head to rest for a moment on the steering wheel. *I need a break, this is all getting to me. It's beginning to affect my judgement. Maybe a couple of drinks and a decent night's sleep.* He found himself actively looking forward to seeing his parents again. *Let them look after me for a day or two. Slow down. Relax.*

The interior of the car was very slightly darker when he lifted up his head. He looked to his left where a car had pulled up alongside him, so close that it was virtually touching his passenger side. The brown gloved finger of the driver was beckoning him to get out.

He scrambled out of his door and across the muddy verge. Two men were already waiting for him on the road. The long black Jaguar quietly pulled up in front of his car.

Two of the men were wearing police uniforms, the other was a civilian. One of the police officers came over and showed him his warrant card. *Police Constable Peter Sutton, Lincolnshire Constabulary.*

'Good afternoon, sir. Do you have any identification upon you?'

He found his Royal Navy identification card in his wallet.

'Lieutenant Owen Quinn, Royal Navy,' muttered PC Sutton, sounding both impressed and sarcastic as he handed the card to the other uniformed officer. He passed it behind him to the civilian in the black coat with an upturned collar, who had been standing a bit further away, impatient.

'Not at sea then, sir?' asked the man in the black coat, looking carefully at the ID card.

Quinn looked around him at the fields and the occasional tree swaying in what was now a fading light. It was going to be dark before he was on the Great North Road.

No, he wasn't at sea – at least not in the way that they meant it.

'Routine stop, sir,' said PC Sutton. 'We have had reports that a Ford Anglia with a single male passenger may be carrying black market goods. We would like to search you and the car, please, sir.'

'What kind of black market goods might they be?' Owen asked.

The two police officers turned round to the man in the black coat.

'Meat and other produce,' he said in a well-spoken and irritated-sounding voice.

'Well, you're welcome to search the car, but I can assure you I have nothing in it that shouldn't be there.'

The man in the black coat walked over.

349

'What have you been up to in this part of the world, sir?'

'Few days' leave. Thought I'd have some time in the country before going back to work in the city.' Quinn smiled.

'Very nice, sir. You're lucky to be able to get hold of enough petrol coupons to get you here and back.'

'I've been saving them up.'

'Very prudent, sir. Now if you don't mind, I just need to search you, so if you could start by removing your coat and your jacket.'

'You're welcome to, but I can assure you that you are not going to find any meat or other produce about my person!' Owen removed his coat and handed it them.

The man in the black coat did not respond. He was carefully going through all the pockets and even checking the lining of the coat and the jacket. Behind him, Owen could see the two policemen thoroughly searching the car, looking under the seats, lifting the floor mats, even running their fingers along the inside of the car roof.

'I'm sorry; I didn't catch your name.' Owen asked the man in the black overcoat.

'I'm with these two officers, sir. If you don't mind, I'm going to empty the contents of your wallet, just need to check.'

'What, for rashers of bacon between the pound notes?'

He said nothing, spilling the wallet onto the bonnet of the Jaguar. One of the policemen had a torch and was looking under the Anglia. When they had finished with the boot they even had a look at the engine. The black overcoat was now subjecting Owen to a very thorough body search.

By the time they had finished it was nearly dark.

'No meat or other produce then?' said Owen.

'No, sir,' said PC Sutton.

'So I can be on my way then?'

The black overcoat stepped forward.

'Can you tell me where you have been today?'

'I've told you, seeing the country. I have been staying in Boston and driving around the area.'

'Have you visited anyone?'

'Today?' asked Owen, trying to buy himself a bit of time as he attempted to judge what was behind this question.

'Yes. Today.'

'No.'

'Sure?'

'Yes. I am sure.'

The man in the black overcoat looked exasperated, as if finally beaten at a long game of chess. He put his gloves back on.

'So I can go then?'

The man in the black overcoat looked past him, well into the distance.

'Yes. You can go now, Lieutenant Commander Quinn.'

One of the policemen had walked back to the main road and was directing Owen as he reversed onto it. They waved at each other and he was on his way.

Probably a coincidence after all. They do stop people they think are handling black market goods. Odd how they had been following him, but he was worrying too much.

He didn't feel quite right about the whole business, nonetheless. For the time being, he was more concerned with getting on the Great North Road and finding enough petrol to get him back to Surrey.

The feeling of elation he'd had before had evaporated. He had worked out his plan. Tomorrow he'd write to André. 'Coming over to Paris early in the New Year,' the letter would say. 'And maybe in the meantime, André, you would like to see if you could trace the whereabouts of a Georg Lange, formerly of the Abwehr in Paris?' He'd wait until he was back in London before posting the letter, in a postbox that was near neither where he lived nor worked. *Best to be safe.*

But it was hard to concentrate. Something was niggling at him about the way he had been stopped, and he could not put his finger on it. Maybe it was nothing to do with being stopped, but everything that was going on, and going back to work next week. It was only much later – as he was driving through Bedfordshire and the pitch-black night enveloped the road and everything around it – that it hit him so hard it was as if the little car had been rammed from behind. He braked hard, the car skidding to the verge of the road just as a roundabout loomed into view.

He sat still, gripping the steering wheel, his heart pounding. He could feel the familiar symptoms of fear. The cold feeling sweeping through the body, the prickling of sweat all over, the sick feeling in the stomach, the tightening of the chest, the suddenly dry mouth and the need to look nervously around. He wound down the windows, breathing in the earthy taste of the country night. The man in the black overcoat. The smug, well-spoken man in the black overcoat who never said who he was and clearly thought he was so clever.

Well, thought Owen, he was so bloody clever that he had made a bloody stupid mistake, hadn't he!

Owen's emotions were all over the place: he was pleased with himself for spotting the mistake, but fearful now that he realised what it meant. Of course, they had not been looking for 'meat and other produce'. Stopping him had been no coincidence. They were onto him. There was no question about it.

It was thinking about going back to work that had done it, and more specifically his Royal Navy identity card, which he had shown to the policeman. The name on the card was Lieutenant Owen Quinn. *But that was the thing.* He had not yet got round to getting a new card, to reflect his promotion a few months ago to lieutenant commander. They had been nagging him at work to get it changed.

But what was it the man in the black coat said a few hours ago in that desolate lane in Lincolnshire?

'You can go now, Lieutenant Commander Quinn.'

If they weren't looking for him, how on earth would they have known that he was really a lieutenant commander rather than a lieutenant, as stated on his ID card?

The shivers were still running down Lieutenant Commander Owen Quinn's spine when he arrived back in Surrey just before midnight.

Chapter 32

Paris, January 1945

Georg Lange.
   Georg Lange.
   Georg Lange.

As soon as he had the name of his wife's Abwehr controller, Owen had felt the urge to go straight to Paris to find him. But the realisation that he had been followed in Lincolnshire had a sobering effect. He now knew for certain that Edgar was not far behind him. He needed to be cautious.

André had replied to Owen's letter by return of post. He would need time to trace Lange, he wrote. When Owen did come to France, he should allow at least a week for his visit, said André. Possibly longer.

Owen devised a plan based on the assumption that Edgar would find out soon enough that he had gone to France, and would follow him. He realised that he needed to steal at least a day on Edgar, ideally two.

He was certain that Edgar knew nothing about André Koln. He realised now just how lucky he had been to get the lift with the Americans from St Omer to Paris, gaining precious hours on Edgar. If he could get to Paris this time without Edgar realising straight away, he stood a chance. So he booked a week's leave at the end of January, telling colleagues that he was going to play golf in Scotland. On a visit to his parents, he borrowed the passport of a cousin with a different surname, but a decent enough resemblance. He explained that the Admiralty needed to see it to get him to the next level of security clearance. It seemed an implausible story to him, but it appeared to play well enough in Surrey.

He knew that word would soon get back to Edgar that he was going away, so he avoided telling colleagues at work that he was going on leave until Friday the twenty-sixth. He had no idea who at work was Edgar's source, but he was determined to make it as difficult as possible for them. He had actually booked the whole of that Friday as holiday, but came into work as normal in the morning. He was thus able to disappear at lunchtime, take the train to Folkestone, and was in Boulogne before half the office had retired to the pub at the end of the day and realised they had missed Owen leaving.

He had thought of calling in on Françoise and Lucien in Boulogne. Their loss had haunted him and made him ashamed of his own self-pity. But he knew he needed to keep moving, so caught the train straight to Paris instead.

André greeted him like an old friend when he met him at the Gare du Nord that evening. To Owen's slight embarrassment, he found himself being embraced by André on the platform.

'How are you, Owen?' Despite wearing a woollen hat, a heavy overcoat, and what looked like at least two scarves, André appeared to have lost weight. 'Excited?'

'Yes – and nervous.'

The station was busy and as they walked to the Metro he had to lean close to André to catch his words.

'The war has not improved this city, Owen. We're having a terrible winter. There's a shortage of everything: food, fuel – and even women! Food and fuel are one thing, but the women! For Paris, that is a problem.

'The worse thing though, Owen, is the atmosphere. You would have thought people would have learned something from the occupation, that they would have realised how fortunate they are. But no. The atmosphere here is terrible; it's like anarchy but without the revolution. So many people are denouncing so many other people, the accusations of collaboration... it makes the air... poisonous.

'You know me. If I think someone is a collaborator, then they should be dealt with. I have dealt with some myself. But Noisy-le-Sec, Santé, Fresnes – all the prisons, they are full of people who have been denounced as collaborators. And the officials – the people who allowed the Germans to carry on as normal – they are still around. You understand?

'I saw my friend Pierre the other day. He said that Paris has become a city of denunciations. Before the liberation people were being denounced, and there was hardly a pause after it for those denunciations to continue. The only difference is who they are being denounced to.'

They took the Metro to Notre Dame de Lorette and were walking to André's apartment in Rue Taitbout. Owen could see what André meant. He sensed that with the New Year, the city appeared to have lost some of its charm and replaced it with an unpleasant edge. When he had last visited in October, the city was still drunk with the euphoria of the liberation two months previously. Now it appeared to be suffering from the hangover. The short day hurriedly merged into a dark night, giving the city an ethereal quality that was not altogether peaceful. The vents set into the side of buildings and the drains and Metro outlets sent up small plumes of steam. Walking along the cobbled streets and boulevards, slippery with ice and slush, it felt as if tiny clouds had descended to the ground and were gently bouncing up again.

The apartment was much less chaotic than he remembered it. The table was clear and possessions were now neatly stacked into large boxes. There were still no photographs on display, but the apartment looked as if an attempt had been made to tidy it. André showed Owen into a small room.

'You can sleep in here. It was Daniel's room. We had a spare mattress. It is safer than staying in a hotel. I won't ask you to register.' He smiled. He put his arm round Owen's shoulder and led him back into the lounge. He sat Owen down on the sofa and he turned an armchair round to face him. As he lit a cigarette he poured red wine into two large glasses which appeared to have been rinsed rather than washed. He handed a very full one to his guest. Owen tasted the wine and noticed the bottle.

'Pétrus. Isn't that meant to be rather decent?'

'You could say that.' André paused while he held the wine glass back to admire it, then sniffed it appreciatively. 'I think it is probably the best Bordeaux. The *collabo* we removed it from was not so decent, I can tell you. Some friends of my parents had been hiding in the Dordogne. When they returned to Paris they found that their former bookkeeper was now living in their apartment and was refusing to move. He told them that he had bought the apartment legitimately. He had a document. It turned out that he had developed a very lucrative business redistributing the possessions of Jewish families. Of course, he never imagined them returning. So I visited the apartment with some colleagues from the FFI—'

'What is the FFI?'

'Sorry. *Forces Françaises de l'Intérieur*. It was the main resistance body. It is still very active. As you can perhaps imagine, it still has a lot of influence. Anyway, we visited the apartment. It was a very successful visit. My parents' friends got back their home, the FFI got their hands on another *collabo*, and I got a case of very good wine. The apartment was a treasure trove of things he had stolen. Maybe this was from a good restaurant. Your health. *Santé.*'

'And what would have happened to the *collabo*?'

'Who knows? Who cares? The jails are full of them at the moment, all pleading their innocence and telling anyone who'll listen that they love France and how it was a terrible misunderstanding. The big *collabos*? Some of them are being put on trial, but not many of them. The ones just below them, like the one who had taken the apartment, some of them are being dealt with. People say that many have been killed, perhaps hundreds maybe even thousands, but who knows what to believe? I daresay that in a few months most of them will have crept back into society. It may be a bit uncomfortable for some of them for a while, but it will soon be forgotten. You'll understand if I sound cynical, Owen, but I saw what happened when the Germans arrived. Life for most people here carried on as normal. Unless they were directly affected, the majority of people did not really care. The collaborators, yes, of course, they were a problem – but the real problem was the silent majority who quietly went along with the occupation, and suddenly appeared on the side of the resistance on the sixth of June.'

André shook his head and was lost in thought, finally lighting another cigarette and finishing his glass of wine. Owen had never tasted anything quite like it. He felt good. He had reached the magic moment which always came to him just after halfway through the first glass of wine, when things begin to feel better.

'I want to know, André. Why are you doing this to help me?'

André leaned back in his chair, balancing himself on his heels.

'Because I like you. Because you have had your child taken away from you, and I had mine taken away from me. Sure, the circumstances are very different, but I know how it feels, and if there was ever anything that anyone could do to get my son back for me, I would expect them to do it. And because it gives me something to do. Look,' he gestured around the apartment. 'I'm on my own here. My only company is my memories, and I can promise you that they are not good company. So I keep busy. I go for long walks. I have projects that interest me. Yours is one of those.'

André looked around the apartment, which showed all the signs of a life interrupted. For a while, he was lost in his thoughts, looking down at the ground, his forearms resting on his thighs, his feet bouncing restlessly up and down. He glanced at his watch, coughed and composed himself. 'We'll go and get something to eat soon, Owen, but first, let me tell you what has happened since I got your letter.

'It was a good job you got that new information. Before that, I realised that it was going to be impossible to find your wife if we had no proper information. The cameo brooch – I have shown it to jewellers and they cannot help. The strange thing is that it is gold, but there is no hallmark. But it is not going to help us find her. The possibility that her accent may have been from Alsace... that would narrow it down a bit, but only a bit. Alsace is a big region, and it was only liberated from the Germans in November. It makes some sense; many people in that area regard themselves as more German than French, but do you think she would have gone back to Alsace in July, when it was still under German control? I don't know. I could have gone to Alsace, but it would have been very difficult. The fighting there has only just stopped. I'd have needed some more information to help me there anyway.

'But Georg Lange – that is different. Very different!' He leaned forward and slapped Owen on the knee. The wine swayed violently in his glass.

'Getting that name made all the difference. I have made a lot of progress. We know that Lange was an Abwehr case officer, his job was to recruit and then look after various agents. We know that he was based at the German Embassy here since 1937, so was probably recruiting agents as far back as then – certainly before the war started. At some stage during the war, he moved from being based at the German Embassy in the Rue de Lille to the headquarters of the SD and the Gestapo in Avenue Foch. That would certainly have happened last year when the SD took over the Abwehr, but he may have gone before. Anyway, it is absolutely feasible for him to have been the person who recruited your wife and would then carry on as her case officer. It all fits very nicely. Have some more wine.'

André leaned back in his armchair and lit another cigarette.

'And how do we find out for sure, André, whether there is a connection between Lange and my wife?'

'It is simple, Owen. We go and ask him.'

André was now smiling. It took Owen a few moments to realise that he was being serious.

'And when do we do that?'

'Tomorrow!'

Early the next morning they were waiting in the street outside André's apartment for a contact of his from the resistance who had helped him track Lange down and had made the arrangements for going to see him. Gaston, André told Owen, had been a leading member of the resistance in Paris and was now involved in the FFI.

'He escaped from the Gestapo twice, he is a very brave man. It is important that we have him with us,' André said as they waited outside the apartment building at seven o'clock, the early morning chill eating into them with a surprising speed.

'As I told you last night, the FFI carry a lot of authority here. Lange is now being held by the French authorities. They look into the background of all German prisoners. If they are not senior officers, or are not suspected of any war crimes, or are not members of the Nazi Party, they will be the first to be released when the war ends. Otherwise, we would have to hold too many German prisoners for too long.'

A silvery-grey Renault with a long bonnet and wide running boards pulled up. A large man wearing a dark coat and scarf got out, embraced André, and shook Owen warmly by the hand. Before they got in the car, Gaston spoke to them on the pavement.

'Look, Émile is our driver today. Don't think he's rude or anything, but he doesn't talk these days. Not a word. He had a terrible time in August and was in a clinic until a few days ago. He checked himself out and we need to keep him busy. Don't worry, he's reliable and very trustworthy. Just don't expect him to be sociable.'

'What happened to him?' asked Owen.

Gaston looked down at the pavement, his hands deep in his coat pockets.

'One of tens of thousands of stories. He was in the resistance here in Paris. Émile was captured at the end of July and tortured in the

Avenue Foch. Émile knew some of the details about one of our key cells in Paris liaising with the Allies, so they really needed him to sing, but he didn't say a word. He had sent his family to the country, near Clermont-Ferrand. Someone told the Nazis where his family were, we have no idea who. So, one evening, Émile was taken to a cell and had to watch his wife being raped by four German officers. The last one, when he had finished, put his revolver inside her and shot her. Still, he said nothing. The next morning they took him to another cell. His two children were in there. His young son was hanging by the neck from a rope. He was dead. There was another rope next to him. They told Émile that unless he told them everything, his little girl would be next.'

Gaston made towards the car. Owen started to speak, but André put his arm across to stop him.

'Don't... don't even think of asking.'

Émile turned briefly as they got in, a dark beret pulled down just above his hooded eyes, which surveyed them through the rear-view mirror. As they headed south through the quiet streets of early morning Paris, Gaston briefed them.

'We are going to a prison for German prisoners of war. Those that are cleared — that is, the non-Nazis — will be sent to a holding camp. They will be released when it is safe, when the war is over. The others, those suspected of war crimes, they will face further justice.

'We managed to track Lange down to this prison. He is being processed at the moment. I have to tell you though, it looks like he is in the clear. There is no evidence that he is a Nazi Party member or has committed any war crimes. He was probably a typical Abwehr officer — not a Nazi. He's clever, apparently. Smart is the word they used to describe him. He was wearing a Wehrmacht uniform when he was caught, and there is no evidence against him. It is not going to be easy.

'We used to have free access to these prisoners. Straight after the liberation, we could even take them away and do what we wanted with them. If it was up to us, we could get the information you want out of him in an hour, probably far less. It would be no problem. But with the authorities, it is not so easy now. We can no longer have open access to the prisoners. That is why we are going early on a Saturday morning. The governor of the prison is away. The senior officer on duty today is very sympathetic to us. He will give us access to Lange, but on one very strict condition – we are not to harm him. Understand?'

Owen had expected the prison to be on the outskirts of the city, but they had driven for some time and Paris was long behind them. They passed Fontainebleau and soon after turned off the main road. The land was flat and covered in a layer of rolling mist, the open landscape broken only by islands of trees and isolated farm buildings. The road had narrowed and was now well above the level of the land on either side of it, which had taken on the appearance of soggy marshland. After about twenty minutes, a large grey building appeared out of the mist ahead of them. They slowed down for a police checkpoint and there were two more before they drove through the main prison gates.

They were ushered into the office of a tall man whom Owen took to be Gaston's contact. From the way they embraced, Owen imagined that they had been *résistants* together at some stage.

He looked at André's pass and nodded, and then spoke in a fast Parisian accent to André, who translated.

'He wants to remind you that there is to be no physical violence against this man. Lange is not expecting us, by the way.'

The senior officer led them through the warren of corridors. It appeared that the building may originally have been a castle, with various prison buildings being added at different stages. The overall effect was of a confusing collection of blocks and rooms, linked by gloomy corridors and courtyards. After walking down a corridor they came to a door which the senior officer unlocked. They were now in a courtyard, surrounded by high, grey walls. The air was damp and oppressive, the stone walls glistened. A group of German prisoners were milling around the courtyard, hunched against the rain, staying close to the walls and what little shelter they offered. They were guarded by three French soldiers.

Owen was shocked. Apart from the German prisoners he had seen clearing rubble while driving through Boulogne, this was the first time he had come face to face with any Germans, despite being at war with them for over five years. Gaston spat on the ground, in the direction of the prisoners. André shot them a mocking smile. But it was not Owen they were looking at, nor Gaston, nor the officer. This group of men with their grey prison uniform and hollow eyes, huddled together in the drizzle against the grey brick, could not take their eyes off André. It was unsettling, as if they recognised him.

The senior officer unlocked a door at the end of the courtyard and they were now climbing down a series of steep steps.

'Why were they all staring at you, André?'

'Don't you realise, Owen? They know my type, they've had years of training. I was supposed to have been eliminated, remember?'

They waited in a narrow corridor while the senior officer went into a small office. The steps had taken them down into what now felt like a dungeon. The only light came from a series of yellow light bulbs, all protected by steel mesh, and the atmosphere was distinctly damp. They were now joined by a guard who led them down another corridor, through further locked doors and into a small corridor with four more locked doors. They paused in the corridor.

'I will carry out the interrogation,' said Gaston. 'Leave it to me. André will translate for you. We do not want him to know at this stage that André speaks German; we may need that later. I will explain that you are from British Intelligence. Under no circumstances must you say anything about your relationship with her. You must remain silent. You are here as an observer. You understand? You have the photographs, André?'

André nodded and turned to Owen. 'Don't worry. We know what we are doing.'

'Let's go.' Gaston signalled to the guard, who unlocked the door nearest to them.

The room was about twenty feet by twenty feet, harshly lit and windowless. Behind a metal table that was fixed to the stone floor sat a well-built man with slicked-back fair hair. A guard was standing to the side of him. In front of the table were three chairs. There was nothing on the table apart from an empty ashtray.

The man stood up as they filed into the room. He was on the short side, and was wearing the same grey uniform they had seen the other prisoners wearing. The guards left the room, leaving just the three of them facing Georg Lange.

André took a packet of cigarettes out of his pocket and tossed them onto the table, gesturing for Lange to help himself. He took out three, placed one in his mouth and two in his top pocket. Then he smiled. André held a lit match for him, and lit a cigarette for himself.

'We are from French Intelligence,' said Gaston, pointing at himself and André. 'Our colleague here is from British Intelligence.' Lange's eyebrows raised, part surprised, part interested.

'We are interested in finding about some of your agents. We are going to show you some photographs of Abwehr agents that we have arrested. We need to establish their true identities. We believe you may have been connected with them. It would be in your interests if you could tell us what you know about them.'

Lange leaned back, so that his wooden chair was resting on its two back legs. One arm was folded across his middle, the other holding the cigarette in front of him, the elbow resting on the folded arm. His eyes narrowed, before he replied in what to Owen sounded like immaculate French.

'What do you mean by in *my* interests?'

'I mean,' said Gaston, 'that if you co-operate then your chances of an early release will be greatly improved. If you fail to co-operate, then you may find that you are a guest of the French Government for many years to come.'

Lange laughed and shrugged his shoulders. 'My understanding is that the Allies play by the rules.' He smiled directly at Owen as André quietly translated. 'I am a prisoner of war, gentlemen. I am covered by the Geneva Convention. I am not obliged to answer any questions. I only have to give my name, my rank, and my serial number. I have done nothing wrong. There are no conceivable grounds for detaining me any longer than necessary once this war is over.'

'You are an Abwehr officer, though.'

'If you look at my file, gentlemen, which I am sure you have, you will see that I am a Wehrmacht officer. I was arrested in Paris on the 25th of August wearing a Wehrmacht uniform. In my file is an affidavit I have signed testifying that I am not a member of the Nazi Party, neither have I ever been a member of it. You will find no record of my being a member of the Nazi Party. I have done nothing wrong. I am very confident I will be released along with all the other Wehrmacht soldiers, because I know that there will never be any evidence that I ever did anything improper. You should not be wasting your energies on me, gentlemen. There are plenty of Nazis who you should be chasing after. Certainly, I worked in the field of military intelligence, but I do not think that is a war crime, is it? You may not choose to believe me, but I was never a Nazi. Sure, I was a loyal German, but never a Nazi. You will find no evidence that I was. I am sorry; I am aware that I may be repeating myself, but what more can I say – other than the truth?' He inhaled deeply, folded his arms, leaned back in his chair and smiled politely.

André took an envelope out of the small briefcase he had brought with him and removed some photographs.

'I am going to show you some photographs,' said André. 'They are of people we have arrested who we believe are Abwehr agents. We believe they are giving false names. We want you to tell us their real names. As we say, if you co-operate it will be in your interests.'

André placed five photographs in front of Lange, as if he was dealing from a pack of cards. They were upside down from Owen's point of view, but he could clearly see that they were of three women and two men. Nathalie's photograph was on Lange's far right.

Lange studied them carefully, picking each one up and tilting it in the light. His face showed no hint of recognition whatsoever. When he had finished he placed them all down again and laid his hands flat on the table, his fingers spread out as he looked once more up and down the photographs.

'No. I am sorry, gentlemen. I do not recognise any of these people. You understand that in military intelligence we had very little contact with French citizens. There was some, of course, but "agents",' he was waving his hand with the cigarette in a dismissive manner, 'agents appear in books. Military intelligence is all about maps, codes and radio intercepts – as I'm sure you know. Very boring, actually. So, I don't think I can help you. If you are looking for spies, then I suggest you try a library.' He smiled at each of them in turn, anxious to convey the impression that he was genuinely sorry.

Lange helped himself to more cigarettes, this time brazenly removing four from the packet and placing three of them in his top pocket. André lit the one in his mouth for him.

Gaston hesitated as if he was not sure what to do next. He had clearly not expected Lange to stonewall them quite so effectively. 'We have different levels of interest in these people. There is one in particular that we want to know about, more than the others.'

'And I imagine that it is this one, am I right?' Owen's heart leaped and he fought to control his excitement. Lange was holding up the photograph of Nathalie. It had been taken in Hyde Park, so she was smiling and clearly out of doors. 'Shall I tell you why? Because the other four have had their photographs taken in a police station. Mug shots. This one, I suspect, is not in custody, as otherwise you would have a custody photograph of her. She is the odd one out. Am I right? Please do not treat me as if I am a fool.'

Gaston appeared to sigh. 'What can you tell us about her then, Lange?'

It was impossible to calibrate, but the pause that followed felt just a fraction too long. It was enough to convince Owen that Lange was hesitating. His face was very still; if anything he was trying just too hard to show no flicker of emotion. He was allowing himself an extra split second to compose an appropriate response.

'Nothing. I have never seen her before, have I? I thought I had told you that.'

'Are you sure, Lange? If we find out that you are lying to us, that will put you in a very difficult position.'

'I cannot see how. If I don't know someone, then I don't know them, do I? Is there anything else that I can help you with?'

There was nothing. They left the prison disconsolate. The idea of placing Nathalie's photograph among a selection of others had seemed a good idea at the time, but it had backfired. Their debrief in the car felt desperate. Lange was smart, they agreed. He might well know Nathalie, but he was clearly not going to admit to it. The rest of the journey back to Paris was conducted in silence. Every time Owen looked up he could see Émile's eyes darting around in the mirror. Owen was devastated. Lange had seemed to be their best bet for finding Nathalie, but he was not going to co-operate. He knew that they had no proof of the connection, so could easily block them. Owen could feel Nathalie slipping from his grasp, after seeming to be so close.

They were dropped off in the Rue Taitbout and André and Owen trooped miserably up the stairs, with the concierge's beady eyes following them from the entrance hall.

For a while, nothing was said. Owen sank into the sofa and helped himself to one of André's strong cigarettes. André paced up and down, at one stage kneeling down by the box containing photographs and glancing at one or two.

Then he seemed to have an idea, turned to Owen and said 'Wait here,' and disappeared.

It was an hour before he came back. When he did, Owen was none the wiser. 'I rang Gaston. He liked my idea. He is going back to the prison to collect something. Then I'll take you into the sewers of Paris.'

Chapter 33

Strasbourg, January 1945

For the first time in five years, the bells of the Notre Dame were able to summon the New Year into a free city. The city had been occupied by the Nazis for nearly four and a half years, longer than almost any other city in France. The bells sounded muted.

There was some shouting in the street, but her mother was asleep and the baby was settling in her arms. She stood at the window, inside the drawn curtains, gently rocking. Over the rooftops, she could just make out the main spire of the cathedral, lit up for the first time in years. In a nearby street she could hear a crowd singing *La Marseillaise*. After the years of silence, you could hardly turn a street corner without hearing that music, she thought. On the table behind her was a half-full glass of white Alsatian wine, its chill long gone. Her mother had insisted on opening a bottle, but she did not feel like celebrating.

–

Her son had been born on an unusually warm Tuesday afternoon at the end of October. It was an easy birth and she had been well looked after by the doctor and the women at the farm. Even the four boys seemed to respond to the baby, spending hours crowding round him, fascinated by every feature. Once the baby was born, the doctor said, the boys began to recover.

Although he had her eyes, when she looked at the baby, she could only see Owen. For most of the time, this gave her great comfort, and she felt an overwhelming love for the baby and its father. When no one was listening, she would talk softly to the baby in English. 'Everything will be all right,' she would assure him.

At other times, she looked at the little one and the enormity of what she had done would hit her. Then she felt distant from the baby and for a few hours would just go through the motions of motherhood, before her mood changed again.

Everyone at the farm had been unsettled by the three men who had appeared near the entrance the night before the birth, but they soon reassured themselves that it was nothing. Only she and the doctor guessed they were Germans, and only she had heard what they said. Their presence haunted the farm for the remainder of her stay there.

She wanted to move on soon after the birth, but the doctor persuaded her to rest. The four boys had repaired enough of the house to make it habitable and, more importantly, warm. To the east, parts of Alsace were still at war. Fighting was raging over the Vosges Mountains and every night the sky was streaked with Allied aircraft.

On the last Saturday of November, the priest from the village came to visit them.

'I have two pieces of news for you. The first good. The second bad.'

They had all gathered around the table in the farmhouse. The priest was enjoying being the centre of attention on a day other than Sunday. He poured a second glass of the rough *vin de table* that was being passed round and continued.

'The good news is that Strasbourg has been liberated. It was two days ago, on Thursday.'

The doctor translated into Polish, German and Yiddish, which she now knew was the language he communicated to Rachel in. The Roma women understood Polish. It was a long process. There were polite nods of approval around the table. They were pleased that Strasbourg had been liberated, of course but, after what they had been through, good news would have to be much more profound.

'Yes. There was a real battle. The Americans and the Free French broke through the Saverne Gap on Wednesday and the French Second Armoured Division entered the city at eleven in the morning on Thursday. General Philippe Leclerc was the commander who liberated the city!'

The others looked at the priest who appeared to be overcome with emotion. They all raised a glass to General Leclerc, of whom none of them had ever heard.

'The second item of news is not so good,' said the priest, deploying his most funereal voice.

'Last Monday a whole family was killed at a farm not far from here, just the other side of the hill behind us. I say last Monday. In fact, that is when their bodies were discovered. They were probably killed some days before.'

The doctor was hesitating before translating. When he started to speak, he kept it very short. He knew that there was only so much bad news the people around the table could take.

'All of them had their throats cut. Mother, father, two sons and daughter.'

The priest shook his head. The doctor did not translate.

'Apparently there are reports of small bands of renegade German troops operating in the area. Probably ones who became detached from their units and have nowhere to go. Usually SS. You had better take care.'

When the priest left, they agreed it was time to leave the farm. The doctor was going to take them all to Nancy, where a proper refugee centre had been set up. She said she was going to head south to join her family in Lyon.

—

She had waited at the farm for just an hour after they left, and then she and the baby headed east. The fighting had only just ceased in Alsace and there were reports of pockets of German resistance, but a mother carrying a baby proved irresistible to the first American truck they saw, and they were in Strasbourg by lunchtime.

It was hardly recognisable as the city she had left four years previously. The damage, she had expected, along with the other physical aftermaths of war. The air of resignation and the exhaustion etched on the faces of the people, she hadn't expected. The city was teeming with French and American troops, and seemingly thousands of German prisoners of war, slowly marching in long lines, enduring the pent-up resentment of a long-occupied population.

It did not feel like she had come home, but she had nowhere else to go. Ever since her son had been born she had understood what was driving her back to Strasbourg: if Owen was ever going to find her, it would be here.

The area where her mother lived was unscathed compared to the centre and some of the outskirts. A neighbour who she didn't recognise helped her lift her bags up the stairs to the apartment while she carried the baby.

Her mother had said nothing when she opened the door. Her lips trembled and she reached out a hand to cup the baby's face before hurrying her into the apartment.

'Do you want to tell me your story now or later, or shall we pretend that nothing has happened?'

She sat down in the familiar armchair. Her son was awake and feeding from her breast.

'Do we have hot water?'

'Is that your explanation?'

'If I can have a hot bath, then I will tell you everything.'

Her account to her mother had been so well rehearsed, so tightly edited and refined, that it did not take long. It had been prefaced with an instruction that there were to be no questions.

'I left in May 1940 because I was afraid. You had already been evacuated, so I couldn't contact you. I thought I would return, but I went to Paris. I came across the identity card of a woman my age. She looked similar to me too, so I assumed her identity. She also had the permit and papers that allowed her to live in Paris, so it was all so easy. I still thought I would return, but life there was not bad. You have to believe that, in many ways, it was normal. I found work in one of the big hospitals. I thought many times of contacting you, but I was afraid that would compromise my identity. If I came back or even risked contacting you, it would all be too complicated. I was worried it could unravel everything. I had a comfortable life in Paris. I was selfish, I am sorry. I am ashamed of that. But I am back now.'

Her mother raised her eyebrows; she appeared unconvinced and certainly surprised at the brevity of her daughter's account of the past four years.

'Not even a letter?'

'I'm sorry.'

'And the baby?'

'The baby was born a month ago in Paris. As soon as I heard that Strasbourg had been liberated, I came home. Here I am!'

She laughed, but her mother remained stony-faced.

'The father?'

She had the script ready. 'A good man. A doctor at the hospital where I worked. But he helped treat injured resistance fighters and had to leave in a hurry. That was at the end of April. I have not heard from him since. I don't know. He did buy me this ring though. If it makes you feel better, you can tell people that I was married to him.'

Her eyes filled with tears for her baby's absent father. Her mother softened and reached over to pick up the baby.

'It all sounds very innocent to me, Ginette.' She was clearly not convinced. 'A few days before I was evacuated, two men came round asking for you. They frightened me. I told them that you were at work, which you were. I never said anything to you at the time. I was going to mention it, but then I was evacuated.'

'Probably from the hospital here.'

Her mother shook her head firmly. 'Probably not, Ginette. If they were, they would have been aware you were at work. The one who did the speaking, he was from Alsace. The other was German, I'm sure of it.'

'I thought you said only one spoke?'

'Ginette, don't argue with me. I know Germans, and the other man was German. I know it. What were you mixed up with? Was it the reason for your disappearance? What about the strange political views you used to have?'

She got up and went to draw the curtains.

'Whatever my views were, four years of the war have changed them. In any case, they had nothing to do with me leaving. I'm home now. Do you want me to stay – *us* to stay?'

She had noticed that her mother had been cuddling the baby, pressing her cheek against his.

'Of course. Where else are you going to go, anyway?'

'If we stay, it is on the understanding that we discuss these matters no more.'

'Is there something important you have to tell me? Like, his name?'

'I was waiting. I thought I would wait until I got home. I wanted you to have a say.'

They agreed on Philippe, after the general who had liberated the city the previous week.

'And what will you do now, Ginette?'

'I'll get a job, mother. The hospital may take me back.'

The room was dark apart from a dim lamp in the corner. Philippe was fast asleep in his grandmother's arms. She knew that her mother did not believe her, but she knew that she would not pry any further.

So life would go on as normal and she would wait.

And wait.

–

The bells of the Notre Dame had finished pealing and Strasbourg was surprisingly quiet. In the next room, she could hear her son begin to stir.

Chapter 34

Paris, January 1945

Gaston returned to André's flat in the early evening and handed a package over to him. Only then did André explain his plan. Up until then, Owen had imagined that they might actually be spending the night in the sewers.

André's idea, he had to admit, was an inspired one. It was risky and could go badly wrong, but he could not think of a better alternative. His real worry was that Lange would be released soon and would then disappear.

'We'll walk,' André said as they turned left out of his apartment block and headed north.

It was a damp night and it was a while before either of them spoke.

'This is Pigalle we are entering. Have you heard of it?' André asked.

'The red light district?'

'If it was only the red light district that would be fine. This is where everything that shouldn't happen does happen. It is where the underworld of Paris gathers. Anything you want, you can buy here. Anything. Even the Germans couldn't tame it in the whole time they were here. You see that guy over there?' They were on the Rue Pigalle, walking past a small bar at the corner of an alley. André was waving at a friendly-looking man in his early forties leaning against the door. Despite the cold, he was in shirtsleeves.

'When he last came out of prison he discovered that his wife had been having an affair with a friend of his. He cut his wife's ears off and made her eat them. I will leave it to your imagination what he did to the friend.'

'And what happened to him?'

André laughed. 'Nothing. Lack of evidence. There is very little evidence here in Pigalle.'

A short man in a full-length cashmere coat was shepherding a young girl out of a long Citroën which was blocking another alley. 'If you have specialist tastes, this is where you come. That is Claude over there. He specialises in young girls, sometimes for himself, but mostly for clients. He did a lot of business with German officers. He was able to pick up a lot of intelligence that way, I am told. Boys you get in another street. Any age you want. The Germans had a taste for fourteen-year-olds, I'm told.'

They darted across the road as an argument started in the alley: a delivery truck was objecting to Claude's Citroën blocking the road.

'Right, we're going into the side streets now, just be careful. If we keep moving fast we will be all right. The pickpockets don't like a moving target. I'm known here anyway, but you look like what you are.'

'Which is?'

'A stranger.'

They had crossed Place Pigalle and turned into a long, narrow alley. At first Owen thought it was covered, but the buildings on either side were no more than feet apart, and the sky was obscured by overhanging balconies that appeared to touch each other. Halfway along, André turned up a small flight of partially concealed steps and then they cut back into another alley, which had no street lighting, relying on the occasional dim light thrown out from the gathering buildings. The alley appeared to come to a dead end, but André opened a creaky wrought iron gate and they found themselves in a tiny courtyard. A statue of a naked lady stood in the middle of the courtyard, surrounded by plants. A spout that had once turned it into a fountain was sticking out of the top of her head. The ground was bathed by low level lights. André knocked on one of three doors opening onto the courtyard.

Owen heard André mumble something, and mumbling in turn from the other side of the door. Then a delay as a series of locks, bolts and chains were noisily unfastened. The door was unusually high and the man who had opened it was unusually short. He stood behind the door, holding it open just far enough for André and Owen to squeeze in, then hastily shut it, putting all the locks, bolts and chains carefully back into position.

Owen had never seen anything quite like it before. The whole of the ground floor and first floor appeared to have been excavated to form one large room. It was just one large space, with no floors other than the ground floor and no dividing walls. The roof beams were exposed and a small bird was flying between the rafters. Owen could not work out what was keeping the building standing if all the supporting walls and joists had been removed. It felt like an urban cave. There were desks, printing presses, drawing boards, shelves of pencils and inks and a door in a side wall that opened into a dark room. On the opposite wall there were three sinks, side-by-side. One was stained black with ink. There was a small table next to another sink, with food and drink on it. The middle sink had a syringe on the side. The back wall had a ladder propped against it, leading to more shelves. A black and white cat stared down at them from one of the shelves, wedged in between volumes of large, torn, leather ledgers.

'Owen. Welcome to the den of the best forger in Pigalle, which also means the best forger in Paris and, of course, in France – if you don't count Marseilles, of course. We tend not to count Marseilles. Makes life easier. What are you calling yourself this week, Louis?'

'This week?' The short man was jumpy and needed to think about the question. 'This week you can call me Bertrand, André. You can still call me Louis, but Bertrand may be safer.' Bertrand could not have been more than five foot tall and had a nervous tick. Every few seconds his head jerked towards his right shoulder in an involuntary movement. Not good for a forger, Owen thought.

'Now then. Bertrand is a genius, aren't you, Bertrand?'

Bertrand nodded.

'If Bertrand can't copy it then no one can. A clever man. But he has also been a naughty boy, haven't you Bertrand?'

Bertrand now spoke fast, in a surprisingly deep voice.

'That is unfair, André. I explained to the FFI and they understand. If I hadn't done what they asked, the Germans would have killed me. It was the tiniest of favours. And I promise you, I didn't do a good job, did I?'

He sounded nervous. André walked over and put his arm round Bertrand's shoulders.

'Bertrand's mistake – Louis, you don't look like a Bertrand, you know – was to forge some documents for an SS officer. All through the war he was so helpful to the resistance and then he goes and spoils it all in the last few days.'

'André, I promise you. I had no alternative. But I made a deliberate mistake. He was caught, wasn't he?'

'So now the FFI have agreed that as long as Bertrand continues to help us, he will keep his balls, won't you, Bertrand? Not that I think you have much use for them, but they are nice to have anyway, eh?'

Bertrand calmed down when he realised he was not in more trouble. He made a big play of shaking Owen's hand and thanking the British. The British passport was the hardest to copy, he wanted Owen to know that. For him, this was clearly the greatest compliment he could pay. The British passport and the Greek passport, but who wanted a Greek passport? A bottle of Absinthe appeared from a shelf and they all sat round a table in the middle of the room while André carefully explained what Bertrand was to do. Owen toyed with his glass but avoided drinking any. He noticed André did likewise. Bertrand made notes of what was being said and asked a few questions, refilling his glass as he wrote. He understood. Once he slipped into the role of forger, he was no longer the nervous little man with the jerking head. He was now calm and sounded authoritative. Owen could see why he was a master.

'And when do you want all of this by, André?'

'Tuesday?'

'Impossible. Some of these documents you want will be very difficult. One of them I have never attempted before. Thursday at the earliest.'

'Wednesday morning?' asked André.

'How about Wednesday evening?'

'No, Bertrand. I'll be here Wednesday lunchtime. If they're ready, you get to keep your balls. For me, that would be a very good incentive.'

Bertrand nodded. There was no need for André to add that the work had better be good. That was taken for granted.

–

He arrived in Paris while his prey was in the forger's den.

He had been seething when he found out that morning that Quinn had slipped the net and had been spotted in Boulogne, getting on a train for Paris. There would be time for recriminations later, Edgar reassured himself as the RAF plane began its descent into Paris. It was simply appalling. He had put enough measures in place to ensure that if Quinn so much as bent down to tie his shoelace, he would know about it. And what had happened? Quinn had booked a week's leave, which, of course, he knew about. He'd even paid for the hotel in St Andrews, they had checked on that. But he'd fooled those bloody idiots by leaving early, and it was more than twelve hours before they could pick up any trace of him.

Now the priority was to find Quinn. He would not lose him this time. He could not begin to contemplate the possibility of Quinn actually finding his wife, and what the consequences would be of that. It really did not bear thinking about. Edgar reached into the pocket of his greatcoat and felt the reassuring shape of his service revolver. That would not happen.

The last time, it had been simply unacceptable that the French police had been so tardy in supplying the hotel registration cards. He bet that they had been far more accommodating to the Germans. Now he had a promise that he would have help from the Embassy. He may have to stay up all night, but he'd be most surprised if he had not found Quinn by the end of Sunday. Then it would just be a matter of keeping a careful eye on Quinn and letting him do all the work.

–

André went on his own to collect the documents on the Wednesday and was back in the apartment by two that afternoon. Gaston was coming to collect them at five. Owen stayed in the apartment as much as possible. He had no doubt that by now, Edgar would be searching for him in Paris. The hotel registration cards would be of no help, so he did not want to give him the satisfaction of finding himself in the same queue for the Eiffel Tower. He felt safe in the apartment.

Émile drove them south of Paris, the journey to the prison taking a bit longer than it had early on the Saturday morning. He had not acknowledged them as they entered the car, but throughout the journey Owen noticed that he kept glancing at them. Gaston's contact had warned them not to arrive before six, when the governor would still be on duty. After seven would be better. All the prisoners would be back in their cells by then.

They arrived at seven thirty and Gaston's friend made a couple of calls while they waited in his office. Ten minutes later the phone rang and they were on their way through the labyrinth of corridors, courtyards and staircases.

Lange was handcuffed to the chair when they went into the same room as they had seen him in on Saturday. He looked confused and a bit dishevelled. His fair hair, which had been carefully slicked back on Saturday, appeared uncombed. He sat behind the table, looking from Gaston to Owen to André, but the look was a nervous, darting one. The air of self-confidence that had been so evident before was absent. André lit a cigarette, making a point of not offering one to Lange, who looked as if he could do with one.

'Is this really necessary?' The German asked, noisily holding up his two hands as far as the chains would allow.

'We'll see, but I think it probably will be,' said Gaston, carefully putting on his reading glasses. 'Do you have family, Lange?'

Lange shrugged his shoulders and gave the slightest of nods, his eyes narrowing.

'According to your file, your wife is Helga. Daughters Charlotte aged... let me see, twelve now? Maria, she'd be fourteen... fifteen?'

Lange eyes blazed at them.

'And what is Mainz like to live in, Georg? I understand it is a historic city. Isn't it where the printing press was invented?'

Lange sat very still, controlling his breathing. Gaston was leafing through a thick file of papers as he spoke.

'And what is sustaining you now, Georg, is the knowledge that in just a matter of months, possibly even weeks, you will be back in Mainz with Helga, Charlotte and Maria, eh? This unfortunate war will be forgotten and you will go back to being a pillar of Mainz society, if there is such a thing. Am I right?'

No reaction from Lange.

'And you did indeed have every reason to believe that. There was no evidence that you were a Nazi or had committed war crimes.'

Silence.

'Your French is excellent, Georg,' continued Gaston, 'so you will have noticed that I used the past tense there. There *was* indeed no evidence that you were a Nazi or had committed war crimes. I have no doubt you spotted that. But now, let me show you the evidence. You will notice that I am now using the present tense. André, please.'

Gaston removed his glasses in a triumphant manner as André got up and walked over to the table. Owen could see why they had asked for Lange to be handcuffed. He spread out the documents on the table and held each one up in turn in front of Lange's face. Lange was shifting uncomfortably in his chair.

'Let me present exhibit A,' said André. 'A Nazi Party membership card. Very good. You didn't join until 1941 by the way, in case you are wondering when you signed up. You left it a bit late, but we thought it best as we only had recent photographs of you. Obviously a wise career move, Lange. Makes sense, it probably stopped you being sent to the Eastern Front. So you are a member of the Nazi Party now, Georg. Congratulations.'

'Bastards.' Lange struggled in his chair.

'Keep still, Georg, the more you struggle the more your handcuffs will hurt. I know that from bitter experience,' said Gaston. There was a pause, before André continued. 'Now then, the Nazi Party card was easy to produce. It is not exactly rare, but these,' he was waving a sheaf of papers in front of Lange, 'we are very proud of. Exhibit B, we will call them. Have a careful look. The first one is dated the 16th of July 1942. You know what date that is, don't you, Georg? Need I remind you? It is the date of the *grand rafle*. The roundup of the Jews in Paris. And before you tell me again that you were not involved in this kind of thing, that you were in military intelligence... Here, we have a series of orders...' André was leafing through the sheets '...signed personally by you, ordering the arrest and deportation of Jews. That is clear evidence of a war crime, would you not agree?'

Lange was shaking his head angrily.

'You know I was not involved in anything like that. This is an outrage, it—' he shouted.

'Shhhhhhh.' André had a finger to his lips. 'Be quiet, Georg, I have not finished yet. And here is exhibit C. We know that you were in Boulogne in June this year. You admitted that yourself in your affidavit, in your very own handwriting. By the way, thank you so much for alerting us to the existence of that affidavit, it was most helpful, as you can see. It is good to have a nice large signature like that. Very useful for a colleague of ours. Anyway, back to Boulogne. You admit you were there in June. A perfectly legitimate place for a Wehrmacht intelligence officer to be based, I am sure. But do you remember what happened on the 7th of June, the day after D-Day in case you have forgotten?'

Lange shook his head.

'Let me remind you then. Two hostages were executed in front of the Hôtel de Ville. In reprisal for the killing of two German soldiers. Do you remember? A mother of two children and a teenage boy. Well, I have news for you, Georg. This document here,' he held it in front of Lange's angry eyes, 'shows who signed the death warrant. Georg Lange.'

André sat down. Owen noticed that he was shaking. It was as if he had come to believe the veracity of Bertrand's forgeries himself, so good were they. Gaston got up and leaned on the table in front of Lange, who had now turned white, perspiration pouring down his face.

'We can do one of three things with this information, Georg. It can go to the authorities and you will face a war crimes trial. I would have thought we are looking at a minimum of ten years before you see Helga, Charlotte, Maria and Mainz again, that is if they'll wait for you that long. Mainz will, of course, but possibly not Helga. And Charlotte and Maria will not remember you in any event. And then that evidence from Boulogne is very damning. They may even seek the death penalty there. There's only one way to find out.

'The second thing we could do would be for you to be transferred from here tonight and your car intercepted on the way by the FFI. Do you want me to describe to you what they would do? No? I can promise you, ten years in prison will be a very attractive alternative, even if it will last a lot longer.'

There was a long pause now, during which Lange lurched forward and vomited down the front of his grey uniform. When he lifted his stained head up, his eyes were red with tears. His mouth was half open, flecks of vomit and saliva dripping down his chin. The cell now had a rank and fetid smell. Lange was trembling violently.

'I can appreciate your discomfort, Georg. Are you ready for me to tell you the third alternative? All of these documents can be destroyed. They would be burned, in your presence, and the minute the war is over you would be released and free to go back to Helga, Charlotte and Maria in Mainz. If it was me, I would see that as the most preferable of the three options. And you want to know how you can get us to do that? It's simple. You tell us everything you know about this woman.' Gaston slapped the photograph of Nathalie down on the table. 'Everything. You have our word that if we find out that you have been telling us the truth, all of this will be destroyed.'

378

There was a long silence as Lange stared at the photograph and the documents laid out on the table in front of him. He was rocking very slightly in his chair.

'And how can I trust you?' Lange's voice was quavering.

'You can't. It is a gamble,' said André. He waited before continuing. 'But I would have thought the alternatives to not trusting us are far worse. It is a risk you have to take.'

'Do you want some time to think about it, Georg?' asked Gaston.

The German looked up slowly and his gaze took in all three of them. Any pretence at composure was long gone. He was broken. His face betrayed a mixture of fear and hatred. Within the space of less than ten minutes he had gone from a sophisticated and professional officer to a broken man.

'Of course not. I'll tell you everything I know. But I want to tell you something first. It was not difficult to recruit her. She came to us.'

–

There was an air of definite satisfaction in the Renault as it headed back to Paris that night and they discussed everything that Lange had told them. It was in marked contrast to the gloom that had accompanied the journey back the previous Saturday. Owen even noticed that there was some life in Émile's eyes as the driver kept looking at them, taking everything in.

Had they not been so tired, they might have been tempted to stop for a drink in one of the bars around the Avenue des Champs Élysées – and had they done that, they could well have been spotted by the tall Englishman in the long dark greatcoat and wide-brimmed trilby. Some of the bar owners had spotted him more than once over the previous days, peering into the bars, looking around but never buying a drink – which was what bothered them most. One or two had asked him his business and he produced a pocketful of accreditation that quickly persuaded them to mind their own business.

Major Edgar was seething. There was no sign of Quinn. He had established that he had arrived at the Gare du Nord, but since then he had vanished. He could be anywhere, though his instinct told him that he was still in the city. There was no joy with the hotel registration cards. Either Quinn was not in a hotel or the French were just being inefficient.

Had someone told him that at one stage that night, as he crossed the Rue du Colisée, he was probably no more than a couple of hundred yards from Owen Quinn, as his car headed towards Boulevard Haussmann, Edgar would not have been altogether surprised.

It had turned into that kind of chase.

Chapter 35

France, February 1945

They did not leave Paris until the Friday, which was 2nd February.

There was good reason to delay their departure. Paris was a city sustained by rumours, most of which arrived with a clamour one day, only to disappear silently and forgotten the next. But the weekend that Owen had arrived, a rumour emerged that appeared to have more substance to it. By the beginning of the week it was confirmed. On the day after Owen had travelled from London to Paris, the Red Army had entered a concentration camp near Kraków in southern Poland. It was called Auschwitz and was where André and his family and most of the other seventy-five thousand Jews deported from Paris had been taken. André was so desperate to find out if anyone from his extended family or any of his friends had survived that he spent most of the Thursday at a Jewish community centre trying to find out.

But the message was confused. The Russians had found seven thousand survivors in the camp, most barely alive. Many other prisoners had been taken away from the camp in the days and weeks before. It would be some time before they knew the names of who was still alive, if that was the right word to describe them.

Early on the Friday morning they set off. André had borrowed a car from a friend and had managed to get hold of enough petrol to get them to their destination 'We may have to push it for the last few miles.' The car was a snub-nosed Peugeot, more reliable than handsome. They headed north east from Paris, which was a longer route, but there had been reports of some fighting just to the south of where they were heading and André wanted to make sure they kept well away from it. For most of the morning they were in the Champagne region, their progress slowed considerably by long military convoys heading east and long lines of German prisoners of war trudging in the other direction. They were stopped at a few checkpoints, where Owen's Royal Navy identification helped. At one checkpoint, some American troops even allowed them to siphon off some petrol from an abandoned German staff car. It meant that they now had enough fuel to be sure of reaching their destination.

By early afternoon they had dropped down into Lorraine, where there was evidence of more recent fighting. Paris had suffered the deprivations of war, but had emerged unscathed in terms of damage. The same could not be said for Metz and the small towns and villages they drove through. If anything, thought Owen, it was worse than the Pas de Calais.

By the time they had driven through Nancy it was getting dark. They decided to press on: they knew that the roads would be difficult, but neither of them wanted to hang around. There was an air of anarchy in the area. Any time the car stopped it was quickly surrounded by people desperate for food and water. Young children pressed their faces against the windows. When they drove off, people would kick out at the car and some stones were thrown at them. They knew if they did find somewhere to stay the night, it would be too risky to leave the car unattended.

The checkpoints were getting trickier now. So far, Owen's Royal Navy identification had helped them through them. But as they drove, they had been discussing to what lengths Edgar might be going to track him down, which Owen was in no doubt he would be doing. What if he had put out an alert for Owen Quinn? It was perfectly feasible that he could put out a notification that he was a deserter, or worse. So they decided to rely on André's cunning and his FFI identification.

As they entered Alsace, the atmosphere changed. It felt as if they were driving through Germany. The road signs and village and town names were only in German and the buildings were noticeably Germanic in appearance.

'I'll give you a quick history lesson, Owen. Alsace has always been a mixture of German and French. Before 1870, it was part of France. Then there was the Franco-Prussian War, which we lost, and Alsace and parts of Lorraine became part of Germany. After the Great War, they came back to France. In 1940, the Germans returned. This area was not part of occupied France or even Vichy. The Germans made it part of Greater Germany. Now, it has come back to France. So if anyone here who was born in the 1860s and is still alive, they would have lived under German rule twice and French rule three times. When the Germans have run the region, they have discriminated against everything French, and I daresay that when we have ruled the area we have not exactly encouraged the German language and culture, not that you can blame us.' He turned to Owen and laughed. 'But it does explain why this is a rather strange part of the world, and why so many people here are so strange. But then, I think you know that, don't you, Owen?'

They entered Strasbourg just before six o'clock. Their original plan had been to seek somewhere to stay that night and try to find Nathalie in the morning. But nothing prepared them for the devastation. The city had been heavily bombed by the Allies and then there had been bitter fighting before General Leclerc's French troops took the city at the end of November.

Although still identifiable as a city, it was only just functioning as one. The damage was everywhere to be seen. People were still huddled in the ruins of buildings, whose darkened shells were lit by dozens of small fires as they tried to keep warm. Owen realised that you needed to be close to the damage to see that war caused more than physical damage and psychological suffering. There was a smell to it, a fetid taste that stuck to the back of the throat.

Enquiries about hotels were met with confused smiles, so they did what all travellers unsure of their final destination do and headed for the centre. Just off the Place du Temple Neuf they found a small café in a narrow street, where the white walls were pockmarked with bullet holes. They were able to park the Peugeot across the street where they could see it from their table in the window.

Owen was beginning to learn that André always had a plan. He was not complaining. André's forgery plan had worked so well that they were now in Strasbourg armed with Nathalie's apparently real name and an address. Lange had also confirmed that she had indeed been a nurse when the Germans recruited her.

As they sat in the café they agreed that their priority was to go to the address that Lange had given them. He had warned them that the address was from before the war and he could not guarantee she would be there. He was certain, though, about her real name.

The owner of the café just shrugged his shoulders and shook his head when they asked him if he knew the road. He eyed them suspiciously as they left the café. None of the passers-by wanted to know.

People were naturally suspicious and Owen noticed that most of them were speaking French with a distinct German pronunciation. André appeared to be having trouble finding directions as they wandered around the centre of the city.

Eventually a couple walked by who were happy to help. Yes, they did know this area, 'but you must realise it was damaged when the Germans invaded in 1940 and it was bombed last year.' Not many buildings had been left standing. 'Come, we'll show you where it is. We're heading that way ourselves.'

The area was barren. There were indeed just a few buildings left standing in the road where her house was meant to be, and none of them intact. They thanked the couple, who hurried along. On both sides of the road, and for blocks either side, there were piles of rubble, punctuated by the jagged remains of trees, whose top halves had been snapped off by the force of explosions or burned by fire. There was no sign of life, other than some children pulling a wooden trolley, laden with wood and scraps. They went over to talk to them, but the children abandoned their trolley and ran off. They drove around the area and eventually came across an elderly lady dressed all in black, walking a skeletal black Labrador.

No, no one had lived in this area for some time. Most people had moved out in 1940 and the few that remained had left when the Allied bombing started. Her French was slow and difficult to make out. André asked whether she would prefer to speak German. She nodded. They spoke for a couple of minutes and then she merged back into the shadows, pulled along by her dog.

'She thought we were from the authorities. Many people here are worried that they may be called collaborators, so people are going to be suspicious of us. She told me she's lived in this area most of her life and didn't seem to recognise the name, but her memory is not good. Maybe there was a family of that name that lived here ten years ago, she is not sure. But if they did, they would have left long ago.'

'We could go to the police,' said Owen, 'they may have a record of the surname.'

'I am worried about alerting her in some way. We just don't know who to trust around here. I mean look at us,' said André, pointing at the two of them, 'a Jew and an Englishman. We don't exactly blend in, do we? As soon as we walk into a police station or the Hôtel de Ville, people will notice us. We need to be cautious. If someone alerts her then you may never see your child. Jean did give me the name of a contact here, but apparently he will not be back in Strasbourg until Monday. Shall we wait until then?'

Owen thought about it. Perhaps they had no alternative. Then it was his turn to have a plan.

André liked it.

—

A few hours after André and Owen arrived in Strasbourg that Friday night, Edgar had his first breakthrough.

Since arriving in Paris the previous Saturday, Edgar had used all the influence he could muster to ensure maximum co-operation from the British Embassy. It worked. When he turned up at the British Embassy in the Rue Faubourg St-Honoré that Monday morning, Edgar was able to see the ambassador straight away. By the end of the meeting he had been promised the full co-operation of the British Embassy. 'No question about it. Winston clearly thinks this is important. We'll do what we can to help.'

Edgar commandeered Embassy staff to help monitor all the hotel registration cards. They spoke to police and any other officials they could find. He had scoured the streets and the bars. But there was no trace of Quinn. There was always the possibility that he had left Paris, but Edgar felt that even if he had only stayed in the city for a day or two, there would be some clue here as to where he had headed next.

The breakthrough came late on the Friday afternoon. One of the military attachés at the Embassy had been speaking to a contact in the resistance the previous day about another matter, and that contact had happened to mention that one of his comrades, a man called Gaston, had been assisting a British Royal Navy officer. The attaché did not think to mention it to Edgar until the next day. Edgar kept very calm. It would not help matters if he held this blithering idiot up against a wall and asked him why, precisely, he had waited a whole day to tell him this? That could be dealt with later. He would arrange a transfer to somewhere more unpleasant than Paris. There were plenty of options. Right now, he needed to track this Gaston down.

It took a couple of hours. Edgar was being cautious. If Gaston had been helping Owen then he may well be better-disposed towards him than the British authorities.

They found out where he lived, which was in the rundown Marais quarter on the eastern edge of the city centre. Gaston was in a nearby bar, in an alleyway off the Rue des Rosiers.

'We appreciate you helping Owen,' Edgar told him. 'He was one of my best agents. He has a lot of problems. You will understand. We need to find that woman before he does. For her own protection. Where is Owen now? It is in his interests for you to tell us. And yours.'

Gaston said nothing. He slid his glass across the zinc-topped bar for it to be refilled. The barman understood and reached for his oldest Armagnac. The Englishman was paying. Gaston was not sure whether to believe him. He had only become involved in the first place to help André, and André had been so unsettled since he returned to Paris that maybe this Englishman was telling the truth. But then, he had liked Owen and he had believed him.

So he decided to give the Englishman part of what he wanted. Not the name or any other details, though. Maybe that was the solution. Something, but not too much.

'They left for Alsace this morning.'

'Do you know where in Alsace?'

'No.'

'Strasbourg?'

'Possibly.'

'And can you give me any details about the name and address they may have been given?'

Gaston shook his head. He was regretting this now. He shouldn't have said anything.

'How did he get this information?'

Gaston shrugged. 'I don't know. I only saw him once or twice. He seemed to have a contact. I don't know whom.'

Edgar gestured to the barman to fill up Gaston's glass again. Maybe that would loosen his tongue. But he ought to have known better. Try as he might, he got nowhere. The Frenchman was polite. He would like to help. But he had told him all he knew and repeated it. 'He's headed for Alsace, possibly Strasbourg.'

Edgar thanked Gaston, gave him a piece of paper with the phone number of the British Embassy on it, and in return Gaston promised to contact him if he heard anything. *Of course.* Edgar left enough money with the barman to pay for Gaston to finish what little was left of the bottle and headed back to the Embassy.

It was late now, gone nine o'clock. He had been promised he would have whatever help he needed and right now he needed a good car and a reliable driver who knew the way to Strasbourg.

Gaston stayed in the bar until late. The Englishman's money was going a long way. He was bothered though. He should have relied on his instinct and not trusted the Englishman. Émile joined him at nine o'clock that night and listened silently as Gaston recounted what had happened.

'Should I have trusted the Englishman?' he asked Émile. Émile shook his head, thanked Gaston for the drink and left the bar in a hurry. Gaston realised that it was foolish to ask Émile. He trusted no one these days. After what he had been through, who could blame him?

–

They found the hospital easily enough. The one large hospital in the city was just across the river that surrounded the old centre, just off Rue de la Bourse. Their good fortune continued. The first doctor they stopped to ask in the corridor came from Paris and was happy to help a fellow Parisian. 'Come with me, let me take you to the records department. I hope you find your friend and that she and her baby are healthy.'

The lady in the records department assumed that because the doctor had brought them along, it was in order for her to help. 'Because otherwise,' she said as she slid her chair over to the right filing cabinet, 'it would be quite irregular for us to pass on records to someone else. T... here we are, T... let's see Troppe, I can't see anything... When did you say it was? October or November? Can't see anything here. Troppe...'

Owen was not altogether surprised. They were assuming that she had come back to Strasbourg. If she was running away, then this could well be the last place she would come to. And if she did, she would probably have used another name.

She carried on searching, encouraged by André. She was still muttering 'Troppe... Troppe' under her breath as she worked through the documents when a nurse came in carrying a bunch of files to leave on the desk.

'What were you saying, Thérèse? That name?'

'Troppe. I am looking to see if a baby Troppe was born here last year.'

'The only Troppe I know is Ginette. Ah well.' She turned and walked out.

André and Owen were stunned. They followed the nurse out of the room.

'You know Ginette Troppe?' André was taking care not to appear too desperate.

'Sure, I worked with her here in Strasbourg before the war. She went to work in Paris during the war apparently.'

'Yes, that is where I know her from,' said André. 'I heard she had returned here and as I was in Strasbourg I thought I would look her up. She gave me her address and you know, I lost it. I knew she was expecting a baby, so I thought maybe I could find the details here. I have some gifts for her, you see.'

'I don't think her baby was born here. But why not ask her yourself. She's back working here now.'

—

After that, it was not difficult. Even though it was late at night, the nurse agreed to check – discreetly. 'Of course, I understand, sir,' she had said, pocketing the folded notes. 'Everyone appreciates a surprise.' Ginette Troppe, it seemed, was due in at six o'clock the next morning. Her shift would end at three in the afternoon.

They found a hotel near the railway station and stayed there that night. Owen registered using his cousin Peter's passport, which he had brought with him from England. They were up at five in the morning. André had already found out which side entrance the nurses used, and they parked the car just down that street, giving them a good view of everyone approaching the entrance.

Owen was slumped in the passenger seat wearing a hat, with a scarf wrapped across his face. André was concerned that he looked like a robber, but at least he was not recognisable. At a quarter to six, the morning shift began to arrive, in ones and twos and the occasional threesome. It was a bitterly cold morning, with frost on the ground, and it would be difficult to identify her if she was wearing the hood of her cape up as some of the other nurses were doing. André decided to get out of the car. He had looked at her photograph often enough, and Owen had described her in detail, so he reckoned he would recognise her. He was just opening the driver's door of the car when she appeared. She was walking alone along the side street where the entrance was. Her cape flowed behind her and she had the hood down. As she walked along, she threw her head back in her characteristic fashion so as to gather her long hair together. As she walked closer to them, she tied it back., and Owen caught a glimpse of her face. Her deep black eyes pierced through the mist. Owen was in no doubt whatsoever. He made to open the car door, but André restrained him. 'Later.'

That was André's plan. *Let her do her shift*. It would cause trouble if they approached her first. *Let her do her shift and then we can follow her home. You need to know where she lives, don't you? You want to find your child?*

They went back to the hotel to rest. André fell asleep and Owen stood at the window, looking out over Strasbourg. Somewhere out there is my child, he thought.

He realised that he had not expected to reach this moment. Until today, he had not expected to find her, so he had not given any serious thought to what he would do when he did. Would he kill her? Could he forgive her? Would he take her back to England and hand her over to Edgar? Would he march her to a police station? Hand her over to the FFI? Would he be able to forgive her and stay with her? He had no idea. And then there was the child. Until the nurse last night had mentioned that she had given birth, he had not known for sure that she had even had the baby. Could he possibly allow her to keep the child?

He stood leaning against the window, working his way through a packet of André's cigarettes, his heart pounding away and any kind of rest out of the question.

André woke at one. Naturally, he had a plan. They would eat and return to the hospital. Although the shift ended at three, they would be in position just before two, just in case she left early. They would need to follow her, which was the only way to be sure of finding out where she lived – and where, presumably, the child was. Owen would drive the car so that André could follow her on foot in case she caught a tram.

As they waited outside the nurses' entrance, the drizzle which had been present since they had arrived in Strasbourg had now turned to a downpour, making it difficult to see. Nonetheless, she was not hard to make out as she swept out of the hospital just after three, much the same way as she had entered it: cape flowing and alone. As she climbed down the steps she unclipped her small nurse's hat and untied her hair, shaking her head, her long hair now flowing loose behind her. They waited until she had crossed the street and turned left into the main road. She walked past one long tram queue, and it appeared that she might be walking all the way home. At that moment, a beige tram appeared from the other direction and she ran across the road, raising her hand for it to stop. André had jumped out of the car even before Owen had brought it to a sudden halt.

The plan entailed Owen trying to follow the tram. If he lost them then he would have to rely on André following her on the tram, finding out where she lived. They would meet back at the hotel.

By the time Owen had managed to turn the car round in the road he was already behind a lorry and another three or four cars. A couple of blocks on, the tram stopped, but neither André nor Ginette, as he now knew her to be, got off. He was able to pull up behind the tram, but lost it again at the next set of traffic lights. By now the traffic was getting heavier and he decided to have one last go, turning into the oncoming lane and accelerating past the cars in front of him. The tram had just pulled away from another stop as he caught up with it again. He glanced to his right, but could see neither André nor Ginette on the pavement, so he carried on. The tram was turning left now, crossing a river, moving in a southerly direction away from the city centre. He nosed in behind, as close as he could without driving on the tram-tracks. If he lost it now, it would probably be too late. Soon after the left turn, the tram pulled into another stop. He held back a bit before pulling in near to it. Sure enough, Ginette got off, closely followed by André, who looked around and saw him. He waited while André followed Ginette round a corner and followed slowly in the car. It was a long side street with apartment blocks on either side. It was a straight road, so he could afford to pull in and still see where André was following her. She stopped at a *boulangerie* and André followed her in. They both emerged a minute later carrying large paper bags. As she crossed the road, she looked towards him, straight in the direction of the car. He huddled himself further down the seat, but she had not seen him. She was making sure it was safe to cross.

André was well practised, Owen realised. He knew how to follow someone. He had crossed the road in front of Ginette and was now walking before her, allowing her to pass him after a few paces as he paused to tie up a shoelace.

A hundred yards or so later, Ginette climbed up the stairs of a small apartment block, taking her keys out of her handbag as she did so. She briefly turned round as André walked straight past the entrance.

Owen caught up with him a bit further on, where André had turned into a smaller side street.

'Well done, Owen, that was good. Now we know where she lives. Are you ready for this?'

Owen nodded, although he was not sure that he was ready. His heart was pounding so loud and fast that he was feeling lightheaded.

'And you are sure you want me to come with you?'

They only had to wait five minutes before an elderly man walked slowly up the steps of the apartment block and they were able to time their walk up the steps to coincide with his. He was very grateful as they held the door open for him and doffed his hat as they followed him into the entrance hall.

There was no concierge here, which André muttered was a good thing. There appeared to be six floors, three apartments to each floor. Apartment five on the second floor had 'Troppe' on the board.

They climbed the flight of stairs to the second floor. Owen's breathing was heavy now, and he must have been walking slowly as André paused for him, putting an arm round his shoulders as he did so.

They waited outside apartment five. At first they could hear nothing and then, through the closed door, there was the sound of two people talking, followed by silence. A minute or so later, the sound of a baby crying. André nodded. Owen knew his plan. He would wait around the corner so that when the door was opened, it would only be the unfamiliar face of André that they would see, for long enough to get the door open.

André rapped on the door. From behind the corner Owen could hear footsteps coming to the door.

'Who is it?' It was his wife's voice.

Chapter 36

Strasbourg, February 1945

It was the Sunday afternoon before Edgar found what he was looking for. He had arrived in Strasbourg in the very early hours of the morning and spent most of that day driving around the city, trying to persuade the police to let him see the hotel registration cards. *Come back later*, he was told.

He checked into a small guest house in the city centre, intending to get an hour's rest. When he awoke he realised that he had slept for more than five hours. It was ten o'clock at night.

The next day he went back to the police station. They had checked with Paris and they *were* going to be able to let him see the cards. Later. It was noon before he was taken into a small office and shown them.

No sign of Owen Quinn. The only British passport holder staying at a hotel in the city was a Peter Sinclair. He was from the same town in Surrey as Owen.

The hotel owner was very helpful. He was most impressed by the array of accreditation that Edgar had pointedly spread out on the reception desk in front of him, along with the photograph of Owen.

'There were two of them. The Englishman – yes that's him, sir – and a Frenchman. Paris accent. Probably... you know, Jewish... not that that is a problem, sir. There were many of them here in Strasbourg. Before the war. The men checked out yesterday. I've no idea where they went. They may have been going to visit a friend though. I remember now that they did ask me for the best route to the University Hospital.'

Edgar thanked him very much and asked if he would be so kind as to give him those same directions to the University Hospital.

'It is Pascal from apartment eighteen on the top floor,' said André. 'I have a parcel for you that came to me by mistake.'

'One moment, one moment.' She sounded annoyed. It took a moment for the door to be unlocked and bolts and chains removed.

The door opened. André pushed it open wider and, as he entered, Owen followed him straight in. He was already in the hall with the door closed behind him before she realised who he was.

She made to scream, but no sound came out. The colour had drained from her face and her eyes were wide open, as was her mouth. She took an unsteady step back and leaned against the wall.

'Owen!' she gasped. 'Oh my God!'

Very slowly, she sank to her knees. Her mouth was open and she was trying to speak, but nothing was coming out.

'Who is it, Ginette?' It was an older woman's voice from behind a door, accompanied by the sound of a baby crying.

'It is all right, mother. Someone from work.' Her voice sounded hoarse.

She glared at André.

'This is a friend of mine,' said Owen.

'I have heard so much about you.' André bowed with exaggerated courtesy.

'Can we talk alone, Owen?'

'Yes, as long as it is in this apartment.'

'Why?'

'Because I have come for my child.'

Another gasp. She rubbed her knuckles against her teeth, desperately thinking what to do.

'We can go into the kitchen.'

'I will wait in the corridor outside,' said André.

'Mother,' she said, trying very hard to sound calm, although her voice was now high-pitched. 'There is someone here from work I need to see about changing departments. We will go into the kitchen. Please do not disturb us.'

He followed her into the kitchen and closed the door. She gestured towards an empty chair at the table and she sat opposite him, nervously pulling at her hair.

'How did you find me, Owen?'

He ignored her question. 'What shall I call you? Nathalie? Ginette?'

She shrugged. 'How did you know about the baby? How could you have known? You must tell me that, Owen!'

Owen was breathing heavily now, the tension and fury mounting up in him.

'No, I realise I wasn't meant to know. I was in such a bad state over this whole business that I was drinking too much and sleeping too little, so I went to see Dr Peacock in September. He let slip that you were pregnant. You can imagine how much better I felt after that visit. But what it did do was drive me to find you and my child. Is it mine? I don't even know if it is a boy or a girl!'

She got up and paced around the small kitchen before going over to the sink to get herself a glass of water. When she sat down again her hands were shaking so violently that she had to hold the glass with two hands. He could hear it clattering against her teeth as she took a few sips.

'It's a boy, Owen...' She paused and sank her head into her hands. She stayed like that for a while, the sounds of her quiet sobs filling the room. She tried to compose herself, but when she started speaking again, her voice was weak. 'He looks like you. Of course, you are the father... I am sorry, I never intended... But, you know... it happened. I only found out just before I came back to France, when I went to see Dr Peacock. I was in a panic. I had not intended to get pregnant, but I wanted to keep the baby. If I was not being sent to France, I think I would have told you. Not just about the baby, but everything, Owen. I had decided that much. I promise you.'

'You can tell me now.'

'What are you going to do with him?'

'With whom?'

'Our son.'

'What is his name?'

'He is called Philippe, after the French general who liberated Strasbourg. It was my mother's idea really.'

She tried to drink from the glass again, but her hands were shaking so violently that the water spilled on the tabletop. She bit her forefinger to try to stop herself crying.

'Tell me everything first. Why did you work for the Germans? Did they make you work for them or did you volunteer? I want to know everything.' Owen was doing his best to sound angry, but his overwhelming emotions were sadness and confusion.

She was crying freely, the tears gathering under her eyes before rolling fast down her reddened cheeks. For the first time since he had met her, she looked vulnerable. When the crying subsided and she began to speak, he noticed that her face reminded him of the time when she had emerged out of the fog on Westminster Bridge in the winter of 1943. He had realised then that for the first time, she looked unguarded. As if she'd always worn a mask before. She now looked as if her mask had been discarded, and for the first time he was able to look at her face with all her true emotions exposed on it.

'My family is from Alsace. We are of German origin, like a lot of people in this region. In the Great War my father fought in the German Army – Alsace was part of Germany then. As far as he was concerned, he was German. He never thought of himself as French. He worked for the railways, and when Alsace became part of France again after the war, he was sent to Lyon to work. We all went there. I had no brothers or sisters. My father was treated very badly in Lyon. People regarded him as a traitor. People did not talk to him at work, we had no friends. In the time we were there, I don't think we were ever invited to anyone else's house. I was too young to realise, but I grew up with this atmosphere in the house. By 1921, he couldn't stand it anymore, so he gave up his job and we moved back to Alsace. I was seven then. He couldn't get any work here in Alsace, so he went to Germany, but things were even worse there, there were no jobs and they treated him as if he was French, so he felt that he did not belong anywhere. He came back to Alsace in 1922 and killed himself in 1923. I discovered his body hanging from a landing over the stairs when I got up during the night to go to the bathroom. I was nine.

'My mother was destitute, but a German cultural organisation helped with my education and gave us food each week. As I grew up, I became interested in politics. I felt that a strong Germany was important. So in 1935, I joined the Nazi Party. It was clandestine, of course. Alsace was still in France then. I didn't think too much about it. Most of the people in the organisation that had helped us had joined it; they had helped fund my nursing training. Maybe I was trying to repay their help. The Germans were the only people who helped us, and the Nazi Party were the only people who cared about Germany. I moved to Paris in 1938, and I was recruited as a spy. That's it.'

395

'Did they recruit you or did you approach them?'

'Does it matter? I wanted to help.'

'You are a Nazi then?'

'I don't know what I was then. I was a young fool. The organisation that helped my mother, it was more political than anything else. Many of those people were involved with the Nazis, so I went to the meetings, and began to feel part of something.'

Silence again in the room. She threw back her long hair in the way that Owen remembered, then harshly brushed it away from her face with shaking hands.

'Owen, please…'

'My friend out there,' said Owen, 'was taken to a camp in Poland with his wife and child and tens of thousands of other French Jews. His wife and son were killed. Millions of people were murdered, they're saying. From all over Europe. When people find out what—'

'Owen, you don't need to tell me. What I have seen since I came back to France…' Ginette hugged her arms tight across her chest. There was a long pause. 'It's terrible. I felt guilty. I have seen such suffering. I had to escape from Lille after an SS officer tried to rape me. I stabbed him. I became a refugee. In Lorraine I was looked after by Jews and Gypsies who had been in one of these camps that you are talking about. A Jewish doctor from Poland, he looked after me. He told me about the terrible things that had happened.'

Until now, she had avoided eye contact with Owen. She would look at the table, at the floor, at the wall around her, or at her hands as she buried her face in them. But now she stared at him, her eyes pleading with him to believe her.

'You have to believe me, Owen!'

'Do I?' With that, he stood up and lashed out. The back of his right hand caught her on the cheekbone, just by the side of her right eye. She did not even flinch. A trickle of blood darted in a surprisingly straight line down her face. She nodded once at Owen, as if to acknowledge what he had done. He had staggered back as if he himself had been hit.

'Ginette. Is everything all right?' It was her mother's voice from the other room.

'It is fine, mother. Please leave us alone for a while.'

He stood up, his knuckles resting down on the table, leaning right over her. His voice was trembling. She was now the more composed of the two of them.

'Why should I believe a word you say? Tell me that! What do I know about you? I know that you are a Nazi spy, that you deceived me, that you married me, became pregnant without telling me, and then disappeared. And now I have tracked you down, you are trying to talk your way out of it. Look at me – I don't even know what I should call you. Nathalie? Ginette? Are there any other names I should be aware of?'

Silence. She sat still, saying nothing.

'Go on, I want to know.'

'When I was in the Pas de Calais I was known as Geraldine. Why do you want to know all this, Owen?'

'And any other names?'

'I also used the name Hélène Blanc for a while, after I left the Pas de Calais.'

'And what should I call you, tell me?'

He was leaning right over her now, his face just inches from hers.

'My real name is Ginette. Ginette Troppe.'

'And so, Ginette Troppe. Give me one very good reason why I don't drag you now to the authorities. You're a Nazi spy. You're on the run and I've caught you.'

'You'll do what you want to do, Owen. I can't stop you. But let me say something. You say I ran away, but that is not true. I came back here, to my home town, to my true identity. I could so easily have disappeared after I left the Pas de Calais. There are so many refugees moving around the country, so much chaos – it would have been easy for me to find another identity and then another one. I could have changed my identity very easily. I could have gone to anywhere in France. This country is twice the size of yours. It would have been very easy for me to make it impossible for you to trace me. Think about that, Owen.'

'What are you saying?'

'That I wanted to be found by you, Owen. That is why I came back here, and that is why I used my original name. Look, I even went back to the hospital that I worked in before the war. I was not hiding from you, Owen, quite the opposite. I was making it possible for you to find me.'

She was staring directly at her husband, her eyes beseeching him to believe her.

'But why... why did you want me to find you?'

'It was not just because of the baby. It was because of you. I don't expect you to believe this, but once I was away from you, when I arrived back in France, I realised that I cared about you. I even started to have those feelings when the British sent me away for training. And since then, I have cared about you more and more. I realised that I love you, Owen.'

'That's a convenient turn of events, isn't it?' he said sarcastically.

'It's the truth, Owen. I was surprised myself at my feelings.'

Owen looked shocked. He started pacing around the small kitchen. As he came close to her he realised that it was not just the sight of her and the sound of her voice that had so unsettled him. It was the smell of her too. He would never be able to describe it, and he had never even realised that she had her own distinctive scent that he had become so familiar with.

'But hang on. You didn't leave a forwarding address, did you? British Intelligence had no idea who you really were. I accept that you may have reverted to your proper name and come back to your home town, but how on earth was I expected to know all that? It was only because of a lot of hard work, and even more luck, that I was able to find you.'

'Exactly.'

'Exactly what?'

'That I thought you would find me. I knew that if you really wanted to find me, you would. There's one other thing, Owen. I left a clue, didn't I?'

He leaned back against the worktop and frowned.

'If you did, it must have been a very well hidden one, because I missed it.'

'The brooch, Owen, the cameo brooch. Did you find that?'

He nodded.

'I knew that I had to leave some message for you. I wanted to leave you something of mine. Did you spot the initials on the back of the brooch?'

'Yes, just. But how would that help me find you? The reason I found you was because I persisted, and because some very decent people stuck their necks out to help me. The brooch didn't help.'

'But it helped you realise that I might have left a message for you? That maybe it was a sign of some affection?'

'Maybe.'

She smiled. It was a smile that he could not recall ever having seen before, and considering that he had committed every smile, every gesture of hers to his memory and then replayed them over and over again – he knew he would have remembered a smile like that.

'But that is the point, Owen! By leaving the brooch for you like that I was sending you a message. You were to understand that it would be worth searching for me. When I left that for you, I wasn't even sure why I was doing it. Deep down, I must have thought it was a way of giving myself an option – that it might help you find me. I'm not sure.'

She spread her arms open, as if to say 'And here I am'. *Voilà*.

'Well, I suppose it worked.' Owen paused. 'Did you ever care for me, when we were together, that is...?' He was sounding hesitant now. 'Or was I only a way of getting information?'

She had composed herself. 'Let me tell you this first, Owen. You asked me whether I approached the Germans, or whether they approached me. I will tell you the truth. I approached them. One of the men I knew in the organisation, he said that because I spoke German and English, I could be of use to the Germans. He made it sound exciting. So I went to Paris to meet a man he knew at the German Embassy—'

'Georg Lange?'

'That's right!' She sounded shocked. 'How did you find him? Did he tell you where I was?'

'Carry on.'

She had gone quiet. Her long fingernails were tracing a haphazard shape on the table. For a moment, their fingertips touched on the shiny surface of it, before they both pulled their hands away in shock.

'So I met Lange. In 1938. I thought I was going to be something like... I don't know... a messenger, nothing much more than that. But it was like when I was a child and I used to go on the slide at the playground. Once you started, you couldn't stop. It was impossible. I was sent to Germany for training and before I realised it properly, I was becoming an agent. I was too involved to do anything about it. I felt like telling them that this was all a mistake; that I was just a nurse. I was even thinking of leaving, but then it became too late. One of the other people being trained with me, a very intelligent lawyer from Poitiers, he announced one evening that he had changed his mind and was leaving. They seemed to let him go, but the next morning they took us to a forest for training and we discovered his body hanging

399

from a tree. They arranged for us to discover his body, of course. To send us a very clear message. It reminded me of my father, the way that the body was perfectly straight, apart from the neck which looked as if it had been rearranged at an unusual angle.'

With the back of her wrist she dabbed at the cut next to her eye. The bleeding had stopped, but a bruise was beginning to appear.

'So, I was caught in a nightmare, but at the same time, I must have been influenced by everything they were telling me. I suppose I could have run away or something, or just disappeared. But at the time, nothing seemed real. I didn't believe that there would be a war and I thought that if there was one, then they would have more important things to remember than me, and that could be my opportunity to disappear.

'When Germany invaded France, it was a terrible shock. Deep down, I must have thought that would never really happen. I knew that I would now have to become involved. So I escaped. Owen, I promise you I did. Ask my mother, she had no idea what had happened to me. Ask Georg Lange. I left Strasbourg and headed west. The French authorities had evacuated much of the civilian population from the city once the war started. I was only allowed to remain because the hospital where I worked remained open. It was the only one that was. I was not sure where to go, so many people were on the roads, sometimes it was hard to move. I made two mistakes. The first was that I headed north, and walked straight into the German invasion. They found me in a town called Abbeville. It's in Picardy. The second mistake was that I used my own identity. That's how the Germans found me. You ask Lange if you don't believe me.'

She was beginning to lose her composure again and started to weep. Owen handed her a handkerchief from his top pocket. Their fingers brushed very slightly again as he handed it over.

'I was trapped, Owen. And I was a coward. When the Germans caught me, I told them a story about how I had to flee Strasbourg because I thought the French police were after me. They must have believed me. It worked out well for them because people were being evacuated from Dunkirk to England at the time, and thousands of French civilians were escaping too. It was not difficult for me to join them. The Abwehr spent a day or two briefing me on my new identity and then I was taken near to Dunkirk. It was not difficult to join the people escaping.'

'What did the Germans ask you to do?'

'My mission was to get to London and do nothing other than establish myself as a nurse. I had nothing incriminating on me. In time, I was to find a job in a military hospital. Then I was to make contact with my radio man. Once I had been cleared in London after my arrival, I thought it was too late. I was a German spy by then. So I just did as I had been instructed. It was purely by chance that I met you, Owen, but when I did… there was nothing I could do. I had my instructions. Please understand, Owen.'

He snorted. 'Do you know that you were used? And so was I, as it happens. British Intelligence knew all about you, long before you came to Calcotte Grange. They found out about you, they discovered that you had requested a transfer to a military hospital, and they set the whole thing up. They even arranged for you to meet me. They even guessed I would fall for you. Of course, I never realised what was going on, so you can imagine how I feel. And all the information that you got through me was deliberately false, although I never realised that. It was intended to mislead the Germans into thinking that the Pas de Calais would be where the main invasion was. That is why you were sent there. You were used.'

'I didn't realise all that. Of course, once the Allies landed in Normandy, I wondered about the information, but—'

'Ask yourself this. Was there an invasion in the Pas de Calais? No. It was only ever going to be Normandy. So, you played your part. You helped the Allies.'

'Owen, if that is true, maybe it is not a bad thing. By the time I left London, I did not want to be a German spy. I was having your baby. I liked people in England. I had developed feelings for you, Owen!'

'Do you know what happened to your group in Boulogne?'

She shook her head vigorously. She held up her hand as if she didn't want to know.

'Françoise escaped. Lucien was tortured but is still alive, although he is crippled. Their children were burned to death along with Françoise's mother by your Nazi friends. Pierre killed himself before they could arrest him and Jean was tortured to death. Lucien was in the cell next to his. He took a whole night to die. Lucien said he even heard him calling out your name that night.'

She was frightened now. Owen noticed that she was trembling.

'You said you had feelings for me,' she said. 'What are those feelings?'

Owen was trembling now. 'I don't know what to say any more, I don't know what to think. I want to see my son now.'

'Of course. I want you to see him. Tell me something. You must have had feelings for me. What has happened to them?'

'You know that I loved you more than anything else in the world. And I will tell you something else that I did not realise until a few minutes ago. I continued to love you. I loved you when I found out that you were a German spy, even though I tried very hard not to. I still loved you when I found out what had happened in the Pas de Calais. I loved you when I saw you walking into the hospital this morning, and I still loved you when I walked into this apartment a few minutes ago. All along, I hoped to reach a point where I could finally stop loving you, but—'

She handed his handkerchief back to him. This time, their brushing of fingers was not accidental.

'I'll ask my mother to go for a walk. Then we can be alone when you meet Philippe. What about your friend?'

'He could do with a walk too.'

'Does your mother know the truth?'

'Of course not. She thinks I was in Paris during the war. She learned from my father that it is best not to ask too many questions.'

Ginette moved into the hall and addressed her mother through the closed door of the back room. Please could she leave her in the apartment for a while? 'Everything is fine, no really. Please, mother. I'll explain later.' Her voice was shaking and she was gripping the side of her nurse's uniform.

Owen spoke quietly to André. He would wait in the car.

When they had both left, she took Owen to his son.

He was a tiny little thing, with Owen's fair hair but his mother's jet-black eyes, which brightened up when they entered the room. Owen sank to his knees and picked him up, holding him close to him. He could feel the baby's warmth against his chest and his own tears rolling down his face. Gently, he pressed the little boy's head under his chin. Nothing had prepared him for this moment. His son's hair felt like silk brushing against his face.

Ginette was sobbing behind him, pacing up and down the room.

'What are you going to do with him, Owen? He is the most precious thing to me. Please, Owen, I will do anything. Don't take him, Owen. Don't take him. I am sorry, I was wrong, I—'

Owen sat down in an armchair, holding the baby in an unsure manner.

'I don't know. I have really no idea. I need to think. What can we do? The British authorities are after you. Don't forget, you're a German spy. We can't pretend that nothing has happened.'

'Maybe they would understand, Owen.'

His son was studying his face, wriggling his tiny fingers as he did so.

He laughed. 'I very much doubt that. Do you know what they do to German spies? They hang them. Even repentant ones. We can't go back to England and think that everything will be sorted out. I can hardly live here, as if nothing happened. We will have to work something out. I'm still not sure what I want to do, to be honest. I don't know what I want to happen to us.'

She came over and knelt by the armchair. The baby was staring into the face of his father, his jet-black eyes darting around to take in every feature. Her arm stroked his and for a while all was silent and serene. Owen was totally captivated by the baby.

The tranquillity was shaken by knocking at the door.

She hauled herself up. 'It will be my mother. I will ask her to go to her sister's for a while so we can be alone for longer.'

He was more at ease cradling his son now. To his amazement, it felt natural. The baby was continuing to gaze into his eyes and Owen was certain that he was smiling at him. He grinned back.

He could hear her unlocking the door and then the sound of a hoarse male voice saying, 'Ginette Troppe?'

After that, his recollection was blurred beyond repair.

There was a noise, certainly. Not too loud – he realised later that the gun must have been held straight against her body – but it was a sharp noise that echoed around the little flat. That was followed almost immediately by the sound of something falling heavily and then a much louder and far clearer gunshot.

There was a commotion on the stairs and he heard André shouting something. From the hall he heard a long groan, that didn't stop. He was frozen in the armchair, the baby's smile now wide and accompanied by a friendly gurgle. His little arms were reaching out.

When he found himself in the hall, the baby was in his arms.

André was kneeling by her side, his hands covered in blood. Her face was grey, her eyes open wide but darting around, having trouble focussing. Her head was moving frantically from side to side.

André was trying to stem the blood flowing from a wound in her stomach, but a dark red patch was spreading fast across her chest.

'Talk to her, Owen, tell her to hang on.'

Neighbours had gathered in the open doorway. 'Ambulance!' shouted André. 'Get an ambulance and a doctor!'

Owen took her hand, which felt like ice. Her breathing was slow and very noisy. She tried hard to focus.

'Tell her to hang on, Owen. Show her the baby. Do something.'

He held Philippe closer to her. Very slowly, she reached out to him, her hand stopping before she could touch him. As the colour drained completely from her face her black eyes stood out in even more contrast against the white skin. A smile began to appear across her face and then froze as a groan came from deep inside her and her body seemed to sink slowly into itself.

André stood up, drenched in blood.

'She's gone, Owen. She's gone.'

–

André was pushing the small Peugeot as hard as it would go as they headed north. They had made good progress since leaving Strasbourg. The lights of Metz were now fading behind them, the road ahead dark and broken only by the occasional passing lights of army convoys. He was not sure about Owen's plan, but he agreed that they needed to leave Strasbourg fast.

Owen was slumped across the backseat, his son fast asleep in his arms.

'You are sure it was him, André?'

'I told you, Owen. I am not certain, but I think it was. I was sitting in the front seat of the car waiting around the corner for you when a large silvery-grey Renault pulled up in front of me. I didn't think anything of it. I was trying to rest, to be honest. A large man got out of the car and walked past. I was a bit unsettled by him, I don't know why. A minute or so later, something clicked in my mind and I got out for a proper look at the Renault. It had those very wide running boards. I am sure it was like the car that drove us to the prison to see Lange. And then I realised who the man was. Émile, the man who drove the Renault to and from the prison. The man whose family was tortured by the Gestapo, you remember? He was wearing a beret too, just like he was when he drove us to the prison. So I ran back to the apartment block. Just as I entered, I heard two shots, definitely two. As I ran up the stairs I collided with him running down. He pushed me out of the way. What more can I say? Revenge is our new religion.'

–

Edgar arrived at the hospital two hours after Ginette Troppe's body had been taken there. He had expected to find a living person, not a corpse.

He had asked for her by name at the reception and was ushered into a side room by a clearly distressed matron. 'Are you here in connection with her death? How has the news got out so soon?'

Edgar must have looked shocked; the matron was very understanding. He showed her the impressive sheaf of documentation that he had from the British Embassy in Paris and explained that she had done some work for the British during the war. 'She was at Dunkirk, you understand.' He had come to Strasbourg to thank her in person.

The matron tearfully explained what had happened. 'Shot, twice. We thought that kind of thing had stopped with the Germans leaving. There had been reprisals of course, but why would anyone want to shoot a nurse? The police have no idea who it was. And she was such a good nurse. Before the war she was a cold person, if I am honest with you, sir, not someone you could warm to. But when she returned from Paris she was a much nicer person. Maybe becoming a mother had changed her. I had no idea she was at Dunkirk. So many people did things in the war that they do not discuss.'

Edgar asked if he could see the body and was taken to the mortuary. He did not want to stay very long at all, especially as he was aware that his presence was beginning to attract some attention. 'If you don't mind waiting, sir, the police may want to talk with you when they arrive… if you could give us your name.' He wanted to be absolutely certain that it was the woman he had first known as Nathalie Mercier.

The room where the body lay was narrow with a low ceiling and it was dark apart from a light hanging directly over the body. He had not expected her head to be exposed, so as soon as he walked in he knew for sure that it was her. The shroud was gathered across the top of her breasts with the edge of a wound just visible, her skin now a marble white and glinting in the bright light.

He had no idea what had happened, and was going to have some trouble in explaining what had gone on. *Had Owen been responsible for her death? What would he have done if he had got to her first?*

There was a knock on the window that separated the room from the rest of the mortuary. The matron was looking anxious. She had explained on the way down that this was most irregular and really she did not have the authority to…

He held up his hand. 'One minute. Thank you.'

He thought of the past four years, and his role in shaping the life of the woman whose body now lay in front of him. He thought of the lives undoubtedly saved thanks to her unwitting help. He thought of her husband, and of what was going to become of him.

More knocking at the window. *I'm coming.*

Edgar turned to look at the body for one final time. He shook his head and smiled. 'You were the best of our spies,' he muttered, 'and you never even realised it.'

Minutes later, Edgar was on his way back to Paris, accompanied by an enormous sense of relief. What could have been a major problem had gone away. The outcome was messy, but all things considered it could have been far, far worse.

Chapter 37

Aftermath

Less than an hour after Owen Quinn had been to visit Captain John Archibald that day in December 1944, one of Edgar's men had turned up, demanding to know whether Owen Quinn had been to the house. He had pushed his way past Mrs Archibald but, by the time he entered the bedroom, Archibald had secreted under his body the notebook which Georg Lange's name was in.

Captain Archibald feigned sleep and the man had to leave. Later that night Archibald managed to get out of bed and burned the notebook in the fire.

His condition deteriorated significantly in the New Year, and everyone said that it was a relief when he died in March 1945.

They used the word 'peaceful' to describe his passing, as was traditional, but Iris Archibald would have described it as anything but. He was often agitated and usually in pain, but what she noticed more than anything else was that he appeared to be full of regret, as if there were matters he still wanted resolved but could not address. In his last few weeks he often asked her whether Owen Quinn had ever been in touch again and she always had to shake her head.

The day before he died, he told her that he wanted to dictate a letter, which began 'My dear Owen…'

He fell asleep after those words and did not wake up again.

His short obituary in *The Times* concentrated on his role in the Battle of Jutland in 1916. Brief reference was made to how he had delayed his retirement to continue service in the Royal Navy during the current war, in what they described as an 'administrative capacity'.

–

Following his arrest in July 1944, Admiral Wilhelm Canaris was held by the SS in Berlin.

In February 1945 he was taken to the Flossenbürg concentration camp in Bavaria, not far from the Czech border. He continued to be tortured until the morning of the 9th April 1945 when – along with his former deputy, Generalmajor Hans Oster and some of the 20th July bomb plot conspirators – he was stripped naked and dragged into the courtyard of the camp and slowly hanged by the SS.

Flossenbürg concentration camp was liberated by the Americans just two weeks later.

The two SS officers responsible for Canaris's detention and execution in Flossenbürg, Otto Thorbeck and Walter Huppenkothen, were never punished by the German authorities after the war.

–

Arnold Vermeulen felt elated as the plane sped over the last few miles of the silver sea and he was able to make out the coastline of mainland Europe in the distance. After five years, he would be home soon.

All in all, Arnold Vermeulen could not really complain at the way he had been treated.

Considering that in April 1941 he thought he was about to be executed, anything since then had been a bonus. Above all, he felt a sense of relief. He had never thought that he was cut out to be a spy anyway. The British seemed to understand that. He had become a nervous wreck, to be honest. He was a victim of the war. People would understand that in time. But once he had come through the interrogation and agreed to be a double agent, life became much easier. He no longer had to worry about being caught, because he already had been. He had no problems about betraying Magpie because, if he was frank, he never liked her. She was always condescending, treating him as if he were inferior to her, which he probably was.

So, all in all, he had been happy to play along with the British. After they set him up as a double agent, they always treated him properly. He never had to deal with the tall Englishman again, which was a relief. Contact with Magpie was intermittent, but he did everything he was told.

He had begun to wonder what would happen at the end of the war and had asked his handlers that on more than one occasion. There was an understanding that he would have to be returned to Belgium, but the authorities there would be told how co-operative he had been. Maybe six months in jail, certainly nothing more than that.

Life changed a bit at the end of April 1944. He never saw Magpie again. They moved him from the safe house in Acton to somewhere in North Wales. It was not a prison they told him. Not at all. But the house they kept him in was in a locked compound, and the house itself was locked and guarded. Soon after that, he heard about D-Day, and then it was just a matter of time before it was all over. Allied troops entered Belgium in the September and he was not sure how he felt about that. Not relief, but not a sense of defeat either. He just wanted this whole, dreadful business to be over and done with. To get back to his old life, his flat, his records and familiar surroundings.

After VE Day in May 1945 he was moved to a house somewhere in England. He had no idea where it was. It was in preparation for being sent back to Belgium, they had said. He had begun to worry, but then that was in his nature after all.

He had heard some dreadful things on the radio. In April, the Belgian authorities executed sixteen Belgian citizens for their part in torturing prisoners during the war. The sixteen were all shot in the back. He could not get the image out of his mind.

In the middle of May, the tall Englishman reappeared. 'You are going home,' he told him. 'Tomorrow.' He had asked the Englishman whether all these assurances he had been given – about how he would be well treated, just six months in prison etc. – whether he would have them in writing. The Englishman smiled and left. Arnold was sure that he nodded.

He saw him again the next morning when he arrived at the remote airfield. He asked him again whether he had those assurances in writing, and the Englishman just smiled and patted his coat pocket. There was just one plane there, no RAF markings as far as he could tell, and not much else around them. The tall Englishman boarded the plane first and two of his guards came too.

And now the plane was descending, much sooner than he had expected, actually. He had thought it would be a few minutes more before they arrived in Brussels, but then he had never flown before, so he was not sure. The plane had started to descend before it had reached the coast and it appeared to be landing almost within sight of the coast. He was worrying needlessly again. He realised that he was unsophisticated. What did he know about air travel? As the plane came in to land, there was just countryside around them, no sign of anything else. He was not worried, just confused. Maybe they were using a small airport, not the main one, and that made sense. The main thing was, he was home. Back in Belgium.

After that, it was all far too quick and dreadful to take in. The plane had bounced along the landing strip and then come to a sudden stop. As he looked out of the window, he saw a van pull up alongside the plane. The tall Englishman got out and he heard a brief conversation going on, but could not make out what was being said or even what language it was in.

Then he was bundled down the steps of the plane and manhandled into the back of the van, which was filthy and smelled of soil. Scatterings of earth and gravel littered its floor. A man had put handcuffs on him and another tied a blindfold round his head. He had not expected to be greeted with flowers and the Belgian National Anthem, but nor had he expected this. He began to worry. The van sped off. They seemed to be driving over rough terrain, certainly not on roads.

It came to a halt and he was roughly hauled out of the back and marched along. The blindfold was removed. He was in a large barn, lit by streaks of sunlight breaking in through the gaps in the walls and roof. Large parts of the barn were charred and it looked as if there had been a big fire in it.

He was led in front of a small trestle table, behind which sat three men. The one in the middle spoke to him in French. From his accent, he was French, not Walloon.

'Are you Arnold Vermeulen?'

'Yes, sir.'

'You were recruited as a Nazi agent in Brussels in May 1940?'

He looked round, his head darting from side to side. If the tall Englishman was here, he would be able to explain. There was no sign of him.

'Yes, sir. But I don't think you understand—'

'And subsequently operated as a Nazi agent in England?'

If the two men had not been on either side of him, he would have collapsed by now. He was not in Belgium. These people were French. He had trouble getting the words out to reply.

'There has been a terrible misunderstanding. You see, *I co-operated* with the British. I promise you. They even said—'

'Did you ever operate as Nazi agent in England?' The man to the left was now speaking, repeating his colleague's question.

'Yes, for a while… But only as—'

'Does the name Magpie mean anything to you?'

'Certainly, but again I—'

The man in the middle stood up.

'It is clear that you worked with the enemy against the people of France. Now you will suffer the consequences.' He nodded to the two men on either side of the Belgian.

They dragged him screaming across the rough floor of the barn to where a long rope had been slung over a beam, with a stool under it. The ground around where the stool stood was blackened with soot and scorch marks. Another man came over and attempted to tie his legs together, but he resisted. One of the other men kneed him hard in the groin and Vermeulen collapsed to the ground, doubled up in agony.

His legs were tied together and an oily rag was stuffed into his mouth. The two guards picked him up and hauled him onto the stool.

A blindfold, he thought. *Why can't they blindfold me?*

The taste in his mouth was indescribable and he could feel himself starting to vomit.

They appeared to be in no rush to tie the noose round his neck, holding him carefully in position as they ripped the collar from his shirt so that the thick rope was in contact with his flesh.

He noticed two things just before they kicked the stool away. The first was just how much sunlight was seeping into the vast barn. And the second was the sight of the tall Englishman, silhouetted in the open door of the barn, his long shadow being thrown almost as far as the stool he was standing on. He would help him now.

When the stool was finally kicked away, it was at least twenty choking seconds before he even began to lose consciousness. And during that time he was sure that the barn was consumed in flames.

The last sound he heard was of screaming children.

–

The German agent known as Cognac continued to move around England for a good eighteen months after the war, frequently changing his identity and appearance.

He considered moving back to Germany, but realised it was probably safer in England.

By 1949 he had settled into his identity as a Czech refugee so comfortably that he felt able to put down some roots.

He married a war widow in Derbyshire and became stepfather to her two young children. It was a happy marriage, though both his wife and stepchildren knew to avoid discussing the war or his life before it. They were aware that it was too painful for him. The Germans had done terrible things to his family, he told them.

Whenever he read that the British had caught every single agent that the Abwehr had sent to the United Kingdom it would cause him quiet amusement and satisfaction. It was just a shame that he could never tell anyone his story. He tried not to think too much about the past, because there was too much of it. But from time to time, he did wonder what had become of the beautiful Frenchwoman he had kept an eye on during the war.

His wife died in 1959, but he continued to work as a wages clerk in a local engineering factory, and he stayed close to the children and became very close to their children, his grandchildren.

He only let his guard down once. When he was dying in 1974, his stepson, to whom he was especially close, asked if there was anything he would like to do before it was too late. He replied 'To see Germany once again.' His stepson looked confused, but he attributed this to the heavy doses of morphine he was taking.

Cognac had always attended the Remembrance Day parade at the town's small cenotaph. It would have seemed churlish not to do so and he was anxious to fit in, not to draw attention to himself. But he made sure to stand on the edge of the ceremony. Be part of it, but separate too. There, but not there. He was used to that. It was how he had lived his life since 1939.

When he died, the local branch of the British Legion placed a wreath on his grave.

—

Georg Lange acted like a condemned man throughout February 1945, utterly convinced that he had been tricked and was going to be tried as a war criminal. However, at the end of the month, one of the Frenchmen who had confronted him returned to his cell and told him that his information about Ginette Troppe had been correct. He was there to show that he was keeping his side of the bargain. A disbelieving Lange watched as the Frenchman produced the false documents and burned them in front of him.

Before he left, Gaston shook Lange's hand. Georg found the whole thing hard to believe and decided it was best treated as a bad dream and forgotten. He was determined never to mention it to anyone. Who would believe him anyway?

Georg Lange was released as a prisoner of war in June 1945 and returned to Mainz to be reunited with Helga, Charlotte and Maria.

He had assumed he would return to the legal profession, but his few weeks of contemplating what he believed could be his imminent death had a marked effect on him. He trained as a teacher and specialised in working with blind children.

He and his wife spent a few days' holiday in Alsace one summer in the early 1960s, and when they stopped in Strasbourg he did think about looking up the name Troppe in the telephone directory. Purely out of curiosity – he would not have contacted her. But he thought better of it. Some things were best left as they are.

Georg Lange died in Mainz in 1988.

–

After he had helped Owen, André Koln returned to Paris.

The concentration camps around Europe were being liberated and the few French survivors slowly began to return, but it was no more than a pitiful trickle. André was never under the illusion that either his wife or son had survived, he knew that was not even a remote hope that he could cling to. He hoped that some members of his immediate family would return, but none did. Both of his parents, his brother, his sister and her family, and all of his uncles and aunts and their children were gone. One or two friends returned, a cousin of his wife's who had survived a death march, and a few acquaintances, but to all intents and purposes, he was alone. He knew that he was not alone in being alone. Less than two thousand of the seventy-five thousand Jews deported from Paris returned. In all, more than eighty thousand French Jews were murdered in the Holocaust.

André did not return to the law. He concentrated on his journalism, his writing popular and distinguished by an angry passion. He married

413

again, twice; to a friend of his wife's in 1946, and to a fellow journalist in 1953. Neither marriage lasted more than a year. He had no more children.

André's journalism took him to cover the wars in French Indo-China, and it was there that he was shot in 1959. Despite medical treatment, he died of his wounds a few days later. Just before he died he asked a nurse to pass him a photograph from his wallet. He died clutching the photograph of Daniel, his son. The doctor who had been looking after him in the hospital wrote to his editor and said that André was unusually resigned to his fate for someone of his age.

Owen Quinn attended André's funeral in Paris. Addressing the congregation, André's editor said he did not understand why André was so reckless. 'It was almost as if he had a death wish.' People shook their heads. They too did not understand. Only Owen did not shake his head. He understood.

-

Owen Quinn had been due back at the Admiralty on Monday, 5th February, but there was no sign of him until that Thursday, when he quietly returned to work, seemingly with neither a care nor a concern in the world.

When he was carpeted for being absent without leave, he demanded to see Major Edgar.

It was the first indication Edgar had had that Quinn was back in London. His trail had gone cold in Strasbourg that weekend. All he had been able to ascertain was that the neighbours had seen a large man in a beret escaping from outside the apartment with a pistol in his hands. A man, who matched Quinn's description, was seen weeping over a woman's body. Soon after, he left the apartment with a baby and another man, whom the neighbours described as thin, dark and French. Ginette Troppe's mother had arrived back at the apartment as they were leaving. She had been in a state of shock ever since. Even allowing for this, Edgar realised that she knew next to nothing.

Quinn, the other man and the baby were seen driving away in a small Peugeot. After that, nothing. No sign, no trace, no hint whatsoever. If there had been an inkling before that Quinn had had these abilities that he had demonstrated in France, thought Edgar, then he would have made a most effective SOE agent.

He fully expected never to see Quinn again, so he was most surprised on the Thursday, which was the day after he himself had returned to London to explain himself, to get a call saying Quinn had turned up and wanted to see him. The feeling, thought Edgar as he strode purposefully across Whitehall, was definitely mutual.

Quinn was sitting in an office when Edgar walked in. He stood up and saluted and sat down again without being asked.

Major Edgar made great play of demonstrating his anger. He removed his leather gloves and trilby and threw both down on the desk.

'Are you going to tell me what happened, Quinn?'

'I needed to be on my own, sir. Clear my head, that kind of thing. I realise I ought to have been back at work on Monday, for which I apologise. I will, of course, understand if I am to be punished for that.'

'And where were you, Quinn?'

'Just driving around the country, sir. Walking. That kind of thing.'

'You're going to have to do an awful lot better than that, Quinn. France for a start. When did you get there?'

Quinn looked puzzled. He hadn't been to France. 'Check my passport, sir. What makes you think I've been to France?'

It went on like this for the rest of the morning and well into the afternoon. Edgar could see little prospect of getting Quinn to admit to anything. He was well versed in playing the innocent. The most difficult interrogation that Edgar had ever had to conduct up to this point was with an Italian living in Glasgow, who they were convinced was a spy, and who probably was. But it turned out that the man was also suffering from some kind of mental illness. He was deluded, the psychiatrists told him. It meant that he was so convinced that he was innocent that he was not having to play a part. Without the man admitting to being a spy, they had no evidence. They had to let him go in the end. Quinn was proving to be as frustrating.

He lit a cigarette and allowed a few moments for the tobacco to clear his mind. What is it that I am trying to achieve here? Edgar kept reminding himself. The objective was neither to punish Quinn, nor even to find out exactly what had gone on in France. The objective was ensuring that there would be no trouble. No difficulties. No noise. Silence was what Edgar was after. That no one would ever hear of Nathalie Mercier, or Geraldine Leclerc, or Ginette Troppe, or whoever she really was again. No one would know what happened. The whole business would be forgotten.

'Your wife, Quinn—'

'I have not seen my wife since last April, sir. I have accepted that I shall never see her again. I am anxious to put that part of my life behind me.'

Edgar stared at Quinn for a very long time to see if he believed him, and for some reason, he was convinced that he did.

'I am gratified to hear that, Quinn. Don't forget, whatever you went through – whatever we put you through – your wife was a Nazi spy. A totally committed one, I have no doubt whatsoever about that. Our small operation helped to save many thousands of Allied lives.'

Quinn sat very still and didn't say a word. After a while, Edgar felt uncomfortable and dismissed Quinn. He asked Quinn's superior that no action be taken against him for being AWOL.

Edgar kept an eye on Quinn from a distance for a year or so, but he never met with him again. Quinn was as good as gold. His people at the Admiralty said that he was quieter than normal, but seemed altogether calmer. 'At peace with himself' was a phrase used in connection with Quinn more than once. By 1946 Edgar considered that it was safe to let Quinn go. He received an honourable discharge from the Royal Navy in early 1946 and trained as a teacher. The last that Edgar had heard was that Quinn was teaching at a boys' grammar school somewhere in west London.

By the end of 1947, Major Edgar ceased to exist, not that 'Edgar' had ever been anything other than a *nom de guerre*.

His war had been a long one. It had started in early 1939, months before the official declaration of war, and he had even been involved in a clandestine mission inside Germany itself, which had come close to breaking him.

He stayed in the field of intelligence for a couple of years after the war, but found the Cold War altogether too chilly. He could not find it in himself to return to the world of finance, in which he had worked until 1939, so he put Edgar behind him and went into politics. He had a successful political career, and was much admired for his compassion and pioneering work in the area of social reform. Once, in 1955, he was speaking at an educational conference in London and could have sworn he spotted Quinn sitting towards the back of the hall. He looked around for him afterwards, but there was no sign.

In his later years he often thought about what had happened to Owen Quinn. Of course, he could have found out easily enough, but what would have been the point? He had liked Quinn. But not once, either during the war or after, did he ever have the slightest doubt that everything they had done had been other than totally justified. There was no question of that.

The image of Nathalie Mercier, which was the name he associated with her, rather than that of Ginette Troppe, was never far from his mind. He only had to pass a beautiful young woman with long, dark hair in the street to be reminded of her. But what was most likely to bring her to mind was whenever he thought about the deception operation, and how its part in winning the war could still not really be spoken of.

One day in 1957, or possibly 1958, he bumped into Dr Clarence Leigh in the Central Lobby of the Houses of Parliament. His old sparring partner from the SOE was now Lord Leigh of Leominster, or it could have been Leamington Spa – Edgar couldn't remember, though he was sure it was somewhere beginning with 'L' in that part of the country. His peerage was the consequence of an easily forgotten report he had written for the Government on adult literacy, or lack of it.

Leigh now had the hunched appearance of a very overweight man, aged before his time, shuffling slowly from the House of Lords as Edgar emerged in a more sprightly fashion from the House of Commons. Leigh paused when he saw Edgar, tilting slightly back so as to be able to see him properly. Behind him was a young man, who could have been no more than twenty, carrying a bag and a pile of papers.

'Anton – my assistant,' Leigh said, by way of explanation. 'How are you?'

Edgar said he was well and the two men walked silently towards Westminster Hall and the St Stephen's exit, Anton a few paces behind them. Leigh's walking stick echoed on the tiled floor.

Leigh paused again, catching his breath, holding Edgar gently by the elbow as he turned slowly towards him.

'Tell me. Whatever happened to that French girl we were involved with. What became of her?'

Edgar hesitated. He was not sure how much Leigh knew. He frowned, as if he were having trouble remembering exactly who Leigh was talking about.

'Oh! Do you mean Nathalie... Mercier, was it? Lord knows. She disappeared. Never heard of her again after that July.'

They resumed their slow progress to the St Stephen's exit. Leigh was nodding his head slowly, not sure that he believed Edgar but not surprised that the truth was being kept from him. He would expect little else.

'Often thought about that operation we were involved in with you – and her. I think I probably owe you an apology, shouldn't have been so doubtful about it. She must have been worth a division or two to us, wouldn't you say?'

Edgar raised his eyebrows and nodded his head, as if that thought had never occurred to him. He let Leigh carry on talking.

'And you say she just disappeared? Probably best that way.'

'Probably,' said Edgar, before shaking Leigh by the hand and promising to have lunch one day.

He never saw Leigh again.

Edgar never once discussed with his wife anything that he had done in the war. As far as she was concerned, he had been in the Far East for the duration, while she had been left on her own to bring up the children in Dorset. The marriage only really recovered, after a fashion, when he retired in the late 1960s.

During his retirement in Dorset he took long walks along the coast every day. He preferred them to be solitary, but sometimes his wife insisted on accompanying him. He would often stand just staring across the Channel, sometimes for as long as half an hour at a time. On occasion his wife would notice that his eyes had filled with tears. If he saw that she had noticed, he would brush them away and make a remark about the 'bloody wind'.

He could see the other end of the Channel, where the sea was always stained with blood. He had an absolute conviction that, but for his work and others involved in the great deception, it would have been flowing with far more blood.

He died in 1979.

Chapter 38

June 1960

The rail ferry *The Maid of Kent* was twenty minutes out of Dover when the teachers finally managed to settle the boys and were able to sit down themselves for a cup of tea. It was going to be a busy day.

Mr Atkinson, the Head of French, had organised the trip. He sat alongside Mr Quinn, one of the geography teachers. 'Understand you speak French, Owen? You kept that one quiet. Could have used you when Madame Robinson had her fall.'

'Well, I speak a bit. Haven't really used it for years now. I get by.'

'Spent much time in France?'

Mr Quinn drank slowly from a chipped teacup and nodded. 'A bit. A long time ago though.'

The staff were used to Owen Quinn. A quiet man. Well respected. Absolutely dedicated to the boys, which made up for not having any children of his own. Had never married. First class teacher. But very quiet. Not exactly unfriendly, but kept himself to himself. 'Reserved' was the word that was most frequently used to describe him.

'Was that during the war?'

'Yes. I was over there at the end.'

'D-Day?'

'Something like that.'

'Navy weren't you? No chance of you being seasick today then?'

Quinn nodded and smiled politely. The ferry was pitching and it was turning out to be a choppy crossing.

'Been back since the end of the war?'

'No. I think we'd better go and check on the boys, don't you? Can't have any of them falling overboard.'

Mr Atkinson finally took the hint and went through the schedule one more time. The other teachers rolled their eyes. This trip was over-planned.

Mr Atkinson's plan for the day had allowed two hours' free time in the afternoon. He and the other French teacher would stay around the old town of Boulogne; the others could have a bit of time to themselves.

Owen had reread all the letters just the night before. More than thirty of them. They wrote to him twice a year, at Christmas and the start of the summer holidays. The letters always contained one new photograph, news of how he was getting on, and grateful thanks for the money they received every month. The letters never failed to end without a heartfelt expression of gratitude for what Owen had done for them. 'You can never imagine,' they once said, 'how you gave us a reason to live again.'

Owen checked his map and soon found his way to the school. No one would give him a second glance now. The tall young naval officer of fifteen years ago was now a middle-aged man, slightly hunched, slightly overweight, slightly balding.

'After school, he always plays football with his friends in the park opposite. Sometimes for hours!'

Sure enough, a group of a dozen boys aged fifteen or sixteen were playing football in the park across the road from the school. Owen walked over.

Even without the photographs, he would have picked him out. It was not so much the fair hair, flowing as he ran at least as fast as Owen had done at his age. It was the eyes. His mother's eyes. Even from thirty yards away, they blazed out. Like jet-black pools, just as he remembered them. He felt the hairs standing up on the back of his neck.

At that moment, the ball ran towards him. Owen ambled over to trap it. As he did so, the boy ran over to collect it. Owen trapped it and flicked it up for the boy to catch it neatly. *My son.*

'*Voilà.*'

'*Merci, monsieur!*'

For a moment, just a moment, the two looked at each other. Owen knew it was fanciful to imagine that there was any connection there as far as the boy was concerned. Just curiosity. But he did look him directly in the eye and flash him the broadest of smiles before running back to join his friends.

Owen stayed for another few minutes. He was blinking back the tears now, the first time he had cried in fifteen years. He moved a bit further away from where the boys were playing, towards the safety offered by the lengthening shadow of the trees.

He was not sure what to do now. The journey that had begun fifteen years ago in Strasbourg had finally come to an end.

As he and André had driven away from Strasbourg that February night in 1945 he could not be sure that he was doing the right thing. He realised that he could hardly just turn up in England with his son. Who would believe his story? Edgar was unlikely to come to his aid, probably quite the opposite. What proof did he have? How could he bring him up on his own? What would his parents say? Everyone would probably treat him as if he was mad. Literally mad. When he thought about it, he realised his son would probably be put into care. Another war orphan.

They had argued in the car. Owen told André the plan that was forming in his head. 'He is your son,' André had insisted. 'You cannot abandon him.'

Owen told André that the most important thing that he could give to his son was the chance of a normal life and he knew where he could get that.

For the past fifteen years he had hoped that he had made the right decision. Now he was sure that he had.

He moved around the pitch, still in the safety of the shade thrown by the tall trees in the late afternoon sun. He was aware that he cut a solitary figure but he did not want to draw attention to himself. Mostly, he felt a sense of relief. His son was clearly healthy and happy. But as he watched him playing with his friends, he could not fail to be reminded of himself at that age. The same build, the same turn of speed, and even his own favoured position on the right wing.

But he also thought of how his mind used to wander when he was that age, returning home after a game of football or cricket. He'd pass the families walking through the park and assume that that would be him one day. That was all he wanted then: nothing more than a beautiful wife and a couple of children.

Be careful what you wish for.

A few minutes later Owen noticed a couple moving slowly to the side of the pitch: Françoise and Lucien. Naturally, they looked much older than when he had first met them in 1944, broken and totally bereft in their house near Boulogne. Lucien was walking, although with the aid of a stick.

They had come to collect their son. They were calling out for him to come and join them.

'Philippe!'

Author's Note

Although *The Best of Our Spies* is a work of fiction, many of the events described in it and some of the characters are based on fact.

At the heart of the book is the Allied invasion of northern Europe which began on 6th June 1944 – D-Day. The Battle of Normandy was ultimately successful but in its early stages, all did not go according to plan. Despite having air superiority and many other advantages, it took the Allied armies far longer to break out of Normandy than the original battle-plan envisaged.

There can be little doubt that history would have been very different had the Germans not split their forces in northern France between the Pas de Calais (where their superior Fifteenth Army and most of their Panzer divisions were based) and Normandy (where the Seventh Army was based). This was due in major part to the dramatically successful Allied deception operation known as Operation Fortitude. Details of Operation Fortitude only began to emerge many years after the war, which is why it is never referred to by name in the book.

There is no doubt that Operation Fortitude succeeded in convincing Hitler and many of his generals that the main Allied landings would be to the north east of Normandy, in the Pas de Calais. The deception was ingenious enough to continue to fool the Germans for a few weeks after D-Day, thereby delaying the sending of reinforcements from the Pas de Calais to Normandy. By the time they realised that there were never going to be landings in the Pas de Calais, it was too late. Arguably, this was the critical deciding factor in ultimately determining the Allied victory in Europe.

Fortitude was a complex operation and there were many aspects to it, including the creation of the 'dummy' army called FUSAG (First US Army Group), apparently based in the south east of England (and referred to in Chapter 21), along with the use of inflatable tanks and deliberately misleading radio traffic. Perhaps the most effective aspect of Fortitude was the use of agents sent to Britain by the Germans and whom the Allies turned into double agents so as to send false information back to the Germans. Perhaps the best known of these was a Spaniard called Juan Pujol, who was known as Agent Garbo.

The London Reception Centre at the Royal Victoria Patriotic School in Wandsworth, the Double Cross Committee, the SOE (Special Operations Executive), the London Controlling Section and COSSAC all existed. F Section of the SOE sent some 470 agents into occupied France, many of whom were flown in by Lysanders of 161 Squadron of the RAF. All the BBC broadcasts on and before 5th and 6th June are accurately quoted. HMS *Gloucester* was sunk on 22nd May 1941, during the Battle of Crete.

Neither the hospital at Calcotte Grange nor Lincoln House where Owen Quinn worked are real places, although Duke Street in St James's was at the heart of a number of organisations related to D–Day. The Free French were based in Duke Street and the headquarters of COSSAC were round the corner in St James's Square. The Chequers Tavern is still there in Duke Street, and Geales restaurant in Notting Hill Gate, where Owen and Nathalie went for dinner in Chapter Fifteen, also exists to this day.

The Nazi concentration camp of Natzweiler in the Vosges Mountains, referred to in Chapter Twenty-nine, did exist. Known by its full name of Natzweiler Struthof, this was the only concentration camp on French territory. Its main purpose was to deal with political prisoners and resistance fighters (a number of SOE agents were murdered there). However, Jewish prisoners were transported there from concentration camps in the east to be murdered in its gas chambers so that their bodies could be transported to the nearby University of Strasbourg. Their corpses were then used for racial medical experiments by August Hirt.

The German agent, Cognac, is fictional. It had long been believed that throughout World War Two, no Nazi agents in the United Kingdom evaded capture. However, in 2006 the Public Records Office in London released papers suggesting that an Abwehr spy called Wilhelm Moerz did operate in Britain throughout the war and evaded capture. Cognac is loosely based on Moerz. The FTP – Francs-Tireurs et Partisans – was one of the most active of the French resistance groups. The details of the treatment and fate of Parisian Jewry are based on fact.

Many of the German characters in the book did exist in real life. Admiral Wilhelm Canaris was head of the Abwehr until early 1944. His opposition to Hitler and his increasing anti-Nazi tendencies, along with contacts with Allied Intelligence, are now well known. The extent to which he was aware that the Germans were being deceived into believing that the Pas de Calais was the main destination of the Allies is unknown. What is clear is that he and many others in the German military (including those involved in the July 1944 'Valkyrie' bomb plot) had realised long before D-Day that Germany was beaten and accordingly felt that it was in Germany's interests for the war to end as soon as possible. The circumstances of his execution, along with his deputy, Generalmajor Hans Oster, are accurate. The Abwehr case officer in the story, Georg Lange, is fictional.

Apart from the major historical characters referred to in passing, none of the other characters in the book existed in real life. Any connection between any of these characters and people who may have existed in real life is, of course, purely coincidental.

The true events around D-Day, Operation Fortitude, the occupation and liberation of France, and the opposition to Hitler will always be more dramatic than any work of fiction. Nonetheless, I hope that *The Best of Our Spies* does, in some modest way, shine a well-deserved light on the sheer brilliance and guile of the deception operation that played such a critical, yet still underrated part in the liberation of Nazi-occupied Europe.

The
Swiss Spy

List of main characters

Henri Hesse – born as Henry Hunter

Marlene Hesse – mother of Henri. Formerly known as Maureen Hunter

Erich Hesse (deceased) – husband of Marlene & stepfather of Henri

Louise Alice Hesse/Hunter (deceased) – aunt of Henri Hesse

Captain Edgar – British spy master

Hon. Anthony Davis – cover name for Edgar

Patrick O'Connor Jnr – cover name for Edgar

Christopher Porter – Edgar's boss

Basil Remington-Barber – British spy chief in Switzerland

Sir Roland Pearson – Downing Street intelligence chief

Madame Ladnier – contact at Credit Suisse, Geneva

Sandy Morgan – British spy in Lisbon

Rolf Eder – Austrian, working for the British in Switzerland

Franz Hermann – Berlin lawyer & British agent. Codename *Hugo*

Frau Hermann – mother of Franz Hermann

Werner Ernst – Generalmajor in German Army High Command

Gunter Reinhart – official at the Reichsbank, Berlin. Married to Gudrun.

Rosa Stern – first wife of Gunter Reinhart. Married to Harald Stern

Alfred Stern – son of Gunter Reinhart & Rosa Stern

Sophia Stern – daughter of Rosa Stern and Harald Stern

Alois Jäger – Berlin lawyer

Katharina Hoch – British agent in Stuttgart. Codename *Milo*

Dieter Hoch – Brother of Katharina Hoch

Manfred – contact in Essen. Codename *Lido*

Gertraud Traugott (deceased) – 'aunt' in Essen

Telmo Rocha Martins – Official in Portuguese Foreign ministry

Dona Maria do Rosario – Secretary at Portuguese Legation in Berlin

Viktor Krasotkin – Russian spy master

Father Josef – Priest at St Hedwig's Cathedral, Berlin

Michael Hedinger – official at Bank Leu, Zurich

Anatoly Mikhailovich Yevtushenko – Russian émigré in Interlaken, Switzerland

Tatyana Dmitriyevna Yevtushenko – wife of Anatoly

Rozalia Anatolyevna Yevtushenko – daughter of Anatoly & Tatyana

Nadezhda Anatolyevna Yevtushenko – daughter of Anatoly & Tatyana

Nikolai Anatolyevich Yevtushenko – son of Anatoly & Tatyana

Prologue

London, 22nd June 1941

'It looks like it's started. You had better come over.'

It was pitch-dark in the room and he was unsure if the vaguely familiar voice next to him was part of a dream or was real and, if so, where it was coming from.

'Are you there Edgar? Can you hear me?'

He realised he was holding the telephone in his hand. He must have picked it up in the middle of a dream, in which he'd been surrounded by men even taller than him, all wearing black uniforms, with gleaming smiles. The menace that accompanied them had suddenly vanished at the sound of a shrill bell and man calling his name.

'Edgar! Are you there?'

He switched on the bedside lamp and leaned back on his pillow. It was Christopher Porter. Annoyingly, Edgar's cigarette case was not on the bedside table.

'Yes, sir.'

'At last. I imagine I've woken you up?'

'At two o'clock in the morning? Whatever makes you think that?'

'You'd better come over. Looks like it's all started.'

'Not another false alarm, I hope.'

'I don't think so: you'd better come and see for yourself.'

He dressed quickly, not bothering to shave. Just as he was about to leave his flat he noticed a half-full glass of whisky on the sideboard. He hesitated for a moment and then drank it. *If what Porter says is true, this may be the last chance for a drink for some time.*

There was a light drizzle as he hurried down Victoria Street and, by the time he crossed Parliament Square, it had turned quite heavy, causing him to run down Whitehall. The city was enveloped in the darkness of the blackout, causing him to step in a few puddles. By the time he arrived at the entrance to the heavily guarded basement under Whitehall his light summer suit was quite drenched, his socks felt soggy and he was breathing heavily. He joined a small queue of people waiting to be allowed in. The pervading smell was a mixture of rain, sweat and cigarette smoke. He edged his way to the front of the queue, ignoring muttering behind him.

'Who shall I say it is again, sir?' The army sergeant glanced anxiously at the men behind him.

'I told you: I was telephoned just before and told to come here. I really do not expect to be kept waiting. You understand?'

The sergeant hesitated: he had strict orders about who he was to allow into the basement and what accreditation they needed. This man was trying to barge his way in. At that moment the door to the basement opened behind him and a man tapped him on the shoulder.

'Captain Edgar is with me: be a good chap and let him through please.'

Five minutes later they had descended several flights of stairs and passed through a series of guarded doorways. Now they were on a narrow platform overlooking a large and brightly lit operations room, its walls covered in large maps. Men and women in a variety of uniforms were either on the phone, writing on bits of paper or climbing ladders to adjust markers on the maps. Another platform on the wall to their left was crowded with senior officers.

'So this is it, sir?'

'Seems to be. It all started just after midnight – our time that is. The Germans launched air raids against key targets in the Soviet controlled sector of Poland. Soon after that, their land forces crossed the border. Hard to be too precise at the moment, but everything we're picking up seems to indicate that this is a major invasion. Some reports say that over one hundred German divisions are involved. Other reports say it could be nearer to one hundred and fifty.'

'Reliable sources?'

'Bletchley say they can barely cope with all the radio traffic: noisiest night of the war, they say. Plenty of good stuff coming through Helsinki too. The Finns are pretty much in bed with the Germans now, as you know; wouldn't be surprised to see them joining the party. They're also well plugged-in to all kinds of sources in Russia, close proximity and all that. Stockholm station is sending broadly the same message. Morgan sent three messages from Lisbon last night saying he thought it was imminent – two different sources apparently, one particularly good one in the Ministry of Foreign Affairs.'

Edgar showed no reaction, as if nothing that he was being told was news to him. He felt in his pockets and realised he had forgotten to bring any cigarettes.

'What does the front look like?'

Christopher Porter pointed to an enormous map of Europe opposite them. 'Starting up there in the north – where that red diamond is – they've certainly crossed into Latvia. Probably the Fourth Panzer Group, we know they were in that area. Then all the way down the border, as far south as the Ukraine. Looks like the Romanians may be involved there, possibly the Hungarians too. See Brest on the map… there? That is where the main thrust may well be, though it is a bit early to say for sure. Between there and Lublin: north and south of the Pripet Marshes.'

'Quite some front.'

'Well, if they really have attacked from the Baltic to the Black Sea then that's well over a thousand miles. Extraordinary if they manage to pull that off.'

Edgar stared at the map for a good five minutes. 'He is crazy, isn't he?'

'Who is?'

Edgar looked down at Porter, surprised that he didn't seem to know who he was talking about. 'Hitler. He's left it far too late. Look how far they are from Moscow, over six hundred miles. Talking of which, much noise coming out of Moscow?'

'Nothing official. Apparently there is talk of their High Command having sent out some kind of alert about an invasion some three hours

3

before the Germans attacked, but we can't confirm that. Obviously didn't have any effect. Certainly there was a very noticeable increase in radio traffic in and out of Moscow last night, but then we know that the Soviets are prone to getting quite noisy every so often. All in all, it looks like they were caught by surprise.'

'Well,' said Edgar, removing his jacket, 'it's not as if we didn't warn them.'

Chapter 1

A shade after one thirty on the afternoon of Monday 14th August, twenty people emerged from the terminal building at Croydon Airport and were shepherded across a runway still damp from heavy overnight rain.

They were a somewhat disparate group, as international travellers tend to be. Some were British, some foreign; a few women, mostly men; the majority smartly dressed. One of the passengers was a man of average height and mildly chubby build. A closer look would show bright green eyes that darted around, eager to take everything in, and a nose that was bent slightly to the left. Along with a mouth that seemed fixed at the beginnings of a smile, the overall effect was of a younger face and an older body: possibly around thirty, perhaps a bit older. Despite the heavy August sun, he was wearing a long raincoat, and a trilby hat which was pushed back on his head. In each hand he carried a large briefcase; one black, one light tan. Perhaps because of his nerves, maybe because of the burden of a coat and two briefcases, or possibly due to his natural disposition, this man walked apart from the group. At first he strayed to one side, and then lagged some way behind it.

At one point he absent-mindedly veered towards a KLM airliner before a man in uniform directed him back towards his group.

A minute or so later the group had assembled at the steps of a Swissair plane, alongside a board indicating its destination: 'Service 1075: Basle'. A queue had formed as the passengers waited for their tickets and passports to be checked.

When the nervous man with the two briefcases presented his papers, the police officer who was checking the passports looked at his with extra care before nodding in the direction of a much taller man who had appeared behind the passenger. The tall man also happened to be wearing a trilby, although his had such a wide brim that it was not possible to make out any features of his face.

The tall man stepped forward and impatiently snatched the passport from the police officer. He glanced at it very briefly, as if he knew what to expect. He then turned to the passenger.

'Would you come with me please, Herr Hesse?' It was unquestionably more of an instruction than an invitation.

'I cannot possibly understand what the problem might be. Can't we sort whatever it is out here?'

'There may not be a problem sir, but it would be best if you came with me. It will be much easier to talk inside.'

'But what about if I miss my flight? It leaves in twenty minutes.'

The taller man said nothing but gestured towards a black Austin 7 that had pulled up alongside them. By now the last passenger had boarded and the steps were being wheeled away from the aircraft. The short journey back to the terminal was conducted in silence. They entered the terminal through a side door and went up to an office on the second floor.

Herr Hesse followed the tall man into the small office, which was dominated by a large window overlooking the apron and the runway beyond it. The tall man sat behind the desk in front of the window and gestured to Herr Hesse to sit down on the other side of the desk.

'Sit down? But I am going to miss my flight! What on earth is this all about? All of my papers are in order. I insist on an explanation.'

The tall man pointed at the chair and the passenger reluctantly sat down in it, his head shaking as he did so. The tall man removed his trilby, but Herr Hesse was little the wiser: the man had no remarkable features and his age could have been anything from his late thirties to his mid-fifties. He had the tanned complexion that someone gets from spending plenty of time out of doors, and dark eyes that had a penetrating stare, but in truth there was little memorable about the man's face. Hesse could have stared at it for hours and still have difficulty in picking him out of a crowd. When the man spoke, it was in accent that could be described as grammar school rather than public school, with perhaps the very slightest trace of a more refined northern accent.

'My name is Edgar. Do you smoke?'

Herr Hesse shook his head. Edgar took his time to select a cigarette from a silver case he had removed from an inside pocket, and went through a lengthy ritual of first lighting and then concentrating on enjoying the first part of the cigarette. He appeared to be in no hurry. He inspected the lighted end of the cigarette, turning it carefully in his hand, admiring the glow and watching the patterns made by the wisps of smoke as they hung above the desk and drifted towards the ceiling. Behind him the Swissair plane was being pulled by a tractor in the direction of the runway. A silver Imperial Airways plane was descending sharply from the south, the sun bouncing off its wings.

Edgar sat in silence, looking carefully at the man in front of him, before getting up to look out of the window and across the airport for a full minute, even timing it on his wristwatch. During that time he avoided thinking about the other man, trying hard to keep any picture or memory out of his mind. When the minute was up he turned round and sat down. Without looking up, he wrote in his notebook:

Complexion: pale, almost unhealthy-looking, pasty.

Eyes: bright green.

Hair: dark and thick, needs cutting.

Nose at a slight angle (left).

Smiles.

Build: slightly overweight.

Nervous, but sure of himself.

A colleague had taught him this technique. Too many of our first impressions of someone are casual ones, so much so that they bear

7

little relation to how someone actually looks, he had told him. As a consequence, we tend to end up describing someone in such general terms that important features tend to be disregarded. '*Look at them for one minute, forget about them for one minute, and then write down half a dozen things about them.*'

A man who at first glance was distinctly ordinary-looking, who in other circumstances Edgar might pass in the street without noticing, now had characteristics that made him easier to recall.

You'll do.

'There are a number of things that puzzle me about you, Herr Hesse. Are you happy with me calling you Herr Hesse, by the way?' As Captain Edgar spoke he was looking at the man's Swiss passport, as if reading from it.

'Why wouldn't I be?' Herr Hesse spoke with an impeccable English accent that had a hint of an upper-class drawl to it.

'Well,' said Edgar, tapping the desk with the passport as he did so, 'that is one of a number of things about you that puzzles me. You are travelling under this Swiss passport in the name of Henri Hesse. But do you also not have a British passport in the name of Henry Hunter?'

The man hesitated before nodding. Edgar noticed that he was perspiring.

'I am sure you would be more comfortable if you removed your hat and coat.'

Another pause while he hung his hat and coat on the back of the door.

'So you accept that you are also known as Henry Hunter?'

The man nodded again.

'Passport?'

'You have it there.'

'If I were in your position Herr Hesse, I think that I would adopt a more co-operative manner altogether. I mean your British passport: the one in the name of Henry Hunter.'

'What about it?'

'I should like to see it.'

There was another pause. Hesse hesitated.

8

'For the avoidance of doubt, Herr Hesse, I should tell you that I have the right to search every item in your possession; the British passport please?'

Herr Hesse lifted the tan briefcase onto his lap, angled it towards him and opened it just wide enough for one hand to reach in. Still taking great care to shield the other contents of the briefcase from Edgar, he retrieved a thick manila envelope, from which he removed the passport. He handed it to Edgar, who spent a few minutes studying it.

'Henry Richard Hunter: born Surrey, 6th November, 1909; making you twenty-nine.'

'Correct.'

Captain Edgar held up the Swiss passport in his left hand and the British passport in his right, and moved them up and down, as if trying to work out which one was the heavier.

'Bit odd, isn't it? Two passports: different names, same person?'

'Possibly, but I very legitimately have two nationalities. I cannot see—'

'We can come to that in a moment. The first thing, then, that puzzles me about you is that you have a perfectly valid British passport in the name of Henry Hunter, which you used to enter this country on the first of August. However, two weeks later you are trying to leave the country using an equally valid passport, but this time a Swiss one and in a different name.'

There was a very long silence. Through the window both men could see Swissair flight 1075 edging on to the runway. Captain Edgar walked over to the window and gazed out at the aircraft for a while before turning back to face the man with the two passports, raising his eyebrows as he did so.

'Any explanation?'

Henry Hunter shrugged. By now Edgar had opened the notebook again in front of him and pulled the fountain pen from his pocket. He took some time to write in the book. He was still writing when he spoke again.

'We can return to the business of flights in a moment. Let us look again at your different names. What can you tell me about that?'

9

'Will I be able to get on the next flight? There is one to Geneva at three o'clock, I think. It would be most inconvenient if I don't get back to Switzerland today.'

'Let's see how we get on with the explanation that you are about to give me, eh? You were about to tell me how you manage to have two nationalities, and two names.'

Henri Hesse shrugged, as if he could not understand why this would require any explanation.

'Terribly straightforward, really. I was born here, in Surrey as it happens, hence Henry Hunter and the British passport. My father died when I was fourteen, and a year or so later my mother met a Swiss man, and married him fairly soon after. We moved to Switzerland, first to Zurich and then Geneva. When I was eighteen I was able to become a Swiss national, and for the purposes of that I used the surname of my stepfather. In the process the name Henry became Henri. So you see, there's really no mystery. I apologise if it turns out to have been in any way irregular as far as the British Government is concerned: I would be happy to clear matters up at the British consulate in Geneva if that helps. Do you think I will I be able to make the three o'clock Geneva flight?'

'There are a few more questions, Mr Hunter. I am sure you understand. What is your job?'

Hunter shifted in his seat, clearly uncomfortable.

'I don't have a career as such. My stepfather was very wealthy and had property all over Switzerland. I would travel around to check on them – keep the tenants happy and make sure they paid their rent on time, that kind of thing: nothing onerous. I also did some work with a travel agency, but most of the time I would travel with my mother. I've managed to keep busy enough.'

Edgar spent quite a while flicking through his notebook and the two passports. At one stage he made some notes, as if copying something from one of the documents. He then consulted a map he had removed from his jacket pocket.

'You said that your stepfather was very wealthy...'

'He died a couple of years ago.'

'And where did you live?'

'Near Nyon, by the lake.'

Edgar nodded approvingly.

'But I see that you now live in the centre of Geneva, on the Rue de Valais I see.'

'That's right.'

'And how would you describe that area?'

'Pleasant enough.'

'Really? From what I remember of Geneva, that is rather on the wrong side of the tracks. Overlooking the railway line, are you?'

'To an extent, yes.'

'Well, either one is overlooking the railway line or one is not?'

'Yes: we do overlook it.'

'Sounds rather like a fall from grace. Wish to tell me about it?'

Edgar had selected another cigarette and smoked most of it before Hunter began to answer. Hunter appeared to be distressed, his voice now much quieter.

'After my stepfather died, it transpired that he had another family, in Luzern. Of course, with hindsight, that explains why he spent so much time in Zurich on business; my mother never accompanied him on those trips. The family in Luzern, it turned out, were the only legitimate family as far as Swiss law was concerned, and therefore had first claim on his estate. I do not fully understand why, but my mother's lawyer assures us that there is nothing whatsoever that we can do about it. The property by the lake near Nyon turned out to be rented, and the various bank accounts that my mother had access to were more or less empty. We quickly went from being very comfortable to very hard up: hence the flat by the railway line. We have only been able to survive as we have because my mother had some funds of her own – not very much. And her jewellery – fortunately there was quite a lot of that. She has had to sell most of it. I do as much freelance translation as possible at the international organisations, but work is not easy to find at the moment. These are difficult times on the continent.'

'As one gathers. So what is the purpose of your visit back to England – to get away from it all?'

'Family business; friends. That type of thing.'

Edgar stood up and removed his jacket, draping it carefully over the back of his chair before walking to the front of the desk and sitting on the front of it, very close to Henry Hunter, placing his knees just inches from the other man's face. He leaned over, so that he was even closer to him. When he next spoke it was in a very quiet voice, as if there was someone else in the room who he did not want to hear what he was about to say.

'"*Family business; friends. That type of thing…*" What you need to know, Mr Hunter, is that we already know an awful lot about you. We have, as they say, been keeping something of an eye on you. It would save a good deal of time if you were to be honest with me. So please could you be more specific about the family business that you mentioned?'

'You said "we". Who do you mean by "we"?'

Edgar leaned back, pointedly ignoring the question.

'You were going to tell me about your family business, Mr Hunter.'

'My aunt died in July. She was my late father's elder sister. I was attending her funeral.'

'My condolences: were you close to her?'

'Not especially, but I was her closest living relative.'

'And you are a beneficiary of the will, no doubt?'

'Yes.'

'And how much did you inherit, Mr Hunter?'

The Swissair DC3 was now beginning to taxi down the runway. A tanker was turning around in front of the building, filling the room with the smell of fuel. Henry Hunter shifted in his chair.

'By the sounds of it, I suspect you probably already know the answer to that.'

Edgar had returned to his chair and leaned back in it so that it tilted against the window. As he did so, he crossed his arms high on his chest, staring long and hard at Hunter.

'What I am curious about, Mr Hunter, is whether my answer is going to be the same as your answer. How about if I endeavour to answer my own question, and you stop me if I say anything incorrect?'

12

'Before you do, could I ask whether you are a police officer?'

'No.'

'If you are not a police officer, what authority do you have to question me like this?'

Edgar laughed, as if he found Hunter's remark to be genuinely amusing.

'Mr Hunter, when you find out on what authority I operate, you will very much regret asking that question. So, shall I tell you my version of why I think you came over here?'

Hunter loosened his tie and turned around in his chair, looking longingly at the door, as if he was hoping that someone would come in at that very moment and explain that the whole business had been a terrible misunderstanding.

'Louise Alice Hunter was, as you correctly say, your late father's elder sister, and you were indeed her only surviving relative.' Edgar had opened his notebook again and was referring to it as he spoke. 'She was eighty-two years of age and had been a resident in the Green Lawns Residential Home near Buckingham for nine years. The matron of the home informs us that you dutifully came over to visit her once a year. You visited her last November, and then again in May, shortly before she died. On each of those visits you were accompanied by her solicitor. Am I correct so far?'

Hunter said nothing.

'I shall assume, then, that you will point out if anything I say is incorrect. Your aunt died on the 24th July and you flew here on the 1st August – which was a Tuesday, if I am correct. You travelled straight to Buckinghamshire, where the funeral took place last Thursday, which would have been the 9th. So far, nothing remarkable, eh?'

Hunter nodded and loosened his tie.

'But this is where an otherwise very ordinary story does become somewhat less ordinary: sordid, perhaps. I am now substantially relying on a statement kindly provided by a Mr Martin Hart who, as you are aware, is your aunt's solicitor and the man who accompanied you on your last visits to your aunt. According to Mr Hart, your aunt's estate amounted to a not insubstantial 8,000 pounds, all of which was held in a deposit account administered by Mr Hart. You are indeed a beneficiary of the will; the main beneficiary most certainly, but – crucially – not the *sole* beneficiary. There were bequests totalling some 1,000 pounds to various friends, staff and charities – but after Mr Hart had deducted fees due to him and duty was paid to the Exchequer, you would expect to receive a sum of just under 6,000 pounds: certainly a handsome sum. Does this sound correct to you?'

'If you say so. You do seem to know a good deal more than I do.'

'But there is a small problem, from your point of view. That money could only be passed to you once probate was granted, which could take many months, perhaps even up to a year. We have already established that you and your mother have serious financial problems. Your inheritance would restore you to a position of financial security. You would once again be wealthy. However, waiting for probate is bad enough, but with the very likely – some would say imminent – possibility of war, you had a quite understandable concern that you might not be able to get that money out of England and into Switzerland for quite a long time. I—'

'You are making a number of assumptions here, Edgar. What makes you think I have done anything improper? I—'

'Mr Hunter, who said anything about doing anything improper? I certainly did not. However, as you raise the subject, let me tell you what the most obliging Mr Hart has told us. According to your aunt's solicitor, he was prevailed upon by you to "cut a few corners", as he put it, and ensure that the entire funds of the deposit account were released straight away. This is not only improper, it is also illegal.'

Henry Hunter shifted in his chair and pulled an improbably large handkerchief from a trouser pocket to mop his brow. Edgar had now removed a pair of reading glasses from a crocodile skin case and, after polishing them for longer than would appear necessary, began to read from a document he had extracted from the desk drawer.

'According to the best legal advice available to me, there is no question that both Mr Hart and you committed a crime, namely conspiracy to defraud. My learned friends tell me that on the evidence they have seen, a conviction would be extremely likely and a term

14

of imprisonment would almost certainly ensue. They say that there is ample *prima facie* evidence to show that you have conspired to defraud His Majesty's Exchequer of the duties that would have been owed to it from your great aunt's estate, and you had conspired to prevent the other beneficiaries of the will from receiving the money bequeathed to them. Fraud, Mr Hunter, is a most serious criminal offence. Confronted with our evidence Mr Hart has, as I say, been most co-operative. He claims that due to a health issue, as he describes it, he allowed himself to be persuaded against his better judgement to release the funds. He admits that he received a much larger fee than he would ordinarily have expected. Apparently—'

'It is not as bad as it sounds; I have to tell you that.' Edgar was taken aback by how forceful Hunter was sounding. 'I told Hart that if I was able to take the money to Switzerland while I could, then I would be in a position to return the money owed to the Exchequer and the other beneficiaries very soon, certainly before probate would ordinarily have been granted.'

'Really? You and Mr Hart cooked up a somewhat clever scheme whereby you were counting on war being declared. Mr Hart believed that in those circumstances, he could apply to be granted a stay of probate until such a time as you were in a position to claim. In other words, Mr Hunter, he would use the war as an excuse: pretend to keep the money in the deposit account until after the war, whenever that is. Except of course, the money would not be in the deposit account, it would be with you in Switzerland. Apparently, he – you – may well have got away with it had not the matron at the home overheard some conversation about it between yourself and Mr Hart and contacted the police.'

'It would all have been paid back, I promise you. Once I deposited it in Switzerland I would have transferred what I owed back. It seemed easier to send the money back from Switzerland rather than wait for probate and then have it transferred from London.'

'Really? All we need to do now is find the money eh, Hunter? Do you want me to hazard a guess as to where it could be?'

Hunter sat very still and stared across the airport as Edgar stood up and walked round the desk. Once in front of Hunter he bent down to pick up the two leather briefcases and placed them both on the desk.

'Keys?'

Without saying anything or appearing to divert his gaze from the runway, Hunter reached into the inside pocket of his jacket and produced a set of keys which he handed to Edgar.

It took Edgar a full twenty minutes to remove all the bundles of banknotes from the two briefcases, assembling the different denominations in separate piles. Not a word was exchanged during this process, which Hunter watched with some interest, as if he had never seen so much money before. By the time Edgar had finished, there were four piles: one pile comprised the bundles of ten shilling notes, another the one pound notes, then the five pound notes and ten pound notes. The pile of bundles of the large, white five pound notes was by far the largest.

Edgar stepped back from the desk and stood alongside Hunter. The entire surface of the desk was covered in money.

'I have only of course been able to do an approximate count, but I would say that there is 7,000 pounds there. Would that be correct, Mr Hunter?'

'More or less. I think you will find it is more like 6,800 pounds. Mr Hart claimed, rather late in the day, that he needed another 200 pounds – for expenses, apparently.'

'Two hundred pounds does not seem to me to be very much, considering the impact this is likely to have on his professional career.'

'It has all been rather rushed, Edgar. As it was such a large sum of cash, we had to withdraw it from a main branch of the Midland Bank in the city. We were only able to get hold of it this morning, which is why I missed the nine o'clock flight.'

'Yes, I'm aware of all that Mr Hunter.' Edgar was still standing next to the seated Mr Hunter, with a hand on the others' shoulder. 'In a moment some colleagues of mine are going to come and take you away. I shall look after the money and all your possessions. We shall meet again in a few days.'

A few minutes later a clearly shocked Hunter was escorted from the airport in handcuffs by three uniformed police officers. In the office overlooking the runway Edgar removed his tie, lit another cigarette and dialled a London number from the telephone nestling between the bundles of banknotes on the desk.

'It's Edgar.'

'I thought it might be you. How did it go?'

'Very much according to plan.'

'Good. We're on then?'

'Yes. Indeed. We're on, as you put it, Porter.'

'And what is he like?'

'Rather as we were expecting. Not altogether the most agreeable of types, but then that is hardly a disqualification in our line of work, is it?'

'Too true... and, um – any hint at all of... you know?'

'No, none whatsoever. He was rather impressive in that respect, I must say. Had one not been aware, one would really have had no idea at all.'

'Splendid. What now?'

'I think he needs a few days on his own: ought to be easy enough after that.'

Chapter 2

London, August 1939

It was early on a blazing hot Monday afternoon – one of the first truly hot days that August – when Edgar stepped out into Whitehall and paused for a good minute or two on the pavement to enjoy the sun. There was an uncharacteristic bounce in his step as he strolled up Whitehall to Trafalgar Square, where he caught the number 12 bus and headed west. He needed some time to think and what, he thought, could be a more pleasant place to do that than the top deck of a London bus?

He stayed on the bus until Notting Hill Gate and then walked over to Kensington Park Road, taking care as he did so to ensure that he was not being followed. He had been about to walk, but a number 52 bus came along and he decided to hop on. He stayed on the bus until it was halfway down Ladbroke Grove. He waited a full five minutes at the bus stop to ensure his tail was clear, then headed north west to where the grandeur of Holland Park petered out in a series of plain and forgettable buildings. He passed a grocery shop with a long and excited queue outside it, and briefly wondered whether he should join it, as one did these days, but a glance at his watch made him realise he needed to hurry.

Edgar paused outside a small alley, allowed an elderly lady to be pulled past him by a pair of yapping terriers, and then entered the alley. At the end of it he pressed a bell and a large iron gate swung open. He was now in a small courtyard; a policeman saluted and unlocked a door, and from there Edgar descended three flights of stairs before finding himself in what was, to all intents and purposes, a small police station.

Minutes later he was sitting in a stuffy windowless room in the basement with a police inspector.

'What I would like to know is what his general mood is like. What he does. How he behaves. What he says. That kind of thing, Inspector Hill. I'm sure you know the score.'

The inspector removed a notebook from the top pocket of his uniform jacket and flicked through a few pages.

'Let's see then… in a pretty bad mood when he arrived here on Monday night, shouting the odds, insisting he had a right to a lawyer. Shut up once he'd had something to eat. Next day he was on again about a lawyer. We kept him in his cell until Wednesday afternoon, when he was brought in here and I read him the riot act: told him that under emergency regulations, he had no right to a lawyer. He asked for a copy of those regulations and I told him it was in the post, which did not seem to reassure him. Thursday: he's still making a fuss so we bring in a couple of the plain clothes boys as you had suggested, and that does the trick. They tell him that he's being done for conspiracy to commit fraud and that, if he pleads guilty and is terribly lucky with the judge, he may get away with five years. Otherwise, he can double it.'

'And how did he take that?'

'Very much as we would have hoped: a few tears before bedtime. He begged to be able to send a telegram to his mother; told anyone who'd listen that there had been a terrible misunderstanding and that he would happily donate the money to charity.'

'And I presume you then did as I asked?'

'Of course: plainclothes boys return on Friday morning, and he provides us with a neat statement, confessing all. I have it here.'

From a drawer in the desk between him and Edgar, the inspector produced three closely typed sheets of paper, each signed with something of a flourish. Edgar carefully read and then re-read the statement.

'Signed on Friday 18th August. Good. And since then?'

'We allowed him to stew over the weekend. Other than being brought to this room and into the corridor outside his cell for exercise

19

a couple of times a day, he has been locked in his cell all day. He hasn't seen daylight in a week. Even so…'

'You're hesitating, Hill.'

'It is just that I would have expected someone like him to be even more affected by his ordeal than he appears to have been. According to the guards he doesn't sleep well, is unquestionably shaken. And he has signed the confession. But despite that he has a resolve about him that I would not have expected. When he was first brought here, he was a nervous character: quite jumpy. But I warn you, Edgar, there is a certain steel about him.'

'We'll see, shall we? Anyway, well done, Hill. Good work. Better bring him in.'

Despite what Hill had said, Henry Hunter looked more worn since Edgar had last seen him, although his smile was still in place. He had lost a bit of weight, and dark rings had appeared around his eyes, along with two or three day's growth of beard. He appeared to be relieved to see Edgar.

'I thought we might meet again.'

'How has your week been, Hunter? Treated well?'

'Well, I haven't been tortured, if that is what you mean. But they wouldn't even let me have a newspaper, and I cannot believe that I am unable to see a solicitor or contact my mother. Is that right?'

'Depends on what you mean by "is that right?", Hunter. While it is *correct*, Hunter, that you have not been able contact either a lawyer or your mother, whether that is *in order* is entirely another matter. You will discover in due course that we have very good reasons for pursuing this course of action. We have, incidentally, taken the liberty of sending your mother a telegram in your name, saying that all is well and she is not to worry.'

'Can I ask, Edgar, whether this a regular police station though? I do seem to be rather… isolated.'

'It is a police station, although you are at present the only person in custody in it. I understand that your predicament has been explained to you by some officers here?'

'Yes. Conspiracy to commit fraud, apparently, and if I am very, very lucky, then I shall get away with five years in prison. I've signed a statement.'

'And did they add that if you are found guilty, or plead guilty, then all of the money that we found in your possession will be confiscated? After the other beneficiaries have been paid and the duty paid, you will be left with nothing.'

'They did not mention that, no.'

'So, all in all, Hunter, a bit of a mess, eh?'

'So it would seem.'

A very long silence ensued, during which Edgar lit a cigarette and wrote some notes in his book.

'I am told that the prison regime is likely to be especially harsh during war time. Most prisoners are required to undertake quite onerous physical labour.'

Hunter said nothing, clearly unsure how he was meant to react.

'However, there is an alternative, Hunter. There is a way of avoiding prison, and even keeping most of your money. You would be able to return to Switzerland and see your mother again.'

Hunter's eyes lit up and, as suspicious as he was, he found it hard to suppress a thin smile.

'Tell me more.'

'Before I can do that, I need to know for sure whether you are interested or not.'

'Yes, of course I am interested.'

'Very well then. This is, to all intents and purposes, the point of no return. Once I tell you what the alternative is, then your options really are very limited. Do you understand that?'

Hunter nodded.

'I work for a government agency whose purpose is to gather intelligence. As you are no doubt aware, this country is perilously close to war with Germany. We urgently need to expand and improve our intelligence networks across Europe; they are in a pretty woeful state at the moment. As strange as it may seem, Mr Hunter, you are very well placed indeed. You have genuine Swiss and British passports and are fluent in German and French.'

Hunter leant forward, his hands touching the desk, eager to hear more.

'What would you require me to do?'

'I had hoped I had made that apparent, Mr Hunter – Henry. To help us gather intelligence.'

'Be a spy?'

'Correct.'

Outside in the corridor a metal gate slammed shut and there was a murmur of voices passing by. Henry Hunter laughed.

'A spy? You must be joking. What on earth makes you so sure I'm up to this?'

'We aren't. We'll give you some training of course, but our priority is to get you back to Switzerland. That is where we need you to be. For us, your dual identity and your ability to move around what may be enemy territory as a Swiss national are invaluable. And don't forget, we have a hold over you.'

'Which is?'

'If you turn down our offer, the alternative is a lengthy spell in one of His Majesty's prisons. Furthermore, there is the question of the money.'

'You mean my aunt's?'

'Yes: the 6,000 pounds that is legally yours, but which you will lose as a result of the court case. However, if you agree to work for us then not only will there be no court case, but you will also receive the money: all 6,000 pounds of it. A bank account will be opened in your name at the Quai des Bergues branch of Credit Suisse in Geneva. If you accept my offer then the sum of 500 pounds will be transferred to that account immediately. Thereafter, we will transfer a further 100 pounds a month into that account for as long as you work for us.'

Hunter frowned, trying to work something out. 'Hang on. At that rate, it could take... I don't know, years for me to receive all of my money!'

'Henry, you are not obliged to take up our offer. We cannot *force* you to be a spy. Look, it may be a while before we call upon your services, but if you undertake any specific mission successfully then we can consider advancing further lump sums of 500 pounds. And of course, we will cover any expenses that you may incur.'

'How about if you were to advance 1,000 pounds? My mother and I have considerable debts to clear.'

'Henry: you are really not in a position to negotiate.'

'Will there be any danger – you said something about "enemy territory"?'

Edgar laughed, standing up as he did so, stretching himself.

'Of course there'll be danger: plenty of it, I imagine. What's the point of being a bloody spy otherwise! But if you ask me, even with that risk of danger, it is still a more agreeable lifestyle than ten years hard labour here.'

'Ten? I thought it would be five if I pleaded guilty?'

'Believe me Henry. If you decline my offer and this goes to court, it will be ten years. Come on now...' Edgar was tapping his watch. 'What is it to be? Are you coming with me, or shall I leave you here with the police for the wheels of justice to start rolling?'

Edgar had expected more questions, more hesitation and more signs of nerves, but with what seemed to be barely a second thought Henry Hunter clapped his hands and allowed his thin smile to become a broad one.

'All sounds most interesting Edgar. I'm ready to join you.'

Chapter 3

to France and Switzerland, November 1939

Henry Hunter's training as a British agent was entrusted to a classics don who had moved from a crumbling Oxford college to a crumbling country house somewhere north of London for the purpose of training his 'special scholars', as he liked to call them. He never tired of telling them that the transition from teaching classics to teaching espionage was a natural one.

'Classics,' he would say, 'is all about war, human failings, chance and intrigue: not so very different to espionage.'

Captain Edgar visited the country house once a week to check on Hunter's progress. He was taking his time: physical fitness was an issue, as was his radio training, but he was regarded as a brilliant map reader, and became proficient with a revolver. It was only towards the end of October that the classics don conceded that Henry Hunter was more or less ready.

'My opinion is that the characteristics of a spy are innate. It is a skill one is born with: it is, I believe, part of someone's personality. You see, we all too often make the mistake of taking someone who appears to have all the attributes of a spy and then train them in the specifics of the job. They could fly through the training with an A plus, but that would not necessarily make them a good spy. I have been looking after, recruiting and training spies for years, as you well know Edgar. Some of those A plus types make hopeless spies once they're out in the field. A truly effective spy will have some personality flaw or such like, which marks them out from most other people. They are used to walking in the shadows, on the other side of the street from most

24

other people; slightly apart from the crowd, but not so much so that people would notice them.'

'Very interesting. But will Hunter make it as a spy?'

'Good heavens yes, Edgar. I don't think I have ever come across someone quite so well qualified. The most dangerous moment for a spy is when they make that transition from what one might call "normal society" into the world of espionage. For the vast majority of people that can be too great a wrench: they have too much to lose. But if you feel that you have never really been part of society, that you have always been on the margins of it, then you are a natural spy. I've rarely come across such a good example of this as Hunter.'

–

One week later, they – Hunter and Edgar – were being driven down a lane on a moonless night when Hunter chose to break the uneasy silence that had accompanied them for the two hours since leaving the country house.

'Can't see a bloody thing in this dark, Edgar – and what has happened to all the road signs?'

'I appreciate that you have been holed-up in that country house for the past three months or so Henry, but it cannot have escaped even your attention that we are now at war with Germany, even if it doesn't actually feel like it. Hence the blackout.'

'And the road signs?'

'No need to help any German spies who are lost, is there?'

'Can you at least tell me where we are, Edgar?'

'No.'

'You are treating me like I am a bloody prisoner.'

'Which, but for the grace of God and my own good offices, Hunter, you actually would be – and for many years. Do not forget that.'

'How could I? You know how grateful I am to you.'

'Less of the sarcasm if you please, Hunter. I can tell you that we have been driving south and we are now in Hampshire, which is as much as you need to know.'

'Any particular part of Hampshire?'

'Obviously Hunter, but you don't need to know any more than that. In any case, you'll be gone within a day or two. Look, we have arrived: better go and get some sleep. We'll start the briefing first thing in the morning.'

–

First thing in the morning for Edgar was around two hours earlier than Hunter had hoped it would be. It was still dark when Hunter was woken up by a knock at the door, followed by the sound of a key turning in the lock and a stiff bolt sliding open. The soldier who woke him – the same one who had escorted him to the room the previous night – announced that he would need to be ready in ten minutes.

Edgar was sitting at a long table in a large office, the room already wreathed in smoke. He was wearing a coat, and a high window was open, letting in the cold morning air and the distinctive smell of recently-turned soil. The table was crowded with files and documents. As Hunter entered the room, he was followed in by another soldier who was bearing a tray with a pot of tea, toast and boiled eggs.

Hunter had little appetite, but Edgar tucked in. He ate in silence for five minutes while Hunter nibbled on a slice of toast and sipped the weak tea.

'Right: now we begin! Tonight you will begin your journey back to Switzerland, Hunter. I need to be very clear, and you need to fully understand that from now on, you are working for British Intelligence. It is a role that carries few rewards and privileges, other than that of serving your country. On the other hand, you will find that this life that has been chosen for you will have plenty of responsibility and not a few dangers. There will be long periods of tedium and you will find that the fact that you can confide in no one makes it a most difficult and stressful existence. I need hardly tell you that the world of espionage is not one of glamour or excitement. The most common emotions are boredom and fear.'

Hunter nodded. This was not the first time he had heard this, but now that his return to Switzerland was imminent he had begun to feel nervous.

'I will spend the next few hours briefing you. I shall remind you of what is expected of you. I shall tell you everything that you need to know.'

And so it continued for many hours. Within an hour, a weak daylight had filled the room, which further filled with smoke as Edgar worked his way through one packet and then another. As noon approached and the sun became brighter, sandwiches were brought in, along with a couple of bottles of beer. Edgar began to appear more relaxed than Hunter had ever seen him.

'Usually in these situations, Hunter, one spends a good deal of one's time making sure that someone in your position is absolutely familiar with their new identity. In your case, however, the Henri Hesse identity is so good that there would be no merit whatsoever in seeking to furnish you with a new and false identity. It is far better to stick with this one.

'You leave tonight, Henry. I know that flying is your preferred method of travel around Europe, but I am afraid that now that we are at war there are no more civilian flights to either France or Switzerland, so you're going by boat. A troopship, the SS *Worthing*, is leaving Southampton this evening. She is taking a contingent of Royal Fusiliers over the channel. She'll dock at Cherbourg early tomorrow morning, and you will travel from there to Paris. You will stay in Paris tomorrow night and then travel by train the following day to Geneva, using your Swiss identity. Do you understand that?'

Hunter nodded.

'Good. Your mother is expecting you: send her a telegram from Paris giving details of your arrival. Once you arrive, you will tell her as little as possible. All the letters that you wrote while you were being trained have been sent on to her, along with two payments of one hundred pounds into her own bank account. As far as she is concerned, you were staying at a guest house in Fulham while you were sorting out your aunt's will. That was the address from where your letters were sent.'

'It is going to be hard to convince her why those financial arrangements took so long.'

'But not as long as it could have been, eh? Do not try and explain too much. Just tell her that it was far more complicated to transfer money out of the country than you had realised, and in the end you had to settle for it being paid in instalments. The initial 500 pounds deposit and the 200 pounds she has been sent should ensure that you can now lead a more agreeable lifestyle, along with the hundred pounds per month, of course.'

'When will I be contacted, Edgar? How will I know what to do?'

'Within a day or two of your arrival back in Geneva you are to go to the Quai des Bergues branch of Credit Suisse, where we have opened an account in your name, as promised. You are to ask for an appointment with Madame Ladnier. Under no circumstances are you to see anyone else there. Madame Ladnier is a senior clerk there and, among other matters, she looks after new clients. You are to go through paperwork with her, and then she will start the account and you will be able to access the money. Madame Ladnier is, very indirectly, a contact of ours, but you must never discuss intelligence matters with her: she is little more than a conduit, a messenger if you like. However, if you need to contact us urgently, you can do so through her. You can do this either at the bank, which is preferable, or on her home telephone number – she will give that to you. That, you understand, is most irregular, so please do be discreet about that. If you need to contact us urgently, simply tell her that you need to change some Swiss Francs into Italian Lira. She will then know to contact us. If there are any changes in your circumstances, such as when you move home for example, you must inform her. Do you understand all this?'

Hunter understood. Edgar got him to repeat it.

'When we make contact with you, it will not be through Madame Ladnier. It could be in anything from a couple of weeks to a few months. Depends on what we need you to do. Chances are that the first job will be something relatively straightforward, probably within Switzerland. Shouldn't be anything too dangerous; a warm up, if you like. What will happen is this: you will be approached in the street by someone asking for directions to the Old Town. What is it you call it in Geneva?'

'The *vieille ville*.'

'This person will be carrying a copy of the previous day's edition of the *Tribune de Genève*. In reply to their question you are to ask them if they would prefer to walk or to take the tram. They will reply that they would prefer to walk, if you can point them in the right direction. You will explain that you are walking that way and they are welcome to follow you. Take any route to the Old Town. At some point after entering it they will overtake you. You are not to acknowledge them, you just carry on walking at the same pace, but now you are following them. When you see them place the copy of the *Tribune de Genève* in a waste bin outside a building you are to enter the building and wait. If no one has approached you after five minutes, you are to leave the building and return home. However, if someone joins you and introduces themselves as Marc you are to go with him. He will take you to meet your main contact. At that moment, your new career will have begun. Please repeat all of this to me Henry.'

–

Edgar's briefing had finished just after one o'clock and Hunter was escorted back to his room. Edgar urged him to try and get some sleep: it was going to be a long night, and he should not count on being able to sleep on the boat. In his room he saw that a case had been carefully packed for him, along with his two briefcases. A change of clothes was laid out on the bed. Edgar explained that everything had been carefully checked to ensure that nothing incriminating was in his possession, in case he was searched.

He was woken at four and the soldier who had been looking after him told him that a bath had been prepared for him. By four thirty he was back in the office where his briefing had been held that morning. The soldier carried his case and Hunter carried his own briefcases. Edgar was nervously fiddling with his leather gloves.

'There is a train from Cherbourg at ten fifteen in the morning, which you're to take to Paris. There is a telegram bureau inside Gare Saint-Lazare: you're to go to it as soon as you arrive and send a telegram with the following message to this address.'

29

He handed a slip of paper to Hunter. The message read: 'Arrived safely Paris stop regards to all stop'.

'Memorise that and then destroy the paper. Then go and find a hotel, and in the morning take the train to Geneva. You know your way around Paris?'

Hunter shrugged. 'I've been once or twice.'

Edgar pointed to the table. 'Here are your British and Swiss passports, which we have been looking after for you. Here is a receipt for the guest house in Fulham to show you were staying there since the middle of August. In this envelope is more paperwork than you could imagine from various firms of solicitors and the Midland Bank, relating to the release of money from your aunt's estate, including a terribly helpful letter from the bank explaining that the money can only be transferred legally to a foreign country in instalments. Can I ask, is your mother the inquisitive type?'

'Do you mean, is she nosey?'

Edgar laughed. 'Well, yes.'

'She could not be more nosey, if I was honest. Always poking about in my things.'

'Good. Don't show all these letters and documents to her then, just leave them for her to find. It will be much more convincing that way, and she then ought to believe your account of why you were kept here for so long. It is essential that she never suspects what you are up to, do you understand?'

Henry nodded.

'Hang on, before you put all that in your briefcase, here is some more money: twenty pounds worth of French francs, which ought to be more than enough for your hotel tomorrow night and the ticket to Geneva, plus meals. And here in this envelope is fifty pounds worth of Swiss Francs, which ought to cover any expenses you may incur in the foreseeable future in Switzerland.'

At five o'clock a car pulled up outside the building and the two men left the office and walked quietly to it. Edgar helped Hunter put his cases in the boot and then joined him in the back.

'I thought you'd like me to see you off.'

Henri Hesse boarded the SS *Worthing* in Southampton before the troops embarked and was taken straight to a tiny cabin in the officers' quarters, which had a bunk bed in it and little else. The captain came in and told him he was to remain in the cabin for the duration of the voyage.

They docked in Cherbourg just after seven the next morning, and at nine o'clock the captain came into his cabin. He was safe to leave, now all the troops had disembarked. A taxi was waiting on the quay to take him to the station.

Henri was shocked at how France had changed. Everywhere there were troops – British as well as French – and people looked pinched, worried and in a hurry – none of which were characteristics he would usually associate with the French. Normally the train journey would have been jolly, with people chatting. Now, it was quiet. People stared out of the windows and said little. It was as if a whole nation was wrapped in its own thoughts, unwilling to share its fears.

The train pulled into Gare Saint-Lazare just before three o'clock: the journey had taken longer than scheduled due to a lengthy and unexplained stop outside Caen. If Cherbourg had been quiet and the train silent, Gare Saint-Lazare was not. Half of Paris seemed to be leaving through the station, and the other half arriving into it. He found the telegram bureau and sent the message to London. He had little doubt that he would be watched at the station: requiring him to send the telegram was a good way of ensuring that. He then walked out of the vast concourse of Gare Saint-Lazare and away from Clichy and its temptations.

The further you walk, the harder it is for you to be followed.

So he headed south and then east, down Boulevard Haussmann where the elegant shops and straight lines afforded him plenty of opportunity to observe every angle around him. He entered a leather-wear shop to look at wallets, and a *tabac* to buy matches. Then, in Boulevard St Martin, he joined a long queue in a *patisserie* to buy an almond croissant. The ten-minute wait allowed him enough time to be certain no one was following him. He decided to look for somewhere to stay around Republique and found a small hotel by the Canal Saint Martin, where he took a comfortable room with its own private bathroom overlooking, as requested, the front of the hotel, and then spent an hour sitting by the window, behind the half open shutters, observing the street below. When he was as certain as he could be that no one had followed him and no one was watching from the street, he closed the shutters and drew the curtain. After a bath and a rest he left his room at six thirty.

Had anyone checked in since his arrival, he asked the *patron* at reception? He was not sure if a colleague was joining him or not. The *patron* said no one had arrived. He understood, he said, with a knowing and even conspiratorial look. Hunter was not sure what it was that the *patron* understood, but he slipped him a generous few francs for what he said was already excellent service, and explained that he may be back late, perhaps very late. Would the *patron* be so good as to let him have a key? *Of course.* And would he also be able to perhaps slip a note under his door to let him know if his friend arrived, or indeed if anyone else checked in or even asked for him? '*Naturally,*' said the *patron*. '*It would be my pleasure.*' Henri knew that, this being Paris, the *patron* would assume that Henri was conducting an affair: in such circumstances it would be his pleasure, indeed his duty as *patron* to do whatever he could to assist.

Henri walked out into the bitter Parisian night air, where a wind had swept up the nearby Seine and was settling over the city. He waited in the entrance of the hotel for ten minutes and, once he was certain that he was alone, he headed south, turning up the collar of his coat as he did so.

The real danger of being a spy is that which you court yourself.

He headed in a south easterly direction, away from his destination. On the Rue de Crussol, just before it crossed Boulevard Voltaire, he found a telephone kiosk. The call lasted no more than thirty seconds, much of which was taken up by a pause by the person who had answered the phone.

'*Very well. You know where to come. Give us one hour. Be careful.*'

So he walked down Boulevard Voltaire, then found a tiny cafe in the Passage Saint-Pierre Amelot. There were four two-seater tables in the cafe, crammed into a space where three would have been a tight squeeze. One of the tables was occupied by a young couple. Hesse took one of the three vacant tables, making sure he faced the door. He remained there for half an hour; dinner was a bowl of soup with bread and an excellent omelette.

It took him twenty minutes to reach his destination from the cafe. The Marais was once swamp-land, then became home to the aristocracy, and now, as far as Hesse could tell, was in an advanced state of decay. It was the kind of area where people would say it had known better days, but no one alive could remember those better days. But Hesse liked the anonymity of the Marais, with its obvious edge of danger, which meant that people hurried along and avoided each other. It was not relaxed and given over to enjoyment of life, like most other parts of Paris. The area had its different groups: the Jews and their synagogues and little shops around the Rue de Rosiers; those too poor to have their own place, living with others in large crumbling houses; the prostitutes who couldn't make it in Clichy; the gamblers, the drinkers, and the anarchists.

He knew the area very well, and picked up his pace, darting up and down little alleys, doubling back on himself, pausing in darkened doorways and making it impossible for anyone to follow him. He emerged into the Rue de Bretagne, slipped into the entrance of a large grey building with enormous shuttered windows, and waited. On the wall inside the entrance was a series of bells, one for each of the twenty apartments. Under the bells someone had drawn a small circle in pencil. On the opposite wall they had drawn a square. It was safe. He pressed a bell and went straight up to the top floor.

–

'You look very well. You have lost weight.'

'Yes, thank you, Viktor.' Henri hesitated. He was about to return the compliment, but nothing could have been further from the truth: the other man was bigger than ever, his face heavily lined and his large nose redder than ever. Viktor had greeted him with an embrace and had held him in it for a while, which made Henri feel less than comfortable. As he slowly emerged from the embrace, the man held him at arm's length by the shoulders – one hand on each shoulder, as if to admire him. For a moment Henri feared the man was about to kiss him on the cheeks, as he was wont to do. He was always nervous in the man's presence, not least after a long gap, as now. Anyone looking at him would have noticed that, for a brief moment, his thin smile had disappeared.

'I was not sure that we would ever see you again. Come, sit down. We have much to talk about.'

They were speaking in French, neither man's native language, which added to a formal, even tense air in the room. Two other men stood either side of the window, keeping watch through half-open shutters. Another man entered the room and announced that it was all clear: no one had followed him. He was sure of that.

'What will you drink? I seem to have everything here. Whisky?'

'No, not for me thank you.'

'Really? That is the first time I have known you to turn down a whisky. What have they done to you?'

The man's look of concern broke into a broad grin as he poured himself a drink and pulled his chair closer to Hunter's. 'This really has been a most unexpected development, most unexpected. And you are certain that they suspect nothing?'

'I am as certain as I can be,' said Hunter.

Viktor shuffled his large frame around in the chair to make himself comfortable. From a side table he picked up a large notebook, expensively bound in brown leather. He produced a pencil from his top pocket and sharpened it with a penknife which came from another pocket, allowing the shavings to gather on the front of his jacket. He made a few notes before looking up at Henri and smiling, as if checking on him once again.

'We have two hours, maybe three. You need to tell me everything.'

—

Henri Hesse returned to the hotel just before one that morning. There was no note under the door from the *patron*. Despite his exhaustion, he slept only fitfully and got up at seven o'clock. He checked out of the hotel an hour later, stopped for a coffee and a croissant near the hotel, and then caught a tram on the Boulevard du Temple down to the Gare de Lyon. He managed to book a good seat on the ten o'clock train to Geneva, where he found himself in a carriage with six other passengers: a formally dressed Swiss businessman, who tutted loudly if anyone came too near him; an elegantly dressed elderly French lady, who spent most of the journey smiling wistfully out of the window and did not remove her leather gloves once; and a couple with their son and daughter who were, as far as Henri could tell, a year or two either side of ten. They seemed to be overburdened with suitcases and other bags, some of which they had had to keep in the corridor. When the children spoke, which was not very often, they did so with strong Parisian accents. The parents spoke to the children in accented French, but to each other in what sounded to Henri like Polish, and also a strange version of High German that he had never heard before. From what he could tell, they were anxious about crossing the border. The wife kept asking the husband if all the paperwork was in order. '*I hope so. Who knows?*' Whenever one of the family spoke the Swiss businessman looked annoyed and disapproving. On more than one occasion he caught Hesse's eye, hoping to share his disapproval with him.

The journey was uneventful until around a quarter to six, when the train pulled into Gare de Bellegarde, the last station in France before the Swiss border just a few miles away. For five or ten minutes, the train just stood still, with no apparent reason for the delay. The businessman looked at his watch and shook his head. The French lady continued to look out of the window, smiling. Then they could hear voices, working their way slowly down the train. Through the window Henri could just make out the shape of *gendarmes* patrolling along the tracks. The voices grew nearer and the parents looked even more anxious.

'Everything will be all right?' the wife asked the husband, in the strange German dialect.

'I have no idea,' the husband replied. 'Speak in French now: only in French.'

Five minutes later two Swiss border guards and a French *gendarme* entered the carriage.

'Papers please: a routine check: we will have you on your way in a minute.' Henri showed his Swiss passport. One Swiss border guard showed it to the other and they both nodded. 'No problem, Monsieur Hesse.' Nor was there any problem with the businessman and the elegantly dressed lady. But for the family, it was very different. Both guards looked at the papers in some detail and shook their heads, passing various documents to the bored-looking *gendarme* behind them.

'These papers are not in order,' one of them said to the father.

'But I was assured that there would be no problem.'

'Well, there is. You have no valid papers here allowing you to enter Switzerland. It is not possible.'

The husband and wife exchanged glances; the wife nodded. *Do it.*

'Perhaps I could have a word with you in the corridor?' He gestured towards the children. *Away from them, please.*

Henri could just make out the man pleading with the guards, both of whom looked stone-faced. 'Perhaps I could pay for the visas now? I have the funds?' Henri could see the man open his wallet and attempt to press a wad of banknotes into the hand of one of the guards, who refused to take it.

'You are denied entry to Switzerland. You have to leave the train now,' he heard one of the guards say. Henri noticed that the other guard grabbed the banknotes.

'You are in illegal possession of Swiss currency. We are confiscating it.'

The *gendarme* shrugged. *This is not my problem.* The father came back into the carriage, crestfallen and defeated. His wife was doing her best not to cry and the children looked frightened, as if they knew what was happening. The gendarme helped them to remove their cases. The elegant lady looked shocked and the businessman annoyed as baggage was removed from around him. A minute or so later, Hesse watched as the family emerged onto the deserted platform and the train slowly began to move again. The businessman shook his head and muttered the word '*juifs*'. The lady had stopped smiling.

The train pulled into Gare Cornavin just before seven o'clock. On the short walk home Henri was hit by the icy blast from the nearby Alps, bouncing into the city from the lake. Despite this, and despite the burdens he now carried, he had the most unusual sensation of arriving somewhere that he could call home.

–

At around the same time that Henri Hesse's train was leaving Gare de Lyon, Edgar took a call on a secure line in his office. It was Hurst from Paris station.

'Well done, Edgar, you've found a bit of a star there. He didn't half give my chaps the runaround.'

'You didn't lose him, did you, Hurst? There'll be all hell to pay if you did.'

'Come on, Edgar, you ought to know my boys better than that. He's very good, but in the end he made the mistake of assuming that one can only be tracked from behind. We managed to keep tabs on him all last night, but only just.'

'Where did he end up?'

'The Marais, as we suspected he would.'

'And the people he met up with: you're sure of who they are?'

'Yes, sir, we're absolutely certain. No question about it.'

Chapter 4

from Marseilles to Moscow, December 1939

Early in the afternoon of the first Monday of December a large man wearing a long dark coat and a smart black fedora marched with surprising agility up from the *vieux port* in Marseilles to his *pension* overlooking the port and the Mediterranean beyond it.

The large man was Russian, but for the purposes of his visit he was a Swedish shipping agent from Gothenburg. He had been hanging around the *vieux port* for a few futile days, hoping to make contact with an Algerian who had apparently contacted a Communist Party official in the city with the promise of some secret documents of an unspecified nature. The Party official had now disappeared and the Algerian never showed up. It was the nature of the job he reflected, as the *pension* came into sight: unlike the fishermen he had been watching that morning selling their catch on the Quai des Belges, a spy had to become used to the prey only occasionally succumbing to the bait.

He had decided to remain in Marseilles for another day or two; a ship was due in from Greece, and Greek crews always offered the opportunity of good contacts. But when he returned to his *pension* there was a telegram waiting for him, sent from the main post office in Gothenburg.

'Mother ill stop return home soonest stop'

The Russian rarely allowed himself the indulgence of emotion, but he did that afternoon, sitting quietly in his room for a few minutes after he had packed, and contemplating what a summons home could mean. He had survived, as he liked to see it, various such calls over the past few years, but feared his luck could not hold out much longer. A sensation of fear swept over him, and it took the remains of the vodka by the side of the bed and a cold bath before he came to his senses. *I have done nothing wrong. No one in the service is indispensable, but I am closer to it than many.*

An hour later he had checked out of the *pension* and stopped at the main post office to send a telegram to Gothenburg, to the effect that he was so concerned about mother that he was returning home.

'love to mother stop'

Then he headed to the port office, where he found the captain of a Turkish steamer leaving that evening for Istanbul, who was more than happy to take a passenger, especially one who was offering to pay so generously. '*We have a light load: with luck we should arrive on Saturday; maybe Sunday.*'

The steamer duly arrived in Istanbul early on the Saturday evening and the captain took his generous passenger straight to the house of his wife's cousin, who sailed his trawler in the Black Sea. *Yes*, said the cousin. *He would be setting off as usual on Sunday morning. Yes, he would be happy to sail to Odessa first. Yes, that is very generous.* 'Thank you, sir!'

Odessa was a day and a half's hard sailing from Istanbul and, encouraged by the Russian's generosity, the skipper made it there late on the Monday afternoon. The Russian went straight to the railway station: the night train to Moscow was leaving at a quarter to midnight. He had time to send a telegram announcing his arrival and then find a cafe where he could eat familiar food and get used to hearing familiar languages around him once again.

It was past midnight when the train noisily pulled out of the station, and as the final leg of his voyage began, the fear that had stuck him in Marseilles returned. It kept him wide awake until they reached Kharkov in the early hours of the morning, turning his stomach into knots and making his heart beat fast. Along with the fear came the doubt: *Should I have stayed in France? I could so easily have disappeared from there.*

39

The train was held in Kharkov for three or four hours. As usual, there was no explanation and no complaints from his fellow passengers. He left the train to send another telegram to Moscow: he didn't want them to think he wasn't coming.

By the time dawn broke on the Wednesday morning they were approaching the outskirts of Moscow and the train had slowed down. The Russian tried hard to compose himself. The cruellest part of this job was not the loneliness or the danger or the stress of swapping identities every few days and constantly having to be aware of who he was meant to be: that was all to be expected. No, the worst part – the part he could never come to terms with – was that the one place you could call home, the place that you risked your life for and suffered all the hardships on behalf of – that was the place you feared most. He would have no idea whether the day which had just begun would end with a bullet in his head in a basement. It had happened to so many others, after all. But then he pulled himself together as he remembered what they instilled into all the new recruits: '*Never question; never discuss; never hesitate.*'

The train pulled into Kursky station at eight o'clock and he was met on the platform by two young men who escorted him to a waiting car, which he decided was a bad sign. It was a glorious day in Moscow and he began to feel quite emotional on the short journey. He resolved that, if he survived this trip and was sent back into the field, he would make plans. Next time he was summoned back, he would disappear. He had worked for the service since 1920; he had outlived all those he had been recruited with, and many more who had been recruited after him. He knew that he was good – but he also knew that he was not indispensable. What mattered most was that he outlived his luck, and now he feared that that had run out on him.

The car drove straight into a basement, which he decided was another bad sign. He could feel his whole body trembling as he walked with his unsmiling escort to the lift. If it went down into the basement, he knew that was the end. Moments later they emerged onto the fifth floor and he had to bite his lip to stop tears of sheer relief. He was steered into a large office where there were half a dozen of them waiting, all of whom seemed to be pleased to see him. From that group, a familiar figure emerged and hugged the new arrival.

'Viktor, welcome home.'

—

He had been so well received that, for a day or two after his arrival in Moscow, he wondered whether this was some kind of elaborate trap. But it wasn't: they were clearly very pleased with him, but most of all they wanted to know about Henri.

'Who would have thought it?'

'Tell us everything!'

'Does he realise how important he could be? Do *you* realise how important he is?'

'We need to handle him carefully.'

After three days in Moscow he was taken to one of the *dachas* outside the city that the service used. For the first time in years he could relax in the silence. A woman came in every day to cook and clean, and a younger woman arrived every evening and stayed with him until the following morning. The service could be brutal and cruel, especially to its own, but it knew how to look after those it was especially pleased with.

Viktor stayed in the *dacha* for a week before travelling to Stockholm, and from there by sea back to France. But not once during that time was he ever in doubt that he owed all this to Henri. '*Do you realise how important he is?*' they had asked.

But Viktor certainly did not need anyone to tell him how important Henri was. An agent he had recruited had, in turn, been recruited by the British.

Do I realise how important Henri is?

Important enough to have kept me alive.

Chapter 5

Switzerland, 1929-1930

It was a filthy evening sometime in late January 1929 when Henri Hesse emerged from the pink-stuccoed building on the university campus. The rain swept into Geneva from every direction: the Alps, the lake, France. He paused at the end of the flight of steps, already drenched and wondered whether to dash into the Old Town through Les Bastions, or go back into the building and wait for the rain to abate.

He was still debating what to do when he felt a hand on his shoulder.

'You are deciding whether to brave the rain? Me too. Who knows when it will stop? When it rains like this in Geneva, it feels like it will rain forever.' It was the last speaker at the meeting, a handsome man in his late twenties with piercing blue eyes, thick black hair which touched his collar, and a distinctive Parisian accent. Henri had never encountered anyone quite so charismatic and mesmerising. He wore no tie, had a silk scarf wrapped stylishly around his neck, and when he spoke it was about the injustices in Europe and around the world and how only the Communist Party had the answer. Henri had felt the hairs rise on the back of his neck; tears had even come to his eyes. 'Europe is in crisis: capitalism is in crisis. The solution is in our hands – your hands,' he had told the thirty or so people sparsely arranged around the large lecture hall.

'My name is Marcel by the way.' The Frenchman's hand was still on his shoulder as he gently steered him back into the building. The meeting had taken place in the Law Faculty, and Marcel guided Henri through its corridors until they found a deserted seating area on the first floor. Marcel unfurled his silk scarf, revealing a white shirt with two or three buttons undone. He smiled at Henri, his teeth white and perfectly straight.

'Maybe in ten or fifteen minutes the rain will stop, but it is good to talk. Are you a member of the party?'

'Not yet,' replied Henri. 'I am thinking about it.'

'Tell me why?'

It was a while before Henri replied, during which time the noise of the rain beating on the windows and lashing the city beyond grew heavier. *When it rains like this in Geneva, it feels like it will rain forever.*

'I live in a privileged and bourgeois world. I've visited Germany and seen areas which are really poor, where people have no jobs and little food. Even in Switzerland you can go from an area which is very rich to one nearby which is completely different, and that just seems to me to be wrong. My mother and my stepfather are always saying that a civilised world relies on having some people making a lot of money and other people working for them. They say the reason that people are poor is that they are lazy and feckless. They blame unemployment on trade unions and socialists. I always find that I disagree with whatever they say about politics, and the people they seem to despise the most are Communists. That got me thinking that if my mother and stepfather are so opposed to communism, then maybe it cannot be all bad – but I know very little about it, so I am reading a lot at the moment. When I saw a notice for this meeting in the library, I thought I would come along.'

'Really? Tell me, what are you reading?' Marcel leaned forward, genuinely interested in what Henri had to say.

'I have read *The Communist Manifesto* of course, and all three volumes of *Capital*, though I can't pretend I found that easy going. Now I am reading *The Origin of the Family, Private Property and the State*, but it is even more difficult.'

'I understand. Engels is not the easiest person to read, but his ideas – they are excellent, do you agree?'

'I do.'

Marcel edged his chair a bit closer to Henri's. 'I can tell from your accent that you are perhaps not from Geneva.'

'No, I lived in Zurich for a number of years. We moved to Geneva last year.'

Marcel switched to German. 'And can I ask what you do? Are you a student here at the university?'

'No... not yet. My mother is not keen on me being a student. She thinks I'll end up mixing with people she disapproves of.'

'Like Communists?'

'Like Communists.'

'I suspect you are not a native of Zurich either? I am not Swiss myself: I am from Paris. I can always tell when someone is not Swiss: they have more... warmth.'

Marcel patted Henri on the knee. *A friend: someone to trust.*

'Actually, I'm originally from England.'

'Really, where?'

'I was born in a place called Woking; it is not far from London.'

'And how do you end up in Geneva?'

'It's a long story and rather a boring one, I'm afraid.'

'No, no – not at all. People's stories are always more fascinating than they realise. Do tell me.' Marcel had edged his chair even closer to Henri's and looked at his companion in admiration. 'Please tell me, Henri!'

'Well, as I say, it is not terribly remarkable. My father was an accountant and a good deal older than my mother. He died suddenly in the February of 1923; he was sixty when he died. My mother was still in her early forties, and although we were not wealthy, my mother had aspirations to wealth. She inherited a life insurance policy upon the death of my father, and as far as I can recall, she set about spending it – furs, jewellery – that type of thing. We spent most of that summer on the French Riviera, and in Antibes she met a Swiss businessman, Erich Hesse. She married him in the November.'

'Rather quick?'

'Indeed: "indecent haste" was how people described it. But my mother was quite unashamed about it. She disliked England and what

44

she would describe as "a provincial lifestyle". She wanted glamour and wealth, and Erich Hesse offered an opportunity for all that. In the short period following the death of my father, she had quickly become accustomed to a certain standard of living. She was aware that there was a limit to how long this could last; the life insurance policy was unlikely to fund her in the long term, not at the rate that she was working her way through it. So, Herr Hesse was an extremely attractive proposition, financially at least. I ought to add that he was also quite a bit older than my mother. I think he was sixty-five when they married.'

'So you moved here to Switzerland?'

'Yes. To Zurich at first, this is where his business interests seemed to be. We lived in Zurich for around five years and moved here to Geneva last year.'

'Why the move to Geneva?'

'My stepfather has property here, though he seems to have it all over Switzerland. I think the main reason was my mother: she always said she found Zurich rather stuffy, but she loves Geneva and the area around it. We live by the lake, close to Nyon.'

'And how did you become so fluent?'

'I turned out to be something of a natural linguist. I was thirteen when we moved to Switzerland, and I had never really fitted in very well in England. I was an only child, rather spoilt, not especially bright academically, I suppose, and bad at sport. As a consequence, I was constantly bullied. One way in which I could deal with this bullying was through mimicry, which I had something of a talent for. I managed to make myself rather popular by impersonating teachers in particular. I was really rather good at it, and the other boys loved it. I was always playing pranks on teachers, phoning them and pretending to be the head teacher, that kind of thing. When I arrived in Switzerland I discovered that this talent for mimicry and impersonation was a godsend for learning languages: not so much the vocabulary and the grammar, which I found to be easy enough to learn. What I excelled at was imitating the accent and nuances of speech. In Zurich I became fluent both in German and Swiss German, and since moving here my French has really come on.'

Marcel nodded and smiled in the right places. He was sympathetic and friendly, someone Henri instinctively felt he could trust. To his surprise, Henri found himself opening up even more to this stranger about the coldness of his mother; his lack of a relationship with his stepfather; his loneliness; his boredom; his curiosity about the world around him, and his frustration at not being able to satisfy that curiosity.

Marcel switched to English, but only after he had looked carefully around the empty room and moved his chair so close to Henri's that the two chairs were touching.

'You are clearly very interested in communism, Henri.'

'Yes.'

'But you have not joined the party?'

'Well, I did pick up this leaflet when I left the meeting.' Henri had removed a damp leaflet from his coat pocket and was showing it to Marcel.

'So, are you going to join?'

'Probably. I'm a bit nervous about what my mother and stepfather would think. I know it is nothing to do with them, but they are so opposed to communism that I think they'd throw me out of the house. But they won't need to know, will they?'

Marcel said nothing, as he leaned back in his chair and looked Henri up and down.

'You don't have to join the Party, you know.'

'What do you mean?'

'What matters, Henri, is that you believe in the cause, that you believe in communism.'

'I'm not terribly sure that I follow you.'

Marcel paused while a man and a woman walked by, their shoes reverberating long after they had passed on the wooden floor. The rain now sounded as if it had turned into a storm. Marcel had lowered his head, and only raised it very slightly when he spoke again.

'Henri, if one truly believes in the cause then there are many different ways of serving it. Joining the party and attending meetings have their place, but for someone such as yourself, there may be other ways... *better* ways in which you can help the cause more effectively.'

46

'I am still not really following you. Why are you so interested in me?'

'Because it is clear that you believe in the cause, and because you are a man of many parts, not all of them obvious. You have a natural caution about you, along with an inquisitive mind. You speak three languages. You have a Swiss passport and a British one. And the only person who knows that you are interested in the Party, and that you came to this meeting tonight, is me.'

'There were other people at the meeting.'

'Sure, but do any of them know who you are? Do they know your name?'

Henri shook his head.

'Exactly. For the time being, can I ask you *not* to join the Party or attend any meetings? In a few weeks, maybe two or three, possibly longer, I will approach you. We will meet, and I may be able to introduce you to people who share our views. In the meantime, I ask you not to discuss this with anyone.'

'But how will you know where to find me?'

Marcel patted Henri's knee. 'You are not to worry: finding you will not be a problem.'

–

Marcel found him in late February, around four weeks after they had first met.

He was in the library at the university, which he travelled into on most weekdays. It got him away from his mother and stepfather, and from Nyon and the home overlooking the lake. He tended to arrive at the library around eleven in the morning and leave around four. On Marcel's advice he had stopped reading political works – 'There is no need to draw unnecessary attention to yourself,' – and was now working his way through the French novelists. On this particular day he was finding it hard to concentrate on Zola's *Thérèse Raquin*, so in the middle of the afternoon he went for a stroll along the corridors, past the crowded notice board where he had first spotted the handwritten poster advertising the Communist Party meeting. When he returned to his desk he noticed that his copy of *Thérèse Raquin* was closed, with a slip of paper poking out at the last page he had been reading. It was a card from a bar on the Place de la Taconnerie and, in neat handwriting, was inscribed '*Ce soir. 6.*'

The bar was in the shadow of St-Pierre cathedral and was little more than a dimly lit cellar in which it was hard to make out the identities of the few other customers. Henri had arrived in good time – well before six – and for thirty or forty minutes he sat at a small table facing the entrance, contemplating what he might have got himself into. Up until that evening, he had thought that Marcel was just an enthusiast who had perhaps got carried away. He was, in Henri's opinion, unlikely ever to contact him again, and he had come to the conclusion that this was very much for the best. Whatever 'serving the cause in different ways' meant, it was not for him.

He did not notice Marcel until he slid into the chair opposite and greeted him warmly, placing two empty glasses on the table and proceeding to fill them both from a bottle of red wine, while holding the cork between his teeth. He gestured for Henri to drink, and it was only when they had both finished and he had refilled their glasses that he spoke.

'I've come from Paris this morning, which is why I am late. How have you been keeping, my friend? Tell me, what you are reading?'

They chatted for a few minutes, and by the time they were on their third glass of wine Marcel suggested that, when they finished it, they go for a walk. They left the bar in silence. By now, a grey mist had descended on the Old Town, making the cathedral only just visible in front of them. They walked in silence along the deserted streets, as if they were the only people in the city. They followed a road round the back of the cathedral before turning into Rue Verdaine. Marcel placed an arm in front of Henri, gesturing for him to wait. They stood still for a while: ahead of them they could just make out the sound of footsteps. Marcel glanced at his watch, angling his hand to try and catch what light there was from the street lamp. He nodded and then looked straight at Henri.

'You do believe, don't you?' When Henri did not reply but only looked at him as if he did not understand, he repeated the question. 'In the cause, I mean. You still believe in communism?'

'Of course.' *What else can I say?*

'Good.' Marcel started to walk forward again, very slowly. He placed a hand on Henri's back so he would join him. 'You will find that, if you believe, that will help. It is difficult enough even if you do believe, but impossible if you don't. My advice to you is that, even in moments of doubt, you must force yourself to believe; otherwise your life will be intolerable. Do not allow yourself to harbour any doubts. If you force yourself hard enough then it will work, trust me.' Marcel said nothing more, but continued to walk on slowly. They had not gone very far when they passed an alleyway on their left and Henri noticed Marcel peering into it. In the shadows he could just make out a bulky figure standing still at the far end of the alley. They carried on walking, but now Henri could hear footsteps behind them. They reached the corner of Rue de la Vallée and Marcel stopped. When they turned round, a large man was standing a few yards behind them. He was wrapped in a long black coat, its collar turned up to conceal the lower half of his face, with much of the upper half hidden by the brim of a large fedora.

Marcel placed a hand on Henri's shoulder: '*Attends!*' Wait. He walked over to the man and they spoke for a minute, no more than that. Henri knew they were certainly not speaking French or German. As far as he could tell, it sounded like Russian or Polish. When they had finished talking, Marcel turned round and beckoned for Henri to join them.

The three of them stood together for a moment, not a word being exchanged. Then, as if on a signal, Marcel turned and walked quickly away, back along Rue Verdaine.

It was the last time Henri would ever see Marcel.

–

As Marcel disappeared into the mist, the man in the long black coat and large fedora moved off in the other direction, making it clear that

49

Henri should follow him. Half way down Rue de la Vallée he stopped by a parked Citroen and opened the rear passenger door, allowing Henri to enter first. The driver turned round, nodded and, without a word being exchanged, they drove off.

The car drove fast through the Old Town, the speed and the mist making it difficult for Henri to work out where he was. As far as he could tell they were heading south through Champel, but then he noticed that they were heading back into the city, driving along the banks of the River Avre. Soon they were in Jonction, a working class district that Henri was quite unfamiliar with. The driver stopped for a while, his eyes fixed on the rear-view mirror and then started again. After less than a minute he braked suddenly and then reversed hard into a narrow alleyway, stopping alongside a large wooden door. Henri was guided out of the car and through the door, and quickly up a flight of steps into a small attic room which smelt of gas and cabbages.

Once he had closed the shutters and turned on the gas fire, the large man looked Henri up and down, his head slowly moving as if checking him out from every angle. He gestured to a pair of chairs in front of the fire and removed his fedora, revealing a lined face that showed no hint of emotion. Once Henri had sat down the man unbuttoned his coat, placed himself opposite Henri, and addressed him in French with a heavy eastern European accent.

'English is your first language, yes?'

Henri nodded.

'And you also speak French and German?'

'Yes, although I am more comfortable with French.'

'We shall speak in French in that case, I understand it better than English. Two foreigners speaking French; the French would like that.

'Henri Hesse,' the man said as he removed his overcoat and pulled a brown leather notebook from one of the pockets. From his top pocket he took out a pencil and sharpened it with a penknife, allowing the shavings to fall on his shirt before he blew them away on to the floor. He squinted as he checked the notebook, the pencil now lodged in his mouth like a cigar.

'I know everything I need to know about you, Henry Hunter.'

'Not too much I hope!' *A nervous laugh.*

Over the course of the next hour, the man delivered a quiet mono-logue. He told Henri things about himself which he had thought no one else could possibly know, and other things which he had long forgotten or hardly been aware of. He gave him the name of the maternity home where he was born; revealed the names and addresses of family members long forgotten or never heard of; informed him of the name of the accountancy firm for which his father worked. And he described in some detail his routine, such as it was, in Geneva: when he left home in Nyon, his route into the Old Town and to the library – that kind of thing. He knew the name of every book Henri had taken out of the library. He knew the names of the bars in the Pâquis that he liked to hang around in, where he cut a lonely figure as he eyed up the working girls without ever quite managing to summon up the courage to approach them. When he had finished, he smiled for the first time, displaying a set of large teeth, half of which seemed to be made of gold. Henri sat incredulous.

'You can call me Viktor, by the way.' A long silence, during which Henri wondered if he was meant to say anything, but had no idea what to say.

'Marcel tells me that you were about to join the Swiss Communist Party?'

'Not quite: I attended one of its meetings. I told him that I was thinking of joining, nothing more than that. We had a nice chat after the meeting and he mentioned something about not joining or attending meetings. He said that there were better ways in which I could help the cause. I was not altogether sure what he meant.'

'You will work for me, Henry Hunter: that is how you will help the cause. You are a Communist, yes?'

'Well, I suppose...'

'You are ideal, Henri. You have two nationalities and three languages. Most people in Europe have just one of each. You are the kind of person who people do not notice too much, if you understand what I mean – you don't stand out.'

'What does working for you entail, Viktor?'

'It means what Marcel said: it is another way of serving the cause.'

From a nearby rooftop a clock struck eight. 'Look, I ought to be getting a move on. I should have been home ages ago, and my mother will be getting worried. Perhaps I could think about things for a few days?' Henri said.

Viktor was smiling again, displaying even more gold teeth than before. When he smiled he looked friendly, but the second the smile disappeared his demeanour became cold and menacing. 'No, no, no, Henry Hunter,' he said, shaking his head. 'It does not work like that I am afraid. I am not advertising a vacancy at a Swiss bank. I am not looking for a man to deliver Swiss cheese. You are already working for me: you started working for me the moment we met.'

–

For the best part of a year, Henri was little more than a messenger for Viktor. At first this amounted to taking an envelope from – say – Geneva to Paris, and then stopping off in Lyons to deliver another one on the return journey. Even Henri, normally naïve, came to realise that these errands were probably little more than tests. About once a month the errands would coincide with meeting Viktor, usually in Paris or sometimes in other cities. He was, he realised, being trained: Viktor would talk at length in either English or French about what helping him really meant. He explained the rudiments of espionage: the need to fit in to any environment or circumstance without being noticed; the need for discretion; the ability to see and remember everything; how to assume different identities to the extent that you *became* that person, for however short a period; the importance of thinking, not just one step ahead, but two or even three, and at the same time not forgetting what you had been doing before – your cover story.

At no stage did Viktor actually say who he worked for, although over a period of time Henri came to understand that Viktor worked for Soviet intelligence or possibly the Comintern, although he was never totally sure which branch it actually was. Henri's instincts told him that the less he knew, the better. Viktor began to talk about the 'service', and that became how they referred to who his new employers were.

There was a travel agency in Petit-Saconnex in Geneva that was a front for Viktor's operation, and Henri became a courier for them. It provided a perfect cover for his trips and meant that his mother, although curious and somewhat dubious as to whether a travel agency was the right job for her son, did not question his frequent absences.

In the spring of 1930 Viktor introduced Henri to a German called Peter, and a week later Henri accompanied Peter to an isolated farmhouse in northern Germany, somewhere between Hamburg and Bremen. There were five other recruits there: two German men; a French woman; and a Dutch couple. All of them were a few years older than him.

On the second day at the farm, the six recruits were taken to a shed and shown a litter of puppies. '*Choose one each: it can be your companion while you are here!*' Having a dog will make your stay here easier, they were told. Henri chose the smallest of the litter, a black puppy that he named Foxi. He would take Foxi for walks two or three times a day, and as with the other recruits and their puppies, they became inseparable.

For the next six weeks they were trained in what Peter described as fieldcraft. They learnt how to create and use secret message drops; how to follow people without being noticed and, in turn, spot if they were being followed and therefore how to lose the shadow. They learnt unarmed combat, and how to use a series of handguns. There was even instruction in making bombs, and other forms of sabotage. And in the evenings there were lectures: 'ideological instruction' was how they termed it. Any hint of doubt about commitment to the cause was spotted and eliminated. By the end of the first week, everyone fully understood that working for the cause in the way which they were meant knowing that there was no room whatsoever for discussion – without total commitment and utter loyalty, they would fail.

Never question; never discuss; never hesitate.

And along with this there were individual sessions. Henri spent hours with first an elderly German man, and then a younger Polish woman. They were intent on teasing anything personal out of him. The German man seemed to be a psychiatrist of some sort, asking a series of apparently unrelated questions and making extensive notes. He seemed to be preoccupied with Henri's relationship with his mother.

Everything about the Polish woman looked severe: her manner, her heavy glasses, and the way her hair was pulled into a tight bun. She insisted he tell her everything about his personal life. Had he ever had a girlfriend, for instance? Henri had blushed and muttered something about there being one or two, but nothing serious. Had he ever slept with a woman, the Polish woman asked – or a man? Henri was so shocked that he readily told the truth. No; he had never slept with a woman. The thought of sleeping with a man, he said, had simply never occurred to him.

That night he lay in bed, unable to sleep as he tried to make sense of what was happening to him. He felt trapped, drawn into a life he would never have willingly chosen, but one which did at least offer some prospect of excitement. He had just drifted off to sleep when he was woken by someone sitting on his bed and turning on his bedside lamp. It was the Polish woman, the one who had been asking him all the personal questions. Her hair was now loose. She was without the heavy glasses, wearing bright red lipstick and a perfume that smelt of lemons. Henri found himself unable to say anything.

She leant over and brushed his face with her hand, then gently pulled his head towards hers and kissed it.

'You told me that you have never experienced a woman.' Henri nodded, still unable to speak. She pulled a face, as if to indicate that he had done something wrong and then smiled. 'That is not good, is it, Henri? How can we let you go out into the world and not know what to do with a woman? That would be… risky. You need someone to teach you.' Henri opened his mouth to say something, but the Polish woman placed a finger inside his lips, holding it in his mouth for a few moments before pulling it slowly away. She stood up and removed her dressing gown, and then her nightie. She was totally naked. She stood for a moment, her eyebrows raised, inviting Henri to look at her. She was standing in front of the bedside lamp, so was lit from behind, in silhouette. Through a gap in the curtain on the other side of the bed, the light of the moon lit up the front of her body.

54

Had she not remained with Henri for an hour after they had made love, and indeed made love for a second time, he would have readily passed it off as one of his more pleasant dreams. But they lay there together and every time he tried to start saying something, which he felt he ought to do, she placed a finger on his lips and shook her head – her long hair brushing his bare shoulders. As the first hint of dawn peered through the half-drawn curtains, she climbed out of bed and got dressed. 'We never discuss this, you understand? This was something you needed to do. There is a saying that there are more secrets to be found in a bed than in a safe. For your first time, you were quite good, Henri, but next time do remember that you don't need to rush so much. Try not to think about what you are doing: it will come naturally; it is the most natural thing we do. At least next time will not be your first time.'

Henri was confused, but at the same time quite pleased with himself.

Never question; never discuss; never hesitate.

On his penultimate day at the farm, Henri was walking with Peter and Foxi in the woods, when the German turned to him and handed him a pistol.

'Shoot her,' he said, pointing at the puppy.

'What!' The puppy's eyes looked up at him, full of joy.

'The longer you wait the harder it will be.'

Henri fiddled around with pistol, hoping that at any moment Peter would stop him.

'Get on with it. You do as I tell you.'

Henri felt himself drift into a trance and, as if from above, he saw himself call Foxi over and cuddle her, allowing her to lick his face before placing the barrel of the gun behind her ears and pulling the trigger.

Afterwards Peter held out his hand for the gun, and Henri did all he could to stop himself crying. *Never question; never discuss; never hesitate.*

When he returned to Geneva after the six weeks near Hamburg, he felt emotionally drained: there was now nothing that his new masters did not know about him. They probably knew more him than he did about himself. It was as if they now possessed his soul. He had come to understand, even before Hamburg, that Viktor had been putting him through a process which meant that there was no going back. Whether he liked it or not, he was now committed to the cause. He knew that his views on Communism were now quite immaterial.

By the end of 1930, the errands, as Viktor liked to call them, became more serious: clandestine trips to the more dangerous corners of Europe; fleeting encounters with wary women and frightened men; switching identity before hurrying out of the country. There were even some trips to Britain, when he used his Henry Hunter identity to enter and leave the country. He was seeing Viktor at least once a month, probably nearer to once every three weeks. Viktor always allowed plenty of time for their meetings; it was as if he enjoyed them. During the course of these meetings it became apparent that Viktor worked for the Comintern, and he would reminisce about the Revolution and his early days as a Comintern agent. He would describe to Henri the dangers he could foresee in Europe. Above all, he seemed to show genuine interest in Henri, in a way that neither his mother nor his stepfather did. He clearly cared, and Henri found himself being frank with Viktor in a way that he was unable to be with anyone else. Viktor began to refer to Henri as *synok*.

It was the Russian for 'son'.

Chapter 6

Switzerland, 1931

The event which would change Henri's life forever took place in the summer of 1931, but its origins came earlier that year in Paris. At the beginning of March, Henri had been summoned to the French capital, to one of the safe houses that Viktor used in the Marais. Unlike his usual meetings with Viktor, this one was more charged and stretched over a period of days. Viktor wanted to satisfy himself that no one — 'not a single soul', as he put it — could possibly have any inkling as to what Henri was up to, or who he was working for. It took four days and three nights of what amounted to an interrogation for Viktor to satisfy himself of this.

A week later, Viktor was in Geneva — the first time he had been there for some months. Over a long dinner in a private room at the back of a seedy Armenian restaurant in Grand-Lancy, Viktor talked about politics. What did Henri understand about events in the Soviet Union, about the dangerous and counter-revolutionary activities of Trotsky and his mad followers? Henri replied truthfully that he knew little, but that his allegiance was very clearly with Comrade Stalin. Traitors such as Trotsky and his ilk were a distraction.

Viktor had nodded in agreement and then spoke well into the early hours of the morning, fortified by an endless supply of strong Turkish coffee and plenty of vodka. Viktor patiently explained the aims of the Left Opposition, how their arguments may have had some merit in their early days, but that they had deviated seriously from the correct socialist course charted by Lenin. Henri needed to be very clear that there was no room for what Viktor described as a 'bourgeois indulgence'. Henri said he understood and was grateful to Viktor for explaining matters so clearly: he had no doubt that Trotsky and his few remaining followers were enemies of the Soviet Union and of socialism, but surely the matter had been dealt with? Had Trotsky not been expelled from the Soviet Union?

It was one in the morning now, and when the exhausted *patron* returned with more coffee Viktor dismissed him sharply in Russian.

'I told him to leave us alone, *synok*; what I am about to say now is most important. Trotsky is indeed living in exile in Turkey, and most of his supporters in the Soviet Union have seen the error of their ways – or at least claim to have done so: even Zinoviev and Kamenev. Others have been dealt with. But the danger posed by Trotsky and those of his followers that remain still exists. There are powerful supporters of Trotsky dispersed around Europe, and as long as they are able to operate, they pose a threat to us, which we cannot tolerate: we cannot put at risk the achievements of the Revolution. You understand that?'

Henri nodded.

'So, dealing with them is a priority for our service.'

Henri nodded again. *Of course.*

A long silence followed, during which Viktor removed his jacket, loosened his tie, and looked at Henri in a quizzical manner, as if expecting him to say something. Henri shifted in his chair, unsure of how to react.

'This is where you are going to perform a vital role for the Service, *synok*.'

–

Henri Hesse spent the first two weeks of July 1931 in a large house on the outskirts of Neuchâtel, overlooking the lake. He had been told to expect to be away from Geneva for at least a month, possibly a good deal longer. As far as his mother and stepfather were concerned, the travel agency he had been working for had acquired a new branch in St Gallen and, as Henri spoke good Swiss German, he was being sent there for a while.

Viktor accompanied Henri to the house and remained there for the first two days. Peter, the German who had taken him to Hamburg for his training the previous year was also present. For two weeks, Peter helped Henri assume a new identity. Just before the end of the fortnight in Neuchâtel, Viktor returned and after a couple more days, he finally satisfied himself that Henri had now become William Jarvis.

According to his much-used British passport, William Jarvis had been born in Norwich and was, at twenty-six, a few years older than Henri. After graduating from Cambridge University, Jarvis had become a teacher, and had moved to Switzerland for a year thanks to a legacy from a recently deceased and much-loved uncle. His aim was to travel and to do some occasional teaching, should the opportunity arise.

That opportunity happily arose in Interlaken.

'They've been advertising for an English tutor on and off for weeks: they'll be delighted that a proper Englishman who also happens to be a teacher applies,' Viktor had told him.

'But I am not a teacher!'

'You don't need to be. They want someone to improve their children's conversational English, that's all.'

The night before Henri travelled to Interlaken, Viktor had given him his final briefing.

'Anatoly Mikhailovich Yevtushenko.' The three of them were sat around a finely polished table in the dining room near Neuchâtel and Viktor had almost ceremonially placed a photograph of a distinguished-looking man in front of Henri. 'Anatoly Mikhailovich Yevtushenko, born Kazan in 1884. Bourgeois family, but became active in socialist politics when he was at university in Moscow. He became a lawyer, and was one of the very early members of the Russian Social Democratic Labour Party, which you may or may not know was the forerunner of the Communist Party. He was active in the October Revolution and began to rise through the ranks of the Party. However, in around 1923 or 1924 he became a confidant of Trotsky, and since then the two have become very close. In 1924 Yevtushenko took up a position in the finance department of the

Party. In early 1928, not long after Trotsky was sent into internal exile, Yevtushenko and his family disappeared while on holiday in Crimea. We lost track of them, but a few months ago we discovered that they were living in Interlaken.'

Viktor nodded at Peter, who opened a folder and produced a series of photographs which he laid out in front of Henri as if dealing from a deck of cards.

'This is Yevtushenko's wife, Tatyana Dmitriyevna,' said Peter. 'We understand that she suffers from a debilitating lung condition, which may well be the reason why they are living in Interlaken. This is Rozalia Anatolyevna, she is seventeen. Nadezhda Anatolyevna is fourteen, and this is the son, Nikolai Anatolyevich. He is eleven.'

'And that is their house?'

'Indeed. A very fine house as you can see, but also a very secure one. This wall runs all around the house and is twelve foot high. It is not altogether unusual for houses to have such security in Switzerland: people like their privacy and Interlaken is a wealthy town.'

Viktor moved the photographs away from Henri. He wanted him to concentrate on what he was about to say. 'We have been watching Yevtushenko very closely. We have come to the conclusion that he is an important source of finance for Trotsky and his movement, something the Service had long suspected. We know now that in the few months before he escaped from the Soviet Union, Yevtushenko channelled large sums of money from Moscow into Swiss bank accounts. Only he has access to them. We do not know exactly how much money is in these accounts, but we believe it could well be in the region of eight hundred million Swiss Francs. As well as the family, these three men live in the house – Peter...' On that command the German produced a series of photos, blurred shots of three different men. 'They are guards, all Russians. They stay in the house and vet whoever comes in or even approaches it. A local woman and her daughter act as housekeepers: they arrive early in the morning and do the cleaning, cooking and shopping. They leave in the middle of the afternoon. The family very rarely leave the house and when they do, they are always accompanied by a guard.'

Viktor took over speaking now. 'Approximately once a fortnight, Yevtushenko leaves the house and travels first to Bern and then to Zurich. He always leaves very early in the morning and arrives back late in the evening. He is always accompanied on these trips by two of the guards. We know that in Bern he visits the Swiss Volksbank and in Zurich he goes to the Union Bank and to the Eidgenössische Bank. Our assumption is that once there, he is able to transfer money from the accounts he controls to the accounts of Trotsky's supporters around Europe or even to Trotsky himself. Our aim is very simple: that money was stolen from the Party and we want it back. In the process, we can starve Trotsky of the funds that are keeping his miserable movement going.'

'And my role is...?' Henri sounded confused.

'To become the family's English tutor, *synok*, and become trusted by them. That may take weeks. Once that happens, we will be able to move to our next stage.'

'And what does that involve?'

'You will find out then, *synok*,' said Viktor.

Never question; never discuss; never hesitate.

–

It had all gone according to plan, as things tended to do in Switzerland, especially when they were organised by Viktor. William Jarvis had taken the trouble to write from England to reserve a room in an inn in the centre of Interlaken. He was on the top floor with a small balcony, from which he could see Lake Thun to the west, Lake Brienz to the east, the mountains of the Jungfrau and the Grindelwald to the south, with the Harder Kulm and Emmental beyond it to the north. Henri, who now had to think of himself as 'William', had decided that this could turn out to be a pleasant enough task.

He waited until his second day in Interlaken before enquiring in the bookshop about the discreet sign in their window seeking an English tutor and that afternoon he telephoned the number the bookshop owner had passed on to him. Two days later he walked through the town and crossed the River Aare, and there on the north bank found the house on the very edge of the rising forest. It was a perfect position, separated from neighbouring houses by trees and surrounded by a high wall, with the front gate set into it. Next to the gate was a small window. Two large men searched him after he rang the bell, and he was then led through to a library.

Both Anatoly Yevtushenko and his wife, Tatyana, were in the room, but the interview was conducted by the husband in passable German. His wife, he explained, did not speak German. Tatyana Yevtushenko was a thin woman, with skin so pale that it was the colour of chalk and, although it was a warm July day, she was dressed for winter. Anatoly Yevtushenko told William Jarvis that the family had moved around Europe but had settled here in Switzerland. 'Because of my business,' he said, in a tone that made it clear that he did not need to elaborate. For the most part, they educated the children themselves, he explained, but they did require the assistance of tutors from time to time.

'Please tell me about yourself, Mr Jarvis.'

William Jarvis remembered what Viktor had told him: '*Tell him just enough, not too much… He will be clever, he will spot any mistakes… Concentrate on how much you would enjoy tutoring his children rather than talking about yourself. Avoid sounding too fluent: be slightly hesitant with dates.*'

Anatoly Yevtushenko spoke to his wife every so often in Russian, evidently giving her the gist of what he had been told.

'Are you interested in politics, Mr Jarvis?'

'I am afraid not, sir. I do hope that is not a problem?'

'No, not at all. And what about foreign affairs, do you follow those?'

'Only what one reads in *The Times* sir, but I have to tell you that my main interest is literature. I would rather read a good book than a newspaper!'

And so it went on. After a brief conversation with his wife, Anatoly Yevtushenko offered William Jarvis the position of English tutor to his children. They agreed the fee, and that he would come for two hours every morning. They would review his position after two weeks.

At the end of the first week William Jarvis was summoned into Anatoly Yevtushenko's study.

'How long do you plan to stay in Interlaken for, Mr Jarvis?'

'A few months, possibly. I hope to learn to ski, so I suppose I am in the right place. It depends on whether I have to work to help pay for my stay.'

'Well that is why I have asked to see you. The children adore you: they absolutely insist that we keep you for as long as possible. For reasons that are too complicated to explain, our life is an isolated one and my wife and I worry about the effect of that on the children. Already we can see how you have been able to help brighten their lives. From now on, we would like you to spend an extra hour every day with each child and to stay for lunch, which will be a further opportunity for you to converse with them in English.'

This was the routine for the next month. William Jarvis would arrive at the house at eleven o'clock every morning, apart from Sunday, and ring the bell on the wall. The heavy metal gates would eventually open and one of the guards would search him before another would lead him through to the library. He would spend the first hour with Nadezhda, who was by far the brightest of the three children. Nikolai would have the second hour, which was hard work as the boy completely lacked discipline, but seemed to be pleased to have William read simple stories to him in English. Then he and the three children would eat lunch together, speaking only English during the meal.

After lunch, he would teach Rozalia for the final hour. Very quickly, he came to appreciate that this was the part of the day he most looked forward to. At first he had seen Rozalia as little more than a child, but on her own, away from her parents and her sister and brother, she was more of a young woman. Her thick, long brown hair fell well below her shoulders and she was constantly sweeping it away from her face. Her skin was not as pale as her mother's, but she had certainly inherited her complexion more from her than from her father. What she had inherited from him were dark brown eyes, with an almost unblinking gaze.

They would spend much of the time in the garden, wandering around, talking in English but more often than not slipping into

German. Her German was not too bad and she did her best to ignore his attempts to speak in English. She was, Henri realised, desperately lonely. She had fled her home country and was now trapped in a house surrounded by high walls. So she confided in Mr Jarvis, as she called him. He found it hard to do other than lend a sympathetic ear, and assure her that if she was patient her life would change for the better. He told her about life in England and what he had seen of Europe on his travels.

'Call me Roza.'

'Very well – and do call me William.'

'What is a short form of William?'

'Bill, I suppose – or Billy.'

Roza preferred Billy and so she and Billy became friends. When they did read from books, she would sit very close to him so that their bodies touched. Roza had a habit, a mannerism even, of touching his arm and allowing her fingers to briefly hold him by the wrist. He had noticed her doing this to the others too, so he did not imagine she meant any special affection for him, but once or twice he tried to return the gesture – placing his hand on top of hers. She would smile and would sweep the hair from her face before gently removing her hand. He knew that what Roza wanted more than anything else was companionship. William's story was that his mother had died when he was young and his father had remarried. This struck some kind of chord with Roza, whose eyes would fill with tears when he told her about being sent to boarding school at the age of six, and how his stepmother did not like him. Henri worried that he may be getting too close to Roza, but then Viktor had told him to make sure that he became trusted.

He knew that he was developing feelings for Roza, but he also knew that he was unlikely to be in a position to do anything about them. She would never be allowed to leave the house without a guard and the house was always busy. One morning, after he had been there for a month or so, the downstairs toilet was being repaired and he was told to use the bathroom upstairs, which he would normally never do. When he opened the bathroom door he was met by the sight of Roza, who had clearly just stepped out of the bath. Despite the steam, and the fact that she was mostly covered by a towel, he could clearly see her breasts, smaller than he had imagined them to be but almost perfectly shaped, with locks of her dark, wet hair hanging down them. There was a very brief moment when neither of them said anything or moved, then he said 'Sorry,' and swiftly shut the door before hurrying downstairs. Neither of them ever said a word about it, but that afternoon she was even friendlier than usual. On Sundays – the only day on which he did not go to the house – Henri would take the bus from Interlaken to Thun, where he would meet Peter in a park. They would walk while Henri would recount what had happened during the week, and Peter would ask a series of questions, occasionally pausing to write something in his notebook. Once he took Henri to a small apartment above a shop in the centre of the town, where Henri was told to draw detailed plans of the house.

In the middle of August he arrived in Thun on a Sunday, only to be taken straight to the apartment by Peter. When they arrived, Viktor was waiting with three Frenchmen, who were introduced as Lucien, Claude and Jean-Marie: the conversation that followed – which lasted well into the evening – was conducted in French.

'*Synok*, Peter tells me that you told him last week that sometimes you and Roza are allowed to leave the house?' Viktor was sitting directly across a narrow table from Henri, watching him carefully. Despite the stifling August heat, the Russian was wearing a heavy jacket. The three Frenchmen were lounging back in their chairs and one of them had a revolver in a shoulder holster.

'Well, yes and no. Roza has a lot of spirit, she seems like a caged animal in that house, but her parents will not allow her to go into the town, certainly not without a guard. However, behind the house is a small wood which is private, just for the residents of the houses around it. It has a fence around it.'

Peter handed a map to Viktor, pointing to a circled area.

'Here?'

Henri picked up the map and studied it. 'Yes, here. You can get into it from a door set into the wall in the garden. Her father agreed that we can go for a walk in there, as long as it is just for a few minutes and we promise not to leave the wood. The guards have the key: At first they would come along to let us out and then in again, but now they don't bother. I have to collect it from them and return it afterwards. I am trusted.'

'And tell me, *synok*, when do the housekeepers leave – is it still in the afternoon?'

'Yes. They make the lunch and then prepare the evening meal. They are usually gone by three o'clock.'

The Frenchmen and Peter all asked questions and Henri must have described the layout of the house a dozen times. Viktor then outlined his plan. It was clever and audacious and by the time he had finished, Henri felt quite sick.

–

Two more weeks. Viktor had decided that another two weeks would help ensure that William Jarvis was even more trusted by the Yevtushenkos and this was important, because if they did not trust him then the plan would not work. The two weeks was also important because Anatoly Yevtushenko's last trip to Bern and Zurich had been just a few days previously. The timing had to be right.

The agreed date was the 1st September – a Tuesday. On the Thursday before that Peter had arrived in Interlaken and rented an apartment on the east side of the town, close to Lake Brienz. Henri checked out of the inn and moved into the apartment with Peter.

William Jarvis arrived at the house just before eleven o'clock on the Tuesday morning. By now the guards were more relaxed with him, even quite friendly. He went through to the library and had his lessons with Nadezhda and Nikolai. By the time they went into the dining room for lunch he was feeling sick with nerves and anticipation. He hardly ate anything, but no one seemed to notice. He managed to keep the children distracted by playing 'I spy'. After lunch he went to the guards' room at the front of the house to collect the key. The guard who spoke the best German handed it to him, with a warning to make sure he locked it properly.

He and Roza wandered into the garden, with Roza struggling to count to one hundred in English. That was the way it worked: complete a task such as counting or naming the days of the week or months of the year and they could go into the woods as a reward. Roza became marooned in the seventies but Henri announced that was good enough. He unlocked the garden door and they spent the rest of the hour walking around the wood. Henri kept glancing around, expecting to see people hidden amongst the trees or beyond the fence, but it was as deserted and as silent as always, apart from the sound of water rushing on the Aare below them.

'Are you all right, Billy?'

'Yes, thank you, Roza. Why do you ask?'

'You are very quiet.' She had switched to German now. 'You keep looking around and you did not eat any lunch.'

'I am fine thank you, Roza. I slept badly last night that is all. Look, you really must speak English. Please try.'

'Why? What is the point? We will never visit England. We will never leave this house. I am a prison, Billy,' she said in English.

'I am a *prisoner*, Roza. That is what you meant to say. A prison is a building in which the prisoners are kept. I am sure you will get to visit England one day.'

They spent much of the hour with Henri doing his best to sustain some kind of conversation in English. As ever, Roza was wrapped up in her thoughts. When they went back into the garden, Henri told Roza to go on ahead while he made a play of locking the garden door. The door appeared shut, but he kicked a stone against it just in case the wind blew it open. After he'd returned the key to the guards' room he went into the library, pausing on the way to remove the bolt on the side door that opened into the garden. His hands were shaking so much that he feared the sound of the bolts being removed echoed around the house.

They'll need to move: I told them the guards usually check the garden door soon after I lock it.

Roza and Nadezhda were in the library. He would hang around for a few minutes, as he had come to do. He could hear Nikolai playing

67

upstairs and the two local women leaving the house. Anatoly was in his study, and he imagined the mother would be asleep upstairs. From the corner of his eye he imagined he caught a movement in the garden, but he did not want to look up. A few moments later there were some sounds from the front of the house, nothing too noticeable at first but then it became more of a commotion and first Nadezhda and then Roza looked up. Seconds later and there was shouting down the hall, and then three loud popping noises followed by a scream and the sound of Anatoly shouting and then scuffling in the hall. Moments later, the door to the library burst open. The first person in the room was one of the Frenchmen, followed by Peter and behind him Viktor and another of the Frenchmen frogmarching Anatoly into the room. The girls screamed and Viktor shouted at them in Russian, waving his revolver at their father's head as he did so. The message was clear: '*Shut up or I shoot.*'

Viktor pushed Anatoly into an armchair and gestured for the girls to sit on the floor. They could hear movement upstairs. 'Go and see what is going on,' Viktor told Peter in French. Shortly after that, one of the other Frenchmen appeared in the room, dragging Nikolai in with him by his hair. Tatyana followed as if in a trance, followed by Peter. Nikolai was shoved on to the floor next to his terrified sisters while their mother was guided to a chair opposite her husband. Viktor addressed the family in Russian, and then in French told Peter to see what was happening at the front of the house. When he reappeared it was with the third Frenchman, the two of them dragging one of the guards. He appeared to be badly wounded: he was groaning and his chest was covered in blood.

'What about the other two?' asked Viktor.

'Dead,' said the third Frenchman.

'And him?' He was nodding at the injured guard.

'Took one in the chest.'

'Finish him off.'

The Frenchman had been holding a revolver by his side. Now he knelt down by the guard and yanked up his head, forcing the barrel of the gun into his mouth. As he did so, the guard seemed to become fully conscious, his eyes opened wide – clearly terrified. The three children screamed and were only silenced when Viktor shouted at them. When the Frenchman pulled the trigger the guard's head slumped, followed by a long silence and then the sobbing of the three children. Tatyana sat very still, clearly in shock and seemingly unaware of what was going on. Henri noticed that Anatoly was staring at him.

Viktor spoke to the family in Russian, pointing at Anatoly and waving his pistol around. They all nodded. *We understand.* Then he spoke in French: 'I'm going to separate them now.' He pointed to the three Frenchmen. 'I'll take Anatoly into the study; he and I have much to talk about. One of you will come into the study with me, the other two had better keep an eye on the rest of the house – make sure one of you stays in the guardroom, we need to keep an eye on the front. Peter, you stay in here. William, you too: try and keep the children distracted. You'll need this.'

It was only when Viktor handed a revolver to Henri that it dawned on the family that he had betrayed them. From the shocked look on the faces of the children and the glare of hate on the face of their father, Henri realised that up until then they must have thought that he too had been caught up as a victim in this nightmare.

Anatoly was hauled up by one of the Frenchmen, who then hand-cuffed his hands behind his back before marching him out of the room. As he passed Henri, Anatoly stopped and looked Henri straight in the eye before spitting out '*Du Bastard!*'

None of the children wanted anything to do with their English tutor. They ignored all his attempts to talk in English. Nadezhda spent most of the time quietly sobbing, sitting on the floor by her mother's chair. Little Nikolai looked confused and terrified, while Roza stared at him with blazing eyes. 'You were the one person I thought understood me. You were someone I trusted,' she said in German, in a quiet but angry voice. 'You know what will happen to us now, don't you?'

'Everything will be all right, Roza, don't worry.'

'You think so do you, Englishman? In that case you have no idea who is paying you.' She shuffled over to him, lowering her voice even more. 'They will kill us all, you realise that?'

69

Peter leaned over from the nearby chair where he was sitting, 'Shut up!' he shouted at Roza. He turned to Henri and spoke in French, 'Don't talk with her anymore.' From the study there was the sound of raised voices in Russian, mostly Viktor, but Anatoly too. The afternoon turned into evening. One of the Frenchmen brought food into the library but, apart from Nikolai, none of the family ate anything. When it began to turn dark, Viktor called Henri and Peter into the kitchen.

'He finally understands that we mean business. I think he realises that he has no alternative but to do what I say. There is a train to Bern at seven twenty tomorrow morning: Lucien and Jean-Marie will go with him. He will be at the Swiss Volksbank when it opens: I have agreed that he can telephone here to be assured that everyone is safe. Then he will transfer all the funds from the Swiss Volksbank. After that, they will travel to Zurich and repeat the procedure at the Union Bank and the Eidgenössische Bank.'

'How do we know he will transfer all the funds under his control?' asked Peter.

'We cannot be totally sure, but we know from following him that these are the only three banks he has ever visited. I managed to persuade him to show me what documentation he had and the accounts amount to just over nine hundred million Swiss Francs: that is more than we estimated. They will be very pleased. By tomorrow night that money will be in accounts controlled by the Party.'

'And what happens then, Viktor?' The German looked nervous, playing with his watch strap and biting his fingernails, glancing first at Henri and then back at Viktor.

'We'll see. I have told him that he will be brought back here and that, a few hours after we leave the town, we will phone the local police to release them.'

'Roza told me that they are all going to be killed. Why would she say that?' Henri asked.

'Don't worry about it, *synok*. We know what we are doing.'

'But—'

Peter leaned over the table and grabbed Henri's forearm, very tight. 'Don't you remember anything? We just do as we are told. This isn't that stupid game you play for days at a time in England, understand?'

Never question; never discuss; never hesitate.

Viktor told them both to shut up. They would keep Anatoly apart from the rest of the family that night. Two of them would guard him while the others stayed with Tatyana and the children in the library, taking it in turns to sleep. Anatoly was made to telephone the housekeepers: '*You are not required tomorrow, please take the day off – we will see you as usual on Thursday.*'

Anatoly was woken up at six in the morning. Henri had been with him in his bedroom along with Peter for the past few hours and was surprised that the Russian had slept at all. They watched while he washed, shaved and dressed. When he was ready he turned round and addressed them.

'Tell him I want to say goodbye to my family before I leave.'

They called Viktor up and there was a short exchange in Russian. The result was that Anatoly came downstairs, went into the library and hugged each member of his family, but said nothing other than a word or two in Russian to each one. When he had finished hugging the last one, Nadezhda, he turned sharply and swiftly left the room. As he passed him in the hall Henri noticed that the Russian's eyes had filled with tears.

–

Viktor spent much of that Wednesday in the study, behind Anatoly's desk. The first phone call came at nine thirty: it was Lucien at the Swiss Volksbank. Peter brought Roza through from the library and put her on the phone to her father.

'Yes, we are all right. When are you coming home? What are they—?' The phone was snatched back from her. Thirty minutes later and Lucien rang again. The money had been transferred. They were now on their way to Zurich. The next phone call came at a quarter to one. It was Jean-Marie to say that they had arrived in Zurich and were about to go into Eidgenössische Bank. This time Nadezhda was brought in from the library to assure her father that all was well. Henri was in the study when Jean–Marie rang again at one thirty to say that the transfer had been made; they were on their way to the Union Bank.

'Wait. Ring me back in half an hour. I need to make a call first.'

Viktor dialled a Zurich number and after a short conversation, in which he said no more than a few words, a large smile filled his face, displaying the familiar gold teeth. 'Good news, *synok*. The funds from both banks have already been transferred to our account in Credit Suisse. Before the close of business today they will have been spread among various untraceable accounts across Europe. We are better at capitalism than the capitalists!'

By three o'clock the business had been done. Nikolai had spoken to his father before the transaction at Union Bank and then Lucien rang to say it had been completed.

'Is Yevtushenko in the room with you?' Viktor was speaking with Lucien. 'Right then, don't say anything, but when I have finished say out loud that you will be on the four fifteen train from Zurich and that you expect to be back in Interlaken by eight o'clock, you understand? You know what to do, Lucien… I will see you in Paris.'

Viktor paused while Lucien responded and then placed the phone back on the receiver, holding onto it for a while after putting it down. He sighed and loosened his tie.

'All good, *synok*. The transfers have taken place. Moscow will be delighted. Now, Trotsky has no more money.'

Henri nodded. 'Is Anatoly on his way back here, Viktor?'

The Russian peered at him as if the sun was in his eyes. 'Tell Peter to come in. You stay in the library with Claude.'

–

The longest half hour of Henri Hesse's life began very soon after that.

He was in the library with Claude, keeping an eye on Tatyana and the three children when Viktor appeared in the doorway. He spoke in Russian and Roza and Nadezhda both raised their hands. Viktor pointed at Nadezhda and gestured upstairs. 'I've asked if they want an opportunity to use the bathroom,' he said to Henri in French. Viktor closed the library door as Nadezhda went upstairs. Viktor said nothing but glanced at his watch and then up at the ceiling, his back against the closed door. After five minutes he spoke to Roza. *Your turn.* She brushed past Henri, looking through him as she went past, pulling her cardigan tightly around her shoulders and across her front.

Ten minutes later, with no sign of either of the girls, there was a knock at the door. Viktor opened it slightly to reveal Peter on the other side. The German nodded briefly but said nothing. Viktor nodded his head approvingly and briefly gripped Peter's shoulder in a friendly manner.

'Go into the guardroom,' he said to Henri, 'and tell Claude to come here. You remain there. Keep an eye on the road. Don't leave until you're told to.'

From the guardroom Henri could see the front gate and the quiet road beyond it. The silence was pierced by a scream, one that was loud but stopped short by a loud popping noise and then the sound of something falling. Henri wondered whether to go and see what was happening, despite Viktor's instructions. Next came the sound of Nikolai shrieking and another popping noise, followed by two more. After that, more silence.

The door to the guardroom opened. Peter was standing there. 'You're to go to the library.' When he got there Viktor and Claude were standing in the middle of the room, revolvers in their hands. The body of Tatyana was thrown back in her chair, her eyes and mouth wide open and a large wound on her forehead. Prostrate on the floor in front of her was Nikolai, two wounds visible on his back and a large pool of blood emerging from under him.

Henri was too shocked to move and for a while could say nothing, until he noticed Nikolai's back moving.

'He's breathing, Viktor! Nikolai's breathing.' Henri felt himself swaying. Claude walked over to the boy and, with his foot, turned him over. Nikolai was breathing very slowly. His face was white, but his eyes were moving as if he was having trouble focussing. Claude looked up at Viktor. *What do you want me to do?*

73

Viktor held up a hand: wait. 'Henri, you finish him off. It is a tradition in our service: everyone on a mission should take part.' The Russian pressed his own revolver into Henri's hand: the barrel was still hot. Henri's hand was shaking so much that the gun was waving around.

'Be careful with that thing please, Henri. You'd better use two hands,' said Viktor. 'And be quick. We need to get out of here.' Henri breathed in deeply. *Never question; never discuss; never hesitate.* He calmly walked over to Nikolai and knelt down by him. The boy's head moved slowly towards him, his eyes locking onto Henri's as his mouth opened, allowing a trickle of blood to form down his chin.

'Come on, quick,' said Claude. Henri released the safety catch and placed the revolver against Nikolai's temple. He noticed that he was trying to say something: hearing him say something – anything – would be more than he could bear. When he pressed the trigger he felt the splatter of blood and flesh on him before he heard the sound. It had been no harder than shooting his puppy. Claude hauled him up.

'Good. Well done. We need to move now.'

–

They left the house just before four o'clock, after trying to make it appear as if a robbery had taken place and gone dreadfully wrong. They opened the safe and made the study look as if it had been ransacked. Henri went upstairs with Peter to help find any jewellery. As they walked past the bathroom Henri stopped suddenly. A girl's leg was poking out of the door. Its shoe had fallen off and was upside down on the carpet in front of him. Peter pushed in front of him as he tried to open the bathroom door, placing himself between Henri and the door.

'You don't need to go in here.'

'I want to see,' said Henri, barging his way past the German.

The bodies of both Roza and Nadezhda were sprawled out on the floor, on top of a pool of dark blood that had spread around the room. The heads of both girls were jerked at an unnatural angle, facing each other, their eyes open and full of fear and very still. Roza's hand had reached out to her sister's, her fingers clutching one of Nadezhda's wrists.

'What...?'

Peter had now pushed past him and was drawing the curtains. He smiled at Henri and pointed at the girls and made a cut-throat gesture.

Henri stood in the doorway for a minute, watching as Peter hauled the bodies of the two girls into the bath and then started throwing towels onto the floor to soak up the blood. He was shocked to realise how un-shocked he felt. His main concern was that he should be careful not to step in the blood.

Henri left the house as normal through the front gate and headed into town, crossing the river and towards Interlaken West train station. He was halfway down Bahnhofstrasse when the car pulled up. Peter and Claude got out and walked towards the station. Henri climbed into the passenger seat next to Viktor.

They drove north towards Bern, but were well past Thun before either of them spoke. 'You realise there was no alternative, don't you, *synok*?' Viktor turned briefly towards Henri, who shrugged. 'We could not afford to have any witnesses.' Henri said nothing. *Never question; never discuss; never hesitate.*

Instead of driving into Bern they stopped briefly in Köniz and then took the road towards Lausanne. It was only then that Henri spoke. 'What happened to Anatoly?'

'I think you can guess, *synok*.'

'Did he know what was going to happen to him?'

'I would imagine so: he has been an *apparatchik* all of his adult life. He knows how we work. He would have known what to expect.'

'So why did he co-operate then?'

'Because I promised him that if he did, we would spare the children.'

'And he believed you?'

Viktor said nothing for a while as he thought about Henri's question. The headlight of an approaching bus caught the Russian's gold teeth as he turned to reply.

75

'Probably not, but what choice did he have? He wanted to believe that I – we – would spare the children and his wife. Look, you are asking too many questions, *synok*. You did well, just leave it at that. You are one of us now. You should be happy.'

Later that night, once he had arrived home in Nyon and he lay in his own bed for the first time in weeks, what most shocked Henri was the realisation of how much he agreed with Viktor. He was now one of them. He was happy. But he knew that it had come at a terrible, terrible price. When he had returned from Germany the previous year, he knew that they had taken possession of his soul.

Now they had destroyed it.

That night, he had the dream for the first time.

Chapter 7

Berlin, January 1940

On a foggy winter's afternoon in the middle of January a tall man with a stooped bearing that afforded him a misleadingly academic air left his office at the Reichsbank on Werderscher Markt in the centre of Berlin, by the canal. It was five thirty, somewhat later than most other people he worked with. The later he left work, he reasoned, the later he would arrive home, and that suited him fine.

Gunter Reinhart had developed a habit of leaving the enormous complex through different exits on different days. Had someone been observing him, which they would have had no cause to do, they might be suspicious. But he did not vary his routine for reasons of security; the truth was far more prosaic than that. It afforded him the opportunity to take different routes home, and on each of those routes lay various bars, where he could further delay his arrival. At least it gave him something to think about during the afternoon.

There was no point in leaving through the Unterwasserstrasse exit, because beyond that was the canal. He liked the anonymity and the slightly rougher edge to the bars round Leipzigerstrasse, but that was further from home. Leaving through Französischestrasse meant heading towards the Unter den Linden, which one could never accuse of offering anonymity. He would, he decided, leave through Kurstrasse and find somewhere to stop off around Jägerstrasse.

These days, stepping out into the street after dark was like descending into a pitch-black tunnel. Gunter Reinhart had very mixed feelings about the blackout that descended upon Berlin at dusk. On the one hand, it conferred an atmosphere of privacy on the city. You

77

felt you were in your own world. On the other hand, there was no question that it made life more difficult. There were no streetlights, buildings were dark and the trams moved around like ghost trains. Cars had just a small strip of paper over their headlights. Any lights that were allowed were covered in blue paper, while low-level red lamps marked danger spots, such as road works. Then there was the phosphorous paint: gallons of the stuff liberally sloshed on the pavements and road surfaces to give pedestrians and drivers some chance of knowing where they were. The effect was quite eerie and unsettling. Berlin at night looked as if it was deserted. There were reports of numerous traffic accidents and people being killed from walking into things or falling over in the blackout. The sister of one of the secretaries in his office had been killed when she stepped off the platform at Kaiserhof station. And then there were the rumours. Berlin thrived on rumours anyway; they had been an essential part of its pre-war diet. Now, rumours were disseminated in more hushed and guarded tones. The latest rumour was that a murderer was taking advantage of the blackout and had already killed a dozen young women. There had even been oblique references to it in the newspapers. Naturally, the police said they suspected the person responsible was Jewish; or Polish; or both.

The few people who moved around the city at night did so tentatively, as if wading through water. Some people had taken to whistling or coughing constantly so as to alert others to their proximity and thus avoid bumping into them. But that was something of a forlorn hope: it was impossible to avoid other people.

Even though this was a route that he knew very well, on nights like this, when there was no moonlight, Gunter Reinhart could not find his bearings.

Just after the intersection with Friedrichstrasse he came across a group of men silently beating up a man on the ground. He paused for a moment, taking in the surreal nature of what he was witnessing before he decided to cross the road. He had learned to keep well away from trouble. Suddenly, a long black car swept past him and stopped. Very quickly, the man who was being attacked was bundled into the car.

Six months previously he would have been shaken to the core by what he had seen, but now it was quickly forgotten. He was more concerned with finding somewhere to drink. Looming out of the dark he spotted the dim blue-covered sign for Das Potsdamer Taverne, a bar that he used to visit at least twice a week, although recently it had become something of a favourite haunt for a group of young SS officers. Given that the whole point of going to the bar was to relax, they were the last people he'd want to find in there.

He walked slowly down the steep steps to the basement, clutching on to the iron railings and keeping a careful eye on the dabs of phosphorous paint on the steps. The bar was quiet and there was no sign of the SS, or indeed anyone else in uniform. The bar had a low ceiling which caused him to stoop. Through the blue-brown cigarette smoke he could see perhaps half a dozen other customers spread out: all of them alone, all smoking, all drinking quietly, all sitting as far as they could manage from each other. Like him, they were avoiding going home.

The barmaid caught his eye as he waited to order a drink.

'How are you, I haven't seen you for a while?'

'A week perhaps? No more than that. I was in here last week.'

That kind of conversation, the kind repeated in bars around the world, between barmaids and husbands who would rather not go home.

The barmaid was a friendly girl with broad shoulders and hair that looked as if it had been dyed yellow. His wife, in her usual waspish manner, would describe her, in the unlikely event of her ever meeting her, by saying that she had 'seen better days', but she had friendly eyes and a seductive voice, with a distinctive Bavarian accent. She kept glancing at him as she pulled the beer, her eyes darting around her. He started to move away, hoping to find a seat on his own. She held up her hand. *Wait a moment.*

When she had finished serving another customer, she leaned over to talk quietly to him.

'A man was in here asking about you.'

Eight words no one wanted to hear in Berlin in 1940.

79

'What man?'

'I don't know, I have never seen him here before. He was very polite and well spoken. A Berliner definitely. Wore a nice coat.'

'When was this?'

She leant back as if trying to calculate the answer.

'Last Thursday, I think; and then again yesterday – Monday.'

Gunter Reinhart pulled up the stool next to him and sat on it. This was bad news. Who could possibly be coming into a bar to ask about him? People knew where he worked and where he lived.

'And what did you say?'

'He seemed like a nice man, Herr Reinhart, but I did not want to say much. On the other hand, I did not want to lie. I just said that you come in here every so often: about once a week these days. Was that all right?'

Not really.

'Did he say anything else?'

'Wait.' The barmaid knelt down and emerged with her handbag, which she rummaged through. 'Here, I've found it. He said that if you come in, I'm to give this to you.' She handed him a book of matches with Das Potsdamer Taverne on the front. He looked at it for a while, puzzled.

'Open it.'

Neatly written inside were two dates.

Den 8 Juni 1901

Den 4 Oktober 1929

'Are you all right Herr Reinhart?'

Gunter Reinhart was evidently not all right. The hand that was holding the book of matches was shaking and the other hand was gripping the bar tightly. Beads of sweat had formed on his forehead. He could feel his chest tightening.

'Pardon?'

'Are you all right Herr Reinhart? You look shaken.'

He put the matches in his top pocket and drank most of the glass of beer in one go, pushed the empty glass towards her and nodded for her to refill it.

'I am fine, thank you. Did this man say how I could contact him?'

'He said that he would be here at six o'clock every Thursday and Monday night until he was able to meet up with you.'

Gunter Reinhart stayed in the bar for another hour and three more glasses of beer before he decided to walk all the way home to Charlottenburg. It was a long walk, but he needed that time to compose himself. He crossed Hermann Göring Strasse, which people would quietly joke was almost as wide as the man himself, and into Charlottenburger Chaussee, the Tiergarten an enormous void on his left.

Despite the brisk night air and absence of British bombers, he found himself becoming increasingly tense rather than composed. He had continuously checked the dates before leaving the bar. There was no question about them.

Why on earth would someone write down the birth dates of his first wife and his eldest son, especially when they were no longer in Berlin?

–

The following morning he took extra care on his journey into work to ensure that he wasn't being followed, not that he was sure what he was meant to do. He was a banker: his knowledge of subterfuge was limited to the world of finance. He could move funds from one bank account to another without leaving a trace, but he had absolutely no idea how to walk from one place to another without being spotted and, in any case, he towered above most other people. It would not be hard to follow him. When he arrived at the Reichsbank he casually enquired of his secretary – maybe a bit too casually – whether anyone had been asking for him: '*Perhaps over the past few days?*' His secretary assured him that no one had been asking after him. She looked appalled at the very thought that someone might have enquired of him and she would not have passed the information on.

His head of department informed him that Funk wanted to see them both the next morning: he wanted an urgent and up-to-date report on some of the new Swiss bank accounts. 'You are not to worry,' he assured his head of department, 'the information will be ready.' Pulling it all together was at least a distraction for Reinhart, but it did mean that his head of department fussed around him for the rest of the day. He was a rotund man, with bad breath, whose suit was always too tight and reeked of mothballs. He had been promoted from his natural level as an assistant bank manager somewhere near Magdeburg simply due to a long-standing loyalty to the Nazi Party, and as a consequence was now utterly out of his depth.

The next day – Thursday – followed a sleepless night: the meeting with Walther Funk proved to be but a two-hour distraction, even something of an amusement. The President of the Reichsbank, who doubled as Hitler's Minister of Economics, was someone else who had been promoted because of service to the Nazi Party rather than any kind of financial competence or knowledge. Reinhart produced a series of complicated balance sheets and lengthy lists of transactions: Funk was impressed and confused in equal measure, but unable to own up to the latter.

The afternoon went slowly and, as the sun disappeared over Berlin, Reinhart wondered whether he was being led into a trap. Maybe he had been a bit too clever by half. Maybe he had upset one too many of the Nazi Party bosses at the top of the Reichsbank, who felt they had cause to distrust him. *Gunter Reinhart, the man who knows everything about the Swiss accounts: time to put him in his place.*

Das Potsdamer Taverne was as quiet as it had been the previous night. He nodded at the barmaid and she smiled, slightly shaking her head: *not yet.*

There was a tiny table wedged into a corner behind the bar, where no one else could fit and he waited as the bar became quieter. He was just wondering how long he should remain in the bar when he caught sight of a man who looked vaguely familiar and who seemed to be glancing in his direction. The man remained at the bar, toying with a glass of beer. A few minutes later he appeared at Reinhart's table.

'Do you mind if I sit here?'

Reinhart was almost certain that this man was a friend of his first wife's family, a lawyer – specialised in banking and finance, rather intelligent and a bit too liberal for his liking: Catholic. First name Franz, if he remembered correctly. He doubted, though, that this was the man who had gone to such lengths to meet him. After all, bumping into an acquaintance in the centre of Berlin was hardly the most remarkable of coincidences. The man produced a packet of cigarettes, took one out and placed it in Reinhart's hand.

'Would you like a light?'

Reinhart hesitated. The man reached into his pocket and found a book of matches, one with Das Potsdamer Taverne on the front. As he opened it he casually angled the packet so that Reinhart could clearly see it. Again, two dates were handwritten on the inside of the packet.

Den 8 Juni 1901

Den 4 Oktober 1929

This time it was in the unmistakably familiar handwriting of his first wife. The man shifted his chair even closer to Reinhart and when he spoke again it was in a quieter voice.

'You remember me, Gunter? Franz Hermann. Just act normally, don't speak too loudly or too quietly. Smile occasionally.'

'I remember you, Franz. I guess it was you who's been asking about me here?'

Franz nodded.

'What is it all about? You've given me a couple of sleepless nights.'

'I fear that I am about to give you many more. You see...'

He paused. A couple of Luftwaffe officers had come into the bar and had moved noisily towards them, looking for somewhere to sit. Franz waited until they moved away.

'Good, this is not a conversation that we would want them to overhear. Stop looking so worried Gunter; you'll draw attention to yourself. Just relax and smile: we are friends who have met in a bar.

Don't look like you're being interrogated by the Gestapo. When did you last hear from Rosa?'

Gunter frowned, trying to remember.

'There was a letter from Paris in October. She sent it at the beginning of October but I didn't receive it until the end of the month: it came via a friend of hers in Switzerland and then through my brother.'

'How come?'

'I don't know if you're aware, but I remarried soon after Rosa and I divorced. Far too soon, as it has turned out. It has not turned out to be a happy marriage, but we have children and it is a situation I am stuck with – I only have myself to blame. Gudrun – my second wife – will not tolerate me having any contact whatsoever with either Rosa or our son, Alfred. As far as she is concerned, I have nothing to do with them. It is safer that she thinks that. She has become a devoted Nazi, like the rest of her family. The fact that I was once married to a Jew and had a son with her is a terrible thing in Gudrun's eyes. I have had to promise her that I have no contact whatsoever with Rosa and Alfred, that I have disowned them. Have you heard from her, Franz: is everything all right? What about Alfred?'

'Gunter, unless you keep your voice down and act normally we are going to have a serious problem. Do you understand? Drink some of your beer. Try and look relaxed.'

Gunter nodded and composed himself. 'I understand, but is there any news?'

'For the time being, they are safe.'

'And they're still in Paris?'

Franz Hermann lowered his head and talked a little more quietly.

'A smile please, Gunter, you need to smile. We are old friends meeting for a relaxed drink. Good, that is better. You need to prepare yourself for what I am about to say. They are safe, for the time being: Rosa, Alfred and little Sophia. But I don't know for how long. They are in hiding you see. Here in Berlin.'

–

Gunter Reinhart had to wait three days before he could see his son and his ex-wife, along with her young daughter. Having to wait that long was bad enough, but visiting them on a Sunday presented added problems. Sunday was the day on which his wife demanded his undivided attention, but he insisted that he had work commitments that were none of her business and he was able to slip out of the house once they returned from church.

'They are living with my mother in Dahlem, Gunter: near the Botanischer Garten,' Hermann had told him at the bar. 'My mother has become quite unwell, unable to look after herself. She insists on staying in the old family home. She needed someone to live in and look after her and luckily with her qualifications and experience, Rosa is ideal. She will tell you the full story. On Sundays, my brother-in-law drives over from Brandenburg and takes her back to their house for lunch. She leaves at eleven in the morning and they bring her back at around four, so you see that will not leave much time.'

Not much time.

'There is no reason to think that anyone will suspect what you are up to, Gunter,' Franz had warned him 'but be careful. Assume you are being followed and take basic precautions: walk at an even pace, don't keep looking behind you – that kind of thing.'

So he walked at an even pace across Spandauer Strasse and caught the S-Bahn at Westend. He did as Hermann had advised: making sure he got onto the busiest carriage and watching out for anyone getting on at the same time as him. The train worked its way south at a Sunday pace. At Schmargendorf he changed to the U-Bahn and then headed south again, getting off at Podbielski Allee.

He was not far now: he had not seen his son or Rosa for nearly six months. He had assumed they were out of the country. His excitement at seeing them was mixed in with the shock that they were still in Germany.

From Podbielski Allee he headed down Peter Lenne Strasse towards the Botanischer Garten. He had memorised Hermann's instructions. '*Write nothing down, Gunter.*'

At the end of the road he turned left into Königin-Luise-Strasse, across the square and then continuing along Grunewald Strasse. 'You

85

know Kaiser Wilhelm Strasse, Gunter? Runs off Grunewald Strasse. Turn into there: first right is Arno-Holz Strasse. The white house on the corner is where my mother lives. I will be there from twelve. If the curtains are drawn in the window directly above the front door, it is safe to approach the house, but please only do so if you believe you have not been followed. Otherwise, head on down to the Botanischer Garten at a leisurely pace.'

He did as instructed. In other circumstances he would have enjoyed his walk on what had turned out to be an unseasonably warm after-noon. The house was as Hermann had described it, the front garden deep and heavy with trees, the walls white and in need of repainting and above the front door, a window. The curtains were drawn.

He looked around him once more, but the streets were deserted. He had not been followed. He unlatched a noisy iron gate and walked down the path. As he approached the porch the front door opened and behind it he could see Franz Hermann, silently ushering him in.

They stood together in the dark hall of a silent house.

'Are they here, Franz?'

'Upstairs. Take your shoes off.'

Gunter ran up the stairs. On the landing, waiting for him in the gloom was his ex-wife and their son. Behind them, peering out from behind a door was Sophia, his ex-wife's daughter from her second marriage.

Alfred flung himself at his father, holding him tight and burying his face in his chest. Gunter could feel his warm tears seeping through his shirt and vest. Rosa came up to him and held his face, kissing him tenderly on each cheek, one hand cupping the back of his neck. He could feel tears welling up in his eyes. Little Sophia waved at him. He waved back.

He held both Rosa and Alfred, unsure of what to say. *The only family I ever wanted.*

It was two thirty when Gunter and Rosa sat alone in a small room on the top floor of the house. Franz had told them he would wait with the children and keep an eye on the front. Gunter would need to be away by a quarter to four to be safe. He and Rosa sat quietly for a while, holding hands.

'I thought you were in Paris, Rosa?'

He was trying hard not to sound angry.

'We were in Paris, Gunter. I wrote to you at the beginning of October. Did you get the letter?'

He nodded. She shrugged.

'Harald was meant to join us in the middle of October: he had remained in Berlin because he needed to make a few arrangements. The idea was that he would get what money he could out of the business – which was not much – and transfer it to Switzerland. Then we would have something to live on and, together with the money you gave us, we may be able to get on to America.'

'That was the idea.'

'I promise you that was the plan. As you know, Harald had been forced to sell the business to two of his managers for a fraction of what it was worth. Both of them were men who had been friends of his, who he had always helped in the past. They had always said that they would help him and one of them did, but the other refused. I don't know exactly what happened, but from what I can gather Harald was reported to the Gestapo for trying to get money out of Germany, which is illegal for a Jew to do. I suspect that the manager he had fallen out with was the person who reported him to the Gestapo. So Harald was arrested and taken to Sachsenhausen – it's a special camp for prisoners of the Nazis. Have you heard of it?'

'Of course I have – near Oranienburg. Are you sure he is there?'

'Believe me, I am sure. Terrible things happen there. I don't like to think about what he must be going through. I know that he is still alive, or at least he was two weeks ago, but I don't know what state he is in.'

'So why on earth did you come back here? What were you thinking of, Rosa?'

'I don't know what I was thinking, Gunter. Please don't be angry with me. I thought that if my husband was in prison here then I should come back to help him. I thought I could get him released.'

'But, Rosa, what about Alfred – and Sophia?'

'I know, Gunter. But remember, we left Germany for France in July. I had no idea how bad things had become. In Paris I borrowed

87

some money from my cousin and I sold all of my jewellery. I thought I could pay a fine or a bribe or something like that and get Harald released. But when I went to the police station they confiscated my passport and wanted to know where I was living. I gave them the address of the old flat in Pankow that we were staying at and they only let me go because I had papers showing I was registered there. I knew that they would come for us, but fortunately, I had left the children with my old colleague Maria in Kreuzberg while I went to the police station. When I left I went straight to Kreuzberg, picked up Alfred and Sophia and then contacted Franz. He took us to his house, which is also in Dahlem, for a few days and then came up with this plan for us to move here in with his mother. It has worked out well: the old lady is almost deaf and cannot climb the stairs, so as long as the children are quiet and stay upstairs, they are all right and she has no idea that they are here.'

'And she doesn't suspect you?'

'She has been told that I am a nurse from Bremerhaven whose husband is in the Navy. Of course, I don't let on that I am a doctor. I can use all my skills to keep her alive. If she dies then we will have to leave the house. I have some papers that Franz managed to get hold of showing that I am from Bremerhaven, but they are not good enough to travel with. Franz comes round most days. The old lady has very few visitors other than that: one or two friends who pop in for an hour every so often, but they always call first. Franz's sister does not know the truth about me but I think she is just grateful that someone is looking after her mother, which means she doesn't have to.'

'And the children?'

'It is terrible for them here; they just have to stay upstairs all day. Poor Sophia has no idea what is going on, other than that her father is in prison and she has to keep quiet all of the time. Alfred knows what is going on, of course. That makes it worse, I suppose. He misses you terribly, Gunter.'

Gunter sat for a while with his head in his hands, deep in thought.

'Why didn't you contact me before now – I mean, once you got back to Berlin?'

Rosa looked at him long and hard. *You don't know why?*

'Gunter – you always said that I was not to contact you directly. You said Gudrun would not allow it. I did not know what your situation is, whether it was safe. I also thought you would be angry with me. I was hoping that we would find a way back to France. Franz was going to see if he could find false papers, but it is impossible. We are trapped here in Berlin, Gunter.'

Rosa was weeping now, her trembling hand holding Gunter's.

'I should never have divorced you Rosa, I was—'

'Don't blame yourself, Gunter. We agreed it was for the best.'

'No, I was being selfish. The three of us should have left after that damn law was passed...'

They sat in silence for a long while.

'It is three fifteen, Gunter. Franz says you are to leave soon. Please spend some time with Alfred before you go. He misses you so much.'

'I don't know what to do, Rosa. Do you need food or money?'

'Yes, but what we really need is to get out: even if you can just save Alfred. As far as the Nazis are concerned, he is only a half-Jew. Could you take him? Would Gudrun not understand?'

Gunter laughed. 'Understand? Even if I said that you had abandoned Alfred and I had found him in the middle of Berlin, she would not want to know. When we got married she made me promise I would never, ever have anything to do with the two of you again. Frankly, I would not put it past her to turn him in. Her brother Norbert, who has all the intelligence of a field mouse but with less of the personality – he's now a big shot in the Nazi Party in Bergdorf, which says everything you need to know about him. The fact that I was once married to a Jew is a terrible secret in that family. Gudrun insists that the children are not allowed to know about it.'

'But what are we going to do, Gunter?'

'I don't know Rosa. Give me time, I'll think of something.'

Chapter 8

Geneva & Bern, June 1940

'*Do nothing unusual and certainly nothing that is likely to draw attention to yourself.*'

For eight long months Henry Hunter, otherwise known as Henri Hesse, had followed Edgar's advice, leading an unremarkable existence. The waiting to be contacted was tedious and living with his mother even more so. The fact that he was now in control of the purse strings was more than she could bear. It was 'intolerable', she announced during a dramatic argument on the night he returned. She could not understand why he had returned with so little of the aunt's money.

He explained their predicament once more, very clearly and very slowly.

'Remember it was your clever idea to bypass probate and for me to attempt to bring all the money back here as soon as possible. That proved to be simply impossible – and illegal: I could have ended up in prison. I have told you what happened: I had to go to London and stay there for all that time to sort out the money. I was tangled up in reels and reels of red tape and then war was declared at the beginning of September, which made matters almost impossible. The British Government simply do not want to release money to go overseas, they say they cannot be sure whose hands it will end up in. You ought to be grateful that I managed to get anything out at all and return in one piece.'

'But it is our money, Henri!'

'*My* money, actually, mother and not all of it, as it turned out. In the end the authorities accepted my explanation that there had been a misunderstanding over the will. I was fortunate. Then it took a few more weeks for probate to be granted. After that, I had to obtain agreement that the money could be released but, as I told you, I don't get it in one sum. You were advanced 200 pounds, I will be able to access a further 500 over the next few days and the rest of the money will then come through at a rate of 100 pounds per month. It is not the amount we had hoped for, mother, but it is enough for us to be able to live far more comfortably.'

Since the death of her second husband, Marlene Hesse's perfectly-formed world had steadily unravelled. She now accepted the changed situation with the minimum of grace. At least they had been able to afford to rent a larger apartment in a much more respectable location just off Quai du Mont Blanc, which was some consolation.

But the wait to be contacted was considerably more trying than his mother. Two days after his return he had gone, as instructed by Edgar, to the Quai des Bergues branch of Credit Suisse and made an appointment to see Madame Ladnier later that morning. In a small office in the basement she went through the details of the account, before handing him a folded piece of paper.

My home telephone number: I only give this to special clients and then only to be used in particular circumstances. You understand?

After that, nothing. As soon as they moved into their new apartment he went to see Madame Ladnier to give her the details. She assured him the matter would be dealt with. He was desperate to ask her if there was any news, but managed to restrain himself.

He began to follow a routine, in the hope that that would make it easier for whoever would approach him: leaving the apartment at a certain time, returning to it at a certain time, an afternoon walk, the shops...

Christmas came and went, celebrated mostly in silence with his still-embittered mother, and January brought the snows down from the Alps, but still no contact. By the end of the month he had started to wonder if he would never be contacted, and to wonder if this would be no bad thing. Perhaps they had forgotten about him; at least the money was still appearing in his account. There was the occasional contact from Viktor, and he always told him the same: no news. Loyalty was proving to be a most complicated business.

At the end of February he received a phone call from Madame Ladnier. Could he come into the bank to sign a document? 'You are not to worry,' she assured him. 'They have told me to tell you that you will be contacted in due course, but it may take a few months. Remain patient – and discreet.'

The same happened at the end of April: 'They want me to assure you that you have not been forgotten. Be patient. It should not be too long now.' Viktor was not surprised when he told him – 'There's no rush, *synok* – that is how people like us operate.'

On the last Tuesday in June, Henri left the apartment off Quai du Mont Blanc as usual at nine thirty. It was already a warm morning, with a light breeze skimming over the lake. As he headed south for a brisk walk before breakfast a woman swept past him before slowing down and studying a map. As he drew alongside her she looked surprised and then spoke in French with a Provençal accent, much faster than the Swiss.

'I am sorry, sir, I appear to be lost! I am looking for the Old Town. Do you know the way?'

It was so natural, so matter-of-fact that Henri was taken aback and thought this could not possibly be the contact, who he had assumed would be a man. It must be a coincidence he thought, but then he noticed that she was carrying a copy of Monday's *Tribune de Genève*. It took him a moment to compose himself.

'Of course. Would you prefer to walk or take the tram?'

She smiled. 'I would prefer to walk if you are able to show me the way to go.'

Another smile and a slight hesitation before Henri replied, 'Well, I am walking to the Old Town myself now. If you wish, you are most welcome to follow me.'

She smiled and theatrically held out an elegantly gloved hand. *Lead on.*

'*Take any route to the Old Town.*'

Henri tried to walk at a normal pace as he headed to the Old Town, unsure what a normal pace felt like. He crossed the Rhône at the Pont des Bergues, allowing himself a glance behind to check that the woman was still following. He crossed the Rue de la Rôtisserie into the Old Town and soon after that the woman overtook him: it was now his turn to follow her. She walked through alleyways, crossed roads, waited on corners and eventually they emerged onto Rue de l'Hôtel de Ville. Her pace did not change, other than when she paused briefly at a shop window. Henri was wondering how long this would go on for, but then they crossed into the Grand-Rue and there on the corner was the Brasserie de Hôtel de Ville and outside it a wastepaper bin, into which she dropped her copy of *Tribune de Genève*. She carried on walking, but Henri knew that his rendezvous would take place here. He entered the cafe.

'*You are to enter the building and wait. If no one has approached you after five minutes, you are to leave the building and return home.*'

He glanced at his wristwatch and the clock on the wall. Within two minutes a man entered the cafe, smoking a cigar and greeting two people sat at a nearby table. He shook hands with the barman and walked straight over to Henri.

'I am Marc. Would you care to join me?'

'*If someone joins you and introduces themselves as Marc you are to go with him. He will take you to meet your main contact. At that moment, your new career will have begun.*'

Henri nodded. Beside the bar was a door which Marc opened. *After you.*

A narrow staircase twisted and turned to the top of the building. When they reached a small landing Marc gestured for him to wait and then knocked three times on a polished oak door.

'It is me, Marc. I have the delivery.'

Henri heard a bolt being drawn and then the door opened. It was a corner room, expensively furnished with an ornate fireplace and a thick carpet: one wall was taken up with a floor-to-ceiling bookcase, many of the volumes leather-bound. On a French-polished sideboard there was an exquisite cut glass decanter with matching glasses on a silver tray. Next to that was another tray, with a teapot and various cups.

The door was opened by a dapper man in his sixties who was wearing a three-piece suit. His iron grey hair, going white at the sides, was slicked back, slightly longer than Henri would have expected.

'Ah, Hunter: welcome! At long last. Welcome indeed. Sorry about all this John Buchan stuff. Not really my idea: seems to be the form these days. Apparently we can't be too careful.' It was a distinctly upper-class drawl.

'Now do come in and make yourself at home. My name is Basil by the way, like the Swiss city.'

'Pardon?'

'Basle, Hunter. The Swiss seems to find it amusing, or at least they would if they allowed themselves the indulgence of a sense of humour. Basil Remington-Barber. There's an "Hon" that goes in front of the name if you're a stickler for that kind of thing. As far as the Swiss are concerned I am a commercial attaché at the British Embassy in Bern. As far as you are concerned I run the station out here in Switzerland. And, if you are still confused, that means I look after all intelligence matters from our place on Thunstrasse. Thought it would be a quiet place to wind up my career. Had rather expected to have retired by now, but I am told there's a war on and someone in London has decided that I am indispensable: helps that I speak the lingo I suppose, all of them as it happens. Had hoped to be hacking my way round some of Scotland's easier links courses by now, but there we go.'

With that, he switched to Swiss German, alternating between it and German. 'Now tell me, Hunter: are you raring to go or had you been hoping that we'd forgotten all about you?' That sentence had been delivered in Swiss German. Henri replied in the same language.

'Well, I can't really say. I imagine that—'

'Bit of both probably, perfectly understandable – not knowing is the worst part. Sorry about the delay, but the good news is the waiting's over. The fall of France has rather spurred London into action, as far as I can gather. We have a little errand for you. But first of all, let us have some tea: milk and sugar?'

Henri relaxed a bit now. The civilised serving of tea, and the promise of a little errand, sounded quite acceptable, perhaps even fun.

What was it Edgar had promised? '*Chances are that the first job will be something relatively straightforward, probably within Switzerland. Shouldn't be anything too dangerous; a warm up, if you like.*'

The Hon. Basil Remington-Barber took a while to serve tea, fussing over Henri's and then his own to check that it was neither too weak nor too strong. When he was satisfied that everything was just right, he leaned back in his armchair and addressed Henri through the steam rising from his china teacup. Henri was beginning to enjoy his morning. His pleasure was to be short-lived.

'We understand that you are very familiar with Stuttgart, Hunter?'

'I beg your pardon?' Henri felt his throat tightening.

'Stuttgart, the German city?'

Henri placed his teacup down on the side table next to him. His hands were beginning to shake and he needed to cover that up, so he folded them on his lap, crossing and then un-crossing his legs as he did so.

'Yes, I know it.'

'Been there often?'

'Once or twice.'

'Really?'

Henri shrugged. *Not sure.*

'*Quite* a few times, we understand, Hunter.'

'Well, possibly...'

'Something that you omitted to tell any of my colleagues back in England?'

Henri hesitated for longer than he knew he should. 'Forgot rather than omitted, I would say.' He was not convinced by his own answer. Nor was Basil Remington-Barber, who shook his head in mild disapproval. 'I rather know the feeling. I seem to forget the odd thing these days. My wife tells me I'm starting to remind her of how her father was just before he went completely potty! The old boy had to be locked up after he shot one of his gamekeepers: thought he was a pheasant, apparently. The point is though, Hunter, that not mentioning Stuttgart is a rather important omission. Perhaps you would like to tell me about it now?'

Henri tried to sound as casual as possible, hoping to convey the impression that his knowledge of Stuttgart was really nothing very important, the kind of thing that one could so easily forget.

'There is not an awful lot to say. My stepfather had some property in Stuttgart. I used to pop up there every so often to keep an eye on things for him.'

'How often would "every so often" be, Hunter?'

'I really couldn't say. Once or twice a year, maybe.'

'My very strong advice, Hunter,' Remington-Barber had dispensed with the bonhomie, 'would be that you are totally honest from now on. You see, your first mission is to go up to Stuttgart, and the more that we know about your familiarity with the city, the better. I do hope you understand that.'

'*Shouldn't be anything too dangerous; a warm-up, if you like.*'

'Edgar implied that my first mission would be within Switzerland.'

'Did he now? Well, that is Edgar for you: an officer but not quite a gentleman. Grammar school, I am told. Now, tell me all about Stuttgart.'

'My stepfather had a fair amount of residential property in Stuttgart, in the best areas: quite a lot in Gänseheide to the east of the city centre and more in the north, Azenberg and Killesberg mostly. He had local agents that looked after them, but he liked me to go up there once a quarter to check everything was in order and to oversee the transfer of his rental income back to Switzerland.'

'So you visited Stuttgart four times a year?'

'Yes.'

'For how many years?'

'Seven or eight, possibly more.'

'Mathematics was never my strongest subject, Hunter, but I make that somewhere in the region of thirty visits to Stuttgart.'

'If you say so.'

'I do. So you are very familiar with the city?'

'I suppose so.'

'Speak the local dialect?'

'No, though I do understand it.'

'And where did you stay?'

'Usually at Hotel Marquardt in Schlossplatz.'

'That is certainly quite an omission, Hunter. Don't worry too much; I am sure that you are about to more than make up for it.'

–

Henri Hesse could never quite see the point of Bern. It was a pretty enough place, with an undoubted medieval charm, and the River Aare leant a certain picturesque drama to the city as it twisted through the centre. But in a typically Swiss way it was rather too aware of its virtues; a little bit too smug. For the past ninety years or so the city had been the capital of Switzerland, and now all roads led to it and, in the case of Hunter's journey there on a windy Wednesday morning, so did the trains.

At the end of their briefing the previous day, the Hon. Basil Remington-Barber had told him to get a move on. Henri had rather imagined that this meant by the end of the month, possibly within a fortnight.

'A fortnight? You must be joking, Hunter. No, this week. Get up to Bern tomorrow, sort out your visa and then I'll give you your precise instructions.'

He explained to his mother that he was visiting friends in Basle for a few days and took an early morning train to Bern, arriving at the station in Bahnhofplatz just in time for lunch. Henri had been pleasantly surprised when Remington-Barber suggested he book into the Schweizerhof, the best hotel in the city and no more than a very short stroll from the station.

'Rather goes against the grain, Hunter, and certainly pushes the expenses, but the point is that you have to stick to your role: as far as the Germans are concerned, you are an affluent Swiss gentleman who wishes to travel to Stuttgart on business. Such people stay at the Schweizerhof, I am afraid. Make sure you're seen out and about in the hotel. There's something like one hundred and fifteen thousand people in this city and I think that if you took the spies away, it would be less than one hundred thousand. Most of the spies hang around the Schweizerhof, so it's good to be seen, just being yourself. Book yourself in for two nights. I just hope London buy it.'

'*Make sure you're seen out and about in the hotel.*' Once he had checked in and changed, he went down to the restaurant. The restaurant manager asked him to wait at the bar, where he found himself along-side two very formally dressed middle-aged men speaking in German. The two Germans greeted him correctly, almost standing to attention as they did so.

'What brings you to Bern?' they asked. Henri explained that he was from Geneva but was here in Bern to arrange a visa: he was hoping visit Germany soon on business.

'Whereabouts?'

'Stuttgart.'

'Very good.' *Was Herr Hesse likely to be in Berlin at any time in the future?*

'Maybe. You never know!'

'You will look me up if you do. There are so many misunderstand-ings about Germany these days. I am sure that you are not one of those people, Herr Hesse, who thinks nothing but bad of Germany; we are, after all, of the same race, yes?'

Henri nodded enthusiastically. *Indeed.*

'But if you are ever in Berlin, I could introduce you to people. You will be pleasantly surprised. I would be happy to be of service.'

With that he presented Henri with a card, bowed slightly and then left. Henri looked at the card:

Alois Jäger
Rechtsanwalt
181 Friedrichstraße
Berlin

A Berlin lawyer; you never know.

The next morning, he visited the German Embassy on Willadingweg. As he planned his journey there, he remembered Remington-Barber's instructions.

'Whatever you do, Hunter, keep well away from where we are in Thunstrasse. There's a good chance you may be seen, the Germans pretty much keep a permanent watch outside our place. You know how you are to get hold of me.'

He breakfasted at the hotel, returned to his room briefly and then strolled casually through the Old City, past the Münster – the enormous Gothic cathedral, over whose main entrance the sculpted participants in *The Last Judgement* gazed down at him, trying to decide whether he was wicked or virtuous.

He crossed the river on Kirchenfeldbrücke and soon found a taxi which took him to the German Embassy, located in a residential street in the east of the city. A large swastika hung limply over the entrance, which was guarded by half a dozen armed German soldiers. In the street outside were two Swiss policemen.

He had expected a short delay, but not the queue which greeted him. The visa office, the man in front of him explained, did not open until eleven. It would close for lunch at one, re-open again at three and then close again at five. The man looked up and down the queue. They do not hurry, he told Henri, but with some luck you may be seen sometime around four. Then you will have to return tomorrow to collect the visa.

He had been standing in the queue for an hour and a half when he heard a familiar voice behind him; Jäger, the Berlin lawyer.

'My dear Hesse, what are you doing in the queue? Come with me.'

To the obvious annoyance of the people in front of him, Henri was removed from the queue and escorted straight into the Embassy.

Wait here.

It was one fifteen now and the visa office had closed for lunch. Ten minutes later Jäger emerged from it with a clearly reluctant man in tow.

'Hesse: Herr Soldner himself will look after you. You could not be in better hands. He has volunteered to curtail his lunch break in order to deal with your visa.'

It was evident that Herr Soldner was no mere clerk, as much as he looked like one. As they marched through the ground floor of the embassy to his office on the third floor colleagues greeted him with a '*Sieg Heil*', which he returned enthusiastically. His office was well appointed, overlooking the gardens at the rear of the embassy. There was a portrait of Hitler on the wall and a large photograph on the desk of Herr Soldner shaking hands with some officers in black uniforms. Next to that was a smaller photograph of Herr Soldner with what he assumed was Frau Soldner and their children. On his lapel was a swastika badge. He gestured for Henri to sit down, removed his spectacles and then read through Henri's form, nodding at times, making notes in the margin in places.

'Please explain the purpose of your visit to Stuttgart, Herr Hesse.'

Henri spoke in standard German, repeating the story that he and Remington-Barber had agreed.

'My stepfather had some business interests in Stuttgart – property mostly. Unfortunately, he died two years ago, and I want to ensure that there are no outstanding liabilities. Tie up loose ends, if you like.'

'Do you have any bank accounts in Germany, Herr Hesse?'

'No.'

'Do you have friends in Stuttgart?'

'More like acquaintances – business contacts.'

'Their names please.'

Henri gave the names of the two lawyers they dealt with, along with the three property agents who handled the various properties.

Herr Soldner wrote each name down. He then put down his pen and put on his spectacles.

'The last name you gave me, Herr Hesse – one of the agents.'

'Bermann?'

'Yes: first name please.'

'Heinz: Heinz Bermann.'

'A friend of yours?'

'As I say, more of an acquaintance, a business associate.'

'When did you last see Bermann?'

'Last time I was in Stuttgart, some three years ago.'

'And were you planning to see him this time?'

'Possibly.'

'Do you realise that if you did so, Herr Hesse, that would be in breach of the conditions of your visa?'

'Really... why is that?'

'The very strong likelihood is that Bermann is a Jew – an enemy of the state.'

With only the briefest hesitation, Henri slapped his thigh in annoyance.

'You don't say! Well that would explain a lot, Herr Soldner. I did not want to say too much before I went there, but we never totally trusted this Bermann. We always suspected that he was being less than honest with us. That was one of the reasons for my visit, to find out whether he owed us money. Typical.'

'If he is still in Stuttgart, Herr Hesse, he will no longer have any assets in his own name.'

He wrote on a plain sheet of paper and attached it to the visa application, placing the complete document in a tray.

'Your passport please, Herr Hesse.'

He handed his Swiss passport over to the German.

'Please wait in the reception on the ground floor. I will call you when I am ready. You will understand that I need to make some enquiries.'

–

'The one thing we could get unstuck on, Henri, is if they delve too far back,' Remington-Barber had told him. 'The only problem would be if they found out that either you or your mother also has British nationality.'

'That would be most unlikely. My mother hated being Maureen Hunter, she thought it sounded common. She has always regarded becoming Marlene Hesse and taking on Swiss nationality as the height of sophistication. She changed her name and her nationality when she married Erich Hesse in 1923 and I am certain that she has not used her English name or British identity since then, which is nearly seventeen years ago. Also, remember we moved from Zurich to Geneva after this happened. I became a Swiss national in 1927, and as far as the Swiss authorities are concerned, I'm Henri Hesse.'

'Well, the Germans would have to dig very deep indeed to find all this out, and they're only going to do that if they suspect anything. Obviously, we hope that they don't.'

Obviously.

–

An hour later Adolf Hitler was once more staring at the man they called Henry Hunter, who was attempting to remain as calm as possible after being summoned back to Herr Soldner's office.

'Your visa is valid for thirty days from next Monday, which is the 1st of July. It expires on the 30th July. You will be in breach of your visa if you are in Germany after that date: do you understand?'

Henri nodded. He was hoping to be back in Switzerland long before then.

'You are only permitted to stay in Stuttgart. While in Germany you must not take part in any political activities; you are prohibited from meeting or consorting with Jews, criminals or other enemies of the state; you will register at a hotel within two hours of your arrival and are not permitted to stay anywhere else during your stay. You are not allowed to approach any military establishments or observe any movements of the armed forces. You are not permitted to take photographs. The only currency that you are allowed to use in Germany is Reichsmarks: upon your arrival you are to go to a bank and exchange your Swiss Francs for Reichsmarks. I should warn you that using the black market is regarded as a serious criminal activity. It should not be necessary for me to warn you that should anyone approach you and ask for your help, particularly in regard to bringing information or messages back to Switzerland, that is also regarded as a very serious criminal activity. You should immediately report any such approach to the authorities. Do you understand?'

Henri did.

'Good. I do hope that you enjoy your visit to Germany, Herr Hesse.'

–

An hour later Henri Hesse entered a cobblers on an arcade on Kramgasse and explained to the bearded man just visible behind a mound of shoes on the counter that he had caught the heel of one of his shoes in the tramline by the station. The cobbler nodded and lifted the counter top, beckoning for Henri to come through.

'Go up the stairs to the very top: He is waiting for you.'

The Hon, Basil Remington-Barber greeted Henri warmly.

'Beauty of this place is that I can get into it through the back of a cafe about five doors along. Now, tell me how you got on.'

Remington-Barber checked the passport and the visa. 'All in order: good.' He was, he said, as certain as he could be that the Germans suspected nothing. For the next hour he gave Henri a detailed briefing on the Stuttgart mission.

'You've got everything, Henry. All clear?'

'Yes, although you say that I am going to be contacted by this Milo. I'm still not sure how I will know that it is him?'

'And I told you – don't worry. Milo will find you: you have memorised the codes, so you will know. The less you know before you meet up, the safer it is.'

'In case I am caught?'

'Exactly, in case you are caught. Remember, you do whatever Milo tells you, you understand?' Henri said he did.

'There's plenty of Swiss Francs in this envelope here: change them into Reichsmarks as soon as you arrive – don't risk hiding any on you. Go back now to the Schweizerhof and check out: there's a direct train to Geneva at six thirty. Before you leave the Schweizerhof ask them to make you a reservation at the Hotel Victoria in Stuttgart, arriving Tuesday the 16th, leaving on the Friday – the 19th. It looks better if you leave a couple of weeks between the visa being granted and you actually travelling there: makes it appear that you're not rushing. Understand?'

Henri nodded.

'One other thing: be careful at night in Stuttgart. There is a curfew on, and few places to eat, so you are to eat in the hotel. On the first night certainly, you should order room service: in my experience that tends to draw less attention to yourself.'

'And how would you like me to get to Stuttgart?'

'On the Monday morning you take the train from Geneva to Zurich: tell your mother you will be there all week. Give her this address; we'll cover any contacts there. Stay overnight at the Central Plaza hotel by Oetenbachgasse, it is very near the station: a room has been booked for you there. On Tuesday morning there's a Swissair flight from Zurich to Stuttgart. It should only take fifty minutes. Here's hoping the RAF doesn't shoot you down!'

Chapter 9

Salzburg Airport, July 1940

Early in the afternoon of the last Tuesday in July, at the height of the Austrian summer, half a dozen men were doing their best to avoid each other in a stuffy room overlooking the runway at Salzburg Airport. The men were all dressed in uniforms denoting high rank in various branches of the German armed forces: two stood by the large window, but well apart from each other; another appeared to be asleep; two others were leafing through their copies of *Völkischer Beobachter*; and another was pacing the room, drawing hard on a cigarette as he did so.

A short while after the clock struck two, a nervous young Luftwaffe officer entered the room. 'A delay: many apologies. The plane was delayed after refuelling in Munich. Departure will now be at three o'clock – four at the latest.'

Much muttering and shaking of heads around the room: the young Luftwaffe officer paused in the doorway just long enough to remember to give a hurried '*Heil Hitler*' salute which was ignored by all the others.

The man who had appeared to be asleep stood up and carefully straightened his Kriegsmarine uniform before leaving the room. Outside was a small lawn with flowers planted neatly around its edges. He strolled up and down and was soon joined by an army officer, one of the two men who had been by the window. The admiral and the general walked in step alongside each other in silence for a while. The general took his time lighting a large cigar before addressing his companion.

'I see we cannot even rely on the Luftwaffe to get us back to Berlin on time! I imagine that Jodl's plane was not delayed.'

'He flew back last night, I understand: soon after the briefing,' said the admiral, looking around as he spoke. 'He probably did not want to hang around too long.'

'Indeed. I assume he wanted to avoid our questions,' said the general, speaking in a louder voice than his companion.

The admiral nodded and looked over each shoulder before he spoke. 'And how is your son?'

The *Generalmajor* paused, slightly surprised by the question. In the circles he moved in, in Berlin, asking questions about an acquaintance's family, especially sons in the armed forces, was a form of code – a way of broaching the sensitive issue of what one really thought about the war. It was the same as discussing food shortages with people. These were questions only asked of people you could really trust.

'Karl is well, thank you; he's an *Oberleutnant* now, based in Poland. And yours? You have two, don't you?'

'One son, one daughter. Ernst joined the Kriegsmarine naturally, but unlike his father, uncles and grandfather, he seems to prefer to be under the water rather than on its surface! He's with the 7th U-boat flotilla based in Kiel.'

The two men paused to watch a Luftwaffe Junkers passenger plane pass low overhead from the south, neatly framed against Untersberg mountain. The plane banked to the left and began its noisy approach to the runway.

'That must be our plane; we could well be back in Berlin this evening after all. Tell me Ernst: what do you make of what Jodl had to say...?'

Generalmajor Ernst turned to face his companion, carefully studying his face. He wanted to be sure he was not being led into a trap.

'You mean about...?' It was clear he wanted the admiral to say it first.

'The invasion plans: what else were we there for?'

'He only wants us to *plan* for an invasion of the Soviet Union, Hans. That is probably prudent don't you think – to make contingency plans, in case...?'

'Come on Ernst: we have known each other for many years! I was watching you yesterday during Jodl's briefing, you hardly looked enthusiastic. It's madness, you must know that better than me. Just imagine for a moment that you were a British general rather than a German one and you had found out that the *Führer* had ordered his high command to turn up in Bad Reichenhall yesterday to be instructed to plan for an invasion of the Soviet Union. You'd be delighted, wouldn't you?'

The *Generalmajor* shrugged. Behind them a plane was noisily taxiing in front of the building where they had been waiting. 'I think our flight will be ready soon, Hans.'

'Come on Ernst, answer my question. If you were a British general you would be very pleased to hear that Germany was planning to break its alliance with the Soviet Union and fight on two fronts, would you not?'

'I think that more than anything, Hans, I would be surprised. So surprised in fact that I would struggle to believe it.'

Chapter 10

Stuttgart, July 1940

'I was only asking what business it is that you have in Zurich, Henri. Surely I have a right to ask? One minute you're off to Basle, then Zurich... wherever next?'

Marlene Hesse had little choice but to accept her son's imminent and largely unexplained departure with her customary lack of grace. Henri had come to learn that these days all he needed to do was tell her what he was doing and then leave it at that.

He arrived in Zurich on the Monday and spent that night in a hotel on Oetenbachgasse where his flight tickets were waiting for him. He left the hotel early the next morning and took the airport bus from Hauptbahnhof station at seven o'clock.

The flight left on time at eight fifteen, the Swissair DC3 banking heavily to the east before climbing noisily through the cloud and then appearing to float as they headed north and crossed the border. The plane landed at Stuttgart Echterdingen just after nine thirty; a few minutes before they had begun their descent the two stewardesses had come round and drawn all the curtains. Henri was in a single seat, but he heard a man sitting in a double seat across the aisle from him explain to his neighbour in French that they always did this. 'It is a military airport now. They don't want us to spy on the Luftwaffe!'

The captain welcomed them to Germany, with a noticeable lack of enthusiasm. 'Please respect all the special security rules in place at the airport. Please follow all instructions. Passengers for the onward flight to Berlin should remain in their seats. Passengers disembarking here in Stuttgart should ensure they have all their belongings with them.

We hope that you have enjoyed flying with Swissair. We wish you a pleasant stay in Stuttgart.'

The plane taxied to a remote part of the airport: outside they could hear shouting and the noise of engines. The passengers were led down the steps to a bus with blacked-out windows that had drawn up alongside it. Henri had no more than thirty seconds to glance around as they were led onto the bus: he could see very little, other than a ring of troops around the plane and a couple of oil tankers nearby.

There were few other passengers in the vast terminal building, although at the far end Henri could see groups of men in uniform hurrying along. At the other end of the terminal were the airline desks, most of which appeared to be abandoned. There were a few people waiting by one of the Deutsche Lufthansa desks, but the only other airline desks that seemed to be operating were Swissair and Ala Littoria. While he waited there were a few announcements made by a woman just managing to suppress her Swabian accent: '*Arriving passengers should wait until they are called; any passengers for the Swissair flight to Berlin are to proceed to the departure gate immediately; a further delay is announced on the Deutsche Lufthansa flight to Lisbon, Portugal.*'

Henri was questioned by two men that stood behind the desk; one in SS uniform, the other in a cheap suit with a swastika badge on each lapel. Behind them was a large clock with enormous swastika banners draped on either side.

They each checked the visa, silently. The man in civilian clothes left the desk at one stage with Henri's passport, but returned a minute later.

'How long are you intending to stay in Stuttgart, Herr Hesse?'

'Until Friday.'

'You have a return ticket?'

Henri handed it to them and they both studied it before returning it.

'And the purpose of your visit?'

'Where are you staying?'

'With whom will you be meeting?'

'Are you aware of the restrictions of your visa?'

All questions that had already been asked at the embassy in Bern: Remington-Barber had warned him of this. *Routine. They will just be trying to catch you out. They'll be looking to compare your answers. Nothing to worry about. Just play a straight bat. Don't smile too much. Don't get impatient.*

'We would like to know more about your business affairs in Stuttgart, Herr Hesse,' said the civilian.

An unnecessarily detailed and complicated account of his stepfather's business affairs in Stuttgart followed. Henri told how he suspected they had been mishandled by a man called Heinz Bermann – at the mention of which there was a knowing look between the two Germans – and how following his stepfather's death – which was probably hastened by the activities of this Heinz Bermann – it was taking time to unravel everything, but he felt it was his duty to come here and see what was going on… and so on. It had the desired effect of making the two officials look bored. Henri hoped to God that poor old Heinz Bermann had managed to get out of Stuttgart: he was a decent man and had always been very charming. It would be a shame if Henri had just added to his woes.

After ten minutes, Henri was taken through to a small side room where he and his bags were thoroughly searched by two policemen. His copy of that morning's *Neue Zürcher Zeitung* was removed from his briefcase and thrown away. Everything else was carefully examined. Nothing else aroused their suspicion, other than the Swiss Francs.

'Are you changing all of these here?' the official in charge of the search asked.

Henri nodded.

'Wait here while I count them.'

The official left the room, returning with the francs five minutes later. Later, Henri would discover that the official had helped himself to some of the money.

He emerged from the side room into the queue in front of yet another desk, but this was a much quicker process. His passport was stamped again and he was now in Germany.

'You are now permitted to cross the border, Herr Hesse. Please go the cashier's window over there and change all money into Reichsmarks. Welcome to Germany.'

Henri changed his money and then joined a queue which had formed just outside the terminal for the bus into the city. The journey took half an hour: again, the curtains were drawn and it was difficult to make out where they were, other than through occasional glimpses through the front window. Henri thought he recognised one or two familiar sights and as far as he could tell, there were few signs of the war, other than a good deal of military traffic on the road. They passed through two road-blocks, at the final one of which three policemen climbed on board and checked everyone's papers.

'*Stuttgart-Mitte*,' announced the driver: The bus pulled into Fürstenstrasse, just off the enormous Schlossplatz.

It was no more than three or four minutes' walk to the hotel and Henri knew the area well, but somehow the city centre did not feel familiar, although it was hard for him to put a finger on precisely why. The buildings were the same, he recognised the street names and knew exactly where he was. But for him, any city had always had a unique atmosphere to it, which was hard to describe, though he knew it when he was there. Despite its familiarity, Stuttgart did not feel like somewhere he had ever been to before, as if he had only ever seen it on film. The city now had an undoubted military edge to it; so many of the people on the streets seemed to be wearing a uniform of one type or another, and there were anti-aircraft batteries on the Schlossplatz. Most of the buildings had large red-and-black swastika flags draped from them.

By the time he had reached the Hotel Victoria on the corner of Friedrichstrasse and Keplerstrasse, and walked through its ornate entrance, he had a better idea why Stuttgart felt so unfamiliar. It was the people and how they behaved, moving around in silence, hardly anyone speaking to anyone else, and all of them appearing to avoid eye contact. A city that he had once found friendly now had a distinctly menacing air to it. Germans had always struck him as being smartly dressed but now, compared to the relative sophistication of the Swiss, they looked drab.

The man behind the reception desk did, at least, look him in the eye. 'Yes, we have a reservation for you, Herr Hesse,' he said, holding up the telegram from the Schweizerhof in Bern. 'You are staying for three nights, correct?'

Henri said that was indeed correct and completed the various forms handed to him by the receptionist. He was then escorted to his room on the third floor by an elderly and evidently arthritic porter. Once he had unpacked, he decided to go for a walk in the afternoon. As tempting as remaining in the relative safety of his room was, he knew that would draw attention to himself, and also would not allow Milo the opportunity to approach him, though he was still none the wiser as to how that was going to happen. Remington-Barber had been decidedly cryptic with regards to that during their meeting in Bern.

'You will be approached by someone using the phrase "We usually have some rain in Stuttgart at this time of year",' Remington-Barber had said. 'You are to reply "That must be the case all over Europe". In response they will say "Surely there must be rain over the Alps". You will reply "There is always rain around the Alps, even in summer", and when they say "How wonderful", then you know it is Milo speaking to you and that it is safe.'

Remington-Barber had asked him to repeat that, many times.

'Good: you are to do precisely what Milo tells you. If they send you somewhere, you go.'

So Henri wandered around the centre of Stuttgart for the best part of an hour and a half and, as far as he could tell, he was not being followed. From Schlossplatz he walked down the Planie, which had now become Adolf Hitler Strasse and then into Charlottenplatz, which was now Danziger-Freiheit. *A different city.* He sat on benches, paused by shop windows – noticing that there seemed to be far less in the stores than on previous visits. He crossed the road and back again, allowing anyone wanting to approach him plenty of opportunity to do so. He was beginning to get a sense of what a country at war felt like: it was as if the horizon was diminished and there was less air to breathe. Less colour, so much quieter and the ubiquitous slogans on buildings and flags hanging from them. From Danziger-Freiheit, he headed north to Neckarstrasse, where one of his stepfather's property agents had their offices. He decided to go in there and then, just in case he was being followed – it was good to be able to show that the reasons he had given for visiting Stuttgart appeared to be genuine. Herr Langhoff took him into his office and was happy to talk for a while: times were very hard; many people had joined the military; Jewish property was being given away, which meant less business for them. No, as Herr Hesse was surely aware, all of his stepfather's properties had been disposed of.

He left the office after half an hour, satisfied that anyone watching would feel that he had indeed been in there to conduct business. A few doors along he found a small basement bar. The barmaid knew better than to ask too many questions, especially when she realised he was Swiss. After a drink he left the bar and walked back across the Schlossplatz to the hotel, concerned at how and when Milo was going to approach him. He could hardly spend the next few days doing little more than hanging around the hotel, going for the occasional walk and eating in his room.

He wandered around the lobby for a while and then returned to his room. He closed the heavy curtains with their view over Keplerstrasse and then ran a hot bath, rested, read a little, before telephoning reception to order his evening meal. There were three dishes on the menu, only one of which was available: sausages and potatoes.

After his meal he left the tray, as instructed, in the corridor outside his room. It was only eight o'clock but he began to think about settling down for the night. He was beginning to think that this trip was no more than a test by British Intelligence to see how he coped – whether he could get in and out of Germany, and no more than that. The more he thought about it, the more sense it made. After all, hadn't Edgar more or less told him that his mission would be something relatively straightforward? Whichever way you looked at it, he told himself, travelling into Germany and meeting with another agent was hardly straightforward. The British were unlikely to risk a novice agent's first assignment on anything too dangerous. Surely they would simply want to see whether he had the nerve to go there and return in one piece?

But what was it Viktor had told him at the weekend? '*Don't think too much, synok: they will know what they are doing.*'

There was an easy chair near a radiator by the window and he sat on it, kicking off his shoes and putting his feet on the small table. He began to recall another conversation with Edgar, when he had implied that they may advance 500 pounds of his aunt's money on successful completion of a mission. Would this count as a successful mission? Maybe he could now afford a car. He watched the patterns formed on the ceiling by the lampshade by the bed when a firm knock on the door disturbed his train of thought. He was annoyed, assuming that they had come to collect his dinner tray when in fact he had left it in the corridor.

'The tray is out there for you,' he called out.

A female voice replied. 'Thank you, Herr Hesse. Please could I come in? We have managed to locate your missing case.'

'I think there must be some mistake, I...'

A car door slammed on Keplerstrasse followed by the sound of a lorry moving down the road.

'There is no need to worry sir, I am the duty manager: if you could open the door please?'

The woman who Henri let into his room was wearing the dark formal uniform of the hotel staff. On her lapel was a badge: Katharina Hoch, Night Manager. She closed the door carefully behind her and then looked him up and down, as if checking him out. 'It is good news that we found your case, Herr Hesse.' She was carrying a small leather suitcase.

'There has been a mistake I am afraid. I have my case here. I only brought the one with me.'

'Are you enjoying your stay at the Hotel Victoria?'

'I am but—'

'And in Stuttgart: you are enjoying Stuttgart? We usually have some rain in Stuttgart at this time of year.'

Henri felt unsteady on his feet. *Milo?* 'I beg your pardon?'

She replied in a pleasant, conversational manner.

'We usually have some rain in Stuttgart at this time of year.'

Henri sat down on the edge of the bed, aware that he was shaking violently. He took a moment or two to remember his correct response.

'That must be the case all over Europe.'

Was it safe to have a conversation like this in a hotel room?

'Surely,' she said, checking behind the curtains and then glimpsing into the bathroom, 'surely there must be rain over the Alps?'

'There is always rain around the Alps, even in summer.'

'How wonderful,' she replied, like she really meant it.

There was a long silence. Another car door slammed on Keplerstrasse; the sound of distant laughter. The woman smiled at him in what in other circumstances he would have taken to be quite a seductive manner. Her mouth was quite beautiful, without any trace of lipstick.

'So, you are Milo?' He was speaking in barely more than a whisper.

'I am Milo, yes – don't look so shocked. Look, I am on duty, so I do not have too long, and we have much to talk about.'

'Is it safe in here?'

'Do you mean are we being listened to? You do not need be concerned. We provide the Gestapo with a list of all new guests, and the ones that they have some interest in we have to put in special rooms on the fifth floor, so you don't need to worry, not for now at least.'

She lifted the suitcase onto the bed and opened it. It was full of men's clothes, along with a hat and a pair of black shoes. 'Have you ever been to Essen, Herr Hesse?'

'Where?'

'Essen. In the Ruhr: north of Cologne.'

'No, I can't say that I have.'

'Tomorrow will be your first visit then.'

'But... surely not? My visa does not permit me to travel outside of Stuttgart.'

'That is what all this is about.' She pointed at the suitcase on the bed. 'Henri Hesse will not be travelling to Essen. You will travel as Dieter Hoch.' She had removed a wallet from the suitcase and emptied its contents onto the bed.

'Dieter Hoch is my brother. Dieter is four years older than you, but the photograph in his identity card here is not a good one, and so we are confident that your identity documents will pass a basic examination. It will work as long as no one has any reason to suspect you. You will only wear these clothes here: they all belong to my brother. Everything that you wear will be German made. There must be nothing on you that could identify you as being Swiss. You will take this suitcase.'

'And your brother is in on this?'

'Of course: we both do what we can to help the British. We are not Nazis; you may have gathered that. Dieter is a manager with the railway here in Stuttgart, which means that he is able to travel more freely on trains. He has worked for the past seven days and finished this evening, so now he is off work until Friday morning. He will remain at home until then and will not leave the house: he will tell my parents he is unwell. That gives you two clear days to get to Essen, complete your mission there, and return here. We want you back in Stuttgart before the curfew on Thursday night.'

'But what about the hotel? Won't people spot that I'm not here?'

'I am the duty manager for the next two nights. I will ensure that all the paperwork is in order. I will also come up during the night to ensure that the room looks as if someone has slept in it. As I say, no one suspects you. The Gestapo is kept busy enough with people that it does suspect.'

'And what do I do in Essen?'

'Do you know anything about Essen?'

Henri shrugged. *Not really.*

'Essen is a major producer of steel and coal. The Krupps family own much of the industry in the town. The steel that is produced there is vital to the Nazi war effort. The British wish to destroy the factories, but their intelligence is poor. Some of the locations that the British are aware of are no longer in use, others have been opened. They are in the process of compiling a much more accurate map of Essen. That is your mission, to assist in that.'

'So I just wander around Essen drawing maps?'

Katharina Hoch looked irritated. 'I will give you the details of how to make contact with someone in Essen. But this is going to be a dangerous mission: you will be required to move around Essen, memorise what you see, and then compile a grid of locations which you will then bring back to Stuttgart. Throughout Germany, life is dangerous, but in Essen especially so.'

Chapter 11

Essen, July 1940

He was woken at five in the morning by Katharina Hoch; a gentle rap on the door so as not to disturb other guests. He washed and shaved, dressed in her brother's clothes and double-checked the minutiae of his new identity: address, date of birth – the details that could trip him up.

He left the room as quietly as possible and descended through the fire exit stairs at the end of the corridor to the basement level, where Katharina was waiting for him.

She looked him over, like a parent checking that a child was properly dressed for school. She asked him to empty his pockets to be sure that he was carrying nothing incriminating: everything was in order.

'This is your ticket here for the rail journey: the train leaves at six o'clock, in twenty-five minutes. The train is scheduled to arrive in Frankfurt at ten o'clock: Dieter says that this train tends to run on time. It is carrying troops so is less likely to be subject to delays. At Frankfurt you should purchase a ticket to Essen: there is a direct service that departs at a quarter to eleven and is due to arrive in Essen at a quarter past two, or fourteen fifteen – that's how they like us to refer to it these days, presumably they think it makes everything sound more efficient. Dieter says he knows less about that part of the DR network, so you may encounter delays. Now you remember I told you last night about the purpose of your visit to Essen, in case anyone asks you?'

'Visiting an aunt?'

'Correct: Gertraud Traugott recently celebrated her eightieth birthday and as you have not seen her in a while, this is a surprise visit. She lives in an apartment in the west of Essen, in Altendorf. This is her address, please copy it down now in your own handwriting and put the piece of paper with the address on it in your wallet.'

She waited patiently while Henri copied down the address, folded the piece of paper and placed it in the wallet.

'But you are not to go straight to that address. When you arrive at Essen station you are to go to the lost property office, which is located behind the main ticket office. You will find that it is well signposted. In the unlikely event that you arrive in Essen before two o'clock, don't go in any earlier. If you arrive after four o'clock, wait outside the office. You have a contact in Essen who is going to help you, and he works in the lost property office. His codename is Lido. He is always on his own there between two and four. Go into the office and enquire if anyone has handed in a gentleman's umbrella, which you mislaid that morning. He will ask you to describe it and you will say that it is black with a carved wooden handle engraved with the initials "DH". He will then ask you to come into the back of the office to inspect the umbrellas. Once there, and when it is safe, Lido will brief you on what is to happen during your stay in Essen.'

'And what if he isn't there?'

'If he isn't there or something goes wrong, you should try and get out of Essen as soon as possible and head back to Stuttgart. Lido has very limited information about who you are or even where you are coming from, so your security should not be compromised if he is arrested.'

Henri tried to take all of this in: the detail was one thing but the sense of fear quite another. He was beginning to shiver, despite the warmth of the basement.

'It is nearly a quarter to six; you need to get a move on. Wear your hat; it will help mask your identity. Carry the raincoat. The next thing I have to say is very important: in the event of you being arrested, your story will not stand a lot of scrutiny. It will not take the Gestapo long to find out that you are not Dieter Hoch, or that Gertraud Traugott is not your aunt. Hopefully, it will not come to that, but if you do find yourself being interrogated by the Gestapo, you must do your best to hold out for twenty-four hours. That will give us enough time to dismantle our cell here in Stuttgart and try and escape.'

Katharina put her arm around his shoulder and leaned close to him. Her mouth looked even more astonishing close up. Her eyes did not blink as she stared straight into his.

'Twenty-four hours, that is all that we ask. Tell them you are a Swiss citizen and your passport is here in the hotel to prove it. They will probably not kill you – the Germans cannot afford to upset the Swiss. But if you keep your wits about you hopefully you will not arouse suspicion. You must leave now.

'There is one final thing that you should know: there is a pencil case in the suitcase, in a zipped compartment in the lid. Under no circumstances should you take it out of the case or open it. You are to give it to Lido. That is very important. Do you understand?'

He nodded that he understood. Katharina led him up a steep flight of concrete steps to a door that led directly onto Keplerstrasse. She motioned for him to wait while she looked up and down the street, and then waved him to come up. She pushed him along with a whispered 'Good luck'.

It was already light, and it was a quick five minutes' walk down Friedrichstrasse to the main station, which was reassuringly busy. He had just enough time to stop at a kiosk and buy a bread roll with cold sausage, and a copy of that morning's *Völkischer Beobachter*.

He spotted the Frankfurt train on platform six, with long lines of troops in black forming to board it. Small clouds of steam floated across the station, and the smell of engine oil and the sounds of metal and whistles and people calling out all felt oddly reassuring. He showed his ticket to the man at the barrier and then a policeman asked to check his papers, but was quick to wave him through. Just as he was about to board the train, he felt a hand on his shoulder and when he turned round it was an officer in black uniform. He noticed the distinctive Death Head symbol: SS. He felt like laughing. He had not even managed to board the train to Frankfurt. It had all been a trap.

'Do you have a light?' The officer was holding an unlit cigarette and smiling. 'I seem to have found myself with a unit where no one smokes. Imagine that!'

Henri apologised profusely. 'I don't smoke either.' *Perhaps I ought to take it up*, he thought as he climbed into his carriage.

—

He was both surprised and relieved when the train from Frankfurt pulled into Essen Main at twenty minutes past two that Wednesday afternoon. The journey could not have gone more smoothly; the Stuttgart train had arrived in Frankfurt at ten o'clock, allowing him ample time to buy his ticket for Essen and still be able to sit in a small cafe on one of the platforms, where he sipped a cup of bitter ersatz coffee and glanced at the *Völkischer Beobachter*. He was able to board the Essen train at half ten when the barrier opened, with the policeman on duty giving his identity card no more than a cursory look. The train was packed all the way to Cologne, so he closed his eyes to avoid being drawn into conversation during the journey up the Ruhr. Inevitably, as he began to doze, Roza appeared before him: gentle at first, as always. Her fingers lightly touching his wrist and a shy smile as she tossed her hair back from her face. And then the fingers grasped his wrist so tightly that he could feel the pain and that was followed by her looking at him with more hate than he could imagine: 'You know what will happen to us now, don't you?' He was about to explain when she began to fade away, asking one further question as she did so: 'Where are you going?' He sat up with a start, concerned he may have said something, but no one in the carriage so much as looked at him. *Where am I going? Where indeed?*

As the train reached Essen, enormous factories loomed either side of the track, with thick plumes of filthy smoke reaching far into the grey sky. The station was not nearly as large as the ones in Stuttgart or Frankfurt and there seemed to be less security. There was a noticeable smell of coal and industrial fumes, and the large swastika flags draped above the platform were streaked with grime. He decided not to go to the lost property office straight away; he needed to get a sense of his surroundings. He studied the timetable on the side of the ticket office. If he needed to leave Essen quickly there was a train to Dortmund in ten minutes and one to Cologne in twenty minutes. There was a cafe on the platform but he felt too sick with nerves to even enter it.

He waited until two thirty and then entered the lost property office. A man in DR uniform was behind a long, low counter, attending to an elderly lady.

'I can assure you that I have looked very carefully and more than once, as you ask. There is no sign of your gloves. They may still be elsewhere in the station: I suggest you try again tomorrow. I will keep a special eye out for them.'

Henri waited until she had left. The man behind the counter looked to be in his late fifties at least, and moved in a slow and quite deliberate manner. The man looked tired, his hair a steely-white. His most noticeable feature was an impressive pair of eyebrows that seemed to join up above his nose and curved up at either end, lending him an owl-like air.

'Can I help you, sir?'

Henri glanced around to ensure that they were on their own.

'I appear to have lost my umbrella.'

No pause, no flicker of understanding, no sign of anticipation from the man behind the counter.

'And when did you lose it sir?'

'This morning: it's black with a carved wooden handle. My initials are engraved on the handle: "DH".'

The man behind the counter shook his head.

'I cannot recall it, but perhaps you would like to come behind the counter and have a look? We have quite a collection of umbrellas here sir: I could open a shop!'

The man lifted up a section of the counter and slowly led Henri to a room at the back of the office. He closed the door and removed his cap, turning to face Henri.

'I'm Lido, by the way.'

'I gathered that: Dieter.'

Lido grasped Henri's hand and shook it warmly, holding his wrist with his left hand as he did so.

'There are some umbrellas over there, pretend to be looking through them. I'll look out of the window in case anyone comes in, but it is very quiet at this time of the afternoon. It is very quiet most of the time now. People don't seem to lose things in the war, apart from their lives.'

Lido spoke quickly and quietly, looking out of the little office window towards the counter as he did so.

'Just wait a moment.'

A woman with two young children had come in and Lido went over to the counter; after a very quick conversation, she left. He came back to Henri.

'Every other person who comes in here thinks we are the left luggage department. It says very clearly that we are lost property. Stuttgart explained that your cover for visiting Essen is to visit your aunt, yes? Let me tell you then that Gertraud Traugott is an elderly neighbour of mine. I live in an apartment block in Altendorf; her apartment is two doors down from me. However, Gertraud Traugott has not been in her apartment for three or four months now. She started to lose her mind a year ago, although she seemed capable enough of looking after herself. In November they took her into a sanatorium near Oberhausen. I went to visit her last month: she tells everyone there that she is engaged to the Kaiser and she is waiting for him to come and take her away. I am not sure how long she will be there – one hears terrible rumours these days about what they are doing to people like her, but that is another story. Now, you need to listen very carefully and I will tell you what you need to do.'

–

At ten to three Henri left the station by the north exit and headed into the centre of Essen. 'I finish work at four,' Lido had said. 'Wait for me by the Hindenburgstrasse exit. I will come out just after five past four. Follow me all the way to Altendorf – I will make sure that I take a route that takes you past as many factories as possible. Make sure you memorise everything. And don't forget to follow me at a safe distance, not too close, not too far. Can you remember all that?'

He could remember all that. He also remembered his training and the need to avoid wandering around a place without any apparent purpose. He used the hour and a bit he was going to spend in the centre of Essen to purchase a gift for his aunt: he was there to celebrate her eightieth birthday after all.

Lido had agreed that this was a good idea. 'Go past the Handelshof Hotel and the Opera House and you'll reach Adolf Hitler Platz. The best places to go shopping are to the north and the west of that – around Vereinstrasse and Logenstrasse. Any idea of what kind of gift you are going to buy?'

Perfume, they had agreed. 'Any woman appreciates perfume; no one is going to think that is an odd gift.'

He followed Lido's instructions: he had plenty of time, so he made sure he did not rush. Lido had said he thought there may be a perfume shop somewhere past Logenstrasse. It wasn't something he ever had occasion to shop for these days, he had said. In an arcade off Limbeckerstrasse he found exactly what he was looking for, a quaint *Parfümerie*: all wooden beams and leaded windows, reached by climbing down a couple of worn steps. There was a sign on the door to ring the bell and, when he did so, it was a minute or two before the elderly owner shuffled along to unlock the door.

'My apologies: when I am preparing perfumes at the back, I lock the door. I have had people stealing bottles in the past. Perhaps I should be more trusting these days. After all, it is not as if Jews come into the shop any more.' Henri noticed that the owner was wearing the distinctive round Nazi Party membership badge on his lapel, a black swastika stark on a white background. The shop was tiny, with all the walls and counters covered in bottles of perfume in every imaginable size and colour. The smell was close to overpowering.

'Now, how can I help you?'

Henri explained that he was looking for a perfume for his aunt, for her eightieth birthday. The owner perused the shelves. 'Maybe something with lavender in it? That is always popular with older ladies – or perhaps bergamot? What kind of a lady is she?'

Henri explained that he had not seen her in a while, this was a surprise visit.

'You do not sound as if you are from this area?'

'No, I am from… the south.'

'I see: whereabouts in the south?'

'Stuttgart,' said Henri, regretting his answer straight away.

'You do not have that dreadful Swabian accent, thank God! You have travelled a long way to see your aunt. Where does she live in Essen?'

'Altendorf.'

'Altendorf? I know it well. I lived there myself for many years, before my wife died and my children left Essen. What is your aunt's name?'

Henri hesitated. There was something about the owner that he found unsettling. It was not the Nazi Party badge, half the population of Germany seemed to wear one of those these days as far as he could tell and it was probably good for business. No, the questions seemed to be pointed and persistent rather than friendly. It was as if he distrusted Henri.

'Maybe I will come back later. I need to do some more shopping.'

'Your aunt's name – you were going to tell me her name?'

'Gertraud. Gertraud Traugott.'

'Gertraud? But I know Gertraud Traugott, I know her very well! Tell me, how are you related to her?'

Henri momentarily considered leaving the shop, but had already revealed too much; Gertraud Traugott's name and Stuttgart. *Trapped.*

'I told you, she is my aunt.'

'But on which side?'

'My mother was her sister.'

The old man nodded as if he was satisfied with the answer. Henri felt a sense of relief. He had overreacted.

'Ah, so you are Hannelore's son?'

'That's right, yes.' He managed a weak smile and felt faintly relieved. The old man leant against the counter, so close that Henri could smell the garlic on his breath.

'Gertraud has no sister. She had a brother, but he was killed in the Great War and had no children. And she has not lived in Altendorf for months. You cannot be her nephew. Who the hell are you?'

The old man's hand moved along the counter towards the telephone. Henri moved fast. He reached over the counter and pushed the man as hard as he could against the shelves behind him. His head struck one of the large glass bottles and he slumped to the floor. A few of the bottles fell on top of him, the glass shattering and the perfume spilling over the old man, who was now groaning. Henri darted over to the door and locked it, turning the sign round so that it would show that the shop was closed. *Geschlossen.*

He climbed over the counter, dragged the limp body into the small room at the back of the shop where the man had been preparing the perfumes and closed the door into the shop. The old man was bleeding from the head and soaked in perfume. Henri could hear someone trying to open the door, the handle turning against the lock and then a knock. The shopkeeper stirred, as if trying to call out. Henri held one hand firmly against his mouth and then gripped his head with the other. The man struggled, so Henri knelt on top of him, one knee pressed hard into his chest; his eyes bulged and his face turned bright red. The knocking stopped and it was quiet outside, but Henri continued to hold the man down. The struggle lasted for what seemed like an age. He could feel something hot and wet against his hand over the man's mouth. Blood was trickling out of his nose.

And then it stopped. The body suddenly slumped, all the resistance had flooded out of it, and Henri knew he was dead. For a few minutes he sat on the floor, catching his breath and gathering his thoughts, watching the old man for any sign of life. The broken bottles of perfume filled the room with the smells of citron, sandalwood and rose. He went back into the shop and drew the blinds on the door and windows. From the till he removed all the notes that were there and left the till open. He turned off the shop lights and went back into the room, taking care to shut the internal door and lock it. He had already noticed that there was another door from the room which he assumed would lead outside. He undid the bolts and carefully opened it just a few inches. Outside was a narrow, enclosed alleyway, the buildings opposite almost within touching distance. He went back inside the shop and removed the old man's wristwatch: this needed to look like a robbery. He was about to leave when he had another thought. From the old man's lapel he removed the Nazi Party membership badge, checked that nothing was engraved on the back and then put it on his own jacket. As he did so, he noticed that his raincoat, which had been on the floor alongside the man, had some bloodstains on the sleeve and reeked of perfume. He bundled it up, hoping to find somewhere nearby to dispose of it.

He carefully opened the door to the alleyway once more. It was dark and, as far as he could tell, deserted. He pulled his trilby low over his face and hurried down the alleyway, eventually emerging into Websterstrasse. Just before he did so, he noticed a large bin that was nearly full. He looked around him and then leant into the bin, pushing his coat as far into it as he could manage, covering it over as best he could with the other rubbish.

Lido was shocked to see him when he appeared in the Lost Property Office. It was five to four and he was preparing to close for the day. Fortunately, there was no one else there. Lido gestured for him to come to the office at the back.

'What the hell are you doing here?' he hissed. 'I thought I told you to meet me in Hindenbergstrasse?'

Henri explained what had happened. Lido sat with his head in his hands.

'I am sorry, but I had no alternative. For some reason, he suspected me. I should never have given him Gertraud Traugott's name of course, but how on earth was I to know he knew her...? What were the chances of that? If I hadn't given a name, that would have looked suspicious too. At least I did my best to make it look like a robbery.'

'That is the problem with this town, everyone knows everyone. Did anyone see you enter the shop?'

'Not as far as I know. It was very quiet.'

'At least you got rid of the coat. That could identify you too. Here, choose another one, there are a dozen or so on the rack over there. It was a dark brown rain coat you were wearing, is that correct?'

'Yes.'

'Choose one of the black ones then. And change your hat too. Choose something different from that trilby. You'd better give me the watch you took from him.'

Lido examined the watch with a professional interest.

'Shame, it is a good watch, but too distinctive. I'll lose it down a drain. My guess is that it will be a few hours at least before he is discovered. You are sure you locked the door?'

'Yes.'

'Let's hope so. We had better go back to the original plan. You leave now and start following me once I emerge in Hindenburgstrasse.'

Lido called him back just as he was leaving the Lost Property Office.

'Did you remove everything from the pockets of your coat?'

'I didn't have anything in them, as far as I was aware.'

'Are you sure?'

Henri left the office without replying. If only he was sure.

–

Lido emerged from the station into Hindenburgstrasse at ten past four. Without pausing, changing his pace, or looking around him, he walked on, turning left at the Krupps Hotel and then left again into what, to all intents and purposes, looked like a factory. Towering above him on either side of the road were vast industrial buildings, whose sheer height shut out much of the daylight. He could feel the fumes fill his lungs, but the most overpowering sensation was the noise: it was not simply the volume – that was to be expected – but more the physical effect it had, sending tremors throughout his body. The buildings on the south side of the road seemed to be denser, and every so often Lido would remove his hat and scratch his head for a moment or two before putting it back on. That was the signal for Henri to take special note of something, which might be the entrance of another factory, usually with a board outside. Most of the entrances had sentries outside them, their gaze following him as he walked past.

It soon became obvious to Henri that goods were moved around the factories and the town by rail: at frequent points on their journey the road was bisected by railway lines and bridges. They had to wait at one or two of these for trains to pass, which gave Henri a good opportunity to look around. He was making mental notes; of where different factories were in relation to one another, their names, where the railway lines went, where any power plants appeared to be located.

After a while he noticed that Lido had slowed down his pace and kept removing his cap, scratching his head. A factory to their left was more or less open to the road, and in it he could see half-built tanks and what appeared to be heavy artillery lined up in a yard. A bit further on they had to pause: a soldier was ordering pedestrians to stand back while a group of workers, all under close guard, were led past them. There were about thirty gaunt men in the group, all dressed in a rough grey uniform. He heard them talking quietly as walked past him: he was sure that they were speaking Polish.

Soon after that, they emerged from the complex of factories, although the smell and the noise lingered on. They were now in the Altendorf district. Lido stopped to tie a shoelace, which was the signal for Henri to drop back further: they were nearing the apartment. Just after a school, Lido turned right into Rullichstrasse, and at that point Henri slowed down even more to allow Lido to get out of his sight. He knew to turn from Rullichstrasse into Ehrenzellerstrasse and then into the apartment block towards the end of the street. It was a large block; four stories high with the apartments opening out onto an external corridor.

'*There are six apartments on each floor, all sharing the same corridor. I am in number nineteen on the second floor. Gertraud Traugott's apartment is just along from mine, number twenty-two.*'

Henri reckoned that Lido had had the five minutes he said he needed to get inside his own apartment, so he climbed the steps to number twenty-two. In common with all the other apartments in the block it was shabby, with paint peeling to reveal warped wood. He knocked on the door, but there was no sign of life. He knocked again and waited. He knocked once more and at that, the door of the apartment next door opened.

A woman in her forties came out. She was wearing a filthy apron with two equally filthy children huddled behind her.

'Who are you after?'

'Frau Traugott,' he replied.

'She's not here, and with some luck she'll never come back. I'd had enough of her frightening the children. Who are you anyway?'

'A relation, from out of town: I'm in Essen on business and thought I'd pop in to see her.'

Lido had now emerged from his apartment and joined them. He nodded politely at the woman and asked if he could help. Henri explained his story again. Lido also informed him that Frau Traugott was not there.

Henri managed to look suitably disappointed. 'I counted on her being here. I was hoping to stay with her tonight. Do you know of a hotel nearby?'

'You'll have to head back into town' the neighbour said, ushering her children back into their apartment. She was sensing she may be called on to help out, and her reluctance to do that marginally outweighed her innate nosiness.

'Manfred will help you. He is an old fashioned gentleman!' With that she laughed and disappeared into her apartment, but not before hearing Lido ask him to join him in his apartment.

Number nineteen was neat and cosy inside. Once Lido had locked the door and checked that all the curtains were drawn, he showed Henri into a small sitting room. There was a table, bookshelves, an easy chair and a sofa: he gestured for Henri to sit on the sofa.

'Let's wait ten minutes. If they were following us, they will come by then. If not, we can relax, if such a thing is possible these days. You can call me Manfred, by the way. I don't need to know your real name; as far as I am concerned, you are Dieter.'

After a silent ten minutes, Manfred removed his jacket, then took Henri's, and then went into the kitchen, emerging a few minutes later with two steaming mugs.

'It's what we call coffee these days. Coffee was my passion. I am assuming that I will never drink proper coffee again.' He sat there shaking his head, sipping at the drink and pulling a face as he tasted it. He removed a bottle of Asbach Uralt brandy from a shelf and poured some into their coffee cups, without asking Henri.

'You will find that makes it more palatable. I will make us something to eat soon. Now you must start making notes of what you saw. There is a false lining to your suitcase. When you have finished with the notes, we'll seal them in there. Before I forget, you have something for me?'

'Pardon?' said Henri.

'Stuttgart should have given you something for me… in a pencil case?'

'Oh yes, sorry. I forgot.' Henri opened the suitcase and removed the pencil case from the zipped compartment in the lid of the case.

Manfred held it carefully with two hands and placed it on the table. He left the room and returned with a small towel, which he folded in half and placed next to the pencil case, which he then slowly opened. From it, he extracted three brass pen-like objects, one by one. He gingerly placed them on the towel, which he then carefully wrapped up. He left the room with it and returned a minute or so later. He handed the pencil case back to Henri.

'What are they?' he asked.

'Those? Oh, they are pencil detonators. For explosives, you understand. I will pass them on quickly to the people who know what to do with them.'

'You mean I carried these detonators with me all the way from Stuttgart?'

'Indeed you did. I am most grateful.'

'But what if I had been searched and they found them?'

'Then you probably wouldn't be here now, would you? We take such risks all the time.'

Henri sank back in the sofa. 'Are there any other surprises?'

'You are the man for surprises, Dieter, eh? You had hardly been in Essen for two hours before you killed one of our citizens. With some luck, the police will assume it is one of the foreign labourers, or a Jew. It is very handy that they blame them for everything. It makes it easier for decent Aryans to commit crimes.'

They both laughed. Henri spent the next hour writing in pencil what he had seen and then they sealed the paper into the lining of the suitcase. Manfred prepared an evening meal and they sat down at the table to eat: a hot stew with more potatoes than anything else.

'How long have you lived here, Manfred?'

'I moved to Essen in 1935. I was a teacher in Dortmund when the Nazis came to power and, as I was a social democrat, I lost my job. Soon after that my wife died and, as you can imagine, I was in despair: on my own and with no job, and an apparent enemy of the state. However, my sister-in-law had a fairly senior position at the local authority in Dortmund and she was able to alter my records. My surname was Erhart and she changed it to the alternative spelling of Erhard. All of my paperwork showed my Christian name as Hans, but she replaced it with my middle name, Manfred. So Hans Erhart became Manfred Erhard: very simple, but very effective. The thing about us Germans, you see, is that we can be too efficient, too methodical. Had I been Hans Erhart then the authorities would have tracked me down, but as all the paperwork is in order for Manfred Erhard, he has no problems. I moved to Essen, got this apartment and a job at the station. As far as people are concerned, I am what I appear to be: a rather lonely railway worker who lives on his own and bothers no one.'

'So how did you get involved in this business?'

'By chance: a couple came to Lost Property who were clearly terrified. They were trying to get out of Essen but the Gestapo were after them. Without having time to think about it, I allowed them to hide in Lost Property office overnight. The next morning they gave me the phone number of a contact of theirs. He arranged to collect them and managed to smuggle them out of the town. A few days later that contact came to see me and asked if I would like to stay involved, to help from time to time. I had no option of course, what could I do? I was already involved. Our main role now is to help gather intelligence for the British so that they can bomb the Krupps' factories. With some luck, the intelligence we give them will be so good that they hit Krupps rather than this apartment block. There are some mining engineers at the Krupps' Maria mine in the north of Essen who are Communist sympathisers: they can get hold of dynamite and, who knows, with the detonators you brought maybe we can do some damage to the factories ourselves, without having to rely on the RAF.'

'Maybe that will be safer.'

'We are a small cell and it is very dangerous work, which goes without saying. So far we have been very lucky, but that cannot last. I am sixty-three now, Dieter, I have little to live for. Helping to resist the Nazis gives me some purpose, but I know I will not survive long. I have a suicide pill: I just hope that when the Gestapo come for me, I have time to take it.'

After Manfred had cleared the dinner plates he returned to the small room and checked the curtains once again.

'Are you ready for some entertainment?'

Henri nodded, uncertain what Manfred had in mind.

Manfred was by the bookcase, on top of which was a Bakelite cabinet.

'This is a *Volksempfange*: a triumph of German engineering. When the Nazis came to power they were so proud of their ability to communicate with us ordinary folk that they had this radio receiver built. It was cheap, this one cost me something like seventy marks, and it works well. It is important for them that we catch all the speeches and fall for their propaganda. For me, I enjoyed listening to the jazz, but they soon banned that. Apparently they felt that it was all Negroes and Jews. So now they expect us to listen to their nonsense, but they failed to take into account this...'

Manfred was moving the dial to the left, stations momentarily bursting into life and then fading away as he went through them. He then settled on one station and turned the volume very low, beckoning Henri to join him crouched by the speaker.

'The BBC,' Manfred was pointing at the dial on the radio. 'We'll listen to their German language service. It is excellent. If they catch you listening to a foreign radio station, you can end up in prison. Goebbels clearly does not like his own propaganda to be contaminated, so now I spend part of my evenings knelt by the radio, with the volume so low that I can only just hear it.'

Henri did not sleep that night, wracked as his body was with exhaustion and fear. Every time he began to drop off, he saw the bulging eyes of the shop owner, or would hear the resigned tone of Manfred, a man who knew his fate. It was another face that would now haunt him, along with Roza, who inevitably appeared before him in the very early hours, her fingers holding his wrist, slowly tightening over the course of what felt like many hours. There was a strong wind that night and the windows in the sitting room, where Henri was trying to sleep on the sofa, rattled viciously. Worse than that was the front door, which shook heavily when caught by the wind: each time that happened, he imagined that the Gestapo had come for them.

The next morning Manfred was up at six thirty and they sat together eating black bread and jam, and drinking ersatz coffee.

'I start work at eight o'clock. You should aim to catch the quarter past nine train to Cologne. We are going to go on a more roundabout route to the station, but it is one which will enable you to see much more of Essen. It is very busy at this time of the morning, so we should be all right, but who knows? Keep an eye on me and make sure you memorise well what you see – and, remember, if you see me remove my cap and put it in my pocket, we are in danger. If that happens, just ignore me and get away as soon as you can.'

Henri watched as Manfred packed his lunch neatly into a tin box, leaving space for the detonators wrapped in the towel. 'I had better be careful I don't eat them!' Both men laughed nervously, grateful for the brief diversion of humour. They left the apartment just after seven and Henri followed Manfred to Altendorf station. They travelled north, allowing Henri ample opportunity to see yet more Krupps factories and the Maria and Amalie mines. At Altenessen they changed trains and took one south: anyone following them would have been immediately suspicious that they were taking such a circuitous route when a more direct one existed, but it was busy and Henri was convinced no one was watching them. Essen was like Stuttgart: people avoided eye contact with each other. The next stage of the journey had the added advantage of being painfully slow, as the train crawled down the track past yet more factories to the North Passenger and Goods station. It was now a quarter to eight and, as arranged, Manfred headed straight to the main station. Henri had more time and walked slowly, taking a slightly longer route so as to take in the power station and the electricity station around Viehoferstrasse.

As he headed towards the station, pleased with his morning's work and relieved to be beginning his journey back, he became aware of a commotion ahead of him. Too late he realised that he was very near Limbeckerstrasse, where the *Parfümerie* was. There were police everywhere, stopping all pedestrians and coralling them into different lines. He thought of turning around, but soon found himself being pointed to a queue. Ten minutes later he was at the front of it. A policeman directed him towards a man in a long trench coat, who beckoned him. *Come here.* The man held out an oval, metal warrant disc: there was the Nazi eagle on one side and the words *Geheime Staatpolizei* on the other. Gestapo.

'Papers.'

He handed over his identity card.

'Where are you heading?'

'The station.'

That seemed to satisfy the man, who did not press him.

'Open the suitcase.'

He rooted around in it for a moment or two but again was satisfied.

'Your watch.'

They'd be looking for the old man's watch. His was fine.

The Gestapo officer seemed satisfied.

'One last thing: let me see your wallet.'

Henri handed it over. He and Manfred had agreed that it would be best to dispose of the Reichsmarks he had taken from the till. 'You never *know*,' said Manfred, 'some shopkeepers mark their notes, or there could be specks of blood on them.' Henri was certain that there was nothing to worry about in the wallet – nothing that would arouse suspicion. He did have the slip of paper, with the name and address in Altendorf of his aunt, but that would appear as innocuous as all the other contents.

But it was as the Gestapo man handed the wallet back to him and told him he could go on his way that Henri had the most terrible thought. He remembered that the slip of paper was not in the wallet: he had transferred it to his coat pocket just before he arrived in Essen the previous day. For some reason he had decided it would be safer there. And now it was in the blood-stained and perfume-soaked coat that he had abandoned, and which there was every chance would be discovered. They would find the piece of paper and go to the apartment block in Ehrenzeller Strasse and start asking questions. The lady with the filthy apron in the next-door apartment would happily tell them about the man who had knocked on Gertraud Traugott's door, and who had been taken in by Herr Erhard in number nineteen.

His legs were shaking as he hurried to the station. The large station clock had edged past ten past nine, and he could see steam billowing from the Cologne train on platform three. There was a good chance they would find the coat any moment now – maybe they had already found it and had already spoken with the woman at the apartments. Maybe they were on their way to the station. He knew he should go to the Lost Property office to warn Manfred, but he also knew that if he did so then he would almost certainly miss the train.

There was movement around platform three, the guard was about to close the gate. Henri ran along and managed to squeeze through in time. He hopped on board as the brakes were noisily released and the train began to ease along the platform.

Every time he closed his eyes on the journey back to Stuttgart, he saw Manfred: he knew he could have warned him and given him a chance to escape, but that would have delayed his own departure from Essen and put himself at risk.

Poor Manfred, he thought: a decent enough man whose remaining ambition in life was that he could take his suicide pill before the Gestapo got to him.

I just hope he manages it.

Chapter 12

Lausanne, Bern, August 1940

Henri travelled to Lausanne on Monday 5th August, following the long weekend to celebrate Swiss National Day the previous Friday. He took the early morning paddle steamer from Geneva and when the *Montreux* docked in Lausanne, a gleaming black Traction Avant was waiting for him.

On the twenty-minute drive to Lutry, the Alps rose high to his left, the lake sweeping below him to the right. That summed it up, he thought: caught between two powerful forces. Not unlike serving two masters.

It took the Citroën a further ten minutes to climb the steep road out of Lutry to an isolated villa high above the town. Henri was led through to a magnificently appointed lounge, with large windows offering sensational views of the lake. The furniture was of the best quality, along with magnificent carpets, and cabinets with enough silver in them to fund a war slightly smaller than the current one.

As with all his meetings with Viktor, it began with an embrace. As Henri extricated himself from it he turned round to admire the room.

'Bit luxurious isn't it, Viktor?'

'The location is very discreet: that is what matters.'

'Do you lot own this?'

'We borrow it from a good friend, *synok*. We have very little time for questions; we need to get to work.'

Henri ignored him and walked around the room, genuinely admiring it. A pair of chairs on either side of the fireplace appeared to be genuine Louis XV: Viktor told him he was not permitted to sit on them. Someone had brought in a tray of what smelled like proper coffee and Henri helped himself to a cup and before sinking into a large armchair opposite Viktor, who had his brown leather notebook on his lap and was sharpening his pencil with a penknife, the shavings scattering on the precious carpet.

'You have not heard from your Mr Remington-Barber yet?'

Henri shook his head. So did the Russian.

'Strange. I would have thought he would have contacted you by now. As far as we can tell, you're not being watched. You certainly weren't followed today. He doesn't seem to be very suspicious, does he?'

'I have no idea, but maybe they are unhappy about what happened in Essen.'

Viktor raised his eyebrows momentarily and looked up. 'And what did happen in Essen, Henri?'

Henri took a deep breath. He had been dreading this moment. He was not sure who he feared telling most: Remington-Barber or Viktor. He closed his eyes and carefully recounted the details of his trip to Germany. He had decided to leave nothing out: the killing of the old man in the shop, and the fact that his carelessness had almost certainly compromised Manfred. Viktor allowed him to speak uninterrupted, carefully taking notes. When he finished, there was a long silence, broken only by the sound of Viktor sharpening his pencil. Henri had leant forward in his seat, his elbows on his thighs, staring down.

'What is the matter, *synok*? You look bothered about something.'

'He'll be dead now, won't he?'

'Who?'

'Manfred – Lido: do you think the Germans would have found him?'

Viktor shrugged. 'I would imagine so. Whatever we think of them, we cannot accuse them of not being thorough, can we? I would be most surprised if they did not find the coat, and that would have led to Manfred.'

Henri shook his head.

'You seem to be upset?' Viktor looked confused.

'Well, I am actually, yes. He was a decent chap, and it was my mistake that probably did it for him.'

'He was a social democrat, Henri: their fate is to end up dead. And now he is a victim of war. How do you feel about killing the man in the shop? Has that upset you as much?'

'Of course not: he was clearly a bad sort – a Nazi. I had no alternative.'

'Indeed. I imagine that it was somewhat easier than with the boy in Interlaken, or the puppy. That is why we train you like that, Henri, so you are used to killing. As far as your Mr Remington-Barber is concerned, it is your first killing.'

'You think I should tell him then?'

'Of course! It is always good to have an agent who has killed in the field. I am not sure whether an English gentleman will approve or not, but he ought to be impressed with it. In any case, he may already be aware of it, and it will not look good if you *don't* tell him.'

It was six o'clock now. Viktor checked back through his notebook, nodding his head at various points. He seemed pleased, though Henri knew better than to expect him to actually say he was. It was now Viktor's turn to speak, in his deliberate and concise manner.

'Listen carefully, Henri: this is what is expected of you... We are satisfied so far, Henri, but there are many difficult days ahead... It is too risky for us to meet on a regular basis... We can keep an eye on you, but we must keep these meetings to a minimum... You must learn to operate on your own, but to do exactly what we want you to.'

It was a quarter to seven when Viktor finished.

'I think we can risk driving you back to Geneva, *synok*. We now need to wait until Remington-Barber contacts you: I imagine that will be soon.'

Viktor stood up and embraced Henri once more. The two men who had brought Henri to the villa had come back into the room. *Time to go.*

'Before I go, Viktor, there is something I need to get off my chest.'

Viktor raised his eyebrows and looked at his watch, clearly irritated. *If you must: go on then.*

'I just wanted to say that I am risking my life now. I've told you what happened in Essen. I am not playing games. I know what I let myself in for, I realise all that. But there is something that has made me very unhappy, and I need to talk about it.'

Viktor shifted uncomfortably and looked at the two other men in the room. He nodded at them and they both left.

'Go on, but make it quick, Henri.'

'I agreed to work with you – for you – because I believe in your cause: I see it as my cause too. You know that.'

Viktor nodded in agreement, unsure what was going to come next. Henri paused to compose himself.

'I agreed to work for you because I was ideologically committed.'

'We know that.'

'And I still am. But now that I have started to lay my life on the line, I cannot understand why we signed that bloody pact with them last year. I mean, they were meant to be our sworn enemy, they stood for everything we despise, and now I have to get used to the fact that they're our allies, our friends even. That seems wrong to me. Whose side am I meant to be on now?'

Viktor sank back into his chair and motioned for Henri to do the same. He leant forward, placed his enormous hands on Henri's knees, gripping them quite tightly.

'What you must understand, *synok*, is that they are not our friends. There is no question of that.'

'But our allies? That is bad enough… perhaps even worse!'

'Hardly even that. It is a non-aggression pact, Henri, that is all – a matter of expediency. I shouldn't quote Trotsky of course, but a couple of years ago he said that "the end may justify the means as long as there is something that justifies the end." That end is the victory over fascism and the triumph of communism. The pact is meant to buy us time to enable us to achieve that. Our feelings about them have not changed, but we need to be ready and this pact allows us to do that. It is not meant to make us feel comfortable; it is meant to protect us.'

'Well, I do feel uncomfortable, Viktor.'

'And do you think you are the only one?' He gripped Henri's knee so hard that he winced in pain. His raised voice meant that one of the men who had been sent out of the room popped his head round the door to check that all was in order. Viktor stood up and leant over Henri, his hot breath was moist and smelt of alcohol.

'We are not permitted the luxury of personal feelings or opinions: they are mere indulgences. Do you understand that?'

Henri edged back in his chair.

'We do as we are instructed, all of us. Maybe we permit you too many bourgeois indulgences, *synok*. Have you forgotten? Never question; never discuss; never hesitate. You would do well to remember that more often than you evidently do. Otherwise, *synok*, you'll be in a lot of trouble.'

–

Henri's journey from Essen to Stuttgart had been uneventful and when he arrived at the Hotel Victoria late on the Thursday afternoon Katharina Hoch had not yet come on duty. She came up to his room later that night to collect her brother's clothes and papers. She insisted that he was not to tell her any details of the Essen trip. 'I don't need to know anything else. Save that for Bern. They will want to know everything.' He couldn't decide whether she had any inkling of what had gone on in Essen, but if she did, she gave no hint of it.

He had removed the Nazi Party membership badge he had taken from the dead man in the perfume shop from his lapel before arriving at the hotel. *You never know*, he thought. He hid it in the lining of his wash bag.

She was right – Bern would want to know everything, although he could not understand why it was taking quite so long. Before the mission, Remington-Barber had told him that he was not to initiate any contact when he got back to Switzerland. 'Just wait, I'll be in touch. Be patient. Apparently it is a virtue.'

Henri had taken the Swissair flight from Stuttgart which landed in Zurich just before four thirty on the Friday afternoon and had managed to catch a train straight back to Geneva. He was utterly exhausted. He had hardly slept for the past week: his plan now was to catch up on sleep that weekend. He assumed that Remington-Barber would be in touch on the Monday, if not before.

But nothing: nothing on the Monday nor the following day or the rest of that week, nor indeed the following one. His visit to Viktor in the hills above Lausanne came and went, and it was the middle of August when he returned from his morning walk to be told by his mother that a messenger had come round from Credit Suisse. There was a letter.

'Whatever can be the problem, Henri?'

It was from Madame Ladnier. Henry tried to read it away from the prying eyes of his mother, who was trying to move behind him.

> *I would like to meet with you today to review recent transactions.*
> *Two o'clock this afternoon, Quai des Bergues. Giselle Ladnier*
> *(Madame).*

At last. He felt relieved. His mother was looking at him anxiously, her eyebrows raised high.

'What is the problem, Henri?'

'There is no problem, mother, none at all. I have a meeting to review my account. It is routine.'

Madame Ladnier was calm and business-like. Henri had arrived at the branch in Quai des Bergues at five to two, and as the clock struck two above the cashiers' counters Madame Ladnier emerged from an office door and ushered Henri into a small office down a long corridor.

'How are you, Herr Hesse?'

'Very well, thank you.' *Do I ask about the delay? Ask why I have not been contacted? Do I mention anything about Germany?*

'Good. Your account is in order. Please now take a few minutes to check your statements and initial each page to indicate you have read them.'

He scanned through the statements, initialling each page. There was no message for him on any of the pages as he thought there may be. He kept glancing up at Madame Ladnier, hoping for a smile or a nod or some acknowledgement of the situation, but she remained as impassive as one would expect of a Swiss bank official.

When he had finished, he returned the papers to her. She checked them and placed them neatly in a folder marked with his name.

'Thank you very much for coming in, Herr Hesse. I am pleased that your account is all in order. I would also ask you to take this pamphlet with you: it explains the various options should you wish to invest any of your funds with Credit Suisse.'

She had stood up now, preparing to leave the room. As Henri stood up she came round to his side of the desk and bent to pick up a piece of paper from the floor.

'You appeared to have dropped this paper, Herr Hesse.'

'I don't think so,' Henri replied.

She handed him the small piece of paper, her gaze making it clear that it was for him. It was a receipt from the cobblers in Bern where he had met Remington-Barber before the trip to Germany. Scrawled underneath the price of a shoe repair were the words: 'Collection Friday 16th August, 1pm.'

Madame Ladnier held a long, manicured finger over her mouth in case Henri was inclined to speak.

He left Geneva on the nine thirty train on the Friday morning and was in Bern in good time for his appointment at the cobblers in Kramgasse. There were no customers, so he entered the leather emporium, where the cobbler glanced up and nodded, holding a few tacks between his lips and a hammer in his hand. He lifted the counter top and pointed the way up the stairs with the hammer. Basil Remington-Barber was standing by the window.

'Good trip?' He sounded as if he was enquiring after a holiday.

'Well, all things considered, yes.'

'All things considered?'

'Well, considering that I was sent into Nazi Germany and then into the heart of the Ruhr carrying detonators concealed in my baggage, yes it was fine thank you.'

'I am not terribly sure what you were expecting, old chap.'

'I was expecting that it would be a bit more of a "testing the water" mission: you know, see how I got on.'

'Which, in a sense, it was. Having said that, we are hardly going to go to the trouble of getting you into Germany and take the risk of

143

exposing some of our very few remaining agents there just as part of a simple training exercise for you, are we, eh?'

'And the detonators?'

'One of the purposes of your trip, Henry: I am told that we British make first class detonators. We managed to get a few into Stuttgart at the end of last year, but we needed to move some to the Ruhr, which is where you came in. Evidently Lido did manage to pass on the detonators to another member of the cell the morning you left, so that is rather good news: with a bit of luck we may be able to do some damage there. Aerial bombing tends to be a bit hit and miss, but if we can actually plant something inside a factory or a coal mine – well, who knows?'

'I think I ought to have been told a bit more about my mission before I was sent on it.'

'Not sure it works like that, old chap. Not to put too fine a point on it, you do as you are told. You remember what Tennyson said? "*Theirs not to reason why.*" You are one of the "theirs", if you catch my drift.'

'Yes, but what worries me is what he said in the next line: "*Theirs but to do and die*".'

'Let's hope it doesn't come to that. No reason why it should. Now then, old chap, care to tell me about it?'

'About what?'

Basil Remington-Barber stared at Henri for quite a long, not in an altogether unfriendly manner, his eyebrows raised quizzically.

'About what led to Lido being arrested and killed: and be a good chap and leave nothing out, eh? It would be safe for you to assume that you were – how shall I put it – observed while you were in Essen. We have a good idea of what happened, even with that shopkeeper chap – but not all of it.'

Henri had already decided to explain what had happened, but confirmation that Manfred was dead caused him to swallow hard. When he regained his composure he began to recount the story in much the same way as he had with Viktor. Unlike the Russian, Remington-Barber interrupted him frequently with little questions to help him on his way or clarify a point. When he finished, he asked Remington-Barber what had happened to Lido.

'You left Essen on the Thursday. As we understand it, that evening he was pulled in by the Gestapo. Apparently they had arrived at his apartment in the afternoon, turned the place upside down and were waiting for him when he got home. Thank heavens the detonators weren't there. From there he was taken to the police headquarters in Virchow Strasse.'

'How do you know this?'

'One of his neighbours – most likely the one you met. Half the neighbourhood heard what happened from her, and one of our chaps there overheard it. As far as the police are concerned, they've pulled in a number of retired detectives while the younger ones are in the army, and another of our contacts heard all this at the bar that they frequent. Manfred was at Virchowstrasse right through the weekend: the Gestapo gave him their standard working over. Not pleasant stuff, Henry: they're bloody barbarians. He was a bloody pulp when they took him to the provincial prison across the road on Zweigert Strasse. The Gestapo had another go at him on the Monday and then, by all accounts, he died that night. Apparently they were due to give him another working over the next day. I suppose in one sense they didn't kill him as such, but of course...'

'Of course...' Henri felt bereft. 'Do you think I should have warned him?'

'Well from what you say, you didn't have time, did you? If you had done that then you would have missed the Cologne train and you weren't to know how long it would take them to find the coat and the trail which would lead to Lido.'

'Good Lord... I don't know what to say.'

'Whatever they did to him, he didn't utter a word. He gave nothing away. If he had sung straight away they may even have picked you up in Stuttgart – possibly even before you got there, but it turns out he was a brave man. We always tell our chaps to hold out for twenty-four hours, although to be frank, even that is pushing it with those animals. But he held out for far longer than that. Remarkable how resilient people can be.'

'And brave.'

'Indeed.'

'And the shopkeeper?'

'What about him?'

'I'm sorry if that turned out to be rather... messy.'

Basil Remington-Barber looked confused. 'Messy? Not at all! You did absolutely the right thing. It would have been messy had you attempted to extricate yourself from the situation in any other way. No, we have all been rather impressed: it was desperately unlucky that the shopkeeper knew Gertraud Traugott. Not your fault. Important thing is that you acted decisively. Don't look so worried, Henry!'

'I rather thought that you'd be... I don't know... angry with me?'

'I'd have been angry had you not told me what happened. And as I said, you were observed in Essen: what you told me tallies with what we already knew. And there's no harm whatsoever in having an agent who knows how to kill, not to put too fine a point on it, eh?'

Remington-Barber clapped his hands and ushered Henri over to a table by the window, on which a large map of Essen was spread out.

'You have brought your notes with you?'

Henri had.

'Good. What we need to do now is fill in all the information you picked up on the ground against this map. It will be like doing a jigsaw: should be rather fun.'

Henri would not have described it as fun. They spent an hour going over the large map of Essen, Henri doing his best to point out the location of factories and other key buildings. For all his bonhomie and apparent diffidence, Remington-Barber turned out to be highly adept at teasing information out of Henri. By two thirty, the map was much more detailed.

'RAF ought to be chuffed with this,' he announced, carefully rolling it up and slipping it into a metal tube. He then stood up and rubbed his hands, as if in excitement.

'Right then! If you hurry, you'll catch the six o'clock train to Geneva: saves us another hotel bill, eh? And talking of money, London are very pleased with the mission. Edgar says to tell you that 500 pounds will be put into your Credit Suisse account next week: says you'll know what all that is about. I hate anything to do with money.'

146

'And what happens now?'

'Go home and wait for us to contact you, which we will do through Madame Ladnier.'

'And when might that be?'

'Good question, Henry. The truth is, I have no idea. Could be next week, could be next year. The only thing I would say is that if London are this pleased with this mission, the next one could be a lot more interesting. Something to look forward to! So don't worry, I'm sure London will want to see you soon.'

Henri was alarmed. 'London! You want me to go to London?'

Remington-Barber frowned. 'Good heavens no! London will come to you.'

Chapter 13

Berlin, August 1940

Berlin in the first full summer of the war was a city of secrets and hushed conversations; a city at the centre of the conflict but a long way from the sounds or more obvious effects of it. The closer to the centre of power, the more secrets there were and the more hushed conversations became. Unless you knew someone very well and were absolutely sure you could trust them, even a routine conversation was guarded and required a circuitous route to reach its point.

For Franz Hermann, such a cautious approach was by no means an alien one. As a lawyer he was used to being careful and non-committal; discretion came as second nature to him. But late in the afternoon of an extremely pleasant Tuesday in the middle of August he was mindful of the need to be even more careful than usual. Franz Hermann was on his way to meet a very important client, a general in the Army High Command.

The lawyer had left his office in Friedrichstrasse to visit his client at his home in Moabit. Hermann headed west, along the north bank of the River Spree and at Lehrter Station turned into Alt Moabit, past the Post Stadion. Four years earlier he had been at the Post Stadion watching Norway unexpectedly beat Germany two nil to knock the hosts out of the Olympic football tournament. His initial disappointment at the defeat had been more than compensated for by the fact that Hitler was at the game and was reported as being furious. He decided that if Hitler was so upset by the result, then maybe defeat was not so bad after all. *Your enemy's enemy...*

Halfway along Stromstrasse he reached his destination: a handsome apartment block, overlooking the Kleiner Tiergarten. A maid, who looked as if she was still in her teens, let him into the apartment on the top floor of the building.

Generalmajor Werner Ernst was in his study, still wearing his uniform. He moved his large head slowly, as if he had a bad neck. His eyes were noticeable for how small they were in comparison to the rest of his face. He smiled politely and pointed to one of two armchairs that were angled towards the window, a small coffee table between them. Behind him were enormous picture windows over the park. A breeze which had not been apparent on the street was causing the tops of the expanse of trees to sway gently from side to side.

'Please do sit down, Herr Hermann. You'll have to excuse me, I have only just returned from work and have not had time to change.'

They paused while the young maid came back into the room, carrying a tray which she placed on the coffee table. Hermann could smell real coffee, an increasingly rare sensation in Berlin.

'Thank you, Anke, don't you worry, I will pour the coffee. And Frau Ernst reminded me that it is your night off. You may leave early if you wish.'

The *Generalmajor* busied himself pouring the coffee and offering freshly baked biscuits to his guest. He waited until he heard the front door of the apartment close before signalling to his lawyer that he could proceed.

For the next half hour Franz Hermann went through various documents with his important client.

'A signature here please... An explanation necessary there... Another signature here, thank you... Just an initial here will suffice... Let me explain this sheet... I have taken the liberty of having this form already witnessed... One more signature there... All is in order. There we are sir. I think you will find that the business of finalising your mother's estate is now complete. I would estimate that the funds will be in your bank account within the month.'

'Thank you, Herr Hermann. You have dealt with this matter most efficiently. I realise that it has taken some effort to sort everything out. I am most grateful to you.'

'A pleasure, sir.'

Hermann began to gather the papers and place them in his briefcase.

'Will you join me for a drink, Herr Hermann? My wife has gone to stay with her sister in Potsdam and it is a pleasure for me not to be ruled by the stopwatch at home for once.'

Without waiting for an answer the *Generalmajor* produced a bottle of Armagnac and poured a large measure for his guest. There was a long silence while he surveyed the drink before putting the glass to his lips and leaning back in his armchair, his tiny eyes first studying Franz Hermann carefully and then closing. It was a while before he opened them.

'Do you have children, Hermann?'

'No, sir.'

'I hope that you do not think it is impertinent of me to ask, but it is something I have been thinking about recently. This may be a strange thing for an army officer to say, but I have noticed among my colleagues that the ones without children seem to have a very different attitude to the war than the ones with them, especially those with sons. My own son is based in Poland, Herr Hermann. He is an *Oberleutnant* and just twenty-two years old. As an army officer I have never held any fears for my own safety. Of course, I have always done my best to avoid making rash judgements that could cause harm to men under my command. But now that my own son is a soldier, I have found that is having an unexpected effect on my attitude to the war: I am more cautious, I worry about the course of the war. It has had a much more profound effect on me than I had imagined. I had hoped that my son would become an architect...'

The *Generalmajor*'s voice tailed off, he seemed to be preoccupied with his own thoughts.

'Hopefully he will not need to remain in the army for too long, sir. Victory will be ours soon!'

The *Generalmajor* looked long and hard at the lawyer.

'You think so, Herr Herrmann? What makes you so sure of that?'

The lawyer shifted uncomfortably in his seat. 'One reads in the papers how well the war is going, that it is just a matter of time before Britain surrenders and—'

'And you believe everything you read in the papers, do you, Herr Hermann? I had thought that lawyers were trained to question things, not to accept matters at face value.'

Franz Hermann shrugged, unsure of what to say and wondering how he had allowed himself to become drawn into a conversation like this.

'Tell me, Herr Hermann: are you a member of the Nazi Party?'

'I am a lawyer, sir. I am not involved in politics.'

'Many lawyers are members of the Nazi Party.'

'I am not one of them, sir.'

Generalmajor Ernst stood up and unbuttoned his jacket, then walked over to the window. The trees in the Kleiner Tiergarten had stopped swaying. The *Generalmajor* shut the window and turned round to face the lawyer.

'Well, if it makes you feel any better, Herr Hermann, nor am I.'

Franz Hermann started to get up, relieved at the opportunity to finish the conversation at that juncture. The *Generalmajor* gestured for him to remain seated and sat down next to him, pulling up his chair alongside the lawyer's.

'You are a clever chap, Herr Hermann.'

'Thank you, sir.'

'You are not just a very competent lawyer, but you are good at managing to appear to be what you are not.'

'I am sorry, I am not sure…'

'You do an excellent job of giving the appearance of being a mild-mannered lawyer, with no interest in politics. You are quiet and you are discreet. You do not draw attention to yourself. But I also know that you have – how can I put this – that you have contacts.'

Franz Hermann could feel his breathing tighten and the room become hotter. He did his best to sound relaxed.

'I suspect, sir, that there must be a misunderstanding here. I am as you originally describe me: a lawyer with no interest in politics. But please be assured that I am a loyal—'

'Please, please, Herr Hermann. I am sure you are all of these things. But you see, I know that there is more to you than that, and you will find that I am not altogether unsympathetic. I know that you have certain contacts and I wish to avail myself of your contacts.'

Franz Hermann said nothing. The *Generalmajor* leaned towards him, so that their faces were just inches apart. He could smell the brandy on his breath and see the tiny red lines in Ernst's eyes.

'Three weeks ago, on the 29th of July to be precise, I was in Bad Reichenhall. Have you heard of it?'

'Of course: a very pleasant spa town in Bavaria, not too far from Salzburg. My parents spent their honeymoon there.'

'Indeed. But I was not there to use the spa, I can assure you. Do you have a good memory, Franz?'

'Yes sir.'

'Werner: please call me Werner. You will make sure to memorise what I say now. Write nothing down.'

Hermann nodded.

'My area of expertise in the army is logistics. It is not a glamorous job, but few people in the high command know better than me how to move our troops around in an efficient manner and then to ensure that they are well supplied. That is perhaps the most underestimated part of warfare. It is one thing to advance fast, especially against a weak enemy, but it is quite another to ensure the integrity of an advance is maintained by ensuring that our forces have good supplies of food and fuel and ammunition. That is what I excel at. But I am not telling you all this to make me seem important. The reason why I was in Bad Reichenhall was because the Chief of Staff, General Jodl, was holding a top secret meeting there on the express instructions of the *Führer* himself. You will have some more Armagnac, Franz? It is quite excellent, one of the more tangible benefits of our conquest of France.' He poured two more large measures. 'Jodl is a busy man, he does not gather senior officers around him in pleasant Bavarian spa towns without very good reason. And the reason he gathered us last month was that, now that France has fallen, the *Führer* has turned his attention to who we attack next. The common belief is that Operation Sea Lion is our priority, and that we will soon launch an invasion of Great Britain. As you know, we started our aerial assault against them over a month ago. But the Kriegsmarine has serious doubts that we will ever be able to successfully invade the British Isles. Our hope is that we win what they are calling the "Battle of Britain" – gain air supremacy – and this leads to victory, but that does not appear likely. The RAF is proving to be a resolute opponent and Churchill shows no inclination whatsoever to surrender.'

With the window closed, the room had now become quite stuffy. The *Generalmajor* stood up to remove his jacket and loosen his collar.

'The *Führer* has instructed Colonel General Jodl to explore other options, in the eventuality that we do not invade Britain. The option that we discussed in Bad Reichenhall was that of invading the Soviet Union.'

During the shocked silence that followed Hermann heard the loud ticking of a clock from the hall. The tops of the trees in the Kleiner Tiergarten had begun to sway again. The *Generalmajor* reached over to a side table and opened a box of cigars, offering one to the lawyer – who declined – before slowly lighting one for himself.

'Invade the Soviet Union? But surely that would be madness! We have a pact with them?'

'It is not as outrageous a thought as you appear to think it is, Franz. That pact was designed to keep our eastern borders quiet while we dealt with Western Europe. Now, I have no love for the Soviet Union but for many of us, Franz – those of us who approach matters from a professional military point of view as opposed to an ideological one – the prospect of invading the Soviet Union is a nightmare. To attempt to invade the Soviet Union would be to ignore the lessons of history. Bismarck himself said that the secret of politics was to "make a good treaty with Russia", which is of course what we did. From a military point of view, invading the Soviet Union has all the potential to end in disaster. Even Field Marshall Keitel is trying to dissuade Hitler from the idea, and he is well known for never disagreeing with the *Führer*.'

'When will this invasion take place?'

'Too early to say, Franz: it may never happen. The purpose of Jodl gathering us in Bad Reichenhall was to get us thinking in theoretical terms about how we might prepare for such an invasion. Such an invasion is so sensitive and so secret that we can do little more than think about it. The final decision will rest with the *Führer*. After the conquest of the Low Countries and France, he is convinced that he is a military genius. He thinks that we older Wehrmacht officers are too cautious, too conservative.'

The *Generalmajor* was now wreathed in cigar smoke, the colour of gun metal. He leant back in his chair, staring up at the ceiling.

'However, Franz, even Hitler knows that the timing of an invasion would need to be very precise if we are not to be caught out in the Russian winter. If we have not achieved our objectives by the start of the winter then we are doomed. So we would need to attack by mid-May at the latest. Then we have a chance of success, although not a very good one.'

'Why on earth are you telling me this?'

'Many of us believe that to invade the Soviet Union would be suicide for Germany. There are groups of us in the Bendlerblock who are of like mind. We believe that we are acting in the best interests of Germany. As you may be aware, the Abwehr has its headquarters in the Bendlerblock. A few days ago, I was talking with an old friend who is a very senior officer in the Abwehr. His mother died a month ago and he asked if I could recommend a good lawyer to take care of everything. I told him about you and that was that. The next day he asked me to go for a walk with him along the banks of the Landwehr Canal. He confided in me that you have come to the attention of the Abwehr...'

'This is preposterous sir. It is simply untrue. I must insist that—'

'Franz, you must not worry.' He patted the lawyer on the arm in a reassuring manner. 'Just be very, very grateful that it is the Abwehr that you have come to the attention of and not the Gestapo. According to my friend, they are aware that you are able to channel information to the Allies. They have permitted you to carry on doing this because they believed that there may come a time when they wished to use this channel. That time has now come.'

Franz Hermann held out his hands in 'what can I say' gesture. 'I am not a traitor, sir. I consider myself to be a loyal German. I happen to believe that Germany should be a democratic country and that this war could ruin us.'

'No one is saying that you are a traitor. Nor am I, for that matter. We all have our different motives. Will you pass on this information, about the meeting at Bad Reichenhall and the possibility of an invasion of the Soviet Union?'

'Of course.'

When he left the apartment there was a cool evening breeze, which was a welcome relief from the stuffiness of the apartment, but it had no calming effect on Hermann. He felt the huge trees closing in on him and imagined that the people around him on the pavement were looking at him. He would have to move fast, he could not afford to think about things.

—

When Franz Hermann was sixteen or seventeen, it had been briefly fashionable among his group at school to root out ancient Chinese proverbs, which they would then quote to each other as if they had stumbled upon words of wisdom which unlocked the secrets of the universe. It was all rather pretentious and it was a phase which did not last long. A couple of their group had continued to grasp at various ancient beliefs long after they had left school, and they were the ones who had become early members of the Nazi Party.

One of the sayings that they had passed around sounded at first like a Chinese good luck wish: 'May you live in interesting times.' The twist was that it was actually a curse. He had never quite understood why hoping that someone lived in interesting times was a curse. All his life he had wished that his life had been more interesting: an obedient student; not fit for military service; a childless marriage; and a worthy but dull career.

Now he was trapped between the gates of heaven and the banks of hell. A chance remark during an unguarded conversation at a dinner party a month after the start of the war had been followed up by a clandestine meeting at the zoo a week later. He and the elegant woman with the Viennese accent, who had slipped him the note as he left the dinner party, had stood alongside the elephant enclosure watching the animals spray each other with water.

'I noticed you made some remarks about the regime. You had best be careful where and to whom you say such things,' she had said, softly. He nodded, he realised he had been careless; his wife had told him as much in no uncertain terms on their way home. Too much good wine had been his excuse. '*But you also said something about tensions in the Nazi Party leadership in Berlin?*' the Viennese woman had whispered. 'Where did you get that from?'

He had waited for two of the elephants to finish calling to each other.

'From one of my colleagues,' he told her.

'And what is his name?'

He had hesitated before replying. The elegantly dressed lady with the elegant Viennese accent was evidently not quite what she seemed. Franz Hermann could have walked away at that point. He could have said that he wanted to take matters no further and would appreciate it if they could both forget they had ever met. She was hardly likely to report him to the Gestapo. But there was something almost seductive about her manner. He found it impossible not to reply to her.

'Alois Jäger: we work at the same law firm. He is some big shot in the leadership of the Nazi Party in Berlin. As far as he is concerned, I am completely apolitical. I pick up a lot of his legal work while he is on Nazi Party business, so he has reason to be grateful to me. And he cannot help gossiping. I hear him talk about Goebbels: he cannot stand him, they just don't get on. But from what I gather, there is a feeling shared among a number of senior Nazis in Berlin that Goebbels cannot be an effective *Gauleiter* of the city and Minister for Propaganda. They think he should concentrate on one or the other.'

'This is very interesting,' she had replied. 'You are clearly in a position to pick up such information. I would like to tell you how you can pass it on to people who need to know this kind of information. Are you willing to do so?'

Franz Hermann said that he was. They walked round to the tiger enclosure and then over to the aquarium. The elegant lady with the Viennese accent had slipped her gloved arm through his as she explained in detail how he could make contact with the right people.

And then his position had become even more precarious in December, when Rosa had turned up on his doorstep. What could he do: turn her away? It made sense to lodge her and the children with his mother, and he was sure it would only be for a few weeks, but that was eight... nine months ago. Now he was a British spy and harbouring a Jewish family, so now he understood why 'May you live in interesting times' was indeed a curse.

–

He would have preferred to walk and give himself some opportunity to compose himself, but time was against him so he took a tram from Alt Moabit into the Unter den Linden, getting off a stop earlier than he needed to at the junction with Friedrichstrasse.

Despite being so near to it, he decided against popping back into his office: had anyone been following him or had spotted him in the street it would have looked normal for him to return to work, but he was in a hurry. He walked along the Unter den Linden for another two blocks before turning left into the Opernplatz.

Although he came to the pretty square at least twice a week and had done so for years, it nonetheless left him with an uneasy feeling. He could never forget what had happened there seven years before, in May 1933, when the Nazis had burned tens of thousands of books. The smell had lingered for days, and for weeks afterwards people would come across tiny piles of ash throughout the area. Even months later it was not uncommon to come across scraps of paper that had somehow escaped the flames, floating around the city in a defiant manner, daring passers-by to steal a look at a word or two that might corrupt them.

His sense of apprehension increased as he entered St Hedwig's, the cathedral he had worshipped at since he was a boy. Although they lived in Dahlem and there were plenty of Catholic churches near to where they lived, his mother seemed to be of the opinion that their piety was increased by praying at the seat of the Archbishop.

Now, the cathedral served a very different purpose for him.

The mass was just coming to an end and most of the congregation were leaving the church. In the old days, people would gather in small groups and chat, but that was not the done thing now. You never knew who might be watching, or listening.

Franz Hermann sat on his own towards the back of the cathedral, watching the small group of priests at the high altar as they began to disperse. Sure enough, the tall and slightly stooped figure of the young priest he was looking for emerged from the little group and walked in long strides towards the confession box that sat on its own to the side.

'*I always take confession after mass on Tuesday and Thursday afternoons. On those days I use the confession box that is on its own, the one near the high altar. Only come to me then. No one can overhear us there. It is safer. Or at least, not as dangerous.*'

Franz Hermann left his seat at the back of the cathedral and walked towards the altar, where he knelt and crossed himself before walking over towards the confession box that the young priest had gone into. An old man with scruffy trousers had just entered the confession box, muttering silently to himself as he did so. The lawyer sat down next to an elegantly dressed lady who had a blue silk scarf wrapped around her neck. She was clutching a photograph of what looked like a boy in Luftwaffe uniform and was dabbing her eyes with a crisp white handkerchief.

The old man shuffled out, still muttering silently to himself and the elegantly dressed lady replaced him, her high heels echoing sharply on the old tiled floor. The confession box was in a perfect position: unlike the ones grouped together on the other side of the cathedral, this one was isolated in a quiet cloister and the chairs were some way from the box: it was impossible to overhear anything, not even the sound of voices in the box, let alone the words.

A few minutes later the lady emerged from the confession box, still dabbing her eyes with the crisp white handkerchief. Franz Hermann walked over to the box, crossed himself, closed the heavy velvet curtain and knelt down.

'In the name of the Father, and of the Son, and of the Holy Spirit. My last confession was two weeks ago.'

He had not been sure if Father Josef was aware he was there, but he looked towards the grill and, at the sound of his voice, he could see the young priest sit up sharply. As Father Josef glanced towards him he caught sight of the priest's bright red nose, as if he had just come in from the cold.

'Go on, my son.'

'I have sinned, Father. I fear I have been treating our maid too harshly because I suspected she may have been stealing some small change left around the house, although I now think it was not her. And I have been guilty of the sin of envy: a friend has been able to find some best-quality cloth material and has had it made into fine suit. You must know how hard that is in these times, and I find it has been the cause of feelings of jealousy in myself.'

'And any other sins, my son?'

'I am afraid that I took the Lord's name in vain: I used it in a disrespectful manner. I am sorry for these and all the sins of my past life.'

'And that is it?'

'That is it, Father.' The lawyer thought he had done quite well to muster three things that he could pass off as sins.

The priest would be decoding his message. The confession of treating the maid too harshly was for security: '*All is well, I am not being followed*'. The sin of envy indicated that he needed to meet his contact. Taking the Lord's name in vain meant that it is urgent.

'I see.' The priest coughed, pausing to take everything in. Through the grill he could see the priest's head bob up and down, the bright red nose most clearly visible in the gloom. 'Say a "Hail Mary" and pray for your sins. She will next be in on Thursday, my son. I will pass on your message. Meet her at the usual place, at the usual time on the Friday. Can you manage that?'

'Yes Father.'

'If she cannot manage that or does not turn up, return here on Tuesday. You had better say an Act of Contrition, my son.'

'I am heartily sorry for having offended you my Lord and I detest all my sins, because I dread the loss of heaven and the pains of hell. I firmly resolve with the help of your grace, to confess my sins, to do penance and to amend my life. Amen.'

The priest replied with a prayer of forgiveness. 'Give thanks to the Lord for He is good.'

Franz Hermann crossed himself and replied, 'For His mercy endures forever.'

He left the confession box. The waiting chairs had now filled. He paused in the main body of the cathedral, said his 'Hail Mary' and a few other prayers and then hurried out and headed home to Dahlem, his reply to the absolution repeating in his mind throughout the journey.

'*For His mercy endures forever.*'

He certainly hoped so.

–

The military attaché at the Portuguese Legation in Berlin was well aware that his secretary attended Mass whenever she could. Although not as devout as he would like to be, this rather impressed the Colonel, as he found religious observance in others somehow reassuring. At least it was a sign that his Dona Maria do Rosario, a reserved woman who shared little of herself, must be trustworthy. He sometimes liked to imagine what sins his secretary had to confess to. She led a pious life: she did not drink or speak out of turn; she was a hard worker and a loyal servant of the Portuguese Government, with a framed photograph of Salazar on her desk.

Berlin was, the Colonel was fond of reminding whoever would listen, not an easy posting, and perhaps the most important of all of Portugal's overseas missions. A neutral country had to lean one way and then the other, depending upon the wind of war. It required him to be fleet of foot and have the utmost discretion, and the Colonel in turn demanded that of his staff. So it was neither unusual nor even unexpected when Dona Maria do Rosario entered the Colonel's office with a neat pile of documents just after five o'clock on the afternoon of Thursday 15th August.

'These letters need to be signed, sir; each one is appended to their relevant file. If you can sign them before you leave I can ensure they are in the diplomatic bag on Friday evening. I am leaving now to go to the cathedral, but happy to return later if you require me, sir. Otherwise I will be in first thing in the morning.'

'That is fine,' the Colonel told his secretary. 'I will sign the papers and see you first thing in the morning.' In truth, she arrived at work sometime before he did. She was invariably in the office by seven thirty, when few other staff were around. He was unsure why she came in quite so early, but he had every reason to be most grateful to her for doing so. He would arrive at work between eight thirty and nine to find all his papers in order and everything neatly set out on his desk, his day already organised for him. Of course, he was technically in breach of protocol by allowing her access to secret documents, but it made life so much easier and, of course, how could such a devout Catholic not be trustworthy?

Dona Maria do Rosario hurried out of the Legation at a quarter past five and arrived at St Hedwig's Cathedral in time for the early evening Mass. It was close to seven o'clock when she finally entered the confession box, a slight early evening chill now around in the cloisters, causing her to pull her light jacket tight around her shoulders.

'In the name of the Father, and of the Son, and of the Holy Spirit. My last confession was one week ago.'

Father Josef looked at her urgently, his face pressed tight against the grill to check it really was her.

'What are your sins?'

She gave the code: a sin of gluttony to indicate that all was well, and a sin of speaking ill of someone behind their back to ensure she had nothing to report. The priest spoke urgently.

'Hugo's been here – two days, ago. He needs to see you as soon as possible. I told him it would be tomorrow, the usual place and the usual time. I hope you can make it?'

Dona Maria assured the priest that she could. 'How are things?' the priest asked her.

Very busy, she told him. 'So much material comes through the Colonel's office that I work late most nights and I'm starting earlier every morning just to find the most important papers. It is getting more and more risky though. I fear that sooner or later someone will suspect me.'

'Maybe moderate your hours. The material you are sending back is so good, I am told, that you should not risk too much. Don't forget, you need to meet Hugo tomorrow and report back on what he tells you.'

'I know.'

'Do you want to pray? Shall I grant you absolution?'

Dona Maria do Rosario was already up and preparing to leave the confession box.

'No thank you, Father.'

As she hurried out of the church she only just remembered to cross herself and pause for a very brief prayer.

–

The following day, Friday, an unusual wind whipped around the centre of Berlin. For some reason, it appeared to linger about four feet off the ground, creating the strange effect of leaves and small bits of litter fluttering around in mid-air. The strange wind was still at play when Franz Hermann hurried out of his office at one o'clock. He was going for a walk, he told his secretary, reassuring her that he would be back in time for his two o'clock meeting. He turned into Behrenstrasse and then left into Wilhemstrasse. In between Wilhemstrasse and Hermann Göring Strasse was a small park, taking up no more than a block, where office workers and civil servants – but not too many of them – liked to take their lunch.

He entered the small park and walked towards the north west corner where a series of old benches surrounded an enormous tree. Perhaps because the benches appeared so uncomfortable, or perhaps because the size of the tree ensured that this little spot was permanently in the shade, this area was deserted, apart from an olive-skinned woman in her late thirties poised demurely on the edge of one of the benches. Her jet-black hair was pulled back from a face that could have been prettier, but for the absence of any make-up and the presence of what looked like a disapproving look. She was eating an apple and an open book was resting on her lap. He sat on the next bench and removed his jacket, taking out a packet of cigarettes from the jacket as he did so. He offered one to the lady.

'No thank you, sir. I do not smoke,' she replied in a foreign accent.

'Very sensible: my wife does not approve.'

'I can offer you an apple in return.'

And so the exchange continued. In the unlikely event of anyone overhearing the conversation it would have sounded like two strangers passing the time of day. But soon they had established that each other was safe; that they had not been followed; and that he had information to pass on.

Franz Hermann shifted to the end of his park bench, so that he was now nearer to the one that Dona Maria do Rosario was sitting on. She had opened her book and was giving the appearance of avidly reading from it. The lawyer was bent forward, his elbows resting on his lap and busy smoking. He was facing the ground, occasionally looking up to be sure that no one else was around. He spoke very quietly, but at a volume that ensured Dona Maria could hear everything he was saying.

'How quickly can you get a message to Lisbon?'

Without looking up from the book she replied. 'It depends how long it is, but there is a bag going this evening. If I can type it up in time then I could get it in.'

'You'll have to, it is urgent. This is what you need to tell them. Colonel General Jodl held a meeting at Bad Reichenhall on the 29th of July. My informant, who is a senior officer in the OKH, was present. I am not giving his name, not at the moment. Apparently they are now entertaining the possibility that Britain may not capitulate after all, and Hitler wants to have alternative plans in place. The purpose of Jodl's meeting was to get senior officers to start thinking about plans for the invasion of the Soviet Union.'

He looked up at Dona Maria. Her eyebrows had risen very slightly and momentarily, as if she had read something interesting in her book, which she was still looking at. She took a dainty bite from her apple.

'My informant says that a lot of the professional army officers are against the idea of invading the Soviet Union as they think it will end in failure,' he continued. 'The thinking is that any invasion will have to start by the middle of May because it would need to be over by the onset of winter. Have you got all that?'

Dona Maria said she had. Franz noticed that her face had relaxed now and she had even allowed herself a slight smile as she briefly turned towards him. He asked her to repeat what he had told her. Her repetition was impressively word-perfect. She would return now to the Legation and type it up in code in time for that evening's diplomatic bag, she said. Was there anything else?

'I think that's enough!'

Chapter 14

Berlin, January 1941

'And finally, one other matter, Herr Hermann.'

These days, Franz Hermann's secretary always seemed to have 'one other matter' that needed to be dealt with. Before the war, there had been enough work for the nine senior lawyers in the firm at 181 Friedrichstrasse to be kept busy and well paid, but not so much that they were overstretched. That had all changed now: one of the senior lawyers had retired and not been replaced, and two others had joined the armed forces, along with half of the junior lawyers. As if that was not bad enough, Alois Jäger now seemed to spend more than half of the time he was meant to be at work on Nazi Party business, which meant that the remaining five seniors had to pick up more and more of Jäger's work. It was not as if they could complain; they just had to go along with it. As far as Franz Hermann was concerned, as distasteful as it felt, at least it afforded the firm a degree of political protection.

'Do you remember *Generalmajor* Werner Ernst, Herr Hermann?'

He had heard nothing from the General since their meeting in August. He had hoped never to hear from him again. He did his best to look as if he was having a lot of trouble remembering who the General was.

'You'll have to remind me, Ilse. Was it something to do with a dispute with his bank?'

'No, sir. That was another army officer. You were sorting out the affairs of *Generalmajor* Ernst's late mother. It was all tied up in August.'

'Yes, of course. I remember now. Doesn't he live near the Kleiner Tiergarten?'

'That is correct sir. He rang today while you were in a meeting. He says that one or two issues have arisen regarding his mother's estate that he would like to see you about.'

'You have my diary Ilse, please arrange the meeting.'

'He said it was urgent, Herr Hermann.'

He knew that Ilse would expect him to protest: matters arising from the estate of the General's mother all these months on could hardly be construed as urgent. He also knew, though, that if the General said he needed to see him urgently, then it was urgent. He could feel himself getting very hot again and was aware that he was drumming his fingers loudly on the desk.

'Very well then, Ilse. He can either come in here during the day tomorrow or I can go to his apartment tomorrow after work.'

'He said that you are to go to his apartment tonight, sir.'

—

Franz Hermann waited impatiently for Ilse to leave work, spending the half hour before she got round to doing so optimistically trying to think of a possible genuine problem with the *Generalmajor*'s mother's estate, which he knew was highly unlikely. Had there really been a problem, it would have emerged some time ago. He feared that the *Generalmajor* was about to entrust him with another secret.

He allowed five minutes to pass after Ilse's departure and then left, managing to find a rare taxi on the Unter den Linden to take him as far as Storm Strasse, from where he walked the short distance to *Generalmajor* Ernst's apartment block. The same teenage maid let him into the apartment, which was now in a state of chaos.

There were packing cases piled up in the hall, suitcases assembled by the door and furniture and paintings covered in dustsheets. A large lady who he took to be Frau Ernst briefly came out of the kitchen to check who the visitor was, but went straight back into the kitchen, where Hermann could see at least one other maid busy scrubbing the sides. *Generalmajor* Werner Ernst came to meet him in the hall.

'Hermann: thank you for coming so soon. I have to go away very soon and need to sort out some annoying paperwork before doing so. Anke, please ensure that we are not disturbed. Follow me, Hermann.'

The study was in a similar state of upheaval to the rest of the apartment, but there were two uncovered armchairs towards the window, which Ernst led his lawyer over to.

'I am sorry to hear that there are problems with the estate, sir. I had assumed that everything was concluded in a satisfactory manner back in August.'

The *Generalmajor* had been rooting around in a nearby packing case, from which he produced a bottle of Armagnac and two glasses. He poured a large measure for Hermann and a considerably larger one for himself. As he sat down he shifted his heavy armchair very close to Hermann's, so that the two armrests were touching. When he spoke, it was in a quiet voice.

'Of course everything was satisfactory, Hermann. You did an excellent job. However, I am afraid that for the sake of appearance, I have had to make a bit of a fuss: I have told Frau Ernst that you have been less than efficient, and I wrote as much in a letter to my son. He has now been transferred to Norway and I assume that the censors may be reading his letters.'

The *Generalmajor* stood up and stretched himself and then walked over to the curtains, pulling them together. Hermann noticed that the *Generalmajor* looked more drawn than before, his tiny eyes slightly bloodshot. He appeared to have lost some weight and his face was more lined. He twisted a half-finished cigarette into an ashtray and took a cigar from a box on top of a packing case, not bothering to offer one to the lawyer.

'Things are not good, Hermann. The atmosphere in the Bendlerblock is terrible. The atmosphere in the whole of Berlin is terrible. Everyone suspects everyone else of conspiring against them – it is hard to know who to trust. The professional soldiers in the High Command and the leadership of the Abwehr are the most distrusted, I fear. Even if you join the Nazi Party, it does not seem to make any difference these days. I felt obliged to join in November, but I still think that people are suspicious of me. The reason for all this upheaval in the department is that I am being transferred to Warsaw. In my view, it is quite unnecessary; I can do my job just as well, if not better, from Berlin. But I think Hitler and Himmler and the rest of them want to dilute any possible sources of opposition to them. Maybe opposition is too strong a word – perhaps what I mean is disagreement.'

'Do you think they suspect you of having passed on information?'

The *Generalmajor* shook his head slowly, at the same time as lighting his cigar. He paused a while as he inhaled deeply.

'No, no, no! Look Hermann, if they did, I would not be here – and nor, I suspect, would you. I was very careful, and I assume that you have been too. The thing is, ever since the meeting at Bad Reichenhall at the end of July, a number of the senior officers like myself who were asked to start thinking about the possibility of invading the Soviet Union have been advising caution. Not everyone, by any means. Too many people feel that they have to say what the *Führer* wants to hear, so they enthusiastically go along with planning for the invasion. A number of others, it should be said, actually agree with invading the Soviet Union. But for people like myself, well, we have done nothing that could be construed as treason. In my case, I have been able to produce very detailed papers about the difficulties in keeping our forces properly supplied during an invasion of the Soviet Union. Tell me, Hermann: do you know how far it is from our border in Poland to Moscow?'

The lawyer shook his head. *No idea.*

'Over 1,000 kilometres. To put that in perspective, from our western border, say near Saarbrücken, to Paris is around 340 kilometres: so an invasion of the Soviet Union would be three times that distance, and let me tell you, the roads in France are considerably better than those in the Soviet Union. And as well as the terrain you also have to take into account other factors, like the weather, and you can see how risky an invasion becomes. That is what I have been saying in my reports – I am very careful to stick to the facts. But it has not done me any favours. They are keeping an eye on people like me. They do not completely trust me, hence my move to Warsaw.'

'So why are you packing up the apartment?'

'My wife does not want to remain here on her own. She and her sister in Potsdam are talking about moving to their family's old hunting lodge near Magdeburg. She says that she will feel safer there. Look, Hermann, there's something else I need to tell you, one other piece of information for you to pass on through your contacts. This will have to be the last information that I give you. It is too dangerous for us to meet again and, in any case, in a few days I will be in Warsaw.'

The lawyer nodded and leaned closer towards Ernst.

'I happen to know that, a week before Christmas, Hitler issued a detailed directive about the invasion of the Soviet Union. The *Führer* is very sparing in the number of directives that he issues, no more than one or two a month. This directive is so secret that I was only able to glance at it in the presence of others, certainly not allowed to take a copy away – which is perhaps another reason why I know that I am no longer trusted. I am only vaguely aware of what is in this directive, though I do know that it talks about the invasion taking place in the middle of May. You must pass this on: will you do that?'

'Yes, but they will want to know more detail, surely?'

'I am sure that they will, they may even want to see a copy of the directive, no doubt, but it is very, very restricted. From what I gather, there were only nine copies. If you only get across that the invasion is still on, and scheduled for the middle of May, that is important. You had better leave now, Hermann. I am glad that we have finally been able to sort out my mother's estate!'

As they left the study, he placed his hand on the lawyer's shoulder.

'I doubt that we shall meet again, Hermann. Maybe one day, if circumstances are very different, we will. But who knows, eh? Good luck.'

As Franz Hermann headed home that evening he could not recall ever having felt more miserable, or so afraid.

–

'And that's the message...? No more?'

Dona Maria do Rosario and Franz Hermann were walking around the enormous tree in the small park between Wilhemstrasse and Hermann Göring Strasse, aware that this was more exposed than sitting on the benches around the tree, but it had been raining and the benches were sodden: sitting on them would have looked suspicious.

'I know it is not long, but it is very important. Remember, Hitler issued the directive a week before Christmas: they are still planning to invade the Soviet Union and they are talking about the middle of May. That's four months away.'

'Yes, I would have hoped even the British would be able to work that one out, thank you.'

–

Franz Hermann had met Dona Maria do Rosario on Friday the 17th of January. The following Tuesday, Ilse came into his office just before lunch. There had been a phone call.

'The man said that he understood you specialised in sorting out estates, especially complicated ones. His uncle recently died in Bremen and he wanted to know if we had an office in Bremen. I said "no" and he said not to worry and that maybe he would call back.'

'Bremen you say?'

'Yes, Herr Hermann. I am not sure why he would think we had an office in Bremen, but there you are. Now, these letters...'

This was only the second time that Father Josef had called him like this. The very fact he was telephoning him at the office meant that something was up. The 'Bremen' reference meant that it was very urgent. He was to attend confession that night.

–

'In the name of the Father, and of the Son, and of the Holy Spirit. My last confession was one week ago.'

Father Josef pressed his face against the grille separating the two men. 'We need to be quick. I have a message from her: she passed on your message and has been contacted urgently. Apparently you talked

170

about a document... don't tell me anything about it, just wait my son... and they are saying they need to see it. That is the message. Do you understand?'

'I understand, Father, but I have not got it. I will see what I can do, but they need to understand that my source has left Berlin. This is going to be very difficult.'

'I am only passing on the message. She said you needed to know before you could meet at the usual rendezvous, in case you can get hold of it. Do your best, my son: I am sure that God will guide you. Do you want to take confession?'

Franz Hermann shook his head.

'No thank you, Father. I wouldn't know where to begin.'

–

In the twelve months since he had been reunited with his first wife and son, Gunter Reinhart had done his best to visit them at least once a week at the house in Dahlem where they were living with Franz Hermann's mother. In one respect the arrangement had held up very well. Franz Hermann's mother could not have been better looked after and therefore the talk of her having to move into a nursing home or even a hospital was long forgotten. Frau Hermann had no idea that her excellent nurse was actually a doctor, and certainly had no idea that she was Jewish and had two children with her. Her hearing was so poor that she never heard the footsteps on the floor above her, or the subdued sound of the children's voices.

But in every other respect, their predicament was an increasingly hopeless one. The situation for Jews in Berlin worsened by the day: although it was still possible for some to emigrate, in reality this had slowed to a trickle, and that was just for people who had all the right paperwork and could afford the punitive taxes being charged. And even then, they needed to find somewhere that would take them. Most of Europe was occupied. There were rumours about Sweden, even Spain. The place most people aspired to go to was Switzerland, but those borders were sealed tight, on both sides.

Gunter, Rosa and Franz had come up with countless schemes to get the three of them out of the country, but all of them had too many risks and too many flaws. Gunter usually visited after work on a Wednesday. That was the day that his wife took their children to their piano lessons in Reinickendorf and afterwards they stopped for tea at a favourite cafe on Holtzdamm. They rarely arrived home before seven thirty, so Gunter found that if he left work at five he could go down to Dahlem, spend an hour and a half there and be home in plenty of time.

He did his best to take some food and money with him and Franz's wife, Silke, always tried to be there at the same time so that she could sit with Frau Hermann while Rosa went upstairs to be with Gunter and the children. On the last Wednesday of January, Gunter arrived at the house to find Franz Hermann sitting in the room upstairs that Rosa used as a lounge. Rosa followed him into the room.

'Where are the children? Is Alfred all right?' asked Gunter.

'They are fine, Gunter. You will see Alfred in a minute. I need to talk with you first.' Franz Hermann was leaning forward on the low sofa, opposite Gunter and Rosa. His head was bowed low. As he talked, he continued to look down at the patterned carpet.

'I am afraid that I have some bad news, Rosa.'

There was an audible intake of breath from her and she gripped Gunter's knee.

'Harald?'

'I am afraid so.'

Rosa Stern lifted her head high and turned to the window, her head resting for a while against the thick curtains. When she turned round again her eyes had filled with tears. Gunter put his arm round her and pulled her close. She let her head fall on his shoulder.

'Tell me everything, Franz.'

'I'll tell you everything that I know, Rosa. As you are aware, we could hardly make a direct approach to Sachsenhausen – "Please can you tell us how Harald Stern is getting on?" – I had begun to hear that when people died at Sachsenhausen, or any of the other camps that they've taken Berliners to, the police turn up at the home of the next of kin. They bring their ashes with them in an urn, along with a bill for the cost of the urn.'

'Do we need all this detail, Franz? Is it really necessary?' Gunter asked.

'No, Gunter, don't be concerned on my part. I need to hear all of this,' Rosa said.

'Of course, you are Harald's next of kin, but fortunately the authorities do not know where you are. You remember a few months ago I managed to track down an address for his elder brother, Paul – in Spandau? I visited him and told him that as far as I was aware, you are in Paris. If he is questioned by the Gestapo about you, he cannot tell them what he doesn't know. He had heard nothing from Harald either, but he did say that he would contact me if he did. I did not give him any of my details; again, it is too risky. But I said I would try and visit him every few weeks and if he had any news, he would then be able to give it to me. I visited him yesterday and he told me the news.'

Franz Hermann paused to remove a handkerchief from his pocket and he noisily blew his nose. His voice was trembling when he next spoke. 'They brought the urn round last week containing Harald's ashes. They say he died of a heart condition – natural causes. Apparently that is what they say with everyone. I am so sorry, Rosa...'

The ensuing silence lasted a lifetime, and as happens in such circumstances, even the quietest, least obtrusive sound reverberated around the room. Rosa cried solidly for the next ten minutes, and then she stood up and walked around the room, deep in thought. When she spoke, her voice sounded resolute. 'I have made a decision, Gunter. Do what you can to get Alfred out. It will be easier if it is just him, no?'

Both men nodded: this is what they had been saying for months.

'We're all doomed if we stay. Alfred will be the easiest to smuggle out. Can you do it?'

Franz Hermann nodded his head, up and down and from side to side, weighing up the chances of success. *Maybe; there's a chance.*

'We can try, Rosa, I promise you,' said Gunter. 'And then we will get you and Sophia out.'

173

It was seven o'clock before Gunter Reinhart left the house on the corner of Kaiser Wilhelm Strasse and Arno-Holz Strasse. Franz Hermann said he would walk with him to the station while Silke looked after his mother, allowing Rosa to stay with the distraught children.

They walked in silence until they were on Königin-Luise-Strasse, each man wrapped in his own thoughts and seemingly overwhelmed by the enormity of the situation closing in on them.

'We must get Alfred out before it is too late,' said Gunter. 'But it is going to be so difficult, Franz – so dangerous. The boy has no papers. If there was any way I could get him to Switzerland then I have a good friend in Zurich who would take care of him, but how can I get him there?'

Franz Hermann said nothing for a while, but Gunter noticed that first he was shaking his head and then nodding it, as if he was having a heated debate with himself. *Pros and cons.* Podbielski Allee station was in view by the time Hermann spoke, although only after he had carefully looked around to ensure that no one was within earshot: that was how people spoke in Berlin these days. 'This is about your son's life, Gunter, so I can absolutely trust you, yes?'

'That goes without saying.'

'Let me ask you a question first: how senior are you at the Reichs-bank?'

'Senior enough: I run a department.'

'And how close are you to Walther Funk?'

'We aren't friends as such, but I am good at my job and he relies on me for certain matters: I handle our transactions with the Swiss. That is very important to him—'

'And the economies of countries we have occupied, do you get involved in them?'

'To an extent, certainly, if we need to move money and gold from those countries to Switzerland. Why are you asking this?'

'I want to know how much you are trusted at the Reichsbank. After all, you were married to a Jew.'

'That was many years ago, Franz. And remember, I divorced her. It is no doubt on a file somewhere, but it is not an issue. I even made sure I joined the Nazi Party. In answer to your question, I am trusted.'

'I have some… contacts, Gunter: people who may be able to help get Alfred out of Germany. But they would want something in return, something that you may be able to get your hands on.'

The two men had now moved to the side of the pavement, standing next to the railing and under a tree whose branches fell to just above their heads. Franz Hermann paused and took a deep breath, about to take the plunge.

'Go on, Hermann, what is it?'

'I am going to ask you about something: if you have not heard of it, please forget I ever asked the question. Do you understand?'

He nodded. The two men waited while an elderly couple and their dog strolled past, nodding in reply to their greeting.

'Have you ever come across a document called Directive 21?'

Gunter Reinhart stared at Franz Hermann long and hard, his eyes terrified. He looked more shocked than when he had met the lawyer in the bar and been told that Rosa and the children were back in Berlin.

'Are you being serious?'

'Yes. Are you aware of it?'

'I am. But how on earth have you heard about it?'

'For heaven's sake, Gunter, keep your voice down. You do not need to know that. Have you actually seen it?'

'I have. Do you know how top secret this is?'

'Tell me how you have had access to it?'

'There is one copy in the Reichsbank. It is kept in a safe in Funk's office, but I have been able to see it because he is very concerned that if this… hang on, Hermann: you tell me what this directive is about – you tell me that before I say anything else.'

'It is about plans to invade the Soviet Union.'

'Very well then: Funk and no doubt many of the others are nothing if not greedy. They are concerned that if – when – this invasion takes place, we should have plans in place to get our hands on what assets we can and get them into our Swiss bank accounts. That is why I am allowed access to the document.'

'Presumably you can't take it out of Funk's office?'

'Yes and no: if I need to see it, I have to put a request in writing to his private secretary, and if he approves then I am allowed to see it in a secure room next to Funk's office.'

'Are you alone in that room?'

'Funk's private secretary is meant to stay in with me, but he is an impatient sort: he will usually stay in the room for five minutes and if it looks like I am going to be any longer he will go and sit at his desk, which is just outside the door.'

Very slowly the two men walked towards Podbielski Allee station, talking as they did so. It was gone eight o'clock before Gunter Reinhart returned to his house in Charlottenburg and the inevitable wrath of his wife. He was, however, oblivious to it.

He had to make a plan.

Chapter 15

London and Lisbon, February 1941

On a blustery Tuesday afternoon at the beginning of February, Captain Edgar was summoned to Christopher Porter's office on the top floor of a building best described as functional rather than in any way elegant. Edgar stood at the narrow window overlooking St James' Square, his back turned to his superior who appeared to be even more ill at ease in Edgar's presence than normal.

'I do wish you'd sit down, Edgar.'

Edgar turned round, leaning against the window ledge.

'You said this was urgent… sir.' There was a pause before the 'sir'.

Christopher Porter cleared his throat and nervously straightened the fountain pen holder on his desk. 'I have to tell you, Edgar, that I am getting all kinds of flak from Downing Street. It is most trying.'

'I am sorry to hear that, sir. Is this in connection with anything in particular?'

'In connection with our intelligence that Germany may be planning an invasion of the Soviet Union. You insisted on it being a complete secret, but now Downing Street have caught wind of it and they are not happy, to say the very least. Their view – and I am informed that this is very much the view of the Prime Minister – is that from the outset we should have shared our intelligence that such plans existed more widely.'

'But we are not obliged to share every shred of unconfirmed intelligence, surely?'

'Indeed, Edgar – but this is more than a "shred of unconfirmed intelligence", isn't it? We knew about the meeting in Bad Reichenhall last July and we know about this directive that Hitler issued in

December, don't we? The Prime Minister is of the view that this is the single most important area of intelligence at the moment, and we must do everything we can to get our hands on it. It has been made very clear to me that our failure to share this intelligence is viewed most seriously: the one way in which we can redeem ourselves is by getting our hands on this wretched document. If—'

'*Get our hands on it?* Are you joking? If that is seriously the view of Downing Street then one has to be most concerned at their grasp on reality. We have been told that there are no more than nine copies of this Directive 21. The idea that we can obtain one of them is ridiculous. How do your chums in Downing Street propose that we go about this?'

Christopher Porter was now busying himself moving the large blotting pad around on his desk.

'You will need to go out there, Edgar.'

'You mean go to Germany?'

'Not if we can avoid it. I was wondering about that chap Hunter?'

'Henry Hunter?' Edgar began to pace the room, turning once again to stare out of the window overlooking St James' Square, deep in thought. 'That is not a bad idea, sir, I'll grant you that. His trial run in Germany last year went well. He's still in Switzerland so has perfect cover to go into Germany.'

'The best bet would be for you to get to Switzerland through Portugal and Spain – can't see another way at the moment. Once you're safely there, we can take a view.'

Edgar stared at Porter in disbelief as it dawned on him that he was being serious.

'Any other country you'd like me to drop into while I'm over there? Italy perhaps, Poland? And how do you propose that I get out there?'

Porter smiled as he unlocked a drawer in his desk and removed a small pile of envelopes.

'That, Edgar, is where I think I can surprise even you!'

'You are being serious then, are you?'

'Indeed I am, Edgar. Not only serious, but also resourceful. You may or may not be aware that there is a scheduled daily air service from Bristol to Lisbon. You won't know how hard this has been, but I have managed to secure you a seat on the flight to Lisbon on Thursday.'

'This Thursday?' Edgar looked surprised. 'And when I get to Lisbon?'

'Well, Lisbon station is very much Sandy Morgan's show. He'll arrange for you to meet up with Telmo, and the three of you can see where we are with regards to our lady in Berlin. After that, Morgan will get you into Spain and over to Barcelona: there are scheduled Swissair flights from there into Switzerland. From Barcelona you're going to have to go into Switzerland with your American cover: no alternative, I'm afraid: the Swiss are terribly jumpy about us at the moment.'

–

Captain Edgar was acutely aware that he appeared to have been cast as a character from one of those Agatha Christie crime novels of which his wife was so fond.

It was midday and he and the other characters were assembled in a draughty room at Whitchurch Airport, just outside Bristol. There were fifteen passengers including a priest, two elderly women wrapped in furs, a woman accompanied by a young boy, and two men speaking Portuguese. Edgar was half expecting to be joined by a Belgian detective with a waxed moustache.

It had been an hour since Edgar had checked in for the flight. For the purposes of the trip Edgar was travelling under a British diplomatic passport in the name of the Hon. Anthony Davis. The 'Hon.', Edgar assumed, was an example of Porter's public school humour. The Hon. Anthony Davis had various letters with him to the effect that he would be spending an unspecified period of time at the British Embassy in Lisbon dealing with 'consular services'.

A few minutes after midday, the passengers were led out of the room and across the apron to the DC-3 that would be flying them to Lisbon. Within minutes they were airborne, heading west along the Bristol Channel and out towards the sea. When the southern tip of Ireland peeked out of the low cloud, the plane changed course, at which point the captain spoke to the passengers:

'*Welcome aboard this BOAC flight from Bristol to Lisbon, where we expect to arrive just after four pm local time. Due to wartime flying regulations we will be flying at a maximum altitude of 3,000 feet.*'

Edgar closed his eyes and tried to rest as the captain continued to speak. He recalled being told that the pilots on these flights were all Dutch: they had managed to fly most of the KLM fleet to Britain just before the German invasion of the Netherlands, and they and their planes now serviced the few remaining BOAC flights.

To his surprise, Edgar must have fallen asleep straight away, because he was woken up by a stern-looking stewardess who was shaking him by the elbow. They were beginning their descent into Portela Airport.

The plane was flying low, hugging the Portuguese coast, the sky cloudless and the remains of the sun lighting up the land to their left. Edgar glanced to his right: across the aisle the priest was fervently praying, the rosary gripped tightly in his hands. The plane banked sharply over the city, buildings rushing by underneath them. Within a minute, Portela Airport appeared below them. The pilot made one pass of the airport, turned one hundred and eighty degrees, and then began the final approach.

–

At the British Embassy just off the Rua de São Domingos, Sandy Morgan greeted him like the old friend that he was. He hurried out from behind his desk in a crumpled white suit and, after grasping Edgar by the hand and warmly shaking it, removed a large bottle of Bells from a cabinet by the window. Two glasses were on his desk, one of which he pushed towards Edgar.

'Now then, old chap, bet you can do with one of these? Good flight, I hope? Beats me how we can get away with it: can't understand how they just don't take a shot at our planes. Mind you, I suppose we'd do the same to theirs, eh? Handy though, can't tell you how much useful stuff we pick up at the airport. We have people watching it the whole time. Germans do as well, so I suppose we cancel each other out. Even pick up their newspapers, which London is rather keen on. Anyway, cheers!'

Sandy Morgan downed his whisky, which had clearly not been his first of the afternoon, in one go and quickly refilled his glass from a new bottle he had produced from behind his desk. Edgar held his hand over his glass and shook his head.

'Now then, quick run through the plan. Idea is that you stay in my place, which is in an annexe of the embassy, so no need for you to be seen out and about. We'll sort your accreditation with the Ministry of Foreign Affairs tomorrow. Correct me if I am wrong, but the story is that you're here to check our consular system?'

'Something like that.'

'Funnily enough, they could do with sorting out, but I can't imagine you're interested in that. That gives you the cover you need: the PVDE keep a careful eye on us, but it is not too difficult to fool them. Idea is that after a couple of days you will come down with something nasty which will keep you in bed for a couple of weeks. The doctor we use is a rather helpful chap; he'll back up any story. That will give us enough time to get you to Barcelona and Switzerland and then back again, and home without the PVDE spotting it. Sound reasonable?'

Edgar nodded, slightly unsure. Sandy Morgan, despite his manner, was a good operator. He was one of the few station chiefs whom he trusted.

'We will meet with Telmo on either Saturday or Sunday: it's quieter then, easier all round. I'll only know for sure late tomorrow. Assuming that goes well, you will head off to Spain on Monday. Madrid station will look after you and get you over to Barcelona, and a flight from there to Switzerland. You'll be using an American cover, I under-stand?'

–

Sunday was warm; it almost felt spring-like. Edgar and Sandy Morgan sat on the balcony of Morgan's small apartment in the Embassy annexe, sipping fresh coffee. Edgar had been aware that Morgan had left the apartment very early in the morning, before six as far as he could tell.

'I wouldn't say that Telmo has got cold feet, but he's nervous, Edgar. Things aren't quite right in this city. Portugal is meant to be our oldest ally, but Salazar trusts no one – not us, not the Germans, and certainly not Spain. He seems to have got it in his mind that Spain has plans to invade this place. Upshot of all this is that everyone is very twitchy. The PVDE are watching everyone and Telmo is worried that they're watching him. He tried to cry off on Friday night, and then again last night, which is why I had to sneak out this morning. He's agreed to meet you, Edgar, but be gentle with him. He is one of us, after all.'

'When and where?'

'This afternoon. Hope you like football.'

Morgan and Edgar left the Embassy later that morning, half an hour apart, and met as arranged at a bar on the Rossio an hour later. They then travelled by tram, taxi, foot, and tram again. By the time they had finished their second tram journey they were part of a crowd heading in one direction. They were, Morgan announced, in Lumiar.

'We're in the north of the city, not far from the airport.'

Twenty minutes later, Edgar was inside a football ground for the first time in his life.

'Quick briefing, Edgar: you're now in the Campo do Lumiar, which is the home of Sporting Clube de Portugal, which is always called Sporting. They're one of the top clubs in the country; some would say the top club, though I daresay Benfica and Porto might disagree. Their opponents this afternoon are Barreirense, so it is something of a local derby.'

They were walking down the stand now, Morgan looking carefully along the rows.

'Just so you don't have to appear too ignorant, Sporting play in green, Barreirense in red.'

'And who do we want to win, Sandy?'

'Doesn't matter, does it? Personally I have a soft spot for Benfica, so I don't mind. Barreirense are quite a good side this year, so it could be a close game. Perhaps best if you don't shout too much anyway. Clap in the right places. Ah... good, there's Telmo; so he turned up after all. Now remember to be nice to him – make him feel wanted. We don't want him turning cold on us, do we?'

At the very end of a row, Telmo Rocha Martins was standing up, waving casually at them. *Here I am.* He was short – about five foot five, bald, with a neat moustache and round, black glasses. A large crowd had already formed in the Campo do Lumiar and Telmo, wrapped in a large, slightly shabby jacket, was just one of them.

It was the first time that Edgar had actually met Telmo Rocha Martins, one of the most important British agents in Portugal. Telmo was a middle-ranking civil servant in the Portuguese Ministry of Foreign Affairs – not regarded highly enough nor ranked so senior as to be considered a diplomat, but the kind of civil servant who ensures that everything runs smoothly while other people grab the glory. This had been a source of increasing resentment to Telmo, one that had led him to approach the British when the war started, with an offer to pass on the kind of information for which money changed hands.

Now, his status and his low profile suited him perfectly. No one suspected this mild-mannered, bespectacled man for a moment. The quality of intelligence that he passed on to the British improved all the time. He had been given a miniature camera, and at first it had been copies of Ministry briefing papers and some telegrams from overseas embassies that were passed on. Then, in early 1940, Telmo asked Morgan at one of their regular meetings whether he would be interested, by any chance, in more material from Berlin?

'*Rather,*' had been Morgan's response, careful to show that he was not too desperate. London had been crying out for *anything* from Berlin, such was their paucity of sources in the city. *And we mean anything: even bloody bus tickets!*

What Telmo came up with was much better than 'bloody bus tickets'. There were briefings from the German foreign ministry, minutes of meetings with German officials, assessments of the strengths and weaknesses of the armed forces, telegrams: half the contents of the diplomatic bag, as far as Morgan could work out. And from what London was telling him, it was all first class stuff. '*Well done. Plenty more of that will do nicely thank you!*'

But Morgan was a cautious chap. He was well aware that this intelligence coming out of Berlin could turn out to be too good to be true, and if that were the case, he did not fancy getting the blame for it. So, one Saturday afternoon, he had taken Telmo out for a drive to Cascais and they had gone for a long walk along the seafront.

'London want to know how come you're getting such good material out of Berlin?'

This was not strictly true: London had been so grateful, they were not questioning the material as much as Morgan was. They had walked for quite a while with Telmo saying nothing, evidently weighing up whether or not to come clean.

'I had been considering raising this with you. If there is ever a problem, will you promise that you will ensure that you could get me to England, maybe on one of your convoys?'

'I'd do my very best, Telmo: what kind of problem were you thinking of, though?'

'If they ever suspected me – that kind of problem. I would like to go to England. I would like to have a house in London. Maybe near to Buckingham Palace.'

'I'd certainly see what we can do. Not sure how near to the Palace, but there are some other lovely parts of London.'

'And if my source in Berlin was to accompany me, would that be a problem?'

'No! Not at all. I'd need to know who this person is, of course...'

'Even if we were not married?'

Which was how Telmo Rocha Martins came to tell Sandy Morgan all about Dona Maria do Rosario. He told him how Dona Maria had been a secretary to his head of department in the Ministry of Foreign Affairs; how they had become close, and eventually became lovers; how it would be impossible for him to leave his wife and remain in his job and stay in Portugal. He told Morgan about how Dona Maria had become proficient in German and had been transferred to the Legation in Berlin, but not before he had confided in her and she had agreed to supply information. In her case, the motivation was personal *and* political. Her fiancée had been imprisoned during the 1926 coup and had died soon after. Following this, she had left Porto and moved to Lisbon, working her way through the various government ministries around the Praça do Comercio.

Telmo had chosen a good spot. They were at the end of the front row of their block, so there was no one sitting in front of them or to the right. Morgan sat between Telmo and Edgar, acting as interpreter.

'We are very grateful to you, Telmo,' said Edgar quietly, pausing while Sandy Morgan translated. 'Very, very grateful. I want you to know how much we appreciate your help. I can assure you that if there is ever a… problem here in Portugal, we will do our very best to get you to London.'

Telmo smiled and nodded his head, not taking his eyes off the pitch. 'I am very grateful. But can you promise me that this assurance will also apply to Dona Maria?'

'Of course…'

They paused as the crowd rose around them: a Sporting player was fouled on the edge of the penalty area. They continued to stand while the free kick was taken and then sat down after it soared over the bar.

'I need to ask you about Dona Maria. She is sending a lot of material. How is she able to do this…? Is she not suspected at all?'

'I assure you she is careful. Because of my job, I am in a position to see the diplomatic bag soon after it arrives at the Ministry, before anyone else has seen it, other than a clerk. I am then able to take the material, which is all in code. It is not possible for other people to spot the material or be aware of any code. If we were suspected, they might be, but no one suspects us. But I have something important to tell you.'

There was another delay as a Barreirense winger beat a succession of Sporting defenders but then shot wide. 'Our defence is too slow today, far too slow. Listen carefully, please: Dona Maria passed on your message to Hugo, about getting hold of this document. A message came through on Friday. Hugo wants you to know that he may be able to get hold of the document: it seems that he has a source who has access to this document. But there is a price to pay.'

'How much?'

Sporting scored and the crowd leapt up around them. Everyone was patting their companions on the back, as if they'd played a part in the goal. Telmo looked delighted.

'Fortunately our attack is much better than our defence. It's not money. It is a lot more complicated. You had better listen carefully.'

Edgar did listen carefully. It was complicated. He would need to get to Switzerland as soon as possible.

He was only shaken out of his thoughts by Sporting's second goal.

The game finished two nil. If only everything in life was so clear-cut Edgar thought as they left the ground and Telmo melted into the crowd.

Chapter 16

London, February 1941

By noon on Wednesday 12th of February, Christopher Porter had been kept waiting in a narrow corridor in a draughty and heavily guarded basement under the Admiralty building in Whitehall for well over an hour past the time of his appointment. When he was finally called into the office outside which he had been waiting, there was neither apology nor explanation, just a mildly exasperated look from Sir Roland Pearson.

'How can I help you, Porter?' Sir Roland Pearson had once been a colleague, but now worked in Downing Street and currently had the ear of the Prime Minister on all matters to do with intelligence. He gave the impression that he was now far too important for his time to be wasted.

'As you know, Sir Roland, we met on the 3rd when you made clear the Prime Minister's feelings regarding our intelligence from Berlin and the directive regarding a possible invasion of the Soviet Union. I subsequently dispatched Edgar to Lisbon, where he met our source, Telmo, on Sunday.'

'Telmo. Remind me?'

'Telmo Rocha Martins: he works in the Portuguese Ministry of Foreign Affairs in Lisbon and has proven to be an extremely useful source of information for us. His main informant is Dona Maria do Rosario, who is secretary to the military attaché in the Portuguese Legation in Berlin. As well as passing on information through Telmo, she also serves as a contact for Hugo – he is Franz Hermann, the Berlin lawyer who is working for us. Any information that he has, or messages that we have for him, comes through Dona Maria in the Portuguese diplomatic bag.'

Porter had now opened a notebook and put on a pair of reading glasses.

'When Edgar met Telmo on Sunday he passed on the latest from Hugo, via Dona Maria. We were aware that Hugo has been sheltering a Jewish family, which we thought was an unnecessary risk and therefore did not wholly approve of. However, it transpires that this family may be critical in terms of our obtaining a copy of this directive. The family Hugo is helping to shelter is a Jewish woman called Rosa Stern and her two children: an eleven-year-old boy called Alfred and a five-year-old girl called Sophia. Rosa's husband is a businessman called Harald Stern, who was arrested by the Nazis sometime in late 1939 and subsequently died – or was killed – in one of their prison camps. Harald Stern was the father of Sophia but not of Alfred. Alfred's father is one Gunter Reinhart, Rosa Stern's first husband. Reinhart is not Jewish: he and Rosa divorced in 1935 after Hitler's law which prohibits marriages between Jews and non-Jews.'

'I hope this family saga is leading somewhere important, Porter.'

'It is, sir. From what we understand, Gunter Reinhart and Rosa Stern remained on good terms and Gunter did what he could to help them. Rosa and the children had moved to Paris, but returned to Berlin when Harald was arrested – it seems that he may have remained there to try and sort out some business matters. Now they are being hidden in the home of a relative of Hugo's. However, Gunter Reinhart works for the Reichsbank, where he occupies a fairly senior position. Part of his job is helping to move money out of countries occupied by the Germans. In this respect, it appears that he has access to a copy of this Directive 21.'

'Good heavens.'

'Good heavens indeed. You see why I needed to give you the background.'

'And this Reinhart – he can supply us with Directive 21?'

'Yes, but...'

'He wants money, I imagine. How much?'

'I only wish it were that simple. His condition is that we smuggle his son Alfred out of Berlin. Reinhart has a friend in Zurich: once Alfred has been safely delivered to that friend, he will release a copy of Directive 21 to Hugo.'

Sir Roland had leaned back in his chair and was staring at the ceiling, as if the solution may be hidden in the cobwebs he had spotted above the coving.

'So how do we get Alfred to Zurich?'

'Even as we speak, Sir Roland, Edgar is on his way to Switzerland. We have an agent there called Henry Hunter. Hunter also has a genuine Swiss identity, and he is able to travel into Germany with it. A year ago we sent him into Germany on a test mission of sorts, which went well. I have said to Edgar that he and Basil Remington-Barber must come up with a plan to get Hunter to Berlin and out again with Alfred.'

'Which will not be straightforward.'

'Indeed, Sir Roland. But we have to get Alfred out – the prize is too great not to attempt it.'

Sir Roland stood up and walked away from the table and over to his desk, from which he picked up a silver box and lit up a cigarette he had selected from it. He removed his jacket and hung it over the back of his chair. On the wall behind him was a map of Europe and for a while he studied it, reacquainting himself with the various locations. With his forefinger he traced an angled line south from Berlin to Zurich.

'And once this Alfred is safely delivered to this friend in Zurich, we get the report?'

'Once the friend has confirmed it.'

'And I presume that Hugo then hands the report over to Dona Maria whatshername and she pops it into the diplomatic bag and we pick up the report in Lisbon?'

Porter closed his notebook and folded up his reading glasses. Twice he started to speak, but hesitated. He was clenching and then unclenching his fists and clearly finding difficulty in knowing where to start.

'Can I be most frank and most honest with you, Sir Roland?'

'I had rather hoped that had been the case up to now anyway, Porter.'

Porter's hands were now clasped as if in prayer. He drew a deep breath before speaking.

'The most obvious route to bring the directive out of Berlin would indeed be through the Portuguese diplomatic bag, I quite agree. But if there is an overriding purpose to us obtaining this document, it is to help prove to the Russians that their supposed allies are not what they seem and in fact have plans to invade them. Correct?'

Sir Roland nodded.

'Up to now, the Russians have chosen to ignore all of these warnings, most especially the ones that can be attributed to us. Frankly, they do not believe what we tell them. They are convinced that our motives are to stir up trouble between them and the Germans. They choose to believe that whatever intelligence we are passing to them is false. Our concern is that if we – the British – show them the directive or tell them about its contents then they will similarly ignore them, as they have all the other warnings. All the considerable effort of obtaining the directive will have been wasted.'

'What do you suggest then, Porter?'

'This is where I have to be very frank. Henry Hunter, our agent in Switzerland who is able to travel into Germany, is not quite what he seems... I think I will have that cigarette after all, Sir Roland.'

Sir Roland rejoined Porter at the table and slid the silver cigarette box across it, followed by a box of matches. He noticed Porter shook slightly as he lit his cigarette.

'We had our eyes on Hunter for some time. He is ideal in many ways: very good Swiss identity, speaks all the relevant languages. Even the Swiss believe he is Swiss, if you get what I mean. We picked him up here just before the start of the war: he was trying to smuggle out some money he had inherited and we gave him the choice of working for us or spending a few years breaking rocks, or whatever we make people do in prisons these days. He chose to work for us.'

'Good.'

'However, what he did not know, and still does not know, is that we know something else about him. That he had already been recruited as an agent: by the Russians.'

Sir Roland had been moving his cigarette towards his mouth. Now he stopped, holding it is mid-air. He leaned towards Porter.

'Really? When did this happen?'

'We think it was around 1930 or 1931, Sir Roland – a couple of years after he moved to Geneva from Zurich with his mother and stepfather. Basil Remington-Barber had an informant in the Geneva branch of the Communist Party of Switzerland. He thought we'd be interested because Hunter had dual British and Swiss nationalities. He had seen Hunter at one or two meetings and then disappeared from view. Normally we would not have attached a good deal of importance to that: plenty of young chaps go to these type of meetings and then lose interest. But Remington-Barber's informant thought that he had seen Hunter chatting to a French chap who was rumoured to have links with the Comintern, and we do know that it is a very well established recruitment tactic of the Soviet intelligence agencies for them to keep an eye open for likely recruits who have joined or try to join their local Communist parties. What happens is they spot someone, and then persuade them that the best way to serve the cause is not to be a party member but to work for them. They leave the party, all records are destroyed and they display no outward affiliation with or interest in communism – often the opposite, in fact. We assume this is what happened with Hunter.'

'And how and when did you get to know that he was a Soviet agent?'

'Not until early thirty-nine. We think he must have been told to lay low until they needed him and certainly the way he was living in Geneva no one would have had any reason whatsoever to suspect him We became very interested in a Soviet spymaster, chap called Viktor Krasotkin. Very bright chap: based in Paris but moves around Western Europe as if he owns the place. Quite brilliant, actually, but our people in Paris were aware of him and for a while had someone quite close to him. This person tipped us off about an English chap with Swiss nationality who was one of Viktor's agents. Once we knew this, we tried to recruit him, and he rather fell into our hands.'

'But what has this to do with the directive?'

'Once Henry delivers Alfred to Zurich and Reinhart gets the green light, Henry can return to Berlin and he can bring the document back to Switzerland.'

'The point of that being...?'

'He will be made well aware quite how important the document is – top secret, et cetera. We know that as soon as he gets back to Switzerland, he is bound to show it to Viktor Krasotkin, even before he hands it over to Edgar. That way, the Russians will know it is genuine. It will have come straight from the horse's mouth, so to speak. They will have to believe it then, won't they?'

Chapter 17

Zurich, February 1941

Under the identity of Patrick T. O'Connor, Junior, a U.S. citizen, Edgar left Muntadas airport in Barcelona just before ten in the morning on Swissair flight 1087. The flight landed on time in Locarno at a quarter past one. Five hours later he was in a small apartment above a hardware shop on Basteiplatz. He was let in by an Austrian called Rolf Eder, who worked for Remington-Barber.

'No need to worry about Rolf,' Remington-Barber had assured him. 'Completely trustworthy: he's an Austrian social democrat. Whitlock recruited him in Vienna sometime around thirty-six. Nazis rolled into Vienna in March 1938 and Rolf rolled out soon after that: hates the Germans more than we do, if that is possible. His fiancée's a prisoner of theirs. When Whitlock had to leave Vienna and he found out that Rolf was here in Switzerland, he recommended him to me.'

–

Basil Remington-Barber and Henry Hunter, otherwise known as Henri Hesse, arrived in Zurich late on the Thursday afternoon and checked into the same hotel on Oetenbachgasse where Henri had stayed the previous February on the night before he travelled to Stuttgart. The next morning Remington-Barber left Henri in his room to rest and met Edgar as arranged on Bahnhofquai. Together they watched a noisy barge make its way up the Limmat.

'Hunter all right, is he?'

'After a fashion, yes: picked him up yesterday morning in Geneva during his morning walk and told him to pack his bags, bid his farewells and we're off to Zurich. It's a year since he was in Germany and I rather think that he assumed we had forgotten about him. Not very happy that I haven't told him what's going on, but then I hardly know myself, do I?'

'And did you give him an opportunity to make contact?'

'Naturally: I told him that we would catch the one o'clock train to Zurich and I would meet him by the platform with his ticket at a quarter to one. That gave him ample opportunity to get a message to his other people that something may be on. Good to dangle bait of some kind in front of them.'

'Good, well done, Basil. Sorry to be somewhat elusive, but I need to track someone down. Come along later this afternoon to the apartment with Hunter.'

–

All things considered, it had not been a good day and a half for Henri Hesse, and it showed no signs of improving.

On the Thursday he had been whisked away from Geneva by Basil Remington-Barber, with little by way of an explanation other than 'We're going to Zurich: pack for a few days. Don't forget your passport.' The subsequent train journey had passed mostly in silence, Remington-Barber declining to answer any of Henri's questions.

Then Remington-Barber had ordered him to remain in his stuffy little hotel room for most of the Friday morning. He had no idea what was going on or what was going to happen, so he was feeling increasingly anxious. There was a small part of him – a very small part, admittedly – which was relieved that, after a year of hearing nothing from the British, at last they now seemed to have plans for him. An even smaller part of him was excited at the prospect of what those plans may involve. He had spent the past year reflecting on the fact that although the trip to Stuttgart and Essen had been fraught with danger, the excitement of having completed the mission so successfully had surprised him. The months since then had been a mixture of boredom and nervous anticipation of when he would next be called upon: added to this was the pressure of serving two masters. At least the 100 pounds was being paid into his Credit Suisse account each month, which was one consolation.

Now Remington-Barber had sent a rather friendly Austrian called Rolf to bring him to a small apartment above a hardware shop on Basteiplatz. It was three thirty in the afternoon and they had been waiting in the sparsely furnished lounge for the best part of an hour. Henri Hesse was sitting on an uncomfortable sofa while Remington-Barber nervously paced the room, darting over to the window overlooking Basteiplatz every time he heard footsteps below. The diplomat had said very little since they had arrived there: 'Sit over there, Henry... Yes, we are waiting for someone... Please be patient.'

Eventually, a bell rang and Remington-Barber sent Rolf downstairs to let whoever it was in. Henri heard two pairs of footsteps ascending the stairs. At first he did not recognise the tall figure wearing a trilby hat who had to stoop as he entered the door. But then he removed the trilby and said 'Henry' – no more than that, just 'Henry' – before taking off his raincoat and slinging it over a chair and then angling the single armchair so that it was directly facing the sofa.

'Sit down, Basil, you're making me nervous. No need to keep looking out of the window: no one has followed me; I can assure you of that. Make yourself useful – pass me that ashtray and then go and sit next to Henry. Either of you chaps fancy a cigarette?'

Edgar lounged back in the armchair, stretching out his long legs so that they almost touched the feet of the two men opposite him. Not bothering to stifle a series of yawns he closed his eyes momentarily and for a while it looked as if he was about to fall asleep. Then he sat up straight, slapped his thighs and then rubbed his hands.

'Right – down to business. Henry, you look rather shocked to see me: understandable I suppose. I imagine you rather hoped that you'd never see me again, eh?'

Henri said nothing.

'And are you keeping well, Henry?'

'I'm well, thank you. And you?'

'Basil tells me that your little trip to Germany last year went well.'

Henri was about to reply but Edgar raised a hand to stop him.

'And the money going in to your account every month as promised, I presume? Along with the 500 you received after your trip.'

Henri replied that it was.

'Which, in a sense, is why I am here. It's time for you to do something more to earn that money. How about if I was to tell you that you're going back to Germany?'

Henri was drumming his fingers on his knees and very slowly nodding his head. 'To Essen?'

'Good heavens, no! We can hardly have the murderer returning to the scene of his crime, can we?' Edgar laughed heartily and Remington-Barber joined in nervously.

'We thought Berlin would make a nice change.'

Henri gazed quizzically at Edgar, as if he was trying to work out whether the man opposite him was being serious.

'Berlin?'

'Yes, Henry, Berlin. Capital of the Third Reich.'

'Really?'

'Yes, really. Look, I could tell you all about it now, but I'd just end up repeating myself later on. We have a chap coming to see us in an hour or so and we'll put all of our cards on the table then. Talking of tables, Basil, how about some tea, eh?'

Basil Remington-Barber headed over to the small kitchen, pausing in its doorway.

'You certain this chap is going to turn up, Edgar?'

'Don't worry Basil. I am certain of it. He really has no alternative.'

–

Captain Edgar had finally approached the man at lunchtime that Friday. It felt as if he had spent half of his life following people, waiting for hours in the shadows of doorways for them to appear, calculating when they would emerge and what would then be the best time and place to approach them. He had learnt through years of experience that most people tended to be unpredictable in their habits, but he could have guessed that if anyone would be a man of precise routine it would be a Swiss banker and Michael Hedinger did not disappoint him.

According to the message that Hugo sent through Lisbon, Gunter Reinhart's friend in Zurich was a man called Michael Hedinger who worked for Bank Leu. Hedinger was apparently aware 'in principle' – whatever that meant – that his friend Gunter in Berlin wanted him to help look after his son, but he would have no idea that he was about to be approached.

Edgar had watched the bank over the past couple of days. It had been founded in 1755 and some of the employees he watched coming in and out looked as if they had been there that long. Now it was one of the 'Big Seven' Swiss banks: not one of the largest, but still big enough to have its snout in the German trough, along with all the others. With the help of a porter at the bank who had been paid generously in return for doing no more than giving a signal when Michael Hedinger entered the building, Edgar had been able to spot his quarry.

Herr Hedinger left the head office of Bank Leu on Paradeplatz at precisely one o'clock, presumably on his way to lunch. He turned into Bahnhofstrasse and Edgar decided that now was the time he had to make his move.

'Herr Hedinger, may I have a word with you?'

Edgar had approached the banker from behind, having got as close to him as possible and making sure he placed himself between the man and the road. It was a well-practised technique, as was the friendly but firm hand on the man's elbow and the enforced shaking of his hand. *Hold one arm, shake the other arm: take control.* That way, anyone watching would assume that it was a chance encounter between two acquaintances.

'I beg your pardon?' Hedinger had replied in German and sounded surprised rather than annoyed. This was encouraging, but Edgar could not assume it would last for long.

'I need to talk you about a rather important matter, Herr Hedinger. Is there somewhere quiet perhaps we could go?' Edgar was speaking German too.

'I don't know who you are. What is this about?' Now Hedinger was beginning to sound annoyed, and a man and woman turned to look at them as they passed by. People were not accustomed to raised voices on the streets of Zurich.

Edgar edged even closer to Hedinger. 'It is in connection with Gunter Reinhart in Berlin, Herr Hedinger.'

Edgar was not prepared for the reaction that followed. He had hoped that, at the mention of Reinhart, Hedinger would relax and want to know more: quite possibly he had expected to be contacted and might even be relieved. What he had not expected was to see the look of sheer panic and fear that spread across Hedinger's face. Edgar could not be sure, but it looked as if his eyes had filled with tears. The banker appeared unsteady on his feet.

'Come with me.'

Michael Hedinger meekly allowed Edgar to shepherd him across Bahnhofstrasse and then onto Kappelergasse, where they settled on a bench overlooking the river. Edgar could see that the man next to him was terrified, a reaction he had not expected. Edgar took his time lighting a cigarette and held the packet in front of the other man. Hedinger shook his head. 'No, I don't smoke.'

'What is your name? What is this about? Please tell me!'

Edgar ignored the first question. 'I told you: it is in connection with Gunter Reinhart. You know Herr Reinhart – from the Reichsbank in Berlin?'

'I am not sure. Why do you ask?'

'It is a very straightforward question, Herr Hedinger. Either you know him or you don't?'

'We are acquaintances, in a professional capacity.'

Edgar had prepared his next line: *Herr Reinhart has asked for help in bringing his son Alfred out of Berlin and he tells us that you are prepared to look after him in Zurich.* But before he had an opportunity to say that, Hedinger gripped his forearm and turned to face Edgar. He was a man of medium height, but with the kind of shrunken appearance reserved for those of especially nervous disposition. With his unhealthily pale complexion, watery blue eyes with scarcely a trace of eyebrow above them, and his few remaining wisps of hair dancing in the wind, he reminded Edgar of an English country clergyman, the type sent to only the most undemanding of parishes. Now he looked like a clergyman who had been caught in a compromising situation and was about to be defrocked. He was utterly terrified. Edgar could smell it on his breath.

'I have always feared this moment and had resolved that if – when – it came about, I would immediately be honest.' Hedinger's voice trembled as he spoke. 'It has all been a terrible misunderstanding... a most unfortunate misunderstanding. Herr Reinhart wanted to divert some of the funds from Germany into a private account in his name and in a moment of weakness I agreed, and in a moment of even greater weakness I accepted some money from Herr Reinhart for myself... for my efforts. I regretted it immediately and in fact my money is held in a separate account. I can arrange to have it paid back to you within a matter of days. I can see to it this afternoon in fact.'

Edgar loosened the grip that Hedinger had on his arm and stood up to face the river. In a world of surprises, it was very rare for one to shock him, but this one had. By the sounds of it, Hedinger and Reinhart were involved in a scheme to smuggle German state funds out of Germany into their own private accounts here in Zurich. Hedinger must have assumed that Edgar was a German official. He turned round: Hedinger was trembling, his feet tapping on the ground.

'I have a young family and I am a good man: I go to church every week. Please understand that I did not intend to keep your money. I am sure that I can have it all returned to you this afternoon – along with the money in Herr Reinhart's private account.'

'Are these accounts with Bank Leu?'

'Naturally.'

'Do you have the account numbers please?'

Hedinger obediently removed a slim black notebook from his jacket pocket and turned the pages with trembling fingers that had the appearance of having been manicured. From what Edgar could see, the notebook was full of numbers, figures, initials and dates. Edgar opened his own notebook and, turning to a blank page, wrote 'Reinhart' and then 'Hedinger'.

'Write the account numbers underneath each name please. Don't forget to put down how much money is in each account. I am sure we can resolve this matter in a satisfactory manner. If you co-operate, Herr Hedinger, then there should be no need for us to take further action.'

Hedinger grasped the bait like a hungry fish, eagerly copying down the account numbers. When he had finished he handed the notebook with its incriminating lists of bank accounts back to Edgar.

'Can I ask you sir, are you from the Gestapo?'

Edgar laughed: the outcome to the encounter with Michael Hedinger had been far better than he could have hoped.

'Well, that is where I think I am going to surprise you, Herr Hedinger.'

–

'How can you be so sure he'll turn up, Edgar?'

'Because he will: because it is not in his interests not to turn up.'

Basil Remington-Barber shook his head and moved away from his spot by the window overlooking Basteiplatz which he had occupied on and off throughout the afternoon.

'Well, I wish I were able to share your confidence. In my experience, things don't always turn out quite as planned.'

'Basil, do stop pacing around and sit down quietly, as Henry is doing. It is now five o'clock. At this moment, our visitor will be leaving his office on Paradeplatz and commencing his short walk here. It will take him six minutes; I timed it myself earlier this afternoon. In fact I walked the route three times and it takes six minutes and twenty seconds, but I would not want you to think that I am a pedant. He will be with us by ten past five at the very latest, mark my words. What is it they say about the Swiss and clockworks? And just one warning: he may tell us things we are already aware of – like the boy, Alfred. Pretend it is the first time we've heard it, eh?'

At seven minutes past five a knowing smile crossed Edgar's face as the bell rang. He gave Remington-Barber a 'told you' look and went downstairs to let their visitor in. Two minutes later Michael Hedinger had joined the three Englishmen around the table.

For a moment the four of them sat in an uncomfortable silence. The newcomer was in a state of considerable nervousness. He had declined offers to remove his coat and had only reluctantly taken off his gloves and hat. He was clutching his bright brown briefcase to his chest and was clearly edgy, jumping at the sound of a car engine backfiring and at a door slamming in an apartment above. Edgar had placed himself at the head of the table: Hedinger was sitting to his left, opposite the other two men.

When Edgar began to speak it was initially to Henri and Remington-Barber.

'Henry, Basil – this is Michael Hedinger. I will speak in German by the way: Herr Hedinger's English is very limited. Herr Hedinger works for Bank Leu, of which more in due course. Perhaps I should explain that when Herr Hedinger and I first met, some four hours ago, there was something of a misunderstanding. It was perhaps a fortunate misunderstanding from my point of view, less so from Herr Hedinger's. Is that not correct, Herr Hedinger?'

The banker looked up in an absent-minded manner, with a 'what me?' expression. He nodded meekly in reply to Edgar's question.

'Not to put too fine a point on it, it turns out that Herr Hedinger here in Zurich and Herr Reinhart in Berlin have been operating a – how can one put it? – a scheme whereby a proportion of the funds that were being transferred from the Reichsbank to the safekeeping of Bank Leu were diverted into private, numbered accounts: one belonging to Herr Reinhart, the other to Herr Hedinger. Is that correct, Herr Hedinger?'

Hedinger began to speak but was stopped by Edgar. 'You will have ample opportunity to talk in due course, Herr Hedinger. A very risky but at the same time very lucrative scheme: Herr Hedinger tells me that of the millions of Reichsmarks transferred through Herr Rein-hart's operation at the Reichsbank to Bank Leu, some twenty-five thousand have ended up in the two private accounts – that is around two thousand pounds sterling. Is that not correct, Herr Hedinger?'

He nodded, avoiding eye contact with anyone around the table.

'And the money is split equally, is it not?' Again, Hedinger nodded.

'Now this is where Herr Hedinger must be kicking himself. When I approached Herr Hedinger earlier today, I knew nothing of this scheme. However, the private enterprise with Herr Reinhart has obviously been on Herr Hedinger's conscience and he assumed that I was an official – a *German* official, would you please – who was investigating the matter. Before I even had an opportunity to explain what I had approached him about, he confessed. Have I accurately summed up what happened, Herr Hedinger?'

The Swiss coughed and spoke in a soft voice. 'I never intended to keep the money but Gunter – Herr Reinhart – is a very persuasive man. He insisted that with the amount of money that was being transferred and the fact that some of it was obtained from private accounts by the Reichsbank, well… he said that it would be impossible for our accounts to be traced. He may well have been correct, but I have been terrified that I would be caught, and that I would lose my job and my house – so much so that I have been a nervous wreck in recent weeks. I felt that it was just a matter of time before I was caught. When you approached me on Bahnhofstrasse I assumed that I had been caught: I was almost relieved, hence my rather too hasty confession.'

He shrugged his shoulders and spread his hands out in a 'so there we are' manner.

So there we are.

'As I told you earlier, Herr Hedinger, I could not care less about the money. Keep it, as far as we are concerned; better that it is in your account and that of Herr Reinhart than in one belonging to the Reichsbank. The money is not our concern. Neither Bank Leu nor the Reichsbank need find out about it: you will keep your job and your fine house. But a happy outcome of that misunderstanding is that our knowledge of it has ensured your complete co-operation, Herr Hedinger, am I correct?'

'Indeed.'

'So now we come to our main business, of which we spoke briefly and of which Henry here is unaware. Herr Hedinger, for the sake of my colleagues here, please tell me again about your relationship with Herr Reinhart.'

The Swiss cleared his throat and paused for a while, clearly giving careful consideration to what he was about to say. His soft voice and the careful way in which he spoke reminded Edgar even more of an English country clergyman – someone more suited to talking to elderly ladies than spies.

'Gunter and I have known each other for some five years. As you are aware, Gunter occupies a senior position in the foreign department of the Reichsbank. He has been involved with the transfer of funds from the Reichsbank to foreign banks, and Bank Leu is, in this respect, one of their main clients. I have been working in the international division of Bank Leu for a number of years and am currently its deputy head. You should be aware that there is a very close relationship between Germany and the Swiss banks. Germany is an important client for us, and we are very important to them – an efficient and discreet way of moving funds in and out of the country. Not all of their funds, it has to be acknowledged, may have been obtained in entirely legal ways. As part of my job I oversee our relationship with the Reichsbank, so over the years I have visited Berlin on a very regular basis, and I think it is reasonable to say that Gunter and I have become good friends. We found that we have much in common; it took us a couple of years to really trust each other but, once we did, we found we could confide in each other. We have been able to talk frankly about our private lives and our worries. About a year ago, when I was in Berlin, he took me into his confidence and told me a secret which he said, if it came out, would cost him his job and quite possibly his freedom. What I am about to say will stay within these walls?'

Edgar laughed. 'We're hardly likely to inform the Gestapo, are we?'

'I realise that, but I am divulging something that was told to me in complete confidence. What Gunter told me was this: he had married a woman called Rosa in 1924, when he was twenty-nine years of age. Rosa, I think, was two or three years younger than him. He describes Rosa as the love of his life. She happened to be Jewish, but was not practising, and Gunter said that their differences of religion

203

were simply not an issue, or at least, not for them. Their son Alfred was born in 1929, so he's now eleven or twelve. Gunter absolutely dotes on Alfred. Gunter describes their life together as idyllic, but that began to change when the Nazis came to power in 1933. Until then, not many people knew that Rosa was, in fact, Jewish, but life became increasingly uncomfortable. Then the Nazis started to bring in all of these anti-Jewish laws and one of them – in 1935, I think it was – banned marriages between Jews and non-Jews. So they had a choice, either leave the country or get divorced. May I trouble you for a drink please?'

There was a pause while Remington-Barber disappeared into the kitchen, emerging a few minutes later with a tray of tea, a jug of water with glasses and a bottle of whisky. Hedinger poured himself a glass of water.

'Gunter says that their original plan was to emigrate: they would have had to leave everything behind, pay a hefty tax, and then find somewhere that would give them an entry visa. Nonetheless, they were prepared to do that. But then it was made very clear to Gunter that unless he divorced Rosa immediately, he would lose his job at the Reichsbank. From what I understand, they both still loved each other and saw the divorce as a temporary measure: Rosa and Alfred would try and go to England or France and then Gunter would join them there and they would remarry. But for reasons of which I am unclear, Rosa delayed leaving Germany: I think it may have been that she really wanted to go to England but she could not get an entry visa. Gunter, meanwhile, was finding life difficult. He met a woman called Gudrun and they married – I think he felt that until he remarried, there would always be suspicion about him, but I believe he has always regretted it. He remained in contact with Rosa, but it was difficult and in 1936 she remarried – a Jewish man called Harald Stern. They soon had a daughter, Sophia. My understanding is that this was all done with Gunter's blessing, because Harald's plan was for them all to move to France, and Gunter just wanted Rosa and Alfred to be safe. Gunter was even helping them financially, and also to try and obtain the right papers.'

'Could he not have had custody of Alfred himself?' asked Basil Remington-Barber.

'A good question: Gunter told me he could have done, and if he had contested custody he would almost certainly have won, although Alfred's status would be a difficult one. The Nazis say that anyone who has three or more Jewish grandparents is a Jew. Someone like Alfred, who has two Jewish grandparents, is what the Nazis call a *mischlinge*, which means a "crossbreed" – like a dog. Nonetheless, Gunter felt he could have taken in Alfred and dealt with that – there are ways, you know. But Gudrun, his second wife, would have nothing of it. As far as she was – and is – concerned, he is to have no contact whatsoever with his first family. Now what I am about to say is complicated and highly sensitive: forgive me if I am unclear as to the exact dates. Essentially, what I believe happened is that soon after war was declared, Rosa did go to Paris with the two children and Harald was meant to follow them. However, he was arrested and taken to a camp for Jews and political prisoners, called Sachsenhausen. For some foolish reason, in an act of utter madness Rosa returned to Berlin with the children, in an effort to get Harald freed. She failed and had to go into hiding, and a few months later she heard that Harald was dead – either he died of natural causes or was killed, who knows?'

'And has Gunter been in touch with them?'

'Yes, since January or February 1940. There is a Berlin lawyer called Franz Hermann who is an old friend of Rosa's. He is hiding Rosa and the children in his mother's house in the city and Gunter is able to visit them. They are trapped there. Hermann is the connection between Gunter and Rosa and the children.'

'And you say that Gunter told you all this last year?'

'Yes.'

'Do you remember when last year?'

'Maybe March… possibly April. In fact, that was when he started diverting the money into our private accounts – he said that the reason he was doing this was that he needed the money to help Rosa and Alfred. I was last in Berlin at the very end of January, just a couple of weeks ago. It was a very brief visit and I only saw Gunter on his own very briefly. He said to me that if he was able to arrange for Alfred to be brought out of Germany, would I promise to look after him in Switzerland? I said yes… what else could I say? That is why he told me about the lawyer, Hermann. He also said that he may even need my assistance in helping to get Alfred out, but that he would be in touch. That was the last I heard – until we met today.'

Michael Hedinger looked less nervous now, as if he was pleased to have got things off his chest. His pale head was wet with perspiration, his strands of hair now plastered to it. Edgar was nodding his head, taking everything in and thinking, while Henri looked bemused, unsure of what his role in all this was meant to be. It was Edgar who spoke next.

'How often do you go to Berlin?'

'Perhaps every other month.'

'And other Bank Leu officials, how often do they go?'

'Hard to say exactly, but on a very regular basis. Look, the Reichsbank is one of our most important clients, but it is a very sensitive relationship. The money that they are placing with us comes from sources that require utmost discretion on our part.'

'What do you mean by that?'

'They have confiscated millions of Reichsmarks from Jews, and also plundered money from the countries they have occupied. They need to move that money around; so much of it comes to banks like ours to be converted into Swiss Francs, which is probably the safest currency in the world at the moment. They are also sending us a lot of gold, not just us – all the Swiss banks. The business we get from Germany is extremely profitable, so we prefer to deal with the Reichsbank in person. We ask very few questions and we leave nothing to chance.'

'Do you send couriers to Germany?'

'Of course! Every week, if not more frequently than that. Documents need to be signed, letters need to be delivered. Couriers are a very important part of our relationship with them.'

'And these couriers are…?'

'Employees of Bank Leu, or people who do this on a regular basis – people that we know and trust.'

Edgar was thinking and looking around the table as he did so. He looked at Henri and smiled while addressing the Swiss. 'Tell me, Herr Hedinger, do you have the authority to decide who can be a courier on your behalf?'

'Yes, in fact only in November I used my own brother-in-law as a courier.'

'I see.' Edgar was still looking directly at Henri as he spoke. Henri was beginning to feel uncomfortable. 'So, Henry here could become one of you couriers?'

'I'm not sure, maybe he—'

'You don't need to worry. Herr Hesse is a Swiss citizen and a regular visitor to Germany himself. I have no doubt that he would be a most capable courier on behalf of Bank Leu.'

–

Michael Hedinger left the apartment at six thirty. Before he left, Edgar pressed him on how soon he could arrange Henri's accreditation as a courier for Bank Leu.

'It is now Friday evening, so obviously I cannot do anything before Monday. It will take me a few days from then. We have a procedure at the bank, you see. Fortunately I am in a position to organise my own couriers, but the paperwork has to be done properly, otherwise we will arouse suspicion. If Henri can give me his passport now, that will speed things up. Also, remember that I will need to sort out paperwork for Alfred. That will not be easy.'

Edgar nodded at Henri, who looked as shocked as he had done when he first heard about the plans for his trip to Berlin. He removed his passport from his jacket passport and handed it over to Hedinger.

'How soon then?'

'By the end of next week, I am sure I can have it sorted by then.'

'End of the week! I thought it could be done in a day or two.'

The Swiss shook his head vigorously. 'No, no, no – I told you, we have our procedures. I need to fill in the form, send it to the correct department, they need to process it, then the form has to be counter-signed by a director, and then I need to arrange Herr

Hesse's registration as an official courier of Bank Leu with the German consulate here in Zurich. I can assure you that it will take a week. Hopefully by next Friday morning it will be sorted.'

They agreed that they would meet again at the apartment the following Friday lunchtime. As well as his accreditation, Hedinger would bring along documents that Henri Hesse would be taking to Bank Leu's clients in Berlin. They waited for Michael Hedinger to leave the apartment and all three of them stood at the window watching him cross Basteiplatz.

'I thought that went rather well, Edgar. Good work.'

'Thank you, Basil. This scheme of his and Reinhart's really is most helpful. I was able to tell him that unless he fully co-operated with us, we might be obliged to inform the Swiss authorities. It means that we have him over a barrel. So, Henry, you're going to Berlin. Looking forward to it I hope?'

Henri had poured himself a glass of whisky which he drank in one go. 'It is madness. You seriously want me to go to Berlin pretending to be a courier for a Swiss Bank and then return accompanied by an eleven-year-old half-Jewish boy? It will never work.'

'Why shouldn't it? Your Swiss identity is perfectly genuine and your visit to Stuttgart last year would have been all in order as far as the Germans are concerned. After all, they have no idea that you went to Essen. If you get questioned you simply say that you now have a job as a courier for a bank.'

'And the boy?'

'We will see what paperwork Hedinger comes up with, but it is in his interests for it to be good.'

'It will have to be more than good, Edgar. I'm not sure whether you're aware of it, but the Swiss are doing their level best to stop Jews crossing the border from Germany. They'll be looking out for the likes of him.'

'Yes, I am aware of it, thank you, Henry. But they'll not be looking out for the likes of you, will they? And the fact that he is with you, in whatever capacity... well that ought to ensure a safe passage. Anyway, that is only half of the story.'

'What do you mean?'

'Obviously I didn't want to say too much in front of Herr Hedinger, but going to Berlin and coming back with the boy is only half of your mission. Once the boy is safely brought to Zurich, Herr Hedinger will send a coded message to Gunter Reinhart. Herr Reinhart has an extremely important document which he will hand over to us once he knows that his son is safe. It is a document that could determine the future course of the war, so it is vital that it is brought out of Germany as soon as possible.'

'How is it going to be brought out, Edgar?'

'By you, Henry!'

Chapter 18

Switzerland, February 1941

After the meeting in the apartment on the Basteiplatz, Henri was instructed to return to Geneva for a few days while Michael Hedinger sorted out all the paperwork.

'Basil will come and collect you on the Thursday. Just act normally until then,' had been Edgar's advice.

As soon as Henri arrived at Gare Cornavin on the Saturday, he walked to a phone booth in a quiet area at the back of the station. The phone call was brief and, as a result of it, he found himself on the Monday evening in the private room at the back of a seedy Armenian restaurant in Grand-Lancy where Viktor had first taken him in 1931.

'So, Edgar himself was in Zurich was he, *synok*?' Viktor sounded incredulous, so much so that he had poured himself another glass of something that, to Henri, tasted like liquorice-flavoured acid. 'I don't suppose he told you how he got to Switzerland?'

Henri shook his head. 'I presume he came on some roundabout route, Viktor.'

'I am not interested in presumptions, *synok*. I am interested in facts. It is quite a feat to travel from England to Switzerland these days, so it was obviously by a roundabout route: he was hardly going to fly direct, was he? I would be curious to know what that route is. You know, it would be a pleasure to meet your Captain Edgar. I think we would have much in common, despite everything. Tell me Henri, this must be important if Edgar himself has come to Switzerland.'

'I have to go to Berlin next week. I'll be using my own identity and acting as a courier for Bank Leu. I have to bring a boy back from

Berlin, a Jew, or a half-Jew to be precise. Once I deliver the boy to Zurich I am supposed to return to Berlin, where I will be given a document to bring back to Switzerland.'

'That's it?'

Henri laughed. 'That's it? Surely, smuggling a Jew out of Germany and then returning to collect a document is enough, isn't it?'

'What I meant was whether you can tell me any more.'

'Edgar said that the document is so important that it could decide the future course of the war. I asked him what he meant, and he was reluctant to tell me at first, but I told him that if I was going to put my life on the line by going into Berlin twice, then I had the right to know. So he told me that it is a document from the very top of the Reich – those were his words – about a proposed German invasion of the Soviet Union.'

Viktor had removed a pencil from his top pocket and had been in the process of sharpening it when Henri said this. He stopped, the knife poised in mid-air, pointing towards Henri.

'Say that again.'

'The document is to do with a proposed German invasion of the Soviet Union.'

Henri could have sworn that the deep lines on the Russian's face grew longer as he took in what he had just been told.

'Edgar told you this?'

'Yes. He seemed to regret having told me as soon as had done so, but I was quite persuasive, don't you think?'

'When you return from Berlin the second time – with the document, that is – did he say where you go?'

'Zurich, because that is where I am supposed to be based – it would look suspicious to the Germans if I went elsewhere in Switzerland. However, once I get to Zurich I'm to hand the routine bank papers over to the contact at Bank Leu and then head straight to Bern to give the document to Edgar.'

Viktor looked worried, lowering his head in thought and then looking up to the ceiling for inspiration.

'Plans for a German invasion of the Soviet Union, you say?'

Henri nodded.

'You don't know what day you will be back in Zurich with the document, do you, *synok*?'

'No. Edgar said that, all being well, I go on the first trip to Berlin a week today, which I think is the 24th. Depending on how things go, I'll probably be back there the following Monday, which would be the 3rd of March, I suppose. So I guess I'll be back in Zurich sometime that week. Maybe the Wednesday: the sooner the better.'

'We'll be waiting in Zurich for you: don't head to Bern until we have made contact with you. Do you understand?'

'Of course: but how will you know when I'm there? Edgar says I'm not to hang around in Zurich: I'm to go from the station to Bank Leu, hand over the bank's papers and then go straight back to the station and travel to Bern.'

Viktor removed his heavy coat and paced around the room. From an inside jacket pocket he took out a small notebook and leafed through it. When he found what he was looking for he wrote on a piece of paper, which he then handed to Henri.

'Here, memorise this number. When you arrive back in Zurich from Berlin, ring it and say "Peter is coming round for dinner". That is all. "Peter is coming round for dinner." They will reply by asking if you are bringing wine with you. If you say yes, we will know you have the document. We will meet you at Zurich Hauptbahnhof exactly one hour after the phone call, you understand?'

—

The journey to Berlin began in Zurich, in the borrowed apartment above the hardware shop on Basteiplatz. A shade after a quarter past one on the Friday, Michael Hedinger arrived, breathless and busily explaining how he had been waiting on one extra document.

'I have to be back at my office by two o'clock for a meeting. I have everything here.'

From his bright brown, leather briefcase Hedinger removed a number of items which he placed neatly in front of him on the table.

He took Henri Hesse's Swiss passport from the top of the pile and handed it to him.

'All is in order, Herr Hesse. Thanks to our excellent relationship with the German consulate here in Zurich your passport now allows you to travel freely between Switzerland and Germany a maximum of six times over the next six months – until the 20th of August to be precise. That is a routine arrangement for our couriers.'

Edgar and Remington-Barber both studied the visa, emblazoned with a swastika and a rampant eagle and made approving noises.

'And here are the documents that you are carrying from Bank Leu to the Reichsbank in Berlin, for the attention of Herr Reinhart: they are, of course, the purpose of your trip as far as the German authorities are concerned. You will see that they are all in sealed envelopes. I would ask that they remain that way until they are handed over. In this envelope...' he passed a long white envelope with the bank's crest to Henri 'is your letter of accreditation from the bank, and here are your rail tickets from Zurich to Berlin: you change at Stuttgart. It is a long journey, but you will travel first class, which is very tolerable. I have taken the liberty of booking you on the train that departs Zurich at six o'clock on Monday morning. You should be in Berlin by six o'clock in the evening.'

Another envelope came over to Henri Hesse.

'In Berlin you will stay at the Kaiserhof: our couriers either stay there or at the Excelsior on Askanischer Platz, but the Kaiserhof is rather charming and is slightly closer to the centre. It is certainly more discreet than the Adlon: everyone stays at the Adlon, it is not private enough I think – too many journalists and possibly spies. Here is the letter of confirmation from the Kaiserhof. The bill will be settled directly by the bank, you do not need to worry about that. Your room will be en suite.'

Henri checked the contents of the latest envelope to come his way across the table.

'Very efficient, Herr Hedinger,' said Edgar. 'I trust you have addressed the somewhat more complicated issue of young Alfred?'

Hedinger nodded. 'I am proposing that he travels under the identity of my own son, Andreas.'

The banker pulled a large white handkerchief from a pocket and used it to wipe his forehead. He hesitated a while before he replied. 'I have to be honest with you, this has been most difficult. I have had sleepless nights over it. I have never met Alfred, but Gunter has shown me photographs of him. Alfred is eleven, or twelve. My own son, Andreas, is ten, but is tall for his age. I would not say that Andreas and Alfred look alike, but I think with a bit of imagination, you could ensure that at the very least they do not look too different, if you see what I mean. Here is his passport.'

The three men studied the passport photo of Andreas Hedinger. His black hair was straight and had a distinctive parting low down on the left side. He wore a pair of round, wire-framed glasses.

'Here are the very glasses that Andreas is wearing in that picture.' Hedinger had brought a spectacle out of his briefcase. 'We bought him a brand-new pair yesterday. I think that if you make sure that Alfred's hair is like Andreas' and he wears these glasses, then you have a chance.'

'Have you told your wife about this?'

'I had to. If this works, we will need to keep Andreas off school until Alfred arrives in Zurich. Also, I have had to tell her about Alfred: he will be coming to stay with us, after all this is done.'

'What does she think of it?'

'Fortunately, Helga is a braver person than I am. She is a very devout woman. She believes that this is her Christian duty. As long as there is no danger to Andreas, then she will go along with it.'

'That's all very well, but why on earth would Andreas be in Berlin – and with me?' Henri was holding the boy's passport. 'What am I to say when I'm asked what I'm doing in Berlin with the son of my boss at Bank Leu? And what about how he got there – won't they spot that he did not come into Germany with me?' Henri sounded annoyed at the fact that no one had questioned this yet.

'Turn to the third page of the passport please,' said Hedinger. 'This is where my relationship with the passport clerk at the German consulate paid off. I asked him to stamp the passport showing that Andreas entered Germany this coming Monday – the 24th. I explained that this was a treat for Andreas. As ever, he was most obliging: given the way that the bank looks after him, he ought to be. In this envelope is the train ticket for Alfred to use from Berlin to Zurich. It is a return, showing that the outward part of the journey – from Zurich to Berlin – was on Monday 24th February. There is no reason why the German border guards should question this and the Swiss ought not to be difficult about allowing a Swiss boy to re-enter his country.'

'And the story, Herr Hedinger?' asked Remington-Barber. 'We always need to have a very good story.'

'A reward! Andreas has done so well at school that I promised him a visit to Berlin. I was planning to take him myself but have been unable to arrange it because I am so busy, so I asked one of my couriers to do so. Andreas is fascinated by everything he sees about Germany, the marching – everything. He is so excited.'

Henri sat very still with his head in his hands. Edgar raised his eyebrows high and looked at Remington-Barber who shook his head.

'Henry, any better ideas?'

'None that I can think of at the moment.'

'Basil?'

Remington-Barber shook his head.

'It's a bit thin, to be honest, but then very few cover stories are quite as watertight as we'd like them to be. We have to rely on no one probing too deeply. I suppose it does at least have the merit of being relatively simple. As long as no one pushes too hard on why a mere courier would be entrusted with taking his boss's son to Berlin. Perhaps we could say that actually Henry is also a close family friend of yours: maybe your wife could write a letter thanking him for putting himself out and all that?'

'That is a good idea, Edgar,' said Remington-Barber. 'Herr Hedinger, you will need to give Henry some important information: your address, what Andreas likes and doesn't like, all about his school, sports – that kind of thing. Alfred will have to learn all that in case he's questioned.'

Edgar sighed loudly, stood up and paced around the room, a trail of cigarette smoke following in his wake.

'Let's be frank. If the Gestapo pull in Alfred and interrogate him, the whole thing will fall apart. We have to hope that we don't get to that point; that no one probes too deep. If none of us can come up with a better legend, I suppose that is it. Herr Hedinger, you had better get back to the bank. Can I suggest that you invite Henry round to your house at the weekend? That way he can familiarise himself with Andreas and your family. Basil, I think you ought to go too.'

Chapter 19

Berlin, February 1941

Henri Hesse arrived at the Kaiserhof hotel on Wilhelmstrasse a few minutes after six o'clock on the evening of Monday 24th February. It was only his second ever visit to Germany's capital, the first being in 1934 or 1935 – he could not remember for sure – when he had accompanied his mother as a late replacement for his stepfather, who had pulled out 'because of business.' He remembered his mother being charmed by Berlin, in a rather naïve way. Utterly oblivious to the politics, she was much taken with what she saw as people's enthusiasm and the enormous swastikas draped from the buildings. She admired the dramatic colours and way that they swayed very gently even in the absence of a breeze. For Henri, the visit was simply an affirmation of what he believed in: he could not wait to get out of the city, vowing never to return.

And now he had returned. The hotel made a fuss of him, assuring him that Bank Leu were most valued clients and would he like to make a reservation for dinner? There were numerous forms and cards to fill in, which he did with the utmost care. He had spent the weekend going through the trip in detail with Remington-Barber and Edgar, and he had been warned about the hotel cards. They were destined for the Gestapo, which had a special office in Berlin where every night the cards of newly-arrived foreigners would be carefully examined against the Gestapo's meticulous records.

Remington-Barber had been quite candid. 'If they've got anything against you from last year's Stuttgart trip, then alarm bells will go off. They'll either haul you out of bed that night or first thing in the morning. That's the bad news, Henry. Good news is that if they have nothing adverse on your file – and there is no reason why they should – then you're in the clear, and that should make the rest of the trip that much easier, relatively speaking.'

Henri Hesse ate little for dinner that night and slept badly, alert to every sound on the corridor as he waited for the Gestapo to come and arrest him for the murder of the owner of the perfume shop in Essen. At four in the morning he was convinced he could hear footsteps in the corridor and finally decided to unlock the door and have a look, but the long corridor was deserted, apart from neat pairs of shoes outside a number of the doors.

He felt a bit more relaxed and drifted off to sleep, only to be visited during it by the familiar face of Roza – her image far more in focus, and its presence remaining far longer than usual. She spent much of the night asking questions, but every time he tried to reply he found that he could not form the words. When he woke on the Tuesday morning he was exhausted, but as he lay in bed his mood lifted. It was a quarter to eight and in the corridor he could hear the chambermaids gathering. At least, he decided, he had passed the scrutiny of whichever Gestapo clerk had been scrutinising the hotel registration cards overnight.

This upbeat mood continued as he went down to breakfast, notwithstanding having to walk down corridors and stairs adorned with a gallery's worth of framed photographs commemorating Hitler's various visits to the hotel, of which there appeared to have been many.

He knew that he was likely to be in Berlin until the Friday. According to Hedinger, it was not unusual for the bank's couriers to have to wait a few days to collect the return documents, and Edgar and Remington-Barber were clear that a few days would be essential for Alfred to prepare for the journey to Switzerland.

'If all goes to plan,' said Remington-Barber, 'you and Alfred will come out on Friday morning. After that it depends on your journey. With a very fair wind you could be in Zurich late Friday, but more likely Saturday. Make sure you send Hedinger a telegram from Stuttgart when you know what train you're going to be on.'

He was due at the Reichsbank at ten o'clock and his instructions were to go by taxi: it was not done to walk the streets carrying important papers. Henri Hesse from Bank Leu entered the Reichsbank through the enormous doors on Französischestrasse. It was ten o'clock and he had been warned to expect delays, and he was not to be disappointed. First he was searched, and then he had to report to reception, which was a tall, polished oak desk behind which a row of serious-looking receptionists peered down. After that he was given a form and sent over to another desk to fill it in. When he returned to the main reception desk, the form was carefully checked and only then did the receptionist deign to telephone Gunter Reinhart's office. 'Herr Reinhart will be with you in due course. Please wait over there.'

'Over there' was a small waiting area where half a dozen other people were sitting quietly. The man sitting opposite was clutching a Swiss passport and a padlocked briefcase. He told Henri he was a courier, from the Basler Handelsbank. He was surprised not to have seen Henri there before, he said: sometimes there could be as many as half a dozen couriers at the Reichsbank from the different Swiss banks.

The man got up and sat himself next to Henri. He was no more than five feet tall and was wearing a dark, formal suit that seemed to be a size too large for him. He stretched up to whisper in Henri's ear.

'I don't know who needs the other more – us or the Germans. I used to work for the SBC in Basel: I cannot tell you how much work they were getting from the Germans. Basler Handelsbank has recruited five of us in the past couple of months. From what I understand it has been even busier for you lot in Zurich, is that right?'

'Indeed.' Henri shifted to his left, away from the man, whose breath reeked of stale tobacco.

'I don't want to know where the Germans are getting all this gold and cash from – but what I do know is that if it wasn't for us, they'd be stuck with it. We're doing them a big favour – and we are making a lot of money in the process. How are things with Bank Leu?'

'Yes... very good, thank you.'

'So, where are you staying? Maybe tonight—'

At that point a secretary appeared in front of them, a gold swastika the only touch of colour on her dark suit.

'Bank Leu?'

Henri stood up.

'Come with me.'

Five minutes later Henri was in the small, deeply carpeted office of Gunter Reinhart. Reinhart had assured his secretary that they would not be needing coffee, and yes, thank you, he had all of the papers he needed. *That would be all, thank you.*

It was silent in the office apart from the ticking of a clock that Henri couldn't see. He and Gunter Reinhart eyed each other carefully. Reinhart waited a moment and then walked over to close the door, which his secretary had left ajar. He gestured for Henri to sit down and held up his hand – *wait*. A minute later he walked softly over to the door again, opened it, looked around, closed it again and came to sit at his desk.

'My secretary is – how can I put it tactfully... very efficient, but nosey. She is the kind of person who likes to know everything. That is bad enough, but in these times – it can be quite a problem. Recently she joined the Nazi Party, and she is forever telling me about how her husband has become some kind of party representative in the street where they live. That means they spy on their neighbours, so naturally I assume that she spies on me. I am very careful with her.'

Gunter had relaxed a bit now, and his manner had become notice-ably friendlier. He reached across the desk and held out his hand to shake Henri's.

'I'm Gunter Reinhart by the way, as you've no doubt gathered. I'm pleased to meet you. You have the documents? It is important that they are here and in order. We don't want people questioning why you came!'

Henri handed over the envelopes containing the Bank Leu docu-ments. Reinhart opened them carefully with a dagger-like letter opener. He glanced over the documents and then put them to the side of his desk.

'I'll deal with them when we have finished. The documents for you to take back to Zurich will not be ready until late Thursday, you realise that?'

'So I understand.'

'It is not unusual for a courier to hang around Berlin for a few days.' He had left his desk now and come to sit next to Henri, speaking more quietly.

'Most couriers seem to end up at the zoo, I have no idea why – I suppose they get bored. It is not as if they can go to a library, not now that we've burned most of the books worth reading! As far as you are concerned, you won't get bored: we have plenty to keep you busy.' Gunter Reinhart paused and coughed. He hesitated before he resumed speaking, this time in an even lower voice. He gestured for Henri had to lean closer.

'I cannot tell you how grateful I am...' Gunter Reinhart looked as if he was overcome by emotion. 'My family situation... has been a source of great stress. It has been explained to you, I take it?'

'Yes.'

'I should never have divorced Rosa. We thought it was for the best. We assumed it would be a short-term measure and that maybe the Nazis would change their minds or go away. How could we have been stupid as to think that? Once we realised that that was never going to happen our plan was that Rosa and Alfred would move to another country, and that I would be able to join them in due course, but it did not turn out like that. We both remarried. At least I believed that they would be safe once they moved to Paris, but to find out that they had returned to Berlin... madness. It was a terrible shock. Now they are trapped here, and I have been desperate to find a way of getting them out. For a while Rosa wanted the three of them to remain together, but once she found out about Harald's death she agreed with me that, at the very least, we must get Alfred out. Once he is in Switzerland, then I can see what can be done with Rosa, and of course Sophia too, even though she is not my daughter. But for now, getting Alfred out of Germany is the priority. That is what I pray for.'

'Does Alfred know about the plan?'

'Not yet. You are going to meet him this afternoon. You will obviously need to spend some time with him. Rosa knows there is a plan, and she knows that something will happen this week, but she does not know the details – neither, for that matter, do I. Tell me briefly what the plan is: if you stay too long then my secretary will become suspicious.'

Henri took Andreas Hedinger's passport out of his jacket pocket and carefully placed it on the blotter pad on Reinhart's desk.

'The plan is for Alfred to accompany me back to Zurich using this identity – Andreas is Michael Hedinger's son.'

Reinhart nodded. *I know.*

'This passport is two years old, so anyone looking at it would not be surprised that the person in the photograph has changed. Also, I have with me the very spectacles that Andreas is wearing in this photograph. You can see that Andreas has quite a distinctive hair style...'

Reinhart had picked up the passport and put on his own glasses. He turned on his desk lamp and studied the passport carefully under it, his face impassive.

'Andreas's hair is much darker than Alfred's. As far as his hair is concerned, Alfred inherited my Aryan genes rather than his mother's. I had always thought that would be an advantage.'

'We thought of how to deal with the question of his hair colour. I have brought some black hair dye with me: it's back in the hotel. If we can use it on Alfred and then style his hair to look like Andreas, it may work: especially with the glasses.'

'It is certainly feasible; there is no doubt about that. But how will you explain that you will be accompanied back to Zurich by the boy?'

Henri drew a long breath, anxious to betray as little of any of his own scepticism as possible. 'The story will depend on us not being questioned too much, but in a nutshell it is that, as well as being a courier for Bank Leu, I am also a family friend of the Hedingers, and that I brought Andreas with me to Berlin as a treat.'

Gunter Reinhart said nothing but stared at Henri for a good few moments.

'That's it?'

Henri shrugged his shoulders. *Yes, I know... don't tell me.*

'You think it will work?'

'Hopefully. On the positive side, the passport is a genuine Swiss one. As long as they're not suspicious, they will probably not push Alfred too hard.'

Gunter Reinhart snapped the passport shut, handed it back to Henri, turned off his desk lamp and walked over to the window. He looked out over the Spreekanal and then turned to face Henri.

'The alternative is to smuggle Alfred out, and that is too dangerous. This plan will have to work. And you know that the document will be released only once I know that Alfred is safe in Zurich?'

Henri nodded.

'Good. You are to meet Franz Hermann at one o'clock. He will escort you to the house where they are all hiding. Let me give you your instructions: you'll need to listen carefully. Incidentally, Henri, are you fond of flowers?'

–

Henri Hesse went from the Reichsbank back to the Kaiserhof, where he sought out the concierge. 'I have an unexpectedly free afternoon. I wonder if you could suggest anything I might do?'

The concierge smiled obligingly. *Please could he have the guest's details?*

Henri recalled what Gunter Reinhart had told him that morning. 'Anything you discuss with them could be reported back to the Gestapo, they like to keep tabs on foreigners – so your plans will need to appear plausible: use them to create an alibi.'

'And what would you be interested in doing, sir?' the concierge asked. 'The cinema maybe? Or shopping?'

Henri shook his head.

'I have been spending so much time indoors that I wouldn't mind some fresh air.'

'The zoo perhaps? It is within the Tiergarten so you could combine the two.'

Henri shook his head. 'To be honest, I'm not very keen on animals. They make me nervous.'

'I quite understand, sir. Do you want to stay in the city?'

'I think so, it will be dark soon.'

'That is true, I was going to suggest a visit to Potsdam, but perhaps that is for another day. Are you by any chance interested in plants and gardens?'

'Yes, I am actually.' He managed to sound just the right side of enthusiastic.

'Well, we have an excellent Botanischer Garten down in Dahlem. It is a quite wonderful haven of peace and quiet in the city, and the gardens are most beautiful.'

Henri managed to look as if he was having second thoughts. 'In Dahlem you say: isn't that far away?'

'Not at all sir,' said the concierge, 'it is no more than six or seven stops on the S-Bahn from Anhalter. The gardens are just a few minutes' walk from Botanischer Garten station. Here, let me show you how to get there.'

–

'*Every minute of your visit will be laced with danger, but no moment will be more dangerous than the one when you drop your guard.*'

Edgar's parting words had been menacing enough, but they hardly began to describe what Henri Hesse encountered at Anhalter. The station was busy, but unnaturally quiet apart from the noise of dogs barking in the distance. Quite a number of people were exiting the station as he entered it, looking over their shoulders and seeming to be relieved to be in the open air. He noticed that there were a large number of troops milling around, dressed in the black uniform of the SS rather than the grey of the Wehrmacht. He purchased a return ticket to Botanischer Garten, making sure to ask the clerk behind the tiny window if he knew how long it would take for him to walk to the gardens from the station.

Continuing to feel pleased with how things had gone, he headed for the platform, which was when he saw them. His first impression was that it was a lot of people waiting for one train, especially at lunchtime. *Maybe an outing?* They were two platforms away from the one he was waiting on, crowded together and hemmed in by the SS men in their black uniforms. Some of the SS had Alsatians with them, holding them on a short leash but allowing them to rear up at the people on the platform, and all the while the non-stop barking, which every so often orchestrated with the sound of a train's whistle or a station announcement.

Henri moved along his platform, trying to get a better view. The crowd of people was very mixed: men, women and children; old and young. They all seemed to be quite well dressed and all of the people were either carrying suitcases or clutching bundles. From what he could see, the SS men were checking what the people had with them, and a few of the bundles ended up being strewn on the platform, with some clothing spilling over onto the track.

He was still trying to make some sense of it when his train pulled into the platform and there was a scramble to board it. Henri positioned himself by a window looking out onto the crowded platform. The window was dirty and it was harder to make out much detail through the screen of soot and grease. With his sleeve he tried to clean his side of the window, and as he did so he caught the eye of a woman who had sat down opposite him. She followed his gaze across the track and then looked down, intently studying the rail ticket she was clutching in her gloved hands. He leaned forward to get a better view, but then the doors of the train slammed, a guard called out and the train lurched forward. Within seconds the crowd of people on the opposite platform became a blur, and soon they were out of Anhalter.

'Do you know who they were?' he asked the lady.

She looked around her before answering. 'You don't know?'

He shook his head.

'Jews. They've started to take them away,' she said in a matter-of-fact tone.

'Where to?'

A ticket inspector had appeared next to them, and they both silently handed him their tickets. She glanced up at him. *Keep quiet.* Over the crackly speaker the driver announced the next station: 'Grossgorsens-rasse'.

The lady stood up, smoothing her elegant coat as she did so. Before moving into the aisle she bent down and, barely pausing, whispered into Henri's ear. 'Wherever it is they take them to, they don't come back.'

He got off the train at Botanischer Garten, crossed the Unter den Eichen, and entered the gardens. He did his best to appear every bit the interested visitor, and made leisurely progress to the Italian Garden, which was actually quite beautiful and, in other circumstances, would have been an ideal place to relax.

If you are not approached by him within ten minutes of entering the Italian Garden, walk back to the station and travel back to Anhalter, and then to the hotel. Just act normally. Just because he does not turn up does not necessarily mean something is wrong.

He had been in the Italian Gardens approaching ten minutes when a smartly dressed man with a broad-brimmed hat came up to him and spoke in an educated Berlin accent.

'Excuse me, sir; could you point me in the direction of the green-houses?'

'I am sorry, but I am not very familiar with the gardens. I can tell you that the lake is in that direction though,' said Henri, sticking carefully to his script.

The man held out his hand and shook Henri's. 'I'm Franz. I am pleased to meet you. Everything appears to be in order. We will spend another few minutes separately in these gardens and then I will head out. Follow me at a safe distance. We will exit through Königin-Luise-Strasse. If at any stage I remove my hat, that is a signal that something is wrong. In that case, keep on walking and make your way back to the station, for which you'll need to take a circuitous route. Assuming that everything is in order, you will see me enter a house – no more than five minutes from here. Allow two minutes from when I enter the house before you approach it. There is a small window above the front door. Only approach the house if the curtains in that window are open. If they are closed, head back to the hotel. Have you got all that?'

Henri nodded.

'Good. Now point me in a northerly direction. I am sure no one is watching us, but just in case they are, they will see you directing me.'

For the next few minutes they strolled apart around the Italian garden. Henri did his best to appear fascinated by the plants. A group of young Luftwaffe officers were also walking around, and he wondered if their presence might cause a delay, but then he noticed the lawyer head out of the gardens. He followed him until he entered the white house on the corner of Arno-Holz Strasse.

'*Allow two minutes from when I enter the house before you approach it.*'

He had slowed his pace right down and allowed himself one quick glance behind him. The area appeared to be deserted. In a house across the street a maid had come out to put something in a bin and was looking at him. He bent down to tie his shoelaces, and a glance at his watch told him that a minute and a half had elapsed since Hermann had entered the house. He would head over now.

The curtains in the small window above the porch were open, and as he walked down the path the front door opened. Hermann was in the hall, gesturing for him to go upstairs. The landing was dark; he could only just make out two doorways in a corridor. One of them opened and at first the person in the doorway was only in silhouette, with the light flooding in behind them. It was a woman and she gestured for him to come into the room. It was a small lounge with two sofas and a table in the corner: a boy and a girl were sitting on the sofa. By now, Franz Hermann had joined him in the room and made the introductions: 'Alfred and Sophia,' – the boy and the girl both stood up and shook his hand, the girl only after being prompted to do so by her brother. 'Herr Hesse is a friend of the family from Switzerland, from Zurich.'

Alfred looked younger than his twelve years: he had a pleasant face that showed signs of beginning to turn handsome and the fair hair that his father had described. He was thin and slightly gaunt-looking, with a pale, unhealthy complexion that no doubt owed much to having been confined indoors for so long. He had a natural smile, but it did reveal a set of yellow teeth.

Henri was unable to gauge whether Alfred's sister looked older or younger than five, but Sophia did share her brother's unhealthily pale complexion. She seemed to hold her head down and stare up at whoever she was looking at with enormous dark eyes, which managed to appear both innocent and knowing at the same time. She had a head of thick, dark hair that fell over her thin shoulders and was a clutching a dirty toy rabbit close to her.

'And this is Rosa.'

Rosa.

Roza.

With long, dark hair that flowed over her slim shoulders and dark eyes that sparkled, this Rosa looked too much like the Russian Roza. In a lesser light she could easily be mistaken for her. And although it was ten years since Henri had last seen Roza, in truth he had seen her image most nights since then, far too stark and far too lifelike to have allowed her to fade from his memory. This Rosa was uncannily like the one in whose murder in Interlaken he had been complicit. She was as he imagined Roza would have grown up to be: the face slightly more lined, the breasts that had been small but perfectly formed now fuller under the blouse and cardigan, the eyes having lived that much longer and experienced that much more. He fully expected her to gently touch his wrist and then, as she was wont to do in the dreams, grip them tightly and admonish him. 'You were the one person I thought understood me. You were someone I trusted,' she had said then, certain in the knowledge of the fate that awaited them. It was what she repeated most nights to him in his dreams.

Roza.

Rosa smiled and shook his hand, and then asked the children to leave the room.

'Go upstairs. I will call you down later. And remember, be quiet!'

The children silently shuffled out of the room. When Rosa spoke again Henri noticed that she did so in such a soft voice that it was barely above a whisper.

'This is the house of Franz's mother. She is very elderly and very infirm and I look after her. In fact, I am a doctor, but as far as she is

228

concerned, I am a nurse. She has no idea that I am Jewish, and nor does she have any idea that the children are here, which is why we have to be so quiet. In fact, her hearing is very bad, but we are very careful nonetheless. The children never go downstairs. We have been here for well over a year and life is barely tolerable. The children have to live in silence: we cannot risk putting the lights on when it gets dark. We are so grateful to Franz, but life is very difficult: we have limited food, despite Franz's generosity. Gunter helps too but he has to be careful as his wife knows nothing. We live in constant fear that someone will find out about us. Apparently, Jews can still technically leave Berlin but, in reality, it is now almost impossible to do so and we would not stand a chance: we have to stay hidden. Gunter feels that at least we should try and get Alfred out; he is insistent about that and I have come round to accepting that, even though it breaks my heart. I understand that you have come to help; I am so grateful. Please tell us everything.'

Over the following hour Henri went through the plan in detail. Rosa was impassive, perched on the edge of the sofa, straight-backed and occasionally asking him to repeat what he had just said. Once, Rosa placed her hand on his, allowing her long, thin fingers to brush his wrist. It was too close to what Roza would do, and Henri must have showed his emotions because Franz Hermann leaned forward.

'Are you all right, Henri?'

'Pardon?' He felt as if he had just woken up, momentarily unsure of exactly where he was.

'Are you all right? You look worried.'

'No, no… I am fine. I was just thinking about what we have to do. There is so much detail to think about.'

They both agreed that if Alfred's hair could be dyed and styled like that of Andreas in the photograph then, along with the spectacles, he would have a reasonable resemblance to the Swiss boy, especially given that the passport photograph was taken two years previously. Even the most rigorous person inspecting it would have to acknowledge that Andreas had aged.

'Alfred is an intelligent boy,' said Rosa. 'I know that most mothers would say that, but he is. I am sure that he will be able to remember the details of the cover story, but how he will act under pressure is a different matter. We simply don't know, do we? He is well aware of how much danger we are in. He knows that he may never see us again.'

Henri only realised that Rosa was crying when he saw that Franz had moved closer to her and had a comforting arm round her shoulder. Henri looked first at the floor and then at the window, awkward and unsure of what to say. At first, he slid along the sofa towards Rosa, thinking that it was his place to comfort her too, but then he checked himself. It would not do to appear too familiar. How could he begin to explain himself?

'In many respects, we are well prepared,' said Franz. 'You have the passport and the rail ticket, and you said something about the Swiss side of the border being potentially the hardest part of the journey. From what I have also heard, that is probably correct. The Swiss are very strict about who they let in: one of their own citizens ought not to be a problem. The Germans will more be concerned with someone who has a German passport trying to leave the country. The priority now is to start work with Alfred.'

Rosa stood up and walked over to the window, drawing the curtain.

'I had better go and check on your mother, Franz. Then let me have some time alone with Alfred. I would like to tell him myself. How long can you stay, Herr Hesse?'

'I suppose I have a few hours?'

'No, no,' said Hermann. 'It will look suspicious if you arrive back too late at the Kaiserhof. There is no question that they will be making a note of your movements; it happens with all foreign visitors. You can have one hour with Alfred and then come back tomorrow, when you will have all day.'

–

It was the Friday, the last day of February, and as the train pulled out of Potsdam station Henri noticed that Alfred, who he now could only think of as Andreas Hedinger, was crying.

It was a very private cry, the silent type where a few tears trickle down the cheek and any sobs are suppressed by a cough, biting the lip and fingers clasped firmly to the cheek as the hands are deployed to shield the face. Andreas had shifted in his seat so that he was looking directly out of the window and neither of the other passengers in the carriage could possibly see his face. Henri caught glimpses of him in profile, along with the reflection of his face on the window.

Alfred had held himself together so far that morning and over the previous two days. Ten minutes previously, he had passed his first major test. Security at the station had been lighter than they had expected, with the main check being to ensure that the tickets were in order. But Henri knew that sooner or later they would be questioned, and that had happened during the wait at Potsdam station when a Gestapo officer had entered their compartment, with two Wehrmacht soldiers waiting in corridor outside.

'*Tickets. Identity documents. Quick.*'

The Gestapo officer's eyes darted from Henri to Alfred and back again and then to the other two men. Both of them appeared to be travelling on business: one to Jena and the other to Würzburg. The Gestapo officer seemed satisfied with their papers. Then it was Henri's turn.

'Your ticket is to Stuttgart.'

'Yes: then we are travelling to Zurich.'

'Let me see those tickets.'

He studied them and then said to Alfred, 'You are travelling together?'

'Yes.'

'You are related?'

'No,' Henri said, quickly. 'Andreas is the son of a friend and colleague. He has been in Berlin visiting while I was on business in Berlin. His parents asked me to look after him.'

'What is your business?'

'I work for a bank: Bank Leu. Here is my letter of accreditation.'

The Gestapo man read every word and then turned to Alfred. 'You: your papers.'

Alfred handed over the passport.

Say as little as possible and when you do, don't speak too clearly: the Germans will obviously expect a Swiss person to have an accent.

'What is your date of birth?'

That was no problem. They had been working very hard over the past couple of days.

Two more questions and I'll begin to worry.

'And where did you visit in Berlin?'

Which is when Henri did begin to worry. Surely the Gestapo man would spot that Alfred was speaking with a Berlin accent, certainly not a Swiss one.

'Pardon?'

'I said, where did you visit in Berlin?'

The carriage door opened and one of the Wehrmacht soldiers came in.

'Otto wants your help in the front – there's a problem.'

Too easy.

Every minute of your visit will be laced with danger.

But that was that. Henri wanted to tell Alfred how well he had done, but all he was able to do was smile.

–

Alfred had been a model student, carefully writing down the details he needed to remember to pass as Andreas Hedinger from Zurich, memorising the story about how he had come to be in Berlin and how Herr Hesse was such a good friend of his parents and was so good to have agreed to take him to Berlin with him.

'*My father is so busy, I hardly see him these days! He kept promising to take me to Berlin and was always cancelling. Herr Hesse has been so very kind!*'

That was the agreed line that they would take if anyone questioned why he was in Berlin with Henri. In an effort to persuade Alfred to believe in the story they all kept up the pretence of how plausible it was. The adults knew that the first line of their defence lay in the paperwork: if that in any way failed to convince then the story would be probed, and Henri knew that it would not stand up to a lot of scrutiny. Their displays of confidence in the story must have worked because, by the time they got on the train in Berlin, Henri had even come to believe in it himself.

Henri had gone to the Reichsbank first thing on the Wednesday morning – the briefest of trips, just enough to be able to show the hotel where he was going. From there he had travelled down to Dahlem and spent the whole day with Alfred. Gunter Reinhart had joined them for an hour in the afternoon: when he left it was to say farewell to Alfred. He had followed the same pattern on the Thursday. Franz had brought Alfred to the station on the Friday morning. Alfred's hair had been cut and dyed and, along with the wire-framed spectacles, the passage of time, and the relatively poor quality of the photograph, he presented more than a passing resemblance to Andreas Hedinger. Alfred stood on the platform clutching his small knapsack with a few clothes and one or two other innocuous items in it. In the pocket of his jacket was the Swiss passport – his lifeline. Franz shook hands briefly with both of them and disappeared into the crowd.

–

After Potsdam there had been a long wait in Leipzig and when the train finally left the city it moved very slowly through Saxony, meaning that they were more than two hours behind schedule when they arrived in Jena. Henri spent the long hours alternating between staring out of the window and closing his eyes, but when he did so Roza was staring at him as always.

By now Henri knew that their chances of getting into Switzerland that night were remote. By the time the train crossed over from Thuringia into Bavaria the rain that had accompanied them since Jena had become incessant. Alfred sat quietly in one position: he had eaten very little apart from a sausage and milk that Henri had bought on the platform at Leipzig. Since Potsdam he had appeared composed.

There was another long wait in Würzburg, and they were joined in their carriage by three new passengers: a woman with a pinched face accompanied by a pretty teenage daughter, and a Waffen SS

Obersturmführer who was one small glass of something short of being drunk. Henri saw the boy tense as the SS officer stumbled into the carriage. At the sight of the girl, who could have been no more than seventeen, the *Obersturmführer's* eyes lit up. For the next half hour he did his best to impress her, but the girl did her best to ignore him, helped by the clear disapproval of her mother.

Then he turned his attention to the boy. 'Where are you from?... Switzerland?... I LOVE Switzerland!... The Swiss are our friends!... YOU are my friend... Where have you been in Germany?... Tell me what you saw in Berlin.'

Henri struggled hard to conceal his amazement as Alfred confidently enthused about everything he had seen in Berlin, not least the soldiers – he loved seeing the soldiers and the marching – it was so exciting, far more exciting than anything we have in Zurich or indeed anywhere in Switzerland for that matter. He would love to return to Germany, maybe when he was older he could even...

Fortunately the SS man seemed to be oblivious to Alfred's apparent lack of a Swiss accent, helped by the contents of a flask, which he had finished since joining the train. Within minutes he had insisted on being called Karl and was showing Alfred his Mauser automatic and describing how he had captured Paris single-handed. 'When you are old enough to meet girls, Andreas, the first place you go is Paris! Which football team do you support Andreas?... FC Zurich?... Ah, Grasshoppers! A good team.'

Just outside the city, still in the blanket darkness of the countryside, the train pulled to a noisy halt. It was seven o'clock. Silence for a few minutes, then shouting and the sound of dogs barking. It took an eternity for the commotion to work its way down the train. When it reached them a Gestapo officer who seemed to be wider than he was tall squeezed into their compartment, breathless and with sweat dripping from his brow. He was wearing a leather raincoat that was so tight that it remained unbuttoned. He looked around and then shouted at Alfred.

'You. Get up... now!'

Henri clutched the seat to stop himself swaying. The boy was so terrified he did not move one muscle, but all the blood had drained from his face.

'Did you not hear me? Come with me now.'

The SS *Obersturmführer* rose slowly and slightly unsteadily, standing directly in front of the Gestapo officer and very close to him. He was at least a foot taller than the other man and used every inch of that to ensure he looked down on him with the maximum effect.

'What is the problem?'

'We have had reports that some Jewish boys got on the train at Würzburg. The police discovered some of the vermin hiding in a cellar and had been chasing the gang: they last saw them in the vicinity of the station. We are checking all youths on the train.'

'Well, Andreas is my friend, and it is impossible that he is Jewish!'

He was shouting at the Gestapo officer, flecks of spit spraying onto the other man's reddening face. When the Gestapo officer replied, it was in a much more uncertain voice.

'And how do you know that?'

'Because he is Swiss!'

The big man wiped his face with his sleeve, clearly puzzled by the *Obersturmführer's* logic.

'I still need to check his papers and question him though…' He held his arm out towards Alfred, beckoning him to join him. The *Obersturmführer* grabbed hold of the Gestapo man's arm and pushed it down.

'You won't need to be doing that.'

'How come?'

'Because I got on the train at Würzburg and Andreas was already on it, so stop wasting your time.'

The Gestapo officer appeared reluctant to argue. By now a pair of Alsatians were barking outside the open door of the compartment. 'Let me have a look at your passport,' he said to the boy.

Andreas passed it to him. Henri noticed that the Gestapo man's hands were trembling as he quickly flicked through the passport, before handing it back.

'That is all in order.'

'Next time, try and serve the Reich in more useful ways,' the *Obersturmführer* spat at him as he left the compartment, defeated.

It was nine o'clock by the time the train arrived in Stuttgart. Henri knew he could have gone to the nearby Hotel Victoria, where he imagined that Katharina Hoch was still the night manager, but it would be too risky. He decided instead that they would stay overnight in the station, where there was a large air raid shelter. The first train to Zurich was at eight twenty in the morning, which meant that he would also have an opportunity to send a telegram to Hedinger.

The air raid shelter where they slept was crowded. The boy was still in a state of anxiety and stress from the events of the day and Henri had to whisper to him how well he had done; how proud his parents would be of him. *'We're nearly there now, you'll be safe.'* They found a corner of a wide bench at the back of the shelter into which they wedged themselves. Henri put his arm round the boy and gradually he felt him relax. Within a few minutes he was fast asleep, on what he both hoped and feared would be his last night in his homeland.

Chapter 20

Stuttgart, Zurich & Berlin, March 1941

For the first few hours in the air raid shelter in Stuttgart station, Henri hardly slept. The spot they had found turned out to have a noisy pipe running directly above it and every time he dropped off he was soon woken by clanging or the sound of air hissing. And then when he did drop off, Roza would appear: her admonishing eyes fixed on him, telling him what he knew all too well. For a full hour she haunted him: she was there if he shut his eyes tight, and still there when he opened them wide, and there when he held his head tight in his hands.

But then the strangest thing happened: Roza stared at him in her familiar fashion, her eyes full of sadness and hatred. But then her face began to dissolve, and when it came back into focus, although the dark brown eyes were there and the dark hair flowing over slim shoulders, now the features belonged to Rosa – and with that, an unexpected calm came over Henri. Rosa was no less sad, but there was the faintest of smiles on her face and a look of pleading in her eyes. And as the very beginnings of an idea began to emerge in Henri's mind, a calm that he was quite unused to came over him, and the few hours he slept between then and when he woke up were the deepest he'd slept for years.

People began to leave the shelter from six in the morning, and by half six it was almost deserted. Henri had hoped to stay in it until nearer to eight o'clock, but when they ventured up onto the main station concourse they spotted that a cafe was open and they were able to remain there for the next hour and a half. At eight o'clock the telegram booth in the station opened and Henri sent a message to

237

Michael Hedinger, who he knew would have gone into the bank that morning as arranged.

> Departing Stuttgart 8.20 stop Arriving Zurich 2.40 stop
> Papers all in order stop

Papers all in order: Andreas is with me, a successful mission… so far.

The train left Stuttgart at eight thirty, but then was held at a red light on the outskirts of the city to allow a military train to pass, its open trucks carrying dozens of tanks. By lunchtime the train had made its steady progress through Swabia towards the border town of Singen, the last stop in Germany before Switzerland. They were held at an isolated platform, where they were told by a loudspeaker announcement that any passengers wishing to travel on into Switzerland should remain in their compartments: all other passengers should leave the train forthwith.

For half an hour there was no sign of anything. There was just one other passenger in their compartment: an immaculately dressed German man with the long, elegant hands of a pianist, and the complexion of someone who rarely ventured outdoors. He had spent most of the journey reading sheet music and attending to his nails, occasionally removing a watch from his jacket with a flourish, studying it with some fascination, tutting and then returning it to his jacket. Eventually, the delay in Singen was too much for him. He was going to see what was going on, he told Henri, and left the compartment, leaving Henri and Alfred. Henri leaned over to Alfred, who he had noticed looked considerably more relaxed than yesterday. 'Don't forget, this is the most dangerous part of the journey. The Swiss border police will be watching for anyone trying to get into Switzerland who shouldn't. Don't make any mistakes. Soon you'll be able to relax. You have done very well, my boy. But be careful now…'

Alfred looked worried and Henri was not sure he had said the right thing. *Maybe I should have just kept quiet.*

Their fellow passenger returned to the carriage. 'They have to wait for the Swiss police to arrive,' he told them. 'I thought the Swiss were meant to be efficient. Ridiculous.'

Ten minutes later the Swiss border police arrived on the platform, where they and the German officers greeted each other like old friends. Working in pairs, one Swiss, one German, they went through the train compartment by compartment.

The Swiss officer who came into their compartment looked no more than twenty. He checked the passport of the pianist, asked to see his return ticket and then handed both to the German policeman. Both appeared to be satisfied.

The officer then turned to Henri. '*Passport.*' It was only when he saw the Swiss passport and said '*Grüezi*' that a fatal flaw in their plan that they had overlooked until now hit Henry hard in the face.

The Swiss border policeman had used the traditional Swiss German greeting, '*grüezi*'. If he was going to speak in Swiss German then the boy would not understand. He and his story would unravel very quickly.

'Where have you travelled from in Germany?' he asked, in Swiss German.

'I have been in Berlin, on business for Bank Leu. Here is my letter of accreditation.' Henri made a point of replying in standard German.

The young policeman took it and read it carefully. 'So how long have you been in Germany for?' Still in Swiss German.

'Since Monday.' Standard German. It had become like a surreal game.

'The boy: is he with you?'

'Andreas is the son of friends. He has been visiting Berlin.' Henri had tried to avoid looking at the boy, but caught a glimpse of his worried face as he mentioned him. He must have feared that he was about to be spoken to in Swiss German, which he would barely understand.

'And you stayed where in Berlin?'

'Jan, I keep telling you! Speak proper German; don't confuse me!' It was the German policeman, standing in the doorway of the carriage and clearly impatient.

His Swiss counterpart shrugged and took the passport of Andreas Hedinger. He checked the visa, looked up at Alfred and back again at the photo, repeating this three or four times, his bright blue eyes darting up and down.

'How old are you?' He spoke in standard German. Alfred gave Andreas's age and date of birth.

'Did you enjoy Berlin?'

'Yes sir, thank you. But I am looking forward to going home.'

—

He was in Zurich for less than forty hours.

They arrived in the city at three o'clock on the Saturday afternoon and were met at the station by Herr and Frau Hedinger. Alfred had shown no signs of relief as they had crossed the border into Switzerland, and by the time they arrived at the station he was in a state of shock, seemingly overwhelmed by what was happening to him. The fact that he was free and safe did not seem to occur to him as he was warmly greeted by the Hedingers. Frau Hedinger led Alfred over to the station cafe for a hot chocolate while Michael Hedinger and Henri found a quiet bench. Henri handed over the papers.

'Everything was in order?'

'Yes, thank you. Your arrangements were very good; faultless in fact.'

A tall man in a trilby was strolling purposefully towards them: it seemed that he had appeared from nowhere, Henri had looked carefully around when they left the train and certainly hadn't seen any sign of this man then. It was only when he was close to them that it was apparent who he was. He removed his leather gloves and shook Henri's hand.

'So that's Alfred, eh?'

'I wondered when you might show up, Edgar.'

'You didn't imagine that I'd miss this, did you? I trust there were no problems?'

'No. Nerve-wracking, but we have arrived in one piece.'

'As I can see. Hedinger, have you sorted your wretched documents out?'

Hedinger took the sealed envelopes from Henri and handed him a few more in return. 'You're returning to Berlin on Monday,' he said as he stood up. 'Edgar will tell you all about it. He has your tickets.'

'You're going to be all right with the boy?'

Hedinger nodded.

'And you'll send the telegram to Reinhart?'

'First thing Monday morning, as we arranged.'

'Won't Reinhart want to know sooner that Alfred's arrived safely?'

'I'm sure he would, but this all has to look proper,' said Edgar. 'It would be odd for an official of the Reichsbank to receive a telegram from an official of Bank Leu on a Saturday acknowledging safe receipts of papers. It will have to wait until Monday. By the time you see Reinhart on Tuesday morning he will know that Alfred arrived safely, and he can hand the other document over to you. Go on, Hedinger, you'd better take Alfred off. Henry, perhaps you want to go and say goodbye?'

Alfred had relaxed by the time Henri met up with him and Frau Hedinger in the station cafe. He had been drinking a hot chocolate and was devouring an enormous cream pastry. He had a big grin on his face.

'Alfred was telling me that he loves dogs but has never had one. He is so looking forward to meeting Mitzi! And guess what, Herr Hesse? She is expecting puppies! I have told Alfred that he can choose one of them to be his very own pet.'

Henri embraced Alfred and promised he would come and visit him. He mustn't worry; everything would be fine. When he released the boy from his embrace he noticed that Alfred's eyes were moist. He kept saying 'Thank you' and, as he disappeared out of the station he turned round and gave Henri a nervous little wave.

–

They spent what remained of the weekend in the apartment above the hardware shop on Basteiplatz. When they arrived there, Basil Remington-Barber was making up a camp bed in the lounge. The three of them sat around the table.

241

'You're booked on the six o'clock train on Monday morning. That got you into Berlin that evening, didn't it?'

'Yes: I was fortunate with the connection in Stuttgart. Coming back yesterday was a different matter. True, we left Berlin a bit later, but whether it was bomb damage or something else, I don't know, but it was a much slower journey: hence the reason why we had to stay over in Stuttgart.'

'I trust that you did not go anywhere near the Victoria?' asked Basil Remington-Barber.

'No, we stayed overnight in the station – in an air raid shelter.'

'Let's get down to business. Here's your ticket for Monday. We want to get you and the document back here as quickly as possible, so the plan is that you go to the Reichsbank first thing on the Tuesday morning, hand the Bank Leu's envelopes to Reinhart, and he will give you the ones to be brought back here. One of the sealed Reichsbank envelopes will contain the document – he will let you know which one. According to Hedinger, neither the German nor the Swiss police have ever tried to open a sealed envelope from any of the banks. I imagine that would be bad for business. I can see no reason why you should not be able to leave Berlin by lunchtime. I know the couriers often hang around for a few days, but we need to get you back here so we will risk it. You won't make it into Switzerland that night, but go to Stuttgart and then take the first train out on Wednesday morning. Does that all make sense?'

'Yes… but shouldn't the document be concealed?'

'We thought of that,' said Remington-Barber. 'If they decide to search you then they'll probably find it anyway. As Edgar says, they don't touch bank envelopes, especially if they are properly sealed. You're booked in the Kaiserhof there – here's the telegram confirming it. You still have the letter of accreditation from the bank? Good. And of course your passport has the correct visas. Tell me, Henry, what is Gunter Reinhart like?'

Henri shrugged. 'He's a German banker, which seems to be rather like a Swiss banker and I daresay British bankers: efficient enough, but what do you want me to say? I'll doubt we'll become close friends, if that is what you mean. Very tall also, for what this is worth.'

'What I think we mean,' said Remington-Barber, 'is what kind of a chap do you think he is? Is he trustworthy? After all, we have used one of our few agents able to travel in and out of Germany to help his son escape. How do we know that this document he is promising us is genuine? Maybe it is a trick...? Has he been just leading us along as a ruse to get Alfred out?'

'I really have no idea,' said Henri. 'He seems genuine enough. I suppose that if the document turns out to be either a fake or not to exist at all then he runs the risk of upsetting us, and that could have implications for his own safety – and that of Rosa and Sophia.'

Edgar and Remington-Barber looked at each other, partially reassured.

'You see, he still wants to help Rosa escape, and obviously that means little Sophia too.'

'I can see why Reinhart wanted to get his son out, but why his ex-wife?'

'He obviously cares very much for her, and to be frank with you, I can see why. She really is the most marvellous woman, you know. She has been holed-up in that house in Dahlem for well over a year now. Poor little Sophia can barely speak; she is so terrified of making a noise. It would be marvellous if we could do something to help them.'

'I beg your pardon?' Edgar was staring at Henri as if he had completely misheard him.

'I was just saying that I thought it would be marvellous if we could help Alfred's mother and sister.'

Edgar sat there open-mouthed. It was Remington-Barber who spoke next.

'Help in what way, Henry?'

'Possibly help them to leave Germany.'

'Has Reinhart asked you to raise this?'

'No.'

'So it is not a condition of his handing over the document?'

'No.'

'So why on earth are you raising the matter then?'

243

'Don't forget I've just come back from Berlin, Edgar. It's like a bloody prison camp, uniforms everywhere. It can only be a matter of time before they are caught. If there were any way we could help get them out before that happens then we would be doing the decent thing.'

Edgar slammed the table with his hand. 'Are you stark raving mad? Who the hell do you think we are – the Red bloody Cross?'

'I was only thinking—'

'Well don't. What has got into you: have you fallen in love with this woman or something?'

Henri hesitated as he realised that was exactly what he had done. He could feel his face reddening. 'No, not at all. I just feel awfully sorry for them.'

'Well don't,' said Edgar, who was no longer shouting. 'In our profession, we simply cannot afford to have those kinds of feelings. Do you understand?'

Until they saw him off early on the Monday morning at the station, Henri was never alone. Either Edgar or Remington-Barber was always near him. When he got up in the early hours of the Sunday morning to go to the bathroom, Edgar was awake in the lounge, sitting in an armchair that he had angled round to face the open lounge door. Henri wondered whether talking about Rosa had caused them to distrust him. He had learnt his lesson.

He was woken at four o'clock on the Monday morning for his final briefing. 'When you get here on Wednesday go straight to Bank Leu on Paradeplatz; hand the envelopes over to Hedinger, apart from the one for us. Understood?'

'Yes.'

'Use the telephone in Hedinger's office to call this number. Both Edgar and I will be in Bern. One of us will answer. Tell us what train you are catching from Zurich and I will meet you at Bern station. You'll be back home in Geneva that evening.'

'Assuming everything goes well,' said Edgar, 'we will put a further 500 pounds into your Credit Suisse account. Two trips in and out of Germany – you'll have deserved it.'

Henri told them how grateful he was. 'Just one thing though,' he said. 'Seems to be the most enormous effort to go to Berlin, bring the boy out and go back again to collect this document.'

'Only way of doing it, Henry. Gunter will only release the document once he is sure that his son is safe in Switzerland. We've already told you that.'

'Must be a damn important document then.'

'That, Henry, is for us to decide. Oh… and one other thing,' said Edgar as they prepared to leave the apartment. 'That Rosa woman: don't be tempted to go anywhere near her. Forget about her. Understand?'

Henri assured them that he understood.

–

Gunter Reinhart had left home just after seven o'clock on the Monday morning and as luck would have it, the U-Bahn and the trams were all running so smoothly that he was concerned that he would arrive at work too early. It would not do to be noticed. So he got off the tram early on the Unter den Linden and walked the rest of the way, and by the time he turned onto Französischestrasse it was twenty to eight, which was still early but hopefully not so early that he would draw attention to himself. He tried to appear as casual as possible as he entered the Reichsbank on Werderscher Markt, but as he found himself alone in the corridors leading to his office his pace quickened.

He waited until five past eight before he picked up the telephone that he had been staring at since he had arrived in his office and dialled an internal number.

'*Yes, Herr Reinhart: a telegram has indeed arrived for you. I beg your pardon? Yes, from Zurich. From Bank Leu. Our messenger starts at half past eight. I will ensure he brings it straight to you.*'

Gunter Reinhart could not bear to wait even for half an hour, so even though it was unusual for him to do so, he went down himself to the telegram bureau in the basement. He did manage to restrain himself from opening the telegram until he was back in his office.

Documentation all in order stop Courier with you again
Tuesday stop All well stop Hedinger stop

He read the telegram twice before folding it up carefully, slipping it into an envelope and placing it in the bottom of his briefcase. He felt a wave of emotion overwhelm him for a minute or so. Alfred was safe in Switzerland. Now he had to keep his side of the bargain.

He telephoned Funk's private secretary at a quarter past nine.

'Why do you need to see it, Reinhart?'

Funk's private secretary was an unpleasant man who had a habit of following his master around like a dog, his hands held in apparent supplication before him, an admiring smile on his face. He took considerable pleasure in controlling people's access to the minister, and generally making life more difficult in an effort to make himself seem somehow important.

'Because Herr Funk has asked that I prepare a paper on dealing with assets that may come under our control should certain events happen, and to complete that paper to the Minister's satisfaction I need to see the document once more.'

'When?'

'This morning.'

'This morning? Impossible: I need to accompany Herr Funk to the Reichstag. In any case, Reinhart, you know that you need to put your request in writing.'

'Very well. Perhaps you would inform the minister that I will not be able to let him have that paper by the end of today.'

There was a long pause, during which Gunter could hear the private secretary's worried breathing at the other end of the line.

'Very well, you can come up now, if you promise to be quick.'

He waited in the secure room behind Funk's office while the private secretary fussed around; making sure the document was in order and signed for. He stood behind Reinhart as he opened the document on the table in front of him. There was a distinct smell of mothballs from the secretary's three-piece suit, a Nazi Party badge on one lapel and a swastika on the other.

'How long will you be?'

'Maybe half an hour, possibly a bit longer.'

'I am meant to remain with you, but I have to prepare for this important meeting at the Reichstag. I will return in twenty minutes. Remember; do not write on the document!'

Gunter Reinhart had practised in his locked study at home over the weekend and he reckoned he could photograph the whole of Directive 21 in ten minutes. He waited for five minutes and then walked over to the door, which the private secretary had left ajar. Through the gap he could see the private secretary busy at his desk at the other end of the outer office. He waited another minute and then pushed the door a bit more, so that it was still open, but only just.

The camera that Franz Hermann had given him was tiny and he had been warned that it was very sensitive, so he had to concentrate on remaining as still as possible as he photographed each page twice. He had placed himself with his back to the door, which would give him a second or two to react but the danger of being caught was still acute.

It took twelve minutes to complete the task and he allowed a further five minutes to check the document was in order, that he had made some notes, and to compose himself. When the private secretary returned, he was able to announce he was ready.

'Would you like to check my notes?'

The secretary glanced at them and then checked the directive carefully. He seemed slightly disappointed that everything was in order.

—

Henri Hesse arrived in Berlin slightly later than he had on the previous Monday, and the staff at the Kaiserhof seemed to be pleased to see him again. The concierge enquired whether he required advice on any trips during his stay, but Henri assured him that this was a much shorter visit: he expected to leave Berlin the next day. He noticed the concierge making a discreet note as he walked away from his desk.

He was in Gunter Reinhart's office by ten past ten on the Tuesday morning. Reinhart carefully opened the sealed envelopes from Bank

Leu and signed a receipt for each one, making a note in a ledger on his desk as he did so.

'Please sit down, Herr Hesse. You are making me nervous standing there; this will take a few minutes more.'

Gunter Reinhart quietly walked over to his office door and opened it, checking that no one was outside it. When he came back in, he silently slipped a lock down. He gestured for Henri to move his chair nearer to the desk.

'Everything is in order,' he was speaking quietly. 'I received the telegram from Herr Hedinger this morning: he told me the package arrived safely. Thank you. Tell me, how was the journey?'

Henri told him that the journey was fine. So was the package.

'It goes without saying that I am indebted to you, but I am now about to repay that debt in full. There are four envelopes here,' he pointed to a pile of bulky envelopes on the desk in front of him, 'for you to take from Reichsbank to Bank Leu. You will sign for these in a moment. This one...' Reinhart pointed to the third envelope in the pile, 'is the one that is to go elsewhere. You understand – I don't need to be more explicit, do I?'

Gunter Reinhart held up the package, which as far as Henri could see was identical to the other three. 'You will see that there is a tiny tear on the flap of the envelope here, can you see? And on the front, this corner of the label has come slightly loose. There is one final way of distinguishing this envelope: the others have a full stop after the word "Reichsbank" – before our address. On this one, there is a comma. In all other respects, it is identical to the other three envelopes. Tell them I had to photograph it: obviously I could not possibly take the original. The document is on film in here.'

–

It was a quarter to eleven when he left the Reichsbank: he would need to be at the station by two thirty, giving him a shade under four hours to do what he had planned. He was cutting it very fine; he would need to hurry.

He walked, neither too fast nor too slowly, down by the canal as far as the Spittelmarkt U–Bahn station. He passed one or two shops on the way, but he didn't want to go into one until he was further away from Werderscher Markt. The journey to Gleisdreieck took twelve minutes; it was a quarter past eleven. He changed lines, heading west to Wittenberg Platz, where he changed onto another U–Bahn line, now heading south. By the time he arrived at Podbielski Allee it was a quarter to twelve. The last leg of the journey had taken him much longer than he had expected. It would take at least another ten minutes to get there and he needed to find a shop first.

He came across a parade of three shops: one had a collection of ladies' dresses hanging forlornly behind a dusty window, another appeared to be some kind of bookshop with more pictures of Hitler than books, and the third was a grocer's. He was annoyed to see a queue of a dozen or so people waiting outside the shop: he was not sure that he had the time to wait.

'How long will I have to queue for?' he asked the man at the front of the queue. The man was wearing a suit and a smart overcoat, but his posture was stooped and he had a sallow complexion. He looked as if he had not understood the question: Henri repeated it. The man said nothing but pointed to a handwritten sign stuck to the inside of the shop's glass door.

Jews may only shop here between four o'clock and five o'clock.

Taped beneath it was a cartoon cut-out from a newspaper showing a Jewish man with a long nose stealing food from angelic-looking children.

'I am sure you can go in now,' said the man. 'It's us who have to wait.'

The shopkeeper had tiny eyes and an enormous belly that appeared to rest on the counter-top. His face was heavily pockmarked and there was a growing layer of perspiration on his forehead.

'I feel like having a bath every time those rats come in here,' he said, gesturing at the queue outside the window. 'Some of them start queuing first thing in the morning, you know? There's not much they can buy these days: not even white bread or vegetables! Good thing too. I'm happy to take their money though, better that I have it than some others: I joined the party before thirty-three, so I reckon I'm entitled to it. Now, how can I help you sir?'

'I need to buy some food, but I am afraid that I have no ration book.'

'No ration book?' The man's tiny eyes narrowed. *A problem.*

'I am from Switzerland, you see. I am visiting friends for lunch and would like to take them some food as a gift. I'd be happy to pay in Swiss Francs, if that helps.'

The shopkeeper's little eyes lit up. *No longer a problem.*

He indicated for Henri to move to the back of the shop, where it was darker and further away from the prying eyes of the people queuing outside.

'Of course,' he whispered. 'You understand that it is hard to charge you the exact rate, because of difficulties, you understand?'

Henri understood. He would be very generous, he assured the shopkeeper.

Five minutes later he left the shop, unable to look at the people waiting until four o'clock before they could enter. The queue seemed to have grown since he had gone in.

Within ten minutes he was knocking gently at the door of the white house on the corner of Arno-Holz Strasse. The interior of the house was dark and he could not hear a sound. He waited a minute and then knocked again. A lady being pulled along by two yapping dogs watched him carefully as she passed by. Still no reply. He knocked once more. It was now past midday and he was beginning to worry. He became aware of a slight movement to his right, where the curtains were drawn on the window of the front room. A few seconds later he heard Rosa's worried voice from behind the still closed front door.

'Who is it please?'

'It is me, Henri!' The door opened quickly and a hand poked out, gesturing for him to enter. *Quickly.*

Since he had begun to formulate this plan, he had imagined that Rosa would be overwhelmed with gratitude to see him. She would be relieved. Instead, she looked horrified.

250

'It's me, Rosa. Henri!'

'I know it is you. You must keep your voice down. What on earth are you doing here? What is the matter? What has happened to Alfred?'

Her dark brown eyes were just like Roza's, but now they were red around the lids, as if she had been crying.

'Everything is all right, Rosa. I came to visit you and Sophia. I have brought food.'

'But what about Alfred? Please tell me.'

'Alfred is safe, Rosa,' Henri moved closer to Rosa as he spoke, placing a hand on her shoulders. She backed away. 'He is in Zurich. I managed to get him there safely. You don't need to worry.'

'You shouldn't have come here. It is so dangerous. Go upstairs quickly. You cannot stay long. I have to give Frau Hermann her lunch. Go upstairs and let me settle her. I'll be a few minutes.'

In the small lounge upstairs there was no sign of Sophia. When she finally came upstairs, Henri asked Rosa where she was.

'In bed: she has been there almost all the time since Alfred left. She misses him so much that it is making her ill. He was wonderful to her, her only companion. I don't think that she has uttered more than half a dozen sentences since he left.'

'Well, perhaps these will cheer her up.' Henri triumphantly emptied the content of his bag on the rug. He placed a pack of sweets and some chocolate to one side and handed Rosa a large cheese, a long sausage, a bag of fruit and another of vegetables. Rosa looked embarrassed.

'I don't know what to say.' Tears were streaming down her face. She knelt down beside him and gently touched his wrist with her fingers, holding them there for a few seconds before busying herself sorting the food. 'Of course I am very grateful, but you coming here is so dangerous. Our only hope is to stay here with no one finding out. Franz does his best to ensure that we get as few visitors as possible, but neighbours spy on each other and watch out for comings and goings. My real fear is that Frau Hermann will die or have to go into hospital and then we won't be able to stay here.'

'Come with me, Rosa – you and Sophia – come with me.'

She looked at him as if she had misheard what he had said.

'Come where?'

'Back to Switzerland, Rosa.'

She burst out laughing. 'Henri – do you think we haven't thought about how we can escape ever since we got here? It is impossible: we have no papers other than our own, and they are useless because I am wanted by the Gestapo. I know you are trying to be kind but...' She held up her hands in a gesture of helplessness.

'But you cannot stay here forever, Rosa. As you say, what if something happens to the old lady? And what about food? People say that it is becoming scarcer. And then the neighbours... someone could inform on you. I could help you. I could get papers.'

Rosa was looking at him as if she had misheard him again.

'How can you do that?'

At that moment there was a weak shout from downstairs.

'I must go, Henri. Frau Hermann wants her lunch.'

Henri grabbed her by the arm and moved towards her. 'I will get papers, Rosa, I will be back. Trust me.'

As she stood up, Henri did too, positioning himself immediately in front of her.

'Henri, please. I have to go to her. You must leave now. In any case, sometimes an old friend comes to see her on Tuesdays. Please let me get through.'

He hesitated for a moment, wondering whether it would be wrong to embrace her. He had expected her to be more grateful. She pushed past him and headed downstairs, beckoning for him to follow her, a finger pressed to her lips for him to keep quiet.

–

He eventually left Berlin on a train for Nuremberg just before three – only a few minutes late – and the journey was much quicker than the one to Stuttgart just a few days earlier. He arrived in Nuremberg at seven o'clock and it felt like a garrison town, troops everywhere. The concourse of the station was a seething mass of grey uniforms, with a sprinkling of black. He could see few other civilians. He joined a long queue of soldiers at the ticket office and had enough time to observe that most of them belonged to the Seventeenth Infantry Division: a gift for Edgar. When he reached the window, he found out that the first train to Stuttgart was at eight twenty the next morning – 'All being well,' added the ticket clerk as he carefully stamped and then initialled Henri's ticket.

Henri calculated that he could be in Stuttgart sometime late morning, and Zurich by mid-afternoon. *All being well.*

The ticket clerk told him that he would find the hotels if he turned left coming out of the station and walked over to the next block. There he found a selection of grey buildings, each seemingly reflecting the ubiquitous uniforms milling around on the street. He went into the first three hotels, each more miserable than the previous one and settled on the fourth only because it was now pouring with rain and he was exhausted.

As the manager laboriously completed the paperwork that would allow him the privilege of being a guest there for one night, Henri had an opportunity to have a look into what the manager called the dining room. If pushed, Henri would have described it as a workhouse, a memory from Dickensian novels read out loud at the end of dark autumn afternoons at school in England.

'You had better go and eat now, the dining room closes in twenty minutes,' the manager said in what Henri thought could be an Austrian accent.

'I am all right thank you,' said Henri, the smell of grease and tobacco settling already at the back of his throat. 'I may eat elsewhere.'

'You'll be lucky: there is no "elsewhere" these days. Leave your case here and go in and eat.'

He reluctantly went into the dining room, having passed up the offer of leaving his case with the manager. There were two long tables in the dining room and each one had six or seven men – only men – hunched around it, all eyeing each other suspiciously and spooning black-coloured stew into their mouths in apparent unison.

Henri found a small space at the end of one table and the man next alongside him very reluctantly moved along no more than an inch or two. No sooner had he sat down than a filthy hand deposited a bowl of the stew in front of him. The thumb and one finger of the filthy hand were dipped in the stew. Henri moved his gaze up the hand and the frayed sleeve just above it: both belonged to a hunched body and pale face flecked with red sores, a woman in her fifties who looked as if she were about to collapse.

A plate of black bread was pushed in front of him, along with a glass of watery beer. No one was speaking to anyone else around the table and Henri was grateful for that.

His night did not become any more comfortable: the room had bare floorboards and just one small threadbare rug by the bed. There was a wash basin with a stained sink by a window that had a crack in the glass and Henri doubted that the sheets had been changed since the last guest but one. As there was no functioning lock on the door, he wedged the single chair in the room against it and lay on the bed fully clothed, his briefcase containing the sealed envelopes under the pillow that smelt of sweat. In the distance he could hear the muffled sound of explosions: he could not tell whether it was bombs or anti-aircraft fire, but when he went over to the window and peeled back the blackout curtain he could see flashes far to the north.

He left the hotel at seven in the morning, the manager and the woman from the dining room confused as to why he declined their offer of breakfast – 'But you have paid for it, sir!'

For the next hour, the station cafe provided a welcome refuge from the all-pervading odour of the hotel. The Stuttgart train left on time and the connection from there to Zurich was good and he arrived at ten past two. He was under pressure now. There was a train to Bern at ten past five, which was the one he would need to catch if Edgar and Remington-Barber were not to be too suspicious about his late arrival. It ought to give him enough time, but only just.

He needed to get to Bank Leu as soon as possible, but only after he had made the phone call. There was a bank of phone booths on the main station concourse, but they felt too public, so he left the station and walked across to the Bahnhofquai, where he found a cafe with phone booth at the rear, well away from the few customers. He rang the number Viktor had given him.

'Yes?'

'Peter is coming round for dinner.'

A pause and a muffled noise at the other end of the line, which sounded as if the person had placed their hand over the receiver and was talking to someone else in the room.

'And will you be bringing wine with you?'

'Yes.'

With that, the line went dead. He checked his watch: it was two twenty-five: according to Viktor's instructions he was to be at the station exactly one hour after the phone call. That would leave him just over an hour and a half to catch his train: he would need to hurry. He left the cafe by the back door and caught a taxi to Bank Leu's head office on Paradeplatz.

Michael Hedinger was apparently in a hurry. He came down to the reception and took Henri up to his office on the top floor. He checked the three envelopes from the Reichsbank for Bank Leu.

'And the fourth envelope is for your friends?'

'Yes.'

'When do you see them?'

'I'm going to Bern now. May I use your phone to tell them what time I'm likely to be there?'

Hedinger gestured at the phone: *Be my guest.*

Edgar answered: '*Welcome home. What kept you?*'

'I'm catching the train at ten past five. I ought to be in Bern by eight at the latest. Where shall I meet you?'

'Don't worry, old chap, we'll meet you.'

That was that. It was now a quarter to three, he had plenty of time. He could even afford to stroll back to the station along Bahnhofstrasse, which would at least give him time to compose himself.

'And all went well?' asked Hedinger.

'Yes... yes, thank you.'

'And I presume you wish to ask me a question?'

Henri had no idea what the Swiss was on about.

'I'm sorry?'

'Alfred! Do you not want to know how he is?'

'Of course, of course! How is Alfred?'

'My wife and the children and the dog make such a fuss of him: it is as if he has been released from prison. He is such a sweet boy and very considerate. We will take good care of him. He is obviously sad though. At night we can hear him sobbing in his room. He must miss his mother.'

–

Arriving too early for a rendezvous is as dangerous as being late for one.

He had arrived outside the Hauptbahnhof at a quarter past three, ten minutes early. Without thinking properly, he had continued into the station, assuming he would find a bar and then go out onto the concourse ten minutes later. This is what he did, but no sooner had he stepped out onto the concourse than he was aware of two men either side of him, marching him out of a side exit. One of them was Viktor, his face impassive but his voice not disguising his fury.

'We said be at the station one hour after the phone call, not fifty minutes. What do you think you are up to, *synok*?'

Henri shook himself from Viktor and the other man, who had now stepped back into the shadows.

'Learn to do as you are told Henri, you understand? Now, follow me – stay behind me. I will go into a shop and through to the back. You are to do likewise. Sergei will be behind you.'

The shop was a narrow tobacconist in a warren of alleys behind the station. The countertop was already open when Henri arrived. Viktor was in a room at the back, along with a shrivelled-looking man half the size of the Russian. The man was dressed in a faded pinstripe suit and peered up at Henri through thick glasses that sat unsteadily on the bridge of a badly misshapen nose.

'Have you spoken with Edgar?' Viktor sounded impatient.

'Yes.'

'Where is he?'

'In Bern: they're expecting me to be on the train that leaves here at ten past five. I have no excuse for not being on that one.'

'Don't worry, you will be. You have it?' Viktor looked anxious.

Henri took the sealed Reichsbank envelope out of his briefcase, but held on to it while he spoke.

'I do, Viktor, but it is sealed. How are you going to open it without Edgar and Remington-Barber realising?'

Viktor passed the envelope over to the man, addressing him in German.

'Arnold, what do you reckon?'

The man took the envelope and held it under the light, turning it very slowly one way and the other, moving it close to his eyes and then running his fingers along its every surface. He nodded and replied into a squeaky, high-pitched voice.

'This should not be a problem. Give me an hour, but I want everyone out of here.'

'Apart from me,' said Viktor.

'Of course, apart from you, Viktor,' Arnold said obediently, half bowing as he spoke.

As Henri left the room he could see the man they called Arnold arranging a large camera, a lamp and various tools on a bench. He was about to operate. Henri spent the next fifteen minutes standing silently in the alley behind the tobacconist with the man called Sergei. When Viktor called Henri back in, he was clearly finding it hard to contain his excitement. Little Arnold was packing away his equipment, the surgery over. The envelope was handed to him. 'Examine it, please. See how perfect it is?'

Henri looked at it carefully. It was impossible to see how it could have been opened. With a huge arm around his shoulder, Viktor shepherded Henri to a corner of the room and whispered into his ear.

'We have made a copy: you have no idea how important it is, *synok*. We will transmit the entire text to Moscow tonight. You have forty minutes before your train, so tell me everything that you can about this man who supplied the document. It is so important that Moscow will ask me many questions about it: I need to have the answers.'

'Before I do that, Viktor, I need to ask a favour of you.'

Viktor looked at him puzzled: a favour? *Henri did not ask favours of them. They asked favours of him.*

'What is it?' he asked, hardly managing to hide his irritation.

Henri looked at the Russian, wishing that he was more sympathetic at times. Even some gratitude wouldn't have gone amiss.

'I don't want to sound like I'm going soft or anything, but I have coped very well in Germany so far and I have this worry that they could send me back there, sooner or later, I—'

'Why, have they said anything about that, *synok*?'

'No, but I get the impression that they don't exactly have a team of agents queuing up at the border waiting to be sent into Germany. I feel exposed when I am in Berlin and I was wondering: do you have anyone I could contact in Berlin – in an emergency?'

Henri shrugged, eager that Viktor should not think the request an unusual one. *What am I to do – tell him that I am determined to go back there anyway?*

Viktor looked at Henri, suspicious at first, but then more under-standing.

'Let me see what I can do, Henri. There's the embassy, but I don't trust anyone there. I do have some people, I'll let you know. Now, tell me about how you got this document.'

Chapter 21

London, March 1941

Edgar arrived at Whitchurch Airport just after twelve thirty on Monday the 10th of March on BOAC flight 777 from Lisbon. A black Humber Imperial with military plates was parked close to the bottom of the aircraft steps, and three hours later it deposited an exhausted Edgar outside the building overlooking St James's Square, where Christopher Porter was waiting for him in his office on the top floor.

Edgar handed over the film of Directive 21 to Porter, who promptly left the room, returning five minutes later.

'We'll have that developed straight away and sent off to the analysts tonight. They've all been told to deal with it as a matter of priority. We'll meet here tomorrow afternoon to hear what they all make of it. But well done, Edgar: something of a coup to get our hands on that. How is our chap Hunter?'

Edgar leaned back in his chair, barely stifling a yawn. 'Turns out to be rather good at his job actually. Not someone you would automatically think of as spy material, but I suppose that's the whole point, isn't it? I remember that Classics don who trained Hunter saying that he looks for people who are slightly apart from the crowd but not so much so that people would notice them. He said that he had never come across someone who fitted that bill quite so well as Hunter. He's survived three missions into Nazi Germany now: if he looked or acted like a spy he wouldn't have lasted more than an hour or two.'

'And his other masters... would they have seen the directive?'

'I certainly hope so. We allowed him enough time in Zurich between going to Bank Leu and catching the train to Bern. One of

259

Basil's men spotted him with Viktor leaving the station, so I think we can assume that they have the document. There is one concern, though…'

'With Hunter?'

'No, with our Portuguese friends actually. When I came back through Lisbon, Sandy was in a bit of a flap about Telmo. He's been rather elusive and Sandy is worried that he may be getting cold feet. Telmo seems to think that the PVDE may be on to him, though there doesn't seem to be any evidence for that. Personally, I think he is just getting twitchy; agents get like that from time to time, as you know. There is what appears to be a well-founded concern about Dona Maria though.'

'The lady in Berlin?'

'Correct.'

'Telmo says that Dona Maria has been transferred within the Portuguese Legation there: she's no longer working for the military attaché, now she's with the first secretary.'

'And is that a demotion?'

'Not as such, but it gives her less access to the kind of intelligence we are interested in, and also less access to the diplomatic bag. Apparently the first secretary is quite high up the hierarchy at the Legation, but his role is more ceremonial. She is worried that they may be watching her: she is certain that her desk was searched recently, and she thinks that she has been tailed on a few occasions.'

'By whom?'

'Not the Germans – security people from the Legation. Also, her home leave has been brought forward to 24th March: which is two weeks on Monday. She is worried that once she returns to Lisbon she will not be allowed back again. Telmo is demanding an absolute promise from us that the minute Dona Maria arrives in Lisbon, we put both of them in hiding and bring them to the UK as soon as possible.'

'And you said…?'

'"Yes", of course. I told Sandy to agree to whatever he asks for. I told him to say that once they get to England they will be given money, a house and new identities. I hope that is in order?'

'Oh, I'm sure the Service will be happy to find them some love nest somewhere or other.'

–

The following afternoon Edgar and Christopher Porter were in a large map room in the basement of the St James's Square office, along with a number of colleagues from the Service and a few men in uniform. Copies of Directive 21 were handed out by a lanky Brigadier from Army Intelligence, who cut a colourful figure with his florid face and a large moustache that appeared to comprise of black and grey stripes. When he spoke it was with a Welsh accent.

'These are English translations, as you will see. The document itself is astonishing, quite astonishing. Let me quote: "The German Armed Forces must be prepared, even before the conclusion of the war against England, to crush Soviet Russia in a rapid campaign." That last bit – crushing the Soviet Union – is underlined. The directive says that preparations for the invasion "will be concluded by 15th May 1941".'

There was murmuring around the room, people looking at each other with raised eyebrows and barely concealed surprise.

'They even have a code name: Operation Barbarossa. However, we must be cautious. The most important question that we have to address is whether the document is genuine, because there is no point in us acting upon it if we feel that, on a balance of probabilities, it is not what it purports to be. We have had all types of experts studying this ever since we got our hands on it.'

The Brigadier removed a pair of reading glasses from a case in front of him and glanced at some handwritten notes.

'First of all, we have had the directive subjected to something called text analysis by a German expert. What he does is compare one text with others, to see if they are from the same source. He believes that this document is very similar to other ones released by Hitler. I quote from his report: "It feels identical in terms of tone, syntax and vocabulary to other documents released by Hitler. The mixture of rhetoric and military detail, the constant reference to himself in terms of orders being given and decisions being made – all that is very familiar. Then there is the question of how feasible it is that Germany would consider breaking its pact with the Soviet Union. The consensus is that this is perfectly likely. The Nazis hate Communists, Russians and Slavs almost as much as they hate the Jews. In fact, they tend to see them as one and the same thing: when they think of a Russian, they see a Jewish Communist. So the pact was a surprise in one respect, but not in another – Hitler was being shrewd. He was buying time, ensuring his Eastern Front remained quiet while he conquered Western Europe and attempted an invasion of the British Isles. So, breaking the pact would not be a surprise, it was only ever a short-term ruse."'

The Brigadier walked over to a large map on the wall behind him.

'So if we accept that this document is most probably genuine, then we need to analyse its feasibility from a military point of view. It is an extremely ambitious plan: one which depends on co-operation from the Finns in the north and the Romanians in the south, which may be a problem, as they are unlikely to be as committed to an invasion of the Soviet Union as the Germans are. It also depends on two other critical factors: a significant element of secrecy and surprise, and the Red Army being utterly ill-prepared for it. We do know that the Red Army is not in a good state, but even so...'

The Brigadier was looking at the map and then at the directive. He peered closely at the map and pointed to a spot around the Polish-Russian border.

'He seems to be talking about concentrating the main German thrust here, around the Pripet Marshes. He talks about having two army groups operating north of the Marshes, and one army group south of it. The key object of the southern army group looks like the Ukraine, with all of its agriculture and industry. The aims of the northern army group, it says here, are Leningrad and Moscow. This is what he says about Moscow: "The capture of this city would represent a decisive political and economic success, and would also bring about the capture of the most important railway junctions".'

A colonel wearing the insignia of a guards regiment walked noisily over to the map, his boots echoing on the floor. After studying it for a while he turned round and spoke unnecessarily loudly, each syllable carefully enunciated. 'Personally, I cannot see the Germans attempting this with less than one hundred divisions – talk about putting all your eggs in one basket. If he thinks he's going to get as far as Moscow the only advice I can give him is that he had better get a move on. Once that Russian winter starts, even the greatest army in the world doesn't stand a chance. From a logistics point of view this would appear to be almost impossible.'

For the next two hours the men crowded into the map room weighed up the pros and cons of Directive 21. All the participants took it in turn to play devil's advocate at every opportunity, but the discussion kept coming back to a point of agreement: on the balance of probabilities, the document was genuine.

It was ten o'clock that evening when Porter and Edgar went up to the office on the top floor. Porter pulled back the blackout blinds and turned off his desk lamp, allowing the light from the full moon to fill the room. For a while they sat in silence, picking at the plate of stale sandwiches on the desk between them.

'And what happens now?'

'Number Ten will be informed first thing in the morning,' said Porter. 'I am told that the Prime Minister and Eden discussed the matter this morning, once they knew the directive had arrived. They agreed that if this meeting concluded that the directive is genuine, we would not waste any time. We would get a copy of it over to Moscow as soon as possible, and Cripps himself will take it to the Kremlin. So, well done, Edgar – you've done an excellent job. The Soviets can hardly ignore Directive 21 now, can they? It corroborates the copy Hunter showed Viktor.'

The two men left the office together and walked as far as Pall Mall.

'You look exhausted, Edgar.'

'I've booked two weeks' leave, sir.'

'Splendid. I expect your family will be pleased to see you. Heading down to Dorset, are you?'

Edgar carried on walking in silence, apparently oblivious to what Porter had been saying. They had now reached Waterloo Place, from where each would be going in different directions.

'Probably not, sir. As far as my family are concerned, I'm in the Far East: it's easier that way. I shall probably sleep for a week and then go walking on my own in Scotland.'

Porter slapped Edgar on the back. 'Understood. Five have an interesting case on at the moment and have been asking for your help, but first, have a good rest. Remember, I don't want to see you for a fortnight, that's an order.'

–

Edgar had gone straight to his small apartment in a mansion block behind Victoria Street and slept most of the next day and a good deal of the day after that, and by the Thursday he felt rested and even slightly bored. He visited the dentist, had his hair cut and began to suspect that two weeks off might be a week too long. He decided to wait until after the weekend before deciding whether to go to Scotland, stay in London, or go back to work. The decision was made for him by a ring on his doorbell early on the Monday morning. It was a driver he recognised from the offices in St James.

'Very sorry to bother you, sir. Mr Porter would like to see you, sir. Now, sir, if you don't mind coming with me. There's a car waiting outside, sir.'

Christopher Porter was pacing up and down his office, managing to look both angry and embarrassed. He told Edgar to shut the door and sit down.

'I thought I was under orders not to see you for a fortnight?'

'You were, Edgar, but those were my orders and I consider that I'm allowed to break my own orders. I'm not going to beat about the bush: there's been a change of heart. It's all Winston's fault – and the bloody Foreign Office. Wouldn't be surprised if Five haven't tried to queer our pitch too.'

'I'm not sure I am following you, sir.'

'Let me lay the cards on the table, and please listen carefully. As you know, we agreed that the copy of the Operation Barbarossa directive that Hunter brought back from Berlin is genuine. It was sent in code to Moscow, and Stafford Cripps took it to the Kremlin and handed it to

Molotov personally on Thursday. Cripps said that Molotov appeared to be angry, but he couldn't tell whether he was angry with him or the Germans, or more likely it was just his usual demeanour. Then last night I was summoned to Downing Street. Apparently they have been having second thoughts.'

'Second thoughts about what?'

'About what we should be telling the Soviets after all. Their thinking – and one has to acknowledge that it does have a certain logic to it – is that the whole business could rebound on us. As things stand at the moment, Hitler's priority is still to invade Great Britain, even though we seem to be doing a rather decent job of defending ourselves. If this Operation Barbarossa turns out to be true, then it will take an enormous pressure off us: Hitler will be diluting his forces by fighting on two fronts and it makes the chances of even an attempted German invasion of these shores – let alone a successful one – very remote indeed. I can hear the tinkle of teacups approaching, Edgar – shall we pause for a moment?'

Five minutes later, fortified by surprisingly strong cups of tea, Porter resumed. 'If the Soviets finally choose to believe the Barbarossa Directive and other intelligence, and accept that the Germans do have hostile intentions towards them, then they will stop trusting the Germans, shore up their defences and reinforce the border. That would make a German invasion of the Soviet Union significantly less likely. The question that Number Ten have been asking themselves is this: would such an outcome be in our best interests?'

Edgar leaned back in his chair and removed a cigarette from a silver case. He was halfway through smoking it when he replied. 'So you're saying that there is now a feeling that it is actually in our interests for Germany and the Soviet Union to go to war?'

'Absolutely: if they go to war with each other then the chances of an invasion of Britain significantly diminish and, at the same time, Germany risks a dangerous war in the east which they could well lose.'

'So when you say that there's been a change of heart…'

'What I mean by that is that they now want us to play down the fact that Germany has plans to invade the Soviet Union. They think we should switch from doing the decent thing and telling the Soviets about the German plans to actually misleading them, telling them quite the opposite. I—'

'Bit bloody late for that isn't it? For Christ's sake! I'm sorry sir, but it has been one of the intelligence coups of the war thus far to get hold of that directive and make sure the Soviets see it, and now you're saying it's all been a bloody waste of time. Jesus...'

'Don't shout, Edgar, please. Remember that I am only the messenger. I—'

'And you said something about them now wanting *us* to play down the reports about German intentions and even misleading them. How on earth are we going to do that?'

'I am afraid, Edgar, it means we now need to provide the Soviets with another report courtesy of your man, Hunter, one which reflects serious German concerns about Operation Barbarossa and talks of its postponement at least, possibly even its cancellation. I have to say that is not entirely unfeasible: you yourself said that Hugo's general admitted there were serious concerns in the army high command about invading the Soviet Union. This report would simply reflect those concerns.'

'And how do *we* get hold of such a document?'

'Please don't be so sarcastic. Naval Intelligence are apparently rather good at this kind of thing. This morning I have asked our people to talk to their people and see what they can come up with. I have told them I want it to be ready by the end of the week.'

'And how do we then get it to the Russians?'

Porter heaped another spoonful of sugar into his tea, sipped it, and then stood up and walked over to the window, looking out of it as he spoke.

'You said that Dona Maria do Rosario has to leave Berlin on 24th March, which is a week on Monday – correct? This report needs to be taken to Lisbon, where Telmo is to get it into the diplomatic bag to Berlin. In her final act of service for us in Berlin, Dona Maria will pass the report on to Hugo. Hunter can then go back to Berlin to collect the report so that he can let the Soviets see it when he returns to Switzerland – as before. I grant you that is a complicated route by which to get it to the Soviets, but hopefully it is one that they regard as at least plausible.'

'By the sounds of it, Porter, the Hon. Anthony Davis is about to return to Lisbon.'

'Correct, Edgar: and thereafter to Switzerland.'

–

Late on the afternoon of Sunday 16th March, Edgar was back in Christopher Porter's office. Edgar noticed that Porter was looking uncharacteristically confident. He had a broad grin on his face. On the desk between them was a black leather-bound book, with an ornate cross on the padded front cover.

'Contemplating the priesthood are you, sir?'

'Now, now, Edgar. You may remember that when we met last Monday I said that we would need to concoct a report purporting to show that the Germans were now having second thoughts after all about invading the Soviet Union?'

Edgar nodded. 'And you want this report to fall into Soviet hands?'

Porter rubbed his hands and tenderly picked up the black leather-bound book and passed it over to Edgar. The words '*A Bíblia Sagrada*' were etched on the cover in gold leaf. Edgar gently picked it up and turned it round in his hands.

'Careful, Edgar. The team that put this together want us to know how much trouble they went to to get hold of a Bible in Portuguese. They've done a pretty impressive job though. Here, pass it to me.' Christopher Porter took the Bible over and opened it at the inside back cover. The thick paper on the inside of the back cover was loose and Porter very carefully peeled it away to reveal a gap, folded into which was a document which he carefully removed and opened: three pages on brown paper, typed in German with some scrawled handwritten notes.

'This is the Rostock Report: it is a note on a meeting supposedly held a couple of weeks ago in Rostock, on the 3rd and 4th of March. If you look here, it lists the various participants...' Porter turned the page.

'And on this page it describes the purpose of the meeting: "To review plans for proposed campaign against the Soviet Union – Operation Barbarossa". The next section is essentially a summary of what was in Directive 21.'

Porter was checking the document against a typed sheet in English. 'It makes the case for the invasion of the Soviet Union and repeats pretty much what was in Directive 21. Then we have a rather clever link from the Hitler Directive to the fake report. We already know that, at the end of the directive, Hitler said "I await submission of the plans of Commanders-in-Chief on the basis of this directive. The preparations made by all branches of the Armed Forces, together with timetables, are to be reported to me through the High Command of the Armed Forces." What follows is, in effect, the Commanders-in-Chief appearing to do just that.'

Again Porter was consulting his typed sheet, the English translation. 'There is a rather long section detailing the submissions of all the different services, I don't propose to go into detail. But then there is a paragraph concluding thus: "It is the unanimous view of the OKW, OKH, OKL, OKM" – those being the High Commands of the Armed Forces, the Army, the Air Force and the Navy – "that for the reasons summarised below, Operation Barbarossa should be postponed until the spring of 1942 at the earliest." It then goes on to give those reasons: are you happy for me to read them out to you?'

Edgar nodded. He was leaning back in his chair, his eyes half shut as if to fully absorb what was being read to him.

'"Number one – we are of the opinion that our intelligence services may have seriously underestimated both the size and the strength of the Soviet forces. The ability of Stalin to motivate the Red Army is significant. Number two – we consider that our own planners may have overestimated our ability to supply our forces adequately if the advance through Soviet territory is as rapid as it will need to be. There is a serious danger that our forces could be dangerously exposed by shortages of ammunition, fuel, and food. Number three – Operation Barbarossa depends on the co-operation of Finnish and Romanian forces. We are of the opinion that this co-operation cannot be taken for granted, and could leave the northern and southern sections of our front vulnerable. Number four – the Russian winter presents a very severe risk to our forces. To achieve our objective of capturing Moscow before the onset of the winter, we would recommend that Operation Barbarossa is launched by early May. At present, factors such as the Yugoslavia campaign mean that this is highly unlikely. The risk of maintaining an offensive during the winter is unacceptable. Number five – Great Britain is proving to be far more resolute than we had expected. We had been of the opinion that either they would have surrendered by now, or would have been weakened to the extent that an invasion could be launched. That is not the case and therefore we have to take into account the fact that we would be fighting on two fronts." There's a bit more about future meetings and such like, but that is the gist of it. What do you think?'

Edgar said nothing but asked to look at the report. As he read through it he nodded approvingly, once or twice allowing a knowing smile to cross his face.

'It's good enough to make the Soviets pause at least. Depends on what mood Stalin is in. That line about his ability to motivate the Red Army is a clever touch – does no harm to appeal to the man's ego. My feeling is that, at the very least, it will confuse the Soviets.'

'And at the very best?'

Edgar glanced again at the report and turned it round in his hands, as if checking its weight. 'At the very best, they'll believe it: it's good.'

'Provided we can make sure they see the damn thing,' said Porter. 'The plan is that we seal the report in the bible – I have even been supplied with special glue for that purpose – and you take it to Lisbon: you have a seat on tomorrow's flight from Bristol. Telmo will have to get the Bible in the diplomatic bag to Dona Maria, and she will pass it on to Hugo. All being well, that will happen on Thursday or Friday. Meanwhile, Basil Remington-Barber has been told to make sure we get Hunter out to Berlin for a week on Monday, where he will collect the report and bring it back to Zurich. Naturally we are counting on him showing the report to Viktor first.'

Edgar nodded approvingly. Porter picked up some other papers on the desk.

'These are for Sandy to show to Telmo. They're the carrot that we're dangling in front of him and Dona Maria. This photograph here...' he handed him a photo of a very pretty cottage, with a broad expanse of wisteria across its front and a thatched roof. 'This is the place we can tell Telmo we have rented for him and Dona Maria to live in once they get here. And this is a statement from Barclays Bank in the Strand confirming that accounts have been opened in each of their names to the tune of 500 pounds each. And then there are various other bits and pieces, all amounting to what we hope is a demonstration of our positive intent towards them.'

Chapter 22

Portugal, Switzerland & Berlin, March 1941

'And what if Telmo refuses? He is so nervous at the moment, he's hardly communicating with me. To persuade him to send this on to Berlin is going to be extremely difficult, Edgar.'

It was late in the afternoon on Monday 17th March and Sandy Morgan was far from his convivial self. In front of him was the Bible that Edgar had told him to get Telmo to put in the diplomatic bag to Berlin as a matter of urgency.

'Tell him it's an order.'

'Yes, yes – I understand that, Edgar, you don't need to keep repeating it. All I can say is that we're pushing our luck. Remember, he is under no obligation to obey our orders.'

'Look, Sandy, you have to make him realise that this is in his best interests. Show him the picture of the pretty cottage the Service has sorted out for him, show him the bank statements and all the rest of it. In short, promise him the earth – anything to make sure he sends the Bible over to Dona Maria and impresses on her to hand it over to Hugo. If he says he wants to play cricket for England at Lords, tell him it's no problem. If he wants tea with the King and Queen at Buckingham bloody Palace, ask him how many sugars he takes. Promise him that the minute Dona Maria arrives back in Lisbon, you will spirit both of them into a safe house – tell him that, Sandy, he needs to hear it.'

'And what about if he's still difficult?'

'Tell him that unless he co-operates you'll go straight to the Rua Victor Cordon and tell the PVDE all about him and Dona Maria. And make sure he knows that we mean it.'

On the Wednesday morning the telephone rang twice in the space of five minutes in the apartment that Henri shared with his mother just off Quai du Mont Blanc. On the first occasion his mother answered and after a minute said '*Pas de problème*,' in a somewhat resentful manner, as if her being disturbed was indeed a problem. *Wrong number.*

When the phone rang a few minutes later Henri answered. A lady was speaking very quickly in French.

'Monsieur Hesse this is Madame Ladnier at Credit Suisse. I need to see you urgently here at the bank: two o'clock this afternoon. Now, please respond to this call as if I have called the wrong number again. Two o'clock.'

'No, it is not,' replied Henri, aware that he was sounding rather aggressive. 'You have the wrong number. Please do not disturb us again.'

At two o'clock he was ushered from the reception in the Quai des Bergues branch of Credit Suisse by Madame Ladnier, through a warren of corridors at the back of the bank and up a staircase to the first floor. She unlocked the door to a small office and then opened an interconnecting door. Lounging on a leather sofa in the room on the other side was Basil Remington-Barber.

'When you have finished, ring me on this telephone. I am on extension eighteen,' said Madame Ladnier.

'Henry, Henry – how nice to see you. Do come in, sit down. Sorry I cannot offer you a drink, but it seems that Swiss banks are not very good on that score. Apologies too for all the subterfuge: I needed to contact you urgently and had to rather prevail upon Madame Ladnier to make the calls. Ah, well – all's well that ends well, eh?'

Henri had sat down on a more formal chair opposite Basil Remington-Barber.

'Look, Henry – little bit awkward this: I know that we promised you a nice long rest but something urgent has cropped up.' Remington-Barber stood up and walked over to the window and then paced around the room, at one stage slapping Henri jovially on the shoulders.

272

'Rather annoying really, but I am afraid that we need to send you back to Berlin somewhat sooner than we had envisaged. We thought there was an outside chance of that, but we didn't imagine it would be quite so soon.'

Basil Remington-Barber had returned to the sofa and seemed a bit less hesitant now that he had passed on the message.

'When would this be?' Henri sounded casual, even rather keen.

'Monday, I'm afraid: Hedinger is sorting things out from the Zurich end, but Edgar wants to see you in Zurich on Saturday. I have to return to Bern this afternoon, but I'll travel over with you on Saturday morning. Apparently some of the Swiss banks have started to fly their couriers in and out; seems less risky if they are carrying important documents, and he thinks that he can find some top-level papers for you to take in. Plan is for you to fly in via Stuttgart on Monday morning, and out the next day by the same route – means you should be back in Zurich early Tuesday evening: hand over the bank papers to Hedinger and then hop on the last train to Geneva, where I'll meet you. With any luck you will be in your own bed by midnight.'

Henri did his best to affect a tone of mild annoyance. 'And what is it that is so important now?'

'Another document, nothing to do with Reinhart this time: this one is even more important than the last one. Hermann will pass it on to you and you bring it back to us.'

–

Friday lunchtime and Henri had just arrived at the luxury villa high above Lutry. He waited for twenty minutes in the magnificent lounge, watching the ferry that had brought him to Lausanne that morning heading along the lake towards Montreux and another ferry steaming in the opposite direction towards Geneva. It was a clear day and he had a good view of Évian-les-Bains on the French side of the lake.

Outside there was a slamming of car doors followed by the sound of men talking in Russian in the hallway. Viktor did not so much walk into the room as storm into it, slamming the door as he did so. He was wearing a long black coat, gloves and a black Homburg hat. '*Get me a coffee,'* Viktor shouted at whoever was outside the room. 'This is urgent, is it, *synok?'*

'Of course, otherwise I would not have contacted you.'

'I was in Vienna,' Viktor said, as if being in Vienna was a reason why he should not have been contacted. The door opened again and one of Viktor's men came in with a tray of coffee and sandwiches. Still wearing his coat and hat, but having removed the gloves, Viktor sat down and began to devour the sandwiches. He indicated to Henri that he should join him. Viktor ate most of the sandwiches and finished two cups of coffee before he removed his hat, tossing it onto a chaise longue on the other side of the room. He was still wearing his overcoat, and from one of its inside pockets he removed a leather notebook. A knife emerged from another pocket and the Russian began to sharpen his pencil in an aggressive manner.

'Moscow is very satisfied with the material you brought back two weeks ago by the way. Very satisfied indeed.'

'Good. I think I may have more.'

Viktor stopped sharpening the pencil and blew the shavings from it off his coat onto the floor.

'Really... from the same source?'

'I am not too sure; it sounds like it is from the lawyer this time, rather than the Reichsbank. But Remington-Barber did say that "this one is even more important than the last one".'

'He told you that?'

'Yes, two days ago.'

'They tell you a lot, Henri.'

'Maybe they trust me.'

'Maybe they do, maybe that is how the British operate. We tend not to be so forthcoming. What are the travel arrangements this time?'

'They want me in Zurich on Saturday – apparently Edgar is going to be there – and then I'm to fly to Berlin on Monday, via Stuttgart. Back the same way on Tuesday. I still have to deliver bank documents over to Hedinger, that's my cover after all, and then catch the late train from Zurich to Geneva, where I give the document to Remington-Barber.'

'All right, Henri. We make the same arrangement as before. When you return to Zurich on Tuesday you go straight to Bank Leu and then to the station. From there we will meet you, and we will go to have the document copied. Are you sure they were not suspicious last time?'

'I'm sure. They seemed to be very pleased with how things had gone.'

Viktor stood up, slowly hauling himself out of the chair and walking over to the window before turning to face Henri. His enormous frame appeared as a silhouette, with the sun behind him.

'Let me tell you, *synok*, it is possible to be pleased and to be suspicious at the same time! But I think that if Edgar is here again, it must mean that the document is at least as important as the last one. But I still find it odd that they don't meet you in Zurich to collect the document.'

'The British don't like Zurich, I keep telling you that. Everyone speaks German there, or their version of it. They feel safer on this side of Switzerland.'

'All right, Henri, you go back to Geneva now, and we will see you in Zurich on Tuesday.'

'There is one thing...'

'What is that, Henri? You want to ask me again if I'm still a believer?'

'In Zurich I asked a favour – if you could give me the details of any comrades I could contact in Berlin, in an emergency.'

Viktor nodded his head: *yes, I remember*. The Russian walked back to sit in the chair opposite Henri.

'I used to run networks in Berlin, Henri. To be honest, it was a surprisingly easy city for us to operate in: even after Hitler came to power in thirty-three I am convinced there were still more Communists in the city than Nazis – and many committed ones at that, very ideological and very disciplined. That is what I realised about Germans: they like to have an ideology, whether it is Communism or Socialism or Nazism or Catholicism. It is a few years now since I operated in Berlin and most of my networks have either been arrested, switched over to the Nazis, left Germany, or the few that remain have been taken over by the NKVD or the GRU boys at the embassy. But I have kept a couple: I am going to tell you how to contact one of them, listen carefully.'

Henri leaned forward in his seat; he was just inches from the Russian and could smell stale coffee on his breath.

'There's an agent called Kato and I have no reason to believe that they are not still in Berlin. Kato was my prize agent; I was never going to give them up. Do you know Wedding?'

'I have heard of it, but never been there.'

'Just north of Charlottenburg, not far from the centre. The important thing about Wedding is that it was always a Communist stronghold, and even now I understand that it is a more amenable part of the city for us, which does not mean that it is safe. Catch the U-Bahn line that goes north through Friederichstrasse and Oranienburg and get off at Leopold Platz. From there walk north along Müllerstrasse and turn into Wannitzstrasse. If you come to Amsterdamerstrasse you will have gone too far. Have you got all that so far? On Wannitzstrasse you will see a row of five or six shops under a large apartment block. One of those shops sells items for the kitchen – pots, pans, plates; that kind of thing. Go in there and ask if you can leave something for a Frau Schreiner in apartment twelve. Tell the person you have come from Dresden to deliver it. The reply that you should expect is that they will say their sister lives in Dresden. You will know then that you are dealing with Kato: hand them the envelope. In it will be a message from me: I will write it now. Once they've read it, they will give you their full co-operation. You don't need to worry about the message by the way, there will be nothing incriminating in it: it will look like a shopping list.'

'And how will I know that the man in the shop is Kato?'

'You will, don't worry. In any case, Kato is a woman.'

–

That same day, at the Portuguese Legation in Berlin, Dona Maria do Rosario had to wait until the First Secretary left the office at five before she could open the Bible which had arrived in that day's diplomatic bag.

Telmo's message the previous day had told her exactly where to look and how urgent everything was. She carefully removed the Rostock Report from the Bible and placed it inside an envelope, which she then slipped into her handbag. After that, she stuffed some blank paper into the gap where the document had been and glued the card back in place before placing the Bible in one of the drawers.

She delayed leaving the Legation until half past five, timing her departure to coincide with that of a number of the other secretaries. She walked with them for a while and then quietly peeled away from the little group and headed for Opernplatz and the vast sanctity of St Hedwig's.

She knew that Father Josef was not due to be taking confession that night, but he would be assisting at the Mass. She would sit towards the front and wear her red scarf: he would know then that she needed to see him urgently.

Father Josef was one of a number of priests on the altar during Mass, and not once did Dona Maria notice him looking at her. When it was time to take communion, Dona Maria chose to join the small queue in front of Father Josef. He bent down when she took the communion and whispered in her ear, 'go to the undercroft; wait for me there.'

The undercroft was deserted and she sat quietly on a narrow wooden bench set back in the shadows. After a few minutes she heard gentle footsteps echoing towards her. Without acknowledging her, but looking all around him, Father Josef walked to the furthest chapel and beckoned her to follow.

'Are we safe here?' she asked him when they were alone in the chapel.

'For a few minutes, with any luck. I rarely see people down here after evening Mass. What is the problem?'

'I have something urgent for Hugo.'

'Very well: I will send a message for him to come to confession tomorrow: then you can meet him on Friday.'

'No, Father! I cannot wait that long, it may be too dangerous. I am returning to Portugal on Monday and I fear for my safety. After today, I cannot do anything else.'

'So what do you want me to do?' Father Josef looked terrified. *A messenger, I'll be no more than a messenger.* That is what he had said in the beginning. Now they wanted him to be more than a messenger.

Dona Maria removed the envelope from her handbag and pushed it into the priest's hands.

'Here, please give this to Hugo, Father.'

'No, I cannot do that.'

'You have to, Father.' At that moment there was the sound of heavy footsteps walking towards them. The priest started to say something and then slipped the envelope into the folds of his cassock and sunk to his knees in prayer. By the time he had finished, Dona Maria had slipped away.

Chapter 23

Berlin, March 1941

Henri Hesse arrived in Zurich on the Saturday afternoon, and throughout that weekend was briefed by Edgar and Remington-Barber on what was expected of him in Berlin. If all went well, he was assured, he would be in the city for little more than twenty-four hours.

Henri tried very hard not to show that he was pleased he was to be returning to Berlin. He felt more relaxed than he had been for over ten years: he was going on his own mission, as well as theirs.

He left Zurich airport on the first leg of the journey early on the Monday morning, and by the time they landed in Stuttgart it was a clear day. It was a year and a month since he had last been at the airport, and this time the plane taxied to an even more remote section, well away from any buildings or Luftwaffe planes, a few of which he could make out in the distance. The Swissair plane came to a halt by an anti-aircraft battery and alongside a Deutsche Lufthansa plane. When all the passengers had left the plane they were counted on the tarmac and then divided into two groups. Those remaining in Stuttgart were to board a bus that would take them to the terminal building; those flying on to Berlin were to transfer to the waiting Junkers Ju 52 plane.

The flight for Berlin took off half an hour after they had landed in Stuttgart and within two hours and twenty minutes they had landed at Tempelhof. Getting through security took almost as long.

For the first hour after he landed he was kept in a small room with the three other non-German passengers. One by one they were taken into a room to be questioned and he was the third one to go in.

He was in there for just under an hour, during which time he was searched, as was his case, and then he was thoroughly questioned. 'How many times have you been to Berlin?... What do you do when you are here?... Where do you eat?... Do you meet anyone not connected with your work?... Why have you flown into Berlin on this occasion?... What views do you have on the policies of our government?... Have you met any Jews while in Germany?... Or Communists?... Please tell me again, how many times have you been to Berlin?... What do you do when you are here?'

Then another wait, this time on his own at the end of an over-lit corridor, followed by a few more questions, and finally he was able to leave the airport. On Edgar's advice, he walked over to Flughafen station, from where he took the U-Bahn north for three stops as far as Koch Strasse. From Koch Strasse station it was a short walk across Wilhelmstrasse to the Excelsior on Askanischer Platz, where a room had been reserved for him. It was an enormous hotel, with well over five hundred rooms and, as far as Henri could tell, eight or nine restaurants. Both Edgar and Remington-Barber felt that the anonymity of the hotel might be more suitable for this visit.

It was two thirty by the time he checked into his narrow room on the third floor, overlooking Saarlandstrasse. The room was overheated, but when he opened the window the noise of the city flooded in and he found himself unable to think properly.

'Stay there until the next morning,' Edgar had told him, which was all very well, but that left no time for anything. Tuesday was going to be very tight as it was: meeting Hugo at nine o'clock to collect the document and then to the Reichsbank to exchange papers with Gunter Reinhart. After that he was supposed to go to Tempelhof in good time to catch the twelve thirty flight to Stuttgart.

Maybe.

He managed to stay in the hotel room for twenty minutes, pacing up and down, still not fully decided on his course of action. There were too many flaws to his plan; it depended too much on chance and it meant ignoring everything he had been trained to do over the past ten years or more. He was truly caught between a rock and a hard place.

His mind still unresolved, he left the hotel through a side entrance and from Stadt Mitte caught the U-Bahn north as far as Leopold Platz. He was in Wedding and he was about to use up the favour he had asked of Viktor. How that went could help make up his mind.

Carefully following Viktor's instructions, he turned into Wannitz-strasse and spotted the small parade of shops with the hardware shop in the middle. He walked past it from the opposite side of the road, and when he noticed a woman leaving, he crossed the road and entered.

The shop was empty: behind the counter was a well-built woman, perhaps in her late thirties, possibly older. She had untidy hair that was turning grey and a face that was noticeable for the thick mascara around her bright green eyes, and the dark lipstick that was closer to black than red. On the wall behind her was a small, framed photograph of Hitler, next to a shelf full of white candles. They smiled at each other and he spent a minute or two showing undue interest in a copper saucepan. He checked the inside pocket of his jacket: Viktor's note was there, in an envelope from the hotel. '*You don't need to worry about the message by the way, there will be nothing incriminating in it: it will look like a shopping list.*'

'Can I help you?' The woman had come round from behind the counter and was alongside him. She pointed to the copper saucepan he was holding. 'This is best quality: a company in Magdeburg manu-factures them.'

'I have come from Dresden,' said Henri, aware that his voice sounded uncertain. He was trying to speak quietly. 'I have something for Frau Schreiner in apartment twelve: please could I leave it here?'

The woman glanced anxiously towards the door and then edged slowly back towards the counter. 'Of course. My sister is from Dresden.'

Kato.

The woman casually walked back behind the counter, smiling at Henri, who smiled back at her. Silence, as she looked at Henri, waiting for him to say something.

'You have something for me, maybe?'

'I am sorry, yes. I forgot.' He handed the envelope to her.

She removed the note from the Hotel Excelsior envelope and momentarily gasped as she began to read it. The hand holding Viktor's note was shaking, her other hand was steadying herself on the counter. He heard her quietly say 'Viktor'. When she had finished reading the note, she indicated for him to wait and went to a room behind the counter. There was a brief smell of burning. She back came out with two lit cigarettes, and handed one to Henri.

'No, thank you. I don't smoke.'

'Smoke it, please: in case anyone comes in. It is better to disguise the smell. So, you are a comrade?'

Henri nodded. *A comrade.*

'I never thought that I would hear from Viktor again, never. I know I am not supposed to ask any questions, but just tell me this – is he well?' Her eyes appeared moist and the hand holding the cigarette was shaking, so much so that she used her other hand to steady it.

She loved him. She still does.

'Yes.'

She looked at him quizzically, hoping he would say more about Viktor, but he just smiled and nodded his head.

'He says you are to be trusted, and I am to help you,' said Kato. 'I have heard nothing from anyone for over a year. There were five of us, all loyal to Viktor. He told us not to trust anyone at the embassy. Two comrades managed to escape to Sweden, another was arrested and died at Sachsenhausen, and one disappeared: she is a Jew and I suspect she has gone underground. I am fortunate that none of our cell went over to the Nazis: that happened with a number of comrades. What do you need? Somewhere to stay? Some money?'

'Is it safe to talk here?'

'Of course! Do you think I'd be doing that if it wasn't? There is no one in the back and I can see whoever comes in. Take the saucepan from the stand and one or two others – we can make it look as if you cannot decide which one to buy: men never can anyway. Tell me what you need.' She was clearly nervous, her hands still shaking while she inhaled deeply on the cigarette, but her bright green eyes danced with a mixture of fear and excitement.

When he had finished telling Kato what he needed, he expected her to say it was impossible, but she acted no more surprised than if he had ordered a new dining set.

'You want this for tomorrow morning, you say?'

'Yes, please.'

'What time in the morning?'

'Around eleven o'clock, possibly a bit later, but certainly by noon. From here?'

'No, most certainly not. When you leave here, we will never see each other again. You should avoid Wedding anyway, the Gestapo have too many people around here. What you want will be ready from eleven o'clock. Will you be around the centre of Berlin?'

'Yes.'

'Do you know Ku'damm?'

He shook his head.

'It is actually called Kurfürstendamm, but everyone knows it as Ku'damm. It is a very well-known street in the south of Charlottenburg: before the war it was very fashionable. Now, nowhere is fashionable. Go to Uhlandstrasse U-Bahn and come out on the Kurfürstendamm exit, then cross the road and head west, for just two or three blocks – not very far. On the corner of Kurfürstendamm and Bleibtreustrasse you will see a kiosk set back in the wall; it sells newspapers, cigarettes; all that kind of thing. Don't be put off by the swastikas and the pictures of Hitler all over. Tell the old lady in the kiosk that you have come to collect Magda's cigarettes: she will hand you a pack of Juno. What you need will be inside the packet, but put it straight in your pocket, buy a newspaper and leave. Carry on up Bleibtreustrasse and take the second left – Niebuhrstrasse. Open the packet when you get into Niebuhrstrasse, there will be a note there telling you which one to go to. Now, I need to check that you have remembered all that.'

–

At six o'clock on the morning of Tuesday 25th March, Henri finally gave up trying to force himself back to sleep, as he had been attempting

283

to do for most of the night. They had all come to visit him during his brief spells of sleep: Roza, of course, but also her brother, the man in the perfume shop in Essen, and even Foxi the dog – all shouting at him. Then Rosa had appeared, and for a brief while she seemed to sit on the end of the bed alongside Roza. He had a bath and then sat on the floor, with maps spread out before him. He had been absorbed in these maps since returning to the Excelsior late the previous afternoon.

He could see the routes; there was no doubt about that. He wandered over to the window. Down on Saarlandstrasse a group of Waffen SS were happily chatting away and slapping each other on the back. Not for the first time since he arrived in Berlin, he felt real fear. His chest tightened and the maps shook as his hands trembled.

I don't have to do this. I am not committed to anything. If I abandon my plans now, no one will know anything.

Back to the maps. During his training by the British he had been told that he was a natural map reader. He could study a map and its contents would come to life. He was immediately able to picture the area as if they were observing it from above, and could envisage different routes and varying permutations of those routes.

First of all, there was the map of Berlin and then that of Germany. It all appeared to be straightforward, he knew where he had to be and how to get there, but he could not foresee the hazards and he knew that there would be plenty of those.

He checked out of the Excelsior at half past eight that morning, assuring one of the over-attentive managers on duty that he had indeed enjoyed his stay, everything had indeed been to his satisfaction, and he would most certainly consider staying at the Excelsior when he returned to Berlin.

There was a light drizzle as he walked to the Opernplatz, where the expanse of St Hedwig's Cathedral rose before him. He reminded himself of Edgar's instructions.

Do not enter the cathedral before five to nine.

He paused at the entrance to Opernplatz. It was ten to nine, and realising that it was too early, he found a stone bench to sit on, despite the rain. He waited, steeling himself to go into the cathedral. He had a passionate dislike of churches, buoyed by a fear that he had first encountered in his childhood – that churches were the one place where secrets weren't safe; even the statues and gargoyles seemed to know all about him.

Five to nine.

'*Enter the cathedral through the main entrance.*'

A few people were coming down the steps after the eight o'clock Mass.

'*And don't forget to cross yourself. Find a seat about halfway along between the entrance and main altar.*'

The cathedral was enormous and there must have been no more than two dozen people dotted around it, sitting alone or in pairs, all in silent prayer.

'*If he has seen that all is clear, Hugo will appear on the same row as you and sit two or three seats away. Do not expect to see him before ten past nine. However, if he has not appeared by twenty past nine, leave the church and walk back to Unter den Linden. Do not look around for Hugo.*'

Ten past nine. The cathedral was much emptier now as the last Mass worshippers had left and people made their way to work. He tried very hard to close his eyes and hope that some spiritual feeling would come to him, something to assure him not to worry, that everything would turn out right. Nothing – but at least the ghost of Roza did not appear. He became aware of a scrape of chairs alongside him as someone moved down his row towards him.

'*Do not look directly at him but do look in his direction so you can be sure it is him.*'

It was Hugo, dressed in a long black coat and clutching a hat and his briefcase.

'*If he places his briefcase on a chair either side of him then that is a sign of danger. Leave immediately. If the briefcase remains on the floor, all is well.*'

The briefcase was on the floor. He saw Hugo remove a Bible from the small wooden receptacle on the back of the chair in front of him and slip something into it.

'*Remain where you are until Hugo has finished and left. Then you know how to retrieve the document.*'

After five minutes Hugo finished praying. He put the Bible where he had taken it from, stood up and left.

'*The document will be folded in the middle of the Bible. Remove it as soon as you can.*'

He stood up and straightened his coat and when he sat down again it was in the seat next to where Hugo had been sitting. He picked up the Bible Hugo had left and opened it. The document was indeed in the centre, folded as if ready to be inserted into a narrow envelope. He glanced around, but no one was close to him or looking in his direction, apart from a reproachful medieval saint or two. Within seconds, the document was inside his jacket pocket.

'*Once you have retrieved the document, remain in your seat for another five minutes. Remember to pray.*'

He thumbed through the Bible and stopped randomly. It was psalm 130 – 'Waiting for the Redemption of the Lord. Out of the depths I have cried to you, O Lord. Lord hear my voice!' A shiver ran down his spine and he looked up to see if anyone was watching him now. He looked back at the psalm. 'For with the Lord there is mercy, And with Him is abundant redemption.'

He found himself shaking and he was so hot that the sweat from his hands was staining the page. He glanced up and saw that a stone angel on a pillar near him looked like Roza. He had never been a religious man; it was alien to his ideology. But he was quite clear now. What he had just read decided him. He was certain. He had to concentrate very hard now to remember Edgar's instructions.

'*Put the Bible back behind the seat and leave the cathedral. Do not forget to kneel and to cross yourself. There is a chapel just before the porch from where you leave the cathedral. Hugo will be in there: if he gets up to leave as you go past and his coat is folded across his arm, you know all is well. He will follow you but do not look round. Leave through Opernplatz and then walk down Oberwallstrasse. If Hugo is certain that you are not being followed he will approach you before you go into the Reichsbank to check that everything is in order.*'

As he walked past the chapel he glimpsed Hugo beginning to follow him out, his coat folded across his arm. He walked through

Opernplatz back into Unter den Linden, and after a block turned right into Oberwallstrasse, which was a long narrow street leading down to Französischestrasse and the Reichsbank. About halfway along, the road was filled with rubble from what appeared to be a bombed building. He paused to look up at it, allowing Hugo to catch up with him.

'Everything appears to be all right. I will walk with you as far as the Reichsbank. You have the document safe?'

'It's here in my pocket,' said Henri.

'Good. Make sure that you get a proper envelope from Reinhart to put it in, along with some other Reichsbank papers – and don't forget to get him to seal it. It is essential that it looks like a normal letter from the Reichsbank to Bank Leu, I am sure you realise that. Then go straight to Tempelhof.'

'Franz!'

A smartly dressed man was striding towards them. Hugo muttered, 'Oh no,' and then under his breath said, 'Give me a minute; I need to get rid of him. I'm giving you directions to the Reichsbank, remember that.'

'What are you doing down here, Franz, you should be in the office. I am on the way there myself.'

Henri had a feeling that he knew the man, but could not place him. He was wearing a formal suit and spoke with a Berlin accent. He had begun to stare at Henri, as if he recognised him too.

'Yes Alois, I too am on my way to the office. I had been at Mass and this gentleman asked me to direct him to the Reichsbank.'

'I think we may have met.' The man Franz Hermann had called 'Alois' had now turned directly to face Henri, positioning himself uncomfortably close to him. Henri was convinced that they had met, but had no idea when or where. 'Are you from Switzerland, by any chance?'

Henri replied that he was. He could now remember the man. Franz Hermann was standing behind him and looking worried.

'Alois – I do need to get to the office. Perhaps you will join me? I am sure our friend now knows his way to the Reichsbank.'

The man called Alois ignored Hermann. 'I remember now! Bern, last June – we met at the Schweizerhof. My name is Alois Jäger. I told you that you should contact me if you were ever in Berlin. Do you recall our meeting?'

Henri noticed the Nazi Party badge on Alois Jäger's lapel. 'Yes...' he said hesitantly, appearing to recollect their meeting from the back of his memory. 'I do remember. Of course I do.'

'You name is Henri, correct?'

Henri nodded.

'And what brings you to Berlin?'

'I am here on business.'

'For whom, may I ask?'

'Bank Leu – I work for Bank Leu in Zurich. I have business on their behalf at the Reichsbank.'

'Ah – a Swiss banker! I am most impressed. I have some good friends at the Reichsbank. Perhaps you know Herr—'

'I should explain, Herr Jäger – I am just a courier. My dealings with the Reichsbank are limited to delivering and collecting documents, I am afraid.'

'Do not worry, my friend. It is all very important. I am told that the support we are getting from the Swiss banks is proving to be a lifeline for Germany: such discretion – we are so grateful. And you are from Zurich, a most charming city, so... proper. But I am confused, Herr Hesse: when we met in Bern you said you were from Geneva? You were travelling to Stuttgart, I think, on business. I recall that because I remember wondering why such a good German speaker was from Geneva.'

Henri could see Franz Hermann's eyes shine with fear. 'Geneva, you say? Ah yes! For a while I did live there, but now I live in Zurich and work for Bank Leu.'

'So you are no longer in business?'

'No, no longer.'

'I see,' said Alois Jäger, sounding unsure. 'And what a remarkable coincidence not only that I should encounter you today in Berlin, but that you should also be talking with my good friend and colleague Herr Hermann. You looked like you know each other – it shows what a hospitable city Berlin has become under the *Führer*. Perhaps we could have dinner tonight – the three of us?'

288

Henri explained that he was leaving Berlin that day. 'In fact, I have a flight from Tempelhof at twelve thirty.'

'Well, I want you to promise that the next time you are in Berlin, you will contact me? We shall have a meal together. What do you think, Franz?'

All three men agreed that this was a most agreeable idea as they walked together to the end of Oberwallstrasse, where they enthusiastically shook hands. Alois Jäger and Franz Hermann were turning right towards their office in Friederichstrasse. Henri turned left towards Werderscher Markt.

Henri was shocked. Alois Jäger was clearly suspicious, and the fact that he was wearing a Nazi Party badge and that Hugo looked so horrified was a worry. He would have had even more cause for concern had he looked round just before he entered the Reichsbank and noticed the formal figure of Alois Jäger watching him from the side of the road.

–

When Henri Hesse presented himself at the Reichsbank reception his heart was racing, his chest felt tight, he was perspiring heavily and beginning to feel quite unwell. It was ten thirty. His options were still open: he could exchange documents with Reinhart, go to Tempelhof, return to Switzerland and please both his masters. But the chance reading of the psalm in the cathedral had made up his mind: he would take a much harder option, but one that he knew would give him peace.

Gunter Reinhart appeared to have aged ten years in the short time since Henri had last seen him and, other than thanking him once again for taking Alfred to Switzerland, he said very little. He took the envelope from Bank Leu, signed for it and handed over the sealed envelope for him to take back to Switzerland.

'I need you to give me another envelope, perhaps with another document in it?' asked Henri. 'I would then like to put something in myself and then ask you to re-seal it.'

The German looked uncomfortable.

'I said to Hedinger, this has to be the last time. I cannot risk this anymore. You took Alfred to Switzerland, for which I am deeply grateful, and in return I supplied the directive. Now I have done you this one other favour. Life is getting too dangerous: if I give any cause to suspect me then not only will I be in danger, but so will Rosa and Sophia, not to mention my wife and children of course. You must promise me this: don't ask me to help again. Don't come back to Berlin. You understand? It is too dangerous, far too dangerous.'

He took another envelope from a drawer, found a few sheets from a tray on his desk and slipped them in. Henri carefully inserted the papers he had taken from the Bible in between the sheets and handed the envelope back to Reinhart to seal it.

He promised Reinhart that they would never meet again, which was not difficult as he had every intention of keeping it. It was unusual for him to make a promise that he intended to keep.

After leaving Werderscher Markt he travelled by U-Bahn to Uhlandstrasse. Kato's instructions had been clear enough. He came out on the Kurfürstendamm exit, crossed the road and then headed west as far as the corner with Bleibtreustrasse.

Sure enough, there was a kiosk set back in the wall, with narrow swastika banners hanging down from either side of a large advertising sign: '*Berlin Raucht Juno*' – Berlin smokes Juno. Lucky Berlin.

The old lady in the kiosk appeared to be wearing two coats and had a scarf wrapped round her head with a woollen hat on top of it. Behind her was a large picture of Hitler at a slightly jaunty angle, and in front of her a small queue of people in a hurry. He courteously allowed a woman in a fur coat to go first so that, by the time it was his turn to be served, there was no one else waiting.

'I have come to collect Magda's cigarettes.'

The old lady glanced up at him and held eye contact for a moment before she scanned the street behind him. He wondered whether he was meant to say anything else: had he forgotten something? He added 'Please' and smiled.

She bent down and from under the counter produced a white packet of Juno cigarettes, which she pressed into his hands, no longer looking directly at him. As he slipped the packet into his pocket he could tell that there was something heavier than twenty cigarettes in it. By now he had been joined at the front of the kiosk by two Waffen SS officers. He picked up a copy of the *Völkischer Beobachter* and placed two Reichsmarks into the old lady's mittened hands. By the time she had pocketed the money she had already turned her attention to the SS men.

Niebuhrstrasse was a quiet street, in marked contrast to the bustle of the Ku'damm. He stood in the doorway of a dress shop and removed the packet of Juno from his pocket. There were only four or five cigarettes in it and he placed one straight into mouth and lit it – it could have looked too suspicious to do otherwise. Tucked into the packet was a car key attached to a small metal disk with the word 'Opel' engraved on it. Also inside the Juno packet was a folded slip of paper, which he unwrapped: 'UTM 142'.

He looked down the street. There were a few cars parked on it, but he could not see the one he was looking for. He walked down the block and the last car on the corner before Schlüterstrasse was an Opel Super 6 sedan – UTM 142. It was a handsome car; four doors, dark green, whitewall tyres, and neither so clean nor so dirty that it might stand out.

He unlocked the door and settled into the driver's seat. The car had a musty smell to it, a mixture of damp and old leather. 'I will do my best to get hold of the various papers you want, but it will not be easy,' Kato had told him the previous afternoon. 'Whatever I can get will be in the glove box, inside the log book.'

He reached across to the glove box in front of the passenger seat and removed the black leather log book, with the word 'Opel' in faded silver on the cover. The back cover of the book formed a sleeve, and within that was what he had asked for: identity cards and a form showing that the owner of UTM 142 was entitled to buy petrol. Tucked behind the log book was something hard, wrapped in a thick, grey cloth.

'The car has been hidden in Weissensee since before the war began,' Kato had told him. 'A mechanic who was a secret Party member has been looking after it. He now works in an SS garage, so he has been able to obtain the correct documentation. I have kept the paperwork up to date. I was keeping it for an emergency, but if Viktor says… The identity cards will not be easy, not with so little time. It is possible to purchase these things though; the black market is very active at the moment. Do you have money I can use, by any chance?'

He had handed her a substantial sum of Swiss Francs and her eyes had lit up. 'That should make it much easier,' she had said. 'I will do what I can.'

A policeman had walked past the car, and now in his rear-view mirror Henri could see him turning around and heading slowly back in his direction. He needed to move, but first he removed from his pocket a tightly-wrapped piece of paper, from which he produced the Nazi Party membership badge he had taken from the perfume shop owner in Essen. He pinned it carefully to his lapel and checked in the mirror that it was at a proper angle. The car started first time, if rather noisily and lurched forward as he selected the gears. He drove slowly down the side streets to get a feel for the car before turning into Kurfürstendamm.

'*Create a commentary: decide your route, write it down and then memorise that route in the spoken form. When you are driving along, keep reciting the commentary, it means you can avoid using a map and drawing attention to yourself.*'

East along Kurfürstendamm, then right into Joachimstalerstrasse, which becomes Kaiser Allee. There was surprisingly little traffic on the road, though he had to be careful of the trams. The Opel was a heavy car but a powerful one, and he had to concentrate hard to keep his speed under control.

'*Through Wilmersdorf and Friedenau. Kaiser Allee leads into Reinstrasse. At the end of Reinstrasse you will see the Botanischer Garten signposted. Turn right into Grunewaldstrasse: you will know where you are from there.*'

It was twenty past eleven. The journey had been quicker than he imagined and the Opel now handled beautifully: he had little doubt that once it got out on the open road it would perform well, assuming they got that far. In Kaiser Wilhelm Strasse he eased the car slowly to a halt in a position where he could see the house on the corner of Arno-Holz Strasse.

At various stages since he had arrived in Berlin he had been telling himself that he did not need to do this, that he could pull out now. No one would know if he did, with the possible exception of Kato. He could drive on towards Tempelhof, abandon the car and still have time to catch the 12.35 flight to Berlin – there was just about enough time – and for a brief moment he hesitated.

Then the image of Roza appeared again, smiling this time, and the sense of calm that he had first encountered in the air raid shelter in Stuttgart station returned.

He left the car and walked over to the house, knowing that there was no going back.

Chapter 24

leaving Berlin, March 1941

Henri Hesse's career as a secret agent ceased the moment he knocked on the door of the house near the Botanischer Garten where Rosa Stern was hiding.

He had been a Soviet spy since 1930, and a British one for a year and half. Serving first one and then two masters had required him to be constantly on his guard, and to be in control and exercise caution all the time. Despite sometimes affecting an air of detachment and possibly coming across as a bit too questioning, Henri knew that he had survived because he had actually always done what he was told.

Now, he was doing the opposite. From this moment on he was ignoring all of his training and turning his back on the obedience which had dictated his life for the previous ten years. He had no intention of forgetting all his training, but would exploit it in his own interests.

When Rosa opened the door, she looked as if she had seen a ghost.

'What on earth are you doing here? I told you it was too dangerous to return: you must leave now! Oh my God, Henri, this is so dangerous. Please go. Please!'

'Let me in, Rosa. I need to explain. You will understand when I tell you why I am here. You know that it is dangerous for me to stand here. Please.'

So she had let him in and hurried him upstairs while she settled Frau Hermann. When she came up to the small lounge on the first floor, she looked flustered and stood by the closed door, her arms folded.

294

'What is it, Henri? And how come you're still in Berlin? My God – what is that?' She was pointing at the Nazi Party membership badge on his lapel, its black swastika stark on a white background. 'You're not...'

'Don't worry Rosa; it is to stop me looking suspicious.'

She laughed sarcastically. 'A Swiss citizen walking round Berlin wearing a Nazi Party badge: you think that doesn't look suspicious?'

'Listen to me, Rosa. You are in danger, you and Sophia.'

'Thank you for telling me that, Henri. Don't you think I am already very well aware of that?'

'No, no... what I mean is that you are in immediate danger. You have to leave the house now!'

She gasped and moved away from the door, moving to the sofa opposite Henri.

'What do you mean?'

'I saw Franz this morning. He told me that he has heard through a contact that the Gestapo have been informed that you are hiding in this area: they have been told that you are in a house in one of the roads just north of the Botanischer Garten. They are planning to search every house. The search could begin at any time!'

'But Franz was here yesterday, he never said a word about this. I would have known if something was wrong, surely?'

'I saw him early this morning: he had only just heard.'

'Are you sure?'

'Of course I am sure. Why else do you think I am here?'

'But Franz had a plan that we would use if we are ever in danger: he would telephone and use a code word, and then Sophia and I would go to Pankow, where a friend of his has a shop and we would be able to hide in the attic. He—'

'There is no time, Rosa. I am sure Franz made all these plans, but maybe he panicked. I told you, they could start the house-to-house search at any time. We have to leave now.'

'We?'

'Yes. I have a car. I am going to take you and Sophia, but we need to leave now.'

'This is madness, Henri. We have no proper papers and what about Frau Hermann? I can't just abandon her.'

'I have papers, Rosa, here – look.'

He handed her the identity cards that Kato had left for him in the car, hers in the name of 'Dagmar Keufer', Sophia's in the name of 'Gisela Keufer'. Rosa studied them carefully.

'The photographs, Henri – they are even not of us!'

'No, of course not – there was no time. But they *could* be of you: they ought to be good enough for a basic check, they're not too bad, and I have a card in the name of Erich Keufer, so we will be able to pretend to be a family. You see that our address is in Frankfurt: we can say that we are driving there.'

'To Frankfurt? Are you mad? We will be lucky to get out of Berlin. And what do we do when we get to Frankfurt – buy a house, join the Nazi Party?'

'We are not going to Frankfurt, Rosa. We are going to Switzerland. I also have Swiss papers for you and Sophia, I had these prepared only last week. They are very good, but I think we can only risk using them when we are much closer to the border.'

Rosa was pacing around the room, almost in a circle, shaking her head and running her hand through her hair. 'I am sorry, Henri, but this doesn't make sense to me. You seem to have got hold of these papers very quickly – I thought you said that it was only this morning that Franz told you he heard that we were in danger?'

'Can I be honest with you, Rosa? When I first visited you here it was apparent that your situation was too dangerous. I thought that something like this would happen but I didn't want to voice my fears to Franz, as he has been so good to you. But I was so worried that I had these identity cards prepared: just in case.'

Rosa sank back in the sofa, looking overwhelmed and confused. She clearly thought that Henri's plan was crazy, but so would be remaining in the house if there really was a chance it was about to be searched by the Gestapo. Henri was sure she was far from convinced, but he was counting on her not risking her life and that of her daughter by ignoring him.

'And Frau Hermann?'

'Make her comfortable and tell her that you will be back later. Franz will come round after work. Rosa, we need to move fast – you need to get Sophia ready. Pack a few things, but nothing that identifies you or Sophia. We also need to take food and some blankets; we may not be able to stop.'

Rosa was back by the door now, her hand on the handle and peering at Henri in a sceptical manner.

'Perhaps I should contact Franz? We have an agreed system to use in an emergency – I telephone him pretending to be a secretary from another law firm.'

'No, Rosa! Under no circumstances! Franz said he thinks they will be listening in to all telephone calls in this area – maybe that is why he has not contacted you himself. If you phone him at his office, it could reveal your location and bring him under suspicion. You must do nothing that would draw attention to this house, do you understand?'

Once Rosa decided that she had no alternative but to go along with Henri, she moved fast and decisively. She gave Frau Hermann her lunch early and told her that she would be back later. She packed a small suitcase for her and Sophia, telling the little girl they were going on a long journey and – if she was a very good girl, did everything she was asked to, and told anyone who asked that her name was Gisela – then she would see Alfred. *'But only if you are good. And only if you remember that your name is Gisela.'*

He decided to bring the car right outside the house rather than risk Rosa and Sophia being seen crossing the road with a suitcase.

–

Although Henri had ceased to be a spy the moment he entered the house, he had no plans to dispense with all aspects of his training. He had excelled at what the British called a 'clandestine driving' course and was now about to put what he had learnt into action, though not to quite the same effect that the British had intended.

'Always see a car journey in the same way as one on foot – as a series of short journeys: a car trip from London to Edinburgh, for example, should

be broken down into a series of shorter stages – London to Northampton, Northampton to Nottingham, Nottingham to Sheffield, et cetera. These are much easier to explain if stopped, as long as you have a very feasible story ready to explain that journey.'

All that and more was racing around in Henri's mind as they left the house in Arno-Holz Strasse at noon. They were just ahead of the schedule he had in his mind when they pulled into a lay-by just outside Potsdam forty minutes later. He turned off the engine and removed a road map from the side of the seat.

'Here, let me show you our route.'

'Where to?'

'To Switzerland, I told you.'

'You're serious, aren't you? How are we going to get that far?'

'Let me show you, I have it all planned.'

Henri opened out the map, allowing it to rest on the dashboard and their laps. He moved towards Rosa as they looked at the map. As he got closer he caught the scent of a delicate perfume. She flicked her hair out of her eyes, looking carefully at the map as he pointed at the Swiss border.

'I do know where Switzerland is.'

'There are two possible routes, Rosa. This one here – I've called that the "east" route. It's a more direct one, we'd go due south west in more or less a straight line: Leipzig; Bayreuth; Nuremberg; Ulm. The plan would be to cross the border around Lake Konstanz—'

'*Attempt* to cross the border, Henri.'

'Attempt to cross the border, then. I understand that the Lake Konstanz part of the border can be a bit less dangerous than some other crossings. However, that would take us through Bavaria and very close to the border with the Protectorate, where apparently security is especially strong.'

Henri had to lean over Rosa to expose more of the map, her hair brushing his face as he did so.

'This is what I call the "west route" – it's much more circuitous. We'd drive to Brunswick and then down towards Stuttgart before crossing the border round Singen, with an option to go over the mountains. It has the advantage of taking us close to Frankfurt, and that is where the identity cards say we are from.'

Rosa studied the map for a while, frowning as she did so.

'I suppose your west route is the lesser of two evils. With all this planning, do you know how long it will take us?'

'From here to Brunswick is just over 110 miles, but I am planning to come off the main roads and stick to the side roads as much as I can. If anyone asks why, just say that you get car sick on main roads. I think we will get south of Brunswick – maybe as far as Göttingen before it gets dark. We can then look for a wood to drive into and hide for the night. We'll be 200 miles from Stuttgart: we can be there by Wednesday night and then drive to Switzerland on the Thursday.'

Rosa said nothing, but shrugged as if in reluctant agreement. Henri re-started the Opel and they pulled out into the road.

'You must drive slower, please – and not so close to the centre of the road. You had this all planned, didn't you?'

'What do you mean?'

'You are too near the kerb now, just slow down a bit. Are you seriously telling me that you saw Franz this morning, and since then you have sorted all this out, including working out how long it is going to take?'

'Yes and no. I told you, Rosa, since I first met you, I had been so concerned at the danger you were in that I had given some consideration to this, but when Franz told me this morning I had to move fast.'

To the surprise of both of them, the journey to Brunswick was uneventful. Where they could they dropped off the main road: the Lower Saxony countryside seemed to be suited for this kind of driving, with plenty of small narrow roads leading off the larger ones. On the occasions that they passed police or military vehicles no interest was taken in them: a husband and wife and their daughter out for a drive. A few miles to the north of Göttingen, with the light beginning to fail, they came across a wood with a track leading into it from the road. Henri stopped the car and managed to open a creaky wooden gate at the top of the track, and then drove as deep into the wood as possible.

When he walked back to shut the gate it was impossible to see the Opel from the road. It was when he returned to the car, feeling quite pleased with himself and almost relaxed that Sophia started crying. It was a soft cry at first, almost a series of sobs, but then it became louder.

'What is it, darling?' Rosa asked.

When Sophia replied she spoke so quietly that her mother had to lean across the front seat to hear her.

'I can't hear you, darling. You'll need to speak up.'

'But I can't, Mama,' she whispered. 'You told me always to whisper. You said people mustn't hear me speak.'

Rosa turned round and stroked her daughter's face.

'It's all right now darling. You don't need to whisper here in the car: only if there are other people around. Now, what were you trying to say?'

'I'm frightened,' each word punctuated by a noisy sob.

'What are you frightened of?'

'The goblins! There are always goblins in a forest.'

'There's no such thing as goblins,' said Henri impatiently. 'And in any case, this is not a forest, it's a wood.'

This only seemed to make things worse and Sophia's cry turned into a wail. Rosa left the front seat and went to sit next to Sophia in the back. After a long cuddle, the little girl calmed down.

'Where are we going?'

'You should rest now, darling.'

'But where are we *going*?' Sophia sounded as if she was pleading with her mother, begging her to answer the question.

'Somewhere safe, darling. Now, please rest.'

'If we are going somewhere safe, does it mean that we will see Alfred there?'

'Yes, darling, I told you we would, especially if you are a good girl. You should rest now.'

'Will we also see Papa in this safe place we are going to? Why don't you tell me?'

Rosa did not reply. Henri glanced back at her. Her head had dropped and she was tapping her teeth with her knuckles as her eyes filled with tears. Sophia was sitting with her legs hunched up to her face, her enormous dark eyes unblinking as they looked up at him from behind her kneecaps. In the gloom her pale skin now appeared chalky white. She gave him the beginnings of a smile and waved one of the paws of the dirty white one-eared rabbit she was clutching at Henri, who waved back awkwardly.

'If you are very quiet, Sophia, and behave very, very well, then I promise you that when we get to this safe place, you will get a present. But you have to be quiet.'

'What kind of present?'

Henri shrugged. 'Chocolates.'

The little girl said nothing but pulled a face.

'What about a new rabbit? That one looks very old – it only has one ear.'

'But I love Mr Rabbit! You cannot take him away!'

The little girl started crying again. Rosa pulled her close.

'No one is going to take Mr Rabbit away darling. Henri meant that we will buy you a friend for Mr Rabbit.'

During the long silence that followed the light dropped dramatically and when Sophia spoke again it was almost dark.

'It will be nice for Mr Rabbit to have a friend, won't it, Mama?'

'Yes darling. You try and rest now.'

'Because we don't have friends anymore, do we?'

'What do you mean, darling?'

'Alfred told me that: he said that the reason we had to be so quiet in the house and not make a noise and not go anywhere near the window is because no one is our friend. Is that true?'

Rosa said nothing, but busied herself arranging a blanket around Sophia, allowing the rabbit's head to poke out of the top of it.

'Here are some biscuits, darling. Eat those and then you must sleep.'

She munched at the biscuits, her eyes looking around the car, apparently unblinking.

'Why is no one our friend, Mama?'

'Don't keep asking questions, darling. Where we are going, everyone will be our friend.'

'Is Henri our friend?'

In the rear-view mirror Henri caught Rosa's face as she hesitated very briefly before replying.

'Yes, darling. Sleep now.'

Henri watched through the mirror, waiting for Sophia to fall asleep. When she finally did so he cleared his throat and turned round to talk. Now was the time, he had decided, to be a bit more honest with Rosa and maybe then she would see him in a better light.

But when he turned round Rosa was fast asleep too and the moment had passed.

–

On the Tuesday morning, before the Opel had even left Berlin, Franz Hermann was becoming increasingly worried. He had been unnerved by the encounter with Alois Jäger in Oberwallstrasse, and even more so by the way his colleague had behaved since then. First of all, Jäger had only walked with him part of the way to the office, then had suddenly stopped and said he needed to go back and check something. Back at the office he had come in to see him.

'If you had not told me otherwise, Franz, then I would have thought that you and that Swiss man knew each other. You looked like you were acquaintances, rather than one stranger giving directions to another.'

He assured Jäger that he was mistaken: he had been to morning Mass and as he'd left the cathedral the man had asked him for directions. He had even gone somewhat out of his way to make sure the man went in the right direction.

'And fancy the coincidence of me having met him in Bern last year!'

Franz agreed with Jäger that it was indeed a coincidence. 'It's a small world, as they say.'

'But so strange. When I was in Bern he was about to travel to Stuttgart on business, and I even helped him with his visa at our Embassy there. He was staying at the Schweizerhof, which I tell you, Franz, is a very expensive hotel. And now look – he is a mere courier.'

'Perhaps he fell on hard times, Alois?'

'Perhaps.'

Both men continued to be uneasy about the encounter. As was the custom on Tuesdays, the senior lawyers at the practice lunched together and the two men eyed each other suspiciously throughout the meal. Franz Hermann was worried that Alois Jäger did not believe him, and Jäger was convinced that Hermann appeared to be nervous. When they went back into their respective offices, each man closed his door and made a phone call. Alois Jäger made his first, telephoning a good friend of his who was in charge of the Gestapo office in Treptow.

'Tell me, Lothar,' he said after a brief exchange of pleasantries, 'you must have good contacts with your colleagues at Tempelhof, no? You are practically neighbours…? Good, I thought as much. Do me a favour will you, Lothar? I am sure it is nothing, perhaps just me being suspicious, but could you discreetly check whether a Swiss citizen called Henri Hesse travelled on a flight from Tempelhof to Stuttgart at around twelve thirty today?'

Lothar asked one or two questions. 'We are very thorough in the Gestapo you know, Alois!' Both men laughed. Lothar checked the exact spelling of the man's name. 'And could you describe him?'

'Perhaps mid-thirties; average height, possibly slightly overweight. Pale complexion, darkish hair as far as I could tell, but he was wearing a trilby hat.'

'I will see what I can do, Alois.'

At more or less the same time, in his office one floor below Jäger's, Franz Hermann was pacing up and down. Something was not right, but he had no idea what he could do about it. He picked up the telephone and dialled his mother's number in Dahlem. At least he could be reassured that all was well there.

–

Captain Edgar and Basil Remington-Barber had travelled to Geneva after spending the weekend with Henri in Zurich. They based themselves at a perfectly decent if somewhat anonymous hotel within sight of Cornavin railway station, where they hoped to meet Henri late on the Tuesday night.

The hotel had been chosen carefully. Apart from its proximity to the station, they had been able to book two rooms on the top floor, set apart from the other rooms on that corridor. Each room had a telephone and they made sure that from the moment they arrived in Geneva, one of them would always be beside it. They did not expect to hear anything until four thirty at the earliest on the Tuesday afternoon, when Henri Hesse's flight from Stuttgart was scheduled to land at Zurich. Rolf would be waiting at the airport to watch Henri arrive and check that he travelled onto Zurich. One of Rolf's men would then be at the station to watch Henri meeting with the Russians, and then catching the train to Geneva. Edgar and Remington-Barber ensured that they were both waiting by the phone in Geneva from four o'clock on the Tuesday afternoon. At a quarter past four, Remington-Barber observed that Henri's flight ought to be landing, and at four thirty he mentioned that they should be hearing from Rolf at any moment.

'It's a tight schedule we've allowed him, Edgar. He has to go to Bank Leu, then meet up with his Russian chap, allow them to copy the document, and still make that last train to Geneva.'

'He'll be fine, Basil. Why don't you sit down and relax? Hedinger will stay on as late as he needs to, and the last train to Geneva leaves at a quarter to eight. Please stop worrying. You can pour us another drink if you think that will help.'

By five o'clock Edgar, if pressed, would have described himself as concerned. Five minutes after that, the phone rang and both men jumped. Basil Remington-Barber answered it. 'Yes, hello Rolf... I see... Yes... No... Are you sure...? And you have checked there...? Do so again please, Rolf... Yes... Probably... Call us back in ten minutes.' As he replaced the phone his hands were shaking.

'Well?' asked Edgar.

'Henry was not on the flight.'

'Are you sure?' Edgar's face was just inches from his colleague's.

'You heard what I said, Edgar. Rolf Eder is no fool, he is one of the best men I have ever had in the field, doesn't miss a thing. He said that there were twelve passengers who came off the Swissair flight and Henry Hunter was not one of them.'

'Maybe he missed the connection at Stuttgart? After all, there was only a twenty-minute gap between the Berlin flight landing there and the Zurich flight taking off?'

'Yes, but they are connecting flights. If the Berlin flight is late, they hold the Zurich one. It is possible that he missed the flight from Berlin, but it's unlikely: he had ample time to meet Hugo, go to the Reichsbank, and then get to Tempelhof.'

When Rolf called back ten minutes later, he said that he had been able to check the flight's manifest with a Swissair contact: although a 'Henri Hesse' had been booked in, he had not been on the connecting flight from Berlin. Edgar snatched the phone from Remington-Barber.

'Rolf? It's me – Edgar. Look, your best bet is to get to the station in Zurich as soon as possible and join your man there. See if you can spot Viktor and his chaps. If Henry's not going to show up, they'll probably get worried at some stage and break cover. Just see what they up to. If we see them looking for him then at least that tells us something.'

'Jesus Christ,' said Edgar, slamming the phone down and pacing the room. 'Basil... you telephone Hedinger and ask if his courier has arrived from Berlin. I cannot imagine that he will have done, but there is a very distant possibility that he may have heard from him, or from Reinhart. In fact, ask him to send a telegram to Reinhart asking if all went well with the courier, and then tell Hedinger to stay on until at least seven. Jesus Christ.'

By eight o'clock they knew little more. Michael Hedinger told them he had neither heard nor seen his courier, and promised to send a telegram to Reinhart that night. Rolf reported that he had managed to get to the station by six o'clock, where he was joined by three of his men. At seven o'clock they spotted Viktor prowling around the station, looking anxious. There was no sign of Henry Hunter boarding the last train to Geneva or any of the ones before it. Viktor had been waiting by the ticket barrier, his face creased in anger as the train departed.

'At least he's let them down too.'

'What do we do, Edgar?'

Edgar continued to pace the room angrily, cursing under his breath. 'It's that bloody woman, I'm sure it is. Jesus Christ. We'd better get on the first train in the morning to Zurich.'

–

The mood in a dingy rented apartment in a narrow side street between the railway tracks and the river in Zurich was scarcely any better. Each of the four men who had been with him at the station were brought in one by one and questioned by Viktor, but as he had been there himself, there was little point in it. Henri had not come anywhere near the station.

'He seems to have disappeared,' said Viktor.

'When we met him last week, he said something about having asked you for the details of any comrades he could contact in Berlin, in an emergency,' said one of Viktor's men.

'So…?'

'So, I was thinking that if you did give him details of any comrades in Berlin then possibly they would know what happened to him.'

Viktor said nothing for a while, thinking how little he could trust even those closest to him.

'You are mistaken: I have no comrades left in my network in Berlin: they've all gone – either escaped, disappeared, dead or become Nazis. I told him to contact the Embassy.'

'Really? I thought you didn't trust anyone there?'

'I don't,' said Viktor. 'I don't trust anyone.'

–

Back in Berlin that Tuesday evening, Alois Jäger finally heard back from his friend in the Gestapo, Lothar. It was six thirty and Jäger had remained behind in his office awaiting the call.

'You say that his name is Henri Hesse and he is a Swiss citizen?'

'Yes,' said Alois Jäger.

'Well, I not only contacted Heinrich at Tempelhof but actually went over there to his office, so I was able to look at all the paperwork. There were three Swiss nationals on the Deutsche Lufthansa flight that left for Stuttgart at thirty-five minutes past twelve, but none of them had that name. The officer in charge of checking the papers as the passengers boarded the plane said that, as far as he can recall, one of the Swiss was a woman and the other two were men in either their fifties or sixties.'

'He was obviously not on that flight then.'

'However,' said Lothar, 'he was *booked* onto that flight, he just did not turn up for it. And furthermore, there is a record of him having arrived at Tempelhof yesterday, on the flight from Stuttgart. What is it that concerns you about this man, Alois?'

Alois thought long and hard.

'I'm not sure, Lothar. Something about him doesn't quite add up. And now, missing his flight like that.'

Very odd, they both agreed – so much so that they decided to meet up the next day to discuss the matter.

–

Franz Hermann had telephoned his mother's house in Dahlem five times on the Tuesday afternoon, and each time the call went unanswered his anxiety increased. By five to five he decided he had to go down to Dahlem to check, but he was wary of Alois Jäger; he decided it would be unwise to leave the office before him. Normally his colleague was so preoccupied with Nazi Party meetings in the evening that he invariably left the office no later than five o'clock, but that day it was six thirty before he left.

As soon as he did so, Franz Hermann made his exit too. It was nearly quarter past seven before he arrived at his mother's house on Arno-Holz Strasse. He knocked on the door but there was no reply, so he used his own key to let himself in. The house felt empty and there was no reply when he called out. The lights were on downstairs but the upper floors were dark. Certain that he was walking into a trap, he headed for the room at the back overlooking the garden, where his mother slept and spent her days.

He found her propped up in her armchair, swathed in blankets with a tray next to her and her eyes red from crying.

'I've been calling her for hours, Franz!' she said in a hoarse voice. 'She said something about going out, but that you would be here later. What does she think she has been up to? I have been on my own all this time. I am desperate to go to the toilet and I haven't had my evening meal yet. The telephone was ringing but I couldn't reach it!'

Setting aside his fear, Franz Hermann acted swiftly. He helped his mother to the toilet and then settled her before going upstairs. There was no sign of Rosa and Sophia, and within half an hour he had gathered up any items belonging to them or that could even be associated with them. He bundled everything into old laundry bags and carried them into the attic, where he locked them in an old trunk, which he then covered with old tennis rackets, a cello case, and other reminders of when life was more normal.

When he came downstairs he telephoned Gunter Reinhart at his home. He knew it was a big risk, but he had no alternative.

'Did your courier visit today?'

'Yes – why?'

'And was he acting normally?'

'I think so. Hard to tell, really. Is there a problem?'

'No, no, no – of course not. I was just checking what time he left you?'

'I'm not too sure, I would say by half past ten. Something like that.'

'Perhaps we will meet tomorrow for a chat?' said the lawyer, hoping the other man would recognise the urgency in his voice.

'Yes, perhaps that would be a good idea,' said the banker.

After that, Hermann telephoned his wife and told her that he would stay tonight at his mother's house as the nurse had been called away. He telephoned his sister with the sad news that the nurse who had cared so well for their mother had been called back to Bremerhaven because her husband had been killed at sea. *It was terrible* they both agreed. The poor nurse had no idea how long she would be there, but in the meantime they needed to sort out their mother. Franz Hermann's sister paused for a while and then said that if he could look after their mother until Thursday, she would then come over and bring her back to Brandenburg. *She can stay with us for a week or so.*

'I imagine the nurse will be back by then.'

'I am sure she will,' replied Franz.

–

It was some time after dawn on the Wednesday, before enough light to wake them had penetrated the dense canopy of the woods just to the north of Göttingen. Sophia was upset again when she woke. The tall trees frightened her and she wanted to know whether, if there was no such thing as goblins, what about witches? Hardly reassured by her mother's promise that there were no witches in the wood, she then wanted to know when she was going to see Alfred.

'Soon, darling.'

'When is soon, Mama?'

Henri had been out of the car for a few minutes and had just returned.

'The sooner we can leave this place – the better,' he said. Sophia must have sensed her irritation, but she was glaring at him.

'Give us a few minutes, Henri,' said Rosa. 'Sophia, eat these biscuits and drink the milk, then we can be on our way,' she said softly.

'And see Alfred and Papa?'

'Maybe not today, but hopefully soon. And remember, darling, if anyone asks, your name is Gisela: Gisela Keufer. We will all play that game until we meet Alfred, do you understand?'

Henri checked the map and tried to show the route to Rosa, but she seemed to be barely interested.

'It is amazing that we have got this far, Henri. Our luck cannot hold out much longer.' She spoke quietly so that Sophia could not hear, but there was no disguising the annoyance and fear in her voice.

'I don't see why not, especially if we keep to the back roads.'

'What if they are looking for us?'

'How would anyone know? Franz is unlikely to report us, is he?'

They waited until seven o'clock before starting off, first heading south through Göttingen and then keeping to the patchwork of smaller roads until they reached Würzburg at lunchtime. They needed to stop for petrol, which was risky, but Würzburg was just seventy miles west of Frankfurt and, according to their identity cards, that was where they were from. They drove slowly through the town centre, looking out for a petrol station. The first one they found had a police van waiting at one of the two pumps, so they drove on. Just before the river they came to a garage with a solitary pump and an elderly owner sitting outside on a bench with a large dog sitting next to him and less than an inch of a lit cigarette protruding from his lips. He asked to see the documents entitling them to petrol.

'If I was minded to be difficult,' he said in a gruff Bavarian accent, 'then I would say that you are only entitled to half a tank.' He smiled, revealing a mouth with no more than half a dozen nearly-black teeth in it. The cigarette stub appeared to be stuck to his lower lip. The man's eyes focussed on the Nazi Party badge on Henri's lapel and swiftly his mood became less hostile. 'But fortunately for you, sir, I am not minded to be difficult. I had a delivery of petrol yesterday – the first for over a week. I will fill you up, but you don't need to tell anyone that. Come inside. It takes longer these days to do the paperwork than it does to repair a car… maybe even longer than it takes to build one.' The man's throaty laugh echoed around the workshop before breaking into a violent cough.

They went over to a counter at the side of the garage. The owner checked the paperwork painfully slowly: he checked the identity card in the name of Erich Keufer and the documents showing that Opel Super 6 sedan registration number UTM 142 was entitled to petrol every ten days. Henri glanced out of the garage and saw Rosa looking worried: this was taking a long time. The owner wrote slowly in a large ledger.

'So tell me, are you returning to Frankfurt?'

'No, we are just on our way from there. We are visiting my wife's family in Nuremberg.'

'You sound like you may not be from Frankfurt?'

'Very well spotted my friend: I have lived all over Germany, which explains my accent!'

The owner nodded and handed back the paperwork, which was now covered in grey grease marks. 'Odd that your petrol entitlement document was last stamped in Berlin.'

When he returned to the car Sophia was asleep on the back seat and Rosa looked pale and tense.

'Why did that take so long?'

'Paperwork,' he said, thinking it best not to mention the apparent flaw in the petrol entitlement document.

–

The garage owner, Jürgen Neumann, was a worried man as he watched the Opel Super 6 pull away awkwardly from the forecourt of his garage not far from the banks of the River Main in Würzburg.

He was not a political man by any means, and nor was he any good at keeping his mouth shut, and that was his problem. In recent months he had rather too openly complained to his decreasing number of customers about the infrequency of his deliveries, the cost of food and the lack of business. This had led to a series of visits, the first from a Würzburg police officer who happened to be a friend of his, and lastly a visit from the deputy head of the local Gestapo, who was no friend at all.

'This complaining has to stop. If you are out to make trouble then be assured we can make plenty of trouble for you. It is about time you were more co-operative with us.'

And that had been followed by a noticeable drop in business, and in the delivery of fuel. So now Jürgen Neumann had decided that enough was enough. Unless he went out of his way to ingratiate himself with the powers that be, he would have to close down his business. He picked up the telephone and dialled the number of the deputy head of the local Gestapo, the man who had recently given him his final warning.

'It is probably nothing, sir, but I did promise to contact you with any information.'

He explained about the car that had come from Frankfurt but whose petrol entitlement document was last stamped in Berlin, and whose driver said they were heading for Nuremberg but had driven off in the other direction. It all seemed rather... odd.

'Do I have the registration number sir? Of course I do!'

–

Only three hours before the garage owner in Würzburg contacted his local Gestapo office, a lady in Berlin rang her local police station and began in a similar manner.

'It is probably of little consequence and I was unsure whether to trouble you, but I thought I would pass on this information in case you were interested.'

The officer who took the call at Dahlem police station was well used to this. These days he seemed to spend half his time taking calls from people eager to inform on neighbours, work colleagues, friends, and even family. This one sounded little different and he took down the details. The lady – a Frau Werner – said that she lived in Arno-Holz Strasse and, although she was minding her own business and was certainly not the kind of person to spy upon her neighbours, she could not help but notice something unusual the previous morning.

'Yes, Tuesday. There is an elderly person who lives opposite me: a Frau Hermann. I hardly ever see her these days, she is virtually housebound. She has a nurse, I understand, who also hardly ever leaves the house. But yesterday, it must have been at around twelve noon, I happened to notice a man leave the house and walk over to a car parked just across the road. He then parked immediately outside Frau Hermann's house. Within two or three minutes, no more than that, I saw the man come out of the house along with Frau Hermann's nurse, and with them was a young girl. They all seemed to be rather nervous, looking around. I have never seen a child going in or out of that house before: never. How old, do you say? Four or five, I'm not sure. They were in a hurry. Do I think they saw me? No. I don't want you to think badly of me, sir, but I was kneeling down on the floor, peering through a gap in the net curtains... As it happens, sir, yes I did. Are you ready? It was an Opel – I am not sure what model, but it was dark green and the registration number was… do you have a pen ready? UTM 142.'

Up until a couple of weeks previously, the policeman in Dahlem would have been more annoyed than he was now by this call, as it would have meant hours of work just to satisfy the whim of a nosey neighbour.

But recently the rules had changed. After one or two unfortunate incidents, the Gestapo had realised that criminals and other people they were interested in were finding it too easy to move around the Reich by car. As these people drove from one town or district to another, there was no proper system of keeping track of them. So the Gestapo brought in a new system: the details of any cars that the Gestapo or other sections of the police were interested in would be passed on to a central control in Berlin.

Suits me fine: more work for them, less for me, thought the officer. He filled in the form and took it upstairs to the Gestapo liaison office in the station. *Still*, he thought, *they will be pleased enough with this one.*

Not often we get a registration number.

Chapter 25

Franz Hermann woke early on the Wednesday morning, checked on his mother, and then walked around the house he had grown up in, preoccupied with the thoughts that had played around in his head all night. He needed to move fast.

Once his mother was settled, he left the house through the back gate. From there it was a swift ten-minute walk to his own home. He explained to his wife what he was planning to do. Before leaving the house, he telephoned his sister and then the office, telling them he would be slightly late as he needed to see a client on his way in.

He rarely used his car these days, but the Daimler started at the third attempt and within two minutes he was back at his mother's house, parked by the back gate he had departed through barely half an hour previously. He told his mother that she would be coming to his house for a day or two, and then his sister would collect her and she would go and stay with her in Brandenburg for a week or so. Hopefully after that the nurse would return and everything would be back to normal. His mother was confused but there was no time to argue.

Once she was settled at his house, he left for work, but not before stopping once again at his mother's house, where he spent an hour checking again that there were no signs that anyone had been there for at least a day or two.

He made a point of leaving the house through the front door and boldly walking over to the house opposite, from where the lady carefully observed all the comings and goings in the street. As he approached her door he noticed the net curtains in the front window twitch. A moment later the door opened, a split second before he had knocked on it.

'Frau Werner, I just thought I'd let you know, in case anyone asks, that there will be no one at my mother's house for a few days. In fact, she has not been there since Sunday – she is staying with my wife and me. Her nurse has had to return to Bremerhaven suddenly – a death, I'm afraid. Her husband was in the navy, he died in the cause of the Reich.'

The woman was very grateful to be told. She told Franz that she had wondered about Frau Hermann because only the previous day she had seen the nurse leave the house with a man... and a young girl. They had been carrying a case and some other things which they put in the boot of a car parked outside the house, and had then driven off.

'Oh really?' He was trying his best to sound confused rather than shocked. 'Could you describe the man?'

With unerring accuracy she described Henri Hesse. Franz Hermann did his best to look none the wiser. 'As I say, Frau Werner, my mother has been staying with us since Sunday. I have no idea about this man; it is possible that he was taking her to Bremerhaven.'

'And what about the girl?'

'As far as I am aware no child has been in the house for a very long time. How old would you say she was?'

'Perhaps four or five, hard to say. I did not get a perfect view, you understand. She was such a slight thing.'

'And are you certain they came from my mother's house? Maybe they were just passers-by.'

She was certain. She just happened to be cleaning the windows at the time – by coincidence.

'I don't suppose you saw what car it was, by any chance?'

'I did, Herr Hermann: it was an Opel, a dark green one. And not only that: I even wrote down the registration number. But don't worry; I have given all the details to the police.'

–

315

When they left Würzburg they headed south. Henri announced that they would head south west, into the Black Forest.

'The Black Forest!'

'Yes, Rosa, the Black Forest.'

'You are crazy! Do you still read fairy tales?'

Sophia started to cry in the back seat. She didn't want to go into a forest. She was afraid of witches. Henri turned round and snapped at the little girl.

'I told you! There is no such thing as witches, or goblins. Or fairies, for that matter.'

Sophia's crying became louder.

'Don't shout at her: she's a little girl. She is frightened, and she is not the only one.'

'Trust me, Rosa, the Black Forest stretches down to the Swiss border – it almost goes as far as Basle!'

'I am aware of that, but do you really think we can just stroll over the border? Maybe the SS or whoever is guarding it will help us carry our cases?'

'Listen to me, Rosa: our Swiss papers are very good, far superior to the German ones. I am using my own papers, and I managed to get papers showing you are my wife and she is our daughter. They are hidden in the boot. When we get near the border we can use them, but we will need to abandon the car first.'

They stuck to the side roads and lanes and, at four thirty, emerged from a long lane onto the main road at Heilbronn, before taking the road to Pforzheim and from there into the Black Forest.

–

Edgar and Remington-Barber arrived in Zurich on the Wednesday afternoon and were met at the station by Rolf, who took them to another of their safe houses, an apartment above a bar on Predigerplatz. On the way up, he collected a bottle of whisky.

'I think it may be a bit early for that,' Edgar said once they were in the small apartment.

'Not when you hear what I'm about to tell you,' said the Austrian. 'I went to see Hedinger this morning, he had just heard from Reinhart. Apparently Henri *did* come to Reinhart's office at the Reichsbank yesterday morning, and collected the documents. Last night Hugo called Reinhart to ask whether Henri had been to his office and they arranged to meet up today, which they did at lunchtime. It seems that rather than heading for Tempelhof, Henri headed for Hugo's mother's house in Dahlem.'

In the shocked silence that followed Remington-Barber looked confused, as if he had not properly heard what Rolf had said. Edgar had heard clearly enough and looked furious.

'No!'

'Yes, I am afraid so. Hugo knows this because he was telephoning his mother's house all Tuesday afternoon, and when there was no reply he went round there after work. His mother was all alone; there was no sign of Rosa or her daughter. This morning he spoke to a neighbour who had seen Rosa leave the house along with a young girl and a man who seems to match Henri's description. They drove off in a green Opel.'

Edgar had declined the offer of whisky until this moment but now leaned over to the bottle and poured himself a measure that, in other circumstances, would be described as excessive. He drank most of it, repeating 'Jesus Christ' quite a few times.

'How on earth has he managed to get hold of a car?' Basil asked.

'Your guess is as good as mine, Basil. The fool probably stole it. Carry on, Rolf.'

'Reinhart is in a terrible state, according to Hedinger. He thinks the Gestapo are about to knock on his door, and of course Hugo is worried sick too, not least because when he was with Henry on Tuesday morning after they left the cathedral, they bumped into a colleague of his who is not only an active Nazi but also claims he had met Henry in Bern a year ago.'

Remington-Barber was watching Edgar very carefully, expecting him to explode at any moment, but he remained calm. Edgar drank the whisky remaining in his glass, removed his jacket, loosened his tie, and walked over to the window. 'Thank you, Rolf. By the sounds of it, Henry decided that rather than return to Switzerland as he'd been instructed, he'd turn his return journey into some kind of adventure: a rescue mission.' Edgar was speaking very calmly, as if everything he said had a perfect logic to it.

'But he is carrying the Rostock Report, Edgar. That is meant to be falling into the hands of our Soviet friends!'

Edgar turned from the window. 'Thank you, Basil, I had realised that.'

—

By March 1941, few people in Germany would have been foolish enough to accuse the Gestapo of inefficiency. When the deputy head of the Gestapo in Würzburg was informed by the garage owner about the 'odd' dark green Opel Super 6, he simply followed procedure. He sent a telex giving the details of the car to his regional headquarters, where, in turn, the duty officer also simply followed procedure and passed on the details of the car to the new central control room in Berlin. Around three o'clock that Wednesday afternoon an officer at the control room in the Gestapo headquarters in Prinz-Albrecht-Strasse was reviewing the 'alerts' received since his lunch break. When he spotted that a dark green Opel, registration number UTM 142, had been added to the watch list he thought there was something familiar about it, so he checked that morning's alerts. Sure enough, the Gestapo liaison office at Dahlem police station had passed on details of that same car: a woman who lived in Arno-Holz Strasse had observed a man, woman and a young girl leaving a neighbour's house and getting into the car. They seemed – according to the neighbour – 'nervous'.

The officer wrote up his notes: the car was seen in Berlin at noon on the Tuesday and just over twenty-four hours later was in Würzburg. It would certainly be worth putting this one out for national alert. He should have been less sceptical about this new system, maybe it was working after all. And thank heavens for frightened business owners and nosey neighbours. What would the Gestapo do without them?

At four o'clock that Wednesday afternoon, Officer Reinhard Goetz left the police station in Pforzheim for a routine patrol, briefed – among other things – to keep an eye out for the dark green Opel. 'Berlin is interested, and it was last seen in Würzburg,' he had been told, 'heading south – so you never know. It's the Gestapo who are interested, so keep your eyes peeled.'

The traffic policeman headed east on his BMW motorbike, and after a while changed direction – south into the Black Forest. At five o'clock he decided that he had earned his first cigarette break so, just before the small town of Tiefenbronn, he pulled into a clearing in an area where the forest started to become dense. He would be able to enjoy his cigarette in peace. But as he turned into the clearing, he noticed a car was already there. A dark green Opel Super 6. He parked his motorbike so that it blocked the path back to the road and walked over to check the registration number of the car.

Henri was on his own in the car when Goetz pulled into the clearing, Rosa having taken Sophia down into the trees to go to the toilet. He watched as the officer parked his bike and headed towards the car. Henri glanced to his left, but there was no sign of Rosa and Sophia. Watching the policeman all the time, he leaned over to the glove box in front of the passenger seat and removed the bundle wrapped in a thick grey cloth from behind the log book. The policeman smiled at him from a distance and Henri smiled back as the policeman moved in a wide arc to the front of the car. Henri held the bundle below the steering wheel and slowly unwrapped it. By now, the officer was at the front of the car, peering down at the registration plate. He looked up at Henri and made a motion with his fingers to unwind the window.

Officer Goetz bent down by the window, his face inches from Henri's.

'Is this your car?'

'Yes.'

'Where have you come from today?'

'Frankfurt.'

'And where are you going?'

'We are just out for a drive – to see the forest.'

'We?'

'My wife and daughter – they have gone to the toilet down there.'

'Have you been in Berlin in the past day or so?'

'Berlin? No, of course not!'

'Or Würzburg today?'

Henri hesitated for too long. He had no idea how to respond. 'Maybe… we stopped at a town for petrol. I don't know what it was called.'

'Right, get out of the car now, I want to check your papers.'

He noticed the policeman's right hand moving towards the holster on his hip and knew he had just seconds to act. The policeman stepped back as Henri opened the car door, and at that moment he heard the voices of Rosa and Sophia emerging from the trees. As the policeman glanced up in their direction Henri pushed the revolver into the policeman's stomach and fired. It was a muffled shot and the man staggered back before collapsing to the ground. He was still conscious and trying to remove his own pistol from its holster. Behind him, Henri could hear Rosa and Sophia screaming. He stepped towards the prone body of the policeman. A large pool of blood was forming under him and he tried to lift his own revolver, but did not seem to have the strength. Henri held his gun no more than a few inches from the man's head and pulled the trigger. In the ensuing seconds, his world slipped into slow motion.

He was aware of a chunk of the man's head flying away, of gore splattering all around him, of the sound of the shot bouncing off every tree in the forest and what appeared to be thousands of birds swarming in every direction, and then Rosa and Sophia standing in front of him, their mouths wide open in silent screams. By now he had sunk to his knees, the gun still in his hand, staring at the body of the third person he had killed.

For a time he could not hear anything other than the ringing of gunfire in his ears. When his hearing began to return, Rosa was shouting at him.

'What on earth have you done? You have killed a policeman!'

'Calm down and get Sophia into the car. We need to sort things out.'

Rosa bundled her daughter into the back of the Opel and came back over to him.

'He was looking for us. He checked the number plate and then asked whether we had been in Berlin or in Würzburg today. He told me to get out of the car and I could see he was reaching for his gun. He was distracted when he heard you and I knew I had to do something. We need to move him and his bike – quickly.'

It took the two of them ten minutes to carry the man's body as deep into the forest as they could manage, covering it with undergrowth. While Henri wheeled the motorbike far amongst the trees in another direction Rosa did her best to clean up the ground where the man had been shot.

'What do we do now?' They were both standing by the car, breathless and filthy.

'We need to get away from here as quickly as possible.'

'Even I could have worked that out. Which direction do we head in? Towards the Swiss border?'

'No, not now – it's too late, and he will be reported missing soon. We don't want to be stuck in the forest or even near the border when that happens.'

'So where do we go then?'

'We'll go to Stuttgart and ditch the car.'

Rosa sniffed. 'And what do you propose we do then – check into the best hotel in Stuttgart?'

'Something like that – yes.'

Chapter 26

Munich, Stuttgart, March-April 1941

'Basil, without in any way wishing to appear rude, may I suggest that you pause, take a deep breath and then start again?'

It was the evening of Friday the 28th of March and Edgar and Basil Remington-Barber had been stuck in the apartment above the bar in Zurich since Wednesday. They had heard nothing further about Henri since Hedinger's report that he had last been seen in Berlin on Tuesday. The circumstantial evidence that he had possibly left Berlin with Rosa and her daughter was bad enough: the fact that he had the Rostock Report with him rather than it being in Soviet hands was disastrous.

Now, Basil had received a phone call from the embassy in Bern – *some news.*

'I am sorry, Edgar; the tension does rather get to one at times. They're in Stuttgart.'

'Who?'

'Henry, Rosa and her daughter.'

'Jesus Christ: I knew it. What on earth does he imagine he is up to? Is he safe?'

'For the time being, yes, although I would say that considering their circumstances, "safe" is a very relative word.'

'And how do we know this?'

'You remember Milo, the Night Manager at the Hotel Victoria? Well, we've heard from her. She contacts us in code by telex to a travel agent in Bern, one with which we have an understanding. It is a safe form of communication – a hotel confirming bookings with a travel agent, terribly routine stuff – if a bit cumbersome. It rather relies on the travel agent passing the messages on to us quickly though, and although Milo sent the telex on Thursday night, the travel agent did not see it until this morning, and for reasons that are not entirely apparent, waited until this afternoon before informing my office at the embassy. They in turn seem to have taken their time before thinking of letting me know. I shall be having harsh words with them about this, I can assure you.'

'So how does Milo know about them?'

'Because they are in her hotel, Edgar.'

–

By the time they left the Black Forest it was five thirty on the Wednesday evening and it took them another two and a quarter hours to reach Stuttgart. It was a quarter to eight when Henri parked at the northern end of the Schlossplatz, as near as he dared get to the railway station. As they parked, a squadron of Heinkel fighters flew low overhead.

'You are sure this is going to work?' Rosa asked him, not for the first time since he had explained his plan.

'No, Rosa, I am not sure. But it is our best hope. They are bound to find the car, and I just hope they will assume that, as it is so close to the railway station, we must have caught a train, and with any luck they will look for people leaving Stuttgart rather than staying in it. And when we walk away from the car, we will look like travellers who have just arrived by train.'

It took them five minutes to walk from the Schlossplatz to the Hotel Victoria, Rosa carrying an exhausted Sophia. Instead of going to the main entrance on Friedrichstrasse they walked into Keplerstrasse at the side of the hotel. It was quiet, the night was drawing in and there was no movement in the street. In a room above them in the hotel – possibly the restaurant – they could hear people laughing and glasses clinking. Henri moved Rosa and Sophia into a concealed doorway.

'Wait here and keep an eye on me. If I can get the door open, watch out for my signal and then hurry along but don't run.'

'And if you can't?'

Henri hesitated. 'Don't worry. I'll think of something.'

Keeping as close to the wall as possible, Henri edged towards the door that led to the basement of the hotel. He had last been there with Milo on the morning of his journey to Essen the previous year. He had no idea whether Milo was still working at the hotel. For all he knew, she could have been arrested, but it was the only plan he could think of.

The door to the basement was stiff, but started to give after a few pushes, and when he used his shoulder it sprung open. He descended the steep concrete steps: the basement was warm and dimly lit. Beyond the machinery he could make out a laundry area. After that was a door that he seemed to remember led to the stairs into the main part of the hotel. There was no sign of anyone down there.

He climbed back up the stairs and gestured for Rosa and Sophia to join him. Once they were safely in, he shut the door and whispered to Rosa.

'We will find somewhere in here to hide, and after midnight I will go up into the hotel and see if she is there.'

'You say this woman is on duty at night?'

'Most nights, but not every night. But I have to tell you, Rosa, that it is nearly a year since I saw her, I cannot even be sure she is still here.'

They found a corner of the basement that was dark and warm, and huddled together. They gave what little food they had left to Sophia and soon she fell asleep in her mother's arms. At midnight, Henri decided to go up into the hotel.

'How do I look?'

'Terrible! Here, let me see what I can do.' Tenderly, Rosa wiped his face and brushed his clothes down and took a brush from her handbag to tidy his hair.

'That's better. You have your Swiss papers with you?'

Henri patted his jacket pocket. A few minutes later he was on the ground floor of the hotel and walking across the deserted foyer to the reception desk, where a young night porter was on his own.

'Can I help you, sir?'

'Yes, I had some dealings before with a most helpful manager. I wondered if she is on duty tonight? Her name was Katharina Hoch, I seem to recall.'

'Fraulein Hoch? Indeed she is, sir. May I ask your name?'

'Herr Hesse – from Switzerland.'

'Thank you, sir. And which room are you in?'

'I beg your pardon?'

'Which room shall I tell her you are staying in?'

Before he could think of what to say, Katharina Hoch emerged from the office behind the reception desk. It was a good job the night porter had his back to her, because her eyes were wide open in fear as she saw Henri. She steadied herself against the doorframe and wiped her brow before regaining her composure.

'Herr Hesse! How good to have such an honoured guest back with us. Please do come through to my office.'

She took Henri down a corridor at the back of the reception and into another office.

'What the hell are you doing here?' she said after making sure no one had followed them.

'Hiding.'

She stared at him for a minute, slowly shaking her head.

'Well you can't. It is too dangerous. Everything is so dangerous now that we do nothing other than pass the odd bit of information on to Bern. As for helping agents and hiding people, that is a thing of the past. You have no idea how much of a risk it is for you to be here. You must leave.'

'I can't.'

'You have to, please. Since you were last here, the situation has got so much worse. Everyone informs on everyone else as a matter of course.'

'But I cannot leave.'

'You have to, I told you. I can give you some money and something to eat and then you go. How did you get in here?'

'Through the basement, you remember you took me there the morning I went to Essen?'

'You must leave that way then.'

'I can't, I'm not on my own. And I killed a policeman today.'

–

Katharina Hoch said nothing as Henri told his story. By the time he had finished she was running her fingers through her long hair. He noticed that she was now wearing a bright red lipstick, which managed to make her lips look less sensuous than before.

'I was foolish enough to imagine that we may be safe,' she said.

'What do you mean?'

'My brother, Dieter – you remember you used his identity when you travelled to Essen – he even joined the Nazi Party after you left, the situation has become that bad. We thought that may help us if there was any suspicion. Now what happens? You kill a policeman and turn up here with two Jews. What do you expect us to do?'

'Help us get to Switzerland. I was hoping to drive to the border, but I cannot use the car now. It is too risky. They are obviously looking for it.'

'And how do you propose to get to the border? They'll be searching for you: hide in the basement tonight, but no longer than that please. I will have to send a message to Bern, but I will wait until tomorrow night. I must talk to Dieter first.'

'Why are you sending a message to Bern?'

'At least we can let Basil know that you're here. He may have an idea.'

–

'Is the only way we can communicate with Milo through this travel agent?'

Edgar was chain smoking now and sitting close to Basil Remington-Barber, as if he were interrogating him.

'It is not the only way, Edgar, but it is by far the safest way. The problem is that it is now Friday evening and the travel agent does not reopen until Monday morning. In the meantime, we could send a telex direct to the hotel, but that is not without risks. At least we know that Milo is on duty tonight and over the weekend so the chances are that she will be the only person to see it.'

Edgar stood up and walked slowly around the room, a trail of cigarette smoke following in his wake.

'The first time I met Henry was in August 1939, at Croydon Airport. I had to remind myself that appearances can be deceptive, that he may have looked and even acted as something of a nonentity, but there was clearly more to him than that. I recall saying that he was actually rather impressive. No hint whatsoever who he was really working for and there was a danger that we could underestimate him. God knows what we're to make of him now.'

Remington-Barber started to speak but Edgar held up his hand. *I'm thinking.*

'What telex machine would you use from this end?'

'One of Rolf's contacts works in a hotel here in Zurich. We can get a message out through her tonight. It's open I'm afraid, but needs must.'

Another pause while Edgar paced the room, deep in thought.

'You ready to write this down, Basil? Tell Milo to tell Henry that he is to leave Stuttgart and get back to Switzerland as soon as possible. He is to come on his own. Under no circumstances should he attempt to bring that woman and her daughter out with him. He's already been told that we're not the Red Cross. That last bit is not part of the message.'

–

Katharina Hoch had come down to the basement in the early hours of the Thursday morning. It was not only for reasons of humanity that she realised she could not turn the three of them out onto the street. It was likely that they would be arrested within minutes, and one of them was bound to say something about the hotel. She realised she would have to hide them until at least she had spoken with Dieter.

At the back of the basement was a narrow corridor, no more than five feet high. It led to a room behind the main boilers and had been used to store equipment. Now the room was empty and never visited. She led the three of them into it. The room was dark, with no lights, a rancid smell and the scuttling sound of mice. Its saving grace was that it was warm and safe, for the time being. Once they were in the room she brought down blankets and some food, and told them to remain there until her next visit – she would come down when it was safe.

It was three thirty on the Saturday morning before they next saw her, holding a torch and carrying a bag with some food in it. She asked Henri to come out with her.

'I cannot stay long. There is a problem with the plumbing on one of the floors and I really need to be around to supervise things.'

They were at the end of the corridor, back in the main part of the basement.

'We have heard from Bern. You are under orders to return to Switzerland.'

'Good! I told you that is where we want to go.'

'Just you: the message is very clear. You are to go back on your own.'

'What – and leave them? Of course not, they're coming with me. What did your brother have to say?'

'According to him, the police at the railway station are searching for all of you. They have your names, but no photographs, which I suppose is something. They found the car naturally, and the fact that it was so close to the station means that they realise you may not be in the city, but that is not the point: as soon as you leave the hotel you will be at risk. The only chance you have is for Dieter to drive you south of the city on Sunday, which is his day off. He may be able to get hold of a van from the railways, so that ought to be safe. He will try and get you as close to the border as possible. You stand a chance if you try and cross at night: alone.'

'But I told you, I'm not going anywhere without Rosa and Sophia.'

–

The next time Edgar and Remington-Barber heard from Stuttgart was on the morning of Monday 31st March. Milo had sent a telex

328

overnight to the travel agents in Bern and this time the message was passed on promptly.

'According to Milo,' said Remington-Barber, following Edgar as he paced around the room, 'Henry absolutely refuses to leave the basement of the hotel without the others. Dieter turned up on Sunday with his van, but Henry would not budge. Milo and her brother are at their wits end. They know that they can't turf them out of the basement because the three of them together are bound to be caught within minutes. But she's convinced it's only a matter of time before someone finds them. If the Gestapo haven't found them elsewhere they'll assume they must still be in Stuttgart, and she's worried they will then search the hotel.'

'Tell her to hold on then. Keep them in the basement and we'll sort something out. Do you still have that cache of German identities?'

'Yes, but I'm down to three, possibly four that I would say I could totally trust.'

'Where are they?'

'In the safe in Bern.'

'Better get them sent here as soon as possible. What about good Swiss identities, do you have many of those?'

'A couple that are watertight, Edgar. I'll get them to send those.'

'How much do you trust Rolf, Basil?'

'I've told you Edgar, he's one of our best, no question about it: type of chap you'd want to open the batting with.'

That's Basil's world, thought Edgar. *Judging people on whether you trust them enough to open the batting with you.*

'And on the train you mentioned something about him having been across the border before – into Germany, I mean.'

'Yes, late thirty-nine it must have been. We needed to get some cash to an agent I was running in Freiburg. We sent Rolf in over the mountains and he came back the same way.'

'You'd better get him up here.'

When Rolf joined them, Edgar gestured for him to sit down. Edgar leaned back in the sofa, opposite the Austrian. Rolf was only slightly shorter than Edgar. With his blond hair and blue eyes he was far closer to the Aryan ideal than Adolf Hitler, his fellow Austrian. Rolf's undoubted good looks were marred by one characteristic though: large, protruding ears which gave him a slightly comical appearance. But he was slim and sprightly-looking, the kind of person who was always moving, but in an energetic rather than nervous manner. He invariably had a pleasant smile on his face, as he did now.

'I understand that you are familiar with Germany, Rolf?'

'I have been many times, though of course not recently.'

'And, excuse me asking, but do you sound like an Austrian when you are there?'

'A good question: I can sound like a Swiss when I am in Switzerland, an Austrian in Austria and a German when I am in Germany. I try to suppress my Viennese accent in Germany, it is too distinctive. Why do you ask?'

'Because you and I are going to Germany.'

To Edgar's surprise, he noticed that Rolf's smile was wider than before.

–

They crossed the border late on the morning of Tuesday 1st April. The German identity papers had arrived from Bern late on the Monday afternoon, and yet another of Rolf's contacts had worked through the night to turn Edgar and Rolf into impeccable German citizens. Rolf Eder had become Ludwig Kühn, an engineer from Landshut, just north of Munich. Edgar became Karl Albrecht, a businessman from Hanover, a city he was not only familiar with after having spent a year at university there, but for which he could also manage the correct accent.

'I hope this chap of yours is reliable,' said Edgar as they drove towards Lake Konstanz from Zurich. Both Rolf and Basil Remington-Barber looked at each other, unsure of who should answer.

'All I can say that he has not let us down so far,' said Remington-Barber.

'And how many times have you used him?'

A long pause. 'Once.'

Edgar said nothing but slowly shook his head.

'At short notice he is our only option,' said Rolf. 'We are paying him a lot of money and he is running an enormous risk.'

They pulled off the main road between the small towns of Rorschach and Arbon and, after a while, the track they had turned onto petered to a dead end and they found themselves surrounded by trees, with the lake just visible through them. They waited for five minutes, and once Remington-Barber was certain that they had not been followed nor were being watched, they set off through the small wood. When they emerged they found themselves at a small jetty, with the black water of the lake lapping high against it and the shorelines of both Germany and Austria clearly visible. Rolf removed a pair of binoculars from his jacket and scanned the lake. He handed the binoculars to Edgar and pointed to a tiny shape in the middle of the water.

'That's her. She will be with us in maybe fifteen minutes. We will wait in the trees until she arrives.'

Twenty minutes later the fishing boat had pulled up alongside the jetty and the three men were scrambling across it. The skipper had a deeply tanned face and a heavy moustache and snatched the thick envelope that Remington-Barber handed to him. He gestured for Rolf and Edgar to go below deck, where despite the noise of the idling engine they could hear the conversation going on above them.

'Don't worry, Paul, it's all here: Swiss Francs and Reichsmarks.'

'And those two – they're not going to cause trouble, are they?'

'Of course not.'

'And promise me they're not Jews.'

'Are you crazy, Paul? What Jews would want to escape *from* Switzerland *into* Germany?'

'Ones who have money hidden there. They still control many businesses you know.'

'No, Paul, I promise you they are not Jews. You had better get a move on. Your brother knows what to do? Don't forget that is why we are paying you so much. It's for the whole journey.'

'Don't worry, he knows what to do. You are getting us on the cheap. I am thinking of putting my price up.'

As the boat pulled away from the jetty and accelerated into the main body of the lake Edgar realised that they had not properly said goodbye to Remington-Barber, which was probably just as well. Sending agents into enemy territory was always the worst part of the job, not so different from pronouncing a death sentence.

They remained in the hold throughout the crossing. They briefly caught sight of the two other crew members, a boy who looked as if he should be in school and a giant of a man who had a permanent grin and seemed to communicate through sign language.

'We have been lucky so far today,' said the skipper when he came down into the hold for a minute. 'The Swiss and German patrol boats are all near Konstanz – there's been some row there about fishing rights at the other end of the lake. The Austrians are lazy: they are just putting out one patrol boat a day at the moment and they seem to prefer to stay around Bregenz. There's a small landing just outside Nonnenhorn – Johannes will be waiting there with his truck. If it's all clear, we will pull in there. If not, we'll continue into port and we'll have to get you off the boat later on, when it is quiet.'

On the first pass there must have been a signal that all was well, because the boat suddenly cut its speed and turned sharply to the shore. Once the boat was tied up, they were called up to the deck, where the skipper had been joined by a man who looked like his identical twin. *Johannes*. Some quick shaking of hands and they were hurried along to a narrow road and into the back of a van waiting there. There was just enough room for the two of them between the crates of fish. Once he was in the driving seat, Johannes turned round.

'I can't pretend this will be anything other than a very uncomfortable journey, but I will get you to Munich in good time, don't worry. And we should be fine if we are stopped: all my papers are in order. You're staying at the Hotel Bayerischer Hof, yes?'

'I am,' said Edgar. 'My friend is staying at a smaller one by the station.'

'That is good.'

'Why is that?' asked Rolf.

'Because I am delivering the fish to the Bayerischer Hof!'

They arrived in Munich just before five o'clock. During the journey Edgar and Rolf talked through their plans. They would have no contact with each other while they were in Munich or on the journey to Stuttgart, so if one was caught there was a chance the other would make it.

'I am not terribly sure why we are taking this route to Stuttgart: it's hardly the most direct way,' said Rolf.

'True, but when we arrive in Stuttgart it will be as travellers from Munich. That should make us far less suspicious.'

Johannes dropped both Rolf and Edgar off in a side street by Munich Hauptbahnhof. It was only round the corner from the station hotel where the Austrian would be staying, and for Edgar the ten-minute walk to the Bayerischer Hof on Promenadeplatz not only meant that he would not be seen getting out of a van delivering fish at the hotel, but also gave him the opportunity for a bit of fresh air and the chance for the smell of the van to evaporate.

On the Wednesday morning both men were on the eight o'clock train from Munich to Stuttgart. They had stood close to each other on the concourse at the Hauptbahnhof, as arranged, but did not exchange a word nor make eye contact. Both men were carrying their small suitcases in their left hands and holding their hats in their right hands, the signal that all was well. They purchased seats at opposite ends of the same carriage so that they could spot if there were any problems, but the journey was straightforward. Their papers were checked as they boarded the train and then once during the journey just after the stop at Augsburg, but each time they seemed more bothered that their tickets were in order.

Both men had bought copies of that day's edition of the *Münchner Neueste Nachrichten* and they made sure they were prominent as they arrived in Stuttgart, where security was far more noticeable. Their papers were searched but neither man was pulled out of the queue for their bags to be searched. They took different routes to the Hotel Victoria, Edgar arriving fifteen minutes after Rolf.

Milo had reserved rooms for the two men close to each other on the second floor and just across the corridor from the back stairs that led down to the hotel basement. Hidden in an envelope taped to the underside of the wardrobe in Rolf's room was a key to the basement and a note as to where to find Henry, Rosa and Sophia. It was one thirty in the afternoon when Edgar reckoned it would be safe to knock on Rolf's door. The two men stood in the tiny bathroom, the tap running to mask their voices.

'You have the key?'

Rolf dangled it in front of Edgar. 'She says that they are hiding in a room at the rear of the basement – here, she has drawn a sketch.' Rolf handed the piece of paper to Edgar.

'I don't like the fact that she took such a risk, putting it down on paper like that.'

'What else was she meant to do? You need to decide. When do we go down? And do we go together?'

'Just let me have another look at that note.' Edgar read it carefully, nodding his head, formulating a plan. 'She says that she comes on duty at eleven o'clock tonight and that we're to wait in our rooms. She will come up to us between half eleven and midnight, apparently. I don't think that we can risk waiting until then, they've been here almost a week already. You have Henry's new identity papers?'

Rolf gestured towards his small suitcase.

'Good. Let me tell you the plan, and then you go down and bring Hunter up here.'

Rolf was impressed with Edgar's plan. It was not without considerable risk and would require nerves of steel, but it was clever. He then left the room and went down the back stairs that led down to the basement. It took him ten minutes to check that the basement was clear and then navigate his way through to the room hidden behind the boiler. When Rosa heard him she cried out in fear.

'It's me, Henri. Rolf. You remember me from Zurich?'

Henri clasped Rolf by the arms.

'It is all right, Rosa – don't cry, Sophia. Rolf is a friend. He's come to rescue us. Are you here on your own, Rolf? When can we leave?'

Rosa had lit a candle in the room and Rolf glanced around, it was cramped, with rusty equipment against the walls and blankets and an old mattress on the floor. The heat was oppressive and there was a foul smell.

'Yes, we have a plan, don't worry. First you need to come with me, Henri, just for few minutes – don't worry, Rosa, he won't be long.'

–

There was only enough space for the three men to stand more or less shoulder to shoulder in Rolf's bathroom, which meant that Edgar and Henri were facing each other. When Edgar finally spoke, after a minute of looking Henri up and down with the makings of a sneer on his face, his voice could only just be heard above the noise of the tap which had been turned on to cover the sound of their voices.

'As much as I am a reasonable man, Henry, and am prepared to give you the benefit of the doubt, I struggle to see how you can possibly manage to come up with a satisfactory explanation for all this.'

'For all what, Edgar?'

Edgar inched closer to Henri, clenching and unclenching his fists as he did so.

'For what? You were supposed to fly from Berlin to Zurich last Tuesday morning and then meet myself and Basil and in Geneva. What happened?'

An embarrassed smile on Henri's face and a shrug of the shoulders. *What can I say?*

'I bent the rules a little bit and decided to rescue Rosa and Sophia at the same time. I thought that if I did so then Gunter Reinhart would be better disposed towards us and provide us with more intelligence.'

'Oh really, Henry? I have never regarded myself as particularly naïve, but I would be bordering on the certifiable if I were to believe a word of what you are saying. You've set yourself up as some knight in shining armour rescuing a damsel in distress—'

'I thought there would be no harm…' Henri shifted uncomfortably, his face now a bright red.

'No harm?' Edgar's voice was raised for a split second before Rolf nudged him. 'You have seriously jeopardised this mission, the purpose of which – in case you have forgotten – was to collect a document from Hugo and bring it back to Switzerland. Do you have that document?'

Henri coughed and stepped away as far as he was able to from Edgar.

'I am afraid not. I know this is going to sound dreadful, Edgar, but after we left Berlin it dawned on me that there was a possibility that we could be caught. I thought that the worst thing that could then happen, from a British point of view, was that the documents would fall into German hands, so I burnt them.'

'Where?'

'In some woods where we were hiding on the Tuesday night. I am so sorry, I know that I failed in my mission, but I felt that the alternative would be far worse.'

Edgar turned around, facing the frosted window. 'Jesus Christ,' was all that he could say and repeated those words a few times.

'We need to get you back to Switzerland as soon as possible. We cannot risk you being caught by the Germans, as tempting as that may be in some respects. Heaven knows what you'd say to the Gestapo—'

'Now, look here Edgar—'

'No, you look here, Hunter. Rolf and I are putting our lives at risk by attempting to rescue you. The very least that you can do is co-operate, you understand?'

'I will, but I am not leaving without Rosa and Sophia. I am adamant about that.'

'So I am told, and we understand that. We will get them out too. Don't worry, we have it all worked out. We have very good German identity papers for you: your photo and everything. We also have new Swiss papers for you, as you can hardly re-enter as Henri Hesse – not after all the fuss you've caused.'

'But what about Rosa and Sophia?'

'We have papers for them too, but you cannot leave together as they will be looking for the three of you together. If you travel separately it will be less conspicuous. You will leave first with Rolf and take the train to Switzerland: your documentation is good enough to risk that kind of journey. We cannot risk Rosa and Sophia being stopped and questioned, so I will drive them to the border myself.'

Henri stared at Edgar, his face full of scepticism.

'Really? You are sure this will work?'

'It's the best way, Henry, believe me. Dieter is sorting out the car: we will be able to hide Sophia under the rear seat and Rosa and I will look like a married couple.'

'But how can I be sure that you will follow on?'

'I am hardly likely to stay on in Stuttgart, am I?'

'You promise me this, Edgar – on your life: that you'll bring Rosa and Sophia out with you?'

'I promise you, Henry. You can trust me. Now we need to move fast. You and Rolf must leave this afternoon. Dieter will bring the car tonight so I will follow with Rosa and Sophia in the morning. All being well, we will meet up in Zurich either tomorrow or Friday.'

Rolf accompanied Henri back to the basement, where he explained the situation to Rosa. He could tell that Henri was uneasy, he had his head in his hands and kept shaking his hands. When Rolf had explained everything, Henri turned to Rosa.

'What do you think?'

'I am not sure what you mean?'

'Should we go along with this? Do as they ask?'

'But what else can we possibly do? They are right: the three of us will never make it anywhere near the border on our own, let alone cross it. Nor can we stay here: it's only a matter of time before we'd be caught. We have to do as your friends suggest.'

There was a brief goodbye, hurried along by Rolf. A few minutes later they were back in Rolf's bedroom.

'It's a quarter to three,' said Edgar. 'There is a train from Stuttgart leaving at three thirty, the last one to cross the border tonight. You and Rolf will catch it, but first you need to have a shave and a bath and

337

get changed: you look a mess and smell like you haven't had a proper wash for days. You'd better get undressed in here while Rolf runs the bath for you.'

As soon as Henri went into the bathroom Edgar whispered urgently to Rolf. The Austrian positioned himself by the bathroom door while Edgar frantically searched Henri's clothes and case. It took him five minutes before he found what he was looking for. He then meticulously replaced everything as he had found it and beckoned Rolf over. Through the bathroom door they could hear the sound of splashing. Edgar was holding three sheets of brown paper with German type on them.

'The Rostock Report!' he announced, waving it triumphantly at Rolf.

'Are you sure?' Rolf was close to Edgar, the pair whispering to each other.

'Of course I'm sure: I saw it in London,' replied Edgar.

'Where was it?'

Edgar was holding a pair of thick, dark trousers. 'Inside the lining, look – that's why I made him get undressed in here, so that I could check his clothes.'

'But how come you knew he had it? He told us he'd burnt it.'

'Keep your voice down, Rolf. When I was talking with Basil the other day I told him how one could very easily underestimate Henry. I simply did not believe what he told us and my instinct was correct. He may have embarked on this mad mission to rescue Rosa and Sophia but, despite everything, he can't risk upsetting his Soviet masters by not delivering this report back to them. All the more reason to get him back to Zurich as soon as possible.'

Through the bathroom door came the sloshing noise of Henri getting out of the bath.

'Are you going to be long?' Edgar asked, as he carefully replaced the envelope.

'Five minutes, no more, I promise.'

'And what do I do with him when we get to Zurich?' Rolf whispered.

'Check him into a hotel, one of the smaller ones around the station. Tell him to stay there while you make contact with Basil. Then leave him, make sure he thinks he is on his own for a while. Have one of your boys keep a watch, but it is vital that he is left alone for a while.'

'Not long now – mind if I use both towels?'

Edgar assured him he could use as many towels as he wished.

Chapter 27

Stuttgart, April 1941

From the window of his room Edgar had watched Rolf and Henri as they left the hotel, both seemingly relaxed and chatting away. They gave the appearance of amicable colleagues. A small group of men in the black uniform of the Waffen SS walked towards them, but there was no hesitation in the step of either Rolf or Henri, and the SS men politely parted to allow the two men to walk on through. Edgar continued to watch as the pair walked down Friedrichstrasse towards the station, eventually disappearing as dots into the distance.

He would have to remain in the hotel that evening. Rolf – Ludwig Kühn – had explained to the receptionist that he had been called back to Landshut. 'So inconvenient, I am so sorry. I insist on paying for my room.'

Edgar had been discreetly watching this as he scanned a nearby notice board. The receptionist had insisted this was not necessary – 'These things happen, Herr Kühn,' – but Edgar knew that if two guests checked out within hours of their arrival it could arouse suspicion. In any event, he needed to see Milo. He would stay the night and slip away in the morning: ahead of the hounds, with any luck.

Edgar ate early in the hotel's ornate but largely deserted dining room and retired to his room. He would wait until Milo came on duty at eleven o'clock.

–

Because he had been in his room on the second floor since eight o'clock, Edgar was unaware of what was happening below him.

The police had turned up at nine: the manager was asked to gather all the staff together in an office. They wanted to know if a family of three – a man and woman in their mid-to-late thirties and a girl, perhaps four or five years old – had been staying at the hotel. Unfortunately, the police told them, they had no photographs, but they had names and descriptions.

'Please think *carefully*. Remember they may have used different names. The man is Swiss; the woman and child are Jews. It is possible that they may have split up.'

They passed around the sheets with the names and descriptions on them. No one recognised them. But at the back of the room was the young night porter, who had just come on duty. He stared at the sheet; gripping it tight in the hope that no one would notice his hands shaking. He looked up and around the room then back again at the sheet of paper, hoping he had misread the name on it the first time he had looked at it. It was still there: 'Henri Hesse, Switzerland.' And then the description: unmistakably that of the man who had turned up the week before asking to see Katharina Hoch.

Even though he had said nothing about it at the time, the night porter had thought there was something odd about the situation. When Fraulein Hoch had taken the man to an office well away from reception, he had checked the register. There was no one staying at the hotel called Hesse. It was not his place to say anything to Fraulein Hoch and he had thought no more of it, until now.

'You are all certain then that you have not come across these people – these criminals?' The police officer in charge looked as if he were in a hurry. 'We need to move on, you are not the only hotel in Stuttgart, you know. Look once more, but remember: withholding information from the authorities is a serious crime.'

At the end of the month he was leaving the hotel, the time had come for him to join the army. What had his father told him, even before the war started? 'Keep your head down. Don't get involved. Don't express an opinion, never volunteer, and do as you're told.'

That was his instinct, to keep his head down and say nothing. But then what would happen if they caught this man and they found out that he had spoken to him that night and he had failed to mention it? *A serious crime.*

The police decided they were going to get no help from the staff at the Victoria and told them to go back to work. One of the officers brushed past him as he left the room.

'Please could I have a word with you, sir?'

'Is it in connection with this matter?'

'I think it may be, yes.'

The officer called one of his colleagues over and the two policemen shepherded the night porter to a quiet corner. '*Tell us.*'

'I am not sure how relevant this is, sir, but a week ago I was on duty at reception. Sometime after midnight a gentleman appeared at reception and asked if Katharina Hoch was on duty.'

'Who is she?'

'She is the night manager.'

'He said his name was Hesse, from Switzerland. I asked him which room he was staying in but before he had a chance to tell me, Fraulein Hoch appeared from her office behind me and greeted the man, who she appeared to know. She then took him down a private corridor to an office well away from reception.'

'Which day was this?'

'Wednesday, so really it was in the early hours of Thursday morning.'

'You have seen the description of the man – Hesse – does it match that of the man you saw?'

'It does, sir, very much so.'

'And what happened after that?'

'He must have been with Fraulein Hoch for a while – I didn't see him again.'

'And is he still staying here?'

'Well, that's the odd thing, sir. I checked his name on the hotel register and there was no record of him staying here that night.'

The officer signalled to the other policemen with him to wait. He spoke kindly to the young night porter, who looked terrified. 'We're not the Gestapo, you know!'

'And Fraulein Hoch – when is she next on duty?'

The young night porter glanced at his watch, the one his grandparents had bought him for his last birthday. 'In just over an hour, sir – at eleven o'clock.'

–

Edgar spent the evening in his room, alternating between resting on the bed and almost relaxing to getting up and pacing around the room, peeking out into the street through the thick curtains or pausing by the door in case anyone may be approaching.

He became aware of a lot of activity below his window, cars pulling up and people entering the hotel and a fair amount of talking. It was, he decided, what one might expect from a busy city centre hotel and in any case, he was not minded to look out of the window and draw attention to himself. He would wait in his room until Milo came up, as she had promised. He waited patiently, even when eleven thirty had gone, with midnight soon after. *Who knows how busy she may be? Another half hour.*

There was no sign of her by half past midnight, when he allowed himself to open his door as quietly as possible and glance up and down the corridor. It was empty and there was no note on the floor. An hour late was worrying, there was no denying that. Edgar stood with his back to the door, surveying the room. He tried to imagine how it would look to someone coming in to question him. It looked ordinary enough, but he was more concerned about his false identity. The papers for Karl Albrecht from Hanover were good enough, but he was not sure how long he could sustain his story if anyone suspected him.

By one o'clock he decided to go down to reception. He would ask if they had any aspirin for a headache. *For some reason I was unable to get through on the telephone!*

He took the main stairs down to the reception. He opened the glass doors onto the landing before the final flight of stairs swept down to the entrance lobby, only to be pushed aside by a uniformed policeman running past him.

Edgar paused and then edged slowly towards the staircase, just able to see into the lobby while still hidden in the shadows of the landing. The area was crowded with police and Gestapo, and in the middle of them was a young woman. She towered above a man in an ill-fitting suit was standing in front of her.

'Fraulein Hoch, you have spent two hours refusing to give a satisfactory explanation as to why this Herr Hesse came to see you.'

'Look, I keep telling you, why do you not believe me?' She sounded annoyed – exactly as Edgar would expect her to do in such circumstances. *Don't come across as defensive: the more aggressive you are the more they may believe you.* 'Look, I keep telling you, I know nothing about him. He was a guest who had stayed here last year. He asked to see me because he said he was staying at the Marquardt on Schlossplatz and wanted to see if he could transfer here, but he did not want to make a fuss about it.'

'At midnight?' The short man in the ill-fitting suit looked confused, unsure whether to believe her. Edgar took a step back into the shadows. He could now hardly see what was going on, but he could still hear clearly.

'Very well,' said the man. 'Remain in your office Fraulein Hoch. Oberg, seal the hotel; make sure there are guards on every floor. No one comes in or out. First thing in the morning we shall thoroughly search this place.'

–

Edgar crept back to his room on the second floor. They clearly knew that Hunter had been at the hotel, but he had no idea how they knew. Had he and Rolf been arrested before they reached the border? If that was the case then it was possible that Hunter would not only have told them about being in the Hotel Victoria in Stuttgart but would also have said something about him – but then if that was the case, they would be looking for him now rather than waiting for the morning.

Edgar went into the bathroom, undressed, and washed his face in cold water. Speculating on what may have happened merely served to stop him thinking about more important matters like what to do now.

344

He changed into his pyjamas and pulled back the sheets and blankets on the bed – if they did come to his room it must look as if he had been asleep.

There was no question now of his going down to the basement, even to warn Rosa. What would be the point? Unless Rosa had heard the commotion and decided to escape they would be found in the morning.

Edgar dozed off in a series of fifteen- and twenty-minute spells during the night. Each time he woke up, he lay still in bed, listening for any hint of a sound. Then he would roll slowly out of the bed and crawl along the floor to the door. By lying flat he was able to look through the inch high gap at the bottom, but not once could he see anyone near his room.

At six o'clock he decided he could not risk dozing off again. Seven o'clock, he decided, was the earliest he could risk leaving the hotel without it looking too early. He checked his small case. There was nothing in it to give him away, apart from his Swiss papers, and they were so skilfully concealed in the lining that they would pass any routine search.

At seven o'clock he did a final check of the room, emptied all of his pockets, looked over his papers for what felt like the one hundredth time, and left the room.

The lobby was beginning to fill with police and Gestapo: it was obvious that the search had begun. All around was the sound of doors slamming and boots moving heavily across corridors and rooms.

'Can I help you, sir?' It was a manager, his face pale and drawn, his fingers nervously intertwining with each other. Next to him was another man, his arms folded, looking Edgar up and down.

'Yes,' said Edgar, placing his room key on the desk in front of the manager. 'I wish to check out, please. If I may settle my account?'

'Most certainly, sir,' said the manager, scanning the hotel register. 'Your name, please?'

'Karl Albrecht.'

'From Hanover, I see.'

'Are you returning to Hanover now?' It was the other man. As he spoke he stepped forward, holding out his Gestapo identity badge. 'Your papers, please.'

Edgar handed over the papers for Karl Albrecht. The Gestapo man looked at them carefully. 'Please can you confirm your address?' Edgar confirmed it, hoping that he was not overplaying his Hanoverian accent. The other man looked over to the register, which the manager was still holding. 'Just a short visit then?'

'Indeed. Thankfully my business here went well.' *He is now going to ask me about this business.* Edgar glanced at his watch.

'Are you in a hurry, Herr Albrecht?'

'Well, there is a train to Frankfurt at seven thirty which I would like to catch, if at all possible; it has a good connection to Hanover.'

'Indeed. Come over here and I will examine and search your case.'

Edgar moved over to a table by the side of the reception desk. As he placed his case on the table there was a noise to his right, beyond the reception desk. It was just a shout at first, followed by the commotion of people running and then more shouting.

'Quick, we've found them!' It was a policeman, running past reception. The Gestapo man who was about to search Edgar looked up and around, clearly eager to join in. He ruffled through Edgar's suitcase, looking up for most of the time in the direction that the noise was coming from.

'Empty your pockets, quickly.' Edgar placed the contents of his pockets on the table. The man shuffled them around, finding it hard to disguise his haste. The noise was getting closer now. Edgar turned round, in time to see a woman and young girl being manhandled across the reception area; they were both blinking and looked terrified. *Rosa and Sophia.* The policemen and Gestapo who had found them brought them to a halt in front of the reception. They were just yards from Edgar. He turned round and looked at the Gestapo man.

'Am I able to leave now?'

The other man was already moving from around the table. 'Yes, yes. Go.'

The senior officer and the short man in the ill-fitting suit moved over to Rosa and her daughter.

'We found them hiding in a room at the back of the basement, sir.'

'What about the man?'

'It was just them, sir.'

'You are certain?'

'Yes, but we are continuing to search the basement.'

'We must search every inch of this wretched hotel. What is your name?'

Rosa clutched Sophia, but a man dragged the child away. As he did so a toy rabbit the little girl had been holding fell to the floor. A policeman kicked it out of the way.

'Dagmar Keufer, from Frankfurt. I have papers. This is my daughter, Gisela.'

The Gestapo officer held his hand out for the papers. He looked them over and snorted, passing them to a colleague.

'A joke! Not even good forgeries – the photographs look nothing like you! You, little girl. What is your name, come on?'

He had bent down in front of Sophia, his hands resting on his knees. Sophia's eyes were wide with fear as she tried to look at her mother.

'Go on. Your name!'

'I don't know.' Tears were streaming down her face.

'You don't know! What girl does not know her own name, eh? It's Sophia, isn't it? Sophia Stern?'

'Yes,' she said, almost sounding relieved. Edgar took his time in picking up everything he had removed from his pockets and putting them back. They were still searching for Henri: he must have got away after all.

'So,' said the Gestapo man, standing directly in front of Rosa. As he shouted, his spit covered her face. 'If this is Sophia Stern, you must be Rosa Stern. I am pleased to meet you.' Rosa said nothing.

'Where is the Swiss man?'

'I don't know.'

'He was here with you?'

She nodded. 'Yes, but he left.'

'When?'

'Yesterday.'

'Where did he go?'

'I don't know.'

'Was he on his own?'

There was a long pause before Rosa replied.

'Yes.'

The Gestapo officer hit Rosa so hard that Edgar could clearly hear the crack of bone. *Leave now, go* – a policeman was indicating. *Go. None of your business.*

'I am not going to tell you anything!' Rosa's voice was defiant, even confident.

'I think you may now!'

Edgar straightened his coat and had moved towards the door. He turned round to see the Gestapo man holding a revolver against Sophia's head, the barrel buried in the girl's thick hair. An officer stepped back and another one held out a hand, as if to restrain the man with the gun.

'You tell me exactly where he is and who is helping you!'

'But I don't know!' Rosa sounded panicked, no longer defiant.

Because he was holding the revolver directly against Sophia's head, neither the sound of the gun nor its echo was nearly as loud as Edgar would have expected, especially in a relatively confined space. Then there was the silence that one would expect, partly caused by the noise of the shot and partly by the shock. Edgar stepped closer to the hotel exit, not certain he could avoid being sick. He noticed a horrified look on the face of a policeman and broad grins on the faces of others. And then the scream came. It was restrained at first, like someone calling from a distance. By the time Edgar reached the hotel entrance it had turned into a wail, so loud that people in the street stopped to see what it was.

By now he had turned into Friedrichstrasse, pausing to compose himself before attempting to quicken his stride as he walked towards the station. With every step that took him away from the hotel, the scream became louder. He turned into a small alley, crouched behind a large dustbin and threw up. The noise drowned out the scream, but for no more than a second or two. He waited a minute and then hurried to the station.

During the short walk, something died inside Edgar. He felt tears welling in his eyes and he pulled his hat down low to hide them. He had never experienced anything quite as dreadful as this and was quite unprepared for the impact it was having on him. He continued to hear the scream long after he entered the station, the noise of the trains failing to muffle it. The scream was still ringing in his ears as he asked the clerk for a ticket; he heard it above the sound of the train that took him south.

It was the last sound he heard as he slipped out of Germany that night and the first sound he heard as he entered Switzerland.

Chapter 28

Zurich, April 1941

Edgar arrived back in Zurich on the morning of Friday, 4th April. He had started out from Stuttgart the previous morning, well aware of how perilous the journey could be, but throughout it he was accompanied a sense of almost surreal detachment, brought about by the shock of what he had seen at the hotel and the consequences of his own failure to do anything.

He had been forced to deceive Henri: he knew that promising him that to help Rosa and Sophia escape was the only way of ensuring he would leave the hotel with Rolf. Trying to bring Rosa and Sophia with him back to Switzerland was always a risk he could simply not contemplate; they would never have stood a chance. Even going into the basement to warn them would have been too great a risk to consider.

But the sight of little Sophia being shot in cold blood had utterly overwhelmed him. For a few hours, his defences were down and his normally pin-sharp judgement was blunted. When he looked back on that day in the months – and indeed years – that followed he realised that for much of it he hardly cared what happened to him. It was not just Sophia: he did not want to contemplate what fate awaited Rosa, and he imagined that Milo, and no doubt her brother, would be unlikely to survive. For all he knew, poor Rolf and Henri may even have been caught after all. It had been an utter disaster, and what would bother London most was that the Russians would not get to see to the Rostock Report. For a few hours that day, it did not bother him at all.

Edgar's trance-like state continued as he broke all the rules by not taking the first train out of Stuttgart. Instead, after buying his ticket he sat in a corner of the draughty station buffet, sipping at an ersatz coffee he had allowed to get cold and nibbling a sausage. By half past eight, a sense of reality slowly began to return to him as the initial shock thawed and he began to think more clearly. Rolf and Henri would have tried to cross the border after Singen and he decided to try a different route, just in case. He chose to wait for a train that would give him other options and caught one heading south at half past nine. The train was crowded, with a large number of soldiers on board. About ten minutes out of Stuttgart a woman brushed past him as she pushed her way down the carriage. Even from behind there was something familiar about her and as she turned to open the door at the other end of the carriage Edgar caught a glimpse of her face. Had he not thought that at that moment she was in the hands of the Gestapo then he would have sworn it was Katarina Hoch.

He did not spot the woman again and left the train at Tuttlingen. It was a quarter to twelve and according to the timetable on the wall of the deserted forecourt there was a train to Waldshut-Tiengen leaving at twenty past two. Waldshut-Tiengen sat on northern bank of the Rhine, with Switzerland on the other side: it would be a safer place to cross the border.

The ticket office was closed, so Edgar walked into the town and ten minutes from the station he came across an inn. The innkeeper was leaning against the bar, seemingly intent on avoiding serving anyone. Edgar had to position himself directly in front of the man and cough loudly to attract his attention. When the man did deign to look at his new customer, it was with a pair of eyes that never stopped blinking.

'Yes?'

'I'm looking for a room please, just for a couple of hours.'

The eyes blinked even faster and then narrowed. 'A couple of hours? What kind of a place do you think we are?'

'I am sorry, there is a misunderstanding. I have been travelling for a long while and I am just looking for somewhere to have a bath and change my clothes before I return home to Geneva. I am catching a train in a couple of hours.'

The innkeeper leaned closer to Edgar. 'But the journey from here to Switzerland will take you just two hours.'

'I realise that, but then I have to travel on to Montreux, which means I will arrive home late. Look, I am happy to pay the full daily rate for the room if that helps.'

Edgar peeled a generous amount of Reich marks from his wallet and slipped them into the innkeeper's hand, whose eyes lit up and stopped blinking for a moment. He smiled briefly, allowing a glimpse of a mouthful of dirty yellow teeth.

'No problem, sir, use room four. Here's the key. Can I send some food up?'

Edgar said that would not be necessary, he would eat later. Once in the room he locked the door, jammed a chair against it and placed his small suitcase on the bed. It took him ten minutes to carefully unthread the lining just far enough to extract his Swiss papers. He was now Marc Rassier from Montreux. What remained of Karl Albrecht was torn up into little pieces and then burnt in an ashtray, the ashes flushed down the toilet. Once he had washed and changed, Edgar went back to the bar and ordered lunch, leaving the inn as soon as he felt it was reasonable to do so.

The two twenty train arrived on time to take Marc Rassier to Waldshut-Tiengen, arriving at the station in the north of the town at half past four. An elderly policeman checked his Swiss papers as he left the station.

'Are you taking the bus across the border?'

He had saved him from asking the question. 'Yes. When does it leave?'

'An hour: you need to register for it though. They have to check everyone who gets on. Wait over there – those ladies are going on it too.'

Edgar waited with two Swiss German women, who were thankfully as reserved as he would have expected them to be, especially when they realised he was French-speaking. At five thirty, a noisy blue bus pulled in front of the station, by which time another four people were in the waiting area. A police car pulled up and a young officer, wearing a smart raincoat and leather gloves checked everyone's paperwork.

'What has been the purpose of your visit to Germany, Herr Rassier? I need to know where you have visited in the Reich.'

Edgar affected broken German. 'I am sorry, my German is poor. Do you speak French perhaps?'

He didn't. One of the Swiss German ladies explained to the officer that this was typical. 'They make no effort. They expect us to speak French but you never hear them speak German!'

She spoke to Edgar in slow French. 'He wants to know where you have been in Germany.'

Edgar launched into a lengthy travelogue, covering as much of Germany as he could manage and speaking quickly. The Swiss German lady clearly did not understand too much of what he said.

'I am not terribly sure, sir,' she told the police officer. 'They speak so fast. He seems to have been in Munich and elsewhere in Bavaria, as far as I can gather. He says he has many documents if you want to check them.'

Behind them the queue had lengthened. The officer checked the papers for Marc Rassier again. 'And you entered Germany where?'

Edgar managed to look irritated and took back his passport. 'Look, it says here – Munich; by train, one week ago.'

'I see. You may board the coach now.'

It was approaching six o'clock when the bus pulled away from the station, driving slowly through the town and over the bridge crossing the Rhine. Once they were on the Swiss side they pulled alongside a narrow building, where their papers were checked by the Swiss police. Half an hour later the bus had arrived in Baden. It was seven o'clock and he was back in Switzerland, but felt little sense of elation.

'What time is the next bus to Zurich?' he asked the driver.

'A quarter past seven.'

'And do I catch it from here?'

'Yes.' The driver had turned off the engine and was locking up the bus, anxious to leave.

Edgar put his suitcase down and settled down on the bench inside the small bus shelter. The bus driver set off, turning round after he had walked past Edgar.

'I wouldn't make yourself too comfortable. It leaves at quarter past seven in the morning.'

–

It was half past eight on the Friday morning when Edgar walked slowly across Basteiplatz to the small apartment above the hardware shop. He knew that Basil Remington-Barber would be waiting there. He had thought about telephoning him from Baden the previous night or when he arrived in Zurich, but he decided against it. His few hours' sleep in the small inn in Baden had cleared his mind, and now the enormity of what had happened was hitting him hard. He needed time to consider quite how to explain this disaster to London. A 'debacle', they would call it, those people whose only experience of danger was dodging the traffic around Trafalgar Square on the way to their clubs. He would probably end up in Wales looking after munitions, if he was lucky.

Remington-Barber answered the door, looking as if he had seen a ghost. If he had, Edgar was the first, because in the lounge Rolf and Henri were sitting around the table. It was a while before anyone said anything.

'Well, this is quite some reunion,' said Remington-Barber finally, sounding quite jolly.

'When did you two arrive?' Edgar asked.

'Yesterday,' said Rolf, who had now come over to Edgar and was shaking him warmly by the hand. Henri was now half-standing, half-sitting, saying nothing and peering beyond Edgar, looking to see if anyone was behind him.

'Plain sailing?' asked Edgar, as he removed his hat and coat and dropped them on to the armchair.

'Surprisingly so,' said Rolf. 'When we arrived at the station in Stuttgart I saw that the train to Singen was delayed until four o'clock, but there was one to Ulm leaving almost immediately. When we arrived there, we found there was another train leaving soon for Friedrichshafen. We booked into a hotel overlooking the lake and yesterday morning we took a bus to Konstanz. We crossed the border there using our Swiss passports and then took a train to Zurich.'

'Where are they, Edgar?' Henri had stood up now and walked past Edgar into the small hallway. He opened the door of the apartment, came back in and walked over to the window overlooking Basteiplatz.

'You promised me you'd bring Rosa and Sophia with you. Where the hell are they?' His voice had an urgent tone to it, louder and more broken than usual.

Edgar signalled to Rolf to stand by the door. 'Sit down, Henry.' He led him over to the sofa and sat him down and placed himself in the armchair. 'I am afraid they are not here. I am sorry.'

'Where are they?'

Edgar hesitated: he had rehearsed various versions of what to say in answer to this inevitable question and he was quickly deciding which one to use.

'I am sorry, Henry, I really am... but they were arrested before I had a chance to get them out of the hotel. I—'

'Arrested by whom?' Henri had stood up from the sofa and only sat down again when Remington-Barber guided him down with a firm hand on his shoulder.

'Don't shout and please do sit down. I promise you this is something I regret just as much as you do, but it was the Gestapo, I am sorry to say. They must have come to the hotel late on the Wednesday night. I am not sure what happened, but because Milo had not made any contact with me I decided to go down and find her at around one in the morning. As I went down I spotted that she was being questioned in the reception area and I heard them say that they were going to search the hotel in the morning. There were police everywhere. I went back to my room and remained there until seven in the morning. If there was any way I could have gone down to the basement I would have, but every time I looked out of the door there were police patrolling the corridor. When I went down to check out, I saw Rosa and Sophia being led away.'

'And you didn't try and warn them or anything?'

Henri was shouting so loudly now that Rolf quickly shut the windows and Basil Remington-Barber closed the lounge door.

'I told you, Henry, I just didn't get a chance, I promise you. The Gestapo were all over the place. I was worried if I went down into the basement I could be caught, and that would alert the bastards to search down there. I...'

Henri had begun to cry. It started as a gentle sobbing but within a minute had turned into uncontrollable weeping, with tears streaking down his cheeks. Remington-Barber stood awkwardly in front of him holding out a handkerchief, while Rolf sat next to Henri and placed an arm round his shoulder, but nothing would console him. He was grief-stricken and everyone in the room knew there was nothing to be said that could be in any way reassuring.

Henri did nothing other than weep for five minutes. By now, Remington-Barber had taken Edgar's place in the armchair. He held a glass of water and in his open hand were two large white tablets.

'Take these, old chap. They'll help you rest and when you wake up it will be with a clearer head.' Henri looked at the tablets and took them one at a time. Within five minutes he was stretched out on the sofa, fast asleep. They waited another five minutes and then carried him into the bedroom, which Rolf locked from the outside.

'He'll not wake up for most of the day.'

'Well, before he does, we need to check something,' said Edgar.

They emptied all of Henri's possessions on the floor and searched them carefully, paying particular attention to the pair of thick, dark trousers they had last seen in the hotel room in Stuttgart. The envelope they had found there was missing. It was nowhere to be found. As far as the Russians were concerned, he would have served his purpose.

'Well, that's a relief,' said Edgar. 'Only told him half of it, you know, Basil?'

'Well, whatever you do, better not to tell him the other half,' said Rolf. 'In the hotel in Friedrichshafen last night we got talking: I was telling him about Frieda, my fiancée in Vienna – about not having any idea of what has happened to her and all that. Henry opened up a bit:

I can tell you he was absolutely set on rescuing Rosa and the child. He regarded it as his mission, the most important thing in his life. I don't think love or romance came into it. He kept going on about how if he saved Rosa then he could save himself. He said something about how saving her was a way of making up for something terrible he'd done in the past. I asked him to tell me more, but he said it was too terrible to talk about it. It tortured him to even think about it, he said. He said that he hoped that, once we'd rescued Rosa and her daughter, he would find some sort of peace. He clammed up after that.'

'Were they killed?'

'The little girl was, Basil. Shot in cold blood, just yards from me. God knows what they have done to Rosa. In the...'

'Are you all right, Edgar? You seem a bit choked up yourself. Would you like a couple of these pills?'

Edgar had moved over to the table, his back to Remington-Barber and Rolf. For a while he said nothing. When he did, it was in an unusually quiet and faltering voice.

'Better not, we need to talk. I'll help myself to this Scotch, if you don't mind, Basil. Rolf, you tell me what happened when you got back here. That's the most important thing right now.'

Rolf and Remington-Barber joined Edgar at the table, both sitting opposite him.

'I did exactly as you said, Edgar. As soon as we arrived in Zurich I booked us into a small hotel on Löwenstrasse. Once we were in the room I told Henry to wait while I went back down to the reception and from there I was able to call Basil and he alerted my watchers. I stayed in the room with Henry for an hour, by which time I reckoned my men would be in position, so I told him I was going out for a couple of hours to find out where Basil was, and to see when it would be safe for us to come here. I said he could go for a walk if he fancied, but not to go far and certainly be there when I got back. I walked off down Löwenstrasse. My watchers say that he left the hotel five minutes later and went into a bar across the road to use the phone. He stayed in the bar for about fifteen minutes and was doing his best to see if he was being watched. Then he left the bar and walked up to the station. He met up with Viktor by one of the suburban platforms and my watchers say that they are sure they saw Henry hand an envelope over to him. They spoke for about five minutes and then Henry made his way back to the hotel. When I got back I told him I had made contact with Basil and that we were to come here and wait for you – and here we are.'

Edgar leaned over and patted the Austrian on the arm. 'Well done, Rolf, well done. Maybe London will not see this as quite the total disaster that I feared they might.'

'I suppose that means that everything has worked out rather well in the end, eh Edgar? Rather against the odds I must say, but the going turned out to be in our favour. I have lost my cell in Stuttgart, which is a damn shame, but then they did last somewhat longer than I thought they would.'

'Can't you see that we still have a serious problem, Basil?'

'Not sure I'm with you, Edgar. Tragic about the little girl, and one would not rate the chances of her mother or Milo and her brother very highly, but surely in terms of our—'

'Think Basil: think. Henry. Henry is the problem.'

'But he handed the document over to the Russians and—'

'Indeed, but consider this Basil: the Germans were clearly after a "Henri Hesse" from Switzerland. They knew he was the man who had taken Rosa and Sophia from Berlin, and who had turned up at the hotel in Stuttgart, and somehow escaped from it. Rest assured that they would have informed the Swiss, who will take a very dim view of this indeed. The last thing they want is one of their citizens using Switzerland as a base from which to cause trouble for the Germans: they are not keen on biting the hand that feeds them, are they?'

'No.'

'Henry entered Switzerland yesterday on false papers, which buys us some time – but that is not a long-term solution. Either he stays hidden for the rest of the war, which to me is not feasible, or he returns to Geneva under his proper identity.'

'I see, Edgar… and get arrested by the Swiss, no doubt.'

'No doubt indeed, Basil. Just think then of the implications for all our work here if he starts to spill the beans. The Swiss will know what

358

we're up to, so will the Germans, and quite possibly the Soviets too, undoing all the good work.'

'*If* he starts to spill the beans, surely.'

Edgar stood up, brushed himself down and loosened his tie.

'I fear that we are not going to be able to take that risk Basil.'

–

They left Zurich in the middle of the afternoon of Monday seventh of April. Rolf had borrowed a Citroen TUB van from another of his apparently endless stream of contacts and he was driving, with Edgar and Basil Remington-Barber next to him in the front. They headed south out of Zurich and then through Luzern, Sarnen and the valleys of Unterwalden.

They drove slowly: they were in no hurry, had no desire to draw attention to themselves, and in any case the van made worrying noises when it felt it was being pushed too hard – 'rather like a woman' Basil had said, but none of them were in much of a mood for humour.

It was only seven o'clock when they arrived in Brienz and despite everything, it was still too early. They would need to buy some time. They found a small inn with enough space for them to park the van at the back, in the shadows and hopefully away from anyone else. They took it in turns to go into the inn, one by one. Although none of them would admit as much, no one fancied being left in the van on their own.

Edgar and Remington-Barber were in the van together at around eight o'clock. The older man attempted to break the silence.

'Rum business this, Edgar.'

The silence continued, although Edgar did nod his head. *Rum business, no question of that. A messy one too.*

'Lord knows what will happen if we are stopped.'

'I told you, Basil. You are a British diplomat: you have your papers. You are on Embassy business. They cannot touch you or the van. Please stop worrying.'

'But if… if… anything goes wrong, all hell will break loose. Heavens know what London will have to say.'

'Basil,' Edgar had turned round to face the other man, 'whatever happens will be more acceptable than the alternative. And in any case, nothing is going to go wrong. Pull yourself together.'

They left Brienz at half past eight, when it felt like it was getting properly dark, and drove along the north shore of the lake, stopping in a side street in Interlaken for another hour for it to get even darker and ensure there was no chance they had been followed.

It was ten o'clock when they pulled out of Interlaken, driving along the track across the north shore of Lake Thun. It was only a few days past the new moon and that, along with the thick banks of trees on either side of the track, ensured they were now driving in near-total darkness. Rolf brought the speed of the van down to just ten miles an hour, the headlamps fighting hard to pick much out in front of them. Shortly after they had passed a sign for Steinbruch they spotted a clearing to their left and Edgar told Rolf to pull in.

'Wait here.'

Edgar checked his torch and revolver and disappeared into the trees. He was only gone for five minutes.

'This will do. The lake is just through the trees and there is a decent slope which will help us. Rolf, reverse as far as you can into the trees and then we can take the dinghy down first.'

Once they had placed the dinghy by the shore they walked back to the van.

'How far out will we need to go?' asked Remington-Barber.

'Thun is supposed to be one of the deepest lakes in Switzerland: five minutes rowing should get us as far out as we need to.'

They struggled from the moment they hauled it out of the back of the van, the three of them manhandling and dragging it through the trees. They paused twice for Basil Remington-Barber to throw up and once they reached the dinghy they had to return to the van for the ropes and the weights. By the time they pushed the dinghy into the seemingly solid lake it was half past eleven and the world was completely silent. Edgar and Rolf rowed, in the end for ten minutes, until they felt they were far enough out.

'You do your best to hold the boat steady, Basil: Rolf and I will do the rest.'

'Shouldn't we... I don't know... say something?'

'Like what, Basil?'

'A prayer perhaps? Seems like the decent thing to do.'

'If you must, Basil. Be quick though.'

Basil Remington-Barber muttered his way through Psalm Twenty-Three – pausing after the words 'still waters' and struggling with the walk 'through the valley of the shadow of death' – sounding decidedly tearful by the end.

And then the deed was done. It took them less than five minutes to row back to the shore, and once they reached the town of Thun they were less than an hour from Bern. No one in the van said a word until they saw the lights of the city ahead of them.

'I didn't know you were the religious type, Basil.'

'I'm not, Edgar. Church every so often and all that, but nothing serious. Why do you mention it?'

'Knowing the whole of that psalm, off by heart.'

An ironic laugh. 'Forced to learn it at prep school. The chaplain would beat the living daylights out of you if you got one word wrong. Never imagined I'd have cause to use it, not like that at any rate. I was thinking while I was reciting it, you know. That reference to the "presence of mine enemies" – who would you say his enemies were?'

It was a long while before Edgar replied, so much so that it seemed at first that he may have ignored the question.

'Everyone, Basil. Everyone was his enemy. That, I am afraid, is a consequence of serving more than one master.'

–

It had taken two days for Henri Hesse, or Henry Hunter as he was also known, to die before they consigned this body to the depths of Lake Thun.

Once Edgar had persuaded Basil Remington-Barber that they had no alternative, they came up with a plan. They woke Hesse up at two o'clock in the afternoon, when he was still drowsy, and made him drink some water, into which they had dissolved seven of the tablets. They were convinced that he would not wake up, but one of them still remained in the room with him all the time. Although his breathing became more shallow and at times he appeared to be on the verge of slipping away, he held on through the Saturday and by the Sunday morning his breathing sounded stronger. They crushed a dozen tablets into a saucer and turned it into a paste with a bit of water which they spooned in his mouth, but struggled to get much of it down him.

But Henri hung on. By the Sunday evening they were convinced that they needed to do something else. Remington-Barber was in a terrible state, red-eyed, shaking and pacing around the apartment. He had convinced himself that something was bound to go wrong and they would all be arrested, creating a diplomatic incident in the process. Rolf suggested he went out for a walk. Edgar and Rolf stood at the window watching him cross Basteiplatz and then nodded to each other. *We need to get on with it.*

Edgar removed his jacket and rolled up his sleeves and the two men entered the bedroom. Henri was now stirring, tossing and turning and making noises as if he were trying to speak. As Edgar approached him, Henri half opened his eyes and his mouth moved.

'Come on, Rolf, quick.'

'He's trying to say something, Edgar.'

'Exactly. Let's get on with it.'

There was an indistinct sound coming out of his mouth now, although just before Edgar put the pillow over his face and Rolf held him down, there was one word they could both clearly hear. *Rosa.*

There was a very brief and one-sided struggle, but they both agreed afterwards that it was probably painless. *He would have been too drugged up to have an idea of what was going on,* they assured each other.

'He couldn't have known a thing,' said Rolf.

Edgar was straightening his sleeves as he turned to reply to the Austrian.

'He knew too much.'

Epilogue

Rosa Stern was taken to the Gestapo headquarters in the old Hotel Silber building on Dorotheenstrasse, just south of the Schlossplatz and not very far at all from the Hotel Victoria. She was in such a state of shock that she did not utter a word. She sat very still in her cell, staring at the wall, her hands crossed neatly on her lap and her mouth slightly open, occasionally breaking into the slightest of smiles. A psychiatrist brought in by the Gestapo assured them that she was not putting anything on. It was, he told them, one of the most extreme cases of catatonia he had ever seen. *Could she, by any chance, have been subjected to a serious trauma recently?*

'So she's gone mad then?' the Gestapo officer asked.

'You could put it like that: I find that it is much more common these days.'

They tried for a fortnight, convinced that when she did speak she would have plenty to reveal. Who was helping her in Berlin? Where had Hesse gone?

But Rosa said nothing, sitting quietly, occasionally swaying very slowly as if listening to a piece of soothing music and once in a while mouthing something silent to the wall. In the end, a Gestapo officer stormed into her cell and held his revolver in front of her, but there was still no reaction whatsoever. When he hit her hard around the face she didn't make a noise and stayed in the same position as she had landed on the floor. When he knelt beside her and released the safety catch she did not blink. He shot her four times, only stopping when his gun jammed.

–

Rosa Stern's first husband, Gunter Reinhart, managed to avoid suspicion. He was questioned on two occasions during that April, but was able to persuade the Gestapo that the man, Hesse, was a mere courier from one of the many Swiss banks he dealt with and his contact with him was confined to the handing over of documents.

'I wish I could help, but I really remember little about him… he was such an inconsequential little man.'

Reinhart assured the Gestapo that he had not had any contact with his first wife since their divorce in 1935, and that it had been many years since he had seen his son. The last he had heard, Alfred was in France. The Gestapo officer assured him that this was one of a number of unresolved aspects of this case.

–

Franz Hermann also managed to avoid coming under suspicion. Because he knew that the woman who lived opposite had already contacted the police, he decided to risk taking matters into his own hands. With his mother safely at his sister's in Brandenburg he went to his local police station in Dahlem and reported that the nurse he had hired to look after her had disappeared.

'She mentioned something about her husband being killed and having to return to Bremerhaven, but now I am not sure… and a very helpful neighbour told me that she saw the nurse leave the house with a man and a young girl and drive off in an Opel. I hope that I am not wasting your time, but I am becoming very suspicious…'

The Gestapo officer in charge of investigating the whole business of Henri Hesse, Rosa and Sophia decided that he believed Franz Hermann's account – after all, had not the lawyer reported the matter himself to the police?

Franz Hermann's good fortune only lasted until July 1944, when he was one of many thousands of people arrested after the attempt on Hitler's life. Although the Gestapo never suspected him of being a British agent, there was enough circumstantial evidence to link him with the resistance to Hitler and he was sent to Sachsenhausen concentration camp, where he was murdered in November 1944.

Edgar and Basil Remington-Barber agreed that, as Marlene Hesse had been unaware of her son's intelligence activities, any contact with her would be counter-productive. She had waited until the second week of April before reporting her son missing to the police in Geneva. They could tell her nothing, but appeared to be very interested in what she could tell them. Could Herr Hesse have perhaps travelled to Germany? Could she provide a list of his associates in Switzerland? She insisted she knew nothing and promised to let them know if she heard from her son.

Marlene Hesse's income disappeared along with her son. Edgar was adamant that it would be too suspicious if any money was transferred from Henri's account at Credit Suisse.

'The last thing we need. What if she tells the Swiss police and they try and track the money? They're good at that type of thing.'

Madame Ladnier was prevailed upon to close the account and ensure there was no trace of it having ever existed.

Her reduced circumstances meant that Marlene Hesse had to move to a drab bedsit in a block in between two railway lines, earning a living as a cleaner.

—

Viktor was not altogether surprised that Henri had disappeared after he handed the Rostock Report over to him at the railway station. He had long wondered when the British would discover that the man they had recruited as an agent in 1939 had been a Soviet spy for many years before that. Moscow seemed to be pleased with the Rostock Report: it reassured them that a German invasion was unlikely and Stalin used it as vindication of his conviction that reports of invasion plans were just the British being mischievous. Viktor was well aware that Henri's disappearance could cast doubt on the veracity of the report, so he decided to say nothing to Moscow. If they were pleased, why upset them?

As far as Henri was concerned, he assumed Edgar had killed him, which was what his service would have done in the same circumstances. It was a shame: he quite liked *synok* and he had been a good agent, and had lasted far longer than Viktor had expected him to. In early June he told Moscow that Henri had been recalled to London.

Viktor Krasotkin's encounters with British Intelligence resumed in early 1944 when he turned up in Vienna, where he remained until at least the end of the war.

–

Rolf Eder continued to work for British intelligence. Edgar had been so impressed by him that when he became involved in plans for a clandestine mission inside Austria he had no hesitation in recommending Rolf. He slipped into Vienna in early 1944 and was still operating there when the Red Army liberated the city in April 1945.

–

Captain Edgar returned to London soon after Henry Hunter's death. The mission was deemed to have been a success by those who pronounced on such things, although they acknowledged it had not been without its more unfortunate aspects. Operation Barbarossa meant that Germany had committed itself to fighting on two fronts in Europe and British military chiefs were convinced this was a fatal error. Edgar was credited with having run a successful intelligence operation, helping to ensure that the Soviet Union was, at the very least, confused as to German intentions and, at best, – thanks to the Rostock Report – convinced there would be no invasion.

Author's note

The Swiss Spy is a work of fiction and, with the exception of a few obvious people referred to in passing, such as Churchill or Hitler, all the characters in the book are fictional and should not be confused with anyone in real life. Having said that, the book is based on actual historical events, and in that respect I have endeavoured to be as authentic and accurate as possible.

There was indeed a high-level meeting of senior German military figures in the Bavarian town of Bad Reichenhall in July 1940, where plans to invade the Soviet Union were first discussed, notwithstanding the fact that the two countries were supposedly bound by a non-aggression pact at the time. Hitler's Directive 21 referred to in the book is genuine and was released on 18th December that year and outlined plans for Operation Barbarossa, the invasion of the Soviet Union. The Rostock Report featured in the book is a work of fiction.

Operation Barbarossa began on 22nd June 1941 and Hitler expected it to have been successfully concluded within just a few months. In the event, it ended in disaster for Germany. They failed to reach Moscow by the time the Russian winter took hold, allowing the Red Army to regroup and push the Germans back. The Germans suffered a crushing defeat in the Battle of Stalingrad in February 1943 and Operation Bagration in June 1944 was the start of Germany's defeat on the eastern front.

There is a good deal of evidence to show that the Soviet Union ignored dozens of credible intelligence reports about the planned German invasion. Many of these came from their own intelligence services, including a copy of a handbook to be used by German troops in the Soviet Union which was passed on to the Soviet Embassy in

Berlin by a German Communist printer. As for the British intelligence, Stalin was convinced that these reports were disinformation, designed to provoke a war between the Soviet Union and Germany. He described them as 'English provocation'. So, although the missions at the core of *The Swiss Spy* are fictional ones, the idea of British intelligence using other sources to inform the Soviet Union would be quite in keeping with what was happening at the time.

I have done my best to ensure that details such as street names, the locations of embassies, railway stations, airports and other named buildings and places are accurate.

Many of the hotels referred to in the book existed and, in some cases, still do. The Adlon in Berlin seems to be the preferred hotel in most Second World War espionage novels, but in fact both the Excelsior and the Kaiserhof, where Henri Hesse/Henry Hunter stayed, were prominent Berlin hotels during the Second World War. Both hotels were destroyed in Allied bombing, as was the Hotel Victoria in Stuttgart, which had been the main hotel in the city.

Readers may wonder whether it really was possible to fly on commercial routes in Europe during the Second World War. The answer is that it was, most commonly if the departure or destination airports were in neutral countries. Muntadas Airport in Barcelona was a major hub for travel around Europe, as was Portela Airport in Lisbon and Zurich Airport. During the war, Whitchurch Airport in Bristol replaced Croydon Airport as Great Britain's main commercial airport: the site is now a housing estate. In June 1943 a BOAC flight from Lisbon to Bristol was shot down by the Luftwaffe over the Bay of Biscay. All four crew and thirteen passengers were killed, including the famous British actor, Leslie Howard. It was one of very few attacks on a civilian flight in Europe during the war. The names of the airlines, the type of aircraft used and the flight details in the book are, to the best of my knowledge, accurate.

The Roman Catholic cathedral of St Hedwig was destroyed in an Allied air raid in March 1943 (it has since been reconstructed). Although Father Josef is fictional, a priest at St Hedwig, Bernhard Lichtenberg, was arrested for publicly protesting at Nazi policies towards Jews and the euthanasia programme. He died while being transported to Dachau in November 1943.

This is probably not the place to go into detail about the considerable complicity of the Swiss banks in the Nazi war effort. However, it is well established that there was an active relationship, to say the least, between the Reichsbank and most of the major Swiss banks, including Bank Leu. Bank Leu was an independent bank until it became part of Credit Suisse in 1990.

To save fellow football fans the effort I had to go to, I can assure you that the match between Sporting Lisbon and Barreirense that features in Chapter 15 did actually take place on the 9th February 1941 – and Sporting did indeed win 2-0.

I would like to thank my agent, Gordon Wise at Curtis Brown and his colleague Richard Pike for their help, encouragement and sound advice. Gordon rightly has an outstanding reputation as an agent and I realise how fortunate I am to be one of his clients. I would also like to thank Rufus Purdy and Alice Lutyens. Rufus first saw *The Swiss Spy* when I mistakenly thought it was the finished article: the fact that he has contributed so significantly to its current state is a testament to his editorial brilliance.

And finally, my thanks and love to my daughters, Amy and Nicole, and my wife, Sonia. It cannot always be easy living with a writer, not least one who wonders aloud how to kill someone and who at times may give the impression of living in a world that existed seventy years ago. As a teacher, Sonia is a very astute and frank reader: draft chapters are returned with plenty of annotations in red biro, the occasional tick more than compensating for the more frequent exclamation marks.